ONE SUMMER AT DEER'S LEAP

Elizabeth Elgin is the bestselling author of *All the Sweet Promises, Whisper on the Wind, I'll Bring You Buttercups, Daisychain Summer, Where Bluebells Chime* and *Windflower Wedding*. She served in the WRNS during the Second World War and met her husband on board a submarine depot ship. A keen gardener, she has two daughters and five grandsons and lives in a village in the Vale of York.

ELIZABETH ELGIN

One Summer at Deer's Leap

HarperCollinsPublishers

HarperCollins*Publishers*
77–85 Fulham Palace Road,
Hammersmith, London W6 8JB

A Paperback Original 1999
1 3 5 7 9 8 6 4 2

A catalogue record for this book
is available from the British Library

ISBN 0 00 651051 5

Typeset in Sabon and Bembo by
Palimpsest Book Production Limited,
Polmont, Stirlingshire

Printed and bound in Great Britain by
Caledonian International Book Manufacturing Ltd, Glasgow

Gratefully to
Patricia Parkin, Caroline Sheldon
and Nancy Webber

Part One

Chapter One

I suppose it was to be expected that someone with a name like mine should one day do something a bit out of the ordinary, like deciding to be a novelist.

I do things by numbers. I'd finished my fifth novel – the other four had been rejected out of hand – and sending it out one last, despairing time was as far as I was prepared to go. One more rejection, and that was the end of Cassie Johns, novelist!

'You'll turn her head with a fancy name like that,' Dad had said when I was born because he wanted me called after his sister Jane, and Mum, who had been wavering and half prepared to agree with him, dug her heels in with uncharacteristic ferocity. And Aunt Jane, bless her, sided with Mum and said that Cassandra would do very nicely, to her way of thinking!

Dear, lovely Aunt Jane was the reason I was here now, a novelist at last, driving my own car and smiling foolishly at a passing clump of silver birches and the foxgloves that grew beneath them, and so stupidly smug and self-satisfied I didn't notice the revs had dropped to a warning judder and I was being overtaken by a farm tractor.

'Don't give in, Cassie,' Aunt Jane had urged. 'Just one more try to please your old auntie?'

So instead of giving in and doing the rounds of the universities as Dad had always supposed I would when I got three decent A levels, I wrote *Till Hell Freezes Over* with a kind of despairing acceptance that my father had been right all along. After working for four years – and four useless novels – on the marketing side of Dad's horticultural business (selling vegetables and flowers at the top of the lane in summer and working in the propagating houses in winter) I posted off the novel for the fifth time, then settled down to accept defeat. And university, if I was lucky.

My last-stand novel was unbelievably, wonderfully, gloriously accepted. One or two changes were needed, said the publishing lady to whom I spoke an hour after receiving the letter. A little editing – perhaps a different title? Could I go to London and talk to her? Would tomorrow be convenient? I'd asked breathlessly.

It was to be two weeks later that I eventually met my editor, because after a do in the local and everybody in the village having a knees-up to celebrate the emergence of an author in their midst, Aunt Jane died in her sleep that same night.

The milkman became concerned because she didn't answer to his knock, and came at once to tell us. We found her curled up under her patchwork quilt with such a look of contentment on her face that we knew her going had been gentle.

Had she been thinking of the three sherries of the night before, or her niece's success? Whatever the reason for that smile, we could only be sorry for ourselves because there hadn't been a last goodbye. For Jane Johns there was only relief that she had gone the way most people would like: peacefully, in her sleep.

She left her cottage to Dad, the contents to me and sufficient money in her bankbook to pay for a good funeral with a decent knife-and-fork tea to follow. And to Mum's surprise and consternation – because Aunt Jane had never been one to gamble – she also left me two thousand pounds in Premium Bonds.

I'm still sad that she didn't live to see my novel, with an eye-catching jacket and its title changed to *Ice Maiden*, hit the bookshelves, and sorrier still she wasn't there the Sunday it made the lists, albeit at the bottom. I wondered if, with a first novel, I hadn't been just a bit too lucky and wouldn't I walk under a bus the very next time I crossed the road, because of it? Then I got all weepy inside and went to the churchyard

4

to tell the one person who really mattered – at least as far as *Ice Maiden* was concerned. And Aunt Jane chuckled and said that with a name like Cassandra she'd always known I'd be famous one day, and how about writing a real hot number next, so I could be infamous?

'*And isn't it about time you cashed those Premium Bonds,*' she said, '*and bought yourself a little car?*'

Aunt Jane and I could talk to each other, not with words, but with our minds, because truth known she and I both were kind of psychic.

'I'll have to cash them – when I get them,' I told her. 'The solicitor said that Premium Bonds aren't transferable.'

'*Well then, that's settled, Cassie girl. You deserve a car.*'

I bought a second-hand Mini with Aunt Jane's money: one careful owner, 20,000 miles on the clock. The bodywork was immaculate, as if the careful owner had spent more time polishing it than driving it. But it was the colour that finally clinched it. Bright red. Aunt Jane would have approved. Even so, Dad felt duty-bound to say, 'You don't get something that looks as good as that thing for two grand. There's a catch.'

I agreed to have the AA send a man to look it over. The little red car had nothing at all wrong with it except that it needed new tyres. It was coming up to three years old and would never pass its MOT with tyres like that, he said.

Something maternal and protective welled up inside me. Mini wasn't an it or a thing. Red Mini epitomized Aunt Jane's faith in me. If I'd been inclined to give it a name, I'd have called it Jane.

'New tyres it is then.' I glared at Dad, who asked me if I knew what a set of new tyres cost.

'Is it a deal, then?' Defiantly I avoided Dad's eyes.

The one careful owner took my hand, patted the car with a polishing movement and said it was and in that moment I knew that no matter how famous – or infamous – or how rich I became, I would never part with my first car. Not even if I kept it in one of Dad's outhouses with a tarpaulin over it for ever!

As soon as Dad had got a lady from the village to look after the stall, I'd taken to writing full time. At first I'd wallowed in the luxury of a new word processor and being able to write when I wanted to and not in snatched half-hours at odd times of the day.

True, the novelty soon wore off and I had to discipline myself to work office hours, and even when the words didn't come properly, I typed stoically on. Mind, there were bonus days when the words flowed. At such times I kidded myself I was a genius, even though the flow days were few and far between.

On the whole, though, I was content. With a contract in my pocket for book two – the make-or-break book, had I known it – my own car and just enough in the bank to keep me afloat until *Ice Maiden* came up with some royalties, I'd felt justified in giving up my daytime job and only helping Dad out at busy times.

So after being overtaken by the tractor, I pulled the car onto the grass at the side of the road and reached for the carefully written, beautifully illustrated directions. Winding down the window I breathed in deeply, then studied the map. Half a mile back I had passed a clump of oak trees; now I must look out for the crossroads, turn right, and after 200 yards on what was described as little more than a dirt road, I would be there.

'It's my sister's place,' said my editor, Jeannie, of whom I'd become extremely fond. 'There's a bit of a do on next weekend and I'm invited. Why don't you tag along, too? You don't live all that far away and it's Welcome Hall at Deer's Leap. Bring fancy dress, if you have one.'

I didn't have fancy dress, and had said so; said too that not all that far on her map was all of fifty-two miles in reality and that Yorkshire was a very large county.

'Oh, c'mon, Cassie. A break from words will do you good,' she'd urged, then went on to remind me that the rather clingy, low-cut green sheath dress I'd worn to Harrier Books' Christmas party would fit the bill nicely. 'Stick a lily behind your ear and you've cracked it. Come as a lily of the field. Nobody's going to mind when they see your cleavage.'

So I'd checked that my green sheath still fitted, then bought two silk arum lilies, one to be worn as suggested, the other stuck down my cleavage. Thus, hopefully, I would pass for a lily of the field that toiled not, neither did she spin and hoped I wouldn't look too ordinary against Cleopatra, Elizabeth Tudor and Isadora Duncan.

I took a peek in the rear mirror. Considering my outdoor upbringing, I wasn't all that bad to look at. My complexion had remained fair in spite of northern winters; my hair was genuine carrot, though Mum called it russet, and my eyes, by far my best asset, were very blue. I wasn't one bit like Mum or Dad or Aunt Jane, and not for the first time did I wonder who had bestowed my looks. Some long-ago Viking, had it been, on the rampage in northern England? Or was I a changeling?

I laughed out loud. I was on holiday. I was going to a house called Deer's Leap and Jeannie would be there when I arrived. To add to my blessings, book two was at chapter seven and with Aunt Jane in mind was becoming something of a hot number. I shouldn't have a care in the world. I *didn't* have a care in the world except that maybe my love life was not all it should be.

'Why are you going to a weekend party?' Piers had demanded when I'd told him on the phone.

'Because I need a break.'

'Then hadn't it occurred to you that maybe I'd be glad to see you? Why can't you come to London?'

'You said you were frantically busy,' I'd hedged.

'Never too busy for you, darling. Come to my place, instead?'

Why didn't he and I shack up down there, he'd said, throwing the two-can-live-as-cheaply-as-one cliché at me.

And iron shirts and do the cooking, I'd thought, and be back to writing odd half-hours again. Besides, Piers wasn't my soulmate. I didn't see us ever making a proper go of it. If my ego hadn't balked at being manless our relationship could well have ended ages ago.

We'd made love, of course. Piers was good to look at; dark and lean and somehow always tanned. His designer stubble suited him, too, though I wished sometimes it wasn't so hard on my face – afterwards.

And that was something else about him and me: the afterwards bit. It never felt quite right for me. When it was over I found myself not liking him as much as I ought to, and to love a man you've got to like him – afterwards. Even I knew that.

'Look, I'm sorry,' I'd said. 'I can't call it off now, and anyway my editor will be there. It isn't just a weekend party; it's business.' Sometimes I tell lies to Piers. 'More to the point, when are you coming north to see me?'

I'd thrown the ball back into his court and he was just coming up with a perfectly reasonable excuse when I heard his bell chimes, quite clearly.

'OK, Cassie. Some other time? Soon?'

He'd put the phone down then and I wondered whose fingertip had pressed his doorbell and wasn't surprised to find I didn't much care.

'Forget Piers for two days and get some living in,' I said to the girl in the rear-view mirror. No time like tonight for dipping a toe in the water, I thought, and to hell with the lily-down-the-cleavage bit!

I wound up the window and set out, smiling, on my way again. Above me the sky was blue, with only little puffs of very white cloud. Around me, and as far as I could see, were fields and hedgerows and grass verges that really had wild flowers growing in them. I was going to a party tonight and I would be a lily of the field and have a wicked time. I wasn't

8

in any hurry to settle down because I'd already decided there would be all the time in the world, *after* the third novel. And wouldn't I know when I met the right man; the man I would love *and* like – afterwards?

Oh, concentrate, Cassandra! The crossroads, then a couple of hundred yards and Jeannie will be there at the front gate of Deer's Leap, wondering where you've got to!

The engine revs changed from their usual sweet-natured purr to an agitated growl so I dropped a gear, put my foot down and concentrated on the lane ahead. I was just beginning to wonder how the house had got its name when I saw a man ahead. He was smiling, his thumb jutted and he was in fancy dress.

All the things Dad dinned into me about never stopping for anyone, much less for a man, went out of my head. He was undoubtedly a fellow guest, who for some reason was standing at the side of the lane and in need of a lift. I slowed and stopped, then leaned over to slip the nearside door catch.

'Want a lift?'

'Please. Could you? I've got to get to Deer's Leap.'

'Hop in!'

He arranged himself in the passenger seat, one long leg at a time. Then he pulled his knees almost up to his chin and balanced his khaki bag on them.

'You can push the seat back.' I lifted the catch to my left. 'Shove with your feet.'

The seat slipped backwards and he stretched his legs, relief on his face. Well, six foot two *at least*, isn't Mini size.

'That's a World War Two respirator, isn't it?' I envied his fancy dress. So real-looking.

'They're usually called gas masks,' he smiled, and that smile was really something across a crowded Mini.

'You already dressed for tonight, then?' I turned the key in the ignition.

'We-e-ll, sort of,' he shrugged, 'and anyway, I'm only on standby.'

'Damn!' A slow-moving flock of sheep ahead put paid to the question, 'What's standby?'

I slowed to keep well back. The lambs were well grown; almost as big as the ewes and obviously not used to being driven. If one of them panicked in the narrow road, we'd all be in trouble.

My passenger stared ahead, intent on the sheep and the black and white sheepdog that watched and nosed and slunk behind and to the side of them, and I was able to get a good look at him.

Fair, rather thin. His hands lay still on his lap though his fingers moved constantly. He'd had his hair cut short, too, just as if he'd been the pilot whose uniform he wore. Three stripes on his sleeve; wings above his top left-hand pocket. His shoes were altogether of another era.

The sheep were behaving. I hoped they would turn left at the crossroads. He was still watching them intently so I read the number stamped in black on the flap of his gas mask and thought my lily of the field would look a bit botched alongside his authentic uniform. He'd obviously gone to a lot of trouble, so with future fancy dress parties in mind I asked where he'd got it.

'Oh – the usual place. They throw them at you . . .'

'*Really?* I'd have thought that get-up would've been difficult to get hold of.'

'Only the wings,' he said absently, his eyes still on the sheep.

I realized he wasn't going to be very forthcoming and hoped for better luck tonight when my lily-gilded cleavage might just get me noticed.

I looked at his gas mask again. On the underside of the webbing strap were the initials S. S. and a tiny heart, and I wondered who had put them there. The original long-ago owner, I supposed, the author in me supplying Sydney Snow, Stefan Stravinsky, Sam Snodgrass.

'I'm Cassandra,' I said. 'Cassie.'

'John,' he smiled, 'but I usually get Jack.'

The flock began to push and surge to the left. The dog nipped the leg of a ewe that wanted to turn right and it got the message.

'Soon be there. Been here before?' We'd turned right onto what really was a dirt road.

'Mm. Quite a bit . . .'

The lane was rutted and I slowed, driving carefully, eyes fixed ahead for potholes.

'There it is.' He pointed to the tiles of a roof above a row of beeches.

'Seems a nice place . . .' Bigger than I'd expected and not so northernly rugged.

'It's very nice. Look – mind if I get out here? I usually go in the back way.' He seemed in a hurry, his hand already on the door handle. 'Thanks for the lift. See you.'

He swung his legs out first, then gripped the side to heave himself clear. Then he straightened his jacket with a sharp downward pull, slung his gas mask on his left shoulder and straightened his cap.

'Bye, Jack. See you tonight.'

'Y-yes. Hope so.' He crossed his fingers, smiled, then made for a rusted iron kissing gate that squeaked as he pushed through it.

He knew his way around, had obviously been to Deer's Leap before. I too crossed my fingers for tonight because he really interested me.

I wondered if there would be music at the party. He'd be good to dance with – dance properly with, I mean. None of your standing six feet apart, sending signals with your elbows and hips, but moving closely to smoochy music.

I started the car, drove another hundred yards to a set of open white gates with Jeannie leaning against them, waving frantically. I tooted the horn, then drove in past her.

'Lovely to see you again. Had a good journey? Lovely day

for it,' she said when I'd got out and stretched my back, then kissed her.

'Fine!' I grinned. It had been a very interesting journey. I unlocked the boot and took out my case. 'I'll tell you about it later, but right now I'd kill for a cup of tea!'

She took my case and I followed with my grip and the large sheaf of flowers I'd brought for her sister. Coals to Newcastle, I thought, looking at the gorgeous garden. Then I thought again about Jack and smiled smugly because already my psychic bits knew he could dance. Beautifully.

'Where is your sister?' I asked when we were seated at the kitchen table, drinking tea. Already I was a little in love with Deer's Leap and its huge kitchen and pantry, and the narrow little back stairs from it that led to my room above. And what I had seen of the hall and its wide, almost-black oak staircase and the sitting room, glimpsed through an open door, were exactly what I had known they would be.

'Beth and Danny'll be back any time now. They've taken the kids to the village hall. Brownies and Cubs on a weekend camp. That's why they're throwing the party this weekend. Not soft, my sister,' she grinned. 'Now do you want to unpack or would you like to have a look round?'

I said I wanted to see the house, if that would be all right with Beth, and the outside too. All of it.

'It's wonderful,' I breathed. 'The air is so – so – well, you can almost taste it!'

'Mm. After London I always think of it as golden,' she said. 'It does something to my lungs that makes me want to puke when I get back to the smoke. Let's go outside first, then you can stand back from it – get an idea of the layout.

'Mind, it wasn't always so roomy. Once, I think, it must have belonged to a yeoman type of farmer, then later owners joined the outbuildings to the house. They connect with a rather modern conservatory. Don't think it would be allowed now by the planning people, this being a listed house. I reckon even the farm buildings would be listed these days.'

'It isn't a farm, then?'

'Not any more. They've only got a paddock now. The rest of the land has been sold off over the years, mostly for grazing. At least some of the farm buildings were saved; Danny uses them as garages now. You can shift your car inside later.'

She closed the kitchen door behind us and I noticed she didn't bother to lock it.

'I envy your sister this place,' I said dreamily. 'I feel comfortable here already. Sort of *déjà vu* . . .'

'Mm. Beth feels the same way. Pity they've got to give it up.'

'Selling!' I squeaked, wondering who in her right mind could even think of leaving such a house.

'No, not them. The lease runs out at the end of the year and the owner is selling. I suppose they could buy but they won't. The children, you see. They're a long way from a school. All very well in summer, but in winter this place can be cut off for weeks. Nothing moves: no cars in or out; no mail, and sometimes electricity lines down in high winds. The kids are weekly boarders in Lancaster in winter – come home Friday nights – but even in summer it's a five-days-a-week job for Beth, getting them to school and back again.

'She's cut up about it – they both are – but I reckon she'll be glad to live nearer a school. Beth has to plan her life round the kids' comings and goings. She adores Deer's Leap; she'd transport it stone by stone to somewhere less out of the way if she could. This coming Christmas will be their last here, I'm sorry to say.'

I felt sorry, too, and I'd spent less than an hour in the place. There was something about it that made me feel welcome and wanted. Even the old windows seemed to smile in the morning sun.

We were standing at the white gates when Jeannie said,

'Let's go round the back way. The land rises a bit and if you go to the top of the paddock, there's a lovely view . . .'

She pushed open the kissing gate, slipping through, waiting for me to do the same, but I just stood there gawping.

'Is there another gate like this one?' I frowned. 'One that squeaks?'

'No. This is the only one. Why do you ask?'

'Because I'd have bet good money that this one was in need of a coat of paint and a drop or two of oil.'

'You sure, Cas?'

I was perfectly sure. It had squeaked not so long ago when Jack pushed through it, I'd swear it had. Yet now it was newly painted and swung so smoothly on its pivot that I knew I could have pushed it open with my little finger.

'But, Jeannie, I don't understand it . . .' I stammered.

'Listen, m'dear. This gate was painted about two months ago and to the best of my knowledge it has never squeaked.'

Then she went on to argue that one kissing gate looked much the same as the other, and wasn't I getting this one mixed up with some other gate? She said it in such reasonable tones that I knew she was humouring me, so I said no more. But tonight, when the airman showed, I was determined to mention it again. I was just about to ask where the other guest was when a car swept into the drive.

'Thanks be! They've got away – eventually – and if you offered me a hundred quid I wouldn't take that lot of screaming dervishes out for a Sunday afternoon walk, let alone endure them for two days and nights!' Beth advanced on me, arms outspread. 'You'll be Cassie,' she beamed, then, having introduced Danny, demanded to know if the sun was over the yardarm yet because she was in dire need of a G and T. A large one, she said, because it was probably the last she'd get before the do started tonight!

So when the Labrador that came snuffling up had had its water bowl filled and Danny, bless the dear man, had placed gin and tonics on handy little tables beside us, I said, with the airman in mind, of course, 'When do you expect everyone to start arriving – and do they all know the way here?'

Danny said of course they did and they all knew to arrive not one minute before seven or Beth would blow her top and how was my second novel coming along?

'No book talk, Dan!' Jeannie warned.

'But we don't often get a famous author at Deer's Leap. Come to think of it, apart from a long-haired youth that Jeannie once dragged in, we haven't had an author at all!'

'I'm not famous,' I said very earnestly. 'I'm what's known as a one-book author. I was lucky with the first one; Jeannie says it's only if the next one is any good that people will start taking notice of me.'

'People as in publishers,' Jeannie supplied. 'And they will! But no more book talk, either to Cassie or me. And isn't the weather just glorious? In summer there's nowhere to beat these parts.'

'Jeannie says you're thinking of moving on,' I ventured, not knowing what else to say and still feeling a mite stupid over the kissing gate.

'Sadly, yes.'

'But it's so beautiful, Beth. I don't know how you can leave it.'

'Come winter when we'll have to go it'll be just about bearable, but on days like this I feel lousy about it. Why don't you buy it with the loot from your next book, Cassie? It's fine if you don't have kids – or can afford boarding school fees.'

'I'll need to have at least three books behind me before I even begin to think of buying a little place of my own – let alone a house this size,' I laughed. 'But I'm going to dislike whoever buys it when you've gone.'

'Me, too,' Beth sighed, draining her glass. 'Now, have you unpacked, Cassie? No? Then as soon as you have you can help me with the vol-au-vents. They're resting in the fridge, ready to go in the oven. As soon as they're done, you can stick the fillings in for me. And did I hear you say you were doing the dips, Sis?'

'You didn't, but I think I'm about to. But let's get Cassie settled in, then we'll report for duty.' She gave me a long, slow wink. 'My sister's quite human, really, but at times like this she gets a bit bossy.'

I followed Jeannie up the narrow staircase that led off the kitchen, feeling distinctly light-headed – and it was nothing to do with the gin either. It was all to do with the lovely summer day, a peculiar kissing gate, a guest who seemed to be keeping out of the way until seven, and an old house that held me enchanted.

'I've got a feeling,' I said as I unlocked my case, 'that this is going to be one heck of a weekend!'

My green dress lay on the bed with the silk lilies; on the floor my flat, bronze kid sandals. Everything was ready. Food lay on the kitchen table, covered with tea towels, and the second-best glasses were polished and placed upside down on a table on the terrace. Danny had seen to the summer punch, then humped furniture and dotted ashtrays about the conservatory.

'It's great now that smoking is antisocial,' Beth had said as we'd filled the vol-au-vents. 'If anyone wants to light up there's only one place they can do it!'

'And the plants won't mind.' I'd dipped into my store of horticultural knowledge. 'The nicotine in the smoke actually kills certain greenhouse pests.'

'Really?' Beth had looked impressed, I thought now as I lay in the bath, the water brackish but soft as silk.

I lathered the baby soap I always use into a froth, stroking it down my legs, my arms, cupping my shoulders, sliding my fingertips over my breasts. I was in the mood for something to happen tonight. I didn't know what, but a little pulse beat behind my nose whenever I thought about it. Beth had invited eighteen guests and catered for thirty. Surely out of all that number there would be someone interesting.

But did I want that? Didn't I just want to flirt a little and forget Piers for the time being?

Deer's Leap got its name, Danny thought, because just above the paddock there was once a little brook and when deer and wolves roamed the area, the shallow curve was where the deer – and maybe predators – crossed. It made sense, I supposed. It was a pretty name and that was all that mattered.

I thought again about the awful person who would be living here next summer and wished it might be me, knowing it wouldn't be, couldn't be. So instead, I thought about my novel and whether the publishers would like it when it was finished, reminding myself that an author is only as good as her last novel, vowing to work extra hard when I got home to justify this weekend away.

I told myself that on the count of four I would get out of the bath, drape myself in a towel, then dry my hair – in that order – yet even as I stood at the open window, hairdryer poised, little wayward pulses of excitement at the prospect of the party still beat insistently inside me.

'Grow up, Cassandra!' I hissed. 'Nothing is going to happen tonight – nothing out of the ordinary, anyway! For Pete's sake, why should it?'

'Because you want it to!' came the ready answer.

Beth was testing the summer punch when I got downstairs, ten minutes before seven. She was dressed in layers of lace curtain and muslin and said that later she would put on her yashmak.

'I'm the Dance of the Seven Veils,' she grinned, explaining it was the best and coolest way to cover up her avoirdupois, which any day now she intended to do something about.

'Sorry about my two lilies,' I said, thinking I should have tried harder. 'I'm a lily of the field, actually . . .'

'You look all right to me!' Danny, in the costume of a Roman soldier, handed me a glass of punch. 'This get-up isn't too revealing, is it? It was all I could borrow from the amateur dramatics that fitted.'

'I think you look very manly.'

'You've got quite decent legs, Danny.' Jeannie, in a long robe borrowed from the same source and with a terracotta jug balanced on one bare shoulder, said she was a vestal virgin and the first one to make a snide remark was in for trouble!

Beth said she wasn't at all sure about the punch, and helped herself to another glass just as the first car arrived, followed closely by four more in convoy – sort of as if they'd all been waiting at the crossroads until seven.

The table with the upturned glasses began to fill up with assorted bottles; there were shouts of laughter and snorts of derision at the various costumes. Someone who was old enough to know better said I could come into his field any time I liked!

Danny put on a Clayderman tape and said there'd be music for smooching later, when everybody had had one or two. Jeannie put down her jug and floated around with trays of food. I followed behind with plates and folded paper serviettes, looking for a pilot with short fair hair by the name of John or Jack. He wasn't there.

'He wasn't there,' I said later when everyone had gone and we were sitting on the terrace, saying what a great party it had been. 'He didn't show . . .'

'Who didn't show?' Danny held a glass of red wine up to the light, saying it was a decent vintage and wondering who had brought it.

'The man I gave a lift to,' I said. 'He thanked me, then disappeared through the kissing gate.'

'When?' Danny took a sip from his glass, and then another.

'This morning, on my way here. He wanted a lift to Deer's Leap.'

'What was he like?' Beth was looking at me kind of peculiar.

'Tall. Fair. Young,' I shrugged. 'I remember wondering at the time if he could dance. His name was John, he said, though mostly people called him Jack.'

'He actually *spoke* to you?'

'Why shouldn't he, Beth? He looked so authentic that I asked him where he got the uniform from.' I slid my eyes from one to the other. They had put their glasses down and were still giving me peculiar looks. 'Listen – what's so strange about giving a man a lift?'

'In a country lane?' Jeannie blustered.

'Now see here,' I said, because something wasn't quite right – the expressions on their faces for one thing. 'I'm a big girl now. I can look after myself.'

'No one is saying you can't,' Beth soothed.

'Then are you trying to say I imagined it – that I was driving under the influence? For Pete's sake, I've just told you I spoke to the man!'

'Then you're the first one who has. Most people round these parts don't stop – quite the opposite. They get the hell out of it if they think they might have seen him.'

'So he *is* real? Other people have seen him?'

'We-e-ll, the hard-headed people around here wouldn't admit it if they had; don't want to be made a laughing stock. He's a ghost, you see, Cassie.'

'A *ghost*! You can't be serious! He was as real as you or me! Have *you* seen him, Beth?'

'Yes. I think I might have.'

There was an awful silence and I felt sorry for spoiling what had been a smashing party. But my mouth had gone dry and my heart was thumping because I knew Beth meant what she was saying.

'I see. And rather than be thought a nutter, you said nothing?'

'Yes – we-e-ll, I only told Danny. But the airman is dead.

That much I do know, Cassie, and he should be left alone to rest in peace!'

'But he obviously *isn't* at peace! You think if you ignore him he'll go away – is that it?'

'Are you a psychic?' Danny asked.

'I think I might be, but I don't dabble.'

'Then in that case you'd attract him, wouldn't you? All we know is that his name was John – or Jack – Hunter, and his plane crashed in 1944, about the time of the Normandy landings. The Parish Council put the names of the crew on the local war memorial. You probably passed it on your way here.'

'Go on . . .' I looked from him to Beth, and she nodded.

'Seems he was a Lancaster bomber pilot. There was an airfield near here once – that much we did find out – but people are reluctant to talk about it.'

'Then they shouldn't be! Can't they see he needs help?'

'You said you didn't dabble,' Jeannie said softly. 'Now isn't a good time to start. Leave it, Cassie.'

'I don't believe any of this!' My voice sounded strange. I felt strange. I really didn't believe they could be so offhand about it.

'Good. Then just keep telling yourself that and there'll be nothing to worry about, will there? No one wants a fuss,' Beth said gently. 'Imagine the tabloids getting hold of it! There'd be no peace around here for anybody!'

'It certainly seems there's to be no peace for Jack Hunter. What did he do?'

'Nobody seems to know. All I could find out was that he was close to a girl who once lived here.'

'And he's still looking for her,' I persisted. 'Then don't you think it's about time someone helped him to find her?'

'Cassie love!' Danny put an arm round my shoulders. 'Have a nightcap, uh? How is he to find her when nobody knows her name, or anything about her?'

'But that's ridiculous! There must be someone in the village who remembers who lived in this house during the war!'

'If there is, they haven't said. And the war was a long time ago. The girl might be dead, even . . .'

'And she'll no longer be a girl if she isn't,' Beth said coaxingly.

'OK. I'll accept that. But someone should find out and tell Jack Hunter, because he doesn't know he's dead. It happens, sometimes, when someone dies suddenly or violently. He's a lost soul, Beth!'

'And you mean you'd try to get on his wavelength again,' Jeannie said incredulously, 'if you could winkle out the girl he's still looking for?'

'I don't see why not.' By now I'd got a hold on my feelings. 'She'd be easy enough to trace without a lot of publicity. Have you ever thought to look at Deer's Leap's deeds? Whoever lived here in 1944 will show there.'

'We've never seen the deeds,' Danny said, offering me a glass of wine. 'We don't own this house, remember. And I know what it's like for you writers, Cassie.'

'What do you mean, *we* writers?' I accepted the glass to show there wasn't any ill feeling, then took a gulp from it. 'Surely you don't think I want to go sniffing around because I think it might make a good story? Book number three, is that it, Jeannie?'

'Not at all!' Now Jeannie was using her soothing voice. 'What Danny means is that he thinks writers are a bit imaginative, sort of.'

'We are, I suppose, though I wouldn't go playing around with someone's love life, even if it happened more than fifty years ago. But if you're prepared to admit that I saw something – or *someone* – and that I'm not going out of my tiny mind, then I'll take your advice and let it drop.'

'I think you saw him,' Beth said softly. 'We all do. But like you said, Cassie, he's a lost soul and there isn't a lot anyone can do about it.'

'You're right. Mind, I wouldn't want him exorcized,' I said hastily.

'He won't be, I'm sure of it, if we don't go stirring things.'

'Right, then.' I lifted my glass. 'Bless you for having me, both of you. It's been great. And if you have a wake before you leave, will you invite me, please, because I do so love this house?'

'What a great idea,' Beth laughed, her relief obvious. 'We'll have a goodbye party for Deer's Leap whilst the Christmas decorations are still up – if we aren't snowed up, that is!'

They'd believed I'd let it drop, I thought as I lay in bed that night, and I knew it was sneaky of me and deceitful because they were smashing people who had made me welcome and were prepared to ask me back at Christmas. But there was a young man looking for his girl and who needed my help. Besides which, I'd found him attractive; had wanted him to be at the party. OK – so he was in love with someone else, but I'd have given that girl at Deer's Leap a run for her money if I'd been around fifty years ago! And I knew, too, that I would never let Piers make love to me again.

'Sorry, Piers,' I whispered, feeling almost relieved.

And then I said a silent sorry to Danny and Beth, because I knew too that I would try to find Jack Hunter again, but secretly, so no one would know – especially Beth and Danny. How I'd go about it I hadn't a clue, but if the pilot really wanted to be in touch again, then I'd find a way.

Or *he* would!

Chapter Two

We left Deer's Leap at six the following evening; three cars, in convoy, sort of. Me to pick up the A59, Beth to take Jeannie to Preston station in an ancient Beetle that was worth a bomb, did she but know it, and Danny in the estate car to pick up the children and their gear down in Acton Carey.

I drove with Danny in front going far too fast for the narrow lane and Beth driving much too close behind. I knew what they were up to. I was being hustled into the village so that if the airman appeared again, I wouldn't be able to stop.

We got there without incident and Danny flagged us down. Then he and Beth and Jeannie gave me a hug and a kiss through my open window and said I really must visit over the Christmas break – if not before – and how lovely it had been to have me.

'Let me have a look at the book, uh, as soon as you can.' The holiday was over. Jeannie was wearing her editorial hat again. 'When you get to chapter ten, run me off a copy; I'd like to see how it's going.'

'Of course. Want to make sure I don't start mucking about with the storyline,' I grinned; 'introduce a good-looking ghost?'

'Now, Cassie,' she said quite sternly, 'I thought we'd forgotten all *that*. You said you'd keep shtoom about it.'

'And I will. Not a word to the parents when I get home. Promise.'

Mum and Dad didn't believe in ghosts anyway; only in things they could touch and see and smell – and in Dad's case, drink from a pint pot.

'That's all right, then,' Beth beamed. 'Mind how you go, Cassie. See you!'

Waving, I pulled out, yet before I'd gone a couple of miles I was planning how I could get to drive past that place again without Beth and Danny getting wind of it.

I concentrated on the winding, tree-lined road that dropped slowly down to Clitheroe, then rose sharply at the crossing of a river bridge. Not far away was Pendle Hill; somewhere not too distant was Downham. Witch country, without a doubt, with wild, lonely tracts of land where ghosts and witches could roam free; one ghost in particular, looking for a girl who once lived at Deer's Leap. A young man who didn't realize he was dead.

Jack Hunter. He had flown, I shouldn't wonder, from the airfield that was probably called RAF Acton Carey. The coming of bombers to that little village must have caused quite a stir, yet now all traces of the base had gone. Even the track that ran round the perimeter of the airfield had grassed over and could only be picked out, Danny said, in an exceptionally dry summer when the grass on it browned and died. You could trace the outline of it then, he said, and wonder about those too-young men who trundled their huge bombers around it before takeoff.

Jack had been one of them, though I'd thought it politic not to ask Danny specifically about him in view of what had happened. He'd looked about my age. I frowned. I couldn't imagine those nervous fingers grasping whatever it was they had to pull back to get that great, death-loaded plane into the air. Lancasters, they'd been. A Lancaster bomber and a Spitfire and a Hurricane flew over London during the Victory in Europe celebrations, fifty years on, yet Jack Hunter was still twenty-four.

A great choke of tears rose in my throat and in that moment I didn't care about broken promises, nor letting well alone nor even about snoopers from the tabloids upsetting the peace of Acton Carey if news of a World War Two ghost leaked out. As far as I was concerned it was, and would remain, between me and Jack Hunter and the girl it seemed he was looking for.

How I would go about it, where I would begin, I didn't know. But I liked doing research; could pretend I was setting my next novel in the countryside around Deer's Leap; might even be able to poke around there if the house stood too long empty and for sale after Beth and Danny had left.

Yet they weren't leaving for six months and I couldn't wait that long.

I noticed I was passing the Golf Balls at Menwith and decided to think about Jack Hunter tomorrow and concentrate instead on the roundabout ahead at which I would turn left to bypass Harrogate, a pretty run through Guy Fawkes country.

I indicated left, then closed my mind to everything save getting home before dark. Home to Greenleas Market Garden, Rowbeck. Safe and sound and ordinary.

Rowbeck is very small. Everyone knows everyone else and their parentage. We've been lucky, with only one weekender in the place. She's a teacher who intends living in the village when she retires, so she has been made welcome and the neighbourhood watch keeps an eye on her cottage when she isn't there.

Rowbeck is on the Plain of York where the earth is rich and black and bounteous. Distantly we can see the tops – the hills of Herriot country – where winters can be vicious and shepherds work hard to make a living.

There's a B road into Rowbeck, which runs round the green in a circular sweep, then out again by the same road; a sort of circumnavigation that takes all of forty seconds, driving slowly.

The only other way out of the village is by a narrow lane at the top end of the green by the church. That's where we live. Half a mile further on the lane becomes little more than a track, then peters out. Only the odd farm tractor passes. It's a nice place to live if you like the back of beyond – which I do.

Dad was doing the evening rounds of the glasshouses when I got back and putting down a saucer of food for the hedgehog that lives in the garden and eats slugs and is worth its weight in gold. Mum said did I want a cup of tea and could I unpack tonight and put out my dirty washing? Mum always washes on Mondays and bakes on Fridays, no matter what. She runs the house like clockwork, with a place for everything and everything in its place. It's because her star sign is Virgo and she can't help it. She's inclined to cuddly plumpness and hasn't a wrinkle on her face.

Dad came in and remarked that the first of the early spray chrysanths should be ready for cutting in about a week, though we could do with a drop of rain. Only when Mum had poured and we were sitting at the kitchen table did he ask if I'd had a nice weekend.

'Dad! That house is just beautiful! I'd kill for it!'

'Out of the way is it, like this place?'

'Greenleas is secluded; Deer's Leap is isolated. They get snowed up in winter, but in summer it's magic. You can look out into forever from the upstairs windows. I've never seen such a view. It's in the Trough of Bowland.'

Dad said he'd never heard of it and I said I wasn't surprised; that it was as if the people who lived there had conspired through the ages to keep it a secret and out of the reach of incomers. Foreigners, I meant, as in Yorkshire folk and people from further north. 'You look over to Beacon Fell and Parlick Pike and Fair Oak Fell and it isn't far from witch country.'

'There's no such thing as witches.' Mum pushed a plate of parkin in my direction.

'I know that, but it's so beautiful; sort of breathtaking. Jeannie's sister is leaving there at the end of the year. It would break my heart if it were me.'

'Seems as if it's made an impression on you. You haven't gone over to the Lancastrians, have you?'

Dad looked a bit put out. The Wars of the Roses may be long over, but in Lancashire and Yorkshire they still keep the feud going, if only over The Cricket.

'Of course I haven't, but I'd love to go there again, just for another look. Beth – that's Jeannie's sister – has invited me for a goodbye party, sort of. Christmas in a house like that would be wonderful.'

'So what's this precious Deer's Leap like, then?' Mum sounded a bit piqued because I was making such a fuss over a house I mightn't even see again and because, I suppose, I could even consider spending Christmas anywhere else but Greenleas.

'We-e-ll, it's stone, and tile-roofed. One end of it has a gable end that's V-shaped and it has three rooms and an attic in it. The middle bit has a huge sitting room, with a terrace outside, and two bedrooms. Then there's an end bit with a big kitchen and dairy and pantry, and a narrow little staircase off it to three rooms above. I suppose the workers slept up there when it was a farm and they wouldn't have been allowed to use the main staircase. The windows are stone-mullioned, and all shapes and sizes. From the front it looks as if it's still in the sixteenth century, though it's been tarted up at the back. It's a smaller version of Roughlee Hall, Danny says.'

'Never heard of that place, either,' Dad shrugged.

'Of course you have! Surely you've heard of the Pendle Witches. Alice Nutter lived at Roughlee. She was a gentle-woman and how she got mixed up in witchcraft, nobody seems to know. She was hanged on Lancaster Moor in 1612.'

'And you believe such nonsense?' Mum clucked. 'All that stuff is a fairy tale, like Robin Hood.'

'They don't seem to think so around those parts.'

'If they believe that, they'll believe anything!' Mum had the last word on witches. 'And I forgot – Piers rang.'

'What about?'

'He didn't say and I didn't ask!'

'Well, he'll ring again, if it's important.'

'Aren't you going to call him back?'

'Don't think so.' As from this weekend, I'd stopped jumping when Piers snapped his fingers.

Mum put mugs and plates on a tray, wearing her button mouth. She placed great hopes on Piers. He was Yorkshire-born, which was a mark in his favour, and even if he had defected to parts south of the River Trent and was earning a living amongst Londoners, she considered it high time we were married.

'Think I'll go and unpack. Then I'll write to thank Beth. By the way, she was really pleased with the flowers.'

'So she should be! Your dad grew them!'

'Won't be long,' I smiled. Long enough, though, to let Mum get over whatever wasn't pleasing her.

I hung the green dress on a hanger, then wondered what to do with the two silk arum lilies, because even to say the words 'artificial flowers' is blasphemy in our house. So I stuck them in a drawer because they were a part of the weekend, and I couldn't bear to throw them away.

I sat back on my heels. To open my case was to let out Deer's Leap and Jack Hunter and the promise I'd made to Beth and Jeannie to forget him. Yet I couldn't, because somehow he was a part of that house; was connected to Deer's Leap in some way, and I had to know how.

Common sense told me to leave it, that ghosts didn't exist. But Beth had half admitted that maybe they did in the very real, very solid form of a World War Two pilot whose plane had crashed more than fifty years ago. A very attractive man and Piers's exact opposite.

Piers. I hoped he wouldn't ring tonight when the spell of Deer's Leap was still on me. Just to hear him say 'Cassandra?' very throatily – he rarely calls me Cassie – would intrude on the magic. For bewitched I was, with the enchantment wrapping me round like a thread of gossamer that couldn't be broken. One gentle tug on that thread would pull me back there whether I wanted to go or not.

And I wanted to go.

By Monday morning I'd sorted out my priorities. All thoughts of the weekend were banned until after I switched off my word processor. I have to set myself targets. The contract said that Harrier Books wanted the manuscript by the end of December, so it couldn't be delivered any later than the first week in January, even allowing for the New Year holiday.

I write in my bedroom. There's a deep alcove in one corner that is big enough to accommodate my desk. My latest extravagance was to hang a curtain over it so that when I'd finished for the day I could pull it across and shut out my work. What I couldn't see, I figured, I couldn't worry about. The curtain has proved to be a good idea.

I had just finished reading last Friday's work and got my mind into gear, when the extension phone on my desk rang. It would, of course, be Jeannie. People had got the message now that up until four in the afternoon it was best not to ring. Only my editor was allowed to disturb my thoughts.

'Hi!' I said brightly. 'You made it home OK, then?'

'Cassandra?' a voice said throatily.

'Piers! Why are you ringing at this time?'

'Do I need a chit from the Holy Ghost to ring my girl?'

'I – I – Well, what I mean is that it's the expensive time. You usually ring after six . . .' I closed my eyes, sucked in my breath and warned myself to watch it.

'I rang yesterday. Didn't your mother tell you?'

'Of course she did.' My voice was sharper than I intended.

'You didn't ring me back.'

'I was late getting home – the traffic. I was tired . . .' I tell lies too, Piers.

'So how did the weekend go?' It seemed I was forgiven.

'It was nice.'

'Only nice, Cassandra?'

'Very nice. Jeannie's family are lovely, though I didn't meet the children,' I babbled. 'They were away at camp and –'

'You sound guilty. Did you have an extraordinarily nice time?'

'Piers! I'm not feeling guilty because I have nothing to feel guilty about! If I sound a bit befuddled it's because I had a whole paragraph in my head and now it's gone!'

'You'll have to think it out again then, won't you?'

'It isn't that easy! Once it's gone you never get it back again – not as good, anyway.'

'Oh dear! I'll ring again tonight if you tell me you love me.'

'Why should I, at ten o'clock in the morning?'

'Cassandra – what's the matter?' The smooth talking was over. He actually sounded curious.

'Nothing's the matter. I'm working, that's all. If I were a typist in an office I probably wouldn't be allowed private calls and I certainly couldn't yell that I loved you over the phone for everyone to hear!'

'You don't yell it. "I love you" has to be said softly . . .'

'Yes, and secretly for preference.'

'Then say it softly and secretly from your bedroom.'

'*Piers* . . .' I said in my this-is-your-last-warning voice. 'I am busy!'

'OK! Pax, darling. I'll ring tonight! Get on with your scribbling.'

I sat back, part of my make-believe world once more, reading from the screen, searching my mind for the lost paragraph.

But it didn't come. All I could think was that for once, in all the four years of our on and off affair, I'd challenged Piers and almost won!

*　　*　　*

'Pop out and get me a few tomatoes, there's a good girl. And tell your dad it'll be on the table in five minutes!'

Once I got back in my stride, and sorted the wayward paragraph, the words had come well; it was going to be a word-flow day, I'd known it. I'd just come to the end of a page when my stomach told me it was lunchtime and my mind told me it needed a break.

I saw Dad at the end of the garden, so I waved and yelled, 'Five minutes!' then went into the tomato house, sniffing in the green growing smell, loving the moistness of it and the lush, tall plants heavy with red trusses. A few tomatoes, at our house, meant a bowlful and not half a pound in a plastic bag. I bit into one, marvelling that half the country didn't know what a fresh tomato was.

I felt very relaxed. Once I'd got into my stride again, nothing intruded on the make-believe world at my fingertips. I had forgiven Piers, I realized, for ringing when he shouldn't have done and I had not thought once about the kissing gate through which a World War Two pilot had disappeared.

Now my thoughts were free to roam again, my self-discipline on hold, and I wondered how I should go about finding the name of the family who lived at Deer's Leap before the Air Force took it and they had to find somewhere else to live.

They might have moved to Acton Carey or further afield. They may even, since losing their acres under a runway of concrete and seeing their trees felled and hedges ripped out, have given up farming in disgust.

It was best I began the search in Acton Carey, but this would be risky, as Danny or Beth would be bound to hear of me doing it. I could not, I realized, visit locally without calling on them and if Lancashire villages were like Yorkshire villages, they would soon discover that a red-haired foreigner had been asking questions in the pub. Villagers close ranks at such times, and mention of anything remotely concerned with the ghost they wanted to sweep under the mat would be sidestepped at once! I would be taken for a journalist, no doubt, and that would be the end of that.

Of course, I could drive past the spot as near to the same time as possible, and I told myself I was a fool for not knowing when it had been. Yet had I known something so weird and wonderful was going to happen, I'd have noted the time exactly and had my tape recorder at the ready! But just a glimpse of a furtive redhead in a bright red Mini on that lonely lane would be worthy of note. I knew how it was at Greenleas if a strange car – obviously lost – drove past.

'I said dinner in five minutes! What are you doing, Cassie?' Mum stood in the doorway, flush-cheeked. 'Composing another chapter?'

I said I was sorry, and pushed the remainder of the tomato into my mouth so I couldn't talk. Composition was the furthest thing from my mind, so I was glad it's bad manners to speak with your mouth full. That way, I couldn't tell any lies.

'Good job it's only cold cut and salad,' Mum grumbled, 'or it would be spoiled by now.'

Monday, being washday, it was always leftovers from Sunday dinner, because that was the way it had been for the twenty-five years of my parents' marriage. It was one of the things I loved especially about Mum – the way nothing changed.

A flood of affection touched me from head to toes and I put my arm round her and said, 'The sky would fall, Mum, if it wasn't – cold cut and salad, I mean!'

She threw me an old-fashioned look, which turned into an answering smile, then said, 'Did I hear you on the phone, this morning?'

'Yes. Piers.'

'And what did he have to say?' She chose to ignore my brevity.

'Not a lot. He didn't get the chance. I tore him off a strip for ringing during working hours.'

'Then you shouldn't have! You're never going to get a husband, Cassie, if you carry on like that. Men don't like career women!'

'Men are going to have to put up with it till I've done my third novel. One swallow doesn't make a summer, Mum, nor two! Anyway, I sometimes think me and Piers aren't cut out for one another.'

'Oh?' Mum's jaw dropped visibly, which was understandable since to her way of thinking I was as good as off the shelf. 'Then all I can say, miss, is that it won't end at a third book. You'll want to be famous, and before you know it you'll have left it too late! I think Piers is very nice indeed, if you want my opinion.'

'Mum!' I stopped, put my hands on her shoulders and turned her to face me. 'I like Piers – very much. And yes, I know you watched him grow up, more or less, and he's considered a good catch around these parts.'

'He went to university!' Mum said huffily.

'Yes, and he's doing well. But he hasn't asked me to marry him, yet.'

'He *hasn't*?'

'No. And if he did, I wouldn't know what to say. Maybe I ought to have gone to live with him in London like he wanted, but I didn't fancy being an unpaid servant and a mistress to boot!'

'A *mistress*, Cassie! Then I'm glad you told him no! Clever of you, that was. Men never run after a bus once they've caught it!'

'I know. I didn't come down with the last fall of snow!' We were getting on dangerous ground, especially about the mistress bit. 'But I want to be married, I promise you.'

'Your dad would like a grandson, you know.'

'I'm sure he would. I want children, too, and after book three I shall think very seriously about getting married.'

'To Piers?'

'Probably to the first man who asks me, Mum!'

With that she seemed happy and we walked in silent contentment to the back door where Dad was washing his hands in the water butt.

'Now then, our lass!' He gave Mum a smack on her bottom and she went very red and told him to stop carrying on in the middle of the day.

It stopped her thinking about her unmarried daughter, for all that, and the grandchildren she was desperate to have about the place. I gave her a conspiratorial wink, and peace reigned at Greenleas.

Jeannie phoned just as I'd pulled the curtain across my workspace, pleased with a fair day's work.

'Hi! How's it going, then?'

'Great!' *It* could only refer to the current novel. 'I must spend the weekend partying more often!'

'Well, Beth meant it when she asked you up there for Christmas. I think she quite took to you!'

'I'd love to go, Jeannie. I keep thinking about Deer's Leap and being sad for Beth that she's got to leave.'

'She doesn't *have* to, but it's best all round they don't ask for the lease to be renewed. The twins will start senior school in September. A good state school will be high on her list of priorities. Boarding in winter costs a lot of dosh, you know.'

I said I was sure it must.

'Meantime, Cassie, you might get to stay there again in exchange for baby-sitting the place. Beth and Danny have hired a caravan in Cornwall for a few weeks in the summer. It'll be the first decent holiday they've had in years. Beth's a bit worried about leaving the house, though. She wouldn't want to come back and find squatters in it.'

'Yes, and there's the dog and the cats to think about, I suppose.'

'Kennels and catteries cost money, I agree. So would you baby-sit the house, Cassie? Wouldn't you be a bit afraid on your own?'

34

'You mean you're really offering?' I gasped.

'You'd get a lot of work done, that's for sure, with nothing and no one to distract you. With luck you could do a fair bit of wordage.'

'I don't think I would be afraid – especially with a dog there, but why didn't Beth say anything about it at the weekend?'

'Because I've only just thought about it. Are you really interested, Cas? I could come and join you, weekends. Shall I mention it to Beth?'

'She might think me pushy. And what if she doesn't like the idea of a stranger in her home?'

'You aren't a stranger. I told you, she likes you.'

I wondered – just for a second – what Mum would make of the idea.

'We-e-ll, if Beth agrees . . .' I said.

'She'll agree. She's sure to worry about the animals and the houseplants, and we could cut the grass between us. I might be able to fix it so I could stay over until Mondays – get some reading done in peace and quiet.'

'Mm . . .' Jeannie has to read a lot of manuscripts.

'Well then?'

'If you're sure, Jeannie?'

'I can but ask. I bet they'll both jump at the chance. It would have to be unpaid, of course.'

My heart had started to thump again, just to think of a whole month there. Deer's Leap in the summer. I could write and write and only stop when I was hungry.

'OK, then. I'm game . . .'

I thought, as I put the phone down, that I was stark, raving mad. For one thing, Mum and Dad wouldn't like the idea and for another, it wasn't very bright of me to go there. Not because I'd be afraid on my own – Deer's Leap would take good care of me – but because I'd be heading straight into trouble. For the past two days I'd been looking for an excuse to get back there without Beth or Danny knowing; to drive down the long lane that led to their house and hope to find the airman again, thumbing a lift. Yet now it seemed it could be handed to me on a plate. I could drive up and down the lane as often as I wanted; could open the kissing gate and find where the path led – and to whom. I could even do a bit of gentle nosing in the village, because once they knew I was living at Deer's Leap they'd treat me like Beth and Danny and the twins – one of themselves.

The thumping was getting worse and a persistent little pulse behind my nose had joined in. I knew if I had one iota of sense I should be praying that Beth wouldn't want me there.

Yet I knew I would go back, because Deer's Leap had me hogtied and besides, there was a pilot who needed my help – not only to find his girl but to be gently told he was a name on a war memorial.

Then the phone rang again and I knew it was Piers.

Oh, damn, damn, *damn*!

Chapter Three

Piers was quite loving on the phone. Not *very* loving – that isn't his style. Piers prefers a hands-on, eyes smouldering approach, which doesn't come over too well on a telephone. But he was very nice, asking if I'd had a good day workwise, and when was he to be allowed to come up and see me – since it didn't seem I was in all that much of a hurry to go and see him!

Then he said that of course he understood that I was a working woman and must be given my own space. He didn't mean one word of it – I can tell when he's talking tongue in cheek – but at least he'd got this morning's message.

'You do want to see me, Cassandra?' he persisted. 'I've got a few days owing; could pop up north any time next month.'

I said of course I wanted to see him and that next month would be fine; by then I'd have finished chapter ten and sent off a copy to Jeannie, I added, and probably caught up with myself. I was a little behind schedule, he'd understand, on the deadline date.

I would also, with a bit of luck, have removed myself to Deer's Leap, and out of his reach. It wasn't that I was being devious or two-faced, I was merely keeping one jump ahead of him, and if I had to tell a few lies it wasn't entirely my fault since Piers is a chauvinist. He always has been, come to think of it. Looking back, the signs were there even when he was at the spotty stage, long before he went to university.

'I can tell your mind is miles away, so tell me you love me and I'll leave you in peace,' he said, throatily indulgent.

'You know I do,' I hedged, putting the phone down gently,

marvelling that twice in one day I'd had the last word. Then I forgot him completely because of far more importance was telling Mum that I might be about to baby-sit a house in the back of beyond, and didn't she agree it was a smashing idea?

Mum didn't think it was a good idea at all.

'You said that house is isolated, Cassie! How can you even begin to think of spending a month there alone?'

'For one thing, I'd have no interruptions and –'

'You can say that again, miss! And you could be lying dead in a pool of blood and no one any the wiser!'

'Mother!' I always seem to call her that when she lays it on a bit thick. 'Of course I couldn't! I can look after myself!'

'Famous last words!' Her cheeks had gone very red.

'Mum! Please listen? I *want* to go to Deer's Leap. I love the place, but if you want a better reason, then I need time alone. This book I'm on with now is the important one, and I want it to be better than *Ice Maiden*. I'd have a whole month to myself. I could even get the first draft finished and after that, editing it would be a doddle!'

'And you're sure you wouldn't be nervous, alone?'

'No, Mum! Of course not! And Jeannie will almost certainly be there at weekends; from Friday evening to Monday afternoon, actually. That gives me almost four days to write like mad and I'd be safer at Deer's Leap on my own than I would in the middle of Leeds or Liverpool – or *London*! Mum – you know it makes sense. And you could ring me and I'd ring you . . .'

'We-e-ll – I'll have to see what your dad has to say about it . . .'

She was weakening, so I didn't say another word.

After that I hovered over the downstairs phone, then over the phone on my desk, willing either to ring, willing it to be Jeannie. I was so exhausted willing and hovering that when it finally shifted itself I stood mesmerized, looking at it.

'Jeannie?' I whispered.

'How did you know it was me?'

'Have you spoken to Beth?' I begged the question. 'What did she say?'

'She's quite taken with the idea. They both are – with reservations, of course.'

'Like what?'

'She's a bit anxious about you being nervous, but I told her you wouldn't be.'

'Is Beth nervous alone there during the day?'

'No, of course not.'

'There you are then. Is it on, Jeannie?'

'If you're sure – then yes, it is. I'm looking forward to a few weekends there.'

'It's going to be quite a thrash, all the way from London. Will you drive up?'

'No way. I'll get the train, then I can work. Lord only knows how much reading I've got to do. Could you pick me up at Preston station?'

'No problem.' The thudding had started again, and the little fluttery pulse behind my nose. 'It's going to be wonderful. I'll be able to get loads of work done too. As it is, I aim to send you the first ten chapters before I see you.'

'Fine. Beth will be getting in touch later. I gave her your phone number. She said it might be a good idea if you were to arrive the day before they go – get to know the geography of the place.'

'Like . . . ?'

'Oh, when the bread van calls and the egg lady. And they've got a water softener. You'll have to know about that. No problem at all, but it recharges itself so she'll explain about the gurgling noises you might hear every fourth night in the small hours. Sure you're still keen, Cassie? If you've changed your mind, now's the time to say so.'

'I want to go. Deer's Leap is magic. I'll be there!'

*　　*　　*

'That was Jeannie,' I said to Mum, who was expecting to be told. 'Beth and Danny are pleased about my going. And I forgot to tell you, the bread van calls, and the egg lady.'

I thought it best not to mention that I already knew that Beth left notes and money for them in a large, lidded box at the end of the dirt road near the crossroads.

'Hm.' Mum was getting used to the idea, I could tell. 'I've never met your Miss McFadden, except on the phone.'

'Then you should. Why don't you and Dad drive up there one Sunday? Surely you can leave the place for a day? Jeannie would love to meet you both.'

Holidays together for market gardeners and their spouses are few and far between. It's like being a dairy farmer, I suppose: a seven-days-a-week job.

'Hm,' she said again, obviously liking the idea. 'When will you be going?'

'Not for a couple of weeks. Beth is really looking forward to a break. They haven't had a proper holiday for ages, Jeannie said.'

'I know exactly how she feels,' Mum said fervently.

'Then a day out would be good for you both. Just pick your time and arrive when you feel like it – preferably when Jeannie's there.'

I wasn't being devious, getting Mum interested and on my side. As soon as she saw the house she would love it every bit as much as I did and see for herself how safe and snug it was.

'I just might take you up on that,' she said, filling the kettle.

That was when I had my first big panic. What if, in the entire month I was there, I didn't see Jack Hunter? What if he only appeared once a year? His bomber had crashed not long after the Normandy landings; probably about the time I'd seen him.

The panic was gone as quickly as it came, because I knew

he would be there. He and I were on the same wavelength, and he had something to tell me.

The birds awoke me at five on the morning of my departure. I focused my eyes on the bright blur behind the curtains, then yawned, stretched and snuggled under the quilt again to think about – oh, *everything*! About my route; where I would stop to eat my sandwiches; about leaving the A59 and driving to Acton Carey on B roads, so I could dawdle and look around me and think about the four weeks ahead.

I had no plan in my mind about discovering who lived at Deer's Leap before the Air Force took it in the war. Nor had I the faintest idea how I would set about finding where they had gone when their home and land were requisitioned without the right of appeal.

Things would work out in their own good time. It stood to reason I'd been meant to drive along a narrow road one summer morning because a lost soul wanted a lift to Deer's Leap. Thoughts of the supernatural didn't worry me at all. I knew no fear except that perhaps Jack Hunter would not be able to tell me what I wanted to know.

How deeply, despairingly had he and his girl loved? Very deeply, my mind supplied, or why should the need of her, fifty years on, be the cause of such unrest? Perhaps they had not said a proper goodbye and her heartbreak had been terrible when she knew she would never see him again. All at once I was glad I had not lived during those times, nor known the fear that each kiss might be the last between me and –

Between me and whom? Not Piers, that was certain. If Piers were to walk out of my life tomorrow I was as sure as I could be that only my pride would be hurt. He and I did not, nor ever would, love like that long-ago couple. I didn't even know her name, yet I was sure of the passion between them. Their lives had become a part of me, and until I could discover what caused such devotion from beyond the grave,

I would never be free – if I wanted to be free, that was . . .

I sighed, and leaned over to pull back a curtain. The early morning was bright, but not too bright. Mornings too brilliant too early are weather breeders. I pushed aside the quilt, and swung my feet to the floor. Best I get up. The sooner I did, the sooner it could all begin.

By the time I got to the clump of oak trees at the start of the final mile, my mouth had gone dry. The day was warm and sunny and I drove with the windows down. My hair was all over the place, but my short, bitty style can be tamed with a few flicks of my fingers.

I could feel my cheeks burning, whether from the heat, or driving, or from the triumph that sang through me, I didn't know. Perhaps it was a bit of all three, with a dash of anticipation thrown in.

I slowed as I neared the place, coughing nervously. I was almost there; about a hundred yards to go. I remembered that first time taking my eyes off the road for a second, then looking up to see the airman there.

I glanced to my right, then gazed ahead. He wasn't there and soon I would have driven past the place. I looked at my watch. I had timed my journey so as to be in the same spot at what I thought was about the same time. I'd gone over and over the previous journey in my mind and decided that the encounter had happened a few minutes before eleven o'clock.

The time now was ten fifty-six and I had passed the place without seeing him or sensing that he was around. He wasn't coming; not today, that was. People like him, I supposed, couldn't materialize to order, but even so, I looked in the rear-view mirror, then in the overtaking mirror, to be sure he wasn't behind me.

But he *would* come. Sooner or later he would appear, I knew it. If I really was psychic, then the vibes I'd been sending out for the past fifteen minutes would have got to him good and strong. I would have to be patient. Didn't I have plenty more days? I smiled, pressed my foot down, and made for the crossroads and the dirt road off it. This time, the road ahead was clear of sheep.

I slowed instinctively when I came to the dirt road, glancing ahead for a first view of Deer's Leap. When I got to the kissing gate I almost stopped, noting as I passed it that its black paint shone brightly.

'She's here!'

Beth's children were waiting at the white-painted gate. Hamish and Elspeth were exactly as Jeannie had described them.

'Hi!' I called. 'Been waiting long?'

'Hours,' Hamish said.

'About fifteen minutes,' his twin corrected primly.

'Have you met Hector, Miss Johns?' The Labrador lolloped up, barking furiously.

'Cassie! And yes, I have – the weekend you two were at camp.'

I'd seen little of the dog, actually; he'd been shut in an outhouse because of his dislike of strange men.

I got out of the car and squatted so Hector and I were at eye level, then held out my left hand. He sniffed it, licked, then allowed me to pat his head.

'He likes you,' Elspeth said. 'We'll help you with your things.'

I smiled at her. She was a half-pint edition of Jeannie, not her mother. Hamish was fair and blue-eyed, like Danny.

'Beth's in the bath.' Danny arrived to give me a smacking kiss, then heaved my big case from the boot.

Carefully I manoeuvred my word processor from the back seat, handing the keyboard to Hamish. His sister took my grip and soapbag; I carried the monitor.

'How on earth did you get all this in *that*?' Danny looked disbelievingly at my little red car. 'Looks as if you've come prepared for business.'

'I shall write and write and write,' I said without so much as a blush.

Beth arrived in a bathrobe with a towel round her hair. Her smile was broad, her arms wide. I love the way she makes people welcome.

It felt as if I had just come home.

When they left, waving and tooting at seven next morning, I watched them out of sight then carefully closed the white gate, turning to look at Deer's Leap and the beautiful garden. It was a defiant glare of colour: vivid red poppies; delphiniums of all shades of blue; lavender with swelling flower buds and climbs of every kind of rose under the sun. They covered arches and walls, rioted up the trunks of trees and tangled with honeysuckle. In the exact centre, in a circular bed, was the herb garden; a pear tree leaned on the wall of the V-shaped gable end.

Uneven paths wound into dead ends; there were no straight lines anywhere. The garden, for all I knew, had changed little since witches cast spells hereabouts, and Old Chattox, Demdike and Mistress Nutter fell foul of the witch-hunter.

For a couple of foolish minutes I pretended that everything between the white gate and the stone wall at the top of the paddock belonged to me. I began rearranging Beth's furniture, deciding which of the bedrooms would be my workroom when I had become famous and a servile bank manager offered me a huge mortgage on the place. Hector lay at my feet; Tommy, the ugliest of cat you ever did see, rubbed himself against my leg, purring loudly. Lotus, a snooty Persian, pinked up the path to indicate it was high time they were all fed. I felt a surge of utter love for the place, followed by one of abysmal despair. I wished I had never seen Deer's Leap; was grateful beyond measure that for four weeks it was mine.

'All right, you lot!' I said to the animals, determined not to start talking to myself. First I would feed them, and then myself. Then I would make my bed and wash the dishes I had insisted Beth leave on the draining board. After that, I would start work.

The kitchen table was huge and I planned to set up my word processor at one end of it. I had decided to live and work in the kitchen and only when I had done a decent day's work would I allow myself the reward of the sitting room, or of watching a wild sunset from the terrace outside it – with a glass of sherry at my side.

I smiled tremulously at Deer's Leap and it smiled back with every one of its windows. Already the sky was high and near cloudless, and the early sun cast long shadows. I thought of Beth, and wondered if they had reached the M6 yet. Then I thought of Jeannie.

My route to Preston station had been painstakingly illustrated by Danny so I could find my way there without bother to meet her train at nine tonight. I felt a contentment that even my Yorkshire common sense couldn't dispel. I had even decided not to drive down the lane to The Place, near the clump of oaks; that I wouldn't hassle Jack Hunter nor feel disappointment if he didn't turn up – or was it materialize? Today would be given to settling in, settling down and getting used to being mistress of Deer's Leap.

Tomorrow, if I could, I would find an excuse to drive into Acton Carey *alone*. I am a writer, so surely between now and then I could come up with a believable excuse. After all, the pilot and I had met on a Saturday, so it was worth a try.

I sighed blissfully. I would potter until ten, when I would start work. Not until four o'clock would I prepare the salad to eat with the home-cooked ham Beth had left for us. Only then would I make myself presentable and meet Jeannie's train. I felt so lucky, so utterly contented, that I wondered when the skies would open and jealous gods hurl down anger against me.

I crossed my fingers, whistled, then rummaged in a drawer for the tin opener. First the cats; then Hector's biscuits and water as set out on the list on the kitchen windowsill. It was all so lovely and unreal that I wanted to laugh out loud.

'That's enough, Cassandra!' I said in my mother's it'll-end-in-tears-before-bedtime-if-you-get-too-excited voice. 'Just take every hour as it comes – then sit back and let things happen!

And happen they would, if I had anything to do with it!

Jeannie's train arrived on time.

'Hi!' she said. 'Good of you to pick me up.'

'No bother. I like meeting trains.' I do, actually. 'Good to see you.'

'How's everything going? Got settled in?'

'All set up and working. I've had a good day. Did you eat on the train?'

'No, and I'm famished.'

'Well, there's ham salad and crusty bread and some rather special ice cream for pudding. There's a bottle of white wine on the slate slab in the dairy, too.'

'I'm ready for this weekend.' Jeannie shoved her grip on the back seat of the car. 'It's been a swine this week at work. Nothing but meetings and interruptions and a pile of manuscripts a mile high to be seen to. I've brought a couple with me.'

'You're not spending your time reading!'

'No. I can usually tell if a book is going to be any good by the end of the third chapter. Now, first of all I must tell you how pleased I am with the chapters you sent me. You're on to a winner if the rest of the book is as good. You seem to be writing with more confidence.'

'I am. It's going well and I've covered quite a bit of wordage today. Beth's kitchen is a lovely place to work in. They got away all right this morning. Beth says she needs a holiday to help set her up for the bother ahead.'

'You mean leaving Deer's Leap and finding another house.'

'Mm. She tells me she'll be thinking, once she's left, about

46

the woman who'll be cooking in her kitchen and cutting flowers from her garden and –'

'And shovelling six feet of snow from *her* back door to the wood shed! Have you been behaving yourself, Cassie?'

'Of course I have! I'm well out of temptation's way there.'

'Not *that* kind of trouble! You know what I mean. No ghost hunting, or anything?'

'Positively not!' I met her eyes briefly and was glad to be able to tell the truth. 'What really interests me, though, is the family who lived at Beth's place in the war and got emptied out by the RAF. I'd have been spitting feathers if they'd done it to me.'

'Me too. But I believe it was different then. There was a war on, so no one made too much fuss. It wouldn't have been patriotic to complain. I remember talking to Bill Jarvis – lives in the village – once about the war. You wouldn't believe what people put up with, according to him.'

'Probably he was romancing a bit,' I said carefully. 'He'll be getting on a bit now?'

'Told me he's nearer eighty than seventy, but he's as bright as a button for all that.'

'And he's always lived in Acton Carey?' Again the casual approach.

'In the Glebe Cottages, by the church. I once spent an interesting couple of hours with him. He opens up after a few pints.'

'Ale-talk,' I said, making a note that Bill Jarvis lived near the church and liked his beer. 'Not far to go now. Think I'm hungry too. I'm going to enjoy this weekend, y'know. Will you be able to make it next week?'

'I most certainly will! Get some decent air into my lungs and a bit of peace and quiet. Don't wake me in the morning, there's a good girl – not even with a cup of tea.'

I said I wouldn't, then concentrated on the road ahead – both sides of it – because we had just passed the clump of oaks.

We reached Deer's Leap, though, without incident or encounter, and I can't say I was all that disappointed. Already I had pinned my hopes on tomorrow, if I could get out alone.

'Why don't you sleep in, tomorrow morning?' I said, sort of offhand. 'I'm going down to the village anyway. There's a post office I hope?'

'Yes. Next door but one to the pub. What do you want with a post office?'

'Phone cards,' I said promptly. 'I'm not using Beth's phone to ring home. Is there a phone box, too?'

'Outside the post office.'

'Fine.' I didn't press the point. 'Be a love and open the gate, will you?'

I felt very pleased with myself. I'd hit on an alibi for tomorrow morning and discovered a World War Two veteran ready and able to talk. Or he would be, once I'd established I was from Deer's Leap and had bought him a pint!

We sat on the terrace long after the sun had gone down, me with a glass of sherry beside me, Jeannie with a gin and tonic. We had piled the dishes in the sink and left them. Evenings such as this were not to be wasted on things banal. It was almost dark, but still warm. A softly shaded lamp in the room behind us lit us rosily as distant outlines had blurred and turned from purple to deepest grey.

Somewhere below us, the headlights of a car briefly lit trees as it passed them. Someone was making for the village, I supposed, which was a scatter of pinprick lights far over to our left.

The birds had stopped singing. Tommy's loud purring was almost hypnotic; Hector snuffled and yawned. He was lying across my feet and to shift him would be to break the spell. Lotus, a night owl, had long ago disappeared over the paddock wall.

'If there's a heaven, Jeannie,' I said softly, 'I want it to be like this.'

'Mm.' She tilted her glass, draining it. 'Look – I'm feeling cold, all of a sudden. Tired, I suppose. Would you mind if I shoved off to bed?'

'Of course not.' I got to my feet and the dog awoke with a surprised snuffle. 'I'll see to the animals and do the rounds of the house.'

'Bless you. Night, love.' She kissed my cheek, then patted the dog. 'D'you know, I haven't unpacked, yet . . . ?'

'Tomorrow is another day. And I won't wake you in the morning – when I go to the village, I mean.'

'Don't dare!'

She climbed the stairs slowly, followed by Tommy, who had already, I supposed, decided to spend the night on her bed.

Beth had found him at the side of the lane with a bleeding paw and fed him. By the time it was healed, he had purred his way into the family's affections. He followed people around, grateful for his new, cushy lifestyle. Jeannie's bedroom door closed with a thud and I wondered if the animal had managed to slip in behind her.

Reluctantly I locked and bolted the French windows and removed the key. I'd already decided to wash the supper things because I didn't want to go to bed yet. Even washing up here was a joy. I squirted liquid into the bowl and idly swished it into suds.

I was happy; indecently happy. It was as if I was establishing a rapport with the house so it would stay unoccupied until I could afford it.

'Grow up, Cassie!' Until fishes flew and forests walked again! In my dreams! I would never get Deer's Leap. Some rich bitch would snap it up as a summer retreat. All at once I was glad I was a bit psychic and wondered if people like me could ill-wish. An awful sadness washed me from nose to toes and I wished that I'd never seen the place. I wanted

49

to weep with frustration, then thought about tomorrow instead.

And about the airman.

Chapter Four

The post office at Acton Carey was well stocked and I bought two phone cards, postcards of local views, stamps, a bag of toffees and a bottle of sherry. I shoved it all in the boot, then rang Mum from the phone box. Almost the first thing she asked was if anyone had called – as in visited.

'Jeannie arrived last night. I left her still sleeping. She plans to come next Friday too.'

I could almost hear Mum's sigh of relief.

'Has Piers phoned, Cassie? He rang here to see if you'd got off all right. He said you'd forgotten to give him your phone number, so I let him have it.'

'I'll ring him tomorrow maybe. How's Dad?'

'Same as always. He says that if we come up to see you it'll probably be midweek. The traffic, you see . . .'

'Fine by me.' Dad has a thing about weekend drivers. 'Just as long as you come. I'd love you to see the place. Tell Dad the natives are friendly!'

We chatted comfortably on about things in general and nothing in particular – you know the way it is when you phone your mum – until the card began to run out. I said I'd ring in the week and sent my love to Dad. She told me to look after myself and be sure to check the doors at night.

I called, 'Bye, Mum. Love you!' just as the line went dead.

Then I looked up at the church clock and realized I had half an hour to kill. If I left at about ten forty-five, I'd figured, I should be at The Place a little before eleven. I decided to walk the length of the village and back, gawping at the pub and the village green as if I were a tourist.

The pub was called the Red Rose, which figured. It looked old and, from the outside, friendly. The village green was ordinary, but the grass was cut short and the flowerbeds either side of an oak seat were well kept. There wasn't a scrap of litter about.

I sat down to waste a few minutes, looking about me, liking what I saw. Sheets blew on a line, very white against a very blue sky; a lady in a pinafore came out to wash her front windows. The Post Office van was making the morning delivery. I supposed that Deer's Leap would be its next stop and wondered if there would be any letters in the lidded box at the crossroads end of the dirt road when I returned. There would certainly be milk and a brown loaf, because I'd left a note there this morning.

There was nothing else to think about now except being at The Place at about four minutes to eleven, even though the airman wouldn't be there; how could he be, just because I wanted it? On the other hand, I had thought about him so much that surely some of my vibes had reached him.

Jack Hunter. A young man with old eyes, piloting a bomb-loaded Lancaster. Young men of my own generation were still kids at his age, fussing over their first car, pulling girls. Once, the Red Rose would have been filled with men from the airfield nearby; women too, because they had had to go to war. I wondered how people could have been so obedient, doing as they were ordered in the name of patriotism. I supposed they'd had little choice.

Would Piers have flown bombers or fighters? Somehow, with his dark, brooding looks, I think he would have been more likely to have been a paratrooper; a swash-buckling type with a gun at the ready.

I pushed him from my mind. There was no place for him in my life for the next four weeks. Correction. There was no place for him, if I faced facts, in my life at all! Piers had served his purpose, satisfied my curiosity. He was nice enough to have around, but in small doses.

I wondered what it would be like to be in love – *desperately* in love – with a man who might any night be killed. I jumped to my feet as I remembered the war memorial, realizing I hadn't seen it yet.

I found it on a triangle of grass outside the church gates. It was in simple stone and on the front were the names of men who had died in the First World War. I counted them, horrified that from so small a village, twelve young men had been killed.

Underneath it, three more names were chiselled; dead from a later war. It made me feel grateful those men had given their lives and then I knew I'd got it wrong. They hadn't *given* anything! Their young lives had been taken, stolen, squandered!

I looked to the side to see the names of seven airmen in alphabetical order and the simple inscription, *In Grateful Memory*. 8.6.1944.

I saw the name J. J. Hunter and reached to touch it with my fingertips.

'Please be there,' I whispered.

The tingling began at the clump of oaks. Until I reached them I had managed to keep my feelings in check. But beyond those trees anything could happen and I was hoping desperately that it would.

Strangely, I was more excited than afraid, because deep down I was telling myself he wouldn't be there. In fact, if Beth and Danny hadn't told me to leave it, if Beth hadn't half-heartedly admitted she *might* have seen the airman and told me the people in the village didn't want the press all over the place, I might have convinced myself he was all in my mind. But Jack Hunter was as real as you or me.

I wound down my window. Then I stopped to lean over and slip the nearside door catch.

'Hop in,' I'd say. 'It's open . . .'

Almost eleven. I started the car and crawled past the spot

I'd first met him, trying to look both sides and straight ahead at the same time. I looked in the rear-view mirror, but he wasn't behind me, either.

'Aren't you coming, Jack Hunter?'

My voice sounded strange, then I let go a snort of annoyance because talking to a ghost that wasn't there was worse than talking to myself!

'That's yer lot!' This was a load of nonsense and he'd had his last chance! If he wasn't interested, then neither was I! He could find his own damn way to Deer's Leap! I'd come here to look after a house and two cats and a dog; to write in peace and quiet and when Jeannie went back on Monday, that was what I would do!

'Men are a flaming nuisance,' I said out loud, and that included ghosts!

I began to laugh. A very real Hector would come bouncing up, followed by a loudly purring cat, when I got out of the car. All very neat and normal. Only Cassie Johns was out of step!

I realized I had slowed, because I was looking for a flock of sheep, wondering if I'd imagined them too. The crossroads was ahead, and the signpost. I turned right, then slowed so I could take the pot-holed dirt road easily.

I could see the roof of the house above the trees. Jeannie was up, because the white gate ahead was open, and I'd left it closed. In front, to my left, was the kissing gate and, oh, my God! He was there! Walking through it! I saw him clearly, and the gas mask slung on his left shoulder.

I slammed on the brake, the engine coughed and stalled. I yelled, '*Jack Hunter!*' then flung open the door as he pulled the gate shut behind him. When I got there, he had gone. The path, which led to the farm buildings, was empty. I ran down it as far as the conservatory, but there was no sign he had ever been there.

Then I turned, and stood stock-still, gawping in disbelief at the iron gate. Now it was black again with shiny paint, yet when I'd opened it I'd swear it had been rusty! And what was more I had heard its grinding squeak as he closed it behind him! I walked up to it, touching it with my finger, and it swung smoothly and silently on well-oiled pivots.

Yet he'd been there. He had! He was still around. It was just that this morning we'd missed each other by seconds – and fifty-odd years!

Jeannie and I ate a lunch of soup and sandwiches, then lazed on the terrace, gazing for miles, soaking up the August sun, breathing deeply on the air.

'Y'know, this shouldn't be allowed. It's positively anti-social to have a view like this all to yourself. I wonder what they'll ask for this place, once it goes on the market?'

'Haven't a clue. I'm used to London prices,' Jeannie shrugged. 'But I suppose that even though it mightn't be everybody's cup of tea, it won't go cheap. Like you say, the view is really something and position counts for a lot.'

'If you like out-of-the-way places,' I said.

'The old ones knew where to build, didn't they?'

'Before planning permission came in, you mean, when they could choose their plot and just start building?'

'Sort of, but they'd have to do their homework first. The most important thing when Deer's Leap was built would be the availability of water, I shouldn't wonder.'

'Danny said there was once a stream, just beyond the paddock wall.'

'Well, that would've been all right for livestock and clothes washing, but they'd have needed drinking water too. Mind, that ornamental well at the back near the conservatory was once the real thing. I believe they only got mains water here after the war. And they still don't have sewers. That's why we shouldn't use too many disinfectants and upset the natural workings of the septic tank.'

'They were very self-sufficient, though.' My mind jumped the centuries to the man and woman who built this house.

Their initials were above the front door: *W. D. & M. D. 1592.* 'Do you realize Elizabeth Tudor was still alive when W. D. brought his bride here? Wonder what they were called – and how many children they had.'

'William and Mary Doe,' Jeannie said, off the top of her head, 'and they probably had ten children and would count themselves lucky to rear half of them!'

'A bit nearer home,' I said cautiously, 'I wonder who lived here in the war, and how they managed. Petrol was rationed, I believe. How did they get about?'

'On bikes, most likely. Or maybe they'd go shopping once a week on the farm tractor. Who knows? And anyway, who's interested?'

'Me, for one.' I looked straight ahead, pretending it didn't really matter. 'Well – I'm an author. I can't help being curious and it would all be grist to the mill – if we found out, that is . . .'

'If it's so important, why don't we go down to the Rose, tonight? They don't get a lot in there, especially since drink-drive came in. I could introduce you to Bill Jarvis, if he's in. Bill knows most people's business around here, past and present. Maybe he could tell you.'

'It isn't *that* important,' I hedged. 'It's just that I keep wondering what it was like here when it was a working farm and before somebody tarted up the buildings at the back, and when there were animals around the place, and manure heaps.'

'Then we'll go to the village, like I said. The beer is good there. The further north you get from London, people say, the better the ale. I fancy a couple of pints!'

'So who's going to drive?'

'You, Cassie. It's your car.'

'And drink Coke and orange juice all night?'

'OK! There are loads of bikes in the stable. What say we pick out a couple, put some air in the tyres, and go supping in style?'

'Can you get done for being drunk in charge of a bike?' I giggled.

'I don't know. It depends how well you can ride one, I suppose.'

We decided to have an early tea. Fresh brown eggs, boiled, and crusty bread, then a huge dollop of the home-baked parkin Mum had slipped into the boot just as I was leaving. After which, Jeannie said she'd better have a dummy run, just to make sure she hadn't forgotten how to ride.

It was all so lovely and free and easy. We were like a couple of kids let early out of school, and in a way I was a bit sad about it because next August, when I was writing book three and on the way to becoming a *real*, time-served novelist, I would look back to how it had been that summer at Deer's Leap, and wonder who had bought the house and if they loved it as much as I did. And I knew they wouldn't, couldn't.

We wore leggings, the better to ride in, and shirts. Then we stuffed cardies in the saddlebags in case it was cold riding home. We pushed the bikes along the dirt road, neither of us being confident enough to brave the potholes.

When we got to the crossroads I said, 'If we meet anything on the road, I'll ride ahead, OK?'

'If we meet anything on this narrow lane, I shall get off and stand on the verge! But there's hardly any traffic hereabouts. What are you expecting – a furniture van?'

I almost said, 'No – a flock of sheep,' but I didn't and we managed, after a couple of false starts and a few wobbles, to get going.

'Don't look down at your front wheel, Jeannie! Look at the road ahead. Y'know, I could get to like this. They say you never forget how to ride a bike.'

Jeannie soon got the hang of it and went ahead just at the spot I'd first seen the airman. I slowed and had a good look around, then told myself not to be greedy; that one sighting a day was all I could hope for.

'Hey! Wait for me, show-off!' I called, then pedalled like mad to catch her up.

The Red Rose wasn't too crowded and we got a table beside an open window. Jeannie said she would get the first round and asked me what I was drinking.

'Bitter, please. A half.'

She returned with two pint glasses, then asked me how I liked the Rose.

'It's ages old, isn't it?' The ceiling was very low, and beamed; the lounge end of the one long room had better seats in it than the other end, where there was a dartboard but not a slot machine in sight.

'I could get to like this place,' I said, lifting my glass. 'Cheers!'

'We're in luck.' Jeannie took a long drink from her glass. 'Bill Jarvis is in the far corner. Would you like to meet him?'

'You know I would! Are you going to ask him to join us?'

'I'll take him a pint and tell him it's from a young lady who would like to talk to him.'

'He's scoring for the darts, but he'll be over in about five minutes,' she said when she came back alone. 'He said thanks for the beer, by the way.'

'This is a lovely old pub. I'm glad they haven't modernized it – made it into a gin palace.'

'There's no fear of that happening.' She raised her eyes to the ceiling, which was pale khaki. 'The last time it got a lick of paint was for the Coronation. When it was first built, in the early fourteen hundreds, it was the churchwarden's house, and I don't think it's changed a lot since – apart from flush toilets outside.'

'I suppose,' I said, 'that at the time of the Wars of the Roses, a churchwarden was quite an important man, in the village.'

'Mm. He held one of the three keys to the parish chest – y'know, social security, medieval style. The other two keyholders would be the priest and the local squire. The parish chest is still in the church, but there's nothing in it. You must go and see it before you go back.'

She was already half way down her glass. My dad, I thought, would approve of Jeannie McFadden.

'There's a lot of things I must see and do,' I said obliquely, 'before I go back. But I think your friend is coming over . . .'

An elderly man made his way to our table, puffing out clouds of tobacco smoke that made me glad of the open window.

'Now then, lass,' he said to Jeannie, ignoring me completely, 'what was it you wanted to know?'

'It's my friend, actually, Bill. She's taken a liking to Deer's Leap and wants to know all about it. She's a writer,' she added.

'Then I'm saying nowt, or it'll all be in a book!'

'I write fiction, Mr Jarvis,' I said, holding out my hand. 'What I'm interested in is the history of the house. I'm not prying. I'm Cassie, by the way. What are you drinking?'

'Nowt at the moment, though I wouldn't say no to a pint of bitter.' Reluctantly he shook my hand.

'I want to know,' I said, when he was settled at the table, 'who lived at Deer's Leap in the war. Jeannie said the Air Force just turfed them out without a by-your-leave. I'd have hated that if it had been my house.'

'Ar, but my generation had to put up with that war and we hated it, an' all. Didn't stop the high-ups from London taking whatever they wanted, for all that. Smiths had no choice but to sell up and get out.'

'And where did they go?'

'Can't rightly say, lass. Got my calling-up papers, so what became of 'em, I never knew.'

'Did they have a family, Mr Jarvis?'

'Not as you'd call a family – nobbut one bairn, three or

four years younger than me. Susan, if I remember rightly.'

Susan Smith, I brooded, then all at once I remembered the initials S. S. and a tiny heart on the strap of the airman's gas mask. The initials stood for Susan Smith. She, likely, had put them there!

'How old was Susan when she had to leave Deer's Leap?' I managed to ask, a kind of triumph singing inside me.

'Now then – I'd just been called up, as I remember. Was twenty-two. Usually they took you afore that, but they'd let a young man finish his training, sort of. I was 'prenticed to a cabinet-maker, so as soon as I'd done my time they called me into the Engineers and taught me about electrics! Any road, that would make the Smith lass about eighteen or nineteen. I'm seventy-six, so she would be seventy-two or -three now – if her's still alive. Fair, she was, and bonny, but quiet, as I remember.'

'It was rotten about their land – especially as the government expected farmers to work all hours to produce food,' Jeannie prompted.

'Ar, but t'farm were no use to Smiths any more. Them fellers from the Air Ministry took all their fields in the end. Nobbut the paddock left them. Then they said they wanted the farmhouse, an' all.'

'That was a bit vindictive,' I said hotly.

'No. Stood to sense, really. The Air Force wanted to extend the runway at the aerodrome, and they took Deer's Leap to billet airmen in. 'Em could do what they wanted in those days. Would have the shirt off your back if they thought it would help the war effort! They couldn't get away with it now. Folk wouldn't stand for it!

'Mind, once they'd no more use for bombers, they soon upped and went! I suppose Smiths could have got their house back and their fields, an' all, but they never tried. That farmhouse stood empty for years. It'd have fallen down if it hadn't been solid-built and a good, tight roof on it. A man who'd won money on the football pools bought it eventually and fancied it up. He couldn't stand the quiet, though, so it's been rented out ever since.'

'I think it's a beautiful house,' I said softly as Jeannie took Bill's empty glass to the bar for a refill. 'I wish it belonged to me.'

'You'd never stand the quiet, lass.'

'I would. I'm there for a month and I wish it was for ever.'

'Ah, well, there's folk in it now, so you can stop your fretting for it. Reckon they'm well satisfied with the place.'

'Yes. They love it.' I didn't mention they'd be leaving it, come New Year. 'I think the view from the front is unbelievable. There's such peace there.'

'Weren't a lot of peace for folk around here in the war. 'Em had an aerodrome, don't forget, on their doorsteps, and bombers overhead day and night. Bits of kids flying them. It's a miracle there weren't more crashes.'

Jeannie returned with a tin tray with three pint glasses on it. Bill Jarvis smiled, and took one of them.

'Crashes?' I probed.

'Oh my word, yes!' He pushed his empty pipe into his top pocket and took a long drink from his glass. 'Mind, those bombers were great big things and needed a lot of room for takeoff, but folk around here could never see the sense in the Air Force wanting more land for longer runways. 'Em thought it was going to be something to do with the invasion; that we had a secret weapon that was going to take off from Acton Carey. But it was the Americans came in the end. Mind, I can't help you a lot there. I was in Italy at the time, on the invasion.'

'I wonder why the Smiths didn't come back. I'd have wanted to,' I said.

'Ar, but talk had it that he was given some fancy job with the Ag and Fish; didn't have to work so hard for his money.'

'Ag and Fish?' Jeannie frowned.

'The Ministry of Agriculture and Fisheries. For once, they took on a man as knew a bit about farming! I never found out what happened to him after that. Was none of my business. Now, I mind when I was in Italy . . .' His eyes took on a remembering look, and I knew there would be no more Deer's Leap talk. But I had made contact, and before we left I had arranged to meet the old man again at the Rose on Wednesday night.

'You're a fast worker,' Jeannie laughed as we cycled home. 'What are you up to with Bill Jarvis?'

'Nothing at all,' I called back over my shoulder. 'But like I said, it's all grist to a writer's mill. Life here must have been a bit tame all round once the war was over.'

'Yes, and a whole lot safer!'

We closed the white gate behind us. It would have been dark by now, but for a half-moon. We hadn't passed one street-lamp. It made me feel good, just to think of how remote we were. Tommy was waiting, purring, on the doorstep; Lotus was away on her nightly prowl. Hector barked loudly as Jeannie unlocked the back door, then hurtled past us to run round and round the stableyard like a mad thing. I switched on the kitchen light, then filled the kettle.

'Want a sarnie?' I asked. 'There's ham in the fridge.'

'Please.' Jeannie kicked off her pumps, then flopped into a chair. 'No mustard.'

'It's been a lovely, lovely day,' I sighed as I cut bread. 'Bet our legs'll be stiff in the morning, though. I haven't ridden a bike in years.'

We sat at the kitchen table. It was too late now to sit on the terrace and watch distant lights. Even the birds were quiet.

'I'm tired,' Jeannie yawned not long afterwards. 'All this country air . . .'

'Me too.' I said I would check the doors and windows. I considered it my responsibility since Beth had left me *in loco parentis*, so to speak. 'Off you go. I'll be right behind you.'

Tommy had settled himself on the bottom of my bed, but I didn't shift him. I cleaned my teeth, washed my face, then lifted the quilt carefully so as not to waken him. Then I sighed and stared into the shifting darkness, glad that Jeannie hadn't wanted to stay up late, talking, because I needed to think.

Up until tonight, things had been a muddle, yet now it was as if I was looking down on a table top with the pieces of a jigsaw piled on it in a heap. I had found the corner pieces of that puzzle and laid them out carefully in my mind.

One was a long-ago airfield – aerodrome, Bill called it – at Acton Carey. It had been the cause of the Smiths – piece number two – leaving Deer's Leap, which was corner piece three. The fourth was Jack Hunter, I knew it without a doubt, and that he and Susan were connected – or why were her initials on his respirator?

I had made a start! Next I must complete the entire outline of the puzzle so I could begin to fill in the story, which was the middle bit. I could rely on Bill for some things because Jeannie had been right: his brain was still razor-sharp. For the rest of it, I needed to talk to a sergeant pilot. Only he could help me with the difficult bits.

Were we to meet face to face again, and talk, or was he to be a wraith, slipping in and out of shadows – and through gates – always just out of my reach?

Susan Smith, I brooded. Born 1924, or thereabouts. Fair and bonny and shy. Jack Hunter – tall and fair and straight, and old before his time. Died in 1944 and a name now on a stone memorial. The really sad thing, I sighed, as my eyes began to close, was that he didn't know it.

What, or who, had he been searching for over the years? I hoped he would tell me . . .

There was a comfortable silence about the place when I got up early on Tuesday morning. After making Jeannie promise hand on heart to visit next weekend, I'd stood waving as her London-bound train snaked from the station the previous evening.

I coughed, and the sound echoed loudly around the kitchen. The quiet was bliss, the only sounds, Tommy's rhythmic purring at my feet and a swell of birdsong outside. Hector lay on the back doorstep, on guard. There was just me and the animals and the view from the kitchen window that stretched into forever.

The phone on the dresser rang, intruding noisily into my world. Reluctantly I answered it.

'Cassandra?'

'Piers! Oh – hi!'

'What have you been up to? I've been ringing all the time!'

'You can't have.' I felt a bit guilty for hardly thinking about him all weekend.

'I phoned on Saturday night. Twice. Where have you been until now?'

'We biked down to the pub on Saturday night. Jeannie had someone to see.'

'What about Sunday?'

'If you rang, then we were probably in the garden, cutting the grass.'

'And last night?'

'Most likely I'd gone to Preston, seeing Jeannie on to the train. Listen, Piers, what the heck is this? Are you checking up on me?'

'No, darling. Sorry if I came over a bit snotty. But what was I to think when you didn't even give me your phone number in the first place?'

'You got it off Mum, didn't you?'

'Yes. After I'd asked for it. Why didn't you ring me, Cassandra?' He still sounded peeved.

'Because!' I said flatly and finally. 'I'm very well, since you ask, and yes, we had a lovely, lazy weekend. Where are you?'

'At the flat. I've just got up.'

'We-e-ll, don't ring any more in the expensive time. Leave it for after six, why don't you?'

I'd be better able to cope with his bossiness then. An upset this early in the day could put me off my stroke – especially when he was making a meal of it, like now. 'You've got to understand this book is important, Piers,' I rushed on. 'I came here to write – what you call my scribbling – and I do wish you would take me seriously. Just sometimes,' I finished breathlessly.

'But, my love, I do take you seriously.' His tone was changing from accusing to placating. 'It's just that you seem to be wrapped up in it to the exclusion of all else. You and me, especially . . .'

'Piers! *Please* not now; not this early in the day! And of course I'm wrapped up in it. It's my work, you must accept that. This novel has got to be good and then Harrier Books might begin to take me seriously.'

'You're set on it, aren't you, Cassandra? You really believe you can make a living from it when most writers need a daytime job too. Don't you think you've been living off your parents long enough? Isn't it about time you took a serious look at the way your life is going?'

'I see. I'd be better shacking up with you, providing all the home comforts, you mean?'

'Now you're getting angry, sweetheart.'

'Don't interrupt!' I *was* angry! Piers would have to learn you can only push a redhead so far! 'I have never lived off Mum and Dad. I pulled my weight at home and only wrote when I could find the time. And yes, I *do* hope to make a living from writing! *Ice Maiden* is doing well; they're reprinting it, as a matter of fact! Oh, don't worry! I won't be going into tax exile just yet, but I'm holding my own! And even if I wasn't, I shouldn't have to justify myself to you!'

I took a deep breath. I expected an explosion or a slamming-down of the phone, but all I got was a silence. Piers is good at pregnant pauses; can stretch five seconds into five minutes.

'Cassie love, don't get upset. I was anxious, hadn't heard from you. For all I knew you could be – well . . .'

'Having a passionate affair with a local yokel? Well, I'm flaming *not*!'

'You seem determined to have a row. What's the matter then – stuck for words?'

'No, I'm not. The words are coming well, but thanks a heap, Piers, for helping me to start the day with an upset! I'm not doing a prima donna, but you narking on the phone I can do without! Ring after six, will you?'

I had meant to end the conversation firmly and with dignity, but I slammed the phone down angrily and now he'd know he'd got me rattled! I could imagine his smirk. Drat the man!

For the next two days I allowed nothing and no one to come between me and my work. Luckily Piers didn't phone again. I existed on sandwiches and coffee, rewarding myself for my labours with a large sherry after I had switched off.

On Wednesday, at six o'clock exactly, I had safely stored two chapters on a floppy disk. I felt drained, but triumphant. Deer's Leap was good to me, wrapping me round to keep out all interruptions.

I rotated my head, hearing little crackling sounds as I did so, deciding I needed to loosen up. My heroine had got herself into a bit of a mess, but she could stew in it until morning, I thought, well satisfied with the cliffhanger at the end of chapter twelve.

I was wondering whether to eat at the Rose or whether to boil the last couple of eggs, when Mum phoned.

'Hullo, there! You sound a long way away!'

'I am, Mum! I've just finished work, actually. I've got two chapters done since I came here! I'm having a sherry, then I'll make myself some supper. How's everything?'

'We're fine, only I'm afraid we won't be able to make it up there this week. I'd forgotten your dad is judging at two flower shows. We'll probably make it the week following. Is that all right with you, love?'

'Come whenever you want to. I'd really like you to see this place. When I win the Lottery, I shall buy it!'

'Ha! More to the point, are you getting enough to eat?'

'I am, though I work while the mood is on me, and eat when I'm hungry. Jeannie is coming up again on Friday.'

'Have you spoken to Piers, yet? I don't suppose he'll be coming to see you?'

'Not unless you give him my address, Mum! I'm here to work. I don't want any interruptions – leastways, not from him.'

'Aah,' she sighed, and I knew I had said the right thing.

'I'm going to Clitheroe tomorrow. There's something I want to look up at the library.'

'You're sure you're all right, Cassie?'

'I'm fine. We've eaten all the parkin, by the way. Bring me another piece when you come up, there's a love? Jeannie really liked it.'

I could feel Mum's glow of pleasure in my ear. Tomorrow, I'd take bets on her making a double mixing, then putting my piece in a tin to moisten. Parkin is best kept a few days before eating.

'Of course I will! Anything else you want?'

'No thanks, I'm fine, and working well. I miss you both. Take care of yourselves, won't you?'

'We will, lovey. And don't go answering the door after dark!'

'I won't. And I've got Hector to look after me. He doesn't like strangers very much!'

'Well, then . . .'

'I'll phone you at the weekend, Mum. We'll have a good long chat, then. Love you!'

I smiled at the receiver as I put it down, deciding to take the car down to Acton Carey, and drink Coke instead of bitter, even though it was unlikely I would meet any traffic on the way back.

The way back. Would I meet any*one*, though? I hadn't seen the airman since Saturday morning at the kissing gate, though I hadn't gone out of my way to find him. I wondered if he was once billeted at Deer's Leap after the Smiths left. At least I now knew the names of those long-ago people.

Maybe, though, Jack Hunter had been quartered somewhere else. He'd said he wanted to get to Deer's Leap, but could he have been going there to meet Susan Smith? Had they been an item – or courting, walking-out as it would have been called in those days?

I put eggs to boil, then sliced bread. Lotus walked daintily into the kitchen, indicating, nose in air, that she would accept a saucer of milk. Tommy tried to share it and was warned off. I put a saucer down for him, then began to time the eggs as they came to the bubble.

That was when the phone began to ring. It was Piers, dammit! I moved the pan from the heat.

'Hullo, darling. In a better mood, are we?'

'I'm fine. Put in a good day's work. I'm just about to eat.' This time I wouldn't let him get me rattled! 'How was your day, Piers?'

'Oh, routine, as always.'

'Hm.' He never explained what went on in that lab he worked in. I suppose that he supposed I wouldn't understand it anyway. 'I'm going out tonight.'

'Oooh! Got a heavy date?'

'Yes, and I'm looking forward to it. He's called Bill Jarvis. I'm meeting him at the pub.'

'Where's that?'

'In the village!' Nice try, Piers!

'And he'll wine you and dine you, I suppose, then have his wicked way!' It was meant to sound like a joke, but I knew he was purring with his claws out.

'In the back of a Mini?' I laughed. 'I'm doing a spot of research, actually. I'm interested in World War Two. For a small village, it must once have been fairly jumping hereabouts. Lately, people seem to have got interested in that period. I might just use it for the next book. And for your information, *I'll* be buying the ale! Bill is a pensioner, Piers. He's seventy-six, and like I said, it's research.'

'Of course. As a matter of fact I thought it would be something like that, Cassandra.'

'Oh, you did! Think I'm only capable of pulling a senior citizen, then?'

'The thought never entered my mind! Have you been drinking? You sound – *peculiar*.'

'Of course I haven't!' I smirked at the empty sherry glass on the drainer. 'I just feel good, that's all.'

'Then it's a welcome change! Usually, you snap my head off. Getting that book accepted has changed you, Cassie.'

'Has it?' I had a vision of him telling it to the long-suffering man in the mirror over the telephone. Piers Yardley was wasted on research! 'Anyway, I'm going to have my tea now. Don't ring again because I'll be either in the bath or out! Take care of yourself, Piers. I'll phone you at the weekend. Promise!'

'Do I only merit off-peak, then?'

'Bye, love!' I ignored the snide remark.

Round two to Cassie Johns!

I parked the Mini at the back of the Red Rose, and, once inside, was glad to see Bill sitting alone, an empty glass in front of him.

'Hi, Mr Jarvis,' I smiled. 'What can I get you?'

He smiled briefly and held up his beer glass, then asked me what the 'eck I was drinking when I sat down beside him.

'I'm on Coke tonight. I'm driving. I want to pick your brains,' I went on without preamble. 'Will you tell me what it was like around these parts in the war? Was it really dangerous, having that airfield so near?'

'Us called it an aerodrome in them days. 'Twas only the Yanks that called 'em airfields. I wouldn't say it was dangerous, exactly. But when you come to think of it, they were nobbut young bits of lads flying those bombers. It must have been a bother getting them into the air. Well, they'd be heavy, wouldn't they, with bombs and fuel?'

He placed his empty pipe between his teeth and sucked on it, reflectively.

'I suppose that was before they made the runways longer?' I suggested, trying to steer the conversation round to the Smiths' fields.

'Before *and* after. Was still a bit hair-raising. 'Em made the chimney pots rattle as they flew over. Noisy, it was.'

'I suppose it was better when they came back from a raid – well, safer for Acton Carey people, I mean. At least their fuel would be almost used, and their bombs would have gone. Landing wouldn't have been so risky, would it?'

I saw Jack Hunter's hands gripping the controls.

'You might think not, but getting back from the raid didn't mean they were home and dry, oh my word, no! Some mornings I'd be biking to the workshop, early, and I'd see 'em, wheels down, circling. Mind, it was when they was circling with their wheels *not* down that the trouble started.'

'I don't understand . . .' I sipped at my drink, and wished it was beer.

'Well, sometimes 'em couldn't get their undercarriages down! Sometimes they'd been got at by enemy fighters; shot up, see, and the wheels wouldn't work. Had to do a belly landing then, and the fire trucks and the ambulances standing by. It wasn't a picnic in the Army, fighting in Italy, but I always reckoned I had a better chance of seeing my demob than those flyers.'

'So there were a lot of accidents?'

'Oh, aye.'

'Where was the aerodrome exactly?'

'Was about two miles from the village, going in the direction of that house you're staying at. Two miles might sound a long way, but it was only seconds in flying time. I was once walking a girl out as lived in a cottage about half a mile from Deer's Leap, though it's tumbled down since. The land rises a bit at the back of the farm and we could look down, summer nights, and see them taking off below us. In miniature, sort of.'

'So if I went to the back of Deer's Leap and looked down, whereabouts would the aerodrome have been?'

'If you was to walk to the top of that paddock, then keep on for about a hundred yards, and look over to your left, you'd have seen it. Mind, there was a wood there once. Sniggery Wood, we called it, and very handy for courting couples. The Air Ministry folk cut down all the trees. They'd have been a hazard, see, for bombers taking off and landing. Things change, lass, and not always for the better.'

'So maybe,' I asked cautiously, 'the people – the Smiths, didn't you say? – who lived there would be able to watch it all?'

'Happen they would, if they'd been interested, but I suppose they had better things to do with their time.'

'And the daughter – Susan – do you suppose she might have known some of the airmen there?' *Some*, I said, trying to make it sound casual.

'Her might've. Mind, it wasn't encouraged. Getting fond of them aircrew lads could lead to trouble. They used to have dances at the aerodrome – had a good dance band there, I believe. Civilian girls were welcome, but my sister were never allowed to go!'

'Why could it lead to trouble?' I found myself sticking up for Jack Hunter. 'I thought girls were sort of chaperoned in those days.'

'You did, eh?' He chuckled, wheezily. 'We aren't talking

about when Queen Victoria was on the throne! Young lasses took notice of what their parents said, I'll grant you that, and they didn't leave home, usually, till they was wed or called up. But he-ing and she-ing went on like it always had and always will.

'What I was trying to say was that if a girl got fond of a flyer, then she could get real upset if he didn't come back from a raid. And there was a better than even chance that he wouldn't. Parents didn't want their lasses to get tied up with them, for that reason – apart from the obvious, of course. They could've ended up in the family way, an' all!'

'I see. That would have been awful for them?'

'Awful? It'd have been a disgrace; a scandal. When a lass got into trouble in those days, she had to take herself off quick afore it became obvious – if you know what I mean – if the young man responsible didn't wed her. I did hear as how one father around these parts just chucked his lass on to the street and told her to be off with her shame. Her jumped in t'river!'

'But women were called up into the Armed Forces as well as men. I suppose parents would be a bit worried, their daughters never having been away from home, sort of . . .'

'Suppose they would be, but they weren't given much of a choice! And not all of them lasses as went in the Forces were all that upset about it. For some, it was an adventure – and they got away from strict parents, an' all!' He began to fidget with his empty glass.

'Can I fill you up?'

'That'd be decent of you . . .'

'Did the Smith girl get called up?' I asked, the second I put the glass in front of him.

'Don't reckon so. Farmers kept their daughters at home on account they worked on the land. Farming was a reserved occupation, remember, for young men as well as for young women. Some folk thought it wasn't fair when their daughters went off to war and farmers' sons stopped at home safe.'

72

'But they left Deer's Leap, you said. Maybe she would have to do war work when they left the farm?'

'Maybe she would. I was called up myself before the Air Force emptied them out, so I never knew what became of them. You seem very interested in t'Smiths.'

'Not particularly,' I shrugged, hoping I sounded convincing. 'It was just that I wondered what it was like for the farmer who once lived at Deer's Leap. I'm interested in all the people who lived there. I suppose it would have been quite some property when it was built.'

'Still is, I suppose. The man as built it would be well heeled.'

'Mm. He'd have had servants and farm workers. I think they would have slept in the rooms over the kitchen. If we could invent a time machine and dial the year we wanted, we'd know exactly how it had been.'

'Won't be long,' he grumbled into his empty glass, 'afore they do, the rate they're going on at! Spending all that money shooting off to the moon and what did they find when they got there? Nowt but dust!'

'Are you ready for another?' His interest was flagging. Mention of a refill revived it noticeably.

'Tell me about Italy?' I asked, returning from the bar.

'Which bit?' Carefully he lifted a brimming glass to his lips.

'Monte Cassino?' I hazarded.

The half-moon of Saturday night was full now. It hung in the sky, large and round and glowing. Was it the harvest moon, or would that be the next one, at the end of the month?

Everything around me looked beautiful and mysterious and aloof. What was it about the moon that made people think of magic? Trees and hedges cast long shadows, and the road was clear and visible for as far ahead as I could see. Maybe it was on nights like this that witches flew. I wondered if the Pendle women had really been witches?

Had a harvest moon looked down when they were hanged, one long-ago August? W. D. and M. D. would have known all about that trial in Lancaster. In 1612, when it happened, Deer's Leap had already stood for twenty years. Mary Doe, as I thought of her, might even have visited Mistress Nutter and exchanged herbal remedies with her, because in those days the woman of the house was responsible for all the nursing and doctoring that was needed within her family. I wished like mad for that time machine. What would Mary Doe make of my bright red Mini that could rush along faster than witches on broomsticks? I threw back my head and laughed out loud just to think of it, and then my smile set on my lips and my laughter ended abruptly.

I could see him clearly in the moonlight, and instinct made me switch off my lights. I braked, and dropped a gear. I wouldn't have expected him to be beside the clump of oak trees; further up the lane, really.

His outline stood out darkly, and there was no mistaking his extended arm, his jutting thumb. My mouth had gone dry and I ran my tongue round my lips. In the slipping of a second I asked myself if I were afraid and knew I wasn't.

He took a step backwards as I stopped beside him. Please, *please* don't vanish, Jack Hunter. I leaned over and pushed open the door.

'I'm going to Deer's Leap,' I said. 'Want a lift . . . ?'

Chapter Five

My heart was thudding; the little pulse behind my nose had joined in too. I felt a choking excitement and, at the same time, an amazing calm. I willed him to get in.

'Thanks a lot.' He took off his cap and pushed it under the epaulette at his shoulder. Then he tossed his respirator on the floor of the car, and sat down. This time he could stretch his legs because I hadn't moved the passenger seat forward. He banged the door shut and I began to wish for a flock of sheep again. Without them it would take less than three minutes to Deer's Leap, and he would take off, I knew it, just as soon as he saw the kissing gate.

'In a hurry, are you?' I said, staring ahead.

'Afraid so. I shouldn't be here really. I'm on standby . . .'

'What's that?' This time, I had the chance to ask.

'It means we might be going tonight.'

'Going?' I prompted carefully, driving slowly.

'On ops. We might go, and then again, we mightn't. I shouldn't be here. When we're on standby, we can't leave the aerodrome – or we *shouldn't*.'

'Security?' I suggested, trying to be with it.

'Yes. And there might be a call to first briefing.'

'And if that happens, you won't be there, will you? What's first briefing?'

I was talking gibberish; talking for the sake of talking so he wouldn't get out.

'First briefing is just that. Pilots and navigators only; the rest of the crew join in later on.'

He was being very patient with me, and I was grateful for the fact that his mind seemed to be on other things. Not that

I blamed him. To Berlin and back in inky blackness with searchlights trying to pick you out and night fighters ready to pounce would have been a bit distracting, to say the least.

'I see.' I didn't really; didn't understand the half of it – only what I'd read in books and seen in films. There had been a lot about his war on television four years back. 'Are you billeted at Deer's Leap?'

'Oh, no. The farmer lives there still. There's a chance that the RAF will take it, though it hasn't happened yet.'

'*They* seem to do pretty well as they like, don't they?'

'Yes, they do.' He turned to look at me, frowning. 'But there *is* a war on.'

My God! Indoctrinated by propaganda about the nobility of the cause! I'd read about it, but I hadn't quite believed it. And I could tell him, I thought wildly, the exact day that Hitler would commit suicide, and about the two atom bombs the Americans would drop on Japan. I could, I thought, horrified, tell him the exact day he would die!

'I hope you won't go tonight; not with this moon . . .'

'The moon's good for fighters. They get above it, then fly out of it, and they're on to you before you've got time to think. We call it a bomber's moon because you could go without a navigator on nights like this. Everything's there, below you, as clear as day. On the other hand, a Lanc makes a great silhouette against the moon. Given a choice, I wouldn't go tonight.'

'Do you know Susan Smith?' I asked like a fool, straight out of the blue.

'Of course I know her! That's why I'm going to see her; tell her I might not be able to make it. I haven't met her parents yet, so we decided it would have to be tonight . . .'

'Only you're on standby,' I finished for him.

'Yes, and I don't want her to think I've stood her up. We always meet at the kissing gate, you see. She'll be waiting . . .'

'Are you both – I mean, is it steady between you?' Oh, but I was pushing my luck!

'If you mean are we in love then yes, we are. Very much . . .'

His voice trailed off again. He seemed never quite to finish a sentence.

'And you're going to meet Susan's parents – ask them if you can get married?' That's what they once did, Mum said. Ask permission.

'Yes. And I call her Suzie, by the way.'

I could see the white gate ahead and beside it, the black-painted kissing gate.

I was annoyed now that I had carefully closed the white gate when I'd left, thinking that if I drove straight up to the front door I might disorientate him; that if he didn't see the iron gate he would stay in the car.

But I hadn't even time to open the door when he said, 'Thanks a lot! See you! G'night.'

I didn't see him leave the car – not physically, I mean – and I didn't see him open the kissing gate, but I saw it open of its own accord and I heard its creak as I'd known I would. He had just dematerialized tonight. If I hadn't heard the gate then I wouldn't have known where he'd gone.

I called, ''Night. See you sometime!' but had no means of knowing if he'd heard me. Shaking now, I went through the motion of starting the car, driving through the gate, then closing it behind me. Only Hector's frantic barking pulled me back to the here and now. I took a deep breath, then fumbled my key into the lock.

Tonight – all of it – was going to take a bit of working out. I thought about the mental jigsaw puzzle and knew I had begun to fill in the outline, though there was a long way to go before I completed it – if ever I did.

Hector greeted me joyfully. I patted his head and he felt real and solid and of this age. Carefully, because I was trying to get a hold on myself, I bolted the front door, top and bottom, then double-locked it.

Only then did I say, ''Strewth, Hector, you'd never believe the half of what's just happened!'

*   *   *

Next morning, I awoke to gloom and the sound of rain pattering against the window.

How *dare* it rain at Deer's Leap! I got out of bed and closed the window. Heavy rain on wheat and barley and oats ripe and ready for harvesting for the war effort, Mr Smith could do well without!

Dammit! I was back to that war again! I was here to write and look after a house, not to dig back half a century because a ghost couldn't find his girlfriend. We were coming up to the Millennium, and Susan Smith and Jack Hunter were history!

But they weren't, the voice of reason whispered firmly. Jack Hunter didn't know he had died more than fifty years ago and as far as I knew, Susan could still be alive. I not only wanted to establish that fact, but deep down I was certain that the niggling inside me would go on until I had found her!

But how do you find an elderly lady – who could perhaps be married and have children – *grandchildren* – and who maybe didn't want to be found? And just supposing the impossible happened and one day she opened her front door to me, what would I say?

'Hullo! You don't know me, but not so long ago I met a ghost who was once in love with you! Over fifty years ago, mind, but I think you should know he still needs to find you. His name is Jack Hunter.' And the poor old thing would look at me vacantly and say, 'Jack *who*?'

I tied my dressing gown tightly around me, glad of the warmth, and switched on the kettle. Then I fed the animals, after which Lotus walked ahead of me, tail erect, indicating at the conservatory door that she wished to spend the morning in there. She was quite intelligent I had to admit, and lost no time showing me where she was in the habit of sleeping on wet mornings.

The view from the kitchen window was a forlorn one. Plants dripped miserably and a mist covered everything, blocking out the view – even the white-painted gate. I decided to bring in logs and light the kitchen fire, then realized that not even that would inspire me to words, for this was not a morning for creativity. I didn't have word block. There really is no such thing. As far as I am concerned, when the words won't come it is because I simply don't want to write!

Having established that, my conscience refused to let me sit idly over a fire, curled up with a book. I would drive to Clitheroe instead. I needed to visit the library to check on something I wasn't at all sure about; I would find it there, in *Encyclopaedia Britannica*, I was certain, but just in case I needed to borrow any books for research while I was staying at Deer's Leap, Beth had left me her library ticket. Decent of her, really. And I must buy a couple of trout to replace those we had eaten for Sunday lunch. Raiding Beth's freezer was not on! Maybe, too, I would buy sausages and bacon and have a comforting fry-up tonight – sitting at the kitchen table beside a comforting fire. After all, a writer needs some time to herself, though my professional conscience would insist I get down to work this afternoon when I got back.

I found a car park in Clitheroe with no trouble. Immediately inside the library, I told myself that once I had established that Dorcas in *Firedance*, as I was beginning to know the book, could have used a phonecard in 1985, I would leave at once. Indeed, I discovered that phonecards were in use as long ago as 1981, and would have cost two pounds for forty units. I was glad I had checked. You have to be so careful. Errors are jumped on at once!

Even though I had already made up my mind not to browse along the shelves, I began to look at the section headed 'World Wars One and Two'. I walked slowly, willing myself not to pick up a book; not even for one quick glance.

Books with tanks, aircraft and submarines on their jackets tempted me, but I walked on. Not until novel number three, which I was almost sure now would be set in that period, would I start dipping into Jack Hunter's war. Yet even as I walked away something hit my consciousness and said, 'Look again!' So I obeyed the tingling at the back of my nose, and did exactly that.

Bomber Command. The title stood out clearly. *RAF Bases in Lancashire 1939–1945.* As I picked it off the shelf, I knew that RAF Acton Carey would be listed there, even though hardly a trace of it existed now.

I made for the desk, determined not so much as to glance at it until tonight when I had had my supper and my time was my own. Supper! I bought sausages from a shop near the castle ruins, then crossed the road to buy rainbow trout. As I walked to my car, I realized the rain had stopped and that a sliver of blue sky had appeared somewhere in the direction, I calculated, of Beacon Fell. I might have known, I smiled, that rain so heavy, so early, couldn't last.

I resisted the urge to buy a coffee, knowing that if I did I would open the book. Thoughts of that war would invade my mind, and I had already spent too much time thinking about the airman. And I had Suzie to worry about now; Susan Smith who might well be there for the finding! Oh, *please*, she would be?

I existed on a sandwich and far too many cups of coffee until nearly five o'clock. The garden looked green, the scent of wetness wafting in through the open window. The earth was dark again, having guzzled its fill, and all was well with my world.

I gathered up my papers, turned off the machine, then stretched long and lazily. The flow had returned, the lost morning atoned for. I felt almost smug as I let Hector into the yard.

First I would feed the animals and cook my supper. Then I would allow myself the luxury of a log fire and curl up with the book, hoping it would tell me something, however small, about how it had once been, at RAF Acton Carey.

I pricked sausages and rinded bacon. I would make fried bread too, I thought defiantly. I felt so pleased with my progress, one way or another, that I knew I would finish the bag of toffees as well, once I was relaxed in the firelight. I felt so good that I fixed the telephone on the dresser with my eyes, willing it not to dare ringing.

I should have let well alone. Five minutes later it rang.

'Yes?' I hoped I didn't sound too cross.

'Hi, love! It's Jeannie. Thought I'd ring you before I left the office. I *am* expected, tomorrow?'

'You are, but this last week has flown! Same train, is it? Will I meet you at Preston . . . ?'

'I'm so looking forward to it. Don't bother making a meal. I'll eat on the train. How's the book coming along?'

'Fine. It poured down, this morning, so I went to the library.'

'*Rain*?' She sounded put out.

'Yes, but it's cleared up now. We'll have another good weekend. Anyway,' said the market gardener's daughter in me, 'we needed a good shower.'

'Anything I can bring, Cassie?'

'Just yourself. See you tomorrow night.'

The fire flickered and snapped. Hector lay sleeping at my feet; Tommy, mesmerized by the fire, blinked and stretched and yawned. By my side was what remained of the bag of toffees; on the arm of the sagging old chair lay the book I had been longing to open since it shouted 'Pick me up!' from the library shelf.

First, I fanned the pages, stopping here and there to look at what had once been amateur snaps of crews and aircraft, and diagrams and plans of airfields – *aerodromes*, the compiler of the book called them.

By far the most important parts, as I saw it, were the runways and the control towers. The perimeter tracks –

which ran right round each airfield – and various blocks of buildings were further away and lower in the order of things, it would seem. I turned to the index. What I sought was there, on page ten.

RAF STATION ACTON CAREY. Completed Oct. 1943. Aircraft consisted two squadrons of Lancaster bombers, Marks I & II.

There followed a history of all the raids from Acton Carey; which shipyard or factory or docks had been targeted and how many bombers were missing after each one. The operations flown from Acton Carey had been many. Each Lancaster carried a crew of seven, and seven young lives became statistics with each bomber that did not return.

I remembered the memorial outside the church, the grateful remembrance and the date. Then I scanned the list of sorties.

On 2 June 1944 a flying bomb site in France had been targeted, and on 3 June another site at Mont Orgueil. Then, right up until 6 June, marshalling yards in France had been raided every night.

And then it was there – 8 June 1944. Flying bomb site at St-Martin-Le-Mortier; a daylight raid on which four Lancasters were lost; one of them piloted by Sergeant J. J. Hunter.

I tried to remember what I knew about flying bombs; bombs with wings, hadn't they been, and launched from France against the south coast and London? Hitler's secret weapon; one which would wipe out the D-Day landings and bring Britain to its knees.

And Jack Hunter had dropped his bomb load on one of the launching sites, because until they were destroyed they were a very grave danger to this country. My history lessons in the sixth form had told me that, yet now I was looking at a list no longer impersonal, and I knew when and from where our bombers took off on so urgent a mission; knew too the name of one of the men who did not return from it.

Jack Hunter. Twenty-four years old and in love with

Susan Smith from Deer's Leap farm, who met him secretly at the creaking kissing gate. Did he ever get to meet her parents, I wondered, or were Jack and Susan never to see each other again?

I read on, fascinated to learn that on 15 July 1944, RAF Acton Carey had been handed over to the United States Army Air Corps, who flew daylight missions from there until the end of hostilities in Europe – VE Day. Those huge American Flying Fortresses needed longer runways to take off and land, and what remained of Deer's Leap fields had been absorbed into the airfield.

Yet now Deer's Leap was once again a place of tranquillity. All that was left were memories, a war memorial in a quiet village – and the ghost of a pilot who waited for his girl; had been waiting for more than fifty years.

Near to tears, I closed the book with a snap. It was history now, I insisted; had ended when my mother was a baby. It was nothing at all to do with me, so why was I thinking about it every spare moment I had? Why did I feel the need to find Susan Smith?

I had no way of knowing. All I could be certain of was that Jack Hunter had latched on to me as his only hope, and I could not let him down.

'I lit a fire last night,' I said to Jeannie as I stowed her bags in the car boot. 'The house seemed a little cold, after the rain. Shall we light one tomorrow night? I've got a bottle of wine – or would you like to go to the Rose again?' I said off-handedly, though I was desperate to talk to Bill Jarvis.

'Go on the bikes, you mean? I'd love to, Cassie.'

'So would I, actually.' The relief in my voice was obvious. 'And we'd be better at it this time. Cycling uses up four calories a minute, did you know?'

'Big deal,' Jeannie grinned, because she ate whatever she fancied and didn't put on an ounce.

'Bill Jarvis might be there. I'd like to talk to him again.'

'It'll cost us, Cassie. Bill never does owt for nowt!'

'It'll be worth it. I want to talk to as many of the old ones as I can – get them to tell me how it was when they were young. Money well spent!'

I indicated right at the next set of lights, taking the Clitheroe road. Soon we would be driving through Acton Carey; passing a clump of oak trees and the spot at which I first met Jack Hunter. I wondered if I wanted him to be there tonight when Jeannie was with me, and decided I did not, because Jeannie might not even know he was there. Not everybody can see, or even sense ghosts.

The matter didn't arise, though. We drove past the oaks and The Place without incident and when she got out to open the white gate for me, I had time to take a look at the kissing gate. He wasn't there, either.

'Thanks, chum,' I whispered as Jeannie waved me through; thanks, I meant, to Jack Hunter for not being there. After all, he was taboo, wasn't he?

Jeannie took her bags upstairs whilst I made a pot of tea.

'It's a lovely evening. Shall we put cardies on, and have it on the terrace?'

Jeannie said it was a good idea, and was there any parkin left?

'We ate it all, but Mum and Dad might come up for the day, next week, and she'll bring some with her. I particularly asked her to. I thought they might've come on Sunday, but Dad's busy, judging at flower shows.'

We sat there without speaking because Jeannie had closed her eyes and was taking long, slow breaths.

'Penny for them,' I said when I'd had enough of the quiet.

'I was just thinking that I could get out of publishing,' she smiled, holding out her empty cup, 'if I could find a way to bottle this air. People in London would pay the earth for it.'

'Then before you do – give up publishing, I mean – I think I ought to tell you that I'm getting ideas about the next book.'

'Good girl. That's what I like. Unbridled enthusiasm. Got anything of a storyline worked out?'

'We-e-ll, what would you say if I told you it would have Deer's Leap in it, and the year would be 1944? Will war books be old hat by the time I get it written?'

'Dunno. Depends on who's writing them, and the genre. Would it be blood and guts, sort of, or a love story?'

'A love story – and tragic.'

'A World War Two Romeo and Juliet, you mean?'

'Mm. I was talking to Bill on Wednesday night. He told me there had been a lot of crashes hereabouts and that Acton Carey wasn't a very safe place to be.'

'And you feel strongly enough about that period to write about it with authority? There are a lot of people alive still who would soon let you know if you got anything wrong.'

'I'll tell you something, then.' It was my turn to take a long, deep breath. 'When I was at the library I saw a book about all the Bomber Command airfields in Lancashire during the war and bombing raids flown from Acton Carey are all listed in it. Someone went to a lot of trouble to get all the details. The Lancasters must have gone somewhere else, because in July 1944 the American Army Air Corps took the place over.'

'I wonder where those squadrons of Lancasters went.' Jeannie was getting interested.

'I don't know. But I did see the war memorial in the village. Remember Danny said the names of a crew that crashed hereabouts were included with the local dead?'

'Yes. But I wonder why one particular crew, when there must have been a lot of crashes . . .'

Jeannie was interested, all right. It gave me the courage to jump in feet first and say, 'I can't tell you that, but I'm going – just this once – to talk about someone we agreed not to talk about again.'

'Your ghost? I knew we'd get round to him sooner or later!'

'His name was Jack Hunter,' I rushed on. 'There's a J. J. Hunter on that memorial and the date is 8 June. It was one of the last raids flown before the Royal Air Force left Acton Carey. In the book it says it was a daylight raid on a flying bomb site in France.'

'So why can't he accept it? Doesn't he know he's on a war memorial?'

'I don't think he's grasped the fact yet that he's dead. I think,' I said, not daring to look her in the face because I didn't think, I *knew*, 'that the girl who lived here and the pilot were – well, an item.'

'And you want to write about them, even though you know he was killed?'

'I'd use different names. No one would know.'

'Except the girl who once lived here if she's still alive. It's just the kind of book she'd be interested in, she having had first-hand experience, kind of.'

'I said I'd disguise it. There *is* a story there, and I'd handle it very gently, Jeannie.'

'Yes, I do believe you would. You aren't a little in love with that pilot, are you?'

'Don't be an idiot! Why would I want to fall in love with a ghost? Be a bit frustrating, to say the least!'

'From what you've said, he seems the exact opposite of your Piers.'

'He isn't *my* Piers. I'll admit we had something going once, but it's wearing a bit thin – on my part, that is. But I don't find Jack Hunter attractive!' I crossed my fingers as I said it.

I lay in bed with the windows wide open, listening to the strange, waiting stillness outside; mulling over what we had talked about. And I thought about Jack Hunter too, and his slimness and the height of him and that I *had* found him attractive. Maybe that was why I wasn't in the least afraid of him – or what he was. Excited, maybe, when he was around, but no way did he frighten me. That pilot was exactly my type. I'd already decided, hadn't I, that if I'd been around these parts fifty-odd years ago, I'd have given Susan Smith a run for her money?

Jack Hunter danced perfectly, I knew it, and I felt an ache of regret that I would never dance closely with him. Then I felt relief that every time we kissed I would never know the fear it might be our last.

'Stupid!' I hissed into the pillow. Not only did I see ghosts, but I'd fallen in love with one!

I plumped my pillow and turned it over. I *wasn't* in love with the man! I only wanted to be, with someone very like him; someone who was flesh and blood and whose kisses were real!

'Deer's Leap,' I whispered indulgently, 'what *have* you done to me . . . ?'

Chapter Six

I awoke early in need of a mug of tea, after which I would throw open all the downstairs windows and doors – get a draught through the house.

August mornings should be fresh, not oppressive. I looked towards the hills as I let Hector out. Clouds hung low over the fells and there was little blue sky to be seen.

I put down milk for the cats and the clink of the saucers soon had them crossing the yard in my direction. Tommy had not slept on my bed last night, but then cats are known to find the warmest – or the coolest – places and he'd probably slept outside.

I drank my tea pensively, trying to push the words out of my mind that were already crowding there. Today and tomorrow were holidays – even if the weather seemed intent on spoiling them.

Did bad weather stop aircraft taking off and landing during the war? I frowned. Fog certainly was bad – it could still disrupt an airport – but how about snow on runways, and ice? Perhaps conditions like that gave aircrews a break from flying; a chance to go to the nearest pub or picture house. Or scan the talent at some dancehall, looking for a partner who might even be willing to slip outside into the blackout. Did they snog, in those days, or did they pet, or neck? Things – words, even – had changed over the years. Words! My head was full of them again; words to find their way into the next book, even though I was barely halfway through the current one!

I showered and dressed quickly and quietly, then told Hector to stay. I was going to the end of the dirt road to leave money for the milkman.

'Good boy.' I gave him a pat, and some biscuits, then shut the kitchen door. If Jack Hunter was at the kissing gate, I didn't want trouble, even though dogs are supposed to be frightened of ghosts. Cats, too.

As I closed the white gate behind me, it was evident that no one was there. The kissing gate was newly painted in shiny black. Perversely, I touched it with a forefinger and it swung open easily.

There were letters in the wooden box, mostly bills or circulars. Only one, a postcard view of Newquay, was addressed to me.

Having a good time. Weather variable. Hope all is well. D. & B.

I glanced up at the sky. The weather was variable in the Trough of Bowland too. What was more, I'd take bets that before the day was out we would have thunder.

When I got back, Tommy was waiting on the step, purring loudly. I could hear Hector barking and hurried to tell him to be quiet before he woke Jeannie.

I stood, arms folded, staring out of the window. If a prospective buyer looked at Deer's Leap on a day such as this, I thought slyly, one of its best assets – the unbelievable, endless view – would be lost. I supposed too that the same would apply if they came in winter, when the snow was deep. The view then would be breathtaking – if they managed to make it to the house, of course. Still, even if we had a storm today it wouldn't be the end of the world. My troubles were as nothing compared to those of Jack and Suzie.

Hector whined, rubbing against me. Lotus was nowhere to be seen, but Tommy prowled restlessly, knowing a storm threatened.

I piled dishes in the sink, then set the table for Jeannie. Like as not she would only want coffee – several cups of it – but laying knives and forks and plates and cups gave me something to do.

Even the birds were silent. A few fields away, black and white cows were lying down. They always did that when rain threatened, so they could at least have a dry space beneath them when the heavens opened. Clever cows!

I turned to see Jeannie standing there, yawning.

'Hi!' I smiled. 'Sleep well?'

'Hi, yourself.' She pulled out a chair, then sat, chin on hands, at the table. 'I woke twice in the night; it was so hot. I opened windows and threw off the quilt then managed to sleep, eventually.'

'Coffee?'

'Please. Why is everything so still?'

'The calm,' I said, 'before the storm. We'll have one before so very much longer. Are you afraid of thunder, Jeannie?'

'No. Are you?'

I shook my head. 'Want instant, or a ten-minute wait?' I grinned.

'Instant, please.' She yawned again. 'You're a busy little bee, aren't you? How long have you been up?'

'Since seven. I'll just see to your coffee, then I'll nip down to the lane end and collect the milk before it rains.'

All at once, I wondered how it would be when it snowed. It took me one second to decide that if I lived here I wouldn't care.

'We won't go down to the Rose if the weather breaks, will we?'

'No point,' I shrugged. 'There's lager and white wine in the fridge. We can loll about all day and be thoroughly lazy.'

'I'm glad I came, Cassie,' she smiled.

'I'm glad you did,' I said from the open doorway. 'Won't be long.'

I didn't expect anyone to be at the iron gate, or even walking up the dirt road, and I wasn't disappointed. Ghosts, I reasoned, were probably the same as cats and dogs and didn't like thunderstorms.

I put a loaf and two bottles of milk into the plastic bag I

had learned to take with me, and set off back. It could rain all it liked now.

I wondered if there were candles in the house in case the electricity went off like it sometimes did at home when there was a storm.

I made another mental note to ring Mum tomorrow from the village, then sighed and quickened my step, glad that for two days I had little to do but be lazy.

Jeannie crossed the yard from the outhouse where Beth kept two freezers.

'I think we might have chicken and ham pie, chips and peas tonight. And for pudding –'

'No pudding,' I said severely. 'Not after chips! And is it right to eat Beth's food?'

'Beth told us to help ourselves – you know she did.'

'OK, then.' I decided to replace the pie next time I went to the village. 'And are there any candles – just in case?'

'No, but Beth has paraffin lamps. Everybody keeps them around here. Are you expecting a power cut?'

'You never know. It could happen if we get a storm.'

'Then thank goodness the stove runs on bottled gas! At least we'll be able to eat!'

'Do you think of anything but food? No man in your life, Jeannie?'

I had stepped over the unmarked line in our editor/author relationship, and it wasn't on. Immediately I wished this personal question unasked. I put the blame on the oppressive weather.

'Not any longer. I found out he was married – living apart from his wife.'

'No chance of a divorce?'

'His wife is devoutly Catholic, he said.'

'He should have told you!'

'Mm. Pity I had to find out for myself,' she shrugged. 'Still, it's water under the bridge now.'

She said it with a brisk finality and I knew I had been warned never to speak of it again. So instead of saying I was sorry and she was well rid of him, I had the sense, for once, to say no more.

The storm broke in the afternoon. We sat in the conservatory, watching it gather. The air was still hot, but Parlick Pike and Beacon Fell were visible again, standing out darkly against a yellow sky.

'This conservatory should never have been allowed on a house this old,' Jeannie said, 'but you get a marvellous view from it for all that.' It was as if we had front seats at a fireworks display about to start.

'Are the cats all right?'

'They'll go into the airing cupboard – I left the door open. Hector will be OK, as long as he stays here with us.' She pointed in the direction of Fair Snape. 'That was lightning! Did you see it?'

I had, and felt childishly pleased it was starting. I quite liked a thunder storm, provided I wasn't out in it.

It came towards us. Over the vastness of the view we were able to watch its progress as it grew in ferocity.

'You count the seconds between the flash and the crash,' I said. 'That's how you can calculate how far away the eye of the storm is.'

We counted. Three miles, two miles, then there was a vivid, vicious fork of lightning with no time to count. The crash seemed to fill the house.

'It's right overhead,' Jeannie whispered.

That was when the rain started, stair-rodding down like an avalanche. It hit the glass roof with such a noise that we looked up, startled.

'Times like this,' Jeannie grinned, 'is when you know if the roof is secure.'

I knew that old roof would be; that Deer's Leap tiles would sit snug and tight above.

The storm passed over us and I calculated they would be getting the worst of it in Acton Carey. Lightning still forked and flickered, but we were becoming blasé after the shock of that one awful blast.

'I wonder if it was like this in the blitz – the bombing, you know.'

'Far worse, I should imagine. Bombs killed people. Are we back to your war again, Cassie?'

'It isn't my war, but there's something I've got to tell you.'

Even as I spoke, I knew I was being all kinds of a fool, so I blamed the storm again.

'About . . . ?'

'About what we agreed not to talk about. Shall I make us a cup of tea?'

I was glad to retreat into the kitchen, to get my thoughts into some kind of order, relieved to find the storm had not affected the electric kettle. When I carried the tray into the conservatory, Jeannie was standing at the door, gazing out.

'You think you've seen the ghost again – is that it?' she said, her back still to me.

'I've seen him. Twice more. Come and sit down.' I made a great fuss of stirring the tea in the pot, pouring it.

'Right then!' She placed her cup on the wicker table at her side, then selected three biscuits, still without looking at me. 'And I don't for the life of me know why I'm so silly as to listen to you,' she flung, tight-lipped. 'You're normally such a down-to-earth person!'

'I know what I saw and heard,' I said stubbornly. 'Do you want to hear, or don't you?' I took a gulp of my tea. 'Well – *do* you?'

'There'll be no peace, I suppose, till you've told me.'

There came another startling flash of lightning, followed almost at once by a loud peal of thunder. The storm we thought was passing had turned round on itself as if it were searching for a way out of the encircling hills.

'I'm getting bored with this!' Jeannie lifted her eyes to the glass roof. The rain was still falling heavily and making a dreadful noise above us. 'Let's go into the kitchen.' She picked up the tray and I followed her, carrying the plate of biscuits. Hector slunk behind me, whining, so I gave him a pat and a custard cream.

'Now.' Jeannie settled herself at the table, back to the window. 'You *are* serious? After all we agreed, you've been poking about again!'

'I have *not*! I went to the Rose on Wednesday night, and I'll admit asking Bill about the people who once lived here. It was natural that since the RAF was the cause of them getting thrown out, we should talk about the Smiths.'

'And . . . ?'

'Look, Jeannie – I didn't tell you, but I saw the pilot at the kissing gate, last Saturday morning! One second he was there; the next he'd gone!'

'When you'd been to the post office, you mean?'

'Yes. You said I was acting a bit vague; asked me if I had a headache.'

'So I did,' she said softly, 'yet you said nothing!'

'I only saw him out of the corner of my eye, but that gate opened of its own accord and I heard it squeak. He *was* there!'

'That gate *doesn't* squeak, Cassie!'

'It did during the war, and was rusty and in need of painting!'

'So when did he appear again?' She licked the end of her forefinger, picking up biscuit crumbs with it from her plate. She was doing it, I knew, to annoy me.

'Last Wednesday night.' I took a deep breath, and she lifted her head and looked at me at last. 'I'd been to the Rose, talking to Bill. I took the car, so I hadn't been drinking! I saw him clearly, ahead of me, near the clump of oak trees. It was bright moonlight, Jeannie. I could've put my foot down, like it seems people around these parts do if they think it's him. But I didn't. I stopped. He seemed anxious to get to Deer's Leap.'

'Like last time?'

'Yes. Just like last time. He wanted to let Susan Smith know he was on standby. And before you ask,' I rushed on, 'standby means they might be flying on a bombing mission. I asked him. Then he said he wanted to tell Susan he maybe couldn't make it that night. Seems he was hoping to meet her parents for the first time.'

'And it was important?'

'Seemed so to me. They wanted to get married, you see.'

'No, I *don't* see. He'd never met her folks, yet they were planning to get married? Is that likely?'

'Bill Jarvis said parents didn't like their daughters dating aircrew because so many of them got killed. Jack and Susan managed to meet secretly.'

'And the pilot told you all that – opened up his heart to you about Susan?'

'Why shouldn't he? Seems I'm the first person in more than fifty years to take any notice of him. And he called her Suzie, not Susan.'

'Well, all I can say is that either you've got one heck of an imagination, or you really do think you've seen him again!'

'I have! And talked to him. And don't try to tell me he doesn't exist. He's real enough for Beth and Danny to more or less warn me off!'

'But, Cassie – he might be something someone hereabouts invented.'

'So who told me then? Bill didn't say one word about him to me.'

'Well, he wouldn't. Nobody round Acton Carey talks about him! Like Beth said, they don't want the press in on it.'

'But if Jack Hunter doesn't exist, why try to cover him up? Why not let the reporters run riot – make fools of themselves?'

'OK, Cas!' She threw up her hands in mock surrender. 'So there have been rumours from time to time about – *something* . . .'

'Too right there have! Beth has seen him. She as good as admitted it.'

'But doesn't he scare you?'

'No. He doesn't groan or rattle chains. You could take him for a real person, except he seems able to vanish into thin air like he did on Wednesday.'

'Where did he seem to vanish to?'

'I don't know, exactly. I got out of the car to open the big gate and when I got back, he'd gone. All I knew was that I heard the kissing gate creak.'

'The one that needs painting?'

'You don't believe me, do you?' I was getting annoyed. How could she be so stubborn?

'I – I, oh, I don't know what to believe. And why does the kissing gate feature so strongly in it, will you tell me?'

'Because to my way of thinking, Susan Smith used to sneak out and meet him there. They'd be safe enough; the blackout would hide them.'

'Except on moonlit nights and in summer, when it was supposed to be light until eleven at night,' she shrugged, determined to play devil's advocate.

'When people are in love and they know they might not have a lot of time, they find a way. I would've.'

'All right. Point taken! So tell me – what is he like, your airman?'

'He's tall and slim – thin, almost. He's got fair hair and it's cut short at the sides. I suppose what they'd call a regulation cut. But it's thick on top, and a bit flops over his right eye. He has a habit of pushing it aside.'

'So what are you going to do, Cassie – about the airman, I mean?'

'I don't know. I want to help, because he's looking for his girl and there'll be no peace for him until he finds her – or more to the point, until she finds him. I reckon, you see, that he's rooted to what was once an airfield.'

'Trapped in a time warp, you mean?'

'Exactly. Look, Jeannie – are you with me or are you against me? I'd like to know.'

'Why? So I can help you?'

'No. It's me Jack Hunter is interested in. Seems I must be a bit of a medium and he's latched on to it. So it's all going to be up to me. But you can help by believing that I'm not going out of my tiny mind.'

'Somehow I don't think you are, Cassie. Your vibes and his must match, I suppose, or why has Beth seen him, and not Danny? She told me about it years ago and swore me to secrecy in case people thought she was bonkers. She was scared witless, though. Like she said, if she sees him again and she's in the car, she'll put her foot down and get the hell out of it.'

'Where do you think I should start? Where did the Smiths go when they had to leave Deer's Leap? If we knew that we'd be some way to finding Susan.'

'If she wants to be found. And, Cassie – you're not going to let this business interfere with your writing, are you?'

'Of course I'm not. Bill's parents might have known where Susan Smith went to, but I don't think they're around, somehow.'

'If they were, lovey, I doubt they'd be able to remember that far back.'

'Don't be too sure! Aunt Jane was born in 1915, but she remembered people going mad when World War One ended. She always called it the Great War.'

'All right then. There just might be someone down in the village who remembers the Smiths – even knows where they went. But how do you go about finding them? Do you knock on every door in Acton Carey, or get the vicar to read it out from the pulpit next Sunday? You'll get nothing out of that lot, Cassie. I reckon they know about the airman, too. Bill knows you're a writer. They'd clam up on you.'

'So that rules out the village. Y'know, Bill figured Susan Smith is about seventy-two or -three, and that isn't old these days. Aunt Jane was eighty when she died, and bright as a button. I've been telling myself that at the worst, Susan Smith might not be alive, but I think she is. All I can hope is that she won't slam her door in my face if I get lucky and find her.'

'You really want to go on with this, don't you, Cassie?'

'Yes. I'm his only hope.'

'Even though he thinks Susan is still living at Deer's Leap?'

'Even so. But just say I did find her – would she be willing to go along with it?'

'I don't know. But take it that she would – what do you both do? Drive up and down the lane until he's in need of a lift? Or do you camp outside Deer's Leap and wait for the kissing gate to start creaking? How long would it take, Cassie?'

'That's anybody's guess. But it didn't take *me* long, did it? He found me the first time I came here. But there's something neither of us has touched on. OK – so we're lucky – we find him first try! How is he going to recognize her? She'll have changed, over the years. She'll be old enough to be his grandmother now, and he's looking for a girl of eighteen or nineteen!'

'It won't be easy, but if he accepts her it might be all he needs to convince him it was all a long time ago; that he's dead, I mean. But what if Susan doesn't believe in ghosts? What if she *does*, and is too scared to give it a try? What if she's happily married? She'll have children, by now, and grandchildren. Do you think she'll want a past love raked up?'

'Yes, I do, because I believe they were desperately in love. No matter how happy she is now, she won't have forgotten her first love. I wouldn't have forgotten him if it were me. He really was something, Jeannie.'

'Oh, *Cassie*! Can't we forget your airman, just for a little while?'

I grinned and said of course we could! Any time at all! And if she didn't mind, I *wasn't* in love with him, though he intrigued me – a lot!

In love with someone who, if he'd lived, would have been old enough to be my grandfather? I wasn't *that* stupid!

Or was I? Because Jack Hunter would never be old. He was a young man my own age, and that was the way he would stay. And he'd go on thumbing a lift to Deer's Leap for ever if someone didn't help him.

'Look – the sun is trying to get through. There are all sizes of wellies in the utility room. Beth never gets rid of any that are half decent. There's sure to be some that'll fit,' Jeannie smiled. 'Let's go and sniff in some nice cool air.'

It was fresh again after the rain and the storm. The sun was shining the raindrops that still clung to everything, and the deep pools of water.

'Let's go puddle-jumping,' I laughed, determined to say no more about the matter that shouldn't be talked about. And anyway, we wouldn't see the airman. Jeannie only half believed in him, so her vibes would be very negative. He wouldn't appear.

'Shall we take Hector?'

'No! He'll get wet through, then shake himself all over us!'

We took him for all that, and sloshed through sodden grass all the way to the end of the paddock, where the land rose. Then we walked on to the top of the adjoining field Jeannie said was called Wolfen Meadow.

'Over there,' she pointed. 'You can't really miss it, can you?'

Below, to our left lay a huge, flat area. It had no trees nor hedges and was fenced all round, as far as we could see, with wooden railings. And just to confirm our findings, a long, narrowing jut of land pointed in the direction of Deer's Leap.

'It's the same shape as the diagram in the bomber station

book. We should have brought it with us,' I said. 'Then we could imagine exactly where everything used to be.'

'Do we want to?' Jeannie said soberly. 'I mean, if there really is such a thing as vibrations, then over there must be thick with them.' She nodded in the direction of where RAF Acton Carey had once been, her face strangely sad.

'Well, I do believe in vibes, and there would be all kinds if we cared to take them in. Relief, at getting back from a raid, for one. And what if a pilot was trying to make an emergency landing? The air would be white with sheer terror, I shouldn't wonder.'

'Do you think that's how Susan's pilot was killed, Cassie?'

'I don't know. According to the book, it was during the daylight raid on a flying bomb launching site. That was all it said.'

'Poor Susan,' she whispered. 'I wonder how it was for her?'

'I think,' I said as I gazed in a kind of trance over that flat piece of land, 'that she wouldn't even be told. They weren't married, so she wouldn't be his next of kin. The telegram would go to his parents. I read, somewhere, that aircrews used to leave letters behind to be sent to people. Maybe Jack left one addressed to Susan Smith at Deer's Leap. I'm almost certain the family was still there on 8 June.'

'Hm. I must have a look at it tonight – take it to bed with me – if you don't want to read it, that is . . .'

'No. Not tonight. You'll find it interesting, Jeannie.'

'I think I will.' She turned abruptly and began to walk towards the stone wall of the paddock. 'And I've had enough of ghosts for one day, if you don't mind. Let's get the bikes out and go to the Rose. We could eat there, if you'd like.'

She laughed out loud, almost as if she were trying to shake off the spell of the past, then set off at a run, calling to Hector, her short-cut hair bobbing with every stride.

'A good idea,' I panted, when we reached the paddock

wall. 'I want to phone Mum, anyway.'

'Good, then that's settled. Let's have a quick shower and get changed? All of a sudden, I'm hungry!'

I thought as we walked back through the wet grass that maybe Jeannie wasn't as blasé about vibes and ghosts as she tried to make out. She was interested in the bomber station book and her eyes had been far away as she looked down to where RAF Acton Carey had once stood. I wouldn't mind betting, I thought as I kicked off my wellies, that if she gave it a bit of effort she'd be quite good at sending out vibes. Maybe I shouldn't be too sure that Jack Hunter wouldn't appear if she were with me.

'Would you be afraid,' I said, 'if you were to see the airman? On your own, I mean . . . ?'

'N-no, I don't think I would; not after what you've told me, Cassie. But I'd be very, very sad, for all that. But let's get ourselves off! I'm famished!'

The Red Rose was quiet when we walked in at seven o'clock. The darts team, the landlord told us, had an away fixture at Waddington and Bill Jarvis had gone on the mini-bus with them.

'No grist to the mill tonight,' I said as we looked at the menu, disappointed that Bill wasn't there. 'Look – would you order for me? Scampi and salad; no chips. And get a couple of drinks in, whilst I phone Mum?' I laid a ten-pound note on the table. 'Won't be long.'

'Cassie?' Mum answered quickly, as if she had been waiting for my call. 'I was wanting you to phone, love. Your dad's just got back from the flower show and he says why don't we pop up to see you tomorrow?'

'Of course you can, but I thought he didn't like the roads at weekends.'

'Well, he's changed his mind. If we set out early we should be with you about ten-ish. Is that all right, or shall we leave it till Wednesday?'

'No! Come tomorrow!' All at once I wanted to see them both.

'No problem. I've got a chicken in the fridge. I'll cook it tonight and bring it with me. Shall I bring saladings?'

'*Please*, Mum. Lots. I don't suppose there'd be any parkin . . .'

'As a matter of fact there is, and I'll bring an apple pie.'

'You're an angel!'

'Sounds as if you haven't been getting enough to eat, our Cassie.'

'I have, but your cooking tastes so much better! Jeannie's here. She'll be pleased to meet you both.'

'We-e-ll, if you're sure it's all right – somebody else's house, I mean.'

'Mum! *Just come!*'

'In that case, no sense wasting money on the phone. I'll give you all the news when we arrive. Dad will work out a route.'

'If you look on the pinboard above my desk, you'll find one there – very detailed. And warn Dad the dog doesn't take kindly to strange men. A few cream biscuits in his pocket should do the trick – OK?'

Sunday was going to be a bright, warm day; I knew it the minute I pulled back the curtains. The grass still looked damp, but the flowers stood straight and looked more colourful against the moist black earth.

I thought with a squiggle of delight about ten o'clock and how much I was looking forward to seeing my parents.

'Pity we didn't get the grass cut yesterday,' said Jeannie, who had got up early in their honour. 'And it's still too wet to do today,' she said with relief.

'I'll do it later in the week. Want some toast?'

'No thanks. Just coffee. What are they like, your folks: what are they called?'

'Lydia and Geoffrey. They're ordinary and direct. Dad has strong opinions about things – Yorkshire-stubborn, I suppose. And Mum fusses and is cuddly. I adore them. Oh, and they'd appreciate being called Mr and Mrs. They don't go a lot on first names until they know people better. A bit old-fashioned, that way.'

'If your Mum brings some parkin, I'll call her Duchess!' Jeannie grinned. 'Now let's tidy the place up a bit – put out the welcome mat!'

'As long as the kettle is on the boil, Mum won't mind.' I felt light-headed and happy and eager to show Mum the house. 'But not one word about the airman, if you don't mind. They don't believe in ghosts.'

'Then who did you get your kinkiness from, Cas?'

'Obliquely, I suppose, from Aunt Jane. We were always on the same wavelength. We still have little chats, sort of. Now, will you be a love and get rid of those dead flowers, and pick some fresh ones?'

I was acting as if Deer's Leap were my own house, which it was, really, until the end of the month. And the end of the month was a long way away!

Chapter Seven

Mum and Dad arrived ten minutes early, which meant I hadn't opened the white gate, nor shoved Hector in the outhouse.

'They're here!' Jeannie called, but it was too late to stop the angry dog rushing out and snarling and snapping from the other side of the gate.

'Behave yourself, dog!' I yelled. 'Just a minute – I'll lock him up!'

'No! Leave him be,' Dad said quietly. 'He's got to learn a few manners! Open the gate, lass.'

'Be careful, Dad . . .' I was reluctant to let go of Hector's collar.

'I've never yet met the dog that got the better of me,' he said, standing feet apart, arms folded. 'Now then, my lad. Stop your noise!'

Man and dog glared at each other. Neither gave way. Dad dipped into his pocket and took out a cream biscuit, tossing it from hand to hand so Hector got the scent of it. Then he dropped it at his feet, standing very still.

Hector's nose twitched; the barking stopped. Then he sidled on his belly to snatch the biscuit, retreating behind me to crunch it. Dad went down on his haunches, then offered his hand. Hector gazed back with suspicion, then with longing at the second biscuit on Dad's palm.

'Come on then, lad. Either you want it, or you don't,' he said reasonably.

Hector wanted it. Avoiding Dad's eyes, he took it warily, then slunk away round the side of the house to reappear later, I shouldn't wonder, in a more friendly frame of mind. And hopefully to be given another biscuit.

'Mum! Dad!' I hugged them both. 'Sorry about the reception committee – and this is Jeannie, my editor from Harriers. My mother and father, Jeannie . . .'

'Lovely of you to come,' Jeannie beamed. 'You've brought good weather with you. Did you enjoy the drive?'

'Aye. Once we got off the motorway, it was real bonny,' Dad said. 'Not a great deal different to Yorkshire.'

'Only the other side of the Pennines,' I said. 'But wait till you see the view from the terrace. I've got the kettle on. Can we give you a hand with the things?'

When the chicken and vegetables my parents had brought were stowed away, I said, 'You didn't forget the parkin?'

'Of course not. I brought one for Jeannie, too, to take back to London.'

'Mrs Johns! You are an angel!' Jeannie opened the tin, sniffing rapturously. 'Can I have just a little piece now?'

'No, you can't!' Mum said. 'It'll spoil your dinner!'

We all laughed. Dad and Hector were friends; Mum had charmed Jeannie. The sun shone benignly. It would be a perfect day.

When the vegetables were cooking, the dining-room table laid and a bottle of white wine placed on the dairy floor to chill, I left Dad and Jeannie together, and showed Mum the house.

'I noticed when we got here,' she said, 'that this place is over four hundred years old. What tales it could tell!'

'Mm. Even going back to the war, there's a story. I could write a series of books with Deer's Leap as the focal point, sort of, starting when it was built until the present day. It was here when the Pendle Witches were tried and hanged, and I don't know whose side it would be on in the Civil War; probably they'd be King's men. I could get half a dozen books out of it if I set my mind to it.'

We walked round, up and down the many steps, Mum marvelling at the solidity of the house and its cosiness.

Then: 'Cassie?' She hesitated in a bedroom doorway. 'Now you know I'm not one to pry, but has anything – well – *happened* since you came here?'

'N-no. What makes you think it has?'

'I can't put a finger on it. It's just that you seem different, somehow.'

'We-e-ll, Jeannie did say she liked the first ten chapters of the book and that I'm writing with more authority, though what she means I don't quite know.'

'Not the writing,' Mum said, very positively. 'It's this place. There are no ghosts here but not far away is witch country, you said. Did a witch ever live here?'

'I'm almost certain not or there'd be some record of it. Anyway, why are you worrying? You don't believe in witches!' I teased, because for the life of me I couldn't tell her about the airman.

'There's something different about you, Cassie, for all that,' she persisted.

'Then blame it on Deer's Leap. I've fallen in love with the old house! But we'd better be getting downstairs or Dad is going to think we've fallen into a priest's hole!'

'Oooh! There isn't a priest hole too?' Suddenly Mum forgot witches.

'Not that I know of, but the house is the right age, and it's very higgledy-piggledy, isn't it? I'll bet you anything you like that if someone tried hard enough, and went round measuring and knocking on walls, they'd find one. Around these parts is priest-hole country. A lot of northern people refused to acknowledge the Church of England and they mostly got away with it because this was such wild country. Catholic priests came and went almost as they wished.'

'It still is wild country,' Mum sighed as we walked through the kitchen. 'I can understand why it's got you bewitched. I wouldn't mind living here myself.'

'If you did, we'd be able to look for priest holes to our hearts' content, wouldn't we?'

We broke into giggles, which made Dad ask us what was so funny and we said, 'Priest holes!' at one and the same time, then refused to say another word on the matter.

After our lovely Sunday, and when I had taken Jeannie to the station next day, the house seemed empty and quiet. I went to sit in the kitchen armchair and Tommy jumped on my lap, purring loudly to be stroked; Hector settled himself at my feet and fell into a snuffling sleep.

Yet I couldn't feel lonely; Deer's Leap was a safe, snug house. And I wasn't entirely alone; not if you counted the airman who was never very far away – of that I was sure.

Yet Mum was right. This house had no ghosts, which made me certain that Jack Hunter could not have met Susan's parents before he was killed. I'd have felt his presence here if he had. Were they ever lovers, even though in those days girls were expected to keep their virginity for their wedding night? I wished fiercely that they had been.

I tutted impatiently. This place had got me hog tied, and the ghost of an airman and an airfield that had long ago disappeared were a part of it. And could a witch have lived at Deer's Leap? Had Mary Doe practised the old religion and never been found out? Did she escape the hangman on Lancaster Common?

All at once I knew I had to read everything I could find about the Pendle Witches and about these wide, wild acres of Lancashire too. There were books in my head and this house had put them there; books spanning the centuries and ending with two star-crossed lovers. I had two weeks left in which to do it, yet *Firedance* must be finished on time, as my contract with Harrier Books demanded. Somehow I had to close my mind to all else but that; only then could I, as Deer's Leap demanded of me, write its story.

And by then it would belong to someone else. It would be too late.

*   *   *

I wrote steadily for two days, not needing to leave the house because I was able to exist on chicken and salad, thick slices of sticky parkin and left-over apple pie.

The words flowed. By Wednesday evening I had completed a chapter and roughed out another. I rotated my head. I had been sitting far too long. There was a tenseness in my neck and shoulders and my eyes felt gritty. The chicken was all gone; only the carcass left for soup, and I'd had my fill of saladings.

A beef sandwich and a glass of bitter beckoned from the direction of the Red Rose. I switched on the kettle to boil and took a bright red mug from the dresser, all the time looking at the world outside.

The sun was still high; it wasn't six o'clock yet, and it wouldn't be dark until almost ten. I could cycle to Acton Carey and if I left early enough, could manage to get back without lights. Though we had tried, neither Jeannie nor I could find any lamps, though it hadn't worried us too much. The road between Deer's Leap and the village wasn't what you could call busy; we had decided we could manage without them.

Mind made up, I fed the animals then changed into slacks and a sweater. With luck, Bill Jarvis would be at the Rose and might, perhaps, tell me how I could get a look at the parish records. I was hopeful he would know everything I needed so desperately to know, if only he could be steered away from the Italian campaign.

Would Jack Hunter appear tonight? Perhaps, I thought light-headedly, he didn't thumb lifts from cyclists. And why hadn't he reacted to the red Mini, asked why it wasn't camouflaged in khaki and green and black? Even I knew that much about World War Two motors; surely he couldn't miss something so startlingly red?

Or did he only react to the *sound* of a car engine? Could ghosts see colours or was everything in black and white? Did Jack Hunter see only what he wanted to see – a car in which he might get a lift to Deer's Leap? I found myself wishing him, willing him to be there, but I reached the Red Rose without seeing him.

I wondered what would happen if I asked him if he knew he were dead; if I told him the war had been over for more than fifty years, showed him today's newspaper to prove it! Would he, shocked, begin to age before my eyes? Would he become an elderly, grey-haired man, then disintegrate as I watched?

'Eejit!' I made for the back door of the Rose. I was hungry, and brain-damaged into the bargain from a surfeit of words! I needed the earthy presence of Bill Jarvis to bring me down from the giddy highs of my imagining.

It was a relief to see him sitting there, and the smile that crinkled his face when I said, 'Hullo, Bill! What are you drinking?'

And when he chuckled and said, 'Nowt at the moment. I was just off home, though I dare say I could sup another!' I knew that for the duration of a couple of pints, the world would be back to normal again.

'It's quiet in here tonight. No darts?' I asked, when we had eaten a plate of sandwiches between us.

'No. Folks is spent up till payday and, any road, they're busy with the last of the harvest; be at it till dark. That storm at the weekend flattened some of the standing wheat, though we needed the rain, mind.'

'I haven't found time to see the church yet,' I said when I had replenished our glasses. 'Is there anything of interest there – like old tombs?'

Or the baptismal register!

'Not that I know of. St James's isn't all that old. Were a cotton man from Manchester as built most of it. Name of Ackroyd. Bought the Hall in my great-grandfather's time. Brass, but no breeding.'

'Oh dear. It looks quite ancient.' I was quite put out by the intrusion of brass into Acton Carey. 'I really thought the church was as old as this pub.'

'He didn't make a bad job of it, I'll say that for him. Added it on to the little church as was already there – or so I believe.'

'But where is the Hall? Is it old?'

'It *was*. Got pulled down in the thirties and the stone bought up by a mason. Weren't no money in cotton no more, with all them fancy fabrics getting invented. The heir couldn't sell the place so he upped and left it. All he hung on to was the land, and a few houses in the village.'

'They wouldn't be allowed to demolish an old house nowadays, Bill. It would be a listed building. Elizabeth Tudor might even have slept there.'

It was a feeble joke which rebounded on me.

'No. Seems she never got this far north; folk in these parts was a law unto themselves in those days and her kept well away. But talk has it that King James stayed there on his way from Scotland to London. Well, that's what my dad once told me.'

'And we'll never know now, will we?' I felt quite peeved that an old house could have been demolished, with people gathering like vultures to cart away timbers and fireplaces and almost certainly the staircase.

'No. But like I said, them at the Hall wasn't real gentry and they weren't locals neither.'

'Foreigners from Manchester, Bill!'

'Aye. But if you want to see inside the church, there'll be someone there on Friday mornings as can talk to you. They alus gives the place a sweep and a bit of a dust ready for Sunday. My sister, Hilda, goes; collects all the news. A right gossip shop, it is!'

'Your sister still lives here, then – the one who knew Susan from Deer's Leap, I mean. The one you said wasn't allowed to go to the RAF dances?'

'She does. Married an airman at the end of the war and he settled here when he got his demob. Got work with a plumber in Clitheroe.'

'But how did they manage to meet if the girls round here weren't allowed to fraternize?'

'Like courting couples alus did – on the quiet, of course! All the lasses round these parts were at it. Creepin' out. Our Hilda used to say she was going to her friend's house.'

'And her friend said the same?' I laughed. 'I suppose it added spice. I should think Susan Smith had a boyfriend too – on the quiet.'

'You seem a mite interested in the Smith lass.'

'N-no. Not really. Only because I'm staying at Deer's Leap. I mean, her living all that way from the village.' I took a drink from my glass, nonchalantly, I hoped. 'Things were different then, weren't they? Young women didn't have the freedoms I take for granted.'

'They didn't and that's a fact!'

He tilted his glass, draining it to the last drop and I felt irritated that I would have to go for a refill just when the talk was getting interesting.

'But girls still got married, in spite of the way it was.' I put the glasses down and beer slopped onto the tabletop. 'In the end, they all made it to the altar.'

'Aye, and some of them in a bit of a hurry, an' all,' he chuckled. 'But as long as they got wed, they was forgiven.'

'So some of them got pregnant beforehand, in spite of everything?'

'Oh, aye. It's the nature of things.' He tapped his nose with a forefinger. 'Alus was; alus will be.'

'Your sister would have known Susan Smith,' I said, trying to keep my voice level.

'They went to the same school, if that's what you mean, though they were in different classes. But those Smiths kept themselves to themselves. Didn't even go to the church here. Was Chapel, see. Got the pony and trap out and went over Leagram way, Sundays. Edwin Smith had no option, come to think of it. His missus was very devout. Eleanor Smith did a lot for the chapel.'

I sucked in my breath, marvelling how easy it had been – how I'd hoped to find some way of seeing the parish records, yet Bill had dropped two names right into my lap. Smiths can be hard to trace, there being quite a few of them, yet now at least I knew I was looking for Edwin and Eleanor Smith. I was on my way. Small beginnings, but I had avoided the disappointment of finding no record of Susan's christening in St James's registers. In a chapel over Leagram way, it would have been.

I felt so lucky I said, 'Let me top you up before I go, Bill. I'll have to be off – don't have any lights on the bike, I'm afraid.'

I bought a half at the counter and placed it more carefully beside him.

'You'll be going, then?'

His face showed disappointment that we hadn't even touched on the fighting in Italy.

''Fraid so. But Jeannie will be here again on Friday – we'll be down at the weekend, I shouldn't wonder.' I drained my glass and got to my feet. 'Night, Bill. See you.'

'You be careful, lass, riding without lights. If you hear a car coming, you'll have to jump off, though it isn't likely you'll meet anything on that road.'

'No. It's very quiet, but I'll be careful. Bye, then . . .'

I smiled at the landlord as I left; a satisfied smile really, because deep down I was hoping I would meet something, someone, on that road.

The village lights were well behind me, and the narrow road ahead was unlit. I blinked my eyes rapidly, making out the dark shapes of trees and hedgerows and, dimly on my right, dry-stone walls. The only sounds were of my own breathing and the soft crunch of the tyres on the gravel at the roadside.

This, I thought, was what it must have been like when a complete blackout covered the entire country, but even as I tried to imagine it, I could see an orange glow in the sky ahead that was probably Preston. Yet during Jack Hunter's war there would be no shine of lights below him as he flew; only, sometimes, the moon which could be his enemy as well as his friend.

I was passing the clump of oak trees, now, and began to look around me. The familiar little pulse behind my nose began its fluttering, and I wondered if it was because he was around and his vibes – his radar – were trying to beam in on me. Or was it myself sending out the signals, calling him to me? And why did I shake with dry-mouthed excitement? Why wasn't I afraid?

Afraid of a ghost I could easily fall in love with? Afraid of a wraith that had no substance; who, if I tried to take his hand, would vanish into the air maybe never to return? Could you, should you, try to touch a ghost?

Something crossed my path just inches ahead of my wheel. It slid, soundless as a shadow and was quickly gone. A stoat, was it, or a rat? I began to shake. I was afraid of rats. Ghosts I could stomach, but not rats!

I attempted a smile. It was all right! Whatever the creature was, it was surely more afraid than I! Concentration broken, my front wheel began to wobble and I swerved across the road, hitting the grass verge on my right.

Fool, Cassie! I pushed both feet down hard and picked up speed, admitting for the first time that it was stupid of me to ride home in near-darkness. Suppose someone had seen me leave the Rose and was following me? It happened all the time. Women were attacked in broad daylight, even, yet here was I, asking for trouble! I was in the middle of nowhere, hoping to meet a ghost! It was completely ludicrous, and if Mum could see me now she would blow her top!

I pedalled harder, wanting suddenly to be safely back, with Tommy rubbing against my leg and Hector welcoming me home; Hector, who didn't like strange men!

As I turned at the crossroads, I realized I had put Jack

Hunter out of my mind, so sudden was my imagined danger. I jumped off the bike, walking carefully, feeling my way cautiously because the last thing I wanted was to trip and fall in the rutted dirt road.

Then I let go my breath, just to see the white gate ahead. It was all right. I was back. In just a few seconds Hector would begin his barking and things would be sane and safe again.

It was then that I heard the laugh; a man's laugh, low and indulgent. My mouth filled with spittle and I closed my eyes and stood there, unable to move. He had followed me; allowed me to reach safety, almost, and now he was laughing.

I straddled my feet either side of the pedals then reached for the gate, wrapping my arms around it as if it could protect me, then waited, breath indrawn. I was rigid with terror. Times like this you were supposed to run, kick out, shout and scream, but I could do nothing.

I heard the laugh again, then a voice said, 'Suzie . . .'

Suzie? My God, it was him; Jack Hunter at the kissing gate! I swallowed hard on the sob of relief that choked in my throat.

'It's Cassie,' I gasped.

'Suzie darling, don't worry. It's going to come right for us. I'll make it come right . . .'

I listened, relaxing my hold on the gate, though my heart still pounded.

'Sweetheart, we *will* be married. They can't stop us . . .' Him, talking again. 'Don't get upset. Tomorrow morning we'll tell them. I do so love you . . .'

Jack, talking to Suzie, only Suzie wasn't there! Jack, reliving one of their snatched meetings at the kissing gate! I felt like a Peeping Tom, spying on lovers, listening. Yet only he was there; I heard only one voice.

The shaking inside me had stopped, my fear gone. No one had followed me home.

'Jack . . . ?' I said, more clearly.

The kissing gate creaked, then silence. I propped up the bike and walked towards the gate, pushing it gently. It swung without effort or noise. He had gone.

'Jack Hunter!' I yelled, but my voice was lost in the night.

It took me several seconds to unlock the back door. For one thing, it was dark and I had no torch; for another my hand wasn't as steady as it might have been. But Hector was behind it, barking, jumping against it.

It was all right. I could have been followed home by a man, had heard a ghost, but it *was* all right! Just how mad can you get?

I slammed the door, pushing home the bolts. Then I bent down to stroke Hector, felt the comforting roughness of his tongue as he licked my face.

I reached for the light switch and Tommy blinked, stretched, then jumped from the armchair to purr against my leg.

I was home, with the safeness of Deer's Leap around me. I would never do anything so foolish again!

'Let that be a warning to you, Cassandra Johns,' I said sternly, loudly, as I drew the curtains, then took down a mug; a sane, safe, familiar red mug.

The heavy old-fashioned key was still in my pocket. I shoved it into the lock, turned it, then hung it on the brass hook at the side of the door.

'Ooooosh!' I let go a deep, calming breath. The airman was still around. I had always thought the kissing gate was their meeting place and he'd been there, talking to Suzie.

'Susan Smith, where are you?' I demanded of the kettle. 'He was waiting for you tonight and you didn't show! I need to find you!'

When I collected the milk next morning, there was a letter in the lidded box from Piers, redirected from Greenleas, and a holiday postcard addressed to Cassie, Aunt Jeannie,

Hector, Tommy and Lotus. It wished we were all there and was signed, Elspeth and Hamish.

I read it again, and propped it on the mantelpiece, then reluctantly opened the envelope bearing a London postmark.

There was only a single sheet, which pleased me – until I read what he had written.

Cassandra love,

I shall be taking the remainder of my holidays starting Monday next. What a pity you'll be wherever it is and I shall be at Rowbeck, bored out of my mind – unless you relent, that is, give me a quick bell and tell me where I can find you. Why is your address such a closely guarded secret? What are you up to?

I will call at Greenleas whilst I am there – and meantime take care and don't do anything I wouldn't do!

Yours,
P.

Feel free, Piers! Try to wangle it out of Mum if that's the way you want it, but she won't tell you!

'And I'm not up to anything!' I said out loud, pushing the letter in my pocket. You'd think I was having an affair in deepest Lancashire, I thought indignantly.

And aren't you, Cassie? Aren't you just a little in love with Jack Hunter and aren't you enjoying it because you know you can never have him? Isn't he the excuse you want to break up with Piers?

'Don't be so stupid, girl! How can you be in love with a ghost? And there was never anything between me and Piers, anyway. Just sex. Not love. Not like the way it was between Suzie and Jack.'

And I was talking to myself now! Roll on tomorrow night when I went to pick up Jeannie!

Jeannie! The cupboard was bare! I would have to go to the village for food, though it might be politic to go tomorrow when the ladies cleaned the church, find Bill's sister, talk to her about Deer's Leap and maybe, with luck, about Susan. A bit underhand maybe, but reporters do it all the time and, besides, I owed it to Jack Hunter. About time someone gave him a bit of help instead of pretending he wasn't around.

I sliced bread, filled the kettle, took a red mug from its hook, because I had long ago learned that flights of fancy – of fiction – are all very well, but they must be turned off, shut down and pigeonholed. Otherwise, people who write for a living wouldn't know what they were about!

At home, at Greenleas, I kept my fictional world in its place simply by pulling the curtain across my writing alcove, knowing it would be waiting there next morning. But here at Deer's Leap, when I turned off *Firedance*, Jack Hunter and Susan Smith were there to bother me, and an old house that had charmed me from the minute I set eyes on it. Now I was obsessed with a house that could never be mine, a creaking kissing gate, and not a little attracted to a man who had been too young for the responsibilities forced upon him.

Imagine being in command of a bomber; of sitting on your parachute because it was too cumbersome to wear in flight, and hoping you could get the thing on if ever you had to jump for it. Imagine wings filled with aviation fuel that allowed the crew just seven more seconds of life if pierced by a shell from a night fighter, and of being responsible for the lives of six other men when all you wanted was to steer clear of fighters, stay airborne and make a safe landing at Acton Carey airfield – *aerodrome*.

The toast popped up with a startling noise and I looked at it almost in disbelief because it was so ordinary compared to a Lancaster bomber on a mission, and seven young fliers trying to stay alive. And they hadn't flown missions. They had gone on ops – operations – in those days! I knew it just as surely as I had heard the roar of four great aero-engines, smelled fear, known the draining relief of getting back to mugs of tea laced with rum, trying all the while to concentrate on the persistent probing of the debriefing officer when all you wanted was sleep. Then to meet your girl, secretly, at a creaking kissing gate. Dry-mouthed, I pulled out a chair to sit, chin on hand, at the table.

I was shaking at the reality of it; of being there in the absolute darkness, flying every mile of the way to the target and back with an airman I loved to desperation. I was becoming a part of a war most people were too young to remember; was living it through the heart and mind of a girl who once lay awake, blessing her lover on his way then willing him back to her. How else could I know such things?

The kettle boiled, bubbled fiercely, then switched off. I spooned coffee into the mug and granules spilled over the tabletop because my hand was shaking so.

I closed my eyes then said out loud, 'Cassie! That war is history! Count to ten, then open your eyes to the real world!'

This was indeed 1998 and somewhere was an elderly lady who was once called Susan Smith. She was still alive, I knew it, because I had just homed in on her vibrations, felt her long-ago fear. And if I didn't stop myself I would know, too, her desperate heartbreak, feel her tearing despair as she came to realize that the bomber that crashed on a June day had been Jack Hunter's!

Then all at once I heard Aunt Jane's voice inside my head; heard it as surely as if she were here in this room.

'Cassie, girl! It'll be all right! Finish your saucy novel then give yourself to Deer's Leap. Write those books, starting with Margaret Dacre in 1592.'

Aunt Jane? I sent out a desperate plea from my heart, my head, but her voice was gone beyond recalling. I took a gulp of coffee, swallowing it noisily. Aunt Jane was right. I must finish *Firedance*, and only then concentrate on the Deer's Leap novels and the women who lived here through the ages, starting with Margaret Dacre. M.D.! *Not* Mary Doe, Jeannie! Now I knew the name of the woman who lit the first fire in this kitchen and hung her cooking pot above it! Aunt Jane had told me!

I smiled, all at once warm with tenderness, because now I had established a rapport with the woman who must have loved this house as much as I did, had likely walked these hills with her man until they found exactly the right spot on which to build; where there was water for the farm animals and a place to sink a well. They would have studied closely the lay of the land and from which direction the wind blew in winter and where to build for shelter from it. But on a distant spring morning, when the trees were green and the hills so beautiful they took your breath away, Margaret Dacre would have opened her arms in an expansive sweep and said, 'This is where it shall be, husband, where the window of my summer parlour must face!'

'So you may sit and look at yon view, Meg, and neglect your chores?'

Meg, he would call her, and as their family grew they would build on more rooms: a snug winter parlour, maybe, and another bedroom. Or did they call them bedchambers when Elizabeth Tudor was queen? And I must try to discover how many babies they had and if they were taken to the tiny church in Acton Carey for christening, before the cotton merchant from Manchester made it bigger and grander.

My heart thudded with pleasure. The Deer's Leap books would be a joy to write. I had been meant to come here – if, sadly, too late. Come another summer, some other woman would be in this kitchen, though she would not hang her cooking pot over the fire, nor salt sides of bacon in the dairy as Margaret Dacre had done.

So I must enjoy the last of my summer days here, then return at Christmas to wish it goodbye and hope that if I was meant to, I would come back to Deer's Leap one day.

The phone on the dresser began to ring and I gasped with

annoyance because it was Piers, I knew it, homing in on my dreams, mocking them, damn him; Piers reminding me he was on holiday, and could he come up and visit?

I drew in my breath then said 'Hullo?' very evenly and normally, though only half of me was yet in the real world.

'Cassie! It's Beth! How are you?'

'How lovely of you to ring!' My relief was enormous.

'Thought I'd better make sure you're all right and not too lonely . . .'

'Not a bit. Jeannie's coming tomorrow.'

'Animals OK?'

'They are, Beth. Lotus leads her own life – I only see her when she's hungry – but Tommy and Hector are never far away. By the way, my parents came to visit last Sunday – hope it was all right?'

'Of course it was!'

'Dad loved the garden and Mum thought the house was just beautiful. How are the children?'

'Brown as berries and never far from the water.'

'We had a storm last weekend, but we're keeping on top of the grass cutting between us, tell Danny.'

'And you're sure you're all right, Cassie?'

'Loving every minute of it!'

'Oh dear. The card's running out. Love to Jeannie when she comes, and take care of –'

The call ended with a click and I smiled at the receiver by way of a goodbye, then plugged in my machine and screen. I would work until I felt hungry; no stopping for coffee breaks.

I had just decided to write one more page and then I could stop for a sandwich, when Hector growled from the back door, all at once alert.

'What is it?' I frowned, but he was gone, barking angrily.

I got up and went to the door. From the direction of the front gate came a furious clamour. A walker, was it, needing to ask directions?

I made for the front gate calling, 'Stop it, Hector!' then gasped, 'Oh, flaming Norah!'

Beside the gate was a red BMW; a few feet back from it stood an angry-faced Piers. On the other side of it, Hector was at his magnificent best when confronting a strange male.

I grabbed hold of his collar then said, 'Piers! What are you doing here? How did you know . . . ?'

'Look – just lock that animal up, will you? The blasted thing went for me as I tried to open the gate!'

'He doesn't like strange men!'

'Ha! You could've fooled me! It nearly had my hand off!'

'Don't be silly!' Hector continued to snarl, despite my hold on him. Hector, when angry, took a bit of controlling and I decided to put him in the outhouse. 'Wait there,' I said snappily, still shocked and not a little dismayed Piers had found me.

'Why have you come?' I demanded as I filled the kettle. 'I mean, I made it pretty clear I didn't want anyone here. I came to work and anyway, this isn't my house. I can't go treating it like it's a hotel. It wouldn't be right.'

'Your father and mother visited – why not me?'

'Mum and Dad are different.'

I could feel the tension round my mouth and it wasn't entirely because I was angry. Piers had been determined to find me, probably annoyed because I wasn't as biddable as I used to be, and wanting to know why.

'And I'm not? I thought we had something going, Cassandra. It was good between us till you got this writing bug.' He was doing it again: trying to belittle what I had achieved. 'Coffee, please. Black, no sugar.'

'I know!' I said snappily, turning my back on him because I couldn't bear to look at the did-you-think-I-wouldn't-find-you smirk on his face. 'Who gave you this address?' I handed him a mug. 'Did you wheedle it out of Mum?'

'Not exactly . . .'

'Then how?' I glared, sitting down opposite.

'I went to Greenleas. There was a postcard of Acton Carey on the mantelpiece.'

'Oh, clever stuff, Piers! So who gave you directions?'

'The postman. I asked him where I could find Deer's Leap. And your mother didn't tell me. She let it slip, accidentally. "Deer's Leap is such a lovely house," she said. "Very old and quaint. Cassie loves it there." I don't think she saw me pick up the postcard, by the way.'

'You're a sneaky sod!'

I went over to the dresser to sweeten my drink and he was on his feet in a flash, arms round my waist, pulling me close.

'Stop it, unless you want coffee all over you! This is neither the time nor the place, so don't get any ideas! You just can't come barging in, upsetting things,' I flung when I had the distance of the tabletop between us again. 'You can't take no for an answer; always want your own way in everything!'

'Answer, Cassandra? I don't recall asking any relevant question.'

'Not questions,' I was forced to admit, 'but you did take it for granted I'd go to London, didn't you? And you've no right to come here, stopping me writing. You know I can't write if I get upset!'

'Ah, yes. You're a creative type. I forgot you must have your own space!'

I almost lost my temper, then; yelled at him to get out. But I took a deep breath and wondered if I should open the outhouse door, let Hector sort him out.

Instead, I said, 'You can't stay the night, Piers. It's not on – not in Beth's house!'

All at once I disliked him a lot, resented the way he could sit there unruffled and make me want to lose my temper. And I resented the underhand way he'd found me.

'I mean it!' I said as evenly as I could. 'If I'd wanted you here, Piers, I'd have asked you. I came to look after the animals and the house for Jeannie's sister, and to write.'

'And I don't merit just one day of your time, Cassandra?'

His expression hadn't changed, his hands lay unmoving on the tabletop. All at once I wished him in a bomber, hands tense, his eyes and ears straining, wanting desperately to live the night through. And he'd soon be told to get his hair cut! He never had a hair out of place; Jack Hunter's fell over one eye and he pushed it aside with his left hand; didn't know he was doing it.

'Come and see the garden, or better still walk with me to the top of the paddock, Piers?'

'Why?'

'I want to talk to you.'

'Can't we talk here?'

'I'd rather walk.' I wanted him out of the house.

'OK. If that's what it takes.'

He got carefully to his feet, shrugging his jacket straight, indicating the door with an exaggerated, after-you gesture and I thought yet again he should have been an actor. I locked the back door behind me and slipped the key into my pocket. 'This way,' I murmured, deliberately walking past the outhouse.

Hector snarled as we passed, and threw himself at the door, and I knew Piers had got the message.

'Isn't it beautiful?' I waved an arm at the distant hills.

'Very pretty, Cassandra.' He was leaning, arms folded, against the dry-stone wall now, his boredom turning down the corners of his mouth. 'So what have you to say to me?'

He didn't yawn. I expected him to, but he spared me that and I was glad, because I think I'd have hit him if he had.

I drew in a breath, then said, 'You and I have come to the end of the road, Piers. We aren't right together. I don't want to see you any more. It's over.'

'What's over, Cassandra?'

'Us. You and me. We couldn't make a go of it.'

'But I never thought we could! Your heart was never in it, even when we were in bed. To you it was just something else to put in a book – how it's done, I mean.'

'And you, Piers, made love to me simply because I was there and available. Another virginal scalp to hang on your belt, was I?'

'I thought you'd enjoyed it . . .'

'I did – at the time.' I had to be fair. 'It was afterwards, though, that I didn't like.'

'What do you mean – *afterwards*?' He was actually scowling.

'When it was over, Piers. I looked at you and found I didn't like you. Oh, it was good at the time, but I think that when two people have made love they shouldn't feel as I did – afterwards.'

'Cassandra! You're making it into a big deal! It was an act of sex, for Pete's sake! You were willing enough. Curious, were you?'

'Yes, I'll admit I was and I was quite relieved it went so well. I was afraid I'd make a mess of it. I'd wondered a lot what it would be like, first time. But I think it isn't any use being *in love* with a man if you don't *love* him too.'

'There's a difference?' He was looking piqued.

'For me there is. Look, Piers – you and I grew up together. All the girls in the village fancied you. Then you went away to university and when you came back to Rowbeck you singled me out. I was flattered.'

'I didn't have a lot of choice. Rowbeck wasn't exactly heaving with talent!'

'Point taken!' Piers was himself again! 'But I always thought that the first time I slept with a man, he'd be the one, you see. And it seems you aren't.'

'Why aren't I?'

'I don't know.'

Oh, but I did. He wasn't young and vulnerable and fair. And his hair wasn't always getting in his eyes – he wouldn't let it! And he wasn't desperately in love with me either, and sick with fear that each time we parted would be the last.

'Piers!' I gasped, because he was staring ahead and not seeing one bit of the beautiful view. 'I just want us to be friends like when we were kids.'

'But we aren't kids. You aren't all teeth and freckles, Cassandra, and mad at being called Carrots. You've grown up quite beautifully, as a matter of fact.'

'Thanks,' I said primly. 'Flattery will get you everywhere – but not today. Sorry, but that's the way it is. I really must work.'

'Work? You don't know the meaning of the word.'

He said it like a grown-up indulging a child and I knew I had made my point at last. I held out my hand.

'Friends, then?'

'OK.' He smiled his rueful smile, then kissed my cheek. 'My, but you've changed, Cassie Johns. Is there another bloke, by the way?'

'No.' I shook my head firmly. 'And you'd best not tell Mum you've been. She'd be upset if she thought she'd given my whereabouts away.'

'So you said she mustn't let me have your address?'

'Yes. I didn't want any interruptions.'

'I see. Would you mind, Cassandra, if I gave you a word of advice? Don't take this writing business too seriously?'

'I won't,' I said evenly, amazed he seemed no longer able to annoy me. 'You'll want to be on your way, Piers . . . ?'

'Mm. Thought I might take a look at Lancaster, get a spot of lunch.'

'I believe it's a nice place,' I said as we climbed the stile in the wall. 'They used to hang witches there.'

'You haven't seen it? Come with me – just for old times' sake – a fond farewell?'

'Thanks, but no.' Deliberately I took the path that led to the kissing gate. 'And thanks for being so understanding – about us, I mean, and me breaking it off.'

He got into his car, then let down the window.

'There was never anything to break off, Cassandra. Like you said, another scalp . . .'

I stood for what seemed like a long time after he had driven down the dirt road in a cloud of dust thinking that, as always, he'd had the last word. But I could get along without him. I shrugged, closing the kissing gate behind me.

I let go a small sigh, straightened my shoulders then walked, nose in air, to let Hector out.

All at once, I was desperate for a cheese and pickle sandwich.

Chapter Eight

Page two hundred and fifty, and the end of chapter seventeen. I rotated my head, hands in the small of my back. Cassie Johns her own woman again, *Firedance* ahead of schedule and the mantel clock telling me it was time for tea and a biscuit.

I felt a surge of contentment, a kind of calm after this morning's storm, waiting patiently for the kettle to boil, gazing arms folded through the window to the hills and the purple haze of heather coming into flower.

I would miss the space, the wideness of the sky, the utter peace of Deer's Leap when I went home. I had just absently plopped a saccharin into my cup when the phone rang again. I had a vision of Piers calling me on his mobile, telling me he was lost in the wilds of Bowland.

'Hi, Cas! It's Jeannie. I'm leaving now. See you tonight, uh?'

'You're taking an extra day? But that's wonderful! What time shall I meet you?'

'It's part business, part pleasure, so I'm driving up. I'll tell you about it when I see you. I'd like to be clear of London before the rush hour starts. Once I'm on the M6 I'll stop at the first caff for something to eat, so don't bother cooking.'

'You're sure?'

'Absolutely! I'll be there before dark. See you!'

'That was Jeannie,' I said to Hector, who had heard the rattle of the biscuit tin. 'She's coming tonight and there's not a thing to eat in the house!'

I took a sip of tea, giving a biscuit to Hector. I would go right away to the village in case Jeannie got her foot down on the motorway and decided not to stop. Anyway, I was low on coffee.

Chicken pie, peas, oven chips – I made a mental list – coffee, white wine and a phonecard. Mum would cluck and scold for not waiting until after six, but she'd be pleased to hear from me. I smiled at the red rose that peeped, nodding, through the kitchen window, feeling almost completely happy, wondering if I wasn't tempting fate, because no one could feel this smug and go unpunished. I looked at the calendar beside the fireplace. Soon, Beth's lot would be home and I would have to give back Deer's Leap. Just to think of it wiped the smirk from my face.

'Want to come to the village?' I reached for Hector's lead and he was at the door with a yelp of delight, tail wagging. I would miss Hector too.

I stopped at the lidded box and left a note for the milkman to find in the morning, then wondered if there would be any sign of the airman. It seemed ages since the last encounter.

Yet the trip there and back passed completely without incident. Even my parents hadn't been in; all I'd got was Mum's posh telephone voice, inviting me to leave a message on the answerphone.

I got back a little after five, just enough time to make up Jeannie's bed and dust her room. Then a quick tidy-up all round and with luck I'd be able to wash my hair before she got here.

The contented feeling was back again. I looked forward to seeing Jeannie and wondered why she was taking the day off, and driving up too. I opened wide the windows and smiled into the pale purple distance, remembering that the big, blowsy poppies Jeannie liked so much were just breaking bud, and though they would quickly open and fall indoors, I decided to pick some for her room.

Jeannie was her usual unruffled self with not a hair out of place, despite the long drive.

'Did you stop to eat?' was the first thing I asked and she said she'd had fish and chips and peas. Mushy, of course.

I helped her in with her things, thinking that if she wasn't such a love, I could hate her for the way she could pig it, without adding an inch to her waistline.

'So what's news?' We were sitting outside with glasses of wine, watching the twilight thicken. 'How come you've driven up, and a day early too?'

'There's a literary luncheon hereabouts tomorrow and I'm minding Susanna Lancaster. You'll have heard of her?'

'Of course. Who hasn't? But what is minding?'

'That, my dear good girl, is the taking care of an author when she's making an official appearance, so to speak. Writers of Lancaster's calibre always get one. She's the guest speaker. It'll be her last time, so Harrier Books want it to go well for her. Her book comes out officially today, and after that she's giving up writing, or so she says.'

'And are you her editor, Jeannie?'

'No, her regular editor is getting married on Saturday, so I volunteered. I tried to get a ticket for you, Cassie, but no luck. Strictly limited, and sold out ages ago.'

'No problem.' For some reason, literary luncheons made me think of poetry readings, and big hats. 'Where will it be?'

'At the Throstle Farm Hotel, about seven miles from here. The great lady will want driving there – it's why I brought the car. I'll have to be up early in the morning to give it a wash and polish.'

'Does she live far from here?'

'Near Lancaster, actually. I believe her house is really something.'

'It follows.' Every one of Susanna Lancaster's novels were bestsellers and some had been made into television dramas. I figured she wouldn't be short of a pound or two. 'What's her latest book called?'

'*Dragonfly Morning*. There'll be books for sale at the

luncheon and she'll do a signing session afterwards. The area sales rep will be there and we'll organize things between us. And when she's had enough, I'll drive her home.'

'Do all writers speak at luncheons and have book-signing sessions?' Just to think of it made me uneasy.

'Quite a few. It's a pity you can't come along, Cas, and see how it's done. There's more to getting to the top of the heap than writing good books, you know. Publicity is important, as well.'

'Mm. Piers arrived this morning,' I said, by way of changing the subject. 'Uninvited and unannounced.'

'Oh, lordy! I thought your mother wasn't going to give him this address?'

'She wasn't – didn't. But he saw a postcard of Acton Carey I'd sent home, and put two and two together. We had words and, to put it in a nutshell, I gave him his marching orders. Hector got so nasty I had to shut him in the outhouse.'

'Well, if it's to be the end of Piers Yardley I can only say I'm not altogether sorry. I got the impression, from things you let slip, that he can be a little bit selfish.'

'He is, but it isn't entirely his fault.' I had to be fair. 'His parents dote on him. From being little, nothing was too good for our Piers. He expects everyone else to bow down and worship too. It's a pity, because he's very attractive, if you like 'em dark and brooding.'

'And all of a sudden you don't?'

'Seems not. Aunt Jane was right, I suppose. She always said you shouldn't settle for second best and that's what Piers would have been.'

'Why, Cassie? Was there once someone else?' She topped up the glasses, avoiding my eyes.

'No. Piers was the first, but I think I always knew he wasn't the right one. Better to end it than let it drift on and fizzle out. Mind, Mum would like to see me married, though I think she went off Piers a bit when she found he'd asked me to go to London and live with him.'

'So we're both fair, free and on the shelf. Spinsters, I suppose you'd call us.'

'Then here's to spinsters!' I said defiantly, raising my glass. 'And just look at that sunset!'

A blazing sun had reddened the sky and the hills stood mistily black against it. At the top of the laburnum beside the front gate, a thrush sang its heart out, and love of Deer's Leap washed me with a sadness that hurt.

'I must take a lot of snaps before I go back, Jeannie – for the Deer's Leap book, I mean. And if Beth asks me here at Christmas, I'll take some winter ones, too.'

'She'll ask you. I'm glad you're still keen on the book, Cassie. I like the idea. I think it would do well.'

'I've thought of doing a succession to take in the whole history of the place. I've worked out I could write four, all linked to Deer's Leap. I'd start with the building of the house, I think, in 1592. There should be loads of good factual background material; the Pendle Witches, the Civil War . . .' I decided not to mention Margaret Dacre.

'OK. Get the current book finished and I can't see why we shouldn't give you a contract. Are you up to four in fairly quick succession? When it's a series, it's better if there isn't too long a lapse between the books.'

'I can do it!' Of course I could. Writing about Deer's Leap would be no trouble at all. 'You know how fond I am of this place.'

'You had mentioned it! And had you thought, Cassie, that the bank just might give you a mortgage on the strength of a four-book contract?'

'Oh, I couldn't!' I felt my face flush. 'I'd be so scared owing so much it would affect my work. I'd dry up, I know it. Besides, I don't even have the deposit.'

'Pity. You could do it, you know, but I suppose it isn't for me to try to influence you.'

'Aunt Jane always said that if a thing is for you, it will come your way in the fullness of time. I suppose I can always hope.'

'Have you seen any more of the ghost?' She changed the subject so quickly I was caught unawares.

'Y-yes,' I admitted, though I'd meant not to mention it. I mean, what would she say if she knew I'd biked back here in the dark, and been scared witless because I imagined I was being followed. 'I *thought* I heard him at the kissing gate, but it was dark. I'd popped out to check that the white gate was shut.' The lie came glibly. 'I thought I heard him talking – maybe to Susan. Imagination, probably.'

'I know. A lot of writers suffer from a fertile imagination, thank God! Shall we see this off?' She divided the remaining wine between the glasses. 'Then it's me for bed. I shall sleep tonight. I always do here. It's so peaceful after London. No street lights, no noise.'

'Before you do, Jeannie, what's the drill for tomorrow?'

'I'll give Susanna Lancaster a ring to confirm I'll be picking her up, and at what time. The lunch is twelve thirty for one, so she'll want to be there a bit beforehand – get her bearings. Suppose I should leave here no later than half-past ten. Don't let me sleep in, there's a love?'

'I won't. I'll wake you with coffee – how's that?'

'You're a good girl, Cassandra Johns,' she murmured.

'Yes, but good girls don't have a lot of fun!'

'I know exactly what you mean!'

So we laughed, which is all a couple of spinsters can do, come to think of it.

'Get yourself off to bed,' I ordered. 'There's plenty of hot water if you want a bath.'

'Bless you.' She finished her drink then kissed my cheek. ''Night, Cassie . . .'

The day lived up to the promise of the previous evening. The morning sky was clear and blue with not a cloud to be seen. I stood at the window, staring, a habit I seemed never to tire of, and felt sad that in ten more days there would be no more hills nor endless skies nor stone walls clinging to the hills in untidy lines. Soon, I would look up from my desk and see only a pinboard on the wall, just three feet away.

I filled the kettle, thinking about Susanna Lancaster; wondering if I would ever have a signing session.

The kettle began to whistle, pushing pie-in-the-sky dreams out of my head. Of more importance was the fact that I had little more than a week in which to do something about the airman, because I couldn't leave here knowing I was in Rowbeck and he was still trying to hitch a lift to Deer's Leap with everyone around pretending he didn't exist.

'But what can I do about him?' I demanded of the coffee pot. 'All things being equal, he just isn't my responsibility!'

'Beg pardon?' Jeannie appeared in the open doorway, bucket in hand.

'Good grief! Couldn't you sleep?'

'The birds woke me so I've been cleaning the car.' She kicked off her wellies. 'Why were you talking to yourself? They section you for that, you know!'

'As a matter of fact, I was trying to straighten things out in my mind – about the airman, actually – and I'm coming to realize that what happened around these parts more than fifty years ago is really none of my business.'

'No. But you've got yourself tangled up in it, love, so I reckon it is. And I'll take bets that if you do the Deer's Leap books, the last of them will be Jack and Susan's story – or as near to it as you can get.'

'You know it will, Jeannie. I'll have to be careful, though. Wouldn't want Susan to recognize it – nor people like Bill Jarvis and his sister. Deer's Leap will have to have another name – right from book one – and Acton Carey too. But I'll worry about that when *Firedance* is out of the way. There's plenty of time. Did you sleep all right – apart from the birds?'

'I just crashed.'

'The coffee's ready. Want to take the pot back to bed?'

'No, thanks. I'll just sit here and empty it. What did they do in your war, Cassie, about coffee? I suppose it was hard to get.'

'It wasn't *my* war. I'm interested in it, that's all. Aunt Jane once said the tea rationing was awful; said you just couldn't brew up whenever you felt like it. And they didn't have teabags. Those came later. But coffee I'm not sure about. Tea was the drink of the masses, I believe. Coffee was more middle class in those days. I wish Aunt Jane were still here. There's so much she could have told me – especially when it comes to writing Jack and Susan's story.'

I decided to talk some more to Bill Jarvis before I left; try to meet his sister too – ask her how it had been to grow up in a war. I might be really lucky, and get her to talk about Susan Smith.

'Cassie – you've got three books to see off before you can get down to the star-crossed lovers. Don't get too tied up with them – not until you have to. Do you find the pilot attractive, by the way?'

'Yes, I do.' If she'd expected a red-cheeked denial, then she wasn't getting one! 'As a matter of fact, he'd have been the type I'd have gone for fifty years ago.'

'Fair, didn't you say – Piers's opposite. Did he put you off Piers?'

'Jeannie! I'm not *that* stupid! Don't you realize if he were still alive, Jack Hunter would be seventy-five, at least! He wouldn't be young and straight and fair – and a little bit strung up.'

'He had a nervous tic, you mean?'

'Not exactly. But he pushes his hair out of his eyes with his left hand. I don't think he realizes he's doing it. But then I suppose most aircrews got a bit stretched at times. I know I would have.'

'So he's young and attractive and you find his nervous

habit endearing. Reckon you were born fifty years too late, old love.'

'Maybe I was, but the matter doesn't arise. He belongs to Susan. After all that time, he still loves her! If Piers had cared for me like that, I'd have eaten out of his hand!'

'If I didn't know you better, Cassie, I'd say you were a nutcase. As it is, I'm half inclined to believe you – about the ghost, I mean. I envy you really, but I'm a down-to-earth Scottish lassie and things like communing with World War Two flyers don't happen to me.'

'Then be glad of it!' I really meant it, because since that first meeting when I'd thought Jack Hunter was one of Beth's fancy-dress guests, he'd been there, waiting to take over every spare minute of my thoughts. 'And I think we'd better talk about the luncheon. Can I do anything to help?'

'No, thanks. The car should be dry by now. I'll just give it a bit of a polish, then I'll ring Susanna – ask directions. Think I'll take the pretty route through the Trough and pick up some honey on the way. If you're making toast, by the way, I'll have a couple of slices. Cut thick, please.'

'One day, Jeannie McFadden, all those calories are going to catch up with you, and when they do, don't come running to me for sympathy,' I laughed, wallowing once more in the contentment that hadn't been far away since Piers drove out of my life in a cloud of dust. 'And if you're to get the speaker there on time, you'll have to shift yourself!'

Jeannie got back at seven, just as I was beginning to wonder if she'd had a flat, or run out of petrol.

'You took your time! Got lost, or something?'

'No. We left the do at four and Susanna asked me in for coffee, then showed me her place. She's a real love. Y'know, if I could guarantee looking like she does, I wouldn't mind getting old.'

'Yes you would, Jeannie. You'd hate it – just like Susanna

Lancaster does, I shouldn't wonder. But tell me about her – and the house?'

'We-e-ll, she told me she had plans, but didn't elaborate. I think she *will* start another book, but it's up to her. That house, though! I'd kill for it. It's just outside Lancaster and pure Regency. Red brick, white doors and windows, and seven steps up to the front entrance. I counted. She must have made a pile!'

'It follows. The television dramatizations alone must have sent her sales figures soaring. Is *Dragonfly Morning* going to sell, do you think?'

'Hope so. It isn't her usual thing; nothing to do with mystery and murder. Seems it's a love story. She said it could have happened to anyone born in the twenties and whose young years had been touched by war.

'Someone asked her if the book was fiction or biography, and she went a bit pink and said it was a bit of both really. I've brought you one – got her to sign it for you and she wrote something rather nice in it.'

'Thanks a lot! What do I owe you?'

'I'll settle for a sandwich. I'm starving!'

'Why? Wasn't the lunch any good?'

'It was fine – but somehow we seemed to talk instead of eat. You know how it is with working lunches? You balk against speaking with your mouth full and the next thing you know it's gone cold and they're pushing the next course at you! I'll just get out of these things – won't be a minute.'

I looked at the book she had left on the table. The jacket was stark and eye-catching; a girl on a bluff, alone against a morning sky, and shaded hills in the background. Her face had a waiting look, her eyes were anxious. The artist had done a good job. I turned to the title page.

> For Cassie, a new author,
> from Susanna Lancaster,
> an old one.

'You told her,' I asked, embarrassed, 'that I was a writer.'

'But of course! I also told her your first novel made it to the bestseller lists.'

'Only just! I made a very little plop in a very big pond!'

'She was impressed, for all that. She knows that most first novels don't do as well as yours. She told me about her very first effort; said it came back so quickly from every publisher she sent it to that she was sure they hadn't even bothered to read it. "Of course," she said, "I know now that it just wasn't good enough." So there's a compliment, Cas. You should give yourself a bit more credit for what you've done. Now, what say we take the dog for a walk?'

So we pulled on wellies and walked way beyond the top of the paddock and up the steep slope behind it so we could look down on Deer's Leap and the space beyond, and I stored a picture of it in my mind in case I never stood there again.

'I rather wish I'd been with you today, Jeannie.' I pulled a stem of long grass, then nibbled the soft white end of it. 'Just talking about it makes me realize there's more to a novel than sitting at home writing it.'

'Couldn't agree more. What it boils down to, though, is selling books. Readers like meeting authors and Susanna seemed to enjoy herself today. I wish you could have seen her house, Cassie. Just to think of what royalties can buy would make you want to work like a dog.'

'I'm looking forward to reading her book. I'm curious about the storyline.'

'Then take my advice and do no such thing! Don't get another author's book into your head whilst you're writing one of your own! Put it in a drawer, then read it when you've finished *Firedance*. Susanna told us she allowed herself little treats for working extra hard. She said she once gobbled five After Eights, one after the other, as a reward for finishing a chapter that had taken ages to get right. It made her seem very ordinary and human.'

'She's made an impression on you, hasn't she, Jeannie?'

'Mm. Pity I can't write. I wouldn't mind ending up like her.'

'Filthy rich?'

'Y-yes. But more the way she looks and is. She's obviously getting on, but it doesn't show somehow.'

We had reached the top of the rise now, and stood without speaking, to stare. The sun was beginning to go down and there was a hint of chill in the air. It made me remember that in a week it would be September, with autumn not so far away.

'Have you taken in all you want of the view?' Jeannie teased. 'Because I think we should start back. It's turned quite cold.'

'Yes, but I'll come here again with a camera.'

Not that I would need reminding of that one summer at Deer's Leap. I would always remember it, and wonder who was living there, and worry too about Jack Hunter and that I hadn't been able to help him find Suzie. How long would he wait at that gate for her? Into forever? It made me swallow hard on the sentimental tears in my throat.

'Hey! You there!' I heard the snapping of Jeannie's fingers under my nose and shook my head clear of the pilot. 'You were miles away!'

'*Years* away, if you must know. Do you realize I've got little more than a week to find where the Smiths went when they left Deer's Leap?'

'So you were thinking about the pilot again?'

'Suppose so. It looks as if I'm not going to be able to help him, for all that.'

'You mean you've been serious all along about finding Susan Smith?'

'I – I've wondered about it quite a bit . . .'

'Then I don't understand you, Cassie Johns! I can't even *think* you'd waste good writing time chasing after a woman who probably won't remember Jack Hunter – even if she's still alive!'

'She *is* alive, I know it! And she won't have forgotten him.'

'But she could have married someone else, for Pete's sake! And if she hasn't, what are you going to say to her, "Excuse me, Miss Smith, but there's a ghost looking for you!"?'

'OK, Jeannie! I agree with everything you say and it *will* be difficult.'

'But if you find this Susan Smith are all your troubles over? The heck they are! Have you just once stopped to think you can't take up residence at the kissing gate with an elderly lady, waiting for a ghost to turn up?'

'We-e-ll, I suppose –'

'No supposing, Cassie! Jack Hunter is none of your business and neither is Susan Smith! You can't go poking and prying into things that don't concern you. Leave it! Take the lid off that one and you don't know what you'll find. Nasty wriggling maggots, I shouldn't wonder!'

'You're right, I've got to admit it, yet –'

'Too right I'm right! Say you'll forget it?'

'OK! I'll forget it!'

'And you *really* promise, Cassie? You'll let well alone?'

'I just said so!'

I stuck my hands in my pockets and whistled to Hector, and it was only when we were manoeuvring ourselves through a kissing gate that didn't squeak and wasn't in need of a coat of paint that I knew I had no intention of keeping my promise, even though I might well be taking the lid off a tin of maggots.

Sorry, Jeannie!

We drove to the village next morning and the familiar feeling took me as we neared the straight stretch of road and the clump of oaks. But the airman didn't show and I was reluctantly glad, because I didn't want Jeannie messing up our encounter, and she would have.

I parked behind the Red Rose and left her to do the

shopping, making for the phone box. Mum seemed pleased to hear from me and straightway asked if Piers had phoned lately.

'Phoned! He turned up on Thursday, bold as brass!' I told her what had happened. 'He left in a huff,' I finished. 'I was so mad, the way he got my address!'

'Mm. Sneaky. Mind, he was always a spoiled child. Maybe you're well rid of him after all! You'll be home, next week?'

'Yes, but I'm not sure when. Is Dad about?'

'He's at the bottom of the garden, pricking out lettuces. Take too long to fetch him. I'll give him your love.'

'Do that, Mum. Anyway, the card has almost run out! I'll ring on Wednesday.'

'Don't bother. I'll ring you. Save you going out. Now don't forget to check the doors and windows at night, and don't answer the door after dark!'

I put the phone down just as Bill Jarvis walked past to stand at the bus stop, and I smiled at the lady by his side.

'Now then, Cassie!' he grinned. 'How have you been lately? This is our Hilda.'

Hilda held out a hand and said she was pleased to meet me. 'You're interested in the Smith lass?' she said without preamble.

'Yes, but not in a nosy way,' I said earnestly. 'More how it was for people like her in the war. It couldn't have been very nice, getting thrown out of your home.'

'A lot about that war wasn't very nice. Mind, I've got to be fair. I found a husband and I wouldn't have done in the normal course of events. Young men were a bit thin on the ground in Acton Carey before the Air Force came. What do you want to know about Susan Smith?'

'Nothing in particular – just anything you can tell me, Hilda. What did the RAF do with Deer's Leap once they'd taken it over? I just can't believe some man from the Ministry could knock on a door and say the occupants had to get out!

There'd be an outcry if it happened now, and protesters everywhere!'

'Happen so, lass, but when there's a war on things are a mite different. Weren't considered patriotic to protest in those days. But it isn't me you should be talking to about Susan Smith. There were two years' difference in our ages and that's a lot when you're young. Lizzie Frobisher as was would know more about her than me. Those two were close; both of 'em went to Clitheroe Grammar on the school bus every day. They'd be about fourteen when the war started. Lizzie's dad worked for Mr Ackroyd at the Hall. She married a curate when the war was over.'

'I see.' The one person who could tell me about Susan could be anywhere now. 'Do you know where she went?'

'Aye. Somerset.'

'Pity. I'd have liked to talk to her. I still want to see the church, though. Will it be all right if I pop in next Friday?'

'Feel free. But about Lizzie. Her name's Taylor now, and –'

'Look! There's your bus!' I cut her short, which was very rude of me but I didn't have a lot of choice. Jeannie was making towards us and we'd agreed that the Deer's Leap affair was taboo. Saved by the Skipton bus!

'What was all that about?' Jeannie frowned. 'Been asking questions, have we?'

'Yes. About the church.' My gaze didn't waver. 'I'm going to look at it on Friday morning – that's when the ladies clean it.'

'And why are you interested in the church?'

'Because anything about Acton Carey interests me.' I didn't blush nor feel one bit ashamed. 'You're in a very suspicious mood, if you don't mind me saying so.'

'No, I don't.' She looked up at the church clock. 'It's a bit early for a drink. Would you like to hang around and eat at the Rose when it opens? We could have a look at the church while we're waiting.'

'No thanks. Best get back.' I was almost sure she was calling my bluff. 'We said we'd cut the grass today as soon as it was dry enough, don't forget.'

'So we did. I feel like a bit of exercise. We can see this off,' she held up a bottle of wine, 'when we've finished. As a reward,' she added solemnly.

Chapter Nine

On Friday morning I drove into Acton Carey, a last, sentimental journey. I would take a look at the church, then buy Bill a pint, if he was around. Say goodbye. Because since this morning I had a feeling that I would never come back, never see Deer's Leap again. And maybe it was better that way; better to forget Jack Hunter and that war, and anyway, I decided mutinously as I drove past the clump of oaks, why should I bother my head about a ghost who didn't have the decency to turn up when he must surely have known I would soon be leaving here. For ever!

I still felt piqued as I parked the car, then made for the war memorial, to stand there, staring fixedly at the name J. J. Hunter, asking silently why he hadn't been there this morning, wishing I had brought flowers as a kind of goodbye. Flowers from Deer's Leap garden; a bunch of the red roses that grew up the wall and peeped in at the kitchen window! It was a very old plant with a thick, gnarled stem that could even have been there when Susan slept in the room above the kitchen! Why hadn't I thought?

'I'm going home on Sunday,' I whispered in my mind to the name chiselled there. 'I'm sorry about what happened to you and Susan and I'm sorry I wasn't able to help you. But I won't forget either of you. One day, somehow, I'll find how it was for you both . . .'

I blew my nose sniffily, then walked to the grandiose church, built to the memory of a cotton broker from Manchester whom almost everyone had forgotten, blinking my eyes to accustom them to the gloom, inhaling the churchy smell of dampness and musty books and dusty hassocks.

'Hullo, love! Over here!'

I turned in the direction of the voice.

'You came then!' Hilda stood beside the lectern, waving and smiling.

'I said I would.'

'Happen you did, but you went off at a right old lick; didn't give me time to tell you that –'

'Your bus was coming.' So too had been Jeannie! 'I hope you didn't think me rude.'

'Nay. All I'd been going to tell you was that Lizzie Frobisher lives in Acton Carey.'

'She lives *where*?'

'At the vicarage. We don't have a parish priest in the village any longer – all a question of money. Any road, there was a vicarage standing empty, so the Diocese made it into four flats for retired clergy. It was nice that Lizzie was able to come back to the village to live out her time. She's over yonder, in the green cardigan.'

Here! Dusting pews no more than ten feet away!

'Susan Smith's friend?' I whispered. 'The one she went to school with?'

'That's the lady you should be talking to. Away over, and have a word with her. She's Lizzie Taylor now.'

'Did you tell her I was asking?'

'No. But there's none better to tell you about Susan.'

'You don't mind? I really came to look at the church . . .'

'Then ask Lizzie to show it to you!'

Glory be! With only two days to go, I'd found Susan's long-ago friend!

'Mrs Taylor?' I coughed loudly and she spun round, looking at me over the top of her glasses.

'It is. And who might you be?'

'I'm Cassandra Johns. I'm staying at Deer's Leap.'

'Ah, yes – you'll want to talk about Susan?' she said matter-of-factly.

'I do, actually. But how did you guess?'

'Ha! The whole village knows. Tell Bill Jarvis and you might as well tell the town crier!' She pulled down the corners of her mouth and I took in her hand-knitted cardigan, the skirt gone baggy round the hips, the thin hair, permed into corkscrew curls. 'Why are you interested in Susan Smith?'

'I – I'm not especially. It's Deer's Leap really. I'm a novelist, you see, and I'm interested in anything to do with the place.'

And may you be forgiven, Cassandra Johns, for lying through your teeth in church!

'Ah. An historical novelist! Then you can't do better than write about Margaret and Walter Dacre – if you dare! Local folklore has always had it, you see, that those two were the worst of the bunch – the Pendle Witches, I'm talking about – but were never found out!'

'Margaret Dacre?' Oh, lordy! Aunt Jane *had* got it right! 'The 1592 one?'

'That's her! Legend has it she worked spells and heaven knows what else. She got away with it too! I suppose people hereabouts were too afraid to shop her to the witch-hunters.'

'But how do you know all this? I've never come across any reference either to her or to Deer's Leap.'

'You wouldn't. Nothing was put on record; just handed down through the generations, sort of. But Mistress Dacre got her comeuppance, for all that. Seems she wanted to found a dynasty; pass that fine house on to her son, but she never conceived. The Lord's punishment on her, if you ask me! But what's got into you? You look quite odd, Miss Johns. Stupid of me talking about witchcraft, and you alone in that house. Let's go outside for a breath of air? I've had enough dusting for one day. Feel like a cigarette?'

'I – I don't smoke.' I followed her in a half-daze.

'Afraid *I* do! A habit I picked up in the war, and never managed to kick!' She settled herself on a bench beside the church porch and dug into her cardigan pocket. 'But we can't all be perfect, can we? Sure you don't want one?'

'Quite sure, thanks. But I really can't imagine a witch ever having lived at Deer's Leap. To me, it's a beautiful old place. I've been alone there for days on end and never picked up one bad vibe – er – funny feeling.'

'It's all right.' She inhaled deeply, eyes closed. 'Vicars' wives know what vibes are! Mind, there was often an atmosphere at Deer's Leap – Mrs Smith's fault, I reckon.'

'Why? Wasn't she happy there? Was it too isolated for her?'

'I don't think so. She just kept herself to herself. Not like in the village. No one locked their doors in those days. People just walked in without waiting to be asked. Mind, Susan's father was a decent chap, though they weren't much missed when they left.'

'Then can you tell me,' I whispered, 'where they went when the Air Ministry took the house off them?' My mouth was suddenly dry and my tongue made little clicking sounds as I spoke. 'You and Susan would keep in touch?'

'Well, that's just it! It was as if they'd done a moonlight! One day they were there; the next day not a sign of them, and the place deserted. I know because I had arranged to meet Susan and she didn't turn up. I went to Deer's Leap looking for her because it was – well – rather urgent.'

'And they'd vanished? All the livestock gone?'

'Everything! I was hurt when Susan never wrote; not one line to tell me her new address, and she and I so close! I wonder to this day why she never got in touch. It was the talk of the village at the time; a nine-day wonder. No end of speculation, but no one ever found out. Susan never came back after the war. I'd have thought she'd have brought flowers or a poppy wreath to the memorial. It was as if Jack Hunter had never existed for her.'

'Jack was her boyfriend,' I said softly.

'He was her whole life! They were so in love; right from the night they met. Mind, it wasn't easy for them to meet,' the way things were. It wasn't on, going out with an airman, so I did all I could – gave Susan an alibi, sometimes . . .'

'And the other times?'

'She'd slip out of the house. When it was winter and dark before teatime, it was easier for her. He'd walk all that way, just to have a few minutes with her at the gate, then afterwards, in the barn.'

'Was the aerodrome far away?'

'About two miles from here. It was nearer to Deer's Leap, actually, than to the village. That's why the RAF took Mr Smith's fields when they wanted to extend.'

I looked at the ash on her cigarette end. It clung there, more than an inch long and I waited, fascinated, for it to drop, thinking how steady her hand must be.

'My mother said that in those days, girls didn't have the freedom my generation has. I can't understand it.'

'I can! A girl obeyed her parents until she was twenty-one. That was when young people came of age in my day. Do you know, there were boys of twenty flying those huge planes. Old enough to drop a bomb-load on Germany and kill God knows how many, but not old enough to marry without permission! It was mad!'

'What would have happened if Susan's mother had found she was meeting an airman?'

'She did know eventually. There was ructions!'

'But couldn't they have met sometimes when Susan left work? Didn't she ever think to say she was working over-time?'

'She never had a job; leastways only at home. She helped in the house and on the farm. Farming was work of national importance; so important it kept you out of the Armed Forces! Susan would have liked to join up, but it wouldn't have been any use her trying. I felt sorry for her. It must have been awful, once she left school, with no one her own age to talk to for days on end.'

'I'm surprised she ever got to meet her young man!'

'She wouldn't have, in the normal course of events, but there was something on in the village, I remember, to do with the church, and she stayed the night at our house. My mother had to practically beg permission. Susan's mother said she couldn't go, them not being Church of England, but Mr Smith said she could. He was a quiet man really, and hadn't a lot to say for himself, but if ever he put his foot down, his wife didn't argue! You'd have thought it was a bacchanalian romp, and it was only a beetle drive in the parish hall in aid of the church choir!'

'They met at a *beetle drive*?'

'No. They bumped into each other – literally – in the village in the blackout. People bumped into just about everything, come to think of it. Lampposts especially were the very devil. You could get a nasty bang from one of those, apart from breaking your glasses, if you wore them!

'Anyway, this airman was full of apologies and insisted on walking us to the transport. *The transport*, I ask you! He thought we were going to the sergeants' mess dance at the aerodrome! The RAF had a dance there every week, and they always sent a lorry round the villages, collecting girls. Lady partners were a bit thin on the ground, you see. Folk around these parts called it the love bus.

'Of course, respectable girls weren't allowed to go. No knowing the trouble they might get themselves into! Chance would've been a fine thing! I don't know what got into the pair of us that night because we followed the airman and he helped us onto the transport. We were the only two from Acton Carey!'

'And that's where it all started – at a forbidden dance?'

'That's where. In a Nissen hut, actually. Not in the least romantic, but it was love at first sight for those two. I suppose you'd call it physical attraction nowadays!'

'That was very daring of you,' I teased. 'I suppose you let him walk you both home!'

'You bet we did! The blackout did have its uses, you know,

and we both reckoned we might as well be hanged for sheep. I lived in one of the lodges at the Hall then, so it was a fair walk. We didn't wait for the love bus because we had to be back before the beetle drive finished. Jack's tail-end Charlie escorted me. Mick, his name was. Lovely dancer . . .'

'Tail-end *what*?'

'Charlie. There were two gunners to each bomber: one amidships, sort of, and another in the tail. Susan and I got to know them all. Mick and I started seeing each other, but we were more dancing partners than anything else. Not like Jack and Susan. Those two were smitten right from the start. He was gorgeous. Tall, fair-haired. Susan was fair too. A golden couple. I'd look at them together and think it was too good to last, and I was right!

'But here's me rabbiting on, and you wanting to look at the church!' She ground her cigarette end into the grass, then brushed a hand across her skirt. 'I'll show you round if you'd like. We'd better get a move on. They'll be finishing soon, and the church has to be locked. When I was young, churches were never locked and the altar silver out for all to see. Thieves left churches alone in those days . . .'

'If there isn't a lot of time left, then I'd rather see the original part of the building.' I felt less breathless now. 'It's ages old, I believe.'

'Built in the thirteenth century, when few could read or write but who believed implicitly in heaven and hell and eternal damnation! It's the Lady Chapel now and so simple it's beautiful. When it was built, so small a church wouldn't have had pews and the faithful would have stood right through the service – all except the Lord of the Manor and his family, who'd have had special chairs. But let me show you . . .'

I didn't go to the Red Rose when I left the church. My head was too full of Susan and Jack, and besides, Beth and Danny would be home the following day and I wanted to clean the house before I went to meet Jeannie's train.

My word processor was already packed in its carrying box; no more *Firedance* until Monday; no more working at the kitchen table with Hector beside me and Tommy curled up in the armchair! Sadness took me just to think of leaving, so I thought instead of Mum and Dad and how pleased they would be to have me home again.

But it was difficult not to think of Susan and Jack and how glad I was to have found a lead in the very nick of time. I'd tried not to appear too interested for fear of arousing suspicion, because far too many people think that anything said to a novelist would appear, completely unashamed and unabridged, in her next book! I'd felt just a little guilty, especially when Mrs Taylor said, on parting, that I had only to write to her or phone if there was anything I wanted to know about the history of the area or about the war. I had her address and phone number in my purse, though at the back of my mind I knew it would be a long time before I would be in touch. *Firedance* must first be completed, and a lot could happen in the space of three and a bit novels – even supposing Harrier Books gave me that contract!

I was snipping red roses when the phone rang, and I ran to answer it.

'Cassie! I'm at King's Cross. Is the minicab available – same time?'

'It is.'

'Beth rang. Said they were taking it easy and would be home late on Saturday night about eight – give or take the odd traffic jam!'

'She rang me too!'

'Fine! See you, then!'

'That was Jeannie,' I said to Hector, who always came to investigate when the phone rang – just in case, I supposed, there was a man on the other end of it! 'I'm going home soon. Are you going to miss me?'

He whined softly and looked at the biscuit tin, which was his way of telling me he would, and the custard creams too, and I felt a sudden ache inside me to think that soon he too would be leaving Deer's Leap. Poor Hector, poor Cassie, poor Jack and Suzie!

'Life's a bitch,' I said out loud. 'And then you die!'

Even when you were hardly into manhood, I thought soberly, and you didn't want to die and your girl didn't want you to either!

Then I thought about Piers, whom I hadn't really loved at all, and promptly burst into tears at the unfairness of it.

On the way back from Preston station, I slowed automatically as we neared the clump of oak trees and Jeannie slid me a warning glance

'You're at it again, Cassie! You're still on the lookout for him! I thought you'd decided to let it drop.'

'Yes, I had.' I put my foot down, because there wasn't a single vibe to be felt. 'And I really meant it at the time, but something happened this morning.'

I told her about going to the church – hand-on-heart only to look at it! – and how I'd met Mrs Taylor who once was Susan's closest friend, and there in Acton Carey all the time!

'What do you mean – living in the village all along? Then why didn't Bill Jarvis mention it? He knew we – *you* – were interested.'

'Maybe it slipped his memory. It all happened a long time ago, and he was older than Susan, didn't he say, and away in the army for a lot of the war. That could be why he wouldn't know about the Smiths' mysterious departure – without a goodbye to anyone. It was a shock to Lizzie. Even she hadn't known when they were going.'

I told her all I'd learned, and said surely Bill would have told us about something that caused such a stir at the time, if he'd known about it.

'Maybe he did. Maybe,' she said over her shoulder as she got out of the car to open the white gate, 'he was rationing his knowledge – with the beer in mind!'

She brought the matter up again, which surprised me, as soon as we were sitting at the kitchen table, a pot of coffee between us.

'Why, all of a sudden, are you interested in Susan Smith, and the pilot?' I asked her. 'It's not all that long ago you warned me off, Jeannie.'

'We-e-ll, things have changed a bit since then. I mentioned the Deer's Leap books at work. They showed quite an interest. Maybe they'll ask you to come to London to talk about them when *Firedance* is finished. How's it going, by the way?'

'Fine. I'll meet the deadline with no problem. And there's something I forgot. Local folklore has it that Walter and Margaret Dacre were up to their necks in witchcraft!'

'You mean W. D. & M. D. – the couple who built the house?'

'You got it in one! There's no record of it – and there wouldn't be since they were never accused and tried – but Mrs Taylor said M. D. was a witch! Mind, things get added to and embroidered in the telling, but I always thought of Margaret Dacre as a happy contented wife with a lot of children. I even imagined them adding rooms as their family grew, but I was wrong. According to Mrs Taylor, the Dacres never had children. That can of maggots you warned me about might go a long way back!'

'Cassie! It gets better and better!'

'Yes, and it's only just hit me! What if Margaret Dacre put a curse on Deer's Leap?'

'But why on earth should she?'

'Well, for one thing she could well have been a witch, so ill-wishing would be second nature to her; and never to have given her husband an heir must have upset her a lot. Imagine building that lovely house for future generations to live in, and no son to inherit it! Maybe the curse was eternal and still applies – if there was a curse, I mean. Susan and Jack didn't have children, that much we do know.'

'Susan and Jack didn't get as far as the altar, but what a theme to run through the books! Every couple who lived at Deer's Leap to be childless! Mind, you'd have to lift the curse eventually – maybe in the final book, Cassie. Y'know, I really do believe we're on to something!'

She was pink-cheeked with excitement which made me feel a bit of a meanie when I reminded her that Susan Smith was the daughter of the house, and Danny and Beth had two children.

'Yes, but they were born in Edinburgh. They came here when they were toddlers! You'll have to think of something for your novels, though, Cas. Can you?'

'You know I can!' Now I was excited too. 'I'd have to do a fair bit of historical research, though. And had you thought – even World War Two is history now.'

'I'll grant you that, but Mrs Taylor is still around and didn't she say you could get in touch with her?'

'Oh, Jeannie. If only I could find Susan! She's around too, I'm as certain as I can be.'

'What you want, I think –' Jeannie was an editor again, all else forgotten – 'is a situation in the last of the books whereby the curse is lifted.'

'Easy! My star-crossed lovers will have a happy-ever-after ending and live at Deer's Leap, and have children too.'

'Only the house won't be called Deer's Leap . . .'

'Think I'm stupid? Of course it won't.' It would mean spending time around Acton Carey and maybe calling back the ghost of a pilot, but what the heck! 'This morning I'd accepted I would never return to Deer's Leap; never see it again after Sunday. I even went to the war memorial to say goodbye to Jack Hunter! Then in the next breath, almost, I meet Lizzie Taylor. Seems Deer's Leap isn't going to let me go, Jeannie!'

'And will that worry you?'

'Of course not.' Bet your life it wouldn't, because hadn't that old house just handed me the plots of at least four novels;

handed them on a plate because it was determined to keep its hold over me! 'In fact, the only awful thing about it is that I'll have all sorts of excuses for coming back here, and it mightn't go down too well. Because by the time I'm ready to start writing those books, Jeannie, someone else will be living in Deer's Leap, and I won't like that one bit!'

Come to think of it, Margaret Dacre mightn't like it either!

The lucky Cornish pixie Elspeth and Hamish hung in the rear window of my car swung from side to side as I reversed out of the white gate and onto the dust road. Beth and Danny stood waving, Tommy beside them, and Hector gazed at me mournfully.

'I have never,' I said to Jeannie, 'seen a dog who could look so sad, yet wag his tail at the same time, the old fraud!'

'You're going to miss him, aren't you?'

'I am.' And the snooty Lotus, who hadn't condescended to see me off, and the view from the kitchen window and, oh just *everything*! I felt very choked up still at having to hand over Deer's Leap, and I told Beth and Danny as we hugged a goodbye that I wasn't turning to look back – not even for one last glance – because it's unlucky and there's a limit to what I can bear without bursting into tears.

So instead I wound down the window, and stuck out my arm in one last wave. Goodbye, Deer's Leap and the animals and the garden and the kissing gate. And especially goodbye to Jack Hunter, who would still be waiting there for his Suzie for all time.

'So!' I let out my breath in a noisy huff. 'That's it!'

'You sound quite full up, Cassie.'

'I am.' So full up that I wished I had never accepted an invitation to that fancy dress party, nor ever seen Deer's Leap nor got myself involved with long-ago lovers. 'Never mind. I'll just chalk it up to experience, Jeannie; grist to the mill.'

'You won't, you know! I mean, how do you know that

Margaret Dacre hasn't put her mark on you? Hadn't you thought she might really want a child to be born in that house!'

'But children *will* have been born there! Dammit, it's against the law of averages for a house to stand more than four hundred years and never have a baby born in it!'

'How do you know, Cassie? Didn't we agree that's how the plots of the Deer's Leap books will be: a house cursed never to know children!'

'But that's fiction we're talking about! And anyway, we don't know that Margaret Dacre was a witch. It's only local tittle-tattle!'

'Interesting, for all that and *Cassie*!' She grabbed the wheel. 'For God's sake, watch it!'

'Look!' I slammed into reverse gear, bumping over the grassy edges of the road. 'He's there! *Look!* Behind you!'

The car went into a skid and I pulled hard out of it, all the time watching the man who stood at the side of the road, willing him, *imploring* him not to go!

I turned the car, throwing up gravel and dust. Out of the corner of my eye I'd seen him on the other side of the road as I drove past. He was still there, looking straight ahead, not one bit bothered by screeching brakes and a car almost out of control.

'Look at him, Jeannie! Now tell me he isn't real!' I inched forward, my heart thudding in my ears. 'And don't say a word! Leave it to me!' I stopped the car, my eyes not leaving him for a second. What could I say to him? 'Hullo and goodbye'?

Jeannie had her hands over her eyes as if my performance had unnerved her. Or was it because she didn't want to look at the airman?

'Jeannie – *please*?' Slowly, carefully I opened the door, got out, then quietly closed it. Jeannie took her hands from her face and stared at me, bewildered.

'There's no one here, Cas, but you and me . . .' Her face

was very white and she ran her tongue round her lips, turning slowly in her seat to look behind her. 'No one at all!'

'Jack,' I said softly, so he would look at me. 'Want a lift? Deer's Leap, is it?'

'Cassie!' The horn sounded, loudly, insistently. Jeannie was in the driving seat, making the most awful noise. Her eyes were wild and frightened-looking. I thought she was going to start the car!

'*Don't!*' I turned to wrench open the door, snatching the keys from the ignition. 'He's there!' I pointed to where he stood. 'Oh, *no!*' I'd taken my eyes off him for a second! 'Oh God! He's gone. Why did you do that, Jeannie? *Why?*'

'Get in,' she said softly, her eyes locking on to mine. She pointed to the passenger seat. 'Get in, and *I'll* drive.'

'No! I – I'm fine. Just fine!'

'Are you coming with me to the station, or aren't you?' Her face was still pale, but her voice was steely calm and very, very soft.

'He was there. He *was* . . .' I sat down beside her, fighting tears.

'Give me the keys, please.'

'OK.' I dropped them into her outstretched hand. 'But I'm all right. I can drive.'

'Sure. But not just yet. Just calm down . . .'

'Why didn't you see him?' I blew my nose noisily, breathing deeply, trying to get a hold of myself.

'Because you can see ghosts and it's obvious I can't! It's as simple as that!'

She turned the key in the ignition, glancing in the rear-view mirror. I followed her gaze as she turned the car without effort in the narrow lane. There was no one in front of us and no one behind us. All I could see was a country road with grassy verges and a lucky Cornish pixie, swinging from side to side in the window behind me with annoying nonchalance.

'I'm sorry,' I said.

'And so am I – that I didn't get to see him, I mean.'

'But you believe me, Jeannie? You believe that *I* did?'

'I believe you. And I'm sorry I pressed the horn.'

'You startled him. Maybe he isn't used to noises like that.'

'Oh, you're so right, Cassie! I bet he hasn't heard anything as frightening as the horn of a Mini!' She looked at me, the corners of her mouth pulled down and I knew the drama was over – until, of course, either of us cared to speak about it again.

'I said I was sorry,' I said shakily.

We were driving through Acton Carey now, past the post office and the Red Rose; past the church and the war memorial.

'I'll pull in at the lay-by – OK?'

'Fine.'

'You're sure you want to drive? No more emergency stops? If you see him, you'll put your foot down?'

'We won't see him now. We're too far from Deer's Leap. But I *did* see him,' I insisted as she flashed left, then pulled in.

She turned to look behind her before opening the door, which was her way, I suppose, of giving me the last word without actually agreeing with me.

'You've got exactly thirty minutes!' she said, fastening her seat belt, 'and if I miss that train you're in trouble, Cassandra Johns. So get weaving!'

'Did you know,' I smiled, all at once calm again, 'that *get weaving* was a World War Two expression?'

'Yes. It meant Get Your Foot Down. It still does!'

We made the station just as the train drew smoothly, snakily, into the platform. I gave Jeannie a hug and said, 'See you, old love.'

'You're sure you're all right?'

'Absolutely.' I really was. 'Will you be at Beth's place at the weekend?'

'No. There's a book fair I want to take in, so I'll be there instead.'

'And I'll be at Greenleas . . .'

It was as if we were closing the door on Deer's Leap, then locking it. I wondered if we would agree to throw away the key.

Doors opened. I picked up Jeannie's case and handed it to her when she had found her seat. Neither of us spoke. There just didn't seem to be anything to say. Soon she would be on her way to London and I would be turning left at the lights and onto the A59.

'Don't wait. Off you go.' Jeannie didn't like being waved out of sight.

'Safe journey, then . . .'

'You too, Cassie. I'll ring you in the morning.'

I walked away. In little more than an hour I would be home, and a big red sun would be sinking behind Beacon Fell. I felt so flat, I wanted to weep.

'It'll be September before we know it!' Mum put a match to the sitting-room fire. 'Would anybody like a cup of tea before I get myself comfortable?'

Dad and I said we wouldn't, thanks.

'Right, then!' Mum picked up her knitting. 'It's about time we got the business over and done with!'

'What business?' I frowned.

'About your Aunt Jane,' Dad said. 'It's about time we –'

'It isn't as if we're doing it in indecent haste. She's been gone more than two years; time we had a chat about what's to be done,' Mum said firmly, 'about her cottage.'

'What about it?' I demanded. 'She left it to you, Dad. Why the urgency? No one's been there for ages.'

'I've been there all the time, opening windows,' Mum defended, 'and I've made up my mind to talk to you about it, Cassie. After all, the furniture in it is yours.'

'And you want it cleared out?' I felt vaguely sad.

'Not necessarily, only several folk in the village have asked what we intend doing with it.'

'It's none of their business!'

'Everything in Rowbeck is Rowbeck's business. Worrying about other folk's business is all they have to do, most times! Anyway, Cassie love, we want you to know what Dad and me have decided – well, *almost* decided. We'd like your opinion.'

'You're not going to sell it!' Not to some townee who would rip out the lovely iron firegrates, and put in double glazing and a functional kitchen, then only use it at weekends! 'I don't think Aunt Jane would like that!'

'Sell it!' Dad looked most put out. 'Oh, no! I was born in that cottage and your grandpa left it to Jane for her lifetime, and then to me. As a matter of fact, Mam and me have made up our minds to live there when we retire.'

'But you aren't thinking of giving up work yet, Dad?'

'Not for ten years, if I have any say in the matter! But the place can't stand idle and unlived in, so we thought we'd give it a spring clean, do a bit of decorating, then offer it as a holiday let. We'll have to get central heating put in before the cold weather is on us again, so we won't make a fortune. But as long as it is lived in and kept warm and aired until we want it, then I think it's a good idea.'

'And you'd use the furniture?'

'Of course – provided you don't mind. People seem to expect old-fashioned stuff these days in country cottages.'

'I wouldn't mind at all.' I felt relieved in fact. 'Mind, there are one or two things we'll have to move – her personal things, and family photographs. And I'd like her sewing machine.'

She had bought it, she told me, long before the war, which made it almost an antique. But it wasn't for its value I wanted it, but because I'd watched, fascinated, as she sewed dolls' clothes on it when I was little and because I'd liked the chuckling sound it made when she turned the handle quickly.

'Take out what you want – it's all yours, Cassie.'

'Then until I need it myself, I think everything should be left the way it's always been.'

'Need it?' Mum's face registered a mixing of dismay and hope.

'Well, I suppose I will – one day. One day I might think of buying a little place of my own if everything goes well. But not for a long time,' I soothed.

'Good! Well, that's settled, then. I'll go and make a pot of tea! Sure you don't want a cup, Cassie?'

'Only if there's a slice of parkin to go with it!'

'And did you ever know the day,' Mum clucked, 'when there wasn't parkin in the cake tin?'

I smiled. I really was home again, Deer's Leap was a long way away and I had given it back to Beth. Yet for just the speeding of a second I was standing at the white gate, gazing up the path, and there were lights in all the windows.

And then, as I stood unseen, the kissing gate creaked, and I knew the airman was there again, waiting for Suzie to creep out to him in the darkness so they could whisper together, and kiss. And then he would tell her he couldn't stay long, because he was on standby . . .

'A penny for them?' Mum put the teapot on the hearth, then covered it with a cosy.

'O-oh – anything and nothing . . .'

'Nothing, was it? Then all I can say is that you had a very creamy smile on your face! Have you got a new boyfriend?'

'No, I haven't,' I grinned. 'I haven't time for boyfriends at the moment. I've got a book to finish first – or had you both forgotten?'

Finish *Firedance*, then start researching the Deer's Leap books. I would love it and loathe it, because by the time I had an excuse to go back there the house would stand alone and empty, a detestable For Sale notice at the white gate. And a stranger would buy it and everything would change, except the stone above the front door with W.D. & M.D. 1592 on it.

Were you *really* a witch, Margaret Dacre?

'Coffee time already, is it?' Frowning, Mum switched off the vacuum.

'No, but I'll make a cup, if you want one. I can't seem to settle down to work,' I shrugged. 'Maybe it's the changeover. I'll get over it.'

'No coffee for me just yet. I'll wait till ten, when your dad has his. If you're a bit restless, though, why don't you pop in on Aunt Jane – she can do with a few flowers.'

It surprised me I hadn't thought of it myself. I needed to get a few things straight in my mind, and when Aunt Jane and I swap thoughts, things always seem clearer.

I waved to Dad, who was packing cucumbers, then took a sharp knife from the potting shed. I felt disorientated, here amongst straight rows and straight paths and not a hill in sight. I let my thoughts go free and I was back in the lane, near the clump of oak trees, sliding my eyes left and right; glancing in the rear-view mirror in case he was behind me. He. J. J. Hunter. Was he there now at the roadside, arm extended, thumb jutting?

I cut ten stems of apricot spray chrysanthemums, then made for the village. The lane between Greenleas and Rowbeck reminded me again of Deer's Leap lane, only there were no oak trees and it was nowhere near so long. I hoped I wouldn't meet anyone I knew, because I wasn't in the mood to answer questions about where I had been and how the book was coming along and wasn't it a pity I'd been away when Piers was home?

I reached the church gates unchallenged, all the time trying to be glad I was home again, wondering why I felt so restless. Was it because I had seen a ghost and talked to a ghost, or was I feeling this way because with the exception of Lizzie Taylor, I had come up against a brick wall every time I'd tried to get a lead on Susan Smith? And Mrs Taylor hadn't exactly been a mine of information, come to think of it. All I could be sure of was that Jack and Susan met at a dance and that for a long time, her parents didn't know about those secret meetings.

'Hullo, Aunt Jane,' I said – with my thoughts, of course. 'Missed me?'

I filled the stone vase on her grave with water, then snapped the ends off the flower stems.

'No.'

Of course she hadn't. She was always as near as she wanted to be; only ever a thought away really.

'The book's coming along fine. I wrote well at Deer's Leap. It's a love of a house; the kind you never forget. It'll go on the market soon, and I can't have it.'

I stuck a stem in each hole at the top of the vase.

'*You'll have it if it's meant to be. All in the goodness of time!*'

'I want to find a lady called Susan Smith, but all I know is that she was in love with a pilot fifty years ago and that she vanished without a word to anyone.'

'*She'll take some finding. There are a lot of Smiths about.*'

'It'll be just my luck for her to be in New Zealand. I've got it in my mind, you see, that she's just about as far away as she can be.'

'*You're determined to make it difficult for yourself, aren't you? Before you start bothering about New Zealand, why don't you look a little nearer to home? Often what we're looking for is right under our noses. You've established, of course, that she's still around?*'

'No, but I'm as sure as I can be that she is.'

'*Then follow your instincts, girl.*'

'I met a ghost at the side of the lane near Deer's Leap.' Best I should tell her. 'I suppose you don't believe me, Aunt Jane?'

'*Why shouldn't I?*'

'Because people don't usually believe in ghosts.'

'Then get yourself off home and write some more of that naughty book!'

'He's called Jack, and he's tall and fair and – and –'

'Handsome, eh, but this Susan person got there first? Find a man of your own, Cassie Johns!'

'I half thought I had, but Piers and me are all washed up . . .'

'Good! He was never any use to you. I never liked him. He was a spoiled brat. Thank you for the flowers, by the way . . .'

'Aunt Jane!' I hissed out loud, forgetting what Mum had said about being seen talking to headstones. 'There's so much to tell you!'

But she'd switched off without so much as a chuckle. Pity, when I'd wanted to tell her about the war memorial and how Jack Hunter had been killed almost at the end of the war and that I was sure there'd be no peace for him until he found his Suzie.

But I would come here another time. Maybe, I thought, ghosts had to get their auras working – charge themselves up before they could make contact. And then I supposed, they disappeared when they were run down; like a battery, maybe.

'Bye, love,' I whispered. 'See you.'

Chapter Ten

September came in mistily, with dew-soaked mornings and warm afternoons. I had settled into a routine again, and *Firedance* seemed to be writing itself. Almost all else blotted from my mind, I worked with stubborn concentration as the final chapter got nearer.

In the gardens, Dad picked the last of the Victoria plums and the first of the damsons and laid apples and pears in the store shed to mellow. In the kitchen, Mum made green tomato chutney and salted shallots ready for pickling.

The pantry looked as it always had ever since I could remember: shelves full of jams, pickles and chutneys, half of which she would give away. And by far the best, four bottles of peaches grown on the south-facing wall and preserved in brandy, for special occasions.

There was no news of Piers, except that he had visited the Leeds laboratory where he'd used to work, and stayed overnight with his parents. He had neither phoned nor written and I felt more and more sure I was free of him; that I was neither missed nor even remembered – except, of course, when he was counting virginal scalps!

'How about you and me going brambling on Sunday afternoon?' Mum asked after breakfast. 'Do you good to get into the fresh air for an hour or two. You've been stuck in that bedroom far too long!' She liked to pick wild brambles before the end of the month because in October, so legend had it, the devil claimed them for himself, and was none too particular what he did on them! 'I'd like to make a few pots of bramble jelly.'

'Fine by me.' She was right. I'd been working like a mad

thing. 'As a matter of fact, I'll be starting the last chapter on Monday morning, so I deserve a day off.'

I would enjoy writing the final pages of *Firedance*, then going back to the beginning again for one last check before I began to run off the pages. I was quite well satisfied with the way it had turned out. It wasn't as explicit as Aunt Jane once suggested; no bodices ripped, though it had almost come to it a time or two. Slightly salacious I suppose you could call it, with things left unsaid, words left unwritten to allow the reader to put her own interpretation on events. I had just pulled back the curtain on the writing alcove when Jeannie rang.

'Hi! How's it going, Cassie?'

'Fine. Only the last chapter to write. I reckon you can have the manuscript by the end of November. I'll edit it page by page, but the worst is over now.'

'And then?'

'I plan to take a week off, doing anything I want but write. I'll probably have a day in York or get into the car and go where the mood takes me.'

'Like Acton Carey, perhaps, or Deer's Leap? It won't look very pretty in November.'

'N-no. But the way I see it, I've got quite a bit of research to do; might as well get stuck in first as last! And I know it might look bleak, but I've got to see both sides of it now, haven't I?'

'I suppose so. After all, you'll have to do a synopsis for book one before Harriers offer you a contract.'

'Never mind the synopsis; they won't be offering anything if *Firedance* doesn't come up to expectations.'

'And will it?'

'I think so. I'm almost certain it only needs editing – the odd word here and there; maybe a few cuts.' I said it cautiously because all at once I realized she was a bit edgy. 'But why do you ask? I thought you liked what you've seen of it?'

'I do, and I've no reason to think I won't like the remainder when I get it, Cassie, only – well –'

'Only Harriers have cut their romantic list and don't want the Deer's Leap books!' It came from out of my mind and I spoke the words without hardly realizing I'd said them. 'No contract – is that it?'

'Of course it isn't! Haven't I just said I shall want a synopsis?'

'So tell me.'

'All right.' She let out a sigh, then said, 'I've got no reason to believe there'll be anything to stop you writing those books, Cassie. What I was getting round to telling you is that Beth and Danny have found a house. In Skipton. They've bought it – subject to all things being equal, of course. Danny saw the For Sale board and liked the place at once. Beth looked at it next day and liked it too. They've agreed a price and the seller wants a quick completion, so there shouldn't be any problems. It's all happened so quickly. With luck, they could be moved in before the worst of the winter.'

'Before Christmas, even?'

'Beth is hoping to. It's so near to the twins' school that in decent weather they can easily walk there. And it's only two miles from Danny's work. They can't believe their luck.'

'How many bedrooms? Is there a garden?'

I didn't care about how big it was or how much land it had. I only asked to give me time to accept there wasn't going to be a Christmas at Deer's Leap. No tree, no cooking smells, no log fires.

'Four, and two attics. And the garden is adequate. Much smaller than their present one. There certainly won't be as much lawn to cut!'

'No. Better for Danny.' I recalled the scent of newly cut grass and Jeannie and I taking turns with the mower. 'But I hope whoever buys Deer's Leap won't cut down the red rose on the kitchen wall.'

'It's a very old rose, Cassie. Danny was saying not so long ago that it had grown very woody. But maybe it'll be as well if they get moved by the end of November – less risk of snow.

I mean, can you imagine a furniture van getting stuck in a six-foot drift?'

'Yes. It couldn't have happened at a better time. I'm very glad for Beth. No more boarding in winter.'

'Mm. And like she said on the phone last night, she'll be able to go to the shops whenever she likes. And there'll be the market stalls in the High Street every week. She won't know what ails her!'

She wouldn't. Beth would be able to spend her mornings window shopping instead of gazing serenely into eternity. And there would be no need for the lidded box at the end of the dirt road. Mail would come through the letterbox, milk would be left on the doorstep each morning and bread would be stacked in rows in the supermarket.

I was still thinking about it long after Jeannie put the phone down. I had looked forward to Christmas at Deer's Leap when I could say a proper goodbye. Maybe, too, I would have met Mrs Taylor again, and Jack Hunter. Now, no matter how good a move it was for Beth's family, I could only feel sad and vaguely cheated. And even though I knew the move was inevitable, I felt so stunned that I sat unmoving, staring at a blank screen for a long, long time.

I had made it: finished *Firedance* by the end of November! I dialled Jeannie's direct line at Harrier Books, euphoria washing over me. *Firedance* was as near perfect as I could make it, and now I felt drained of all emotion but relief.

'Hi! It's Cassie!' I said, when finally she answered. 'I'm posting the manuscripts in the morning!'

'Clever girl! You haven't packed them up yet, have you?'

'N-no . . .'

'Then why don't you bring them tomorrow? A day in the big city will do you no end of good. Leave as early as you can – I take it you'd be coming by train?'

'What do you think?' Driving in London was not for me!

'So how about arriving here about noon, dumping the scripts, then I'll treat you to lunch – OK?'

'Can you spare the time?' Jeannie seemed always madly busy.

'I'll make time. A couple of hours off will do me good too! We can talk about the Deer's Leap books without interruption as well. You are still keen on them, or aren't you?' she demanded when I remained silent.

'Of course I am. But if you must know, I've tried not to think about Deer's Leap. I suppose Beth and her family will be moving out any time now?'

'Tomorrow. First of December. It seemed as good a day as any, Beth said.'

'Of course.' So tomorrow, when I was sitting on the train with two copies of *Firedance* in my holdall, the furniture vans would already be parked outside the white gate, and Tommy and Lotus in special carrying baskets and Hector shut in the shed – going mad, I shouldn't wonder, at all the commotion and the sound of strange male voices.

'So see you tomorrow then. Cassie? Are you there?'

'I'm here. Just thinking about that poor old house. Tomorrow, it'll be all lonely and deserted.'

'Yes, but you'll see it again. You'll be going up that way to do some of your research. Nothing to stop you saying a quick hullo over the gate!'

'Yes – and see the new owner looking out of the kitchen window. She'll probably have a yappy little dog that doesn't like strange women! But I shall want some winter snaps of the area, so I'll have to go.'

'We'll talk about that tomorrow. Any idea when you'll be arriving?'

'I think there's a train at eight something. I'll check with enquiries. I'll most likely be with you about eleven thirty.'

'Fine. Just arrive. We can have a good old chat then. And thanks for getting *Firedance* finished in such good time.'

So that was it. London tomorrow and hopefully another

contract. October's royalties on *Ice Maiden* had been more than I'd expected. For once, I had money in the bank; the worst was over. The financial worst, that was, but what about me, Cassie Johns? Twenty-four, almost, and manless. All my friends were either married or in relationships; only I still lived with my parents out of the whole gang of us. Mind, certain things had had to go by the board. I'd understood and accepted that when I made up my mind to write. Trouble had been, though, that I hadn't known how hard it is to get a book accepted. Only my stubbornness had kept me going; that, and Piers's ever-so-lightly veiled sneers. Piers could sneer and smile at the same time, like a cat purring with its claws out. Piers wasn't nice, truth known. The day I finished it between us hadn't been a day too soon. Yet I wanted a man in my life. I'd be peculiar if I didn't!

I pushed back my chair and went to stare in my dressing-table mirror. Good cheekbones, if freckled; a decent nose, and the pale, easy-to-flush complexion that often comes with red hair. Very blue eyes; pity about the pale lashes.

There were blue rings under my eyes, but that was to be expected after glaring at a screen almost non-stop for the last three weeks. And my hair needed cutting and shaping. Otherwise, not bad. Nothing there that a week of lazy indulgence wouldn't put to rights. Because I was really tired – physically and mentally drained – and Beth's leaving Deer's Leap so suddenly hadn't helped. I had so looked forward to Christmas there – maybe get the lowdown on Margaret Dacre and see Lizzie Taylor and Bill again. Or even have one last sight of the pilot. I had so needed to tell him I'd really wanted to find Susan, then maybe say goodbye. Goodbye to a ghost! What a title for a novel!

I turned to look out of the window, half expecting to see fells and fields and sun-slanted moors. Instead, I saw leafless trees and stacks of wooden boxes and a mist that was taking a long time to lift.

That one summer at Deer's Leap was long over. Tomorrow it would be December. Tomorrow that lovely old house would stand empty, its windows like sad eyes gazing across to Parlick Pike.

Would Margaret Dacre know it was empty; know that the house she set such high hopes on all those years ago was up for sale? Would her spirit take it over so that all who came to see it said what a cold, unfriendly place it was?

The man who bought it after the war – the one who'd won a lot of money on football pools – hadn't stayed long. Too isolated he found it. He'd rented it out, in the end, and Beth and Danny had lived there almost ten years. Margaret Dacre hadn't been able to get rid of them, had she? But then Beth was happy there, and happiness is a powerful antidote to evil. Margaret Dacre hadn't been able to cope with that!

But witches or not, I wanted Deer's Leap. I wouldn't care if there was a coven of them battering at the door, flying low on their broomsticks and making the chimneypots rattle. That house had cast a spell over me that had nothing to do with witchcraft; only the simple fact was that I loved it. Desperately. And I couldn't have it.

I switched on the lights and drew the curtains against the gloom. I was acting like a child; a spoiled brat. There would be other houses and one day, when I could afford it, I would find the one for me. Hadn't Aunt Jane said so?

'Besides,' I said, 'there are no such things as witches!'

Of course there wasn't, and anyway, Hallowe'en – the night when spirits and ghosts and hanged witches have one final fling before they settle down for the winter – had been and gone a month ago. If there had been any goings-on around Pendle, they would be over with now.

I shut the door behind me and made for the saneness and safeness of Mum's kitchen and a fire piled high with spitting, crackling logs.

'I'm going to London tomorrow,' I announced. 'Jeannie

wants me to take the manuscript down, have lunch with her, and a chat.'

'That'll be nice. I suppose London will be all lit up for Christmas,' Mum said without glancing up from the apple pie she was making for tea.

'I'm not sure, but the shop windows will be lovely. I got an idea for a book whilst I was at Beth's place – four books, in fact. Jeannie will want to talk about them. And, Mum – I won't be going to Deer's Leap at Christmas.'

'I see. What made you change your mind?' Mum beamed.

'I didn't. If I'm honest, it was changed for me. Beth has got another house. They're moving into it tomorrow.'

'Well, it'll be more like Christmas when we're all together!' Mum was still smiling. 'She'll be sad to leave that house, for all that. I was real taken with it.'

'Me too, Mum, but come tomorrow it'll be standing empty.'

'Not for long! It's a grand house for a family.'

'With no schools for fourteen miles, and the nearest shop more than a mile away! It would be fine for young children. They could run free. But as soon as they were old enough for school it would be a different matter. Beth's had to be weekly boarders in winter.'

'But it's a lovely house, for all that.' She put the pie to bake in the old oven that was heated by the fire. There was an old fire oven in the kitchen at Deer's Leap, though Beth never used it for anything but drying out kindling and logs.

It flashed through my mind that a day out in London would be a good thing; might keep my thoughts from an empty house. And then I realized that I was going there to talk about four books, and all of them about Deer's Leap – or a house exactly like it, with a fictional name.

'If there's nothing you want doing, Mum, I think I'll look out something to wear tomorrow; see if it needs pressing.'

Mum said there was nothing at all, thank you; and I knew

171

her magnanimity sprang from the realization that her only chick would be home, after all, for Christmas!

My bedroom was warm and normal again; maybe because the central heating had switched on for the night, but probably because I had got control of myself and my imaginings.

I decided to go casual and wear my best jeans, trying them on to make sure I could pull up the zip, because I could never be sure, what with Mum's cooking, and all that sitting on my behind!

They fitted, and I sorted out a top and jacket, pleased I could have a second helping of apple pie. Then I decided against it, because I always comfort-eat when I'm on edge. And I was edgy because something was wrong with my life and I didn't know what.

OK. So I was a bit drained. I'd worked all-out on *Firedance* and it was to be expected. Yet there was more than fatigue to be faced up to, and sorted out – like there was no man in my life, now. Yet to be fair, it was I who made the break, so what was I complaining about? That Piers wasn't fair and twenty-four, perhaps, with wings on his tunic and an endearing habit of pushing his hair aside with his left hand?

Oh, for Pete's sake! Who in her right mind would be attracted to a ghost? Who, if she had her wits about her wouldn't be tickled pink that out of a crazy encounter in a lonely lane had sprung the plots for at least four novels? No-one at all, truth known, but Cassie Johns, who chatted to an aunt in the churchyard and let herself become completely bewitched by an old house!

If I had any sense at all, I would insist that enough was enough; that I would *not* write books about Deer's Leap nor go near the house again! Nor would I worry about Susan Smith and where she was living, nor about a World War Two pilot for whom time had stood still! I would wash my hands of the whole shebang, find another storyline for my third novel and stop acting like a nutcase!

I should, but I wouldn't, because sense doesn't come into it when an old house, a woman who once practised witchcraft and an airman who was twenty-four, touching eighty, had put their mark on me and there wasn't a thing I could do about it!

The train pulled into King's Cross exactly on time, and I was making towards the underground when I saw them; Piers, with a very beautiful woman. He was holding her hand as they pushed through the surge of people in the station entrance. She was dark-haired and slim and he looked down at her and smiled indulgently; almost a look of love!

I watched them until they were lost in the crowd, though it was obvious they were making for the Glasgow train. Getting off at Leeds, perhaps, or York? Was he going north on business or was he taking her to Rowbeck for parental approval?

I didn't know and what was even more pleasing, I didn't care! To see him with another woman hadn't upset me. I was free of him; free to have affairs with the heroes in my books, flirt at parties, throw my cap over the windmill! Piers had been my first love – no, wrong! – my first *lover*; had taken my virginity, but so what? It didn't bother me one iota because couldn't something – *someone* – really marvellous be around the next corner. I was Cassandra Johns, author, with two books under her belt and a whole new scenario ahead of her. In a rush of magnanimity, I wished Piers all the luck in the world because I had the feeling he was going to need it!

'Farringdon, please.' I smiled at the man in the ticket office, then followed the pointing arrows to the Circle Line.

'Lovely to see you!' Jeannie, her smile as bright as ever, took my holdall and guided me to the lift. 'Had a good journey? I'll just dump these in my office, then we'll have a lovely long lunch. There's a carvery place on the next block, so we can walk there. Let's get out of it before that dratted phone rings!'

She put the two copies of *Firedance* into a drawer, turning the key in the lock, and it wasn't until we were settled at a corner table and had lifted our glasses to the success of *Firedance*, that I said, 'I saw Piers at King's Cross. He had a woman with him and she was absolutely beautiful. He seemed besotted.'

'That didn't take him long!'

'No, but I've got a feeling she's been around for some time, only I didn't know about it. I only saw them in passing, but she looked very expensive.'

'Did seeing him with someone else bother you?'

'Not a bit! Actually I felt relieved, almost.'

'Good! So can we talk about the first Deer's Leap book before we eat? You still want to go ahead with it?'

'Yes, though last night I tried to tell myself I didn't; that I'd got too tied up with the place. But I shall write them. I've got to get that house out of my system. I was thinking about it on the train. I'll probably call the first one *Witches Hey*, though I haven't found a name yet for Deer's Leap.'

'So shall we drink to the Deer's Leap books?' she smiled, lifting her glass.

'And to Beth and Danny. They'll be almost on their way now. Good luck in their new home.'

'To the new house. And may God bless her, and all who sail in her! And to the new book too!' Solemnly, she clinked her glass with mine.

Almost on their way. The furniture packed and one last look round, maybe? Going from room to room ostensibly to check that nothing had been left, but really to whisper a goodbye?

'I think,' I said chokily, 'I'd like to eat, now . . .'

So we ate splendid beef and drank red wine and talked about books and contracts and sometimes, when we were off our guard, about Deer's Leap and the time we had spent there together.

Yet it wasn't until we were leaving that Jeannie said, right out of the blue, 'So now that you're taking time off, are you going to read the book I gave you?'

'The one of Susanna Lancaster's?' It had taken a while for the penny to drop. 'D'you know, I'd forgotten about it.'

'Then I think you should allow yourself the luxury of curling up with a good book. I've read it.'

'And . . . ?'

'You'll like it. In fact, I think you won't be able to put it down, so be warned!'

'It's *that* good, Jeannie?'

'Just read it, Cassie, like I said.' I couldn't see her face, because she was standing at the edge of the road, scanning the slow-moving traffic for a taxi to take me back to the station. 'I guarantee it'll make you sit up and take notice!'

It was to be two more days before I took *Dragonfly Morning* off the shelf. I smiled, loving the smell, the feel of a new book. Susanna Lancaster's name was printed large in gold letters and, beneath it, the title. I flicked it open to read the names of her previous publications. Nineteen were listed there; *Dragonfly Morning*, her twentieth, featured on the page opposite, with her name above it and at the bottom of the page, the name and logo of Harrier Books. The following page bore the dedication:

> *To Memories*
> *And to Say Goodbye*

Goodbye to what, or whom? Smiling indulgently, I began to read.

SUSANNA LANCASTER

———

Dragonfly
Morning

Harrier

To Memories
And to Say Goodbye

ONE

1942

It was frightening, if you let yourself think about it too much. Rosamund Kenton stood at the gate of the cow pasture and looked over to her left, to where giant machines ripped and chewed at hedges. And after the hedges, every tree would be felled, and their roots dragged out by a tractor and chains.

Soon, all the land *They* had taken from Fellstead, the farm next to theirs, would be nothing but a flat waste, because aerodromes must be flat so that planes could take off, and there must be no hedges nor trees to hinder their landing.

Already, Fellstead farmhouse was empty. The farmer had had to leave – the Air Ministry insisted on it – because when the aerodrome was finished, the farmhouse, standing on the very edge of the runway, would no longer be safe to live in. So land farmed for 150 years by generations of one family was taken for an aerodrome without so much as a by-your-leave. It was not only frightening, it was heartbreaking too, because before so very much longer it would happen to Laburnum Farm, though to a lesser degree.

Laburnum could keep half its acres, said the slab-faced man who had first told them about it. And they could keep the farmhouse too. Rosamund supposed they were lucky, really, though her father had demanded to know how a man was to make a living with his best arable land gone! His wife had been the first to come to terms with it. They could still manage without culling any of the milking herd, though they would have to buy fodder instead of growing it themselves. They would concentrate on milk, she said, and crops such as potatoes – upon which the government paid a large subsidy – would have to go by the board.

Rosamund watched as the cows began to walk towards her. They knew it was milking time; their bags, full to the point of tenderness, told them so. She quite liked milking; could rest her forehead against the side of a cow, and think – or not think – as the mood took her. This afternoon, when the milk was hissing into the bucket she held between her knees, she would wonder how long it would be before the man from the Ministry called again, giving them, if they were lucky, a month in which to evacuate the fifty acres Laburnum Farm would be losing to the aerodrome.

Very soon now, because those giant machines moved like hungry monsters, pulling and chewing and flattening everything in their way. Fellstead fields had been stripped of everything that grew save grass. And then they would gorge themselves on Laburnum Farm's acres. It would hurt a lot, because mature beeches would be felled, their trunks carted away, their branches sawn and chopped into logs to be used as fuel for the war effort. It wouldn't matter that those beautiful beeches had been growing for years and years and had given pleasure to all who looked at them and shelter to birds and small animals.

Next year, nothing would be left of them, and great ribbons of concrete would be laid from north to south and from west to east. And there would be rashes of ugly huts and hangars too, she shouldn't wonder.

'Coosh, coosh, coosh,' she called to the few beasts who lingered for a last pull of grass. 'Coom on, pet; coooom on . . .'

Silly creatures. She opened the gate wide so there would be no pushing and heaving. People thought cows were gentle as their soft moist eyes, but they could be vindictive, shoving younger beasts aside, kicking out viciously with hooves that looked too dainty to bear their bulk.

Now more than ever, the herd was their support, because when the machines had finished at Fellstead, they would let loose their destruction on Laburnum's fields; probably, her father said, without giving them time to harvest the hay that was almost ready for cutting.

She hoped not, because since the war started, hay had become as important as food, in a roundabout way. Hay fed the herd in winter and would be expensive to replace. If they started cutting tomorrow, she calculated, they could have it turned and dried and cocked, and carted into the hayloft. Perhaps her father wouldn't wait; perhaps, if the weather held good they would make a start on it just as soon as he was able to borrow men from other farms.

Finding labour was a bother now, because young men had gone to war, and all unmarried women had to register at the labour exchange and be sent anywhere the mood took *Them*, the faceless ones. Even into the Armed Forces!

'It's a crying shame,' her mother said. 'Young girls, gently reared, being pitchforked into uniform. And they'll be serving with men parted from their wives and –'

She stopped then, and Rosamund had finished the sentence for her. Mentally, of course.

'– missing the comforts only a wife can give!' That's what her mother would have said if her daughter hadn't been in the room.

Mildred Kenton. Devoted to home and family; hardworking and thrifty; so prim it bordered on narrow-mindedness! Procreation was never talked about, even though they lived on a farm where animals did it all the time.

'Come on, lazy creature!'

Rosamund slapped the side of a heifer that hung back because it wasn't yet its turn to walk through the gate. Cows were like that. There was a pecking order in every herd, with the sharp dig of a horn to remind any that stepped out of line.

She dug her hands in her breeches pockets, leaving the gate open because the herd would return, after milking, to spend the night in the field. She walked slowly behind the lumbering beasts, who matched their pace to the undisputed leader, an old shorthorn, big with calf.

She wondered how procreation was – how it *really* was. Something that came as part and parcel of being a married woman and the mistress of her own kitchen, her mother had hinted, and strictly between husband and wife in the privacy of their bedroom.

Yet Bessie Drake's cousin had done it on a haystack and had

a lovely time with a soldier; hadn't got pregnant either! There was more to it, she and Bessie had long ago decided in the back of the school bus, than grown-ups were prepared to admit.

But now she was seventeen and had given up trying to learn about *things*, putting it down to the fact that in all probability her mother was reluctant to admit she and Dad had done *that* – in the privacy of their bedroom, without doubt – in order to get their only child.

Yet surely you fell in love and children came naturally as a result? She had seen enough films, read enough books, indulged in sufficient daydreams to know that one day she would fall in love, even though it wasn't going to be easy since Laburnum Farm was a good mile from the village, and young men to fall in love with weren't exactly thick on the ground in Laceby Green. Three! That was all!

It had been better at school. There were loads of boys around, then, though to be seen talking to one, let alone caught walking with one to the bus, merited a grave warning in the Head's study and the promise of a letter to the miscreant's parents for a second offence! Which all boiled down to the fact that talking to boys was a rather nice, rather daring thing to do!

She pushed procreation from her thoughts. There was a war on, and winning the war was more important than anything. More and more government posters appeared on walls and in shop windows, asking everyone to Dig for Victory, Save for Victory and inviting young men to fly with the RAF and report to their nearest recruiting centre and join an aircrew. And always to remember that Walls Have Ears.

Aircrew. They would be coming to the aerodrome when it was finished. There would be bombers flying over all the time and the peace of Laburnum Farm would be gone until the war ended. And heaven only knew when that would be.

Her father was crossing the farmyard with a pail of steaming water as the cows lumbered into the shippon. Dad always washed the cows' udders before milking began and it was Rosamund's job to put cattle cake into the troughs. Just the noise of it made the beasts hurry to their stalls. Each knew its own position as if it could read the name above it. Cows really were quite intelligent. She went down the line of nodding heads, fastening neck-chains, then hurried to the dairy to collect washed and scalded pails.

Only when they were settled on low, wooden milking stools did she say, without looking up, 'They've made a start on Fellstead. It's in a terrible mess.'

'Aye. It'll be our turn next, lass. No rhyme nor reason to it.'

'No. But they aren't taking all our fields, and they don't want our house.' It wasn't considered patriotic to complain.

Bart Kenton lapsed into silence, concentrating on the hissing milk that hit the sides of the pail then ran into a froth in the bottom. God only knew what would have happened if the Ministry people had said they wanted the house too. Laburnum farmhouse and the paddock behind it was their own; not rented, as their land was, from Laceby Hall. That house was Mildred's joy, had cost them every penny of her inheritance. He remembered the look on her face as they'd gone from room to room, inspecting it. Rosamund had been a baby then, and himself a herdsman on a farm near Ribchester. Marrying Mildred turned him from labourer to master. He had been grateful to her; always would be.

'What on earth are we going to do with such a big place? How are we to fill it?'

Furnish it, he'd meant, but she shot him a glance and said they would take what the good Lord sent. Mildred trusted implicitly in the Lord – her shrewd business sense coming a close second.

There had been only one child, and Bart planted a climbing rose outside the kitchen window for the little lass they'd called Rosamund. A red rose, it had to be, for Lancashire. It gave them one beautiful flower that first summer, then took hold and rampaged up the wall, and as long as it flowered and thrived, Mildred said, so would Laburnum Farm.

With the help of the bank, they kept their heads above water. Laburnum's thick packet of deeds had been handed over to secure money to buy stock and farm implements, all acquired at farm sales at knockdown prices. They had furnished the kitchen and the bedroom above it, and that was all. The baby's cot stood beside their bed. Even though there were bedrooms enough for ten bairns, there hadn't been a spare penny left over for their one little lass to have her own room.

Farming was a risky thing in those days. They couldn't have moved in at a worse time, 1926 being a bad year, with the country in turmoil, and the have-nots standing shoulder to shoulder against the haves. The promises made to the men who survived four years in trenches were forgotten. Heroes sold matches and bootlaces in the streets and Authority turned a blind eye on what amounted to legalized begging.

'What's that, lass?' His daughter was speaking to him.

'I said things seem to be going better – the war, I mean.' She had tired of the silence and said the first thing that came into her head. Things *were* better now than they had ever been. Sixty Spitfires – *sixty*, mind you! – had safely arrived at Malta and were giving German and Italian bombers a pasting; the Russians had halted the German advance and American soldiers were arriving in England by the shipload.

But by far the most heartening thing of all had been another 1,000-bomber raid on Germany. The entire country had listened in amazement to the announcement on the wireless, telling of the first one, because no one had thought we had that many bombers! Then last night, on her birthday, came the second great raid, though 31 aircraft had not returned from it. More than 200 young men reduced to statistics. It was awful even to think about.

It was why, she supposed, the RAF was building yet another aerodrome only a mile from this very place. Mr Churchill had promised more and more raids with more and more bombers. It stood to reason there must be more and more aerodromes. Yet did they have to put one here, on this most beautiful part of Lancashire? Until now, nothing disturbed the peace. They hadn't even heard an air-raid siren, except on newsreels at the picture house in Clitheroe. Nor had they heard the crash of bombs, crept from the shelter to find their home blasted and burning. They didn't need a shelter at Laburnum Farm. The cellars were deep and all the protection they would need, because there might be raids now. It stood to reason the aerodrome would be bombed.

'How long do you think it'll take to finish it?' she called. 'The aerodrome, I mean . . .'

'Not long. It never does, when t'government sets its mind to things.'

'How long is not long?' How many more months, she really meant, before the bombers came?

'Talk has it they can get a place like that up and running in a year. Mind, the new 'dromes aren't like the ones we had before the war. Jerry-built the thing'll be. Everything prefabricated.'

Prefabricated. A new word. It meant, so far as Rosamund could make out, things built in sections, then transported to wherever *They* wanted them, and slotted together. Flimsy things, really. Easily knocked down when they were no longer needed. When the war was over . . .

They had roast pheasant for their evening meal. Pheasants were out of season, but one had been offered and Mildred gave two shillings and six eggs for it, squaring her conscience by insisting that Ned Loftus had five mouths to feed and that since the Ackroyds no longer lived at Laceby Hall they wouldn't miss the odd gamebird from the covers.

'I could smell that pheasant roasting right across the yard,' Bart Kenton teased. 'It's a good job there isn't a house nearby or they'd know we were eating off the black market!'

'Pheasants aren't on the ration!' Not like beef and mutton and pork. 'And they don't have to be brought here by sea either!' Mildred Kenton could not have put a foot inside the chapel if she had been guilty of something as black as that! 'And those Ackroyds have done all right out of us over the years. It isn't as though we owe them anything.' The rent on their fields was paid every quarterday to the solicitor in Clitheroe who managed what was left of the estate. 'And if it goes against your conscience, Bart Kenton, then don't eat it!'

'It doesn't. I was only teasing. Pass the bread sauce, Milly.'

Rosamund let go her breath. It was all right; there wasn't going to be words, or a silence, which meant she would be allowed to go to Laceby Green, to Bessie's. Bessie once had a job in the little workroom that had turned from making ladies' blouses to shirts for ATS girls, Waafs and Wrens. She had been so bad at machining that she was put in the office, so that when the wages clerk was called into the Armed Forces, as he soon surely would be, there would be someone there who had an idea of how wages got into packets. Bessie earned twenty-five shillings a week, and was allowed to keep half of it.

'Do you suppose, that now I'm seventeen, I could have wages?' It came out in a rush and it made her cheeks bright red to ask it. 'Well, I do work on the land, and land girls are paid wages.'

'I see. Everything comes down to money in the end.' Mildred stared fixedly at the bread-and-butter pudding she was dividing into three. 'Why do you want a wage, tell me? You have your keep and your pocket money, and I buy your clothes.'

'I – I was thinking of a rise, Mum. After all, we aren't as hard up as we were. The government pay us subsidies, and nowadays we can sell everything we grow – as well as the eggs . . .'

'Hard up! We were *never* hard up!' Oh, my goodness, had it shown? 'When have you ever wanted for anything, miss? You live in comfort in one of the finest houses around, and the land more than pays its way!'

Now it did. Ever since war threatened, when Mr Chamberlain said it was to be peace for our time, the government all at once became interested in farmers. Once, the country hadn't cared, and had imported all manner of foreign muck rather than eat what British farmers produced.

'I know, and I'm sorry! I wasn't being ungrateful. But I – I don't suppose you could make it ten shillings?' She was almost on the point of remarking that Bessie had twelve and six a week, but thought better of it, because didn't she want to go to Bessie's tonight?

'Eight shillings a week was all your father ever earned until he came of age! Have you no idea at all, Rosamund, of the value of money?'

Bart chewed overlong on his pudding, willing himself not to

say that money wasn't everything, though there were some who thought it was! Then he felt shame, for hadn't Milly provided the house they lived in; worked long hours on the farm and taken the pony and trap to town every week to sell pats of home-churned butter, jars of cream, eggs and vegetables? And hadn't it been a grand day when things took a turn for the better and they were able to bring home the deeds of Laburnum Farm, so long held by the bank as security.

'I think,' he said evenly, 'that your mum and me will talk about it later; though I'll grant you, lass, you work as well as any land girl would.'

'Better!' Milly snapped. 'Rosamund was brought up to farming, which is more than those land girls were!'

'Look – I'm sorry!' Rosamund saw her trip to Laceby Green flying out of the window. 'I shouldn't have asked. It's only that now I'm seventeen –'

'Seventeen is no age at all. You're a child still.'

'You can join the Women's Forces at eighteen.' She regretted the words even as they slipped out.

'Indeed you can!' Mildred Kenton's eyes had narrowed; her mouth formed itself into a tight moue. 'With permission, that is, and your dad won't give his!'

'Mum, I don't want –'

'Farming is work of national importance. They'd show you the door at the recruiting office once they found you were working on the land!'

'I didn't say I want to join anything! I was only pointing out that eighteen is considered old enough for a girl to leave home now!'

'Leave home! When there's a war on and air raids and men in uniform everywhere, not knowing what to do with themselves!'

'I don't want to leave home, either. I want to stay at Laburnum! I didn't mean to start anything, honest I didn't!'

'We know you didn't, lass, and your mum and me will have a word about a rise for you. For my part, I think you deserve it!'

'And so do I, only I'll not be blackmailed into it,' Mildred flung, 'just for the sake of peace and quiet!'

'Don't quarrel. Please don't quarrel. I've said I'm sorry . . .'

'We aren't going to quarrel, Rosamund; not over a few shillings. Now why don't you get your bike out and go for a ride?'

He wanted her out of the way! This was one of the times Dad was going to square up to Mum, and he didn't want her around!

'A – a ride? We-e-ll, I wouldn't mind going to Bessie's. I'll do the dishes first, though.'

'Oh, off you go! I'll see to things!' Mildred realized she was outmanoeuvred. 'But don't be late. I want you home well before dark!'

Before dark, Rosamund smiled, as she passed the clump of oak trees. Tonight, being June, it wouldn't be dark till well past eleven – and God bless the man who thought of putting the clocks forward *two* hours, and calling it double-summertime! Nights were so light for so long now that it didn't seem natural. Yet it was better than the blackout in winter! The blackout was more unnatural than light nights! So dark, it was as if you needed to brush the denseness of it aside with your hand. It hurt your eyes too, staring into it, and you couldn't see cars or lorries coming either because they weren't allowed headlights!

But tonight the air was warm, the breeze soft. Around her the grass verges at the side of the lane were thick with wild flowers and the scent of honeysuckle was heavy on the air. Over to her right, the evening sun lay lower in the sky, casting black shadows over the hills. It was so beautiful here that she clung to her mother's words, and was glad she worked on the farm and would be labelled reserved when she was eighteen and had to register for war work at the labour exchange. She would rather remain at Laburnum Farm and work till she dropped than be sent away from home.

If she stopped now, at a spot just past the clump of oaks, she could look to her left down a little valley where, so Dad said, the stream that once supplied their farmhouse with water had slipped and splashed over cobbles to join the River Hodder. Why it had dried up, no one seemed to know, and only old people in Laceby Green, whose grandparents remembered paddling in it to catch minnows, could vouch for its authenticity.

But it was gone, and soon the path of its bed would be grown over and gone too, like Fellstead's hedges and trees. And soon, Laburnum Farm's beech trees as well.

It was because of their beech trees that Rosamund didn't stop to gaze and wonder, because she knew that when the time came, just to hear the death cries of those trees would go through her like a knife. Trees were living things and could feel pain just as humans could. She was sure of it.

She pedalled slowly through the village, past the post office and the White Hart pub and the church with its triangle of grass at the gates; past the war memorial with the names of the dead of the Great War on it, then turned sharply to her right onto the bumpy road that led to Bessie's house. Only it wasn't a house, exactly. Bessie Drake lived in one of the gate lodges belonging to Laceby Hall. The Ackroyds, who'd once lived there and got very rich from cotton and, some hinted, out of the slave trade too, were gone, and their big house razed to the ground and hardly a stone left standing. Only the cellars remained, to be filled with rubble and rubbish, then sealed over. If you went there at Hallowe'en, Bessie said, you could hear the screams of the Pendle Witches, cursing the witch-hunter and the gallows-man with their last breaths.

Rosamund didn't believe it, though, because she knew it was a story put about to keep the village children from taking fruit from the orchards that still stood there, and to stop them making a nuisance of themselves in the ploughed-up parkland on either side of a carriage drive that led to nowhere.

Through great iron gates, Rosamund traced the windings of that drive, wondering about the people who had driven up it in coaches drawn by at least four horses, with uniformed postilions astride them. She liked to make up stories and often did, mostly to invent siblings. Laburnum Farm would not have been so lonely with a sister to share it.

Bessie had two brothers in the Royal Navy, which made her virtually an only child too. It pleased her no end, she said, though really she missed them, and worried about them, and sent letters every week.

Bessie's mother was weeding in the front garden, and she smiled her wide welcoming smile and said, 'Hullo, Rosamund. She's upstairs – as usual! Go on up!'

Bessie's mother laughed a lot too. Nothing upset her. She would laugh, some said, if the roof fell in.

'It's me.' Rosamund poked her head round the bedroom door. 'What on earth are you doing?'

'Plucking my eyebrows, as if you didn't know! It doesn't half make your eyes water!'

'Then why do it, if it hurts so much?'

'Because everybody does it. My eyebrows are like hedges and I'm trying for a shape like Lana Turner's. And it's all right for you to smirk. Yours don't need plucking.'

Everything about her friend was near-perfect, Bessie thought, returning her agonized gaze to the mirror, tweezers poised.

'They're working like mad things on Fellstead fields.' Rosamund collapsed on the bed with a dramatic flounce. 'It's awful. Just think of it, Bess. We'll be able to go to the top of the paddock soon and look down on that aerodrome. It'll spoil everything.'

'Sorry, old love. There's a war on, so you'll have to put up with it!'

'And supply them with mugs of cocoa, whilst they rip up our land too!'

'Dad says you'll get good compensation. And you'll get your fields back, when They've done with them.'

'All covered with concrete and huts? Thanks a bunch! Talk has it that it's going to be for bombers. Big ones. I don't think I'll like having tons of high explosive flying over Laburnum all the time.'

'So look on the bright side! Before you know it, there'll be RAF bods all over the place! Hundreds of 'em!' And a great improvement on the present position, Bessie gloated, with two of Laceby Green's eligibles already called up, and the third about to go! 'I can't wait to get my hands on one of those lovely pilots! Why is it that aircrews are always so good-looking?'

'It's their aura of glamour, I suppose. All the call-ups want to fly.'

'Dave and Joe say the Navy is the senior service. They call the RAF the Brylcreem Boys! Are you really worried about having an aerodrome so near, Rosamund? I think it'll be quite an improvement. Might liven the place up a bit.'

'I'm not worried, exactly, even though it'll be nearer Laburnum than it is to the village. But are you really looking forward to them coming, Bess?'

'You bet! It'll be great when the blokes get here!'

'And will your dad let you go out with them?'

'Don't suppose so. You know what fathers are like. But Mum will only laugh and tell me not to let him catch me. And not to get myself into trouble either, I shouldn't wonder. Ha! Chance would be a fine thing!'

'Funny you should say that. I was thinking this afternoon about babies and how they get there.'

'But you know how they get there, you daft hap'orth!' Bessie let out a laugh exactly like her mother's. 'Marjie says it's a lot of fun when the fumbling starts.'

'Marjie? That's your cousin – the one who went on a haystack?'

'The one who *did it* on a haystack!'

'I wouldn't dare!'

'You would if you loved him: I'll bet you anything you would!'

'Hm.' She was prepared to take Bessie's word for it. Bessie was seventeen and seven months; not a lot older, really, though Rosamund supposed you could learn a lot in seven months. 'I'd be worried about getting pregnant. Imagine the talk in Laceby! They'd stone you out of the village as a scarlet woman!'

'They would, if you were daft enough to let it happen! There are ways, you know. The chargehand in the machine room was telling one of the girls who's getting married.'

'Ways like how?' Rosamund could feel herself blushing.

'She didn't tell *me*, softie – but she would if I asked her. Talk has it that she once got rid of a baby!'

'Have you finished your eyebrows? Shall we go out?'

Rosamund changed the subject. She had to, because there was a lot she didn't know about *things* and just to think about it made her feel stupid, though maybe in another seven months she'd have learned a bit more. Perhaps as much as Bessie knew now.

'Out? OK, if you want to. Where shall we go?'

'Would your dad be mad if we walked up the drive as far as the ruins?'

It was accepted around Laceby Green that Mr Drake acted as unofficial caretaker of the Hall, reporting to the solicitor in Clitheroe if anything was amiss. It was the least he could do, he said, since they lived in one of the estate houses, and the rent hadn't gone up in years.

'Course he wouldn't! But what's so interesting about the place? You always want to go there!'

'If you must know, I think it's a shame that lovely old house was knocked down. You'd have thought those Ackroyds would have rented it out instead. I'll bet there are dozens of boarding schools on the south coast, looking for somewhere safer.'

'Not any more. Dad says Hitler's had his chips in Russia and he won't be invading us now. I must admit I'm relieved about that. I wouldn't have liked Nazis jack-booting it up and down the village!'

'Bess! They could try for the duration and still not find Laceby Green! There's nothing around here that's worth bothering about – well, not of strategic importance.'

'But there soon will be!'

'Mm. Soon.' Funny, these days, how the aerodrome was on everybody's mind. 'Come on. Let's get going. I've got to be in before dark.'

The Aerodrome. RAF Laceby Green she supposed it would be called, Laceby being the nearest place of habitation. If they came, that was. If They didn't decide against it at the last minute!

But They wouldn't. Already she could hear the cries of the beech trees.

It was late August before the machines had flattened Fellstead's fields and were ready to move on to Laburnum Farm's land. Something to do with drainage had held them up. Bart Kenton not only got his hay safely lofted, but harvested the wheat and barley too, though it was a shame, he said, that he'd had to leave the sugar beet and late potatoes. But then wasted crops meant nothing to the people at Whitehall.

Rosamund stood outside the front door, looking over the moonlit fields to the fifty acres They were taking. Everything was very still, a silhouette in silver and black. She had come here for a last look, and because it was almost nine o'clock, the sacred hour at which the wireless must be turned on and the measured, unemotional tones of the announcer brought the war into their kitchen. Most times she could pretend the war hadn't happened, so isolated were they; so cut off at the end of a lane. But at one o'clock and again at nine, the war became very real, and most times frightening.

Rosamund shut her ears to the news bulletins more than ever now, because any day the machines would come to Laburnum's fields. She was glad of the harvest moon that shone golden in the sky, because this was the picture she would carry in her memory of the way it had been. Tomorrow, or the next day, the war was coming nearer and there was nothing she could do to stop it. Just as she knew there was no way she could cling to her childhood. She was in her eighteenth year; womanhood was just around the corner because at eighteen, *They* said you were a woman! Not long ago, her parents had said as much too.

'You're a young woman now, and Dad and I have decided you are to be treated as such.'

It was why, her mother said, there would be an end to pocket money. Henceforth, she was to have a wage every Friday, and it would be recorded in the farm accounts. It had taken Rosamund some weeks to realize that such generosity had its roots in down-to-earth reality. When the time came for her to register for national service, it would have been on record for almost a year that she was employed as a farm worker; there in black and white, in her mother's careful handwriting, proof positive. Yet at the time of her elevation to wage earner, she had thought of nothing save that she was to be paid a pound a week! Twenty shillings, if you please! Seven and sixpence more than Bessie got!

'I shall expect you to buy your own clothes, now, and –' with lowered voice and eyes – 'things of a personal nature,' Mildred had said.

Things of a personal nature were bought discreetly, and only when the chemist's lady assistant was behind the counter. She could take care of that – but buying her own clothes? How far did forty clothing coupons a year go, when shoes needed five, pyjamas took care of eight more and a winter coat gobbled up fourteen! She thought of the beautiful cotton dresses Marks and Spencer sold for four and eleven, and felt it a shame that now she had the money, there was the matter of seven clothing coupons to prevent her buying one.

She shut down her broodings and looked instead at a moon that changed from gold to silver, the higher it rose in the sky. And she told herself that when the machines came to Laburnum Farm to gobble and tear and destroy, they would fell the beech trees she had known all her life. She must think about it so often that when the time came, she would be able to watch as the last of them fell with a sickening crash; watch, and not weep. It was a part, she supposed, of growing up. She wanted to close her eyes and wish that none of it was happening, but full-moon wishes didn't count. Only new-moon wishes were any good.

She turned abruptly, because if she stood here any longer she would cry; not only for the beech trees but for herself and the strange brooding inside her she couldn't put a name to. It was as if she were standing on the edge of something of such enormity that she wasn't sure she could cope with it – whatever it was and whenever it happened. Maybe, she decided as she pushed aside the small swinging gate that opened on to the path leading to the farm buildings, it was because all the safe, sane things she had grown up with were slipping from her, along with her childhood. Or maybe it was because it was the time of the month, and nothing more complicated than that! She walked carefully along the narrow path, because even though the moon threw a slanting light along it, it got very little sun and was often slippy underfoot, even in summer.

All at once she wanted to run, across the farmyard, across the paddock and on and on until she was so breathless she had to sink, drained, to the moon-touched grass.

And demand of herself what she was running from.

The early November morning was cold, but bright. On days such as this you could see everything crisp and sharply outlined, and the hills, their summer softness gone, etched sharply against a metallic sky.

Rosamund let her eyes linger on the enduring skyline. Once, only a few years before the foundations of Laburnham Farm had been laid, the people of Bowland had lit a bonfire on Beacon Fell to warn of the coming of the Spanish Armada. And those around had seen the leaping flames and closed their eyes and prayed for England. Exactly, she supposed, as they'd prayed in chapel after Dunkirk, when Britain was threatened again.

People prayed a lot in wartime. The Germans would be praying too, for their soldiers in Russia, because already there the winter snows had started. Sworn enemies, each begging the same God for victory, so who did He listen to? Did He toss a coin?

She shifted her gaze to the fields below, to the devastation that once was fifty acres of living, growing things. Now the tracks of caterpillar tractors sank deeply into the soft, sodden earth, throwing it into the air to fall as mud. She hoped that one by one, those tractors became bogged down in the muck of their own making, so they weren't able to drag out the tree roots.

The scream of chainsaws filled her head as they sliced through branches. Even from so far away, their noise reached out to mock her. It was like saying goodbye for ever to summer meadows and fields of corn. They would grow there no longer, their hedges already gone, burned on the fires lit every morning to get rid of unwanted rubbish. And then, at the coming of darkness, those fires were doused with water because of blackout regulations, and rekindled next morning with sump oil thrown over them to help start another blaze.

Mud, acrid fumes, screaming saws. Armageddon had come to

Laburnum's far fields; the war getting ever near. But the entire world had been pulled into the fight: Australia threatened with invasion by Japan, Stalingrad digging in for another winter of siege, 2,000 Jews gassed in Treblinka and our own merchant seamen being killed all the time, trying to get tanks and guns to Russia. Did the ever-demanding Stalin understand that for every two ships that left for Archangel and Murmansk, only one would get home safely? How many more despairing winters before peace came? And in those years, how many men and women were to die?

A hand touched Rosamund's arm and she drew in a startled breath.

'Now then, our lass . . .'

'Dad.' She slipped a hand into his, glad of the closeness. 'I didn't think it would be as awful as this.'

'It's like they say: things get worse afore they get better.'

'I'm waiting for the tree.' Only one beech remained, etched black and leafless against the pale sky. It stood tall and proud as though it looked down on the crawling creatures beneath it with the contempt of a hundred years of living and being and growing. 'Look at it. It's as if it's cursing them! Where is Mum?'

'Taking a jug of tea to the tree-fallers . . .'

'She's giving them tea? *Our* tea, that's rationed? I wouldn't give that lot the time of day!'

'Nor me, lass. But there's nowt we can do about the trees, nor the land, and your mother said she wanted her hands on some of those logs. Coal is scarce now. You can't blame her.'

'But those are *our* trees! She shouldn't have to ask!'

'Not any longer, Rosamund. They were part and parcel of the compensation the Air Ministry agreed on – well, told us we would get would be nearer the point.'

'*Looooook out . . .*'

They heard the faraway shout clearly as the tree began to fall. It went slowly, reluctantly, then fell with a crash of branches and boughs and twigs, all spread-eagled on the muddy earth.

'That's it then, Dad – the biggest and the best of them.'

'It went proudly.'

She hadn't wept as she thought she would. She had watched unflinching the destroying of something she loved, never taking her eyes from it, so it would know it wasn't alone; that she shared its pain. And when it lay there, felled, she knew her childhood had gone with it.

'Bart! Rosamund!' It was her mother, running, red-faced.

'I thought you were taking tea to the men!' Rosamund said, too quietly.

'Oh, *them*! I've been and come back! Now listen!' She stood there, gasping for breath. 'On the light programme! Gave me quite a turn when he interrupted the music for an important announcement. Said it had just been released by the Ministry of Information. There's a battle going on in North Africa! Guns and tanks and men! Started last Thursday night, it seems! Anyway, he said it was the battle for El Alamein and there would be more about it on the one o'clock news!'

'It'll be good news, won't it, Dad? They wouldn't break into a programme for something bad?'

'Reckon they wouldn't. It's about time we won something, come to think of it! But we'll find out in a couple of hours.'

They began the downward walk to the paddock, and over the stile to the hen arks spaced around it.

'You shouldn't have given tea to those tree men, Mum; not after what they did.' Rosamund was determined to have her say.

'Oh, you wouldn't? Then listen to me, my girl! Coal is on the ration – one bag a week, which doesn't even keep the kitchen fire going! Those were Laburnum Farm's beeches, and we've got a right to some of that wood!'

'True,' Bart said quietly, making it clear whose side he was on.

'But, Mum –'

'No *but Mum's*! The gaffer said that all he was interested in was the tree trunks; seems they've already been sold. But the rest we could do what we liked with, so I reckon we'll get the tractor out, and the chains, and drag all we can into the yard! I want that wood shed full, Rosamund – yes, and more besides! You'll not complain in winter, will you, when it's freezing outside!'

'You're right, I suppose. If we don't take the wood, someone will. But I'll think about those trees every time we put a log on the fire.'

'Then let's hope you never have anything worse to think about!' Mildred stuck her nose in the air and walked on alone, her back rigid with indignation.

'Let her go, lass.' Bart put a restraining hand on his daughter's arm. 'Your mother is right, no matter what. We can do with all the logs we can lay our hands on. There's nothing to be done now. The beeches are gone and our acres, too, for the duration. I know you were fond of those old trees, but there's a war on, remember, and your mother will be all right once she's heard what the wireless has to tell us.'

'I'm acting like a child, aren't I?'

She knew that at Laburnum, they were lucky. They eked out their rations with eggs and milk from the farm and killed a pig each January to salt for bacon and ham, when most other people had to make do with four ounces a week! And there were rabbits and pigeons and wild game for the taking, whilst people in towns had to manage with one-and-twopenceworth of meat a week each! Until the coming of the aerodrome the war had been a long way away, sheltered from it as they were by the very isolation of Laburnum Farm.

Shame washed over her, because she knew there were far worse things than the cutting down of trees, and she must think of all the merchant seamen who would be killed today trying to get through to Russia, and the men who had died, and were still to die, in the battle for El Alamein.

She closed her eyes, and whispered, 'God, this is Rosamund Kenton, and I'm sorry.'

TWO

—

1943

Because Bessie's eighteenth birthday fell on a Sunday, and because Mrs Drake had sent a plea in the form of a carefully worded letter, promising that Rosamund would be taken good care of were she allowed to stay the night, and returned safe and sound the next morning, Mildred Kenton had given her permission after much prevarication.

'Mind, you'll have to help Dad with the morning milking and go to chapel as usual,' she told her flush-cheeked daughter. 'It isn't right you should get there until after Sunday dinner, anyway . . .'

Ill-bred and inconsiderate to expect to share the family's midday dinner, rationing being what it was. 'And you'll leave for home on Monday morning as soon as it's daylight.'

'I will, Mum, and you're sure you don't mind doing the afternoon milking for me?'

'Of course she won't mind, will you, Milly?' Bart Kenton urged. 'Your mum's a good milker, for one not brought up to it.'

Milly's father had worked at the council offices in Skipton, and his Aunt Mildred, a maiden lady, had left her entire estate to the little girl he'd shrewdly named after her.

The house and furniture had been sold and the money banked until Mildred came of age, upon which she confounded everyone by marrying a farm worker from Ribchester way, and setting him up in quite the grandest farmhouse, fifteen miles the other side of Clitheroe.

She had taken to farm work with an ease that stemmed from a necessity to work or go under, and her inheritance with her.

She learned to milk cows, pluck chickens and skin rabbits all the quicker because of it, and Laburnum Farm to keep its head above water until the coming of a second conflict with Germany caused it to prosper overnight.

'Careful how you go,' Bart murmured as Rosamund kissed her parents dutifully.

She felt especially happy as she pedalled along the narrow lane that led to Laceby Green. In her saddlebag were six eggs, carefully wrapped in newspaper, a large loaf and a teacake – both home-baked – a jar of plums and a screw-topped lemonade bottle filled with milk, which was also rationed.

In the wicker basket at the front of her cycle were her pyjamas, a change of underwear and a little bottle of saccharin tablets to use in her drinks so as not to take any of Mrs Drake's rationed sugar, even if it were offered.

In her coat pocket was a birthday card into which she had tucked a pair of fully-fashioned silk stockings, bought with two of her own clothing coupons. She would have liked to give Bessie something more glamorous, but living at the back of beyond gave her little chance to join lipstick queues, or stand in line for a pot of cold cream. Living on a farm they ate better than most, but fared badly with the extras to be had from time to time in the shops.

Given a choice, Rosamund would not change a thing, even though Bessie had the best of both worlds by living in the village and working in Clitheroe, where lunchtime queuing was a part of her life.

'Mother's gone to church,' she said when Rosamund had unpacked and pushed her cycle into the wash house at the back of the lodge. 'I was excused because you were coming and because it's my birthday.'

Evensong in St Mary's, Laceby Green, was held at three each Sunday afternoon, because its lofty windows were near impossible to reach, let alone fit with blackout curtains. Only in summer, when days were long, could evening worship be held at the proper time. Almost everyone attended church or chapel now, because almost everyone had someone close to commend to Divine protection.

'For you. Happy birthday.' Rosamund offered the card and Bessie hugged her and said thank you and that only the dearest of people gave up her clothing coupons for a friend!

'What does it feel, being eighteen?' Rosamund held her hands to the fire.

'Just the same as yesterday, when I was seventeen. I won't feel properly grown up until I'm twenty. Whilst you're still in your teens, nobody takes you seriously.'

'The government does. Won't you have to register soon?'

'I suppose so. I'll be reserved, though, because I'm doing war work – if you can call working in a shirt factory war work!'

'If the shirts are for the Armed Forces, then it is,' Rosamund reasoned. 'Would you like to join up?'

'I think I would, but I wouldn't like them bossing me around. And I'd hate to have to salute people. Makes you subservient, sort of . . .'

'You wouldn't be saluting the person; only their rank.'

'Same difference. Anyway, when push comes to shove, if I'm really truthful I want to stay at home if I can. Joe takes a Wren dancing when his ship is in Plymouth, but he says it's a dead loss, her having to be in by half-past ten. Imagine? *Half-past ten!*'

'But we don't stay out that late, Bessie!'

'Only because there's nothing going on around here, but when the RAF arrives, it'll be different!' She closed her eyes, and sighed ecstatically. 'How's the aerodrome coming along, by the way?'

'It isn't – at least not what I can see of it. Dad says they won't lay concrete runways until the risk of hard frost is over. Everywhere is flat; sort of soulless. All *They* seem to have done is put a high wire fence round all the land they've grabbed.'

'They'll get cracking before so very much longer – at least I hope so. The war's going to be over if they don't get a move on!'

'You think so, Bess?'

'No, not really. But things are going a bit better for us now.'

'Leningrad being relieved, you mean? It must have been

terrible, there. Imagine being so hungry you'd eat cats and dogs. But you've got to feel just a bit sorry for those German soldiers, dying so far from home and their bodies left there, because the ground was too frozen to dig graves,' Rosamund sighed.

'Sorry my foot! It was their lot started it! And surely Hitler had grabbed enough, without invading Russia.'

'Yes, but maybe they aren't all Nazis. Mum said it wasn't decent, them not having a Christian burial.'

'Rosamund Kenton, I'm surprised at you! Of course they're all Nazis, though Dad says you can't blame them for listening to Hitler in the first place. We really humiliated Germany after the Great War.'

'Wars are stupid. But let's not be miserable today. Mum said she would have liked to send some cream to eat with the plums, but cream is illegal now, and she daren't make any. Remember when we always had cream on Sundays?'

'Mm. Big dollops of it on tinned peaches. But there aren't any peaches now, nor cream biscuits, nor Christmas cakes . . .'

'And hardly ever a lipstick in the shops. Once every Preston Guild, if you're lucky. And did you see it in the paper the other day? A girl nearly blinded herself using black boot polish on her eyelashes. It said to brush Vaseline on them until mascara is back in the shops.'

Which was all very well, Rosamund accepted, but her mother forbade makeup anyway, except for parties and dances. And who had food for a party, these days, and when did she last go to a dance, even in Laceby parish hall?

Yet in spite of its remoteness, Laburnum Farm was a lovely old house, though they hadn't as yet got a bathroom; not one with running water. Nor could they hope to get mains water till the war was over, with building work forbidden and only the most urgent repairs to bombed houses allowed.

Meantime, the well in the stableyard never ran dry, nor the pump, which gave them drinking water, though just to turn on a tap and have water at your fingertips and not have to bucket it everywhere would have been nothing short of marvellous.

'What on earth are you thinking about?' Bessie broke into

her dreamings. 'You were miles away! You were thinking about boys, weren't you?'

'I was thinking about bathrooms! You don't know how lucky you are, having one here.'

'*Lucky?* Our bathroom is freezing in winter and you can't get bath salts or scented soap now. Baths are a dead loss, especially when you can't have more than six inches of water in them. Six inches doesn't even cover your bottom! You're the lucky one. At least you get your baths in front of the kitchen fire!'

'I wonder who thought up the six inches lark, and why . . .'

'Some chinless wonder in Whitehall, I suppose, though water *is* vital to the war effort. When London was blitzed, there wasn't enough water to put the fires out, if you remember. It must have been awful, seeing everywhere burning, and not being able to do a lot about it.'

'I suppose we should count our blessings,' Rosamund said softly. 'There's nothing here to bomb, is there?'

'Not yet. But there soon will be.'

'Bess – can't we forget about that aerodrome?' It still hurt to think about the beech trees and the desolation their far fields had become.

'OK, let's talk about blokes; droves and droves of them – *when* they come – and getting asked on dates. And they'll hold dances, I shouldn't wonder, and drink at the White Hart. I can't wait!'

'Bessie! Don't you ever think about anything but men?'

'Of course not! What else is there to think about, when we might all get killed tomorrow?'

And when you thought about it, Rosamund admitted, there was no answer to that!

Three taps on the window; three knocks on the kitchen door. Mildred put down the sock she was darning.

'Who is it?' she demanded firmly.

'It's me, missis – Ned Loftus.'

'What on earth do you want at this hour of the night?' she demanded, opening the door only a little, because of the blackout.

'A bit of business,' he whispered.

'You'd better come in then, and be sharp about it!' She slammed the door, pulling the long curtain over it. 'What sort of business?'

'Was out for a bit of a walk, and came across this.' He pulled a pheasant from beneath his coat. 'Thought I'd give you first refusal.'

'One of these days the law's going to catch up with you, Ned Loftus, and then where'll we all be!'

'I doubt it.' He let go a wheezy laugh. The law, around Laceby Green, was partial to roast pheasant too.

'How much?'

'The usual. A couple of bob and a few eggs will do nicely.'

'Sorry! It's cash or nothing. Hens don't lay well in winter!'

He settled, in the end for half a crown, because eggs were all very well but, rationed or not, they weren't legal currency in the White Hart.

'Will that be all?' she demanded, when he stood his ground.

'As a matter of fact, there *is* summat else . . .'

'Then you'd better sit down.' She motioned to a chair, which he drew up to the table, then propped his chin on his hands.

'Where's the gaffer tonight?'

'In the shippon. There's a cow calving down and she's having a bit of bother. Why do you ask?'

'Because this is women's business really.' And because he didn't want Bart Kenton's opinions on selling things you weren't entitled to sell. 'Clothing coupon business.' He sucked air through his teeth.

'And you've got some to get rid of?' Stood to reason. Apart from his wife's scrubbing and the money he got from poaching and thieving, it was common knowledge they lived from hand to mouth.

'Reckon I might have. In very short supply, though. Would fetch a pound apiece in London.'

'But this isn't London, Ned Loftus, and folks up here aren't so daft with their money. Anyway, Bart wouldn't countenance buying clothing coupons. I could end up in prison.'

'So could we all,' he said with relish, 'if we were daft

enough to get caught. What do you say to five bob apiece, then?'

'Not even a shilling!'

'You'll regret it, Mrs Kenton. You know they've been cut from forty to thirty-six!'

'Of course I know!' Just eighteen coupons to last for six months was plain ridiculous, because not for anything would she go stockingless as a lot of women did now. Not even in summer!

'It isn't breaking the law,' he wheedled. 'Not when I've got no need of 'em, and you have money to spend on clothes!'

'You'd have money enough if you'd shift yourself and find work.'

'Can't work now; me breathing's bad. And anyroad, work's hard to find.'

'Not these days it isn't! Not with a war on!' She looked him up and down. A work-shy scrounger, in need of a shave and a haircut and a change of linen, an' all!

'I'm hard put to it, Mrs Kenton.' He was almost whining now, she was pleased to see. 'Five bairns and a wife to feed! How's a man in my state of health to do it?'

'Your state of health didn't prevent you fathering five! Don't you ever stop to think that bairns are to feed and clothe?'

'Aye, *clothe*! And here's me with nigh on two hundred coupons and nowt to do with them.'

'Yes, and I'm right sorry they're going a-begging, but I'll not buy on the black market!'

Imagine it – Mildred Kenton getting caught with illicit coupons! What a field day folk in Laceby would have! Her at the big house up before the magistrates!

'Then I'm right sorry, because there's our Betty with the offer of a job, and nowt to wear to it. Work at the vicarage minding the bairns, and seven-and-six a week and her keep. She's desperate to go and live there. Says she wants a bed of her own, and respectability. But what's a father to do?'

'You tell a fine tale, Ned Loftus! But I'm sorry for your girl. She deserves a chance. How old is she?'

'Fifteen, though inclined to be small for her age . . .' He gave her a meaningful glance then held her eyes with a steady stare, so she would get the message.

Smaller than Rosamund! Mildred Kenton got the message.

'What would your girl need?'

'Just about everything, but a warm winter coat and a pair of shoes wouldn't come amiss.'

'Then if I was to have a poke around the attic and see what I can come up with . . . ?' She never threw anything away.

'Our Betty would be right grateful.'

He slid two fingers inside his jacket pocket and brought out a sheet of coupons. A whole sheet! *Twenty!* Two long nightdresses and two pairs of stockings!

'You know you can't spend loose coupons.' They had to be in a ration book. Shopkeepers weren't allowed to accept them otherwise.

'I can give you a list of shops as'll take them, no questions asked!'

'And you'd give me one or two coupons for some of Rosamund's clothes?'

She was fighting her conscience now. In one ear she heard the hissing urges of the wicked one.

Take them! Who's to know? You're giving him clothes in return, aren't you?

Using clothing coupons that aren't rightly your own is a sin! the voice of the Minister thundered in her other ear. 'And it's against the law!'

Against the law to *buy* them, surely. But what about fair exchange?

'*Exchange for second-hand clothes?*' The Minister again. '*But you know that coupons aren't required for second-hand clothes!*'

But clothing wasn't brought here by sea. By doing business with Ned Loftus she wasn't putting the life of a merchant seaman at risk, was she? The only risk was to herself, and getting caught with them!

'Come tomorrow morning.' Bart would be at the market then. 'Maybe there'll be one or two things Rosamund has grown out of . . .'

Her conscience squared, she let him out as Bart crossed the yard.

'Ned Loftus just left.' She nodded towards the pheasant on the table. 'Cow all right, is she?'

'Aye. A bull calf, after a bit of a struggle. Just in right time for the market tomorrow.'

There would be little sleep tonight. The animal would be bawling till daylight for its calf, Mildred supposed. A cow made a terrible noise when its calf was taken away, but it would be back with the milking herd tomorrow morning, calf forgotten. That was the way of it on a farm. She had soon learned to push her scruples aside.

'Seems Betty Loftus has the offer of a job at the vicarage, but the lass has nothing decent to wear.'

'Then can't you find a few bits that Rosamund's grown out of? I don't think Betty would be too proud to accept them.'

'I'm certain she wouldn't!' The entire family was clothed at jumble sales, though people thought twice and thrice now before throwing clothes out. 'I said he was to come up in the morning when I'd had a chance to root something out!' She made no mention of the clothing coupons. 'Get yourself washed down, Bart, and I'll make us a sandwich.'

Come to think of it she cogitated as she sliced bread, she shouldn't get herself into a tizzy over a few under-the-counter clothing coupons, because hadn't *They* taken Laburnum's acres without so much as a by-your-leave? If the government could take things willy-nilly, then so could Mildred Kenton!

All that mattered now was how many the rascal would be prepared to part with . . .

Laceby Hall lodge was almost as old as Laburnum Farm, Rosamund thought as she sat in the parlour with Bessie and her mother, listening to the Forces programme. Not for anything would Bessie's mother turn over to the Home Service, and the nine o'clock news, because she listened to the one o'clock news and that, as far as she was concerned was enough, with the government giving people a bit of good news with one hand, then taking it away with the other!

'Can we have Lord Haw-Haw on at half-past nine, Mum?' The man who broadcast from Hamburg every Sunday night had become something of a star turn, though no one admitted listening to him. His voice was harsh and nasal – it was how he got his name – and for a long time what he told the British people caused nothing but laughter and derision.

'We have sunk your *Ark Royal*!' he sneered. HMS *Ark Royal* had been sunk so many times it had become a music-hall joke.

'Haw-Haw? No, we *can't* have him on! That man's British and he's gone over to Hitler! When this war's over they'll hang him along with the rest!'

'But we always tuned in to him after the nine o'clock news!'

'Not any longer we don't!'

Now Elsie Drake had two sons in the Royal Navy for the duration, and the jibes and taunts of Haw-Haw the traitor no longer made her laugh.

'Do you really think all the top Nazis will be tried for war crimes after the war, Mum?'

'That's what Mr Churchill said, and I hope they hang the lot of them for what they've done! In the Great War, a soldier could get shot for desertion, and Haw-Haw has deserted to the enemy, which is far worse! But I'll say no more about that creature!' She wouldn't let him spoil her Sunday, which she thoroughly enjoyed, especially when her husband worked late shift, as he was doing tonight, at the factory making aircraft components. He earned good money now; much more than Mr Ackroyd had paid him as handyman before the war; before the Hall had been pulled down.

Yet she would change it all for the pinchpenny days when her bairns were young and a dratted nuisance with their tree-climbing and fighting and getting caught by the head gardener at the Hall, scrumping apples in Mr Ackroyd's orchard.

'You've gone all quiet, our Mum! Penny for them.'

'I was thinking we could all do with a cup of tea and that you and Rosamund should make it! And we'll all have a slice of Mrs Kenton's teacake whilst we're about it. And I never thought to ask how your mother is, Rosamund. Well, I hope, in spite of that business with the aerodrome.'

'They're both fine. I think they've accepted it now, though it was an awful shock at the time.'

'I should think so, too. They do what They like, these days. A man came one day from the Ministry of Agriculture and Fisheries and said all that beautiful parkland around the Hall had to be ploughed up and put to better use. When the Ackroyds lived there, sheep grazed it and they kept a herd of deer there – pretty little things. But the man from the Ministry wanted potatoes grown, and if anyone had protested they'd have been called unpatriotic! But off you go and make that tea, then I just might let you tune in to Haw-Haw – though not a word to a soul, mind!'

Rosamund pedalled quickly, her woolly scarf wound round her neck and over her ears, for the morning had come in bright and sharp. She had enjoyed staying with Bessie. They had talked and giggled long into the night, snuggled in the big bed, and she thought it would be good to have a sister.

They breakfasted off boiled brown eggs, with Mrs Drake saying she had forgotten what a decent fresh egg tasted like!

'You tell your mother those eggs were a real treat and I won't say a word to a soul about her sending them.'

'You better hadn't, or we'll end up in Preston jail,' Rosamund laughed. 'And thank you for having me, Mrs Drake. I enjoyed Bessie's birthday, even if she couldn't have a party.'

'She's getting a bit old for parties, now. Suppose the next one will be her twenty-first – if the war is over by then, and food rationing has been done away with . . .'

If. Such a little word, but surely the most used, nowadays. *If* the war is over by then; *if* the shops have food in them; *if* Dave and Joe can get leave; *if* the Nazis don't use their secret weapon against us and bring the country to its knees.

Last night, Lord Haw-Haw hadn't mentioned the defeats in Russia. All he spoke of was Germany's secret weapon, and how it would crush Britain into submission. But Mrs Drake laughed, and said she wondered why they hadn't used it before now, them being in so much trouble on the Russian Front.

'Secret weapon my foot!' she had said. 'Who does he think he's kidding?'

Of course the Nazis didn't have a secret weapon, Rosamund echoed as she pedalled into a wind that stung her face. Hitler was bluffing. He had to be, unless he intended using poison gas.

Yet by the time she was halfway home and passing the clump of oaks, she had completely forgotten secret weapons, because she glanced across, almost in passing, to where the aerodrome would be, then stopped to stare in amazement at the distant activity.

The flatlands had come to life again. Men and machines were everywhere. She leaned her cycle against a tree, then watched the lorries, at least a dozen of them, piled high with rubble. Brick rubble, it looked like from a distance, and it was being tipped in a straight line than ran from west to east. The foundations of the runways were being laid, and what they were using was probably blitz rubble. There had been heavy raids on Liverpool and Manchester; in all probability it had come from there. She turned her back on the scene below her, saddened that work had begun again on the aerodrome. There was no chance now that it wouldn't happen. Within a year it might well be finished, and bombers would be using the runways.

The only good thing, if you thought about it in a practical way, was that when those aircraft took off to carry the war to Germany, it would be from a runway made partly from homes the Luftwaffe had blasted to the ground. Manchester, Liverpool, Clydeside, Coventry and London, all fighting back in a roundabout sort of way. Poetic justice, really . . .

When she got to the crossroads, a slash of winter-blue sky appeared and beneath it a lightening of the clouds, as if the sun were trying to break through. Then she rode to the other side of the road, jumping off to wait the passing of Laburnum Farm's truck, which slowed and stopped.

'Hullo, our lass! Had a nice time, then?' asked Bart.

'Smashing! Going to the cattle market?'

'Aye. Taking the calves . . .'

'Then have a look as you pass the six oaks. They've made a start. I think they're putting the runways down. There was a convoy of lorries dumping rubble, and there are steamrollers there, too.'

'We knew it would come, Rosamund. It's the way things are when there's a war on. Your mum is in the dairy, seeing to the milk. Give her a hand with the churns, will you?'

She said she would, then stood to watch him out of sight. Dad didn't seem to mind her growing up; it was Mum who kept reminding her she was still a child. And she wasn't. If Mum knew some of the things she thought about there would be big trouble. She always thought about *things* when she and Bessie were together. Bessie brought out the curiosity in her and convinced her it wasn't dirty to think about falling in love and getting babies; that she'd be very peculiar if she *didn't*!

When she was with Bessie, she felt normal. Only when she was at home and watching everything she said did she accept that it was better to think like a child and act like a child, if only for the sake of peace and quiet, and keeping her mother happy.

A bitter, north-easterly wind hit her as she turned into the dirt road. Just a few more weeks, she sighed, and the worst of the weather would be over. They had had a long, dark winter. Everyone was tired of it and longed for warm days and long, light nights. Summer wouldn't make the war go away, but at least it would be more bearable.

And when summer came, she would be eighteen!

The milk churns were loaded ready for her to take down the lane to the standing from which they would be collected. The cheque that came each month from the Milk Marketing Board was their main support now they had lost the fields. Yet her father said she wasn't to worry; that he intended increasing the herd and that her mother had plans to get more hens, and to fatten cockerels for the Christmas market. And the compensation from the Air Ministry – when it came – would be a nice little sum to put by, and earn them interest into the bargain.

Dad was a love. If she had to say, hand on heart, which of her parents she cared for most, it would have to be her father. Mum was fine, but she had high ideals that took a bit of living up to. To her, things were either black or white, right or wrong and there was nothing in between. No grey areas, no white lies. Mum never wavered in her opinions. She was, Rosamund supposed, very dogmatic, and sadly she would never change.

'Hi! I'm home!' She hugged her mother extra hard and kissed her extra warmly to make up for her unfilial thoughts. 'Bessie's mum was very pleased with all you sent, especially the eggs. She said she'd forgotten what a good egg tasted like. We had some for breakfast.'

'Hm. Can't expect her to feed you, not with food being what it is. What did you do?'

'Nothing, really.' She knew her mother would expect a detailed account of everything done and said, if it was in any way interesting. 'We sat by the fire and talked about the war. Dave and Joe are very well, and Bessie's dad was working lates and we'd gone to bed before he came in. I'll nip upstairs and get changed, then I'll see to the churns. You shouldn't have loaded them onto the trailer, you know!'

'Someone's got to do it! Your dad wanted to be at the market early, and I hadn't finished putting the milk through the cooler when he left. And it wouldn't be the first time I've heaved churns!'

'No, Mum.' Her mother was being self-righteous, which meant she had either something on her mind, or something had upset her.

'Anything bad on the early news?'

'No! Why should there be?'

'I just thought – I mean I . . .'

She shrugged. Mum had been more quiet than ever since They had taken the fields. Maybe, Rosamund thought, it would be as well if she didn't mention that work had started again on the aerodrome. She had just lifted the sneck on the staircase door when something caused her to turn and stare. Funny she hadn't noticed it when she came in.

'What are those?' She nodded towards the pile of clothes on the table.

'You know what they are! Some of your old things. I'm giving them to Betty Loftus.'

'But they're *mine*!' Frantically Rosamund searched through the pile, checking what had been taken.

'They're only your school clothes! Surely you didn't think I'd go in your drawers!'

She nearly said, 'I *know* you would!' but bit on her tongue and said instead, 'I think you might have asked me first!'

'And why should I? Wasn't it me paid for them?'

'I know you did, but there might be things I'd want to keep. My hockey badge, and my school hat – sentimental things.'

'Your badges are of no interest to Betty Loftus and I certainly wouldn't give her your hat. She never went to the grammar school and she isn't entitled to wear it! All I've given her is your gabardine and some shoes and gumboots. And one or two blouses and your last school skirt. And there's a cardigan, an' all, that'll never fit you again! Betty Loftus has been offered a place at the vicarage and has nothing decent to wear, and I think it most unchristian of you, Rosamund, to begrudge the lass something you aren't in need of!'

'I still think you should at least have mentioned it to me first! I'm sorry, but –'

'And I'm sorry too, that I can't do what I want in my own house without having to ask my daughter! Now get yourself upstairs to your room, and don't come down until you're sorry – and are prepared to say so!'

'No! I won't! Not until you tell me what I'm to be sorry for!'

'For back-answering your mother!'

'But I didn't back-answer! I only said that I'd liked to have been told about my things being given away!'

'Don't you think you're being just a little childish, Rosamund?'

Her mother's tone had changed. Now her voice was soft and coaxing; the one a grown-up used when talking to a wilful child. It offered Rosamund the chance to climb down, say she was sorry, but she didn't say it because defying her mother and getting away with it was heady stuff!

'Childish? Yes, I suppose I am, but if you treat me like a child, then you mustn't be upset if I act like one!'

She felt her cheeks burning and her mouth had gone dry, but her eyes met those of her mother and held them steadily. The unspoken challenge was like a gauntlet thrown down and Mildred Kenton did not pick it up, being saved the climb-down by a knocking on the kitchen door.

'Well, go on then, girl! Answer it!' She held her hands to her cheeks, drawing in a calming breath, knowing she had been the loser; promising herself it would be the last time Rosamund would be allowed to stay the night with Bessie Drake if that was the mood she came home in!

'It's Mr Loftus,' Rosamund said quietly before walking head high across the kitchen and taking the back stairs with her nose in the air. And when she came down, dressed in working trousers and a thick sweater, the garments had been stuffed into two bags and Ned Loftus was handing over a sheet of clothing coupons.

Both he and her mother looked sheepish and seemed relieved when Rosamund walked out of the kitchen without saying a word, and Rosamund, out of harm's way for the time being, climbed onto the tractor, her cheeks still burning, in spite of the coldness of the morning.

Had she gone out of her mind, then? Would she ever be forgiven for cheeking her mother? And what would her father say when he'd been given chapter and verse of her fall from grace? Dad would be shocked. It would hurt him far more than his wife's sharp tongue, because Mum could be waspish when the mood was on her!

Rosamund stopped the tractor beside the platform, unloading the churns, tilting them slightly, rolling them carefully into position for the lorry driver to collect about noon. Then she would return before evening milking to onload the empty churns he would leave behind him, and though they would be clean and sterile, still her mother would insist on washing them out again because her mother trusted no one, and nothing would change her. There were two ways of doing a thing: Mildred Kenton's way and the wrong way! For the first time in her life, Rosamund wondered how her father had managed to live for nearly twenty years with such perfection.

She knew the answer, of course. Dad was grateful to her for buying the farm, and though Rosamund had never laid eyes on the deeds, it would not surprise her to find they were in her mother's name only, and not held jointly with her husband.

She parked the tractor beneath the Dutch barn, then made for the storeroom to fill a bucket with wheat and another with water for the hens. The ground was cold underfoot, the sliver of blue sky gone, but feeding and watering the hens – all twenty arks of them – was to be preferred to her mother's disapproval.

Climbing the stile into the paddock, she wondered when the time would be right to ask her mother's pardon, and was shocked to realize she did not want to, and nor would she, save for peace and quiet. She was almost a woman. In a few months' time she would be ordered to register for war work at the Ministry of Labour office. Not even her mother could prevent it happening and she was tempted, when the time came, to register as unemployed – and that would put the cat among the pigeons!

But she knew she would not do it. She wanted to remain at Laburnum Farm.

What would happen when she registered, she was still in too much of a bother to think about. Yet of one thing she was sure: she had challenged her mother for the first time, and won! From this day on, her childhood was behind her.

And she didn't want it back!

THREE

They had got their tabs on her. The announcement had been in the daily papers and on news bulletins too. All females born between 1 January and 30 June 1925, must report to their nearest labour exchange to register for war work.

Rosamund had reported with the G to K group, on Friday, 11 June and her name and address, identity number, date of birth and present occupation noted. It came as a relief to be told that if the particulars given were correct, she would almost certainly be exempted from call-up. She would hear from them in due course. Meantime, she must not change her occupation without first obtaining permission from the Ministry of Labour.

Two weeks later, in an envelope bearing the words 'On His Majesty's Service', her exemption was confirmed. She was to remain at Laburnum Farm and was again reminded she was not to leave it without permission.

Quite unnecessary really, since she had no wish to leave home. Nothing would change. She would continue to help with morning and afternoon milking, look after the poultry, and muck out and hose down the shippon twice a day as she had always done. Helping to produce milk, eggs and wheat and barley was as important, her mother said, as serving in the Armed Forces or working in a munitions factory or down a coal mine. And let no one say it wasn't!

Now her official exemption stood behind the clock on the kitchen mantel, and since nothing had changed, she opened the pasture gate and called, 'Coosh, coosh. Oy! Oy! Oy!' as she had always done.

The cows were slow today, but she didn't mind. Once the

first was through the gate, she would walk to the far end of the pasture to round up loiterers, and get an uninterrupted view of what was going on in the distant fields. Only they were no longer fields, and it still hurt that Fellstead Farm was gone, and half Laburnum too. And that for the duration, that cruel intrusion was to be called an aerodrome!

Two feet to the other side of the hedge that now formed the new boundary of their farm was a chain fence, eight feet high, and right beside it, and as far as she could see, a track wound round the outermost edges of the aerodrome. On it, at intervals, was an apron of tarmac, which she now knew would provide standing for bombers, though whether Lancasters or Halifaxes was still being debated in the White Hart. But they would have crews of seven, and would go off on raids. Operations, they were called.

'They'll make your chimneypots rattle, when they take off,' Bessie once teased, even though they both knew it wouldn't be anything to joke about when it happened.

Rosamund squinted into the afternoon sun. It was easy to make out what was what. Two runways of soulless concrete crossed each other at a point where the last of the beech trees once stood, and if she reached on tiptoe and looked over to her right, she could see the control tower, angular and ugly and painted in camouflage colours of green and black and khaki. It was two storeys high and had a gantry with railings running round it – probably to prevent people toppling off in the dark, because it would be night-time when those planes took off. Now the Americans bombed by day and the Royal Air Force took over when it was dark. Round-the-clock bombing. Cruel, but necessary.

She shifted her eyes in the direction of two massive hangars and the Nissen huts clustered around them. Ugly things, those huts, yet men and women would live in them; each had a little chimney sticking through the low, rounded roof, which could only mean that each had a stove.

A tractor crossed the line of her vision. The workmen had levelled out every dip and hollow because, she supposed, if a bomber ran off the runway it would need firm, flat ground beneath its wheels. They'd used a tractor-hauled cutting machine on that grass, which had made her father very cross.

'Men cutting grass! That's war work, is it? Our lass could sit on a tractor and do the same! Any girl could!'

'But *our* girl is going to stay at home and drive *our* tractor on *our* land – or what's left of it. She isn't being taken for the war, so I wouldn't bother my head about what the Air Force is doing!' her mother had said.

Her mother, Rosamund realized, thought that if she ignored it that hastily built sprawl would go away. She had coveted Laburnum Farm for its isolation, so she and her husband and child could live their lives without outside interference or distraction. As far as she was concerned, that was still the way she wanted it, war or not.

Rosamund turned her back on the aerodrome. What the Air Force did was none of her business. She was a land girl now, only she didn't wear a uniform and didn't live in a hostel with other land girls. She had her own bedroom still, at the top of the back stairs that led off the kitchen, and her life hadn't changed one iota.

She caught up with the herd as the last cow walked through the field gate, and matched her step to their plodding clumsiness. This was now her war work. She was very lucky. She had never watched her man go to war, nor put her children on a train to be evacuated to a place called Somewhere in England. And it could never happen, because she had neither husband nor children. There would be time enough, her mother said, to think about a young man when the war was over; one who wasn't going to get killed! Couples of no age at all were rushing head first into wedlock, and all because of the war. Girls married a man handsome in his uniform; what would be their feelings, Mildred Kenton stressed, when he was a civilian again, and jobless, like most men after the last war? Where would the glamour be then?

She made for the barn where the cattle cake was stored, shoving a scoop deep into the sack, throwing the pieces into the bucket with a force that made a satisfying clatter. She would fill two buckets, carry them across the yard, then feed the pieces in equal amounts to each cow to munch on as it was milked; would do it twice each day for ever and ever, she thought with sudden apprehension. She would do it automatically, like a girl on an assembly line who pushed bits into holes as they came past her on a conveyor belt, the only difference being that women in factories had *Music While You Work* twice a day to help take their minds off the repetitive task. Girls in factories had someone their own age to talk to as well.

So had you forgotten, Rosamund Kenton, that there's a war on and that thousands of people do boring jobs too? What's so special about you then . . . ?

And she hadn't forgotten − not really. It was just that for a little time *that* feeling had returned, as it did more often now; a feeling not of discontent, but of wondering what was the matter with her and what exactly could be the cause of it.

She made up for her unpatriotic and thoroughly selfish feelings by being extra nice to her father, and by offering to wash the supper things, pans and all, then ask of her mother if there was anything else she would like doing before she went to meet Bessie at the halfway place this evening.

'You didn't mention you were going out tonight,' Mildred Kenton frowned.

'I thought I had. I'm meeting Bess at six oaks. She got a skirt in the sales − a good one, not utility − but it needs taking up a bit. I said if she would unpick the hem, I would pin it for her − if that's all right with you?'

She *had* mentioned it, she was sure! Why was her mother so awkward these days? Was she still bitter about losing their fields, or was it because she was tired of the war? Yet most people were sick to the back teeth of it. It had gone on nearly four years, and the end nowhere in sight!

'I suppose it'll have to be all right! I was looking forward to a sit-down and a bit of peace and quiet!'

'Then if you like we'll go to Bessie's. Have you a head-ache, Mum?'

'No! Why should I have? It's just that you seem always to be wanting to be off out!'

'Milly!' Bart Kenton looked up from the form he was filling in. 'Surely the lass is entitled to go out once in a while? She hasn't been anywhere this past week,' he said reasonably.

His wife did not reply. Instead, she laid down her knitting and made for the door, letting it close behind her with a bang.

'Dad! What did I say? Doesn't she want Bessie to come? We can go upstairs, if you like. We won't make a noise . . .'

'Bessie is welcome. Now off you go and meet her. Your mum will be over it, by the time you get back.'

Rosamund did just that, running across the yard for her cycle, leaving by the path that ran down the side of the farm buildings, overlooking until she got to it the impossibility of pushing a bike through a kissing gate!

'Damn!' She wasn't going all the way back and risk meeting her mother getting over *it*!

With a strength she didn't know she had she heaved the cycle high, then dropped it with a clank and a bounce on the other side. Then she pushed aside the creaking, rusty gate, stepped to the side, and was through it and into the lane.

'I'd almost given you up!' Bessie was waiting at the fieldgate beside the oak trees. 'Have trouble getting out?'

'No more than usual. I washed up after supper without being asked! Sorry I'm late. Dad said I could come in the end . . .'

'I don't think you should have to ask! You *are* eighteen, now! I just tell Mum I'm going and she says, "Don't be late," and that's it!'

'Well, I'm here now. Have you brought your skirt?'

'Y-yes, but do we have to go to your house? Mum's at the WI, and Dad is going to the pub. We'd have the place to ourselves. And there'll be Geraldo on the wireless . . .'

Bessie threw in Geraldo as added bait, because she knew Mrs Kenton wasn't overkeen on dance music.

'I – I don't see why not, then Mum will be over it by the time I get back.'

'Over what? Isn't she well?'

'Not really. I don't think she's been the same since *They* took our fields.'

'Well hard luck! *They* took my brothers, but you don't hear Mum going on and on about it!'

'Look – don't get me wrong, Bess. It's just that sometimes she gets a bit protective. I suppose that's what comes of having an only child!'

'Sometimes? Rosamund, she's *always* at it!' Bessie was astride her high horse now! Just because she lived in a big house, Mrs Kenton thought she was Lady Muck! 'Anyway, I'd prefer to go to our place – OK!'

So Rosamund, who wasn't one to argue, said it was fine by her and it wasn't until they were in sight of the village that she said, 'I was in the far field this afternoon, and I felt kind of queer. It was as if I was looking at the aerodrome – *the war* – only I wasn't a part of it; that our hedge and the new mesh fence were keeping it out, sort of. It was as if, now I've registered, my war has been taken care of.'

'What do you mean exactly?'

'Like now I'm officially in a reserved occupation, Bess, I'm immune to it all. It's as if the war – the bogeyman – can't get me now.'

'I see. Then what do you think it's going to be like once the bombers arrive? The war is going to be at the bottom of your fields, and when that happens, no fence is going to keep it out!'

She began to pedal furiously, having dropped her bombshell and not expecting a coherent reply.

'Wait for me!' Rosamund yelled, pushing the aerodrome and all it entailed out of her mind. 'Bess! Wait on . . . !'

Rosamund pedalled idly along the lane that led to Laburnum Farm, riding from side to side in big, swooping curves, turning Bessie's words over in her mind.

'I don't believe it! I can't! You can stand there and say hand on heart that you aren't good-looking, Rosamund Kenton? Haven't you ever looked in a mirror?'

'Of course I have!' Everyone looked in mirrors! 'I only remarked on your legs.'

She had said, as Bessie stood on the kitchen table, turning slowly round to make sure the hem was level, that her friend had lovely long legs, and that if *she* had legs as good, she'd be taking her skirts up too! Whereupon Bess asked her tetchily what she meant!

'But *you've* got good legs and kitten hips and real blonde hair! And your eyebrows don't need plucking and your nose is just like Hedy Lamarr's! In fact, you're so damn perfect, Rosamund Kenton, that if I'd any sense at all, I'd ditch you and be friends with Freda Barnes!'

Freda was cross-eyed and wore glasses. She had bitty hair too.

'Then why don't you?' Crossly, because it was vain to think you were good-looking, Rosamund removed pins from her mouth and stuck them peevishly, jab, jab, jab, in the pincushion, for truth known she *had* once or twice thought she was quite pretty.

'Why? Because before so very much longer, the blokes at the aerodrome are going to buzz around you like bees round a honey pot, and I want to be there to take my pick of the leftovers! Besides, I like you!'

'Then if you are really my friend, Bess, don't say anything like that when Mum's around, will you? She'd blow her top if she thought I was thinking about men and she doesn't like vanity either.'

'Is there anything she *does* like?' Bessie jumped off the table as her mother lifted the sneck of the back gate.

'Isn't that a bit on the short side?' Eyebrows raised, Elsie Drake looked at the skirt.

'Oh no, Mrs Drake,' Rosamund said earnestly. 'Not if you've got good legs like hers!'

'Well, I'll be blowed!' She threw back her head and laughed. 'Good legs, has she, Rosamund? You'd better not let your mother hear you talking like that!' Mrs Kenton would never stoop to such banalities! Folk sometimes wondered how that cold unsmiling woman had ever got pregnant with Rosamund! 'Any road, have you signed up yet for the make-do-and-mend class? It'll be starting in September. I did hear they show you how to save fourteen coupons, making a winter coat out of an army blanket – if you can lay hands on one!'

'Out of a *what*?' Bessie shrieked. 'Mother! I wouldn't be seen dead in anything like that! Army blankets are an *awful* colour!' And scratchy too, she shouldn't wonder!

'You would if it was the middle of winter and you hadn't a decent coat and all your clothing coupons spent, my girl! Anyway, I'm going. The lady seems very good; teaches you to make all kinds of things from stuff you'd normally send for jumble. I'm all for giving it a try, and it'll be a night out. Now get the kettle on, our Bess. I'm dying for a cup of tea!'

Women's Institute meetings weren't half the fun, she reflected sadly, now there was no longer an interval for tea and cakes – home-baked, of course, and always from best butter. Nowadays, she yearned, butter was a luxury, the amount They allowed you barely sufficient to spread on your Sunday toast! No one baked with it. Stood to sense on the two miserable ounces that must last a week!

Sighing for the bad old days, Bessie's mother shook a spoon of tea leaves until it was level, then slid it almost reverently into the smallest pot, thinking that Hitler had much to answer for!

Then she remembered her sons at sea, and pushed Hitler's hated face from her mind to send her love to her sailors in warm, motherly gusts.

'Someone told me tonight,' she said, 'that it's almost certain there'll be bombers on our back doorstep before winter.'

'They'll be a lot nearer to Laburnum Farm!' Bess had said dolefully.

That was when Rosamund realized she had stopped pedalling and was looking across from six oaks to the aerodrome where even at this hour men still worked and would continue to work, until the light faded completely. Bessie's mother had been right. It would soon be finished, but how to get to meet any of the airmen there, much less have them buzzing around her, Rosamund couldn't for the life of her imagine.

'Oh, *dammit*!'

She jumped on her bike and pedalled furiously homeward.

'And where have you been until this hour?'

'I've been to Bessie's. You know I have!' From the set of her mouth, she knew her mother was still upset.

'I know no such thing! You said you were meeting the girl halfway, then coming back here!'

'Well, we decided to go to Bessie's. Nothing wrong in that, Mum.'

'Nothing at all, except that I've been worrying about you and if anything had happened to you!'

'But what *could* happen? I've biked up and down that road hundreds of times. I met nothing at all and anyway, it's still light!'

'Then wait till *that lot* get here; our lives won't be worth living! Have you for just a minute stopped to think, Rosamund, that there'll be no peace for us when they do? Planes taking off and landing all the time, and there'll be airmen swarming over our land, breaking fences, stealing chickens, like as not.'

'Of course they won't steal from us! They'll be decent young men like Bessie's brothers.'

'And they'll be speeding up and down the Laceby road in their trucks and lorries!' Milly Kenton urged, determined to have her say.

'They won't come anywhere near our stretch of road. All the exits are on the Preston side. You won't know they're there,' Rosamund coaxed.

'Of course I'll know! How can you *not* know there's a bomber flying over your head – and loaded with bombs!'

'That's why they're called bombers, Mum!' Almost at once, she knew the joke had misfired.

'Don't get cheeky with me!' Milly Kenton looked up from the bread dough she was kneading with clenched fists.

Rosamund looked at the tightly rounded mouth, the flush to her mother's cheeks, the almost fanatical way she pounded the dough, and knew something was very wrong.

'Why are you baking bread at this hour, Mum?' She made a conscious effort to move to safer ground. 'It's got to rise, then bake. You won't be in bed till midnight!'

'So who else is there to do it, with you gallivanting off?'

'It would have waited till morning. And haven't I the right to go out sometimes?'

She was treading on eggshells, she knew it; knew she could put an end to the atmosphere with an apology and a plea for forgiveness, but tonight she too was angry, with unspoken words choking her throat.

'Right? There's a war on and nobody's got rights any more! *They* think They can do as They like; take your land without a by-your-leave; take young girls from their mothers and only the Lord knows what's going to happen to their innocence! But I don't have to justify myself to you, miss! Whilst you are under my roof you'll do as you are told! There'll be no more going out for the rest of the week!'

'And are you going to tell me why?' Rosamund whispered, dry-mouthed.

'Because I say so! And especially you'll not speak to any of those airmen when they get here! I don't want them taking advantage of you!'

There was a wildness in her mother's eyes, and for just the speeding of a second Rosamund was almost on the edge of capitulation. But defiance had taken hold of her.

'Why *should* they take advantage? They'll be mostly ordinary young men from decent homes, not rapists on the rampage.'

'*Rapists!* What kind of language is that! But you're always the same when you've been with Bessie Drake! You're not to see her any more! I won't have her in my house, do you hear me?'

'But she's my friend!' Rosamund recoiled at the verbal slap. 'We grew up together!'

'Then she's your friend no longer! That girl was brought up far too liberal, if you ask me!'

'*Liberal!* Is that what you call being normal! Is being liberal having a mother who laughs sometimes!' She was on the brink of tears; angry tears. 'But you'd like to lock me up, wouldn't you? Why don't you padlock me to the table leg? That way I'll never meet anyone, fall in love. That's what this is all about, isn't it?'

'*Fall in love!* You're much too young to know what love is!'

Mildred laid tins of dough on the hearth to rise; did it with a slam and clatter so her daughter might know the anger that was in her. 'Love is being faithful and working hard together in a Christian marriage and – and . . .'

'Is that all, Mother? But you can do those things without getting married! You don't need the Minister's blessing for that!'

'What do you mean – *without getting married*? You and that Drake girl have been talking about *things*!'

'I know about *things*!' Rosamund's cheeks blazed with shame and anger. 'I should do! I'm a farmer's daughter!'

'I'm talking about things between men and women! You know what I'm on about!'

'Yes, I *do* know! I've known about *that* for ages. We talked about it at school. It's life, Mum; you can't shut me away from life! And I won't have you calling Bessie *that Drake girl*! The way you talk about her you'd think she was a trollop!'

They were quarrelling. She and her mother were having a row for the first time! And what was so awful, Rosamund thought with dismay, was that she didn't care! She lifted her chin defiantly, then turned to stare out of the window. Afraid as she was, she must brazen it out. There could be no going back. This outburst had been simmering inside her far too long!

It was then she became aware of the silence. Her mother had ceased her tirade of words, yet her anger hung on the air still, and was more frightening than the bitterness she had hurled at her daughter.

'Well, go on, Mum!' Slowly, willing herself to be calm, she turned around. 'Say something!'

'What's to be said against talk such at that! Where did you learn it? Do you know what a trollop is?'

'It's a bawd who's no better than she need be! Mother! Do you think I came to earth with the last fall of snow? I'm normal and ordinary and as curious as the next girl about life. But I'm not going to get myself into trouble the minute you cut the cord and let me free!'

Mildred gripped the sides of the kneading bowl, her knuckles dangerously white. Then she took a deep breath and said, too softly, 'Trouble! Well, all I can say, Rosamund Kenton, is if ever that day comes, you'll not be welcome in this house! Land yourself in trouble and I'll show the door! Now be out of my way! I've got things to do! Get off to bed and think on about what you've said. And then you can ask my pardon in the morning!'

'I won't go upstairs and I won't say I'm sorry either,' Rosamund gasped, wide-eyed. 'Not unless you say sorry as well!'

There was a ringing in her ears and her heart was beating very quickly but she stood her ground, even as her mother pushed past her without another word and made for the front stairs.

The fury of that passing was like a cold shock, an angry slap to her face, but still she stood there. As the bedroom door slammed shut she closed her eyes and whispered, 'I am *not* sorry. I will *not* say I am sorry.'

She opened her eyes to the quiet around her, wishing her father were here now, and not helping on a nearby farm.

But perhaps that was why her mother was angry; perhaps having her man helping cut some other farmer's hay when Laburnum's fields were gone had upset her?

Yet they were only fields, Rosamund reasoned. Bessie's mum had two sons gone to war and sons were more precious than all the acres in Bowland!

All at once she needed to be out of the house. And to stay out, too, until she knew her father was home! Her mother was unreasonable, bad-minded; had such a fixation about *things* that it was unnatural. It was dirty too, because things between men and women were good and loving. Humans weren't like animals; men didn't act as her mother's thinly veiled hints would have her believe! Mind, things between men and women could be tempestuous, she knew that Bessie's folks often had rows, but they kissed and made up, Bessie said, in bed!

So why weren't there ructions sometimes at Laburnum Farm and why didn't her mother and father kiss and make up afterwards? Why were her parents so polite to each other, and why did her mother imply that doing it – *loving* – was only for getting children?

She let go an impatient gasp, then left the house by the dairy door, walking across the cobbled yard. The shippon was empty of cows and from the sties came a snuffling that told her the pigs had settled down for the night. Over the hills, the sun was sinking big and blood red, promising another good day to come. It threw long shadows to darken fields and fells, changing them from green to black.

The sight of it made her hug herself tightly. Everything she could see was precious and enduring and she wanted to gather it to her and defy anything to harm or change it. But war fed on fear; gobbled young lives and soiled everything it touched. Who, then, was Rosamund Kenton to want to be different? She, who had so much, did not have the right to question the way things were. She had a mother and a father and the war had allowed her to stay with them in a safe old house that she loved. Wasn't that enough? Wouldn't any one of the war dead change places with her without a second thought? A girl of eighteen in a concentration camp; a young soldier, gunned down on Dunkirk beach; a sprog pilot, on his first and last op?

Drained of energy and bitterness and defiance, she walked to the top of the paddock, checking each hen ark as she passed it. Then she turned and looked down into the dim distance, far over to her left.

The workmen had gone. The aerodrome was still now; a silent silhouette of dark shapes, its quietness seeming to make it less threatening. Without men to give it mobility it was a helpless sprawl, yet tomorrow they would be back and soon airmen would come and lorries and trucks and massive warplanes. And bombs.

She leaned against the paddock wall, its stones cold and rough beneath her shoulders. She was calmer now, and wiser, but she wouldn't give in. She was almost a woman. The child in her was gone, and childish thoughts. She needed to know about life and loving and belonging; would not let her mother stifle her thoughts and her dreams. She clenched her teeth until her jaws hurt in an effort not to give way to tears, telling herself silently, fiercely, that tears were for children.

It was time to go back. Not to seek out her mother and lie

about being sorry, but to wait at the end of the dirt road for her father's return. The light was fading. He would be on his way home now.

She walked slowly, making for the foldyard and the path alongside it that led to the little iron kissing gate. And when he came, she would tuck her arm in his and brush his cheek with her own, glad to be with him.

She closed the gate carefully, but it still creaked. She stood still, fearing that an upstairs window would open and her mother's voice demand to know who was outside. But all was quiet, and she walked slowly to the crossroads and heaved herself onto the staging where tomorrow's milk churns would await collection, to sit, legs swinging, pulling in breaths of hay-scented air. She would wait as long as it took, because she didn't want to face her mother alone; not tonight.

Because tonight, for the first time, she hadn't given in.

August came in a blaze of golden heat, ripening corn promising a good harvest. Warm days gave way to cooler evenings; rosehips swelled in the hedges and elderberries hung in thick, green clusters. It was a busy month for country people; squirrelling away whatever they could against a dark winter of food rationing.

The aerodrome began to look more solid. Buildings were hastily roofed, paths began to branch out from the main roads and the runways, lorries delivered crates and boxes, all of them disappearing into the hollows of the hangars.

The machines still cut the grass and the peculiar mound of concrete-covered iron girders that stood alone and apart, was hidden under load after load of earth, then finished off with sods of grass. It looked like an unnatural hillock, an ancient burial mound, Rosamund thought as she stood at the far end of the cow pasture. She went there at least once a day, usually when she collected the cows for milking. It was essential that she should; that nothing should happen without her knowing about it. She told her father about the strange mound of earth, and he said that without doubt it was the ammunition dump and was glad it was as far away as it could be from Laburnum Farm.

'It won't be long, will it, before they come?' she whispered, all at once apprehensive

'Not long, lass. I reckon they'll be in business well before Christmas.'

She told Bessie what her father said. She went out now almost without asking, but was always polite about it, for all that.

'Will it be all right if I pop down to the village? I'll be back before dark.'

And usually, her mother supposed it would have to be, though her father always smiled and told her to be careful on her bike.

'You'll have to be cutting down on your outings, once it's dark early,' was the only protest her mother made. 'I shan't like it if you're out till all hours once the blackout's back.'

The blackout had never gone away. It was just that in summer you hardly noticed it. Light, bright mornings and the sun not setting till eleven in June. You could almost forget the war in summer.

'You did right, telling your mother where to get off,' Bessie had said.

'I didn't *tell* her anything!' No one ever did that – not even Dad. 'I only refused to say I was sorry.'

'What about?'

'Oh – anything and nothing. Mum was in a bit of a mood, and things just flared. She was annoyed about the aerodrome really. Said the airmen would steal from us. I stuck up for them, and I suppose that was the start of it. Anyway, I didn't apologize. After all, I was only expressing an opinion.'

'And at eighteen you're entitled to an opinion!' Bessie defended. 'Your mother should realize there are girls of our age in uniform.'

'Yes, and taking orders from corporals and sergeants instead of their parents!' Rosamund giggled.

'And getting to work with loads of lovely fellers . . .

'Bessie Drake, you are man mad!'

'Yes! And *madly* curious!'

Which made two of them, Rosamund had thought, though she wouldn't have admitted it for anything. Not even to Bessie.

★　　★　　★

When September came softly on a trail of misty mornings and mellow afternoons with clouds shading the hills to darker greens and the days growing shorter, the war slipped into its fifth year.

An uneasy truce still existed between Mildred and her daughter. On the surface, things seemed better with all forgotten, if not forgiven, though there were times when, through a mirrored reflection or on turning suddenly, Rosamund found her mother's eyes on her, narrowed in unspeaking disapproval.

She did the work expected of her and more besides, and usually announced her intention of going to the village within her father's hearing. It was sneaky, really, because he always said, 'Don't be late back, lass,' before her mother could draw breath to say she couldn't go. It meant as well that she could get away without too much fuss. She knew it was wrong to force her father to take sides, but she needed his support if she was to hold on to the small measure of independence so hard won.

These days she always went to Bessie's house, her friend being no longer welcome at Laburnum Farm. Now, after such visits, Rosamund was careful never to voice an opinion or make any remark that could be pounced upon by her mother. Yet as the month drew to a close – it was Michaelmas, actually – she carried home news of such importance that it had to be told.

'The RAF is arriving tomorrow – well, *some* of them . . .'

Her father lowered his paper, her mother's knitting needles clicked out a slower rhythm, though she did not speak.

'You're sure, lass?' Bart Kenton at least thought it worthy of his curiosity. 'Who told you?'

'It came from the White Hart. An airman was in there and he told Bessie's dad that twenty-five of them and two officers had already arrived – twenty from the RAF regiment and the rest to do with administration. The RAF regiment guards aerodromes, and the advance party is checking out security, the airman said. They've already got the guardroom manned, and the perimeter fence is patrolled at night. Mr Drake said they'll all be here soon, he shouldn't wonder – then the bombers will come.'

'Your friend's father seems very free with his information,'

Mildred said sourly, 'and the airman too! Hasn't anyone told them that careless talk costs lives?'

'Oh, I hardly think they're telling state secrets. We've known there was to be an aerodrome for nigh on eighteen months,' Bart offered reasonably.

'Yes, and there'll be no peace for anyone now!' Mildred closed her eyes with a shudder, seeing in her imaginings a plane hurtling out of control in the direction of Laburnum Farm. 'And you can't insure against war damage. What if our home goes up in smoke?'

'Mildred! Just walk over to the window and look out! There's miles and miles of space! How come they're going to pick on this place? And just supposing they did – and it's pretty certain they never will – would all the insurance money in the country compensate us for the loss of Laburnum?'

'Look, Mum – I'm sorry I mentioned the aerodrome. I shouldn't have,' Rosamund whispered. 'I thought you'd be interested. And Dad's right. *If* there is going to be an accident, it might just as easily happen to any house in Laceby. If a bomber overshot the runway, the village would catch it.'

'Yes! And the other runway, if they chose to use it, points directly at our two laburnums! Is your head so full of nonsense that you can't see what is staring you in the face!'

Rosamund made no reply because she knew what her mother meant by nonsense. Men! Men wolf-whistling girls on bikes; men dating girls and dancing with them; doing what normal young men who might not live to see tomorrow needed to do. But nonsense to her mother also meant *things*. Dirt. Men lusting after innocence; wanting to know how it was because of tomorrow or the next tomorrow. Couldn't she, just once out of charity, realize they needed to live a little before it was too late? You couldn't blame them. Young women were just as curious, as anxious, only they knew what would happen if they did *that*. Young women had to say no!

'And was there any more news from the village?' Bart steered the talk away from runways.

'Joe Drake is coming on leave next Thursday, then he's going on a course to Plymouth Barracks. He's been at sea nearly six months. Mrs Drake is really looking forward to seeing him.'

'I'll bet she is! You'll be sending them a few eggs, happen?'

Bart looked at his wife meaningfully, but she glanced down at her needles and began counting stitches.

'And happen not! The hens will be going into the moult soon.' Moulting hens did not give eggs.

'But the young birds are coming into the lay. The pullets won't be moulting, will they?'

'No. And Mrs Drake won't pay our fine if They catch us giving folk eggs off the ration!'

'It hasn't stopped you before – letting one or two have a few from time to time . . .'

'No. But it's stopping as from now! All the eggs are to go to the egg packers in future!'

'Then you'll remember that, won't you, Mum, when you slip a few in your bag next Sunday,' Rosamund hissed. 'Like I said, I shouldn't have mentioned the aerodrome, nor Joe Drake. He'll bring a ration card with him and there'll be an egg on that, I shouldn't wonder! I'll going to bed now. Good night, both!'

She opened the stair door, then carefully closed it, feeling her way with her toe up each steep step, because she had forgotten her candle and not for the world, having delivered her exit line, was she going back for it.

'Lass!' The door sneck clicked. 'You've forgotten to take a light!'

Her father handed her the candlestick, then struck a match and held it to the wick, his eyes searching for hers.

'Thanks, Dad. Good night.' She shaped her lips into a kiss and mouthed, 'Love you.'

''Night, Rosamund. God bless.'

It was in that moment of candlelit intimacy she realized how very much she loved her father and that she would never willingly do anything to hurt him.

But as for her mother . . .

FOUR

Rosamund stood shivering at the open window to gaze over towards the fells; to where, on any normal Guy Fawkes night, she would have seen distant clusters of red stars and bursts of silver and gold and green shimmering in the wide night sky. Yet all she saw now was a blackness that made her want to reach out and push it aside; an unnatural darkness. No bonfires now. Any kind of light after dark was forbidden. For the duration.

But we were winning the war at last. Leningrad and Stalingrad were free again. Heaps of rubble, both, but free. All North Africa rid of Axis soldiers and Allied armies on Italian soil, and marching through Naples.

Was the invasion of Italy the second front Stalin was constantly demanding? Her father said not; that there was a long way to go yet.

'How long is a long way, Dad?'

Bart Kenton had not known, but she must remember, he had said, that almost all the world was at war, and when peace came to Europe there would be another war to face, in the Far East.

She pulled down the blackout, drew the rose-printed curtains across the window, then felt for the candlestick and matchbox.

The flickering flame made the room cosier, and the dark corners seemed to form a barrier that shut out that world at war. Here, in the little room above the kitchen, she felt safe enough to let her thoughts go free again, to remember the shock of seeing the bombers four days ago.

She had been standing at the far end of the cow pasture, watching the comings and goings of trucks and tractors and airmen. Yes, and women airmen, too. Waafs.

Then she felt a shiver of apprehension as her eyes were drawn to a shape, no bigger than a sparrow in flight, high in the sky. And as she watched it grew bigger and the sound of its engines could be heard. Four engines. She could see them distinctly, now, because it was dropping, slowing, obviously looking for the runway below. Then it circled, wheels down, and she knew it was the first of RAF Laceby Green's bombers. Operational before Christmas, local opinion had it. For once, it seemed, gossip had got it right. Two more were already in sight.

She ran, heels pounding across the pasture, forgetting to close the gate behind her; ran across the foldyard and past the pigsties and the brick dovecote, hurtling into the kitchen.

'There's one of them landed and two more circling! Lancasters!'

She stood there, gasping on her breath, waiting for her mother to run to the front of the house and watch. But she didn't. She only said, 'Well, we knew they would – one day.' Said it with a fateful acceptance, then closed her eyes, as if briefly praying.

'Yes. We knew.' Rosamund went to stand at the window. She couldn't see the bombers, but their noise filled the air with a great growling, as they came in to land. 'Was there a letter from Mrs Drake this morning?'

'Are you expecting one?'

'Yes. Hasn't anyone brought the post in?'

'Not yet. You'd better go and collect it. What's it about?'

'She'll be asking if I can stay there on Saturday night. There's a do on in the parish hall – something to do with the choir . . .'

The choir. Her mother would approve if the church choir had a hand in it, she thought as she lifted the lid of the post box at the end of the lane. Her mother would say yes – especially as Bessie's mum had taken the trouble to write; make it official.

The letter was there, and she hurried to give it to her

mother, placing the remainder of the post on the mantel behind the clock.

'Well – go on! Open it!' she said when the envelope lay untouched on the table for what seemed an age.

'Haven't you work to be getting on with, Rosamund?'

'Plenty. But can I go, or can't I?'

'I'll read it, child. Later.'

'It's in aid of the choir . . .' Dammit! Why should Bessie's mum have to go to the bother of writing? Why couldn't a young woman of eighteen stay the night at her friend's house without permission from the Holy Ghost? The eighteen-year-old Waafs at the aerodrome would be allowed sleeping-out passes; she'd take bets on it.

She sighed, determined not to make an issue of it, and went in search of her father. Dad would be all right about it, though it made her feel guilty that she so often asked him to take sides. She found him sweeping out in the foldyard.

'I'll give you a hand, Dad . . .'

With the coming of colder nights and the risk of ground frost, the milking herd spent the night in the shelter of the yard. Soon, they would spend both night and day in it and be no end of a bother. Milk cows were tender creatures, to be guarded against the cold so they shouldn't start coughing or, worse still, go down with bovine TB. Tuberculosis in a herd was a nasty thing.

She picked up a brush and said, without preamble, 'Mrs Drake has written to Mum. I want to stay the night at Bessie's on Saturday. There's a do on in the parish hall in aid of choir funds.'

'And what did your mother have to say on the matter?'

'She hasn't even opened it! She's doing it on purpose because she doesn't like Bessie.'

'We-e-ll, you sometimes get a little bit defiant when you've been at Bessie's . . .'

'You mean I've expressed an opinion of my own, like any girl of my age is entitled to? D'you know, Dad, I'll bet you anything you like that some of those Air Force girls at the 'drome are no older than me, yet nobody thinks they're up to something when they want to stay out the night!'

'And will you and Bessie be up to anything?' He smiled as he asked it.

'Dad! Don't you think chance would be a fine thing! What on earth is there to get up to in Sin City? Carryings-on with choirboys?'

'There are a lot of strange young men around now.' Bart Kenton felt duty-bound to warn his daughter of the recent influx of strangers. 'They say you can't get near the counter, some nights, at the White Hart.'

'I wouldn't know. Did you see the bombers, Dad?'

'I did. And a right noise they made, an' all.'

'What's it going to be like when there's a whole squadron of them and they start flying ops?'

'I reckon there'll be a few disturbed nights for people around these parts.'

'Mum for one, you mean?'

'Mum,' he laughed. 'But I dare say we'll get used to the din.'

'I dare say we'll have to. They're here for the duration. And maybe when Mum realizes they aren't going to crash on Laburnum, she'll learn to put up with it.'

'Don't say things like that, even in jest!' The gentle face was all at once serious. 'Planes have been known to crash on houses.'

'Not on ours they daren't, and anyway, Bessie's dad says they'll mostly be taking off over the village, that being the direction of the prevailing wind.'

'Happen they will.' He studied his pocket watch. 'Did your mother have the kettle on? I reckon it's just about time for drinkings.'

The kettle had boiled and the brown pot was covered by a knitted cosy when they opened the kitchen door, yet the letter still lay on the kitchen table. Unopened.

It wasn't until Rosamund had cleared the supper table and washed and dried the pots and pans that she felt entitled to ask, 'Well, can I go to Bessie's on Saturday or can't I, Mum?'

'I think not, Rosamund.' Mildred Kenton's mouth took on a belligerent set. 'You know I don't like you going to *that* house.'

'*That* house! You'd think I was asking to stay the night at a brothel!'

'There now, Bart! Did you hear that? It's always the same whenever the Drake girl's name is mentioned! Tell her she's not to go!'

'I'll do no such thing! And the Drake girl has a name, Mildred! Tell me, will you, what has the lass done to offend you so?'

'Nothing.' She laid aside the sock she was knitting. 'And everything. Those Drakes are far too free and easy for one thing, and for another –'

'For another, you simply don't want Rosamund to go?'

'There'll be the blackout. I don't like her out in the blackout . . .'

'Laceby's blackout is no different to ours! Take a flashlight, lass,' he looked meaningfully at his daughter, 'and check the foldyard.'

Ostensibly he was making a point, Rosamund realized, though really he wanted her out of the kitchen because there was going to be words.

'Oh, for goodness' sake! I won't go if it's going to cause trouble!'

'Off you go,' Bart said quietly, nodding in the direction of the door, 'and take the dog with you.'

Without a word, not looking at either parent, Rosamund left the kitchen groping for the flashlight that always stood on the dairy window ledge, and lit her way to the yard door. It wasn't pasted over with brown paper as regulations demanded, with just a small, circular hole in the centre to give a pinpoint of light. Its beam was long and strong because no one, her mother said, would notice it up here. Up here was Mildred Kenton's undisputed kingdom; her refuge from people and especially from a war she wanted no part of.

Rosamund swept the beam to the dog kennel and the

black and white collie blinked and whined, his chain rattling.

'Come on, Shep.' She bent to release him. 'Good boy, then.'

Silly, she supposed, having a sheepdog when they had no sheep. But Shep barked a lot at strangers and marauding foxes, and was a nice old thing, really.

She fondled his ears then switched off the light, her eyes accustomed now to the denseness of the night, walking slowly to the foldyard to lean on the gate. Her father didn't really want it checking; no point in disturbing the herd. All he wanted, she sighed, was to reason with her mother; insist that it was all right for their daughter to spend a night away from home.

There would be no words, as such; no shouting or fists banged on the tabletop; Bart Kenton always made his point quietly. It was why, on the rare occasions it happened, he always won. Her mother knew it too, though there would be a price to be paid. No one could act as hurt and offended as her mother, Rosamund thought bitterly. Her silences could last a week and ordinary, normal people called it sulking.

The dog pressed against her calf as if it understood.

'It's a queer old world, Shep,' she said, and her voice sounded small and forlorn in the great, wide darkness.

She blinked her eyes rapidly. She always blinked when she wanted not to weep and tonight especially, she was determined not to give way to tears.

She sniffed loudly, then focused her eyes in the direction of the aerodrome. The sky above it was dark, though she knew that if she walked through the paddock and up the incline, she could have an uninterrupted view of it. Perhaps then she would see brief pinpricks of light or the flaring of a match but that, apart from dim blue lights atop the control tower and the hangars, was all there would be to give its position away. Only on moonlit nights did it stand out black and angular against a silver sky.

She wondered if the three bombers had been towed into the hangars or if they had already been given their dispersal points and were now guarded by men with rifles.

She looked down at her watch, clucking impatiently because she couldn't see it. Had she stood here long enough? Was it all over in the kitchen? Perhaps she should wait a little longer; best she shouldn't walk in to a cold silence. Cold silences were worse than a shouting match.

The night was chilly. She decided to count to a hundred and one, then walk slowly back making sure to bang the dairy door to warn them of her coming.

When finally she stood blinking in the sudden glare of light, her father sat alone, the morning paper on the floor at his side. Her mother's knitting, four needles protruding awkwardly, lay on the other chair. The mantel clock ticked loudly in the silence and she saw it was almost nine o'clock.

'Where's Mum?' She held her hands to the fire.

'Gone to bed, with a bit of a headache.'

'My fault, wasn't it?' She knelt at her father's feet and reached for his hand, laying her head on his knee. And because they were alone, he stroked her hair in a rare gesture of affection.

'Nobody to blame. I think it was the bombers coming that upset her. She'll be herself again by morning.'

'Maybe tomorrow there'll be more of them.'

'Aye. Turn the wireless on, there's a good lass.'

She rose to her feet. Sulking or not, her mother would expect the nine o'clock news to be listened to. Every word. It was the only time she willingly allowed the war into Laburnum Farm.

Rosamund did not mention Mrs Drake's letter. She knew that her father had put his foot down, as he did from time to time when he felt strongly about something.

'I don't think I want to listen to the news tonight, Dad. Shall I make us a cup of tea?'

'If you think the rations will run to it . . .'

He placed his empty pipe between his teeth. Bart Kenton never smoked it; just used it for comfort occasionally. Tonight, Rosamund thought, must be one of those stress times, even though he had won.

'I don't think Mum will miss a spoonful. I'll use the little pot,' she smiled. 'Shall I cut us a slice of teacake?'

'Might as well go the whole hog . . .' He removed his pipe to smile at his daughter and she thought that once, her father must have been quite a good-looking man. Before the frown lines came, that was, and the grey hair, and an almost perpetual quietness.

'Dad,' she whispered, 'I'm sorry. I really am.'

But he merely said, 'Whisht,' and nodded towards the kettle.

'You're early!' Bessie grinned. 'I didn't expect you yet!'

'Mum said she'd milk for me. Said she didn't want me riding in the dark.'

'To tell the truth I'm surprised she let you out at all!' Bessie rolled up the last curler and snapped it shut, because even a beetle drive in the cold parish hall merited an effort. 'What did you have to do? Grovel?'

'No. But Dad put his foot down. It was him said I could come.'

'Your mother is queer. She gives me the shudders. If people believed in witches these days, she'd be one!'

'*Bessie!*' Rosamund giggled. 'And she isn't queer, exactly. Just a bit funny-peculiar sometimes.'

'I expect she's in the change. Mum told me about it. Women can go quite ga-ga and imagine all kinds of things.'

'Let's not talk about Mum. Did you see the bombers, Bessie?'

'You mean the eleven that flew in on Wednesday? I was at work. I missed it. What was it like?'

'Noisy. I was helping shift the poultry arks and Dad and I got a marvellous view. They flew in all together, then circled and got lower, and landed one by one.'

'Lucky dog. Mum said they're big things. I believe they've been flying round quite a bit, but it seems all quiet today.'

'I suppose they were testing, sort of.'

'Mm. It's called circuits and bumps. Doing one or two rounds of the aerodrome then landing again,' Bessie said knowledge-ably, folding a flimsy scarf around her head, because it didn't do to be seen with curlers in your hair; not even by your best friend.

'Who told you?'

'Dad. The flight sergeant he drinks with told him. They're becoming quite buddies, those two. He told Dad about the women pilots too.'

'*Women* pilots! You've got to be joking!'

'No. Honestly. Those first three Lancasters that came were flown by women! And all on their own! They're called ferry pilots and they deliver planes all over the place. Fighters or bombers; they just get in them and take off! Those three were straight from the factory. Brand-new.'

'Bessie! That's a dangerous thing for a woman to do! They might even get shot down!'

'So they could. But they're in more danger, I believe, when they land.'

'Really? The one I saw touch down did it very well.' Had she but known, Rosamund frowned, that women were piloting those planes, she would have stayed and cheered like mad!

'No! Not that! Predators, I mean. Wolves. Randy blokes . . .'

'Well, I reckon,' Rosamund giggled, 'if they can fly a Lancaster, they can take care of themselves all right! It's amazing, though, just what women can do when the occasion demands.'

'Work in the wages office of a shirt factory, for one! And talking about the RAF, we've been making shirts for Waafs, all week. Such a lovely blue. I think if I joined anything, it would be the WAAF. Sometimes, I wish I could.'

'Me, too.' Not so long ago, when her mother was being sniffy about Mrs Drake's letter, Rosamund would have taken the King's shilling without a second thought. 'So what are we going to do?'

'Well, I said I'd see to the supper tonight. Mum won't be back from Preston till six, so I'd like to have it all ready for when she gets back. Buses always give her a headache. The vegetables are done, and there's a rabbit casserole ready cooked. Remind me to pop it in the fire oven, will you, in about half an hour?'

'You were lucky, getting a rabbit.'

'Not really. We get one every week. Ned Loftus lets us have

it for nothing. Dad turns a blind eye, you see, when he does a bit of poaching in the Hall grounds. Haven't you ever had things off Ned?'

'N-no. Well, he wouldn't walk all the way to Laburnum, would he, with a rabbit?' Rosamund blushed deep red and was glad Bessie was staring into the dressing-table mirror.

'It figures. I can't see your mother taking anything under the counter. She's very religious, isn't she?'

Rosamund thought of the pheasants and clothing coupons and eggs carried secretly to chapel most Sundays, and declined to comment.

'Shall we go downstairs and get the supper on?' Bessie's bedroom was colder than the snug little room at the top of the kitchen stairs. 'And what time will we be leaving tonight?'

'It starts at half-past seven. I hope enough people turn up for four tables. If the choir didn't get the parish hall free, they wouldn't make a profit. Ooooh! I hope there'll be some blokes there from the aerodrome.'

'Bess! Can you see any red-blooded young man sitting all night, shaking a dice and drawing beetles on pieces of paper? Even if HM Forces do get in half-price!'

'A girl can but hope! I'll bet you anything you like that those Waafs at the aerodrome aren't short of dates, the lucky things!'

A girl can but hope. The phrase might have been especially coined for one Rosamund Kenton, virgin of this parish. What wouldn't she give, right now, to be one of the Waafs at RAF Laceby Green!

'Give me your hand, Rosamund.' The fog, which had caused Mrs Drake's bus to be late, was even denser as the two set out for the parish hall. 'As if the flippin' blackout isn't enough!'

They walked slowly, blinking rapidly. Bessie trailed her hand along the stone wall until she was sure of their bearings, then pulled her friend's arm through hers, walking with more confidence.

'Watch the kerb.' She felt for it with her toe, felt too the iron grid of the water drain and knew the little stone hall would be about twenty paces ahead. She had learned to find her way around Laceby after dark by counting steps and memorizing things like gates and fences. 'Just take it easy. Not far to go.' Bessie was still counting.

'I'm fine. I can see a bit now. How on earth, Bess, can bombers take off in this?'

'They can't. If the met. people tell them there's going to be fog, they call off the flying. Bet the aircrews aren't half glad. There might be one or two at the beetle drive – oooh! Hey! Steady on, mate!'

She sidestepped to miss the bulk that loomed at them out of the blackness, but Rosamund took the full force of the encounter.

'Ouch!' Her handbag went flying and she would have followed it had not a hand grabbed her arm.

'Sorry! I was looking for you! I could hear you but I couldn't see you. The transport's over there . . .'

'Hang on! My friend has lost her bag.'

'OK. Stand still, and I'll look for it.'

A thin beam of torchlight touched their feet then circled the path, and in it Bessie could make out trousers and boots.

'Which transport?'

'The one for the dance – at the aerodrome. We put notices up . . .'

'My bag!' Rosamund wailed. Her purse was in it, and her only lipstick.

'Got it. It's still closed; nothing's spilled out. Look, better stick your arms in mine, both of you, or there'll be another collision.'

'But we're going to the –' Rosamund's protest was silenced by a dig from Bessie's elbow.

'Where's this dance going to be held?' Bessie was quick on the uptake.

'In one of the huts. Not very glamorous, but at least it's empty. There are one or two musicians at the camp; they've got a band together,' the voice hastened. 'We-e-ll, the place is hardly up and running yet. I'm glad you're coming. We're short of partners, and –'

'Sounds good.' Her friend, Rosamund thought, was positively purring. 'Are you in the band, by the way?'

'No. As senior sergeant in the mess I was put in charge of the transport. A dance isn't a lot of good without girls, and I was ordered not to go back without some!'

He had a nice voice, Rosamund thought, trying desperately to convince herself that this was a good idea.

'And how many have you got?'

'The two of you make seven, but if it goes well tonight, the word will spread. We plan to hold dances every Saturday night.'

'You mean if you aren't going off bombing?' Bessie demanded. 'Do you fly, by the way?'

'Yes. But here we are. Hang on and I'll give you a hand up.' He shone the light into the interior and Rosamund was relieved to find that there were indeed five girls there. A hand guided her to a wooden bench. A voice whispered, 'You'll have to hang on to the side when we get going. It's a bit bumpy . . .'

'Think there'll be any more?' the voice asked.

'Shouldn't think so.' Bessie's reply was prompt, as if she wanted to be off before she had second thoughts. 'What time does it finish?'

'Eleven-ish. We'll have you safely home long before midnight.'

The tailboard banged shut and was made secure; the transport started with a lurch.

Rosamund whispered, 'Well, I hope you know what you're doing, Bessie Drake! Supposing there's someone there who knows us?'

'We're the only two from Laceby Green. It'll be all right. Anyway, it's too late now,' Bessie giggled nervously. 'Oh, c'mon. Live dangerously!'

Dangerously, Rosamund echoed silently, nervously. Oh, my goodness!

The Nissen hut was bare and smelled of newness; the floor was covered in brown linoleum. Chairs lined the walls; thick blackout curtains covered the small windows

'How many did you get, Skip?' a voice demanded.

'Seven.'

'Only *seven*! S'truth, there'll be a riot!' At the far end of the floor, a group of musicians talked earnestly. Beside them, straight-backed, sat no more than a dozen girls in WAAF uniform. Grouped in the middle of the floor, airmen worked out that the odds on grabbing a dancing partner were three to one against. Someone wolf-whistled as seven civilian girls blinked in the sudden light.

'Hallelujah!' Bessie whispered throatily. 'We'll be danced off our feet!'

'Jonathan – Jon – Hunt.' The voice assumed an identity. Rosamund gazed, embarrassed, at the wings above the pocket of his tunic. Then she raised her eyes to the knot in his black tie, to his chin and finally his eyes. Blue eyes.

He was holding out his hand and she whispered, 'Rosamund Kenton.'

'Rosie,' he said firmly, smiling, holding her hand, still; looking down into her eyes.

His hair was thick and fair, his smile unbelievable. He was very tall and slim; someone a girl could fall in love with. This very minute.

'No one calls me Rosie,' she choked, mesmerized.

'They do now, and I'm keeping hold of your hand because I want at least one dance. And just in case we get separated, I want the first waltz. And the last one.'

'Yes. OK . . .'

She was making a fool of herself. Why couldn't she be like Bessie, who was hanging on to an air gunner for dear life?

'This is Mick,' Bessie grinned. 'He's *his* tail-end Charlie.'

'*He* is called Jon,' Rosamund said breathlessly, 'and what's a – er – tail-end Charlie?'

'Mick is my rear gunner.' Jon was still looking into her eyes. 'Harry is our other gunner but he's on a forty-eight-hour Compassionate. He's just become a father.'

'I see. Do you really think we should be holding hands like this?' Why was she making such a fool of herself?

'Yes, I do. I rather like it and anyway, any minute now they're going to start.'

To a roll of drums a quickstep was called and he pulled her to face him, his hand behind her back.

'No fancy footwork,' she whispered. 'I'm not very good.'

He was still looking at her; right into her eyes. She wished she could look away.

'Just follow me,' he said comfortably. He guided her onto the floor and their steps matched at once. It was as if they had danced together before tonight; lots of times.

But then, of course, they had. She smiled up at him, all at once relaxed, because they'd been dancing together, in her dreamings, for a long, long time.

She smiled again because he was good to be with; good to touch, to hold closely. She was glad he'd asked her for the last waltz and that she'd said yes.

'Oh, lordy!' She stood stock-still in the middle of the floor, so they stumbled and bumped into another couple. 'We can't have the last waltz! We'll have to be home long before eleven. We aren't supposed to be here, you see. We were going to a beetle drive in the parish hall . . .'

'Oh, Rosie! And I grabbed you both in the blackout . . .'

'We-e-ll – yes.'

'But I didn't hear either of you protesting.' Laughing, he began to dance again.

'If Bessie had, I would've, too.'

'But Bessie didn't!'

'No. And if I'm truthful, I wanted to come here.' She closed her eyes, pleased she was getting the steps right, and that he wanted to dance with her again.

'Why weren't you supposed to be here, Rosie?'

'Because we didn't know about it and because we wouldn't have been allowed to come, even if we had. Well, I wouldn't.'

'Your parents are strict?'

'Yes. We-e-ll, Dad is all right, but Mum is worse than strict. And she thinks I'm still a kid, and I'm not!'

'How old are you, Rosie?'

'Eighteen. And a bit . . .'

'Then you are most certainly *not* a child. Some of the Waafs on the station are quite young – but old enough to be in uniform.'

'I was envying them tonight – being away from home, I mean. But I'd miss Laburnum if I had to go away. Laburnum Farm, I mean. It's about a mile outside Laceby, to the north. You might have flown over it and not known.'

'I think I know where it is. At the far end of the north/south runway. A stone house.'

'That's it! You can't miss it, Jon. It's a straggly house, and our land reaches down to the perimeter fence, actually.'

'Then we're neighbours! I'll give you a wave, next time I'm flying over!' The dance ended, and he took her elbow and guided her to the furthest corner of the hut. 'I think the next one will be a waltz. It's mine, don't forget.'

Mine. Delight tingled through her and for a little time she forgot about being found out, and punished.

'I don't think anyone will ask me; not whilst you're holding my hand so tightly.'

'Don't you like having your hand held, Rosie?'

'No one has done it until now. Not a young man.'

'I asked if you liked it.' He was looking at her very seriously, and she knew that if she said she didn't like it, then that would be the end of things between them. She raised her eyes to his.

'With you, I like it very much.'

'Good.' He smiled again, and an unfamiliar, wonderful feeling sliced through her.

'Tell me about yourself, Jon.' If tonight was to be the first and last time, she must know all about him. 'How old you are, your brothers and sisters, where you live . . .'

'Age nearly twenty-three.' He moved closer, letting go her hand, laying an arm on the back of her chair. 'Born in my aunt's house in London – 19 January 1921. Parents both gone – next of kin my Aunt Lottie.'

'No parents? Jon – I'm sorry.'

'Don't be. I never knew them. When I was three months old, Mother and I went to India to join my father. I don't think she wanted to go.' He shrugged, pushing aside a lock of hair that fell over his eye. 'Anyway, it seems she couldn't or wouldn't get used to the life – became very unhappy. In the end, my father pushed off with someone else, asked for a divorce, said he'd give her grounds . . .'

'*Divorce!*' Divorce was a wicked word at Laburnum Farm. 'What did your mother do?'

'Took an overdose.'

'*Killed* herself!'

'Suicide.' He said it matter-of-factly. 'I suppose you could say it saved the mess of a divorce.'

'But that's awful!'

'I guess it is – *was* – at the time. But you did ask and it happened long ago, when I was two. I was put in charge of a ship's nurse and sent home to England, to Aunt Lottie. I don't remember much until my fourth birthday really. I was given a tricycle. You don't forget your first bike!' He was smiling again.

'And you don't resent what happened to you?'

'Why should I? And anyway, it happened to my parents. I had a good life. Aunt Lottie worked on a newspaper and gave it up when she was landed with me – went freelance. My father sent an allowance until I was through university. We haven't heard from him for over a year.'

'What about your uncle?' The music had started again, but still they sat there as if, she thought, they were getting things straight between them. Right from the start.

'There was no man about the house. My aunt never married. Her young man was killed in the last war. She never wanted anyone else. I think she looks on me as the son they might have had together if things had been different.'

'So you were happy, Jon, as a child?'

'Very. Happier than I'd have been with my parents, I shouldn't wonder. How about you?'

'Can we dance?' All at once she wanted to tell him about the way it really was and if they were dancing, she wouldn't have to meet his eyes. 'It'll be better, if we're dancing.'

'Why?' He rose to his feet and held out his arms, but she did not go to him.

'Because – well, I don't know how to say it. It's a bit embarrassing.'

'You've got a boyfriend,' he said flatly.

'Lordy! No!' She laughed because that really was funny. 'Quite the opposite. Mum and Dad treat me like a child – Mum especially. If it wasn't for Bessie, I suppose I'd still be thinking they'd found me under a gooseberry bush. No! That isn't fair.' She was blushing furiously, already regretting what she had said. 'I know about *things*. I should do; I'm a farmer's daughter and I'd be daft if I didn't. But Mum doesn't talk about it at all; you know – between men and women. That's why I'm pretty dim, really, about men. I'm not a pushover, though.'

'Want to go outside, Rosie – talk . . . ?'

'*No!* We-e-ll, yes. It might be best. But I'm not –'

'Not a pushover,' he said gravely. 'You'll be perfectly safe. I'll keep my hands in my pockets, I promise.'

He held out a hand and they walked towards the door, side-stepping the dancers. She looked up to see Bessie, who winked at her over the air-gunner's shoulder and mouthed, 'Naughty.'

The cold outside slapped into them as they stood still in the darkness for the usual fifteen seconds, blinking, peering into the blackness, feeling the dampness of the fog on their faces.

'Are you all right, Rosie?'

'I'm cold. I should have brought my coat.'

'Green, isn't it, with a brown collar? I'll go back and get it.'

'No! Don't bother.' She didn't want any fuss.

'Come here, then.' He unbuttoned his tunic, wrapping her into it, pulling her close. His body was warm beneath his shirt and she marvelled that it was the closest she had been to any man. 'That better?'

'Mm. Lovely.'

'So tell me, then?' He laid his cheek on her hair.

'I don't know where to start, really. And anyway, it's sort of personal . . .'

'You've got a wooden leg?'

'Idiot! I – I suppose, really, that it's only fair you should know you're the first man I've ever dated – if you can call bumping into a man in the blackout a date.'

'A blind date, sort of?' She could sense the laughter in his voice.

'What I'm trying to say is I'm no good at kissing, and all that. Not like Bessie.'

'Do you want to be kissed?' He pushed her a little way from him, cupping her face in his hands, but she shook it free.

'Of course I do, but I just told you, I don't know how!'

'But it isn't a question of knowing, sweetheart; it's all about wanting to. It isn't something you have to learn. It's something you want to do, so it comes easily.'

'I suppose you've kissed a lot of girls, Jon?' How had she got herself into this mess?

'Heaps.'

'And did you like doing it?'

'Very much.'

'So you've had a lot of girlfriends?' she whispered, dismayed.

'Dozens. But I've never fallen in love – was always too busy, I suppose.'

'Doing what?'

'Oh, playing games – football, tennis. Swotting for exams; getting a scholarship to university; more swotting. Joining the RAF . . .'

'You've packed a lot into twenty-two years. I haven't done anything.'

'That, Rosie, you seem pretty keen to establish! So why don't we do something about it? Close your eyes!' He placed a finger beneath her chin, tilting her face. 'And open your lips – just a little . . .'

Bemused, she did as he asked, pulling in her breath, waiting, deliciously afraid, for his mouth to touch hers. And when it did, his lips were warm and firm and she let go a keening sound like a lovesick mouse! Why hadn't she moaned softly, dammit, like they did in the movies?

She pulled away, but he put a hand behind her head, so she closed her eyes without being told to and parted her lips, and the second time it came right and she wrapped her arms around his neck so he wouldn't stop.

'Ooooosh!' She let go her indrawn breath, then laid her lips to his, very gently. 'You were right,' she whispered. 'It's all a question of wanting to. Snuggle me close again, please?' She clasped her arms around his waist and he wrapped his jacket around her again and the nearness of him seemed right and safe and dizzy-making. 'Tonight, when it's all over, will you think I'm a bit of a nutcase?'

'Tonight, before it's all over, I shall ask you when we're going to meet again. You do want to, Rosie?'

'I want to; I really do – but how?' Falling in love, she supposed, was much, much easier than sneaking out to meet a man. 'Mrs Drake had to write a note to Mum to make it all right for me to sleep at Bessie's place. I'm hardly ever allowed out, Jon. I suppose really you can't blame Mum, us living so far away from the village, but she's going to get suspicious if I keep wanting to stay with Bessie. And anyway, it mightn't always be convenient for Mrs Drake.' Dismay wrapped her round and she wished she had never come to the dance; never met Jon Hunt.

'Then why don't I call for you? Surely that would make it all right?'

'It wouldn't. You don't know my mother! She doesn't want me to have anything to do with men – especially men from the aerodrome. Time enough to think about that sort of thing, she said, when the war is over.'

'And is that what you want – not to fall in love, I mean, until it's safe; till you know he won't be killed?'

'Jon! No! I shouldn't have said that!' Aircrews were always getting killed! 'Mum didn't mean anything by it. What she really meant, I suppose, was that I'm too young to know my own mind, so it would be better to wait till I'm older – twenty-one, sort of.'

'And is that what you want, Rosie?'

'No.' Her voice wobbled with tears. 'My mother is very practical – not a bit romantic. But she's a good woman, in her own way. It's just that at times I feel sorry for Dad. Sometimes, I wonder how they got me.'

There! She'd said it! Now he'd know what a funny family she came from. It made her want to weep, almost, because all at once she knew her parents never kissed now, and even when they had, her mother had probably taken the back of her hand across her mouth to wipe the kiss away. Mentally, that was.

'You know how they got you! What you mean, I suppose, is how much joy was there in it?'

'Joy. Yes. Loving should be a joyful thing, shouldn't it?'

'Oh yes, Rosie Kenton! And mind-boggling and wonderful! And tender and warm and passionate!'

For a while she didn't speak, then she drew a deep, steadying breath and said soberly, 'You seem to know all about it!'

'I know how I want it to be – but it's got to be with the right girl!'

'And will you know when you've found her?'

'Meet me tomorrow night and I'll tell you!'

'I can't, Jon. You know I can't.'

'Couldn't you slip out for ten minutes?'

'You'd walk all that way, just for ten minutes!'

'I like walking. Look – you're cold. Let's go back inside and talk ways and means.'

'Only if we can talk first about Bessie and me getting home by half-past ten!'

'For a kiss, I might . . .'

This time she knew exactly how it was done, so she lifted her chin and closed her eyes and parted her lips. And it was easy, and wonderful. And absolutely right.

When they had all decided it would be politic to leave the dance at ten and walk to Laceby by way of a short cut Bessie was familiar with – even in the blackout – Mick said, 'OK, Skip, that's settled then. We'll meet up outside at ten.'

He looked quite cheerful about it, Rosamund thought, but then he and Bessie had danced together all night. And she wouldn't mind betting that if he asked Bessie to meet him in Clitheroe or Preston, she would be able to make it, because her mother would say she could, but not to let her father find out, and to get herself home by eleven.

But imagine, Rosamund frowned, saying, tomorrow morning when she walked into Laburnum kitchen, 'Mum! I met the most wonderful man at the areodrome last night and he walked me back to Bessie's. Can he come to Sunday tea?' Imagine the horror, the disbelief, the accusations of deceit. Going to a dance at the aerodrome, when she had said – and Mrs Drake too, in her letter – that she and Bessie would be at the parish hall! And that would only be the start of the silences and sulking and strange sideways glances!

'Jon – are you sure you can find your way to Laburnum in the dark?'

They were dancing, cheek on cheek, bodies touching, their feet moving in small, slow circles. Someone had turned off the main light, and the half-dark lent itself to intimate moving.

'Dearest girl, I can find my way to Germany and back in the blackout. Finding your place will be a piece of cake!'

'You've flown ops before, then? I thought the squadron was a new one.'

'It is, mostly. But a few of us have been operational before. One pilot is on his second tour of ops.'

'You mean he's started his second thirty? And how many have you done?'

'Seven – lucky seven, they say it is. The first op is a bitch – I can vouch for that – and if you make it home, then the next six are dicey. But when you've done lucky seven, then you've got a good chance, so aircrew folklore has it, of making your tour of thirty. I must, in all honesty, admit that not a lot of crews do.'

'Jon! Don't say that! Don't ever say that again!'

'I had my fingers crossed, Rosie! You always cross your fingers when you take a swipe at Fate!'

'Where did you fly from before?'

'Leeming. That's the other side of the Pennines. I flew a Halifax, then, so I'm on what you might call a conversion course right now. Lancasters are good planes – ours is *J-Johnnie* – and I think I've been lucky in my crew.'

'Your new crew?'

'Mm. My first lot are still flying – had done their twenty-sixth, last time I heard. I had a spell in hospital blue, you see, so my first crew got a replacement pilot.'

'You were wounded, Jon!'

'No. Laid up for three months with a broken leg! I did it playing football. No heroics. My squadron leader played merry hell with me! Anyway, I've got myself a decent bunch, though none of them has flown ops before. A pilot chooses his own crew, usually. No one to blame but himself, then, if he picks a wrong 'un. I was lucky. I got a navigator who was a failed pilot.'

'Why is that lucky?' Her lips were close to his ear and she wanted, very much, to kiss it.

'Because if anything happened to me, at least there'd be one bod on board who had an inkling of how to get the plane down. An insurance, really. He'd done a fair few landings, actually, before they failed him. So he became a navigator, and I grabbed him.'

'Tell me about them.' She must know everything about him!

'Well, you know about Mick and about the other gunner who's on Compassionate.'

'Yes. Harry . . .'

'Well, my navigator is called Richard, though he gets Dick, and the wireless op is Sammy – he's Canadian, from Manitoba. The flight engineer is Willie MacBain – Mac – and the bomb-aimer is –'

'Tom! It's got to be Tom!'

'Right! Tom, Dick and Harry! That's got to be lucky.'

'Does luck come into it, Jon?'

'You've got to have your fair share, I suppose. But really it's down to all of us to make sure we get back in one piece. My crew seem to have a lot of faith in me. Maybe it's because they know I've been there and back a few times. They're a good crowd. We'll be just fine.'

'And what is your lucky mascot called?' Aircrews always had a lucky mascot, didn't they?

'We don't have one, though one'll turn up, bet your life on it.'

The music stopped and they linked little fingers and walked back to their corner. Then she turned to him, smiling.

'Y'know, Jon, we've known each other less than three hours, yet it feels like I've always known you.'

'Maybe you did, in another life.'

'You believe in reincarnation? Don't you think it's a bit unchristian?' Her mother wouldn't believe in it!

'No.'

He was very firm about it. He wanted to say that when you aren't yet twenty-three and it's odds-on there's a Messerschmitt pilot with your name on his list, reincarnation is a very good thing to believe in; a second chance, sort of. But he didn't say it, because right now, come hell or high water, he was going to do his tour of ops and come off flying for a year at least and by then, who knew what would have happened between them? Because tonight wasn't a one-off. Tonight, when finally he saw her, could put a face to the voice in the blackout, he knew he'd been meant to meet her. She was the girl he'd been waiting for since ever he could remember. Fair, blue-eyed and beautiful. A virgin too.

'Well, I mean –' he floundered, when she didn't speak. 'Wouldn't you want a second chance; maybe get it right next time around? Or maybe do the same, only more so. I don't know why I believe in it and I haven't had any fearsome flashes of a past life either. I don't think, though, that you can just snuff out a soul.'

'Don't! *Please*. Let's talk about tomorrow? Will you be flying tomorrow night?'

'Not if this fog keeps up – and our met. boys think it will. I don't think we'll be on serious ops for a week or two yet. We've got a lot of sprog pilots and you can't just throw a squadron in at the deep end. I reckon we'll have a few milk runs, first – easy ops, I mean. Shall we try to meet? About eight-ish?'

'Could you make it a little before nine? Mum and Dad always listen to the news. I'd have a better chance if the news was on.'

'So give me instructions from Laceby village then?'

The band began to play a waltz.

'This'll have to be the last one, Jon. It's almost ten. But getting to Laburnum is fairly straightforward, if you take the right fork at the pub. Can you lay hands on a decent torch? You'll need one if it's foggy. You pass six oak trees on your left, then keep on to where the road turns sharp left. Got that?'

He said he had, and drew her closer.

'The left-hand road is to Lancaster. To get to Laburnum you turn right. It's just a dirt road really, and about a hundred yards to a big wooden gate. To the left of it, there's a little iron one. Wait there. Don't push through it because it squeaks, and the dog might hear you. Wait there, and I'll come to you. Even if it's only for a minute, I'll get out somehow!'

'I'll be there – fog permitting. I'll hang around for about half an hour. If you can't make it tomorrow night, I'll be there again on Monday – same time. That all right?'

'If you're sure you want to . . .'

'You know I want to.'

'All right, then,' she whispered. 'And Jon – I want to as well. Very much.'

FIVE

'All right, Miss Goody Two-Shoes! Tell! The lot!' Bessie blew out the candle, snuggling bouncily beneath the bedclothes. 'There's you, draped all over that pilot . . .'

'He's called Jon!'

'. . . draped all over him like there was no tomorrow! And where did you get to on the way home? We were waiting ages at the gate for you!'

'You weren't, Bess. We were right behind you. And don't spoil it for me? I still can't believe it!'

Only now, safely in bed, could they talk about the dance.

'Well, I only hope we weren't missed at the beetle drive.' In a village the size of Laceby Green, someone was bound to let the cat out of the bag, Bessie fretted, by demanding of her mother where she and her friend had been.

'So do I!' The more she thought about it, the more Rosamund realized what a foolish, risky, marvellous thing she had done. 'But I wouldn't have missed it for anything. Jon is – oh, he's just wonderful. I'm seeing him tomorrow . . .'

'You are *what*? And just how are you going to get out? Mum can't keep on writing letters. Even she's going to get suspicious before very long!'

'Not a date, exactly. But he understands. Said he didn't mind the walk. He broke his leg, you see, and walking's good for it,' she whispered throatily.

'Now listen here . . .' Bessie groped for the matchbox, relighting the candle. There was some explaining to be done, and she wanted a light on the subject! 'Tell me, will you, just how you're going to manage it? Your mother won't let you – even I know that! And where is he supposed to walk to?'

'To Laburnum.'

'To *your* place? Have you gone out of your mind, Rosamund Kenton?'

'I think I have and what's more, I don't care!' Maybe in the morning, when she had got her breath back and the stardust had blown away, she would wonder what she had done. But not tonight. Not when her body tingled from the nearness of him and her lips still felt his kisses. 'And he isn't calling at the house, exactly. I'm meeting him outside.'

'But *how* for Pete's sake?'

'I don't know. But Jon understands the position. I told him about Mum, and how – well, *protective* she is . . .'

'And how suspicious-minded and snotty as well?'

'Now would I say that?'

'Only if you want to frighten him off – and I can't think you do. So tell me?'

'Jon said he'd be at the gate around nine, when the news is on; I think I'll be able to slip out then.'

'But how long do you think it'll be before you're missed?'

'Not long. But I can get away with five minutes, I'm sure of it.'

'The poor bloke is going to walk all that way in the blackout on a cold night, for *five minutes* at your gate? Well, all I can say is that he must have got it bad – or he's having you on!'

'He'll be there.' She wished she could be as sure as she sounded.

'Did you ask him if he's married?'

'Of course I didn't and of course he isn't. He's twenty-two, that's all!'

'That's more than old enough, Rosamund! If I were as attractive as he is and on ops, I'd be married – or something.'

'By *something* you mean he's bound to have a steady girl?'

'Well, wouldn't you, if you couldn't be sure which night you'd cop it up on? I mean –' She stopped, all at once contrite. 'Oh, drat my big mouth! That was an awful thing to say! And me with two brothers at sea! But you know what I mean, love?'

'I know. Think I'm stupid? But my mother *is* protective and she can be suspicious-minded, too. In fact, up until tonight, I thought you only did it once to get a baby. Like a bull and a cow. That's what I'd been led to believe, though I knew loving had to be better than that. And now I know it is! The way I feel about him, I know there's more to *that* than laying back and thinking about England! I think doing it with someone you love, isn't – well – dirty.'

'Well, of course it isn't, and it's wrong of your mother to let you think it is!'

'I know that now. I wish she were more like yours, Bess, so I could really talk to her. But she seems to be obsessed with keeping my mind off men; as if she doesn't want me to have anything to do with them till the war is over. It's like she thinks the men I'm likely to meet these days are fly-by-nights and only after one thing.'

'Some of them are. Mick is a marvellous dancer and gorgeous with it, but I'll bet he's been around, for all that. And you can't blame a tail-end Charlie for wanting to live a little, can you?'

'So you wouldn't, Bess – not with Mick?'

'Wouldn't let him, you mean? No way – unless we were engaged, and there's no chance of that! But he's fun. I'm seeing him again next Saturday. There'll be another dance if they aren't on ops.'

'Jon's one of the few there who's done any active flying. Most of the squadron are sprogs and he said they wouldn't be thrown in at the deep end just yet. He thought they'd do a few easy ops first.'

'Let's hope so, though I don't suppose any op is easy. Just getting one of those bombers into the air and back on the runway would give me the shakes. Sometimes I'm glad I'm in a reserved occupation, but now I think I'd like to have joined the WAAF. It's more glamorous. "What did you do in the war, Mummy?" "Worked in a shirt factory, dear." At least you can pretend you were a land girl, Rosamund.'

'I am a land girl, though not an official one. I wish I could be. There'd be a chance of getting sent to a hostel to live, and I could get out at night without having to tell lies or cause bother at home. How am I going to make it to the dance next Saturday?' And why, she wanted to know, did they have to live so far from the village that her mother had a good excuse in winter to keep her in? 'I wish we were on the phone.'

'Well, you can't be now. You can't get the phone put in for love nor money till the war's over. You should have got one before they went under the counter.'

'I don't suppose we could afford one when the war started.'

And even if they could, it wouldn't have been allowed. Telephones made it easy for people to get to you. Her mother would think they were an intrusion into their life. Her mother didn't want people. It was why they lived at Laburnum Farm.

'Bess, *how* am I going to get out next Saturday night? I can't keep saying I'm going to a beetle drive and your mother can't keep asking me to stay the night at your place.'

'You've got it bad, haven't you? We're going to have to do a bit of thinking about this one.'

'Like what?'

'You'll have to ask me to your place. We'll find an excuse.'

'We won't, you know.' Bessie wasn't welcome at Laburnum Farm. 'Anyway, it isn't as if you can call by chance – pretend you were out for a walk.' Nobody went for long walks in winter. 'I hate the blackout. It's as if it takes your life over . . .'

'Aircrews have to fly in it. There and back in the pitch-black.'

'Jon's flown seven ops.'

'Now we're back to the pilot again!'

'I know. He seems to be all I can think about. Sssssh . . .'

A knocking on the wall reminded them that Mr Drake was on earlies, and needed his sleep.

'We'll talk about it tomorrow,' Bessie whispered, blowing out the candle. 'Maybe we can get Mum on our side. Now snuggle up and close your eyes. Night, love. Sleep tight.'

But Rosamund couldn't, wouldn't, didn't want to sleep. She needed to stay awake and live every marvellous minute again. Because it had been wonderful to dance close, and whisper together, and kiss. Especially kissing. Properly. Not like screwing your mouth up and touching someone's cheek, but real kissing that took your breath away and made you want to be closer, and touch and fondle.

Doing *it* with Jon would be unbelievably beautiful. Jon would know what to do, like he'd known how to kiss. Jon would make it easy so neither of them was embarrassed.

She thought of her mother and father and squeezed her eyelids tighter, because she knew she hadn't been conceived in love. And then she thought about the bull in the cow pasture and her mother saying she must never watch because that was what animals did and she was too young to understand.

But she had watched and it had been very ordinary. The bull stumbled clumsily away from the cow afterwards, and the cow had gone on cropping grass. It was why she had believed what her mother told her about *things*. Until now, that was.

She lay very still. It had been easy to dance with Jon; once she relaxed her body, the pressure of his hand on her back told her what to do. Easy too to dance close, hardly moving their feet. And it hadn't mattered one bit, because every couple in that bare, stuffy hut was doing it. Her mother would have – She pushed her mother from her thoughts. Tonight belonged to Rosie and Jon.

Rosie. No one had been allowed to call her that; had received a sharp correction if they'd ever tried. But Rosie Kenton was a different person. Rosie went to dances on the sly and stole outside into the blackout to kiss.

Kissing was wonderful with Jon. Walking the short cut across the fields to Bessie's house had been wonderful too, because they had stumbled a lot in the dark, and had had to cling tightly.

Jonathan. Rosamund. Jon and Rosie. Would things come right for them or would they spend the rest of the war meeting at the gate? Meeting, kissing, parting. But never mind the rest of the war – how was she to get to the dance, next week? Lies and more lies, or would Mrs Drake help? Mrs Drake was scatty and laughed a lot. Why didn't her mother laugh? What was so awful in her life that laughter seemed out of place at Laburnum Farm?

She turned carefully to lay on her back because it was useless trying to sleep. How could she sleep when Jon might be awake, and thinking about her? She sent her love to him, then closed her eyes, the better to see him. And to beg him silently to be there tomorrow night.

A tear trickled down her cheek, and plopped into her ear. And why, in heaven's name, was she crying when tonight was the most important, wonderful, most mind-boggling night of her life? At a little after half-past seven they had met – *bumped* – and by eight they were talking, laughing, dancing as if they'd known each other since ever they could remember and had a lifetime of Saturday nights ahead of them. Another tear trickled and plopped and she wondered if people really did cry when they were happy. Or did they cry because they had fallen in love and wanted to go to the aerodrome dance again next Saturday night. And couldn't . . . ?

'Hullo, both! I'm back!' Rosamund closed the shippon door quickly behind her because even cowsheds must be blacked out. She had left Bessie's house very early so she could insist on doing her usual stint of milking; had made up her mind to do everything possible to put her mother in a good mood so that tonight she wouldn't ask her where she was going when she got to her feet a few minutes before nine o'clock. 'I'll just get into my overalls . . .'

'No need. We're nearly finished. Put the kettle on and make a start with the breakfast, will you?'

Her mother sounded quite cheerful, she thought thankfully, wishing it hadn't come down foggy again; glad that it had because there wouldn't be any flying at the aerodrome tonight.

She built up the kitchen fire and filled the kettle, sorry she had thought such awful things about her mother – about her father too – determined this morning at chapel to pray extra hard about the dance on Saturday night; beg that some small miracle might make it possible for her to go again. She just had to. She couldn't bear it if she couldn't, and Jon danced with someone else.

She shut her mind to something so awful and busied herself

with laying the table, getting out bacon and eggs ready for the pan. She cut three thick slices from the loaf so that when the fire burned red again, she might toast them. Marmalade and saccharin. She ran to the dairy and filled a jug with milk. Oh, please let Saturday night happen . . .

'I'll pour you a cup, Mum.' She was surprised how steady her hand was. 'Sorry I was a bit late – the fog . . .'

'You can't be blamed for the fog. How did everything go?'

'Oh, fine. Just the usual, you know. Mrs Drake's bus was late back from Preston; she had a headache and had a lie down on the sofa. Mr Drake has to work today – earlies.'

'Not right, that, but I reckon soldiers have to fight on Sundays; sailors too. Happen working on a Sunday is to be forgiven if it's for the war.'

Rosamund noticed that her mother didn't include the Royal Air Force in her absolution. She was good at ignoring things she didn't approve of. But wait till the fog lifted and the circuits and bumps started again, and bombers coming in so low to land that her mother cringed and closed her eyes tightly and said, 'Heaven help us! Why don't they just come in through the front door, and have done with it?'

'You won't be putting the cows out, Dad?'

'No, lass. Not in weather like this. Best leave them in the foldyard. Put some fodder down for them after breakfast, will you?'

She said she would, and was glad there was no more mention of the beetle drive. And since her mother had registered their ration books with a Clitheroe grocer, there was little chance of her going into Laceby in the near future and finding out exactly who hadn't been at the parish hall last night.

Rosamund said a silent thank you, then began to cook breakfast, always ready to remind herself how lucky she was to have bacon and eggs every day, and count her blessings as her mother was always insisting she should.

Listen, God! I'll count them fifty times a day if only you'll make it all right for Saturday night!

★　　★　　★

Bart Kenton harnessed the pony into the trap, then left it outside whilst he changed into his Sunday suit. Mildred Kenton felt almost content as they set out. She looked forward to Sunday service and meeting people of like beliefs. St Mary's at Laceby Green was very High Church, and there was too much bowing for her liking. It was why she went to chapel.

Rosamund closed the gate behind them as she always did, then climbed up to sit beside her mother. It was very cold, and she pulled her muffler round her ears and stuffed her hands into her pockets.

The fog seemed to be lifting, though nothing could yet be seen of the aerodrome. She marvelled that Jon was so near, and that had he been able to walk the perimeter track, he could get to the far end of the cow pasture in no time at all. But then he would come up against the high, steel-mesh fence, so there was nothing for it but to walk the long way round. And that didn't seem fair for five minutes!

The pony began to trot, the wheels turned faster. She wished her father would get a car. Cars were cheap now because of petrol rationing. Most people kept theirs in the garage for six months of the year to eke out their coupons. She could drive the tractor, Rosamund reasoned, and would soon get used to driving a car. And all you had to do now was to apply for a licence, because driving tests had been suspended for the duration.

A car, just a little one, would be the answer to everything, even if they were the very devil to drive in the dark with lights so dimmed-out they were useless. But just imagine being able to drive into Laceby to meet Jon . . .

And why was she making such a fuss when it was obvious Jon wouldn't be there tonight. Why should he be? Tonight he'd be off to the nearest civilization with the rest of the crew, because who in his right mind would trudge all that way in the blackout to spend a few minutes with a girl as naive as Rosamund Kenton? Mind, *Rosie* was a different proposition entirely, and a quick learner. Maybe Rosie was worth the long, cold walk. She closed her eyes tightly, despairingly, then opened them wide to reality.

Idiot! Of course he wouldn't be there! He would stand her up; nothing was more certain. A good-looking man like him, with wings up, too, wouldn't waste his time on a farmer's clodhopping daughter. Pilots were glamorous, and every girl's pin-up. Jon could take his pick of half the females in Lancashire; girls whose parents let them go out on dates! They shouldn't have gone to that dance. There'd have been none of this soul-searching if they'd stuck to the beetle drive.

Nor would she have met Jon Hunt, and fallen deeply in love. It was a sobering thought.

The day was one great anticlimax of doubt and torment, and the niggling worry that Jon was writing to his girl at this very moment. Or his wife. But she would forgive him for not turning up, because last night had been wonderful and something to remember always; the night she learned that kissing the right man is giddy-making, once you've learned how it is done.

So chalk it up to experience, she insisted silently, carefully wiping clean the day's egg collection, and be thankful that Rosie had a brilliant time and danced all night with the best-looking man in the room.

She had been very well-behaved at chapel; had smiled extra sweetly at the minister's wife and whispered her prayers most devoutly. Especially so when they'd prayed for the King and Queen and all members of the Armed Forces – Allied Forces, of course – and asked a blessing on all who mourned or were sick in body or mind. It was only then that she'd slipped in a quick one on her own behalf and begged most earnestly for just five minutes at the iron gate tonight. With Jon.

After dinner, she washed dishes and cleaned pans without even being asked, then straightaway helped with the afternoon milking which, on winter Sundays began at three o'clock. By five, she had put the milk through the cooler, hosed down the milking parlour, and found there were still four hours to be lived through.

'Think I'll check the hens,' she said to no one in particular, taking the torch which wasn't blacked out. She wasn't afraid of being alone in the dark and walked past the pigsty and the foldyard and through the yard gate to the paddock.

She checked that each ark was secure, then walked to the dry-stone wall, switching off the light, breathing softly so she might listen to night sounds; a hunting owl, the distant bark of a dog, the cry of a vixen.

She gazed in the direction of the aerodrome, but could make out only one dim blue glow. No other light showed; no sound came to her on the wind. Marauding enemy fighters would find it near impossible to find RAF Laceby Green, so complete and secure was its blackout.

Switching on the torch again she made her way down past the hen arks, pausing to speak to Shep, who lay head on paws in his kennel, and who blinked as she shone the light on him.

'Don't bark tonight, will you?' she whispered. It made her insides churn just to think about getting out, so she stood quite still, closed her eyes, crossed her fingers and wished: not just that Jon would be at the gate tonight, but that with the help of a small miracle so too might she.

Her parents were sitting in the front parlour when she got back. Because of the fuel shortage, a fire was only lit there on winter Sundays. In summer it was used all the time, with the windows open to the long evenings and the view from them so heartachingly beautiful that you had to believe in God. And on this dreary Sunday, she longed for the freedom of sunlight and warmth, because November was the month of the dead, some said, when unshriven souls roamed free.

'Everything's all right outside,' she whispered to her father's newspaper. Sunday papers were allowed now at Laburnum Farm because they were so skimpy – usually no more than six pages. War news took precedence and there was no space left for the reporting of divorce cases, and sleazy goings-on in hotel rooms in which intimacy had taken place. The Forces programme was allowed too, because if it was good enough for our fighting men (no mention of women!), then it was good enough for Laburnum Farm.

Her father gave a grunt of acknowledgement; her mother

nodded. She was turning the heel of a sock and had come to the fiddly bit so she didn't even bother to glance up.

Rosamund liked the low-ceilinged room with its ages-old hearth piled with spitting, flaming logs, but tonight she remembered they were beech logs from five proudly beautiful trees, and thought of the day she had watched their destruction.

On the wireless, Vera Lynn was singing and after that would be music from the Grand Hotel. Then it would be time for the news and Big Ben would chime nine – recorded, of course – and when the booming was over would come the Minute for Reflection, though tonight she would be too jumpy to reflect upon any of the things she ought.

She felt fidgety. She wanted to talk, but feared her words would come in a babble that would make her mother look up, narrow-eyed. Instead, she closed her eyes, counting the slow ticking of the mantel clock, trying to breathe evenly and deeply.

Where was Jon now? It was almost half-past eight, so maybe he had left Laceby behind him and was making for the clump of oaks on the left-hand side of the lane, wanting to reach the gate early, just in case . . .

No! He would be in the mess, drinking. Or writing to the VAD girl who helped nurse him when he was in hospital blues, or to the aunt who had taken the place of his mother. He would *not* be passing six oaks! It stood to reason. Why should someone like Jon Hunt fall for a milkmaid, because that's what she was! If ever he sneaked up on her and put his hands over her eyes and said, 'Guess who?' she would smell of milk and cowhide and ever so slightly dungy! Even if she were the only female for miles around, she doubted he would fall for her as crazily and completely as she had fallen for him.

She opened her eyes and looked at the clock. Twenty minutes still to go. She wondered if she should speak, but her father was still reading and her mother still counting stitches.

Her heart was making a terrible noise and she wondered why they seemed not to hear it. But hearts apart, what would she say when nine o'clock came?

'I think I'll go upstairs and tidy my drawers.' Not allowed when the news was on!

'Would either of you like a cup of tea?' Neither was the indiscriminate wasting of the tea ration.

'Excuse me – I'm just popping across the yard.'

Even the hallowed news could not prevent her needing a wee. And thank heaven for an outside lavatory, cold and uncomfortable though it was! It would be the perfect excuse, though just to think of it made her want to giggle hysterically. Just how romantic could you get!

The minute hand of the clock – and she would swear it was so until her dying day – stopped at a quarter to nine; at ten minutes to and again, five minutes before nine. She bit on her lip, determined not to look at it again for an hour, by which time she would switch on the wireless in time to hear Big Ben.

Her father lowered his paper, turning the page. It made a terrible noise and reminded her to look again at the clock.

'Excuse me,' she said croakily. 'I'm just popping –'

'Ssssssh,' her father said softly, nodding towards the chair opposite.

'Sorry,' she mouthed. Dear sweet heaven! Her mother was asleep, fingers still, her mouth ever so slightly open. 'Won't be a minute . . .'

Bart Kenton let the paper slip to the floor, folded his arms over his stomach, and closed his eyes.

Oh, glory! It had been so easy it was as if it were meant to be! Quietly she closed the kitchen door, then groped her way to the windowsill where the torch always stood, taking her coat and muffler from the peg, shrugging into them. Then she closed the back door and walked softly to the kennel.

'Good boy, Shep. It's only me.' She stroked his head, then walked in the direction of the yard gate, blinking rapidly as she went.

She held out a hand, trailing it along the wall to her left, then drew in a steadying breath.

God! This is Rosamund Kenton. Thank you . . .

She turned the corner into the narrow path that skirted the

farm buildings, then hurried to the iron gate – and please, please don't let it squeak tonight.

She let go a nervous cough, then relief coursed through her as she heard a movement ahead of her.

'Jon . . . ?' She began to run, wanting to shout out with joy, knowing that if she did, it would end in a sob of disbelief. Arms took her, pulled her close and she closed her eyes, not able to speak because of the noise in her ears; a great chorus of hallelujahs, with stars exploding all over the sky.

She felt the remembered roughness of his uniform, then laid her cheek on his. His face was cold and she whispered her lips across his chin, his eyelids. She was shaking so much she had to cling to him tightly.

'Please kiss me,' she whispered when the turmoil inside her had died down, 'then I'll know it's really you.'

'You thought I wouldn't be here?' he demanded huskily.

'Yes. I wanted you to be, but common sense told me you wouldn't turn up.'

'So see how wrong you can be about airmen who pick you up in the blackout?' he murmured, kissing her again.

'Hold me tightly?'

'How did you manage to get out?' He unbuttoned his greatcoat, then folded her inside it.

'Said I was popping out to the lavvy – it was the only thing I could think of!'

She began to giggle, because outside lavatories just weren't a part of shooting stars and music in your ears and falling in love.

'And how long can you make it last?'

'About three more minutes, though Mum was asleep so she won't know when I went.'

'Then let's live dangerously, and take five? Shall I come again tomorrow night?'

'Do you want to?' she whispered incredulously. 'All that way?'

'All that way, and back,' he said firmly.

'Then shall we make it eight, tomorrow night – vary it a bit?'

'If that's what you want – but what about Saturday?'

'I'll be there,' she said recklessly. 'And it's ages since you kissed me.'

She offered her mouth, and small, wayward pulses beat behind her nose and in her throat and the giddy feeling was back again, and the need to be closer.

'This is a stupid thing to say.' His lips were still on hers. 'But all at once I believe in love at first sight. I thought about you – *us* – half into the night; told myself it was just that you were attractive and the sort of girl I wanted to be seen around with. But it's more than that, Rosie . . .'

'I know. I want it too – want us to be lovers. I couldn't stop wondering what it would be like with you. I've never thought such a thing before. Does that make me common?'

'No, darling. And what was it like, with me?'

'Oh – nice and gentle. And easy. Just like it was when we first kissed. Right, somehow . . .'

'We're mad, aren't we? I've known you just a day, yet it seems like for ever. And we haven't got for ever, Rosie.'

'Yes, we have. I love you so much that nothing can harm you! We're special, you and me. And, Jon – it's such a relief to be normal. I thought there was something wrong with me before last night.'

'There is nothing wrong with you. You are absolutely perfect. You do believe in love at first sight?'

'Mm. And in reincarnation too. I've got to now. One lifetime together won't be enough. There'll have to be another life after this one and we'll come back and fall in love all over again.'

'That's a promise. And, my lovely girl, we've had our five minutes. I don't want to leave you.'

'It's all right.' She closed her eyes and lifted her lips. 'There's all the time in the world for us. Two worlds. Kiss me good night, then shove me in the direction of the foldyard?'

'I'll walk with you.'

'No! Say good night here, at the gate. Shep'll get wind of you if you walk up the path.'

She snuggled into his coat, wrapping her arms around him, loving him so much it was like a song inside her.

'Good night, Rosie Kenton. See you.'

'Tomorrow, at eight. Is all this real, Jon?'

'Yes, and I love you.'

'I love you too. When will it happen for us, darling?'

'When the time is right. We'll know . . .'

Her mother and father were both asleep when she tiptoed into the living room. The fire had burned low, and she knelt to place logs on it. Then she turned on the Forces programme with the volume very low and went to sit in her chair as if she had never been to the kissing gate and told Jon she loved him and promised to meet him again tomorrow at eight. If they weren't flying, that was, and why should they be? How *could* they be, even on a milk run?

She kicked off her shoes and tucked her feet beneath her, curling into a ball, hugging herself tightly because already she missed his arms. Tomorrow night, at the iron gate. And Saturday night, outside the parish hall, waiting for the transport to pick them up. Because nothing would stop her going to the dance. For the first time in her life she felt free and wholesome, and the things she thought about love and loving *were* normal. It was her mother who'd got it wrong.

She raised her head. Her mother hadn't moved. The knitting lay on her lap and her mouth was a little open still. Her father was sleeping too; each completely unaware that their daughter had given her heart away at the rusty gate. Rosamund had crept out, but it was Rosie who returned, and nothing could be the same again.

She could still feel Jon's mouth hard on hers, and touched her lips gently. She was glad he was the first; that no one had ever kissed her with passion before, nor taken her. She was his entirely. They had collided in the blackout because on the day Rosamund Kenton was born, Someone-up-there wrote in her Book of Life that on the first Saturday in November, in the year 1943, she would meet the love of her life. There was nothing anyone could do to change it. Not even her mother could order Fate about!

Comforted, she curled into a ball again, closing her eyes

tightly to live again their minutes at the gate. Tonight, when she went to bed, she would take his kisses and his arms and the nearness of him with her. And dream of him all night.

When the alarm jangled her awake next morning, she realized she had not dreamed, and when she lit the candle and got unsteadily to her feet, she saw her bed was crumpled, as if she had tossed restively all night. And in the cold November darkness, when the stardust had gone and she felt lonely and alone, she wondered how she was to make it to the aerodrome dance.

Her foot touched something soft and cold. On the floor lay the rag doll that sat astride her bedhead; had done so since ever she could remember. Matilda Mint, with eyes carefully embroidered beneath her fringe of bright yellow wool, and surprised eyebrows almost touching it. Matty, who wore a green cotton frock and white apron and who, until Rosamund went to school, was her inseparable companion. She had grown out of Matty, of course, but had never discarded her. 'Oh, Matilda Mint,' she picked up the doll; 'I know what I'm going to do with you!'

The doll smiled at her in the candlelight and all at once everything came right, and the stardust was back. She gave a little laugh, all doubts gone, then reached for her clothes, pulling on her thick sweater, tucking her trousers into bright red, knee-high socks.

A light shone beneath the door of her parents' bedroom; they were not yet up. She padded down the kitchen stairs and into the dairy, pulling on gumboots; shrugging into the jacket that smelled of the milking parlour.

A box of matches rattled in her pocket; first one up always lit the hurricane lamps and hung them in the shippon. She took a deep breath against a wind that blew from the north-east and hit her face like a slap; a wind that arose in the night to blow away the fog. She bent to release the dog, and it yelped gratefully, then made for the barn and the warmth of the hay. For the first time in many mornings she could see stars, and her first fearful thought was for the crew of *J-Johnnie*.

By the light of a torch, she lit the lamps. Her mother always kept them filled with paraffin and the wicks free of soot. One day, when electricity came to Laburnum Farm, there would be instant light in the shippon, and lights in the foldyard and over the back door, her father said. But the war had put paid to all that, because electricity had to be used sparingly and anyway, most electricians had been called up. But one day, when the war was over and things were back to normal again, they would have an electric cooker, even, and a wireless that didn't need batteries. And why she was thinking such stupid things when all that mattered was that the sky was clear, and tonight could well witness RAF Laceby Green's first operational flight? She made a mental note to ask Jon – if he came tonight – exactly where *J-Johnnie* had its standing and if it would have to pass the end of the cow pasture in its way to takeoff. He wouldn't be able to see her in the darkness, but he would know she was there, sending love to him, wishing them all well. And a safe return.

When her father came bleary-eyed to the shippon, Rosamund was happy with hope again, the shippon was lighted, milking pails and stools at the ready, and the first twenty cows herded from the foldyard and chained in their stalls.

'Morning, Dad.' She kissed his cheek. 'Has Mum got the kettle on?'

'Aye. She'll be over with drinkings afore long.' He yawned, and even in the gentle lampglow, he looked older than he had any right to.

'Are you all right?' They only had half a farm now. He shouldn't look so tired.

'Just fine, lass. But I woke up in the middle of the night and couldn't get back to sleep again. Happen I'll try to get a bit of a doze before afternoon milking. I'll be as right as rain then.'

When she returned with a bucket of broken cow cake, Rosamund said softly, 'You aren't worrying about anything, Dad? The farm, I mean, and all the forms? Are we managing, now They have taken our acres?'

'Of course we are! The Air Force took away half of our workload too, don't forget, and we don't have to pay rent on the fields they requisitioned. We get regular cheques from the egg packers and the Milk Marketing Board; we're better off than we've ever been, though it took a war to do it! What makes you ask, Rosamund? After a rise in your wages?'

'No, Dad. Of course not!'

Mind, she would settle for a night off sometimes; time of her own she didn't have to ask for, or cause an upset to get. Just sometimes, she would like to be like other girls and have dates. Bessie could manage it, if she wanted to. But she had missed her cue. When asked if she wanted more money had been the perfect time to say she wouldn't mind a night off, a couple of times a week.

Best leave it for the time being because her father looked tired and worried, and the confrontation, when it came, would have to be with her mother. No more involving her father. About time she stood on her own two feet and spoke up for herself! Tomorrow, as soon as she got the chance, she would tell her mother she wanted to go out again on Saturday; with or without permission!

Without permission – words to send fear shivering through her. Until this morning, that was! Why not, she thought as she made her way along the stalls, clattering feed into the troughs, go the whole crazy hog and say she wanted to go to the aerodrome dance? Since she'd met Jon, she was light-headed enough to do it, an' all!

No! Wrong! Rosamund was silly enough to jump in with both feet! Rosie, though, was altogether different; was a woman in love and had left the ordered, sheltered days of her childhood behind her. And Rosie was going to the dance next Saturday night!

'No need for you to milk this morning, Mum,' she said when Mildred Kenton arrived with mugs of tea. 'And I'll see to the cooler and the churns, as well. After all, I do owe you one. You milked for me last Saturday, don't forget.'

'If you're sure . . . ?'

Her mother too looked tired. Perhaps she had not slept either. Had there been words between them in the night?

True, her parents seemed never to quarrel, but maybe they saved their grudges for the bedroom.

'I'm sure, Mum. Me and Dad'll see to it.'

'Aye, Milly. Off you go.' Her father added his weight to hers.

'Mum looks as if she could have done with a lie-in too,' Rosamund said when her mother had closed the shippon door behind her. 'What kept you both awake?'

'Nothing that I know of. But you must bear with your mother, lass. She's at a funny age for a woman, and losing our fields didn't do anything to help.'

'But we'll get them back after the war?'

'We'll get summat back when it's over, that's true.' Bart turned to face his daughter, though his fingers still squeezed and pulled rhythmically. 'But are they going to shift all that concrete first? We were given nothing in writing to say they'll make good what they did. All they ever said was that they wanted our fields. You don't argue with the Air Ministry, nor ask for guarantees.'

'I suppose not. People in the Forces can't ask either. I suppose they just take each day as it comes,' she whispered, her voice all at once trembly, 'and hope like mad they'll be lucky.'

'Like I used to hope. And the day that Armistice was signed, I vowed I'd never grumble again.'

'Sorry, Dad . . .' How stupid of her, and thoughtless! Her father knew what living from day to day was like, had spent three years in the trenches. Not that he ever talked about it. No one she knew who'd been in the Great War ever said much. 'Was it awful for you?'

'Awful? No. Just plain bloody hell. Folk say there isn't a hell, that you make your own here on earth, Rosamund. Well, my hell is called Ypres. But what's got into us? There's fifty cows to be milked and we're wittering on like there's no tomorrow!'

'Sorry.' Chastened, she took a pail and milking stool. She had never before heard her father swear and suddenly realized he had been a person in his own right before he and Mum were married; had been Bartholomew Kenton, soldier and herdsman. Then he and Mum met, though neither of them once said where or when, and she had never once thought to ask.

She tucked her hair into her milking cap, then wriggled herself comfortable, head against the side of the cow, trying to concentrate on the job in hand, thinking instead of Jon and wondering what he was doing and if, perhaps, he was thinking of her.

Then her lips moved into a small secret smile, because she knew Jon would still be in his RAF-type, black-painted iron bed, with Air Ministry-issue blankets on it. His hair would be tousled, she thought fondly, and his chin would be scratchy with fair hairs. She wondered what it would be like to spend the whole night with him and opening her eyes to find him still beside her. Was heaven too of our own making?

'No, idiot! Heaven,' she whispered very, very softly, 'is eight o'clock tonight, at the iron gate.'

Amazingly, she was there on time and amazingly she had not used the lavatory excuse.

'I'm going up to the big attic to look for something,' she said, three minutes before eight o'clock. 'Is the blackout all right?'

She knew it was; that the skylights had been covered with several coats of black paint and only heaven knew how they would get it off when the war was over.

By rights, all attics and roof voids should be empty. Because of air raids, nothing was to be stored in them in case of incendiaries falling through the roof. Fire bombs were far easier to put out when you didn't have to plough through years of rubbish to throw sand over them. But their attics were still full of junk, because Mildred Kenton chose not to empty them. Laburnum Farm was hers and not even Winston Churchill told her what she might and might not keep in her own roof space!

Rosamund took a candle, then closed the kitchen door behind her, running noisily up the front stairs as far as the half-landing; walking quietly down again to where she had left her coat.

She hated the deceit and lies, but if she had to, she would

lie with her right hand on a stack of Bibles if that was what it took to see Jon.

She slipped out of the side door, letting go her indrawn breath in a huff of relief. The wind blew scuds of dark clouds across a half-moon. On her left she could pick out the dark bulk of the farm buildings. Just about twenty steps away – you always counted in the blackout – Jon would be at the little gate, though if he were not, she didn't know how long she dare wait.

Jon was there. She had known, deep down, that he would be, and went into his arms to stand close, kissing urgently.

'I've brought something for you,' she said when they drew apart. 'It's something you want – need . . .'

'You, on a plate?'

'No. She's to be your mascot. You're to take her with you always when you fly. She's called Matilda Mint, and I've had her ever since I can remember.'

'A *doll* . . .' She could hear the laughter in his voice.

'A rag doll. She went everywhere with me till I went to school. She got so tatty Mum said I should throw her away, but I couldn't. She's been hanging on my bedpost for years, so I want you to hang her in *J-Johnnie* and then a part of me will be with you,' she finished breathlessly.

'Thank you,' he said gravely. 'I'll take good care of her.'

'And I promise she'll take good care of you, Jon. You don't think it's sissy, grown men taking a doll along?'

'Not a bit. At my last station, one crew always took a teddy bear called Maurice. One of the WAAF drivers knitted him a little scarf. Maurice wouldn't fly without it. Tell me something?'

'I love you, love you. You won't be flying on Saturday, will you – the dance, I mean?'

'I don't know. But if we do go, there won't be a dance anyway. You'll know if there's an op on. You'll hear us taking off.'

'Promise you'll always be careful?'

'Promise. I've got my girl to come home to now.'

'Mm. And it just might be a milk run. What are milk runs like?'

'Short. Sometimes to drop window – fine, metallic strips to muck up their radar. And sometimes a squadron will create a diversion to draw enemy fighters away from the main bomber stream. Not so much risk . . .'

'You're to take care, for all that.'

'We mightn't go. I wouldn't want to push my luck, but I've a feeling there'll be a dance on Saturday. You'll be able to make it, Rosie?'

'All taken care of.' It wasn't, but she knew exactly what she would do and say. She didn't want to defy her parents but she would if she had to. 'I'll be there.'

'Do you think,' he whispered many kisses later, 'that we're a couple of fools – falling head over heels and not knowing the first thing about each other?'

'No, but if you like, I'll write down everything I can think of about me. Bad things, good things – the lot – and you're to do the same. That way, we're going to save a lot of kissing time. And I want especially to know what your Aunt Lottie's surname is and where she lives.'

She reached on tiptoe to kiss his chin, marvelling how two people could be so right, so good together.

'Where are you now, Rosie? Gone to the lav again?'

'Tonight, I'm in the attic, looking for something. And I don't like telling lies, Jon. Don't think I do. But I'll get something sorted soon, and that's a promise.'

'Hope so. I'd like to meet your folks, and I want you to come and meet Aunt Lottie next time I get a seventy-two-hour pass.'

'I'd like that a lot, but I don't think I'd be allowed. We-e-ll, not just yet.'

Imagine, she brooded, throwing it at her mother, all off hand: 'By the way, Mum, I met an airman when I was supposed to be at the beetle drive. We're very much in love, and he wants me to meet his aunt.'

'How nice, Rosamund. But I think you'd better bring him to Sunday tea, so we can meet him.'

But no way would her mother invite Jon to tea – or even allow him to call at Laburnum. She would even forbid Saturday night. A pound for a penny, she would!

Distantly, a dog barked, and it reminded Rosamund that she had been away too long.

'That's Shep, darling. It might be Dad, checking the foldyard, or it might be a fox. We often get a vixen in the rocks above the paddock this time of the year. It's getting near their breeding season. I'll have to go, Jon. I'll want desperately to see you, but don't come tomorrow night – it's much too far.'

'It isn't. But if I don't make it by eight, you'll know why.'

'Take care, sweetheart.' She clung tightly, not wanting to leave him. Then she pushed him from her and turned abruptly. 'See you. I love you.'

She left him then, unbuttoning her coat as she ran, all at once realizing that someone else might have heard Shep and gone to investigate. But the foldyard and the stackyard were quiet; the dog too. A fox, surely, or maybe a wild cat.

'I heard Shep barking,' she said as the closed the door behind her.

'I heard him too but it was nothing,' Bart said comfortably. 'Found what you were looking for, lass?'

'No, but it isn't all that important. Just a school photograph – my last year . . .'

'It's in the desk drawer in the parlour,' her mother supplied. 'You should have asked.'

'No bother. I quite enjoyed myself.' She smiled brilliantly, shocked at the ease the lies slipped off her tongue. 'It's surprising what you find when you go rooting. Anyone want a drink?'

'Please, but it'll have to be cocoa. We're a bit short of tea. I'll have to put a smaller spoon in the caddy.'

'Why is tea rationed, Mum, and not cocoa?'

She could talk about cocoa, she marvelled, when not two minutes ago she was in Jon's arms in another world!

'I've no idea, child. The government does what it wants and it isn't for us to reason why. I suppose it'll go on the ration once some bright spark at the Ministry of Food realizes it isn't. And make it with milk, will you?'

Rosamund made for the dairy, jug in hand, marvelling that, for once, her mother seemed quite relaxed. Maybe, she frowned, tomorrow would be a good time to bring up the matter of the Saturday dance.

She set the iron pan to boil on the fire hob, all the time worrying what would happen if her mother flatly refused to allow her out, then shook so awful a thought from her head because if she had to climb out of her bedroom window she would be there on Saturday!

As she spooned cocoa from the tin, she was dismayed to see that her shaking hand had spilled the dark brown powder over the much-scrubbed table top.

God? Let it all come right for us? I love him so much!

SIX

Tuesday was mild, and by midday the sun broke through with an amazing warmth, for November, prompting Bart Kenton to empty the foldyard of cows.

'Walk them to the pasture – let 'em have a bite of grass. We can give the yard a good swill down while they're gone.' And after all, he reasoned, such warmth so late on in the year could only be a weather breeder. Tomorrow it might well be snowing!

It was why Rosamund was in the cow pasture at three, when the nip was back in the air, and a round, red sun beginning to set

'Cush, pet, cooosh . . .' Silly creatures! Why was there always one lingerer at the far end of the field?

It was then she remembered with sudden pleasure that at the end of the pasture was the high, steel-mesh fence and beyond it the aerodrome. And somewhere in all that sprawl was Jon's billet. Perhaps, they could meet at the fence sometimes; just for a minute to whisper, 'Hullo. I love you.'

She laughed out loud, wondering why neither of them had thought of it, making for the wayward cow. Then her laugh died abruptly, and she stood staring at the bomber, so near on its standing that she could read the squadron markings on its fuselage and the letter S. For *Sugar*. It wasn't Jon's Lancaster, but it was having its tail-end gun fitted, whilst amidships men in overalls fed ammunition into the gun that Harry, who had just become a father, would fire, had *Sugar* been Jon's plane.

All at once the awfulness hit her. The bombers were being made ready for operations. They were going tonight, and someone who had a baby less than a week old would fly into darkness and danger with Jon. There would be no meeting at the gate tonight; she would be here instead, watching heavily laden bombers lurch clumsily past; hoping to recognize Jon's Lancaster, willing him to know she was there, loving him, wishing him well.

'Get a move on!' Peevishly she brought the flat of her hand down on the rump of the cow. 'Don't you know there's a war on?'

Of course it didn't know. It went on dropping a calf every year, being milked twice a day, cropping grass and chewing its cud. Nothing else mattered. A cow didn't have feelings except briefly, when its calf was taken from it. None of the herd even flinched now when a bomber flew low over the field. For cows, the war didn't exist.

She closed the fieldgate behind her. She had started to shake and her mouth was all at once dry.

'I'll make a start, Dad. Can you see to the feed?'

Bart Kenton looked up sharply, because his daughter always secured the cows in the stalls and put out scoops of cattle cake. 'Everything all right, Rosamund?'

'Sure.' She pulled on her milking cap, then jammed the bucket between her knees. 'It's just that I'd like to go out sometimes . . .'

'But you do go out.'

'Not in winter. Not without causing an upset.'

'We-e-ll, that's between you and your mother.'

'I know. I don't want to involve you, Dad, but it's time Mum and I got things straight and she stopped calling me *child*.'

'Habit, lass.' He paused beside the cow she was milking. 'What's brought all this on?'

'Nothing in particular. It's just that I enjoyed being at Bessie's and I think Mum should let me go out every Saturday night – if I want to, that is.'

'Seems reasonable enough to me, but like I said –'

'You don't want to get involved. And I don't want you to. I've got to learn to stand up for myself!'

She didn't look at him when she spoke, but kept her head

down, watching the milk hit the sides of the pail. She loved her father very much, and not for anything would she let him get mixed up in her troubles. Because trouble there would be!

She was crossing the stackyard when she heard the noise. It sounded like a distant, spluttering bark. Then it came again and she knew it was the engine of a bomber.

She stood stock-still and the noise became louder as other engines started up. The pilots were running their engines and soon *J-Johnnie* would bump around the perimeter track to the top of the runway. Then a green light would stab through the gloom from the control tower, and Jon's bomber would be hurtling down the concrete strip.

And when they were airborne, when the undercarriage had come up with a thud, they would all let go a gasp of relief as they flew on and upward. She knew exactly how it would be, and hoped Matilda Mint was with them.

Be lucky for him, Matty Mint. Take my love with you.

Then defiance took her, and she began to run. Across the yard, down the path at the side of the farm buildings and through the creaking iron gate.

She would go to the fence; watch as the bombers trundled past on their way to takeoff. It was dark, but a half-moon would show outlines, even if she wasn't able to read the bombers' markings. She would stay until every plane had taken off; wish every crew good luck, and a safe return.

She climbed the gate of the cow pasture, wondering if instinct would tell her when Jon's Lancaster passed by; whether the love between them would make him know she waited at the high, forbidding fence.

She stood there a long time, hardly moving, fingers entwined in the cold steel of the fence. Eleven lights flashed green; eleven bombers hurtled down the runway with a strange, roaring reluctance. She could not see takeoff but saw each bomber as it climbed through a shaft of half-light, and up, up into the sky.

The sound of climbing, circling bombers beat in her head. Soon, they would make formation and head south, or south-east. Was this to be a milk run, a diversionary raid like Jon said, or was it the real thing? Would they drop bombs instead of tinsel shreds?

'Take care, Jon,' she whispered, sending her love high and wide into the uncaring sky. 'Come back safely?'

She turned abruptly and walked across the cow pasture, eyes accustomed to the darkness. Eleven Lancasters had taken off. From the distant noise of one lone engine to the fast-fading roar of eleven bombers, their despatching had taken little more than twenty minutes. So quickly gone, so suddenly and finally.

She moved briskly, all at once aware of the shaking inside her, though whether from cold or fear she wasn't sure. Both, she shouldn't wonder. She felt wretched and useless. She, who loved Jon so much, must wait helpless until she could begin her counting again, all the while sending her love in great warm gusts. It was all she could do for him.

All at once she wished she were a limp rag doll.

'Where is Dad?' Rosamund made for the warmth of the kitchen fire.

'With the heifer. It's started. It was all that noise upset the beast, I shouldn't wonder! Your father could be in the shippon the best part of the night!'

'It's nothing to do with the bombers, Mum. The heifer has been restless all day. Dad likes to be there when it's a first calf – you know he does.'

'So where have you been, Rosamund? Your supper's in the side oven. Ruined, I shouldn't wonder!'

'I was at the bottom of the pasture, watching the bombers.'

'Don't you think that's rather stupid?' Mildred Kenton's head came up sharply. 'Those things are full of bombs and suchlike, and they're only the other side of the fence! Anything could happen! Since that lot came, my nerves have been in shreds!'

'But why? We're safe enough here. If the Air Force had thought we were too near, they'd have made us leave, like at Fellstead Farm.'

'Never mind Fellstead. It's us I'm thinking about! You're not to go there again when those bombers are taking off. It's too dangerous!'

'Only for the aircrews, and Mum – I'd like to go out on Saturday.'

All at once, she was angry; with the war, with the RAF for sending young men on bombing raids and with her mother. Especially with her mother for being so self-centred.

'Out? And where to, for goodness' sake? Off to town, spending your money?'

'How can I spend money when everything is on ration? And I'm saving my coupons for a coat and shoes, anyway. I'd just like to go out for a change. Everybody goes out Saturday nights.'

'*Everybody* doesn't live at Laburnum Farm.'

'I know, and that's the trouble. I live here, work here and sleep here. It was fine when I was at school. I had company my own age. But all at once I'm not to go out in winter! It's because of the aerodrome, isn't it?'

'No, it isn't! It's because I say so! And are you going to eat your supper? There's a war on, don't forget. It's wrong to waste food!'

Rosamund opened the heavy oven door and a wave of warm air hit her. 'So are you going to tell me why I can't go out? What kind of a life is it for me, do you think?'

'A life of luxury, compared to some. You live in a beautiful home and you eat better than most. Why, all at once, is the company of your parents so unbearable?'

'Mother!' She dropped her knife and fork with a clatter. 'You're just twisting things! Being here isn't unbearable and I know how lucky I am. But I get lonely sometimes. I'd like someone of my own age to talk to. Why are you making a big thing of it?'

'It's the Drake girl, isn't it? Whenever you've been with her there's trouble!'

There were bright red spots on her mother's cheeks and her mouth was tight with anger, but Rosamund was past caring. All right! She needed to go out to be with Jon! What was so terrible wanting to go on dates? And why couldn't she tell her parents about him; ask if he could call for her?

Because if your mother thought you wanted to go out to meet a man

*she'd have you locked up! You'd never get beyond the lane end, till
the war was over!*

'The Drake girl has a name, Mother! Bessie — remember?
And she doesn't put ideas into my head. She's just nice to be
with. I went to school with her for years, so why suddenly is
she so dreadful?'

'Nobody said she was dreadful! All I'm trying to say is that
Bessie Drake has brothers and knows about men, and their ways.
You haven't. There is so much you don't know, child!'

'Mum! I know about *things*! I live on a farm! I'm not entirely
ignorant of the facts of life!'

'I'll grant you that. But you weren't brought up to think and
act like an animal, Rosamund Kenton! And as for the facts of
life — you'll soon learn *those* once you're married!'

'Oh, I give up! There's just no talking to you, is there,
Mother?' Angrily she got to her feet, sending the chair spinning
across the floor. Tight-mouthed she picked up her plate, taking
it into the dairy, scraping the food into the pig-swill bucket.
Then calmly as she knew how she said, 'I *am* going out on
Saturday night!'

'And I shall speak to your father about this!'

'You do that, Mum! Bring Dad into it, as if he hasn't worries
enough!' She took a candle from the sideboard. 'But you'll be
wasting your time, both of you!'

'So you'll go to bed on your anger?'

'If I have to — yes!'

She turned and would have climbed the stairs, but a hand
took her arm and she was flung round to face her mother, her
cheeks wet with tears.

'You're up to no good, miss! What's going on? I want
the truth!'

'Mother! The whole world is at war! There's fighting in
Russia and the Pacific and the Far East and Italy! And that war
is at the end of our land now! Why can't you stop pretending
that Laburnum Farm isn't a part of it? And why do you treat
me like a child? There are girls of my age at that aerodrome,
in uniform; away from home!

'You managed to keep me at home by saying I worked on

the land, but we haven't enough acres left to justify three people being exempted! You and Dad could manage Laburnum and I could do something really worth while!'

She shook away the restraining hand, even though she felt sick inside at the sight of her mother's tears. She had never seen her mother weep before.

'So that's it! You want to be in uniform! Have you gone out of your mind?'

'No! I don't want to join up,' Rosamund said wearily. 'And I'm going to bed now.'

'Without saying sorry?'

'Wanting to go out next Saturday calls for an apology, does it?'

She walked up the narrow stairs in the darkness and didn't light the candle until she had shut the door of her room behind her. She was shaking, and there was a ball of panic tight in her throat that made her want to be sick, because her mother had been right. Something *was* going on, but things had come to a pretty pass when you'd met a man and daren't let your mother know.

She blew out the candle flame, then drew back the blackout curtains to stand at the window, staring out until her eyes hurt. Clouds had covered the moon and she couldn't see the aerodrome. Everything was so still it was hard to believe that not an hour ago bombers had snarled and roared into the sky.

Yet Jon was somewhere out there and she would stay awake, for no matter how long, until he came back; would count the Lancasters in as she had counted them out. Jon would be all right; would be at the kissing gate tomorrow night – oh, *please* he would be?

She emptied her mind of her mother's fury. Jon was all that mattered. Not until she knew he was safe would she worry about tonight's bitterness.

She lay in bed, wide-eyed and cold. She should have taken a hot bed-brick from the fire oven where it had been warming all day, but her hasty, angry exit had not allowed it. The bottom of the bed was very cold, so she curled herself into a ball and pulled the blankets up to her chin.

Below her, she heard the closing of the kitchen door, and voices. Her father was back from the shippon; the young cow must be all right.

She breathed quietly, trying to hear what was being said, but the voices were low. At least they weren't arguing, probably because Dad agreed with her mother this time. Maybe because she had slammed up the stairs without a sorry or even a good night, she had lost an ally. Dad didn't hold with bad manners.

Quietly she got out of bed, wincing as her feet touched the cold linoleum. Slowly, carefully, so they should not hear her footsteps, she tiptoed to the window and closed the blackout curtains, lighting the candle so she might see the time on her watch.

It was only ten o'clock; was going to be a very long night. Below her, she heard sounds of the fire being raked and made safe for the night. Then the kitchen door closed and she heard steps on the main staircase. They were going to bed; leaving her to stew in her own juice. Neither was going to tap on her door and ask if she were all right – offer a truce. And she didn't care. Soon she would creep downstairs for bed-bricks. She was so cold she didn't care if they caught her.

She opened the oven door to find two smooth, shiny bricks on the top shelf. Gasping with relief, she wrapped them in pieces of blanket kept especially for the purpose, then hugged them to her. She would place one at her feet and cuddle the other, then think of Jon; be with him every mile of the dark, dangerous way.

She got gratefully into bed, her bones aching with cold. It would be icy in *J-Johnnie*, but the crew would have warm boots and thick flying jackets and helmets plugged into the intercom so they could speak to each other. Jon had told her how it would be.

Her shivering stopped as the bed began to warm, and she tried to think of something really awful so that sleep should not steal up on her. But her mind went blank because the most awful thing that could happen was that Jon wouldn't make it back, and such thoughts were never to be allowed.

I love you, Jon. Last week I didn't know you existed, yet now I can't get you out of my mind. Please, now that I've found you, don't leave me?

She wondered, yet again, if Matilda Mint was with him.

She awoke suddenly to hear Shep; not his usual sharp, guarding bark but a soft, mournful howling. Why was he making such an awful noise? Did he know something was wrong?

The howling stopped suddenly and she lay, hardly daring to breathe lest there was some small sound she should miss. She lighted the candle again and blinked at her watch. Five minutes to two. Seven hours since the bombers took off. Had she missed them? Had they landed whilst she slept?

She sat up in bed, wrapping the eiderdown round her. All was so quiet she felt she could brush the silence aside with a sweep of her arm; a brooding silence, like stillness before a storm.

Then she heard it and hurried to open the window. The cold hit her like a slap, but it didn't matter. Out there in the darkness was the first of the returning bombers! Shep had heard it long before she.

The sound drew nearer and became a roar. Across the fields she could see an orange glow. They had lit the flares that lined the east west runway. The bombers would come in low over Laburnum Farm and Laceby to start their touchdown. She heard the splutter and cough of engines and knew that one bomber at least was safe.

Then all was quiet again and reason told her that though the bombers had taken off only minutes apart, they would return in ones and twos, straggling in as best they could.

She stood there, not feeling the cold, determined to wait until all eleven returned. She knew what the homecoming would be like. Wireless operators would switch to home wave, and each Lancaster would be talked down by a voice from the control tower. Or maybe told to circle until the runway was free. Nobody, Jon had said, minded that last delay because they were all thankful to have notched up another op and soon they would be in the debriefing hut with mugs of sweet hot tea laced with rum. It was almost worth it, he had laughed, just to feel that tea biting your throat; convincing you that you'd really made it there and back! And touched down without pranging your plane.

It wasn't until an hour of waiting that Rosamund knew eleven Lancasters had landed. Then the glow that lit the runway flickered and died and she closed the window, relief thudding through her as she snuggled beneath the blankets, reaching with her toes for the bed-brick. Eleven had taken off; eleven were home. Jon was safely back, and tonight at eight he would be waiting at the little creaking gate. Tonight he would kiss her and tell her he loved her; hold her close and laugh as if he hadn't flown into danger and back, nor ever would again. She closed her eyes and let go a sigh that was almost a sob.

God! This is Rosamund Kenton. Thank you; oh, thank you!

The alarm awoke her at five and she hurried, eyes gritty with tiredness, to the shippon, surprised to find the lamps already lit and cows lumbering into their stalls. A whistle told her that her father was in the calf shed, and she hurried to find him.

'What was it?'

'A nice little heifer.' He spoke without shifting his gaze from the newly born calf.

'We'll be keeping her then?' Only bull calves went to market.

'Aye. She's a good 'un.'

'I'll get on then – see to the feed.' She had no wish to stay and talk. Last night had to be explained and apologized for, but not just yet.

'Rosamund!'

She stopped, unspeaking.

'You upset your mother last night.' It was a statement that demanded an answer.

'I'm sorry. But all I did was ask to go out sometimes. That's all it was, but she tried to read something into it. She blamed Bessie for putting ideas into my head, so I answered back. You didn't get the brunt of it, did you?'

'No, but it took me long enough to calm her down. She was crying.'

'Mum never cries. She was putting it on.'

'She cried herself to sleep, for all that.'

'That was because I stood up for myself for once.' Anger flushed Rosamund's cheeks. 'Mum doesn't want me to grow up, doesn't want her chick to fly the coop.'

'But you were threatening to leave home! Wasn't that a bit thoughtless? You know you can't without asking the Labour Exchange first.'

'Mum got it wrong. I said that I'd be better off doing something more worthwhile. She must have thought I wanted to join up, and I don't. I just want to be allowed out sometimes without an inquisition. Mum's afraid I'll meet a young man.'

She made to return to the shippon, but her father laid a hand on her shoulder.

'And have you met someone? Is that what it's all about?'

'No, Dad! When do I ever get the chance, will you tell me?' She despised herself for lying so glibly, especially to her father, who was entitled to the truth. But she couldn't tell him about Jon because he would feel honour-bound to tell her mother. 'Look, I'm sorry if there's been an upset, but girls my age do go out to the flicks and dances.'

'I know, Rosamund. It's just that Laburnum's a bit far out in winter.'

'But it's always been out of the way! I grew up with a mile between me and civilization. And anyway, what's wrong with my bike?'

'The blackout, for one thing, though I'll grant you there's very little traffic about.'

'Mum said our road would be alive once the RAF moved in, but it hasn't been. I don't suppose they know Laceby Green or Laburnum exist, except when they fly over. But there'd be no problem at all if we had a car, or even a phone. I can drive the tractor; a little car would be easy. And secondhand cars are going begging now.'

'There are no phones for civilians for the duration, you know that. And as for a car – well, we did talk about it a while back, but there's no chance now; not when our income was cut by half when we lost the fields. We'd only just got on our feet, an' all, when They took them.'

'Dad! I'm sorry!' She threw her arms around him and laid her cheek to his. 'You must have a terrible time of it, between Mum and me and the war, and all the form filling.'

'When you've been in the trenches, lass, you don't grumble overmuch about this war; and I'm satisfied enough with the way things are. Your mother is a good woman, Rosamund, and a caring mother, think on.'

'I know.' Her mother would cross the yard soon with mugs of tea and a pail of hot water for scrubbing up. There was no escaping her mother's caring. 'Think we'd better make a start.'

'Aye. But just one thing more. I think both you and your mother should be prepared to meet each other halfway. I reckon that if you were to tell her you were sorry about your outburst of temper last night –'

'*Temper?* All I want is to go out sometimes! Why should I apologize?'

'If you were to say sorry,' he continued softly, 'she might be a bit more understanding about you going out weekends. And you're right, we'd best make a start.'

'Dad! What did you say to her!' she gasped. 'Can I really go out on Saturday?'

But Bart Kenton had said his piece, diplomatically as he was able, and indicated the matter was closed, which was just as well because the bobbing light from a torch told her that Mildred Kenton was crossing the yard and it might be politic to be busily engaged at the far end of the shippon. Because even if her father hadn't fixed it for her, she thought resentfully, she was determined to go to the dance, no matter what the outcome.

'Good morning, Rosamund,' her mother called.

'Morning, Mum,' she said as cheerfully as she knew how, then disappeared into the cooling shed to get stools, pails and milking coats. Brave though she had been, she was not yet ready for another confrontation. Her mother offering an olive branch was like Greeks bearing gifts and made her shake inside, though whether from relief or triumph she couldn't be sure.

She had denied Jon when asked if she had met someone, and she would go on denying him if that was what it took! She wished she were twenty-one, and could please herself what she did; could leave home or get married without permission. Funny, really, when you thought that a lot of men in the armed forces were not of age, yet they could be shot down, torpedoed, blown up by landmines or shells. Old enough to be killed or maimed, but not old enough to marry without parental consent. It was crazy!

All at once she felt sickened that her parents' generation had endured the most awful war imaginable, yet stood by and let it happen again only twenty-odd years on. Just to think how stupid old people could be made her feel less guilty and even more determined to meet Jon whenever and wherever she could.

And lie and cheat without batting an eyelid to do it!

Jon was waiting at the iron gate, and she ran into his arms whispering, 'Darling! I've missed you. Sorry I'm late . . .'

'It doesn't matter. And I wasn't sure if it was eight or nine. I'd have hung about.'

'Are you all right? Tired?'

'No. I slept till four.'

'Where did you go?'

'A diversion over the Dutch coast – kept their fighters away from the main stream. They went to Berlin, to drop a few.'

'Yes. It was on the news. I was at the end of the cow pasture. Did you see me?'

'Hell! Didn't think to look. Too much on edge, I suppose.'

'It doesn't matter. I counted how many took off and as soon as I knew eleven were back, it was all right. I meant to stay awake all night, but I dozed off. Shep woke me. He heard the first plane five minutes before I did. Did you take Matilda?'

'Of course! She enjoyed it. Tell me you love me.'

'I love you, love you, love you.' She whispered it provocatively, her lips on his. 'Will you be flying on Saturday?'

'Wish I knew.' He pulled her closer. 'I reckon we'll go on Thursday; maybe a long one, now the sprog pilots have been blooded. The CO went last night, though normally he doesn't – too old. But he flew dicky with one of the new pilots – was the first to take off. Decent of him really. *J-Johnnie* followed – did a good takeoff, thank God. I'm considered the old man of the squadron having flown seven – *eight*. If we don't fly on Saturday, there'll be another dance. Can you make it, sweetheart?'

'Yes, but I won't be staying at Bessie's so I'll have to leave early – be in by eleven. I'll bike down to the village and back.'

'Then I'll come with you. There are loads of bikes at the 'drome, airmen for the use of; it being such a big place from end to end. I'd rather walk you home, though, the long way round!'

'Me too. But it'll be better once the light nights come. Last night I got the idea to meet you at the boundary fence. It would save you a lot of walking.'

'A good idea, but how do you kiss your girl through a steel fence? And I couldn't climb it . . .'

'It was just a thought. We could meet there sometimes though – at midday, say – just for a quick hullo. I miss you so much. I want always to be with you.'

'I'll get a seventy-two-hour pass every six weeks now I'm back on ops. Come with me, and meet Aunt Lottie?'

'Jon! You know I couldn't. The folks don't know about you, and I'm not going to tell them!'

'Why not? They'll have to know. I'm serious about us, Rosie.'

'So am I, but Mum isn't. Men are taboo for the duration. Sometimes I think she's got some farmer's ploddy son lined up for me.'

'Tough! You're spoken for. Will you marry me?'

'Yes I will! The day I'm twenty-one!'

'Can't wait till then . . .'

'We don't have to, Jon. You know we don't. And make it

nine, tomorrow night, will you? Vary the times a bit. Are you going to get fed up, meeting like this?'

'No, but I'd like us to be together more. Any chance of an afternoon off?'

'I'll try. I'll think of something. And there'll be Saturday.' She crossed her fingers, searching with her lips for his. 'Let's not talk?'

She thought about it in bed that night; about how she had been away from the kitchen for almost fifteen minutes, yet no one remarked on her absence. She'd had an excuse ready, of course, the words carefully thought out so they would slip easily off her tongue: 'Been, Mum? I felt like a breath of fresh air, that's all. Everywhere looks so beautiful in the moonlight.'

A blatant untruth, but Jon was worth all the lies, though she wondered how she would feel and act once they were lovers. Probably it would be so wonderful she wouldn't care about the deceit. Or the risk.

'I love you, Sergeant Hunt. Kiss me again?' she'd whispered from the heady suffocation of his nearness, though she knew, even as she said it, that kisses were no longer enough.

They met briefly, passionately, on two more nights. Nothing was ever said on her return to the kitchen, as if Tuesday's bitterness was being ignored as her mother ignored everything she was powerless to change

Then on Friday she had to go to Laceby to phone the vet. One of the sows had aborted its litter and because such a thing had never happened before, her father wanted the veterinary's advice.

Had things been normal, Rosamund would have said yet again that it was a pity they had never had the phone put in, but it suited her that morning to go to the village.

A bomber took off as she pedalled past six oaks. It came at her so suddenly and so low that she flinched. Then another took off, and by the time she reached the phone box, several planes were in the air. The noise was deafening, its implication clear. They were flight-testing, and tonight Jon would be on ops.

Willing herself not to think about it, she rang the surgery, then dipped into her pocket for three more pennies and the piece of paper bearing the number of the shirt factory.

'Lune Valley Manufacturing,' said a voice. Rosamund pushed button A, and the pennies fell into the coin box with a clatter. 'Can I help you?'

'Is it possible, please, to have a quick word with Miss Drake?'

'Of course it is! Hi, Rosamund! What's up, then?'

'Bess! I didn't recognize you!'

'You wouldn't. That was my phone voice. Where are you?'

'In the village. Are you going to the dance tomorrow night?'

'You bet – if they aren't on ops.'

Rosamund almost said she didn't think they would be; that it would be tonight. But you didn't say things like that on the phone, because careless talk really could cost lives.

'Let's hope not, because I'm going. I told Mum I wanted to go out on Saturday and –'

'You didn't tell her about the aerodrome?'

'Of course I didn't! I just said out, but I'll be at the dance. Shall I meet you in the village, or come to your house?'

'Come to ours, and if Dad's around be careful what you say. Mum knows where I'm going, but Dad doesn't. Are you sure you'll be able to make it, Rosamund? How on earth did you get permission?'

'We-e-ll – no one has actually said I can go yet – but they haven't said I can't. Anyway, I'll make it, though I won't be able to stay out late. Will Mick be there?'

'I'm hoping so. Said he'd see me inside. What about Jon?'

'Fingers crossed he'll be there, too. But I'll give you all the news tomorrow, Bess. See you! Bye!'

The bombers began taking off early, just as afternoon milking was finished, and in half an hour, twelve Lancasters were airborne. As each one flew low over the farm, Rosamund had sent her thoughts high and wide.

Take care, whoever you are. Good luck. Come home safely. And if that was Jon, I love you, my darling . . .

'They're off again,' Mildred Kenton remarked sourly as Rosamund stood at the kitchen fire, warming limbs that shook with cold. 'I swear they fly low on purpose!'

'They fly low, Mum, because they're loaded with bombs and their wings are full of fuel. It's a miracle those pilots get them off the ground at all!'

'That's exactly what I mean! There'll be a terrible accident one of these nights and we'll all be dead!'

'You're determined that every pilot in that squadron is hell-bent on crashing onto Laburnum Farm, aren't you, Mum? Has it never occurred to you that those crews want to stay alive as much as we do?'

'I didn't ask for that aerodrome to be built, you know!'

'No, and I'm sure those airmen didn't ask to be sent there either! And I'm sorry you're upset, but everyone is sick of the war – especially those crews who have just taken off! But there isn't anything we can do about it.' She turned to smile at her mother and was shocked to see how pale and pinched her face was. 'Cheer up! We're winning! It won't be long now!'

'Then I hope to God I live to see the end of it!' She covered her face with hands that shook. 'Is it too much to hope that one morning I'm going to wake up and find it's all been a bad dream? All I want is to live my life without interference from anybody!'

'To shut us all away; make sure we keep ourselves to ourselves?' The wash of pity she had felt for her mother was gone. 'Then when you're getting upset with the war for disrupting *your* way of life, will you spare a thought for all those men and women who are never going to wake up at all? I'll bet every single one of them, if they could, would be glad to be as miserable as you are, Mother! And before all this soul-searching develops into a row, I want to remind you that I'm going to Bessie's tomorrow night.'

'You'll do as you wish, I suppose, with no thought for anyone else!' Mildred Kenton turned abruptly to lift the lid of a pan that simmered on the hob. 'Just like the rest of your generation! Selfish as they come!'

'My generation, Mother, is fighting a war!' Slowly, carefully, she walked to the stair door and though she was shaking inside and wanted to scream out her anger and contempt, she took a deep breath and walked unspeaking to her room, groping her way across it to draw the blackout curtains. Then she trailed her fingers to the bedhead and from there to the candlestick that stood beside it, lighting it, taking in deep gulps of calming air, flopping on the bed, eyes closed tightly against tears.

Then she thought of Jon and his crew, and Matilda Mint, who flew with them, and her lips lost their tautness and relaxed into a smile. She looked into the mirror, and eyes gentled by candlelight smiled back into hers.

'Guess who I love?' she whispered, but the girl in the mirror smiled secretly, and said nothing.

SEVEN

'I'll be off, then,' Rosamund said as normally as she was able. As if, she thought, going to Laceby on a Saturday night was run of the mill. She paused briefly at the door, expecting a protest from her mother, or a warning to be back before bedtime and to think on what she was about. But only her father spoke.

''Night, lass. Take care, in the dark.'

'There's still a moon. I'll be fine . . .'

She tried to smile, but her mouth was stiff because she had thought that the worst moment would be walking out through the barrier of her mother's disapproval. But it wasn't. Since last night, there were far worse things to contend with.

The worrying had begun when she'd awakened without reason, to lie unmoving and tense for several minutes. All had been still; silence hanging over the house like a blanket. She lit the candle, blinking the face of her watch into focus: half-past two.

She burrowed beneath the clothes again, all at once alert, calculating that the bombers had been gone for more than eight hours. She wished she knew the flying speed of a Lancaster. She must ask Jon. You could ask a lot, say a lot, in three long, lovely hours.

She closed her eyes to remember the feel of his arms, his smile, the wayward lock of hair, his lips; the way the little pulse behind her nose began its fluttering when he whispered that he loved her. She had stretched her body languidly, sensuously, needing his nearness, turning her head on the pillow to smile as if he were beside her.

It was then the dog began its howling. Shep had heard the bombers, and soon she would hear them, too. All at once apprehensive, she had blown out the candle, then wrapped the eiderdown around her, feeling with a toe for her slippers. Pulling aside the curtains, she opened the window. Soon, she would see the distant glow of the flarepath lights. Twelve Lancasters had taken off . . .

Twelve, she thought miserably now as she wheeled her cycle down the dirt road. And eleven had come back.

Ten landed in fairly quick succession then, much later, another bomber circled and landed. She was beginning to will and wish the last one home when the runway lights went out. A cold gust of air hit her face and she had shut the window, hurrying into bed, hugging herself into a ball.

One of our aircraft is missing. In her mind she'd heard the controlled voice of the newsreader as if she were downstairs and it was nine o'clock. One Lancaster from Laceby, which wasn't expected, because the runway lights had been turned off.

She had tried to imagine the huge blackboard in the film about a Wellington bomber. Everyone had been to see *Target For Tonight*; had flown with that crew, sat in the smoke-filled gloom of the picture house and willed them a safe landing.

There were people in the control tower in that film, and in the operations room, talking the wounded Wellington back, watching triumphantly as the aircraft's number and the name of its pilot were written on the blackboard as it landed.

It would be like that now in Laceby's operations room she'd thought. There would be Waafs standing round the plot and the controller sitting in front of another huge blackboard and a man – or maybe a woman – standing ready with a piece of chalk. But she wouldn't write in the plane and the pilot because one of their Lancasters had not come back.

God! Listen! Not Jon? Please not Jon?

Yet why should it be Jon? It had happened to someone else; some other pilot's plane was missing, not his. Matilda Mint had flown with *J-Johnnie*. How *could* it be Jon? She had lain cold and wide awake and there had been a pain in the pit of her stomach as if she hadn't eaten for days.

She pulled back her thoughts to here and now, turning on her front and rear lights with stubborn defiance, telling herself that Jon would be there, exactly like last week, only this time she would not bump into him because tonight there was a moon. And they would kiss as he helped her into the back of the transport and she would wonder why she had spent the entire day in misery.

She began to pedal furiously.

'I've left my bike round the back, Mrs Drake; is that all right?'

'Of course it is. Come in do. You look frozen. Bessie's upstairs, doing herself up. Sit by the fire and tell me the news.'

'*What* news? Nothing ever happens at Laburnum. We had a heifer calf the other day and the sow aborted her litter. Oh, and sometimes a Lancaster flies over a bit too low, and Mum goes mad. She hates having the aerodrome so near.'

'Talking about the aerodrome – and we can, 'cause Bessie's dad is out – I hope you realize there'd be ructions if he ever found out about the dance!'

'There'd be ructions at home, too, only it would be Dad who'd be all right about it, and Mum who'd hit the roof. Yet *you* don't mind, Mrs Drake.'

'I can't say I approve, exactly, but Bessie knows right from wrong.' She tapped her nose with a forefinger. 'And it isn't a lot of fun growing up in a war. I did, so I know what I'm talking about.'

'It's good of you to be so understanding. You'll never let it slip that I went to the dance, will you?'

'Course I won't. And you'll mind what I told Bessie, won't you, Rosamund? Never do anything you'd be ashamed to tell your parents about – like *that* sort of thing!'

'Oooh, I wouldn't't! And Bessie wouldn't either!'

I tell lies too, Mrs Drake, because it's all I've ever thought about since Jon kissed me.

'That's all right, then! Bessie's dad is inclined to be strict, see, her being a girl. I've told him many a time that he'll drive the

304

devil *into* the lass, not out of her, if he doesn't stop acting like a Victorian father! Bessie said you'd met a lovely young man.'

'Mm. He's a pilot – Jon Hunt. And it's marvellous to be able to talk about him. At home, I've got to watch every word I say. I slip out for a few minutes at night to be with him.'

'Then the pair of you must have got it bad! Are you sure you can't tell your mother about him, Rosamund? Creeping out like you're doing something wrong doesn't make a lot of sense to me.'

'I'm sure. Mum would tie me to the table leg if she found out about him.'

'Now I wonder why? I got the impression he was a well-spoken young man – educated too.'

'He is, but Mum says it's stupid to get fond of someone when there's a war on because something might happen to him – you know . . . ?'

'Yes, I do know. And I can understand some of the crews at the aerodrome wanting to have fun whilst they can – do a bit of living. There's more than a grain of sense in what your mother says.'

'Sense doesn't come into it as far as I'm concerned. I can't stop thinking about him.'

'Then in that case, Rosamund, remember what I just told you! Don't do anything you might regret. Count to ten, think on!'

Rosamund was spared the red-cheeked embarrassment of a reply by the arrival of Bessie, curled and quiffed and powdered.

'Hi! Will I do?'

'You look great, Bess!'

'I still think that skirt's too short,' Mrs Drake sniffed.

'Are we ready, then? Best be a bit early. We don't want to be left behind, do we? And how are you going to get home, Rosamund?'

'My bike's round the back. Jon said he'd borrow one from the 'drome, and ride with me.'

'So how can he do that, eejit? It's going to be no end of a bother, shoving a bike over the fields in the dark, hadn't you thought?'

'We-e-ll . . .' She *hadn't* thought!

'Oh, for goodness' sake, he'd better have mine! That's all right, isn't it, Mum?'

'Course it is. He can leave it in the wash house on the way back. Tell him not to make a noise, though.'

'Good! That's settled. Let's be off!' Bessie kissed her mother soundly. 'Won't be late, Mum!'

'You better hadn't be! I want you in before your dad gets back from the pub. No later than half-past ten, don't forget!'

'It's exciting, isn't it – knowing we might get caught, I mean!' Tonight the sky was clear, and they could make out the outlines of walls and lampposts.

'No it isn't! And, Bess, they were flying, last night.'

'Yes. It was Berlin. It said so on the news.'

'One of Laceby's lot didn't come back. I counted.'

'Oh, my Lor'! You're sure? Could you have missed one? Maybe two of them landed together.'

'That's one thing they don't do! They aren't Spitfires!'

'OK! Don't get shirty! And why should it be Jon's plane? It's twelve to one against that it isn't! Jon'll be with the transport when it arrives; bet you anything you like he will!'

But Sergeant Jon Hunt was not with the transport that pulled up outside Laceby Green Parish hall. A corporal jumped down, calling, 'Anyone for the love bus?' at the top of his voice, and to get on board sharpish, if they didn't mind!

'Where's Sergeant Hunt tonight?' Bessie demanded of the man with two stripes on his arm.

'Never heard of him! All I know is that Flight told me to collect the bints, and that's what I'm doing!! Now do you want a hand up, or don't you?'

They said they did, and the corporal pointed his flashlight towards empty spaces in the far corner of the truck. Last week there had been seven girls for the dance; this week, Bessie thought dully, the transport was almost full. Word had got around about the free dance where men outnumbered women by three to one. Well, they'd better keep their hands off Mick!

'What'll we do, if . . . ?' Rosamund left the question hanging in the air.

'*If* they don't show we'll leave pretty damn quick, because Mick won't be there either. How'll I find a partner with all this lot there!'

'We aren't talking about dancing,' Rosamund hissed, not caring who heard her. 'It's Jon, and it's serious!'

'But we don't know yet, do we? Bet you anything you like it wasn't *J-Johnnie*!'

'Women for the aircrew dance!' yelled the corporal when they stopped at the guardroom.

'How many?'

'Gawd knows! About twenty!'

The red and white pole lifted and they lurched past, driving more slowly, skirting tall buildings and hangars. Then the truck stopped abruptly, throwing everyone inside sprawling.

He was doing it on purpose, Rosamund thought. The corporal was a nasty little man. She had taken a dislike to him the minute she'd set eyes on his two stripes, though probably it was because she had expected to see Jon there like last week. She took the hands that were offered, then jumped to the ground. She could see the rounded roof of the Nissen hut and stood rooted, staring at it.

'Bess! I'm going to be sick!'

'Don't dare! Sick smells awful!'

'But I can't go in there, I *can't*! I couldn't bear it if –'

'Rosie . . . ?'

Hands reached for her, arms cradled her, pulled her close.

'Jon! I thought – oh, darling, you're all right!' She began to shake and the words she wanted to say got mixed up with a choke of tears. 'When you weren't with the transport, I thought it was true!'

'What are you talking about?'

'The bomber that didn't come back! I thought – I was sure –'

'It was *J-Johnnie*?'

'Yes. I don't know why, but I was so certain – just having found you, I mean. But I shouldn't be glad, should I, that it's someone else?'

'It was *B-Bertie*, Steve Grafton's Lanc.'

'It's all wrong, isn't it? Here's me, cockeyed with relief, yet some poor woman is going to get a telegram soon.'

'Not quite! She'll likely get a phone call from him. He's all right; made an emergency landing down south. Hydraulics got shot up; the undercarriage wouldn't go down. The plane's a write-off, but the crew got out with only a broken arm and cuts and bruises between them! Mind, they'll be a bit shaken, now it's finally sunk in how close they came to getting the chop.'

'Has anything like that ever happened to you, Jon?'

'No, thank God. Pancaking is a dicey business! So do you want to go in or stay out here?'

'Both! Kiss me, please. We're wasting time!'

'Talking about time,' he said, many kisses later, 'I've got a bike. Saw one outside the admin block so I took it and hid it behind the hut.'

'Yes, but Bessie pointed out that we'll have to short-cut across the fields to Laceby. A bike is going to be a bit of a nuisance.'

'I'll manage. I want to see you home!'

'And you will. It's all arranged. We'll do a quick nip across the fields to Bessie's. You can borrow her bike – as long as you put it back quietly.'

'Great! So let's go inside. I want to look at you – properly.'

'It was Berlin last night, wasn't it?' she asked as they danced. 'Was it awful?'

'Bloody awful! I've never done Berlin, though I knew it was a nasty run; thick with flack and fighters. But I hadn't reckoned at them coming at us from all sides! I tell you, darling, after last night nothing can be as bad again! If you can survive Berlin, you can survive anything! I reckon the gods love me!'

'I love you, too,' she said slowly, not caring that anyone looking at them could read the words. She wanted the whole place to know. Watch my lips! Rosie Kenton and Jon Hunt are in love! She was crazily, dizzily happy. She wanted to laugh out loud because it had all come right again. 'Do you know how much I love you?' she whispered, lips close to his ear.

'I'm willing to be shown,' he smiled. 'Let's go outside? And this time, don't forget your coat!'

Neither minded leaving the hot, crowded hut, where cigarette smoke hung in drifts against the corrugated roof; where the band played lustily and the laughter was loud and too high.

They left the aerodrome, slipping beneath an unguarded fence to the fields beyond. The moon was higher now, and threw long shadows across their path. They stumbled over tussocky grass, paused to kiss, to touch. The still night was cold and bright and very beautiful.

'Ride with me as far as six oaks,' she whispered, as they crept out of Bessie's back yard with the bicycles. 'I'll be all right from there.'

'Where is six oaks?'

'Just a little way from our lane end.'

'I'll take you all the way; see you in.'

'Shep might bark, Jon.'

'I shall see you to the gate,' he insisted, so she giggled and said she adored him when he was bossy. It was all she could think of to say, because she was high-as-a-kite happy, and desperately in love.

They stopped at six oaks because they hadn't kissed or touched for an eternity and because she wanted the clump of trees to be one more place that was special.

'Next Saturday, we won't be able to see the oaks. There'll be no light at all. It'll be the dark of the moon. That's when witches work – at moon-dark.'

'Idiot!' He kissed the tip of her nose. 'No one believes in witches!'

'If you live around these parts you do! A witch lived at Laburnum Farm. Margaret Dacre. She and her husband built it in 1592, though it was called Wolfen Place then. She practised witchcraft, so legend has it, but was never caught. There isn't even a mention of her in any of the accounts of the Pendle Witches. I think she must have had friends in high places!'

'And you believe it, Rosie?'

'Why not? It isn't everyone can say they live in a witch's house! But we'd better hurry. It was just that I wanted to kiss you at six oaks, so that every time I pass there and you aren't with me, I can close my eyes and pretend you are.'

'Tomorrow night, sweetheart?' They were standing at the rusty gate. 'At nine?'

'Am I truly worth all the bother?'

'Yes. And more.'

'I'll have to go now. See you, Jon. Take care.'

They kissed hurriedly because they were parting, and such kisses are sad kisses, and best over quickly. The gate creaked as she pushed it aside. Distantly, Shep barked a warning, and she ran down the narrow path to the yard gate.

'Hush, Shep. It's only me!'

Her mother looked unspeaking at the mantel clock when she got in.

Her father said, 'Hullo, love. Mum's just going to make a drink. Want one?'

'Please. But I'll see to it.'

'Had a nice time, then?'

'It made a change, Dad. We listened to the wireless, and talked.'

'Make my cocoa with milk, will you?' Tight-lipped, as if it hurt, Mildred Kenton broke her silence.

'Milky cocoa for three it is!'

Don't make a noise, Jon, when you take the bike back Already, in the loveless chill of Laburnum kitchen, she was missing him. *Take care. See you tomorrow. And tomorrow, and tomorrow . . .*

The shortest day came and went. Winter was half over. From 22 December, Rosamund thought, the days would start to get longer. Blackout curtains were drawn at five o'clock, and remained drawn until half-past eight next morning. Mind, if They hadn't been messing around with the hour, it would have been an hour earlier, in both cases. In winter, because of daylight saving, clocks were at summertime; in summer they were at double-summertime, and two hours ahead. Bart Kenton did not agree with it; nor did his dairy herd. It was interfering with nature, and the milk yield went down for at least a week whenever They altered the clocks.

To which Mildred replied, 'Nonsense!' arguing that it didn't affect the herd at all! Cows didn't know there was a war on; nor could they tell the time. Her parents, Rosamund sighed, never agreed on anything these days, except perhaps that the Allies were going to win the war. Even so, they disagreed about *when!*

Sufficient to know that Churchill, Roosevelt and Stalin had met in Tehran to make plans for another landing. Italy apart, they had agreed on a second front, though where and when was the deepest secret.

Newspapers lifted spirits by speculating upon the timing of the second front, and where the Allies would land. On the Dutch coast some said or Cherbourg or Calais or, more appropriately, why not at Dunkirk? Amazingly the Ministry of Information did nothing to censor those meanderings, since they could only serve to irritate an enemy already in the freezing deeps of another Russian winter.

Some still tuned in to Lord Haw-Haw, who passed on ugly little Goebbels' rantings about the secret weapon that would bring the British to their knees. But people only laughed, demanding to know why, if it existed, it wasn't being used on the Russian Front, where the German army seemed in desperate need of it.

'Steady, now.' Rosamund tightened her knees on the pail as the cow kicked out peevishly. 'Steady, girl . . .'

She cleared her head of all thoughts of last night. Milking was monotonous; making it easy to let her mind wander, and she often gave way to fantasies or recalled words spoken between them.

This afternoon, though, she tried to push Jon from her mind because now he would be miles away on a crowded, dimly lit train; going home to Primrose Cottage, Lower Sellow, to where his aunt had removed herself in 1941, for two reasons: the lease on her flat had run out and, more importantly, London was being bombed, though why she had lighted upon faraway Cheshire was still a mystery.

Jon was elated about his leave at first. Jammy, he'd called himself, landing ten days at Christmas; probably because he had just flown his thirteenth op and thirteen, come to think of it, had always been lucky for him!

'You should be coming with me.' He was all at once serious. 'It's time you and Aunt Lottie met.'

'You know I can't!'

'Couldn't you manage a weekend even? No, you couldn't,' he said flatly when she didn't speak. 'Hell! What a mess!'

'I'm sorry, Jon. I'm making a fool of you, aren't I? Why did you get yourself tangled up with someone like me? You could have any girl you wanted, yet –'

'Rosie! You know why we got ourselves tangled up – because we were meant to! Just think that in the whole of Lancashire in a fog in the blackout, it's you I bump into! And as for having any girl I wanted – why bother, when I've found her? But it *will* come right for us!'

'It's got to, Jon. We'll just have to be patient, that's all.'

'No! When you want someone as much as I want you, patience doesn't come into it! It's all of seven weeks, and still we're no further forward. I want you like crazy, Rosie, want to have you the right and decent way. For Pete's sake, how long have I got, will you tell me?'

'What do you mean – *got*? Got to wait? Listen! I don't want to wait either. We'll be lovers, Jon. That's enough for me!'

'But *when*, because I was talking about living, not waiting!'

'All right, then! *Now*, if you want!'

'Hell, girl, it can't be turned on to order! There's such a thing as being in the mood – both at the same time! But we can't either of us relax! We're snatching all the time: ten minutes here at your gate; a few hours at the dance. You should be coming with me to Cheshire!'

'I know! In the normal course of events I should be but I'm not normal, am I?'

He heard the tears in her voice and pulled her closer, settling his cheek on her head, hushing her.

'I'm sorry, sweetheart. The last thing I want is to make you cry. But I want us to be married. We can't go on like this! When I get back from leave I'm going to see your folks!'

'Jon! We've known each other six weeks and four days! They'll say we don't know enough about each other! Love at first sight? They'll say there's no such thing! *Lust*, more like!'

'But there *is* such a thing! I fell in love with your voice in the darkness, and then I saw you, and it all clicked into place. I thought: Hell! It's her! The one! Love at first sight, Rosie, and lust, too, because before I'd even danced with you, I'd stripped you naked with my eyes and wanted what I saw! So either they let you marry me, or –'

'Or we'll be lovers. We agreed we would, ages ago.'

'I want to call you wife. I want it to be all above board.'

'And if it can't be, Jon?'

'Then it'll have to be a hole-in-the-corner affair – finding somewhere to go; me making a tart of you, putting you at risk!'

'But aren't there ways and means . . . ?'

'Of being careful? Oh, you wouldn't have to worry, Rosie. You get all that guff dinned into you when you join up. They call them hygiene lectures, but what it all boils down to is making sure you don't catch something nasty and not getting the lady pregnant at the same time! Hell! I'm sorry, darling. How can you know about such things?'

'I know about VD, Jon. We talked about it at school. But why are we going on like this? Tomorrow you'll be on leave and I won't see you for ten days! I'll be so miserable I'll have to keep telling myself that at least you'll not be flying!'

'Sorry. I'm being selfish, aren't I? But I get het up, sometimes –'

'And do you think I don't?'

When they were apart, she longed for his touch, his kiss; when they were together kisses were not enough. She wanted him, yet she was afraid of the moment when he would take her, because she would get it wrong or do something stupid. She wanted to be with him always, yet there were times when need of him was so like a pain inside her that she wished they had never met.

'Don't be sad, Rosie. It's all going to come right for us

313

because I'll make it! The minute I get back from leave I'm going to knock on your front door and introduce myself!'

'No, darling. Let me tell them first; prepare them. I'll do it before you get back – promise I will!'

'On my life do you promise?'

'Jon Hunt! *Never* say a thing like that! I won't promise *anything* on your life! I just give you my word that I will!' She reached up to kiss him. 'I'll tell Dad first. If only one of them will listen to reason, it'll be him. Dad's our best hope . . .'

'Rosamund? Are you all right?'

Her father, crashing into her thoughts.

'Of course I am. Why do you ask?'

'Because you were miles away. I thought you'd dropped off. You've milked that cow dry.'

'Sorry, Dad. I *was* miles away. Can we talk do you think – just you and me?' It had to be now! If she left it any longer her courage would fail her! 'It's you especially I want to talk to – not Mum.'

'Secrets, is it? Mum's birthday . . . ?'

'N-No. More serious . . .'

'I see. Then can it wait? Happen we can have our talk whilst we're mucking out.'

'Fine, Dad.' But it wasn't fine! The moment had gone! It had had to be *then*; that very moment when the words were there, ready to tumble off her tongue. Yet now she must wait to tell her father of her love for Jon whilst the shippon floor was awash with cow muck and the stink was awful; tell him of something precious and special and golden on a freezing morning when her nose was red and drippy and a wind straight from Siberia blew through the window slats! 'It's just that I keep wondering why we have to be different from everyone else. And why don't I have any grandparents?'

It came out in a rush because it was the only thing she could think of to say, and she closed her eyes briefly, and begged Jon's forgiveness.

'Aah! Now, all at once, you ask?'

'Not all at once, Dad. I've often wondered.' She had. She wasn't telling lies.

'Then like I said, we'll talk about it – after . . .'

'OK.' Eyes downcast, she carried her pail to the dairy, emptying milk into the cooler, miserable that she hadn't been able to do it; glad she hadn't promised on Jon's life. She shivered, then settled herself beside the oldest cow in the herd. 'You take the heifer, will you, Dad?'

Best leave the newly calved young cow to her father. His hands were gentler than her own, his patience infinite. It being a first calf, the heifer had only now joined the milking herd and hadn't been given a name, yet, nor a number in the herd book.

'We'll have to settle on a name for her,' her father called from two stalls down. 'Any ideas?'

'Not at the moment. I'll think of something . . .'

Later, that was. When her mind was calmer and tears weren't there in her throat, needing to be shed.

'Now then – what's all this about grandparents?' her father said as they cleaned the shippon.

'I just wondered, that's all. It seems silly, even if they aren't alive, not knowing what their names were.'

She glanced sideways to see her father stick his empty pipe between his teeth.

'It's no great shakes, Dad.' The pipe had warned her to go carefully. 'It's just that I've often meant to ask . . .'

'And you had every right to wonder – especially on your birthdays and at Christmas.'

He laughed briefly, though his eyes were still sad. And guarded now.

'It wasn't anything to do with getting presents. That was the last thing I thought about.'

It really was. Absent grandparents had long since ceased to bother her. Until this moment, that was, when she'd blurted out the first thing that came into her mind. Ships, shoes, sealing wax. Did it matter what else they talked about?

'But why do you ask now, Rosamund? Why is it suddenly important?'

'I really don't know.' *Liar!*

When she was very little, she had accepted that some children had grandparents; some did not. Yet by the time she was old enough to realize that everyone *had* to have grandparents, she was old enough to have worked out that there was some reason why she hadn't been told about hers.

Sometimes she had thought – in her imaginings, of course – that it was because her maternal grandfather had been in prison, or that her grandmother secretly drank gin.

Dad's parents she had dealt with more kindly because they were obviously good souls, as was her father. Good, but simple and not half posh enough to figure in her mother's plans. So, for her sins, she had asked nothing, because even as a child she had known how far she could go; how deeply she could delve.

'I had always meant to tell you, lass, but I kept putting it off.'

'Why?' Had she *really* needed to know, when she seemed to have managed perfectly well without grandparents? Did she need to know now?

'Because of the way things were; just you and mum and me. A family, I suppose, up against it and too proud to admit it – we-e-ll – admit it to your mother's parents, that was.'

'Admit what? Did you have to get married or something?'

'No. Nothing like that. But your mother had squandered her inheritance; they made it quite plain!'

'Squandered? She bought this beautiful house with it!'

'I'll grant you that, lass. But every penny she came into went to buy it, and farming was in the doldrums in those days. A bad move, they thought, and I got the impression they wanted more of a hand in things; a say in where the money went.'

'But it was Mum's money! Did they want to get their hands on it or something?'

'Between you and me, I fancy they did – or a hand in the spending. And I fancy they thought she'd married beneath her because I was only a herdsman. Anyway, one day there was a right old row and things got worse. Soon, your grandma stopped visiting. You couldn't blame her because after the big row your mum didn't even ask her in if she called.'

He looked down at the pipe in his hand as if he were considering whether or not to put it in his mouth again; but Rosamund knew it was because he didn't want to look at her.

'So they fell out? But lots of families have rows. Why didn't one of them apologize?'

'Because Milly had no intention of climbing down! She'd never been over fond of either parent, it seems. They expected her to live her life as they thought fit, and marrying a labourer when she could have flaunted her inheritance and taken her pick from half Skipton wasn't what they'd intended.'

'Yet Mum tells *me* what to do – when I shall find myself a young man and settle down, and when I'm to be allowed to go out!' The shippon floor and the dairy were finished. Soon, their time would have run out, because supper was always at six. 'But what about *your* parents, Dad? Didn't Mum want them around either?'

'Mine weren't a lot of trouble. My mother died when I was young and there were six bairns to rear. My father soon got wed again – you couldn't blame him – and I got myself a living-in job on a farm as soon as I left school. Better, that way. I wasn't over fond of my stepmother.'

'You had brothers and sisters?' She turned abruptly away, making great play of hanging buckets on hooks and cleaning the shovels, all at once bewildered because somewhere there must be aunts and uncles and cousins – lots of them! 'Why didn't you keep in touch?'

'Because we'd bought Laburnum and had to work from morning till night just to keep our heads above water. And because your mother wanted to be left alone to sink or to swim. The farm and you and me were all she wanted, she always said.'

'In that order?'

'Sometimes I had reason to think,' he said so softly that it sounded like an apology, 'that that was the way it was – *is*.'

'Dad! What a way to live!' She blew out the lamps, then linked her arm into his in the darkness. 'Mum can't keep the world out, nor the war either! And all these years she's been so busy keeping herself to herself that she won't even go into Laceby unless she's got to. She knows people there think she's stuck up, especially now that farmers are making a lot of money because of the war! After Laburnum, all that seems to matter is her religion.'

'I knew your mother was a devout Methodist when I wed her,' Bart corrected softly. 'I went into it with my eyes open and I've had no cause to complain. And, Rosamund,' gently he removed her arm as they neared the house, 'there's no need to mention our little talk, eh? Your mother has a lot on her mind. Wars upset women. They don't like rearing bairns, then having them taken away to fight.'

'But I'm still at home! Mrs Drake has two sons away, yet she doesn't make people miserable because of it!'

'Aye, though happen you'd best not talk overmuch about the Drakes either!'

'Because Mum doesn't want them intruding into our lives, nor Bessie influencing me? She doesn't want me to know what a normal family is like! But don't worry, I won't talk about grandparents nor the Drakes – at least not in front of Mum.' She reached up to brush her lips against his cheek. 'Though I can't begin to understand why we've got to live like this.'

'Nor me, Rosamund. Reckon it's best that we count our blessings, though, from time to time; try to understand that what your mother does is out of thought for her family – for you and me.'

He opened the kitchen door and motioned with his hand for her to walk through ahead of him. He did it firmly, as if to tell her that what they had talked about was over and done with; as if it had been brought out from a dim, secret place, dusted, then pushed back again. But it wouldn't be like that when she told him about Jon, because tomorrow she would be done with dithering and come right out with it! She would have the words ready!

I want to tell you about Jon Hunt, Dad. He flies one of the bombers, at Laceby. I've been meeting him whenever I could, and we want to be married!

And when he had told her mother, which he would have

to do, there would be no going back, no being swayed by the anger, the pleading, the disbelief. If they said she couldn't marry him, then she and Jon would be lovers, make their own marriage, because once it was all out in the open, not even Dad dare be on her side.

'Aaaaah . . .' Jon Hunt sighed with pure pleasure. Ten days at home and not a uniform in sight!

Fireglow lit the room, warming every picture, every piece of brass and copper it touched. The saggy chair in which he sprawled moulded itself to his body, made him want to spend the remainder of hostilities in this higgledy-piggledy little house; never shift his behind until Hitler had surrendered. Unconditionally surrendered. It went without saying, though he probably wouldn't be around to see it. He had long ago admitted it was pushing his luck to think that *J-Johnnie* would still be flying at the end of the war. Right from that first terrifying raid over Bremen he had accepted that the euphoria of putting up his wings was over, and that now it was him against them; doing his damnedest not to go for a Burton. Thirty ops was what he must aim for. Some crews got away with it, with a whole lot of luck.

'Asleep?'

'No. Just being thoroughly lazy and enjoying the quiet.'

'You had a very peculiar look on your face.'

'Probably because I was thinking that I've done almost half a tour of ops.'

'And that's good?'

'It's a heck of a lot more than some bods do.'

'It isn't right!' Charlotte Martin flopped into the chair opposite, holding her hands to the fire. 'Once you'd finished university, it should have been plain sailing. All things being equal, you should be sowing your wild oats now; not flying damn great bombers!'

'And what do you know about wild oats, Aunt Lottie?'

'Enough! I'm a hard-headed journalist, don't forget. You and I wouldn't have survived, if I hadn't been!'

'And you're managing all right?'

'Sure. I sell my fair share of articles; still got a few friends in Fleet Street – and the column I do for the local paper butters the bread. But what I really want is to write novels – when the war is over, that is, and things get back to normal.'

When things get back to normal. When you can buy as much meat as you can eat. When the shops have things to sell again. When people made a bonfire of their blackout curtains. Phrases said so often they had become clichés.

'What kind of a novel? Romance?'

'No. I'm more of a thriller writer, I think.' She reached to pick a sheet of paper from the floor. 'Writing a letter?'

'No, but be my guest. Read it.'

'You're sure?' She put on her glasses. '*Things You Should Know*. What on earth is it meant to be?'

'Just what it says!' He was teasing her with his eyes, laughing. 'It's for Rosie.'

'And who is Rosie?' The sheet of paper was laid aside.

'She's my girl. I intended telling you. I was doing a potted history of my life for her. There's so much about each other we don't know, you see, and we get so little time together. So I said I'd write it all down. Stupid of me, I suppose . . .'

'So tell me about her, Jon?'

'She's called Rosamund Kenton. Their farm is on the other side of the boundary fence at the aerodrome. Trouble is, her folks are very strict; she can't let them know about me.'

'Well, *that's* a fine romance, if you like!'

'You can say that again! She manages to get to the aerodrome dance, and we meet for a few minutes at night when I'm not flying. I'm hoping things will be better once the light nights come and she's allowed out more.'

'*Allowed out?* How old is she then?'

'Nineteen – in June . . .'

'Going on nineteen, and she can't get out! Don't her folks know she's old enough to be called up into the Armed Forces?'

'She's reserved. She works on the farm – got exemption when she registered. But she's going to tell them about me – tell her father, anyway. He's more likely to be on our side than her mother is.'

'And *will* she tell them, do you think?'

'I've told her if she doesn't, I'm going to knock on the front door, introduce myself, then tell them I want to marry their daughter! It's a fine old mess, isn't it?'

'Hey! Chin up!' He sounded so forlorn that she went to sit on the arm of his chair, pulling him close as she had done when he was a small boy. 'I'm on your side too! There's a war on; things change! You are considered old enough to have command of six crew and a deadly bomber, and your Rosie is old enough to do war work. Why doesn't she put her foot down, stick up for herself a bit?'

'She does. She got as far as telling her parents she wanted to go out Saturday nights, though if they knew she was meeting me they'd put a stop to it. Well, her mother would . . .'

'So you'll both have to go carefully – be patient.'

'*Patient*, Aunt Lottie! So how long do you think we've got – *I've* got? Like I said, I've done thirteen ops, but the next one might be –'

'Stop it! Don't *dare* say that! I won't have it!'

'It's a fact of life, though! Rosie and I collided in the blackout and I thought she was going to the aerodrome dance, so I helped her onto the transport. Only she was going to a beetle drive in the parish hall! Reckon we were meant to meet.'

'And how long has it been going on?'

'Since early November, and I can't get her out of my mind. Even when I'm flying she's there.'

'Less than a couple of months. Can you both be sure you want to marry?'

'Yes. That night we met – when we danced – I was already wondering what it would be like to make love to her.'

'Then let's hope you both don't get curious at the same time!'

'I'm hoping we do; so is she. Do you think we're mad?'

'Why should I? Just because I'm an old spinster doesn't mean I don't know what it's like to be in love in wartime!'

'Were you and Guy lovers, Aunt Lottie?'

'No, but I wish we had been! And don't think we didn't want to, because we did! We didn't get around to it, though.'

'Because he might have been killed and you might have been left holding the baby?'

'He *was* killed, so we never knew – not even once. I wish we had and that I'd got pregnant! Oh, people would have pointed the finger, called me a slut and a tart, but at least I'd have had something of him left! And I'd have kept the baby too. I wouldn't have let them take it from me!'

'So do you think that Rosie and I are wrong to want to?'

'That's something I can't give advice on. It's up to the two of you to work it out between you. I wish you'd been able to bring her with you. Is she pretty?'

'She's adorable. Blonde, and blue-eyed. She's sort of fragile, yet she heaves milk churns and drives a tractor. It's quite a walk to her place, but it's worth it just to have a few minutes together. That's why I was writing that list for her – we don't waste our time talking!'

'Then all I can do is wish you luck and tell you I really do understand. This war is a bitch, isn't it?'

'So was yours . . .'

'Yes.' She turned to the table beside her, taking a photograph in her hands. It had faded over the years and the features blurred a little, but it was still possible to know the soldier was too young to die. 'Lieutenant Guy Ward. We were going to be married on his next leave; were counting the days. And then the telegram came. They were terrible, those little yellow envelopes. His mother came to tell me . . .'

'Don't, Aunt. I'll be taken off flying for a time, when I've done my thirty.'

'And do you think Rosie's parents will let her marry you once you're not operational?'

'Not really. Reckon we'll just have to take things as they come – hope for the best.'

'But you'll be careful – you know what I'm talking about?'

'If we both can't count to ten, you mean? I'll take care.'

'That's all right then. And enough pontificating! Why don't

I make a cup of tea? I got a half-bottle of whisky last week – was saving it for Christmas Day, but what the heck? What say we have a snifter in our tea – live dangerously!'

'Sounds like a good idea.'

'Right! I'll get the kettle on and you can finish your *Things Rosie Should Know*. If you're quick about it, you'll catch the five o'clock post. She *is* allowed letters?'

'Wouldn't know. I've never written to her before. But she picks up the post every morning when she takes the milk churns to the collecting point.'

'Then make sure she's got my name and address – phone number too! It might be nice to hear from her once in a while. And Jon – thanks . . .'

'Whatever for?'

'Oh, for being you and growing up into such a fine young man. And for being the son Guy and I never had.'

Tears trembled on her words and he took her in his arms, hushing her softly.

'Don't get upset. I'm going to be all right, I know it. We're winning the war now – once the second front gets going, it could all be over by next Christmas!' He dried her tears, smiling gently, even though he knew there was still a long way to go; still a lot of takeoffs and flack and night fighters to contend with and that thirty ops was going to take some doing. 'Bet you anything you like it will!'

In spite of all the shortages and most young men being away at war and the Post Office staff cut by almost half, there was a delivery of letters on Christmas morning.

Rosamund saw the envelope at once; not only because it stood out white against the OHMS buff-coloured ones, but because she had known it would be there. He had promised to write.

She held the letter to her cheek, then pushed it into the back pocket of her overalls to stay there, deliciously tantalizing, until she could be alone to open it.

'Happy Christmas, sweetheart,' she whispered.

A bomber flew over low, and she flinched at the suddenness

of it, and closed her eyes as the noise it made beat inside her head.

'*No!*' They couldn't be flying ops! Not on Christmas night? Surely, for just twenty-four hours the bombers could be grounded!

She started the tractor, revving it into an answering roar, glad that Jon was on leave. She wriggled herself comfortable on the cold iron seat, and the letter crackled intimately beneath her bottom.

'Did I wish you a happy Christmas, Sergeant Hunt, darling? *Did* I . . . ?'

It was not until afternoon milking was done and Christmas dinner eaten and her parents settled either side of the parlour fire, that Rosamund was able to open the letter. Decently, that was. She could have snatched at it, reading the odd line then pushing it out of sight again, but that wasn't the way it must be. The reading of Jon's first letter should be an occasion, a ritual, a rite. It should be opened carefully and each word savoured because as she read them with her eyes, his voice would be saying them inside her head.

The mantel clock struck six and she knew that her parents would be listening to the news because her mother was still anxious about Mr Churchill, and how soon he would be home from Tehran. His illness there had caused consternation and if it hadn't been for the miraculous penicillin, he might well have died, in a foreign country, of pneumonia. Britain – the world, even – could not do without him, her mother insisted, and when he got safely home he should be made to take a long convalescence and give up cigars until his chest was back to normal!

Rosamund closed her eyes, counted to ten, then took a knife from the dresser drawer. For half an hour, whilst the announcer droned immaculately on, she had the kitchen to herself, to read and reread the letter. She peered at the postmark – Chester 6.30 p.m. 23:XII:43, then carefully slit the envelope to pull out a single sheet of paper. She laid it open on the table top, smoothing a hand over it as if she were touching Jon's hand, then smiling indulgently, she began to read and to listen to his voice with her heart.

Happy Christmas, my Rosie,

I miss you already. I love you, I want you. I began to write you a detailed account of things you should know about Jonathan James Hunt way back as far as I can remember; about when I stopped believing in Santa and the tooth fairy, right through to university and getting my wings up. But it seemed like line-shooting and none of it is relevant, anyway, because all that happened before we met were only milestones along the way to Laceby Green, and groping around in the dark to find a girl's handbag.

It really began on a Saturday; on 6 November 1943, at half-past seven, and when I saw you (with tremendous relief, actually, because I had been waiting for you a long time) I knew you were my girl.

I want to marry you, have children with you, grow old with you, and because I love you so much and one lifetime cannot possibly be long enough to contain our loving, we shall come back and meet again and love again. So, my darling, you are stuck with me for ever; right through eternity until time is no more.

I will be back on 1 January. It's a Saturday, and the first day of a new year; new beginnings, too.

I love you with all my heart.

Jon

'And I love you too,' she whispered, relieved he hadn't asked if she had told her father about them. Because she had not been able to say the words, even though they were there, carefully arranged in sentences inside her head. She had said them until she knew them by heart, sure in the knowledge that when the time was right, they would slip out easily. But the words were still unspoken because after that first fumbling attempt, the time had never been right. It made her feel as if she had betrayed him.

'I *will* tell Dad; I *will*!'

Yet even as she said the words she knew they had no substance because deep inside her she had already accepted that not only dare she not tell her father about them, but she must persuade Jon it would be foolish if he were to call; that the only way they could continue to see each other must be in secret – and wasn't a secret love better than none? Wasn't it asking too much of any parents, much less her own, to be anything but shocked that their daughter had been carrying on – because that was what her mother would call it – behind their backs, and wanted to marry a man they hadn't known to exist!

'Marry our daughter! And who might you be, young man?'

The door would be slammed in his face, the inquisition would follow and she would be treated like a criminal. And not just herself, but everyone remotely connected would come in for their share of blame. Bessie, and the RAF too, just for being there, and Jon! Jon would bear the brunt of it for slyly coveting their daughter! She laid the letter to her cheek as if asking for understanding, and forgiveness, then slipped it into her pocket.

I'm sorry, Jon. I love you so much I would die for you, yet I'm not brave enough to let my parents – my mother – know about us; can't risk losing you. Because that's what would happen once she knew.

Tears filled her eyes and she slammed the flat of her hand down hard on the table top, exactly as the door opened and her mother stood there, demanding to know why she was crying.

'What is wrong, Rosamund? Aren't you well?'

'I – I don't know. I hurt all over . . .'

It was all she could think of to say, because her mother had beamed in on her thoughts, then crept in without a sound to witness her misery.

'Hurt? Is it *that* time of the month, because if it is, a dose of laxative is what you need!'

'No! It isn't that. It's sadness, I suppose, and being sick of the war and –'

'Then for shame, Rosamund Kenton! You should try to think of those who are far worse off than you! Now dry your eyes and make your father and me a pot of tea. We'll have a slice of Christmas cake too!'

'Yes. All right. And I'm sorry.' She dabbed hurriedly at her eyes, then blew her nose noisily. 'I'll bring it through to you. Won't be long . . .'

Mildred Kenton banged out of the kitchen, back ramrod straight, and in that moment Rosamund felt hatred towards her. Not for seeing her tears nor even for not giving her a hug and a bit of sympathy, nor for cheating and churning illegal butter to make a Christmas cake, but because she had equated her feelings for Jon to the level of laxatives and painful periods!

I hate you! Eyes narrowed she aimed her thoughts at the kitchen door. *You are small-minded and narrow-minded and yes, Mother, you are bad-minded, too! Tell you about Jon? I'd rather have my tongue pulled out!*

She took a deep breath, then set the kettle to boil. Her mouth felt tight as a trap, her tears were forgotten. In that moment she knew she was doing the right thing; that all the lies she must tell in the future and all the underhandedness and deceit would lay lightly on her conscience. They wouldn't let her marry Jon – not if she begged them on her knees – but wasn't marriage merely the words of a priest, and a piece of paper to prove he had said those words? Why must it be right because a priest or a minister said so? Why, if two people were in love, could they not be lovers?

Because society said it was wrong before marriage! The act of love was taboo, until the magic words had been said! And after that, not only was it right, but was *expected* of them!

Cant! Hypocrisy! Old people who were no longer capable of loving, denying it to those who were – until they had been through the rigmarole of the Ritual of Words, that was, and received the smirking approval of society!

Anger thudding inside her, she filled a jug with milk, sliced pieces of forbidden cake and placed them on the best china plates, laid the tray with a clean white cloth. There was no pain inside her now, no self-recrimination. Just bitterness towards her mother – and her father, too, for letting himself be henpecked and led by the nose, just because his wife's name stood alone on Laburnum Farm deeds.

A week from now, Jon would be back and she would tell him she had not been able to confide in her father; explain why. And Jon would understand, and they would be lovers.

More than anything else, she wanted to belong.

The parlour fire was lit again on Boxing Day and piled with beech logs. The work of the farm had gone on as it always did; morning milking, pigs and poultry feeding, egg collecting, evening milking, mucking out. There were no days off for farmers.

Bart Kenton dozed. In the chintz-covered chair opposite, his wife knitted. Another pair of socks in the same dark grey. Sock wool was rationed. One clothing coupon must be surrendered for two ounces of wool and men's socks cost three coupons, bought over the counter. It gave Mildred Kenton great satisfaction to save a coupon by knitting her husband's socks, and the prim pleasure of saying to anyone who cared to listen that not once since she and Bart were wed had he worn a pair of shop socks!

'Are you doing anything, Rosamund?'

'No, Mother.' Only staring into the fire.

'Then you'd better hold this skein whilst I wind it. I'm running out of wool. And switch the wireless on, will you?'

The mantel clock, which was always a minute fast, began nine silver chimes, and when it was finished the announcer would say, 'This is the BBC Home Service. Here is the nine o'clock news, and this is Alvar Lidell reading it.' Or maybe it would be Stuart Hibberd. They seemed to take turns about, reading good news and bad in the same level, unemotional tones. Funereal voices, Rosamund thought.

She knelt at her mother's feet, thumbs jutting, hands held wide for the skein of wool. The Greenwich time signal pipped six times, then gave way to the Moment for Thought.

It was Stuart Hibberd's turn tonight. No one spoke, because

news bulletins were important and the one at nine especially so. Rosamund thought it strange that the war outside should be so regularly welcomed into their home since, at all other times it was kept firmly where it belonged – behind the chain fence at the end of the cow pasture!

A statement had been released, read the announcer, that General Dwight D. Eisenhower had been appointed Supreme Commander of the Allied Expeditionary Forces; our Russian allies, had begun their third offensive of the winter. The Eighth Army, meantime, was advancing steadily in Italy, having taken Ortona.

In the Adriatic, a motor torpedo boat of the Royal Navy had sunk a German light cruiser and on Christmas night, aircraft of Bomber Command completed a successful raid on Berlin. Eighteen of our aircraft did not return.

It was said in the same clipped tones, Rosamund thought miserably, and added at the end as something of an afterthought; as if it were the only piece of bad news in an otherwise splendidly optimistic Boxing Day bulletin.

'I must say that I didn't expect an American to be given precedence over Field Marshal Montgomery!' Mildred tossed the ball of wool into her knitting basket. 'But Americans can be very pushy.'

'We were glad enough of them in my war.' Bart opened an eye.

'That's what I'm trying to say. They join in when we have almost got the war won! And if you want my opinion, they'd have stayed neutral this time if the Japs hadn't sunk their fleet at Pearl Harbor.'

'Our lot had almost lost the war when they joined us in the trenches! We were right relieved to see them, I can tell you! None of us thought them pushy, Milly!'

'Be that as it may, Hitler got a fine Christmas present from *our* lot! I'll bet Berlin never expected a raid on Christmas night!' She said it gleefully, eyes bright with malice.

'No, Mother. And I don't suppose our bomber crews expected to be sent there either. A hundred and thirty men aren't coming back – ever! There'll have been a lot of telegrams today. "Happy Christmas, Madam! Sorry to have to tell you that your son was killed last night over Berlin!"'

'There's no need for sarcasm, Rosamund! It's war, and everyone suffers! Think of the mess it's made of our lives! Half our acres taken, and no right of appeal!'

'Granted. But I haven't gone to the war, and if I'd been born a boy you'd have been able to keep me out of the fighting too! We eat better than most. How many families had a Christmas cake this year? Who but you was able to scrape enough out of their rations to make one!'

'I – I save sugar. We none of us take it in drinks. I can put a little by every week!' Startled by the ferocity of her daughter's attack Mildred faltered. 'And – and we have our own eggs! Surely I can take a few for a cake at Christmas? And I had a bit of black treacle in the bottom of a tin.'

'And butter, and dried fruit? You kept milk back and churned it into butter, and I know you swapped eggs for some raisins!'

'Rosamund! I churned barely half a pound of butter! Does that make me a criminal?'

'When there's a war on, yes! All our milk should go to the marketing board. You know it's against the law to separate it into cream, or make butter! But you did.'

'Now that's enough! I won't have you speak to your mother like that, Rosamund!'

'I'm sorry, Dad, but this war hasn't touched us at all! We've got plenty of food and we've given no one to the fighting!'

'We've given half our livelihood!' Mildred had got her breath back. 'They took our fields!'

'Then if that's the worst of it, Mother, I don't think you've got a lot to worry about! And don't offer me a slice of that cake because it would choke me!'

She jumped to her feet, flinging open the door, slamming it behind her, making for the kitchen. She'd had enough, cooped up here all over Christmas, seeing no one at all, because you couldn't blame Bessie for not calling!

She flopped miserably on the three-legged stool beside the hearth, not bothering to light the lamp. The fire had been banked down with a mixture of coal dust and damp dead leaves, but there was a glow underneath. She held her hands to it, for comfort, because she had gone too far. She was unhappy and missing Jon and had taken it out on her parents – her mother, especially. But her mother was smug in her out-of-the-way farmhouse; could pretend the war was a thousand miles away, except when a bomber flew over to remind her!

'Lass?' The kitchen door opened. 'Are you all right?'

'Yes thanks, Dad.'

'There's no call to sit here in the dark.'

'I'm going to bed . . .'

'Then don't you think that before you do you might say good night to your mother and maybe tell her you're sorry for what you said?'

'Sorry? But I'm not! I only spoke the truth! We *are* well off here, and Mum *did* do a black-market fiddle to get that cake. There won't be a Christmas cake at Bessie's house!'

'I wouldn't mention the Drakes if I were you. They seem to upset your mother!'

'*Everybody* upsets Mother if she doesn't get her own way. And, Dad, I'm sorry if I upset you, but I won't apologize to Mum.'

She rose to take a candlestick from the mantelpiece. Then she lit it, and touched her father's cheek gently with her fingertips.

'Good night, Dad. Sleep well.'

'Well?' Mildred demanded of her husband as he closed the parlour door behind him. 'What did she have to say for herself?' Her knitting needles clicked at speed, her mouth was set tightly.

'Nowt. She's gone to bed. I don't think she's in the mood to eat humble pie tonight. Happen tomorrow, when she's slept on it, she'll tell you she didn't mean it.' He sat down wearily, then pushed his slippered feet to the fire.

'There's something wrong, and I'm going to get to the bottom of it, Bart!'

'There's nothing wrong with the lass that company her own age and a bit of warmth and sunshine wouldn't put right. Folk are sick and tired of the winter. Leave it, Mildred? And you've got to admit, she didn't go out Saturday.'

'Saturday was yesterday – Christmas Day! Of course she didn't go out!'

'And she stayed home today – didn't get on her bike and go to the village.'

'I should think not! This is a farm and a farm is for seven days a week! But there's something going on, I know it. There's been nothing but back answers, and for a long time now! Does she think she's grown up or something, just because she's registered?'

'She registered because the powers that be think she's grown up enough to do war work! They could have sent her to Preston, on munitions, or into the Army.'

'Well, they *didn't*! She's still at home, and till she's twenty-one she'll do as I say! And I'll have an explanation out of her in the morning; find out what she's about!'

Oh my word, yes! Because no matter how much her husband sat there shaking his head, there would be questions asked – *and answered* – tomorrow!

EIGHT

H ad all things been equal, Monday would have officially been Boxing Day, and an extra day's holiday. But official-dom insisted that factories on war work should not come to a halt over Christmas, and it was made clear that those who were unpatriotic enough to expect three days off would have to make do with two!

Bessie's father worked over Christmas without a break, the production of aircraft components being of the highest importance. Bessie's factory, on the other hand, put in extra hours without pay before Christmas, so that for three days the machines were stopped for maintenance and any necessary repairs, which was a good way as any to ease their conscience, Bessie said, glad to go along with it.

'What brings you to Laceby, Rosamund?' She was pleased to see her friend.

'To see you, because if I hadn't got out for an hour, I'd have gone screaming mad!'

'And to post a letter?'

'Two, actually. To Jon. He's back on Saturday. Hope there'll be a dance.'

'I don't see why not. There wasn't one last Saturday.'

'There wouldn't be, on Christmas Day – and anyway, they were flying. Makes you sick, doesn't it, crews being sent out on Christmas night. Eighteen missing, too.'

'Laceby's lot got back all right, I heard. I'll walk with you to the pillar box.'

'I've had two letters from Jon,' Rosamund confided when they were clear of the house. 'Has Mick written?'

'No, but I don't expect him to. We're just friends and dancing partners. He kisses me good night, but his heart isn't in it. I think he's got a steady girl at home.'

'But have you never thought to ask, Bessie? He might be married, even!'

'He might be, but it wouldn't matter. I haven't fallen for him. He's a marvellous dancer, though, and I'd be a bit miffed if some other girl grabbed him. Is Jon spoken for?'

'You know he isn't! He was tied up with work till he got his degree, and then he went straight into the Air Force. It's rotten luck he's got himself landed with someone like me; someone who hasn't got a normal family.'

'So define a normal family for me.'

'One like yours, I suppose.'

'What!' Bessie shrieked. 'Our lot are mad! Dad's always laying the law down about being careful with men; when the brothers were at home, Mum yelled at them all the time for not changing their socks and leaving their room in a mess, and now that they're in the Navy, she nags Dad instead, for going to the pub. And Dad moans at Mum for always wanting more housekeeping money. If that's normal, I'm Betty Grable!'

'Yes, but your mother laughs a lot and she isn't narrow-minded. And you can get out on dates without having to lie about it.'

'I lie to Dad, though.'

'So? I lie to both my parents. At least I do now, since I met Jon.' Rosamund slipped her arm in that of her friend, then whispered, 'We want to get married, Bess.'

'Married!'

'Sssh! Keep your voice down! And don't say we've only known each other two months! I fell for Jon the minute I saw him, and it was the same for him, too.' She slid the letters into the pillar box, smiling them on their way. 'Oh, well – best get back . . .'

'What's the hurry? Why don't we walk to the end of the village?' Bessie scented news of importance. 'Are you sure you want to get married? Isn't it because he's the first bloke you've fallen for – and glamorous with it?'

'I'm sure.' Rosamund gazed ahead, fixedly. 'I want him to make love to me and it's best you're married before you let anything like that happen.'

'But your folks won't let you! Don't suppose you've thought to ask, because you *do* need permission!'

'Think I hadn't realized that? I was going to tell Dad about us, so he'd be on my side, but I've decided I'm not going to. Mum would go raving mad and he'd have to side with her. His life wouldn't be worth living if he didn't. I wouldn't want to land him in it. I'm very fond of Dad.'

'But not your mother?' Bessie hissed, warming to the drama.

'No. Sometimes I think I hate her. D'you know, I'd just read Jon's letter and got a bit weepy when she came into the kitchen and caught me; said I needed a laxative! How can you tell someone like her that you're in love?'

'So what will you do? You'll have to be careful, Rosamund! You know what I'm talking about, don't you?'

'If – *when* – it happens, Jon knows how. You don't have to get pregnant. Your cousin didn't, did she, on the haystack?'

'N-no. Well, all I can say,' Bessie choked, round-eyed, 'is that you and Jon are going to have to find yourselves a haystack – pretty damn quick!'

Rosamund thought about haystacks all the way home; about why she hadn't thought of it before, and how warm it would be and how far away from the house their own hayloft was. It would be perfect, if Shep didn't start barking. And soon it would be spring, and the days warmer and the nights lighter. The hayloft would do, until they could find somewhere better. Her cheeks burned, just to think of it.

Then her elation left her, because Jon wasn't the sort to do something like that; not on her own doorstep. He would think it cheeky and much too risky! She was stupid even to entertain the idea. Yet as she pushed her cycle into the stable, she looked longingly across at the tall, red-brick hayloft. Come to think of it, it was quite a way from Shep's kennel too.

Her father crossed the yard as she closed the stable door and he smiled and asked her if she'd enjoyed her bike ride.

'Yes, Dad. Blew all the cobwebs away. Just went as far as the village – called in on Bessie. I'll get into my overalls, and start the milking.'

'I must say, lass, that it's brought the roses back to your cheeks.'

Roses? Oh, Dad, if only you knew!

She made for the house, wishing she didn't like her father so much; wishing she wasn't such a deceitful little bitch and that her mother was more like Bessie's mother. Then she thought about Jon's arms and his mouth on hers and the scent of summer hay all about them, and all her doubts were gone.

'So you've decided, then? You're going back a day early?'

'Do you mind, Aunt Lottie? I know I'm officially on leave till midnight, Saturday, but if I get the overnight train on Friday, I'll be back in camp before midday – get my head down for a couple of hours, then –'

'Then you'll be seeing Rosie?' She smiled with her eyes at the young man who had been hers since he was little more than a baby, and wanted with all her heart to beg him never to go back! He had grown up so well; should have had a future. Now, everything was uncertain, because the young fool had volunteered the minute he'd finished university, and for aircrew, too! And the way things stood now, he had only a fifty-fifty chance of making it through the war! Just to think of it filled her with dread.

'All your washing is done, and I've sponged and pressed your uniform.' She said it matter-of-factly, as if she were absolutely sure she would see him again after tomorrow night. It was just bearable now because he was wearing old trousers and a sweater and looking like a civilian, but the minute he put on that uniform he would belong to the war. 'And don't forget to get a decent haircut before you go back! That RAF barber scalps you!'

'Has anybody told you, Miss Martin, you can be a very bossy lady at times?'

'I'm entitled. I'm your mother, aren't I?'

'Funny, but I've never called you Mum.'

'Thought it best you didn't, and me with no wedding ring!' She forced her lips into a grin. 'And you'll ask your Rosie to write to me, won't you? If she can't come and see me, at least we can send the odd letter.'

'She'd like that — so will I.'

'Good! By the way, has she got a photo of you — a decent one?'

'Afraid not, nor me of her.'

'Then I think you'd better take her this.' She handed him a framed photograph. 'And pack it carefully; I don't want the glass broken.'

'Good grief! Me, when I was a sprog pilot! Seems like years ago!'

'You reckon?' She didn't say it was little more than a year, taken before he went to Canada to do his night-flying training. He hadn't earned his sergeant's stripes then, nor sewn up his pilot's wings. The young man who smiled into the camera had worn a white flash in his cap to show he was training for aircrew. 'I'm giving you this one because you didn't sign it. Think you'd better put Rosie's name on it. Will that be all right, Jon?'

'It's a great idea. Thanks a lot!'

She would probably keep it at the bottom of a drawer, he thought sadly, because she couldn't have a photograph of a man who doesn't exist beside her bed.

'And, Jon — whilst I'm laying down the law — I do understand the way things are between you; understand better than you know! Be careful, uh?'

She wanted to tell him that if anything went wrong and he didn't make it, his young lady would have one hell of a time with that mother of hers! She bit on the words, though, because you didn't say such things when there was a war on.

'You know I will. I care for her too much — but thanks for understanding.' He reached for her, pulling her close, laying his cheek on hers. 'And I care for you too — you know that, don't you?'

'Reckon so. Now for Pete's sake, let's have done with all the soul-searching! I feel like a lazy night, listening to the wireless. And there's still some whisky left; what say we finish it? And no more war talk! We won't even listen to the news!'

'Fine by me,' he smiled, grateful for her understanding.

Yet for all that, he couldn't deny that tomorrow night couldn't come soon enough and that on Saturday, at about eight, Rosie would jump down from the back of the transport and straight into his arms.

The thought filled him with gladness and sadness, because he had never thought to love and want someone as desperately and unashamedly as he loved and wanted her, which was a bad do, really, because men like him lived one day at a time.

Rosie! Wherever you are, whatever you are doing, I love you.

He sent his thoughts high and wide, so they would reach her, though he knew exactly where she was, what she was doing. Rosie would be in the shippon, milking, and counting the hours until Saturday night at eight. Just as he was!

'I'll be going out tomorrow night,' Rosamund remarked as she toasted bread at the kitchen fire. 'Probably to the flicks. It's *Casablanca*.'

'Well! If that isn't the absolute end!' Mildred Kenton, ignoring her daughter completely, folded the morning paper angrily. 'They're cutting the clothing coupons! Again! All we're to have is twenty-four to last till the end of June! We'll be running around in skins, next!'

She closed her eyes, shuddering. Two warm nightgowns, three pairs of stockings and four for yardage for a blouse, had put paid to her last allowance of coupons, and the new issue already spoken for because she needed knickers. Those she was wearing were so darned and dishevelled, she hardly dare hang them out on washday! Three pairs she would need, which meant six coupons, and not a thing to show for it!

'What about the coupons you got from Ned Loftus?' Rosamund demanded, turning the bread on the fork; black-market coupons which should have been hers by rights since they'd been swapped for *her* clothes!

'Those coupons were used to buy working boots and warm

trousers for your father! Surely you didn't think I was giving them to you to waste on fripperies!'

'As a matter of fact, I could have done with a few, but I don't begrudge them to Dad.'

Yet for all that, just five of those illicit coupons would have provided the wool for a cardigan; she was desperate for a blue cardi!

'And what is more,' Mildred rushed on, deep in self-pity, 'those Germans *have* got a secret weapon!'

'You've been listening to Haw-Haw,' Bart teased. 'Shame on you!'

'I have not! I heard it yesterday in town. There were two women in the queue in front of me, and they'd read it in the paper!'

'Don't you think it was *our* invention they were on about – that plane without propellers, the one that flies on jets?' Though jets of what he hadn't yet fathomed.

'No! Those women called it a rocket, I tell you, and they said it was a plane without a pilot. Seems the news came from Sweden.'

'Now what would the Swedes know about it? They aren't even in the war!'

'I'm only telling you what I heard. It sent me cold all over. Sending poison gas by rocket, that's what Hitler'll be doing!' Close to tears, she dropped her knife and fork with a clatter. 'I've had as much as I can stand of this war!'

'So have we all.' Briefly Rosamund laid a hand on her mother's shaking shoulders. 'But we are winning now, and I'll bet you anything you like those rockets are only propaganda, put out to upset us. Do you honestly think that if Hitler really did have a secret weapon he'd tell anybody about it?'

'Then the papers shouldn't print such lies!'

'Oh, Milly Kenton,' her husband laughed, 'wasn't it your very self who said we should never believe a thing the newspapers printed except the date? And only then when we'd checked it for ourselves with the calendar!'

'Dad's right. Mind, the papers do get the blackout times right – and guess what: tonight we don't have to black out till six o'clock! We'll get afternoon milking finished before it's dark. And I saw snowdrops yesterday at the end of the lane.' *And please, Mother, please, wipe the gloom and doom from your face?* 'It's 1944, and this year we're going to win. Just think of it – before another new year, the blackout could be gone for ever and we'll light the biggest bonfire you ever saw on Beacon Fell!'

'You think so, child?'

'I'm *sure*, Mother.'

And, God, I'm sorry for lying through my teeth, saying things I don't believe, but she goes on and on and upsets everybody. And forgive me for wishing her in deepest Siberia . . .

Jon Hunt quietly closed the door of the Nissen hut his crew shared with the crew of *Z-Zebra*. It smelled of sweat and damp and stale air. At the far end, seven men lay on black-painted iron beds, snorting and snoring beneath grey blankets. Around them, carelessly discarded, lay flying jackets and boots and battledress tops. *Zebra* had been on ops last night, Jon figured, and now its crew slept the sleep of the pardoned; the lucky sods who had made it back to Laceby Green.

Slowly, as if reluctant to acknowledge he was a part of it again, he hung his respirator and greatcoat on the peg beside his bed, then pushed his case beneath it. He was the first back of *Johnnie*'s crew; the remainder, he supposed, would arrive at the very last minute, and Harry would either bore everyone to tears with the amazing progress of his new daughter, or be moody and quiet, announcing that anyone who sang, 'You've had it chum, you've had it, never mind' would have his features rearranged, so bloodywell watch it!

Leave was great; returning from it was a bind. People who reminded you you'd had it for another three months were not popular.

Jon shivered. He was cold and tired, his eyes felt gritty and his uniform had the stink of the dusty train on it. He needed to wash away the overnight smell, but a shower would revive him and he desperately needed to sleep, first savouring the fact that if Laceby's crews had been on operations last night, there was a fair chance of making it to the dance tonight.

Someone at the far end of the hut grunted and turned over with a creaking of bedsprings. The cold struck unmercifully through the concrete floor. No one had bothered to stoke up the stove, and it had gone out. On his bed lay three grey blankets and it made him think of his bed at Primrose Cottage with its soft blankets and blue eiderdown.

He draped his uniform on a hanger, then shrugged out of his underwear, wrapping a blanket round himself, pulling the remainder over him. Then he closed his eyes to shut out the cold, trying not to let the roughness of the blankets irritate him into wakefulness.

Instead, he thought about Rosie; about her small, round breasts and the feel of her mouth beneath his, shutting down his thoughts at the first kiss; fearful that if he allowed himself to undress her, sleep would elude him.

He pulled the blankets over his head, tried hard to control his cold, shaking body and whispered, 'See you, darling. Soon . . .'

Ten days, which had seemed an eternity, were as seconds at the meeting of their lips. Neither spoke. Being together again was all that mattered.

Presently, her mouth close to his ear, she whispered, 'Don't ever leave me again, Jon?'

'I won't. Promise. Tell me . . . ?'

'I love you.'

'And I love you, Rosie Kenton.'

The transport had driven off; those it carried headed for the heavily curtained door of the hut. Jon and Rosamund were alone now in the frosty darkness, and a sudden, spiteful slap of wind hit them.

'Shall we go inside?'

'Kiss me first, Jon. And there's something I have to tell you.'

'Like what?' His voice was all at once sharp.

'Ssssh. I haven't stopped loving you, but –'

341

'But we can't meet again – is that what you're going to say? Did something happen whilst I was away, Rosie?'

'That's just it – nothing at all happened. But I want to tell you I love you and ask you to marry me because it's 1944 now, and leap year. Mind, you can always turn me down, but it'll cost you a silken gown!'

'Then I'd better say thanks a lot, and yes, please, I'd like that very much. Would tomorrow suit you?' He smiled indulgently, eyes teasing.

'No, thanks. A week tonight would be much better. I mean it, Jon. We agreed, didn't we – you still want it to happen for us?'

'You know I do! Are *you* sure, darling?'

'Absolutely. So shall we go inside and find a corner, and talk?'

They pushed, blinking, through the heavy curtain and into the smoke-filled hut, where a conga chain lurched crazily around the floor and the band played loudly and out of tune, sidestepping the heave of bodies to find corner seats. He pulled her close, kissing her, not caring who saw them.

'So tell me about next Saturday?' He twined his fingers in hers, moving closer.

'I've found somewhere, darling; a hayloft. *Our* hayloft . . .'

'*Your* place? You've got to be joking! Of all the damn-fool things I ever heard, that's it!'

'So you don't want to?' Her body went tense with apprehension.

'You know I do,' he hissed, 'but at Laburnum Farm? If you think I'm risking a thing like that – well, it just isn't on!'

'I see. Most ungentlemanly, I suppose, even to consider deflowering a wench right under her father's nose!'

'Rosie! What's got into you?' His voice was rough with disbelief.

'You mean have I been drinking; reading dirty books . . . ?'

'You know what I mean.' He spoke more quietly because the music had stopped and the dancers were returning, red-cheeked and gasping, to their seats.

'But I *don't* know, Jon. I only know I've thought it all out

– thought about nothing else since Bessie suggested it. I was telling her about us, you see, and how we wanted to be together, especially as there's no chance of us getting married.'

'So your father said no – or more to the point, you didn't tell him about us.' He said it matter-of-factly, as if he had known all along she would not.

'That's right . . .'

'Then maybe it's as well. I'd half expected it, began to think when you hadn't mentioned it in your letters that something had gone wrong.'

'It has. I was too scared, decided against it; daren't risk them stopping me seeing you. I'm sorry, but I realized all at once it'd be like hitting my head against a brick wall – would get me nowhere.'

'So instead you discussed us and our future with Bessie?'

'Not exactly. But I did tell her how we both felt about wanting to be married, and that it wasn't any use asking Dad's permission. I said the only thing now was for us – well, to be lovers, and she agreed with me; said it wouldn't be a good idea at all telling them about us, because Mum would put the kibosh on it!' She stopped, all at once breathless, then whispered, 'Bessie is right, Jon. She knows what my mother is like. It was why she said it looked like you and me were going to have to find ourselves a haystack. And I wondered why I hadn't thought of it myself.'

'So Bessie is *au fait* with haystacks?'

'No, but her cousin is . . .'

'Oh, darling!' The tension and disbelief left him and he laughed out loud. 'You are so – so *innocent!*'

'I couldn't agree more, Jon Hunt! And if you won't at least let me tell you about the hayloft, innocent is the way I'm going to stay! I love you very much, you see, and I don't want to wait until I'm old enough to marry you!'

'You mean it, don't you?' He smiled gently, wonderingly, into her eyes. 'You really want us to!'

'They'll never let us get married, so it's the only way.'

'Then maybe we better *had* talk about haylofts?'

'Talk seriously, Jon?'

'*Very* seriously. About what could happen, for a start. Had you thought about what could go wrong? Do you realize you could be left holding the baby?'

'What do you mean – holding the baby!' Her voice was shrill with alarm. 'Are you getting cold feet? Now you can have me, are you suddenly not interested?'

'Rosie! Ssssh! You know I want you! And I was talking about us, too, to Aunt Lottie; told her how it was between you and me, and she said she and her fiancé were desperately in love too, but decided to wait until his next leave, when they'd have been married.'

'And he was killed, wasn't he?' she said flatly.

'Just before his leave was due. She said she was sorry they hadn't been lovers; said she wouldn't have cared about getting pregnant, nor what an upset it would have caused. That's what I'm trying to say, I suppose – what if you got pregnant, Rosie?'

'If something went wrong, you mean? Well, you'd have to marry me then, Jon. I wouldn't care if people knew we'd had to get married. Come to think of it, my mother would have us down the aisle so fast, our feet wouldn't touch the ground,' she giggled nervously.

'Darling – be serious. What if I got the chop one night, then you found you were having a baby? Could you take it; your parents' anger, the sneers, having to bring up a child alone – seeing people point a finger at your brat? Because the child would suffer too! Have you thought it all out – the risks?'

'You *won't* get the chop, Jon. You're going to do your thirty ops and be taken off flying for a year. And by the time you crew-up again, I'll be of age. But if it happened to us like it did to your Aunt Lottie and her young man, then I'd do exactly as she'd have done. I'd want your child, and no one would make me give it away. I love you. It's as simple as that'

'And I love you, Rosie. I always will. And you won't get pregnant. I'll take care of it.'

'Then don't ever say such a thing again! We're going to be married one day and have children and grow old together – I promise you we are. Don't forget I live in the house a witch built! I can see into the future!'

'Idiot!'

'Let's leave now – go back to Laburnum, Jon. We can do a recce along the side path. Let's try getting to the hayloft – see if Shep hears us, and barks. I don't think he will, though. It's quite a way from the house. Surely it's worth a try?'

'And if we don't get away with it . . . ?'

'Then we're back to square one again, and I'm stuck with my innocence!'

She thought about it that night, triumph singing through her, making sleep impossible. They had opened the little iron gate, slowly and carefully so it shouldn't squeak, then walked up the long path, past the backs of the shippon and the cooling shed and the stables, she trailing a hand along the wall to guide them in the darkness. And Shep had not barked, even as they'd lifted the wooden latch of the small side door and crept into the sweetly smelling barn.

'There are wooden steps at the far end, leading up to the loft,' she whispered. 'I should have brought my bike lamp and shown you.'

'And there are no windows, or anything?'

'No. Just ventilation bricks in the gable end walls.'

'So we'd be safe, here?' He'd kissed her in the darkness.

'As safe as anywhere.'

'Next Saturday, then? Here?'

It had been like, she thought hugging the pillow, a problem solved, a worry gone, the way ahead all at once clear for them. A decision made; a coupling agreed. There would be no priest, though, to bless them, make it respectable, acceptable, moral.

But it didn't seem to matter.

'So what's it all about, then?' Bessie pulled out the chair opposite, sitting down with a dramatic flop. 'What's so urgent that it's life and death?'

'It isn't. Not any more. And I know Friday is your busy

day, with the wages, an' all, but I panicked, Bess, and rang you because I was so worried.'

'What about? Your period late, or something?'

'No! How can it be? I told Mum I was meeting you at the British Restaurant for lunch and that I had things to buy – you know, *personals* – so she didn't make a fuss. I got the eleven o'clock bus from the village and I've been waiting here, trying to keep a seat for you.'

'Then if it isn't life or death you can pay, Rosamund!'

'Oh, I will!' British Restaurants weren't allowed to make a profit. A fair-to-middling meal could be had for one-and-sevenpence. She could afford it.

'OK. We'll go and get our food, then you can tell me what was so urgent.' Bessie was piqued there was to be no drama. 'Do you think we'll be able to get the treacle sponge? Hope it hasn't all gone! So tell me . . . ?'

They stood in the queue, trays at the ready, taking small soups, shepherd's pie and carrots and, thanks be, treacle sponge with saccharin-sweetened custard. They refused tea, at a penny a cup, and Rosamund handed over three shillings, smiling at the elderly cashier.

'Sorry I made it sound urgent, Bess, but I was really worried. Jon didn't turn up on Sunday night, nor Monday nor Tuesday and when he didn't come on Wednesday night, I thought I'd blown it.'

'But they were flying on Wednesday night! You couldn't miss it.'

'I know. Jon was at the gate last night and I was so relieved. They'd been on standby for three nights, but the ops were cancelled. He couldn't get out, though. No one could've. I thought I'd gone too far, you see, and he'd decided he'd had enough of me.'

'But he's mad about you!'

'Yes, but when he wasn't at the gate for *four* nights, do you blame me? I thought I'd frightened him off.'

'I haven't the slightest idea what you're on about,' Bessie said loftily.

'Bess! Remember the haystack?' She lowered her voice.

'Well, I found one. Our hayloft, actually. That's why we left the dance early. We went to see if we could get there without the dog barking and –'

'*Your* hay barn! You're out of your tiny mind, Rosamund Kenton!'

'*Ssssh!* Keep your voice down. I suggested it, you see, and that's why I thought he'd had enough – that girls who offer it on a plate are common! And when I got to thinking about it, when he didn't turn up, I mean – I had to admit that I'd made most of the running. I was frantic with worry, then there he was last night, full of apologies and loving me just as much. And nothing has changed. Officially I'll be with you tomorrow night, but we'll be –'

'In your hayloft,' Bessie gulped. 'Oh, Rosamund – are you sure you know what you're doing?'

'No I don't. I shall probably make a mess of it, never having done it before! But if you mean am I sure about, well – *that* – yes, I am. There isn't a hope of us getting married so you can't blame us, can you?'

'No. If I'd fallen as badly as you have, I think I'd be very tempted myself. But you'll have to be careful; tell Jon not to go all the way to Preston – get off at Clitheroe, sort of.'

'Jon will take care of it. Nothing happened to your cousin, did it?'

'N-no. But she only did it once, I think.'

'Once is usually enough, Bess.' It was with animals, anyway. 'But I've got something to show you. Jon gave it to me last night.'

Carefully she took the photograph from her shopping bag, offering it with a tremulous smile.

'Hm!' Bessie read the inscription. '*To my Rosie. Always, Jon.* And what is your mother going to say when she sees it?'

'She won't. I'm keeping it in a drawer she hardly ever goes in. I pop upstairs whenever I can and look at it.'

'Your mother has no right to go fishing in your drawers, Rosamund. Serve her right if she went rooting and found it. She'd have a fit!'

'She won't find it. I'll make sure she doesn't.'

'And what about the hayloft? Are you sure you can get away with that, too?'

'We'll have a darn good try. And it won't be for ever. The light nights will soon be here and I'll be able to get out more often. We'll find somewhere else.'

'Well, I can only say for Pete's sake be careful? Promise you will?'

'I will. The main thing is for us not to get caught!'

'The main thing,' Bessie whispered as they got up to leave, 'is that you don't end up in trouble, because God help you, girl, if you do!'

'I know what I'm doing!'

Famous last words, Bessie thought, though she didn't say it. But she thought about Jon and Rosamund all the way back to the factory, and wished like anything something as mad and mind-boggling and wonderful could happen to her. Because it was awful, when you were touching nineteen and curious, still . . .

The crew of *J-Johnnie* sat in their usual places, staring at the curtain that covered the wall map, willing it, as they always did, to have route ribbons stretching to the coast of Holland and back; a diversionary op, flying high out of the reach of enemy fighters, yet drawing them away from the main bomber stream. Or maybe a spot of mine-laying in coastal waters, which was almost a milk run.

'It'll be a nasty one,' Mac said to Tom and Harry.

'Oh?' the bomb-aimer Tom shrugged. 'So where are we going, know-all?'

'Dunno. But half the squadron will be stuck with a big bastard. I saw six of them being loaded.'

They didn't carry 22,000 pound bombs for fun; they'd be away to the Ruhr, like as not; to happy valley that was snarling with fighters and searchlights and flak, he thought gloomily.

'You're a miserable bastard, MacBain,' Harry snarled, wishing now he was a father never to have to fly again. He crushed out his cigarette, then lit another.

Tom wound his lucky silk stocking around his neck, knotted

it firmly, then said, 'It'll be a piece of cake. This one's our fifteenth – halfway there – and Skip has flown twenty-two, don't forget. We aren't exactly a sprog crew!'

Dick had a fair idea of their target. He and Jon had already attended first briefing for pilots and navigators; would know, soon, if their inspired guess was correct.

Sammy, the wireless operator, said nothing, tapping his wedding ring on the edge of the table, because tapping out SOS was a part of the ritual of briefing and takeoff, and the rest of the crew didn't complain.

The air was thick with cigarette smoke. Smoking too much was also a part of the briefing ritual and almost everyone did it. Cigarettes soothed and steadied, were drawn on as if that particular one was the very last and which, according to the gospel of MacBain, it might turn out to be.

The Station Commander entered the room and there was a sudden hush, then a grating of chairs as everyone stood.

'Good evening, gentlemen.' Briefing had begun. 'Please be seated . . .'

Gentlemen, Mac thought miserably. They were always gentlemen when being sent to their deaths over the Ruhr.

The curtains were pulled apart, the map of Europe revealed. The tapes stretched to Berlin. Sodding Berlin!

'Our target for tonight,' said the Station Commander, 'is Berlin . . .'

Dick winked sideways in Jon's direction. Jon nodded, already having prepared himself for the worst target of all. Sammy, whose left hand had been briefly still, began tapping again. There was the slightest of groans, then lighters flicked furiously and a fresh cloud of smoke rose to the ceiling.

OK! So it was Berlin tonight. They'd been there before, hadn't they, and made it back all right? They weren't sprogs. They knew Berlin by night like the backs of their hands!

Harry whispered, 'Holy shit!' but no one laughed.

They ate a flying supper – almost always bacon and eggs and bread and butter – and swallowed one mug of sweet tea. No more than one, or you wanted to pee all the way there and back, and using the Elsan toilet in flying kit was more trouble than it was worth.

They drew their parachutes, then, making the same stupid joke. 'What if this chute doesn't open, Corporal?' Answer. 'Bring it back. We'll gladly replace it!' It wouldn't have been takeoff without the joke, at which the Waaf parachute girls always laughed.

The trucks to drive them to dispersal were waiting outside, and they climbed clumsily in, clutching parachutes. This, Jon thought, was like going to the dentist. Once you'd rung the bell and the door was opened, there was no going back. But it was the walking-up-the-path-to-the-door bit that was the worst, and to Jon, being driven to *J-Johnnie* was the path; seeing the Lancaster, bombed up and fuelled up, was like ringing the doorbell.

After that, climbing the steps into the belly of the aircraft was less traumatic, almost the point of no return. Placing his parachute on his seat, settling himself down on it, patting Matilda Mint, who hung behind him, was like sitting in the dentist's chair and opening wide. After that, it was in the lap of the gods, and he tried not to think that no matter how awful a filling was, the dentist never tried to kill you. Staggering a bit, clutching your throbbing cheek, you *always* walked down the path again! It followed, then, that flying to Berlin and back, carting a bomb load beneath you and wings full of fuel, was not a bit like having a particularly nasty filling. It was a million times worse!

He drew a deep breath, held it as long as he could, then let it go in little huffs. Then he began his checks, switching on the microphone on his helmet, going round the crew in turn, as calmly as he could.

Pilot to navigator . . . to rear gunner . . . speaking to all six, always leaving the bomb-aimer until last. Tom was a mad sod and always lay in the nose, face down, at takeoff, giving a commentary as they went.

'Bomb-aimer to skipper. There's that little blonde Waaf waving her knickers again!'

Tom always liked to see the Waaf, who stood at the side of

the perimeter track near the control tower for every takeoff, waving her knickers for luck. It boded well for the operation, he said, even though they all knew she waved a white scarf.

'Bomb-aimer to Skipper.' They were halfway round the perimeter track now, lurching clumsily to takeoff. 'Just passed your little milkmaid. Did you see her?'

'I saw her, bomb-aimer.'

Neither of them had, of course, but in the gloom, each glimpsed the white handkerchief she always tied to the fence.

Tom liked to see Skip's milkmaid, too, all shadowy through the perspex of the window, and ran his forefinger round his neck. It was like touching his girlfriend's silk-stockinged leg; his own good-luck gesture, made just before the green light flashed and they hurtled, engines snarling, down the runway past the point of no return. The Lancaster tilted slightly as the tail wheel left the ground; then they were airborne with a sickening lurch, and roaring over Laceby Green.

The wheels retracted with a loud clunk, and Jon sent his thoughts to the steel-mesh fence as the Lancaster climbed steadily, sweetly.

I love you, Rosie. So long, sweetheart. See you tomorrow night. At eight . . .

'I'll make the toast, if you like.'

Rosamund padded into the kitchen on stockinged feet, glad that milking was over. Despite the milky warmness of the cows' bodies, it had been bitterly cold this morning in the shippon, with an east wind blowing viciously through every hole and crack.

The coals in the fire-bottom glowed redly through the bars and she knelt before them, grateful for the heat that would scorch her face long before the plate of bread at her side was toasted.

'Where is your father?' Mildred Kenton broke eggs into the frying pan. 'It's almost ready.'

'Coming. He went to let Shep off the chain.'

Rosamund did not want to talk. This morning, until the

aching cold that gripped her had gone, she wanted to gaze into the fireglow, dream dreams, think about tonight, at eight.

She was tired; had been awake several times during the night, and as soon as the bombers began to return she had left her bed to stand at the window, peering into the blackness.

Last night, ten bombers took off from RAF Laceby. She had stood at the perimeter fence counting, the handkerchief she had knotted onto the fence blowing in the early evening air.

Her mother never asked her where she had been, now, when she disappeared for almost an hour; knew she would be standing at the fence. She always did, these days, and her mother had got used to the laconic answer, 'Watching them take off; wishing them luck . . .'

'One of those things'll crash one night, and then where will you be, eh?'

'Spattered all over the cow pasture, like as not, in very small pieces.'

So no questions were asked, now; no answers given. Doubtless her mother had decided she was either a patriotic little fool, or maybe just curious; it didn't matter.

Jon could not see her as his Lancaster taxied past the bottom of the pasture, but he knew she was there, wishing him well, loving him, and that she would awaken when he returned, to listen and to count.

Last night, she was particularly anxious, because she had seen the huge bombs some of the planes would carry. She had thought herself lucky, because both parents were out for the afternoon. It rarely happened that she was left alone, but her father was in need of a haircut and it was her mother's Friday for collecting the grocery and meat rations. Rosamund supposed, as she had waved them off in the pony cart, that now they only had half a farm, she could be trusted with it, and to get the cows into the shippon and make a start on the milking on her own. It also meant she was free to spend more time at the fence; gaze over towards the aerodrome for tell-tale signs of activity.

This afternoon she wished she had not been there, because what she saw made her very afraid. She had never seen those bombs before; not such big ones. She knew about them; their size had been reported in all the newspapers and their terrible powers of destruction. But she had never expected to see one so close to, nor the trailers on which they rested being towed by tractors driven by Waafs. By *women*! Young women sitting there as calm as you please, with tons of death behind them!

She had not known whether to burst with pride or burst into tears, and chose the latter as she fled for the safety of the kitchen to crouch in front of the fire, all at once glad she had never towed anything more deadly behind their own tractor than milk churns, or a load of hay to feed to the cows in the foldyard. Hay . . . She and Jon in the hayloft, tonight at eight.

She heard her mother's meaningful sniff, realized she was burning the toast, and quickly turned the bread on the long brass fork.

Forget tonight at eight, she urged silently. Until then she must live through twelve hours of excitement and worry and fear. Fear would be uppermost in her mind all day because already she was afraid she would make a mess of it; make Jon think she was frigid. And she wasn't frigid. She loved him, wanted more than anything for them to belong to each other. It was, she supposed, as she scraped the blackened piece of bread to a more acceptable shade and texture, that she was not so much afraid, as apprehensive; fearful of getting it wrong and spoiling it for Jon, and –

'I think,' her mother said tartly, 'that you'd better throw that piece into the swill bucket, and do another!'

Aaaagh! There was nothing like burned toast and acid asides to bring a girl down to earth again!

At a quarter to eight, Rosamund laid aside the stocking she was darning and said, in a voice not a bit like her own, 'Think I'll be off now . . .'

'Out?' Her father raised an eyebrow. 'I thought when it had got to this time, you'd decided to stop in, lass.'

'Did you? Er – sorry.' She gave him a surprised half-smile.

'What your father means,' said her mother with too much emphasis, 'is that you are usually away by seven on a Saturday night.'

'Doesn't matter if I'm late. We aren't doing anything special. Bessie will be expecting me when she sees me, I suppose.'

She was so amazed at the glibness with which the lie slipped off her tongue that her heart began to thud and she had to take a deep breath and concentrate hard on her bicycle lamps, switching them on and off with studied care.

She had rehearsed in her mind all day what she would do and say, and at what time; been over it until she was word perfect and everything would seem Saturday-night normal. She would take her handbag as she always did, check her bike lamps, tie a scarf over her hair, then shrug on her short coat. 'Night, Mum, Dad,' she would say, like always. 'Won't be late and yes, I'll take care in the dark!' Yet not once, she realized, had she allowed for the time, though her mother had been on to it like a terrier onto a rat!

'Well, then,' she said softly, placing the lamps beside her handbag, reaching for her scarf, 'I'll be off.' She buttoned her coat carefully, smiling, 'Night. Won't be late!' closing the kitchen door behind her, leaning briefly against it because she was shaking so.

She took a deep, steadying breath, feeling her way across the dark dairy, opening and shutting the door noisily. And she must remember to bang the door of the small barn in which she kept her bike and do everything exactly as she would have done it had she been going to Bessie's, even calling to Shep as she passed his kennel.

Then she would turn on her lamps in case her mother decided to go upstairs and watch her, and push the bike slowly and carefully in the direction of the top of the lane.

Downright deceitful? Of course it was, but Jon was worth all the lies, and anyway, what else could she do with such bad-minded parents?

Parent! Dad wasn't bad-minded nor suspicious; didn't measure her against his own narrow yardstick. Dad, if he hadn't let himself be ground down by her mother, might even be master in his own house and say yes, of course she could bring her young man to Sunday tea!

She banged the stable door defiantly, half expecting her mother to call her back, then thought that if she knew where her daughter was going and what she intended doing, that was just what she would do!

It didn't make her feel any better about her bare-faced lying, but it pleased her when Shep began to bark, that her voice sounded normal as she called, 'Quiet, boy! It's only me!'

Calmer now, she pushed her cycle to the top of the lane, then switched off the front and rear lights, turning in her tracks, making for the narrow path that led to the little iron gate, the worst over. All she had to do now was push her cycle out of sight, then walk slowly to where Jon would be waiting – oh, *please* let him be there?

Then relief and happiness washed over her as she ran, not caring about the darkness, nor the slippiness of the path, into the safety of his arms.

'Darling! You came!'

'Did you think I wouldn't?' He took her face in his hands, kissing her softly.

'I've been thinking about it all day. I wanted you to be here so much that I was afraid you wouldn't be!'

'So you still – want to?'

'Yes! But I've been a bit worried about it.'

'Why, Rosie?'

'Because I don't know how to. I've never – we-e-ll – not before . . .'

'Well, I *do* know, because I have.'

'Jon! You said there was only me!' Dismay hit her like a slap.

'I said I'd only ever been in love with you.'

'So now you tell me there have been other girls in your life!'

'Best you should know, darling. It's you and me from now on. The first day of the rest of our lives. Best the slate is clean.'

He searched for her mouth, but she jerked her head back, gasping, 'Who was she? You *must* have loved her!'

'Ssssh! I didn't, and she didn't love me. She was a corporal in the ATS, on a gun site outside Cambridge. We met at a dance. She was missing love – her husband was overseas – and I hadn't a clue. I only knew I was desperate to get a bit of living in, have a taste of what life was all about before I got the chop! I'd already passed the medical and been accepted for aircrew; I was as good as in, though the RAF let me take my finals before they called me up. Have I hurt you, darling?' he whispered, when she didn't speak.

'N-no. It's a bit of a shock, though I suppose it was stupid of me to think someone as attractive as you hadn't been around. How many were there?'

'Just the one. Pamela.'

'And did it last long between you?'

'Not long. She was promoted to sergeant and drafted to Scotland. And she wasn't in love with me, nor me with her, Rosie.'

'But if she had stayed . . . ?'

'It wouldn't have made any difference. She was in love with her husband, and lonely.'

'I see. And you wanted to lose your virginity. You haven't forgotten her, though, have you?'

'I don't think of her every spare moment I've got, like I think of you, darling. I must admit, though, that she was a very nice person to lose my virginity to. I hope you'll always remember the man who took yours – well, if you still want to?'

'Hell! You know I do! But are you still in touch? Do you write?'

'Haven't heard a word from her in two years. We parted as friends, though.'

'And it's me you love now, Jon?'

'Only you. Ever. You're the first and the last. I loved you the minute I saw you. Actually, it's exactly two months ago, give or take a few minutes. Am I allowed to say happy anniversary, Rosie? Am I forgiven?'

'Oh, yes! And yes!' She wrapped her arms around him, searching for his lips, loving him, not caring about Pamela who'd been married to someone else, anyway. 'Clean slates, like you said, though sadly I have nothing to confess!'

'I didn't think you would have,' he laughed softly. 'Not with the dragon lady around! I suppose I should be grateful to your mother.'

'Yes, you should!' She laughed, happy again. 'Did you bring a torch? Shall we go then?' She took his hand, walking carefully. 'I've left my bike a bit further along – I'll take the lamp off the front.'

'Did you have much trouble getting out?'

'Not really.' They were whispering. 'No more than usual. But we'll soon have the light nights and I'll be able to get out more. I could even bike down to the village every night; ring you from the phone box – save you walking all the way here.'

'Sorry!' He took her in his arms. 'The walk is worth it and come summer, you'll be able to stay out longer, though there'll be no blackout to hide in – and it'll be goodbye, hayloft!'

'First things first!' Carefully Rosamund lifted the latch; inch by inch she pushed open the small side door of the hay barn. The latch did not snap open, the door did not creak and Shep did not bark. She turned on her lamp, pointing the way ahead. 'All the hay is used, now. There's only a bit left in the loft.'

Jon's torch had a stronger beam and picked out the wide wooden steps that led to the gantry above.

'Up there?' he whispered. 'Shall I go first?'

'No, better let me.' She had climbed those steps a thousand times; could have done it in the dark. There were twelve. She had climbed them even before she could count; when they had been forbidden to her because she was too little and might fall. Now she took them one step at a time, slowly and carefully. Her heart thudded, small pulses beat insistently behind her nose and at the hollow in her throat. This, she supposed, was her wedding night and her wedding, all in one; the night she would remember for the rest of her life. When she walked down the twelve wooden steps again she would be a new person, would be Jon's, and nothing could harm them ever again after tonight, because their love would be special, and sprinkled with stardust.

'I love you, Jon Hunt.'

'And I love you, my Rosie; so very much . . .'

He folded her in his arms, kissing her eyelids, her cheeks, the tip of her nose, her mouth; pulling her closer, hands on her buttocks.

She sighed softly, no longer uneasy. Jon would be patient with her, would forgive her gaucheness. Jon knew what to do. It was going to be all right.

'I think,' she whispered, as he kissed the hollow in her throat, 'that I ought to be grateful to Pamela.'

'Me, too.' His laugh was soft and indulgent. 'Shall we find somewhere . . . ?'

The hay was soft and sweet-smelling; the scent of the June day on which it was cut reminding them of warm afternoons and high, blue skies and wild flowers and green-cool woods with bluebells for a carpet. All at once, the war was shut out and tomorrows were two a penny; no one would ever again be killed or blinded or maimed. All at once, only being in love mattered, and sharing love.

'Are you cold, darling?'

'No.' She took off her jacket. 'Are you?'

'No. Didn't know hay could be so warm to lie on.'

'I wish I could see your face, though.'

'When the light nights come . . .' he said softly, unfastening the buttons on her blouse, cupping her breasts in his hands as he had wanted to do since the first night he'd met her and undressed her with his eyes. 'Y'know, I thought I'd feel rotten about this – about us being here, but I don't.'

'Nor me, though I suppose when I come here in the morning for fodder, I won't ever think of it as the hay barn again. After tonight, it'll be the most precious place I know.'

'We're fools, aren't we? In a couple of hours you'll leave me and I'll go back to the 'drome and we'll be two separate people again.'

'After tonight, we'll never be separate people. And we'll be together as often as we can, I promise. And if we've only got two hours, we're wasting time!'

Unsteadily, because she still couldn't believe it was happening for them, she unfastened the brass buttons on his jacket, then slid her arms around him, moving nearer, and he pressed her shoulders into the hay, laying close beside her. Then he took off his tie, his stiff, starched collar and opened his shirt and she laid her head on his chest, her fingertips gentling his body, feeling, exploring.

'Don't you wear a bra, Rosie?'

'Yes, but not tonight.'

She pulled down the zip of her skirt, sinking her heels into the hay, lifting her buttocks so she could slide it off.

'There, now,' she whispered, wishing she could see the love in his eyes when he took her.

He pulled her to him again, feeling her skin soft and warm and the flatness of her stomach as she arched towards him, offering, asking silently.

'You're sure about us, Rosie?'

'Very sure.' She took his face in her hands, her lips a kiss away from his. 'And I want you now . . .'

She felt his hardness against her, then relaxed so he took her easily, gently, as if they had been lovers before. And she wondered at the pulsating joy of it, and knew at once that loving was right and decent.

Sinking her fingertips into his back, she strained closer, whispering, 'Kiss me?' and that kiss was their wedding vows, the hand raised in blessing, society's approval. Jon and Rosie, always.

They did not speak again for a long, long time.

'Do you know where your torch is, Jon?'

'Mm. In my greatcoat . . .'

He extended an arm, feeling for it in the darkness, dipping a hand in the pocket. Then he pulled the heavy coat over their nakedness, and switched on the light.

'Hullo, sweetheart.'

He looked at her face, soft with loving; at eyes that gazed, slightly surprised, into his; at the spread of hair, tangled in the hay.

'Hullo yourself.' Her voice was low and husky, as if she were close to tears.

'You'll have to comb your hair,' he said softly, 'before you go in.'

'Ssssh.' She shifted her hand into the pool of light, to look at her watch. 'It's only half-past nine.' She snuggled close, kissing his throat, his chin. 'Tell me?'

'I love you, darling.'

'And I love you, Jon. I wondered if I would still love you – afterwards, I mean – and I do. And I thought I'd feel embarrassed, but I don't. All I feel is – is –'

'Married?'

'Mm.' Her body ached from loving him. 'Why can it only be Saturdays?'

'Soon, it'll be different – the light nights, remember . . .'

'Maybe then we'll be able to spend a whole day together.'

'Or a whole night.'

'Don't, darling.' She wanted, all at once, to speak in a whisper so the Fates should not hear and be jealous. Yet for all that she felt strong and sure; a woman. She was Jon's, and his love was wrapped around her like a warm, shining blanket. Nothing could harm her now; she belonged.

'Why not? It's possible. Anything is possible. It's you and me now. We'll make things happen for us.' His hands gentled the rounds of her shoulders and he thought, incredulously, that she was his! All of her! 'God! I love you!'

'Oh, I know you do!' She said it with teasing smugness, laughing softly, sure of herself, of the new creature she had become.

'I want you again.'

'Good. Leave the light on, Jon.'

Rosamund squared her shoulders, then opened the kitchen door. She had thought her parents would be in bed; that she would have time to compose herself, to blink the love out of her eyes and tell herself that Jon had gone, and that she was Bart and Mildred Kenton's daughter again, biddable and obedient.

But they were sitting at either side of a dying fire, and she knew there would be no going back, that they must never call her *child*, again.

'What time do you call this?' her mother said, too softly.

'It's late, and I'm sorry. But you shouldn't have waited up.'

She wondered if her love for Jon was printed large across her forehead or if her eyes would give her away.

'It's *half-past eleven*! Where have you been?'

'I'm only half an hour late.'

'I said *where – have – you – been*?' The words were thick with innuendo, demanding an answer.

'I – I've been out. You know I have.'

She raised her head to meet her mother's eyes and saw a face that was bitter; looked across at her father who sat unmoving, hands on the arms of the chair. His eyes bore a look of resignation as if he had tried his best and been overruled by his wife's anger. And in that moment she felt sudden pity for them both because she knew they had not, never would, know a loving like hers and Jon's.

'*Where*, until this time? And I want the truth!'

'Very well. I've been out with a man; an airman. He's a pilot at the aerodrome, and he's called Jon. Jonathan Hunt.'

There was a shaking inside her, but it felt as if her hands were in Jon's hands and his kisses still on her lips, and a courage she didn't know she was capable of swept through her.

'A man! I knew it all along! I told you, didn't I, Bart Kenton? She's up to no good, I said, but you did nothing about it!'

Her mother's eyes gleamed with fury and her mouth was set tight as a steel trap. She looked as if any moment she would burst out screaming, or hit her, Rosamund thought.

'I'm sorry, Dad. I should have told you.'

'And what about *me*, lady? Am I of no consequence in this house? Now I want to know that man's rank and number – everything you know about him. Then I'm going to ring the aerodrome and speak to the man in charge!'

'If you do you'll turn yourself into a laughing stock, Mother. And I shall leave this house!'

'You can't! You're still a minor! And the Ministry of Labour won't let you, anyway!'

She's mad, Rosamund thought. She really is mad! And she's going to have a heart attack!

'Mother, please calm down? You're going to be ill!'

'*Ill?* And who'll be to blame for it, eh?'

She collapsed into the chair, shoulders heaving, hands clenched into fists, and in that moment Rosamund believed in reincarnation just as Jon did; knew that if Margaret Dacre's soul still roamed unshriven, then it was here, now, inside her mother!

'I think we all get what we deserve. If I have deceived you, then I'll be punished for it. But some of the blame will lie at your door, Mother, because I didn't dare tell you. I tried to tell Dad, then knew it was no good; that you wouldn't let me bring Jon home.'

'Home! Bring a man into my house who's been carrying on with my daughter behind my back! How dare you even think such a thing?'

'How, indeed?' Rosamund went to stand beside her father's chair. She wanted to show she cared for him, sympathized with him. Behind her was the little door of the stairs that led to her bedroom, and she wanted its safeness close at hand so that if her new-found courage failed her she could bolt upstairs and lock the door of her room behind her. 'Crazy of me, wouldn't it be, to tell you I love him very much, because you don't know the meaning of the word, Mother! And I was mad to think you'd let us get married! Because I want us to be married. All right – so I've known him just two months, but I knew the minute we met that he was right for me!'

'Ha! Met!' Mildred Kenton jumped to her feet and began to pace the floor. 'And where did you meet him? Bessie Drake has a hand in this, hasn't she?'

'Bessie had no hand in it. Do you think I'd be stupid enough to involve her? I met Jon in Laceby; bumped into him in the blackout and we got talking. We've been meeting ever since.'

No need to go into detail; tell about the aerodrome dances, nor the meetings at the little iron gate. And she must never let her mother find Jon's photograph, look at it with hatred. Witches ill-wished, and tonight there was such evil about her mother that if she let herself, Rosamund knew she could be very, very afraid.

'Then it's going to stop, do you hear me! You are not to leave this house after dark! And you're to stop seeing that man; forget all about him, because he won't ever be welcomed into my house! And you can stop your foolish thoughts, an' all! You're a child still; don't know your own mind! Married, indeed!' She glared at her husband. 'She's known him eight weeks, and she wants to be wed! Well, with a bit of luck his plane will crash, and serve him right!'

'*Mother!*' Red flashes of rage blinded Rosamund and hatred took her, shook her into action. She lunged at the woman, the witch who tormented her, pushing her, sending her sprawling into the fireside chair. 'How *could* you? How could anyone be so evil as to wish a young man dead?'

'Rosamund! Mildred! That's enough!' Bart Kenton was on his feet, snatching at his daughter's flailing fists, pulling her away.

'Stop it, Dad! Don't get involved. She isn't worth it! She's wicked!' Rosamund tore free of his hands, then turned to face her mother again. 'Well, you can ill-wish Jon all you like but you won't harm him, because ill wishes rebound on the sender and it'll be you who'll be dead!

'And I'm going upstairs now, Mother, because I can't bear to be in the same room as you, but before I do, let me just tell you this. I know it isn't any use my asking you to meet Jon, much less let us be married, because I know you wouldn't so much as listen. But I'm not ashamed of deceiving you and I'm *not* ashamed of loving Jon, only of not telling you about him before now! And I'm sorry, Dad, but I won't apologize to her, not even if she never speaks to me again! I'm just sorry she's my mother, though how you both got me, I'll never know!'

To her mother's scream of outrage, Rosamund slammed shut the stair door, then flung into her room, turning the key, groping for the candlestick and matches at the bedside.

The candleflame dipped and guttered, then grew, lighting

the area around the bed, leaving dark corners. She dropped to her knees, opening a drawer, taking out Jon's photograph, needing the comfort of his nearness. She folded it in her arms, rocking to and fro, fear surging through her.

'I'm sorry, Jon,' she whispered through a choke of tears. 'They know about us now. I had to tell them and it was stupid of me because now she has ill-wished you!'

Just an hour ago they had been together with everything golden and shining and wonderful beyond believing, yet now it was as if their loving was wrong; that evil had touched it and fouled it.

Below her, she heard raised voices, and tears flowed afresh; not for what she had done nor the upset she had caused, but because her mother's anger was now being hurled at her father; now it was his turn to suffer.

Doors banged, and she heard footsteps on the staircase, then no more. She drew in her breath and listened, but the argument was not to be continued in that big, double bed. Perhaps, for once, her father had ordered her mother to be quiet!

But it would all be there in the morning, she thought despairingly; her mother's eyes following her, accusing her silently, ill-wishing her too, maybe. And her mother's mouth would be button-tight and she would go around with her pained look; her after-all-I-have-done-for-this-family look. And life would not be worth living for Dad.

She fished for her handkerchief and blew her nose as quietly as she could, then drew in a sighing gulp of air, holding it as long as she could, letting it go in little calming puffs. Then she looked at the photograph again, touching it, thinking about their loving, their coupling, and the wonder of it. And all at once she knew she would fight like a hellcat; take on the entire world if she had to, because nothing and no one – not even the force of her mother's hatred – would keep them apart!

Tomorrow she would tell her parents that nothing would prevent her from seeing Jon, and that if she had to she would go to the Ministry of Labour office and tell them she wanted to change her war work – beg, if that was what it took! And from this night on, she would meet Jon in Laceby, do it openly, be with him as often as the war allowed! And if her mother so much as thought again of getting in touch with his commanding officer, she would be reminded that people who dealt in black-market eggs and clothing coupons, and who churned butter when buttermaking was illegal, should put their own conscience in order before telling other people what to do!

'I hate you, Mother, and if anything happens to Jon, I shall spend the rest of my life hating you!' she whispered to the shadowy corners of the room. 'You spoiled tonight for me, and I'll never forgive you for it!'

All at once she wished she had gone completely mad and told them that she and Jon were lovers; hurled it at them defiantly, but she knew it would have played into her mother's hands. And anyway, what did her mother know about loving?

She closed her eyes and shuddered to think of the manner of her getting, and wished with all her heart it need not have been so; that her conceiving had been immaculate, or even that they had found her under a gooseberry bush. Anything but *that*!

She laid her cheek to the photograph, wondering if Jon were back in camp yet; if he were in bed in the hut they shared with *Z-Zebra* and if he was thinking about her, wanting her, loving her still.

'I love *you*, my darling,' she whispered to his smiling image. 'I won't let anyone spoil it for us; I promise.'

Slowly she undressed, dropping each garment to the floor. Then she carried the candle to the dressing-table mirror and looked at the body Jon had taken; called back his mouth on her shoulders, her breasts, her lips; wondered at the joy of belonging.

Then cold shivered through and she pulled on her pyjamas, debating if she dare go down to the kitchen and take a hot brick out of the fire oven, then defiantly pushed her feet into her slippers.

Of course she dare! She was Jon's now, and touched with everything that was magic, and even if she were still in the kitchen, her mother could not hurt her!

Quietly she walked down the stairs; carefully she opened the oven door, taking a brick, wrapping it in one of the pieces of blanket that hung, precisely folded, on the wire beneath the mantelshelf.

Then she closed the staircase door behind her and it was as if she were shutting out all the accusations and angry words, and the evil in her mother's eyes.

Tomorrow was a new day, and she would take it as best she could. But what remained of this night belonged to lovers and all she wanted was to creep into bed, go over it all in her mind, live again every kiss, every touch, every word of love.

'Good night, my darling. See you. And by the way, I love you . . .'

Smiling, she placed the photograph beside her bed.

Rosamund awoke with a start and lay quite still, listening. But nothing broke the silence; Shep had not barked; there were no returning bombers.

She lit the candle, then saw Jon's face smiling at her through the pale, flickering glow, remembering last night, and coming home to the awful things that had been said in anger and malice and spite.

It was five o'clock. Best she should get up; make a start on the milking, collect her thoughts before her father came into the shippon at half-past.

Slowly she dressed, pulling on trousers and warm socks and a sweater. She did it as she did it every morning; automatically and half asleep. She didn't really come to life, mornings, until her mother brought mugs of tea to the shippon.

Her mother. She stood quite still, eyes closed, demanding of herself if the white-hot hatred she had felt was still inside her, and knew it was.

'See you,' she whispered as she laid Jon's photograph in the bottom of the drawer; said it defiantly, like a promise. Then she ran downstairs on stockinged feet, pulled on gumboots and a thick jacket, jammed a woollen beret on her head.

She gasped as the cold air outside hit her, and hurried to the shippon to find her father already there, lighting hurricane lamps, hanging them on roof hooks. She stood in the doorway, not knowing what to say.

'Shut the door, lass. We don't want to be done for the blackout.'

'Dad?' she whispered, grateful that he had broken the brittle silence. 'Last night . . .'

'Last night is over and done with. Best leave it.'

His face was pale and tired-looking and she felt ashamed that she had been the cause of his sleepless night.

'No, Dad, it isn't. And I can't – *won't* – say sorry to her, because of what she said! It's a terrible thing to wish someone dead. I won't ever forgive that. And when she brings the tea, I won't speak to her!'

'There'll be no tea, this morning. The kitchen fire is out and your mother asleep. She was awake a long time, last night. Lass, why did you have to come out with it like you did? Couldn't you have bided your time?'

'No, I couldn't. It had to be said. I tried to tell you about Jon, remember? I was going to ask you to be on my side and persuade Mum he could come to tea. But I couldn't say it and I asked you about my grandparents instead.'

'Aye. Well, talking of that, I never got around to telling you I still keep in touch with my father. Only on his birthday, mind, and at Christmas. I slip him a pound or two inside a card, so he'll know I think of him, even if it's only twice a year. But I wish you'd told me. Is he a decent lad, then, this pilot?'

'Like I said last night – I love him. I was going to ask you to let us get married, the day we talked about grandparents, but I knew it would be hopeless. And anyway, how can I know my own mind? To you I'm a child still! But I'll tell you something! On Friday I was at the fence, watching the aerodrome, and there were some of those big bombs on trolleys, and young Waafs in charge of them! Nobody calls *them* child, when they're towing one of those blockbusters behind them! And the Ministry of Labour didn't call them child when they sent them into the Armed Forces! Why won't my mother let me grow up? Why does she throw a fit, if she thinks I've been within spitting distance of a man?'

'I don't know, and that's a fact, Rosamund. Your mother was never one to share her thoughts with me. But I don't want a repetition of last night's behaviour. I've said as much to your mother and I'm telling you, an' all. Your mother was out of order, and so were you. I thought you were going to hit her!'

'Then it's a pity you stopped me, because I wanted to! She said she hoped Jon's bomber would crash! How can anyone be so rotten?'

'It was said in the heat of the moment, lass. Happen she's sorry now.'

'Yes, and happen she isn't, because she meant it, I know she did! But if I caused trouble for you, Dad, I'm sorry. You know I wouldn't do anything to hurt you – not deliberately. But I *won't* be kept in! I'm going to see Jon again tonight if he isn't flying, and Mum had better not try to stop me!'

'At about nine, maybe? I wondered why you popped off so regular when the news came on.'

'Well, now you know. Jon walks all the way from the aerodrome just so we can have a few minutes together. And on Saturday nights, I meet him at the aerodrome dance. Bessie does know about him, but I don't want Mum to know that. She thinks Bessie's a bad influence, and she isn't.'

'And where do you meet this young man every night, then?'

'Not every night, Dad. Two or three nights he's flying, but when he isn't he waits at the little gate. He wanted to come to the house; knock on the door, he said, and introduce himself, but I said he wasn't to, that I would tell you about him first. He didn't want for us to seem to be carrying on, as Mum put it, behind her back!'

She stopped abruptly, because her father had been kind to her, tried to understand, and his sympathy brought back last night's tears. She stood for a moment, fighting them, taking deep breaths, shaking her head because she didn't know what else to say or to do.

'There now, lovey. Don't take on so.' He gathered her into his arms, patting her back, hushing her as he hadn't done since she was little. 'It's a fine old kettle of fish, and no mistake, but we'll have to try to sort a bit of sense out of it, see what's to be done . . .'

He gave her his handkerchief and she dabbed her eyes and swallowed hard, turning her back on him, because she despised herself for the way she was hurting him.

'Thanks, Dad. But don't get involved? This is between me and Mother, and it's about time I stood up to her. I'm not giving Jon up, no matter what, and if anything happens to him it'll be her fault! Doesn't she know that bad wishes can rebound? Can't she realize *she* could die instead, or you, or me? How can she pray in chapel? How can she even put a foot over the threshold?'

Her voice rose again to near hysteria and she pulled her sleeve over her eyes.

'Rosamund!' Bart Kenton's voice was harsh as he took his daughter's arm and pulled her roughly to face him. 'I have never in all my life lifted a hand to a woman, but if you don't calm down and get a hold of yourself, I'll slap you! I will!'

'Oh God, I'm sorry.' Suddenly she felt limp and drained of all feeling. 'I'll be all right. Just give me a minute? I – I'll get the stools, and pails. And I won't mention Jon again. There won't be any more trouble, I promise, unless Mother starts it. Only don't either of you try to stop me seeing Jon!'

She turned, gasping on her breath, willing herself not to weep, wondering what had gone wrong with her world when last night she had been so happy.

'I love you, Jon Hunt,' she whispered. 'Love you, love you.' And she went on saying it until the pain inside her eased, and she was able to face her father again.

NINE

Mildred Kenton announced she was too upset to go to chapel; that her eyes were too puffy and swollen and she didn't want people asking her if she'd had bad news; because bad news came often these days in small yellow envelopes, and travelled fast. 'I can't face people. We'll have to give it a miss this morning.'

Rosamund concentrated on her food, thinking about Jon, wondering what he was doing. Church parade, or a morning in bed, perhaps? Aircrews were spared a lot of the bull, he said, that most others had to put up with; could get away with murder at times.

She swallowed hard on the egg she was sure her mother had deliberately overcooked, mopped her plate with the last of her bread because it was unpatriotic to waste food, then rose to leave the table with a scraping of chair legs.

'I'm going to see to the poultry,' she said to the teapot. 'I'll do the dishes later.'

It was a relief to get away, she fretted, filling buckets at the pump in the yard. Anything was better than meeting her mother's eyes, seeing anger in them still; evil, too.

She walked to the paddock, water slopping over her gumboots. Hens drank a lot of water; it would take three trips just to fill the water troughs. Then when she had thrown feed into each ark, she would collect the eggs, place them carefully in a bucket, lined with hay.

Hay. From the loft. Ordinary hay from an ordinary loft that had become the most precious place in the world.

Jon! I love you. Please take care and please be there tonight, at the gate?

She was in the dairy wiping the eggs when she heard the faraway growl of engines being revved and she closed her eyes and whispered, 'No! Oh, no!'

They were going, tonight. Soon, there would be no mistaking it because the sky would be full of the sight and sound of bombers taking off, flight-testing their engines, checking instruments. Then landing, and taxiing back to their standing on the perimeter track, being worked on by riggers and mechanics and electricians. And later, armourers would fit the guns and load the belly of the aircraft with bombs, and fill the tanks in the wings with fuel.

Gently she laid the eggs on trays, ready to be collected on Tuesday by the lady who drove the egg packer's van. She would leave empty trays behind her, and payment for last week's eggs in an envelope. The egg money belonged to her mother; always had. In the bad days, when every penny did the work of two, hens provided the housekeeping money.

Her father came into the dairy and she smiled and said, 'That's the eggs done and dusted; just the churns to see to. I – I'd thought I might go to the village this morning, since we aren't going anywhere. I don't suppose I could take the tractor?'

'No, lass, you could not! Fuel is rationed, and that tractor is strictly for business. And don't you think that before you do anything else you should have a word with your mother, tell her you're sorry?'

'What for?' Her reply was so glib it sounded impudent.

'You know what for! It's up to you to make the first move, lass, and then we might get back to normal again. I don't like all this frostiness and frowning.'

'Like I said, I'm sorry if what happened last night upset you, Dad, but I'm not going to apologize for Jon. She just wants to see me grovel, but I won't! Not even for peace and quiet!'

'Then all I can say is that you're storing up trouble for yourself, Rosamund. Isn't there enough upset in the world without you adding to it?'

'My mother wished Jon dead. I can't forgive that,' she said flatly, finally.

'I told you, she said it in the heat of the moment.'

'She *said* it, and that's enough for me. Look, Dad, there's nothing you can say that's going to make me stop seeing Jon, so please don't get involved. If I give in to Mum over this, I'll never be able to call my life my own! I'll be nineteen soon. I'm old enough to go to war, so I think I'm old enough to have a young man – and one of my own choosing!'

'You might be right, but did you have to go at it like a bull at a gate, lose your temper like you did? But I've had my say, and from now on it'll be better if I keep my oar out of it. Trying to come between two fratching women is like trying to separate a pair of fighting dogs. Best leave 'em to get on with it!'

'Bitches!' Rosamund tried hard to smile. 'You got the gender wrong! And you're holding up the war effort. Have you loaded the churns?'

'Aye. Be off with you!'

He watched her climb on the tractor, reversing it, trailer and all, as if she had been born to driving. She was a lass to be proud of, he thought, wishing that Mildred would leave her be, stop trying to put her own narrow ways into her daughter's head.

He smiled and held up his hand, returning her wave, and in that moment he knew that far from keeping out of it, he would line himself up with her, might even suggest, when things had settled down a bit, that the young man should call at the house one of these nights instead of waiting at the gate like a leper.

When pigs flew, he thought gloomily.

'So where did you get to last night?' Bessie raised a teasing eyebrow. 'You didn't, did you? Ooooh, Rosamund, do tell?'

'Hey! If you think I'm telling anybody about Jon and me, then you're wrong!'

'But *did* you?'

'Ssssssh! They'll hear us!' Rosamund hissed, pink-cheeked, even though it was bliss to almost admit it.

'It's OK. Mum has gone to church and Dad is in bed. Shall I make a cup of cocoa, or shall we go out?'

'Cocoa, please.' Rosamund settled herself at the fireside. 'I just had to get out. The atmosphere at home is unbearable.'

'Thought you'd be at chapel . . .'

'No. My mother is too upset to go. She's been weeping and didn't want people to see her.'

'What about?' Bessie sensed drama.

'Me. I was late in last night and she got nasty. Only half an hour, but she was waiting there with the sarcasm. So I told her about Jon. It just came out. I said I'd met an airman in the blackout and we'd started talking and been meeting ever since!'

'*Oooooh!* Bet she went berserk!'

'She hit the roof! Said I wasn't to go out after dark any more and that she was going to get in touch with Jon's CO! Then she said she wished Jon's Lancaster would crash, and that it would serve him right!'

'She said *what*?' Bessie's eyes were round as saucers. 'But I told you she was a witch, didn't I? Well, God forgive her, that's all I can say!'

'May He indeed, because I never will. Y'know, Bess, if I had somewhere to go I'd leave home, ask the Labour Exchange to let me change my job. It's Dad I'm sorry for. What did he ever do to deserve my mother?'

'Married her for her money – well, that's what some say. But what about *you*? If I were in your shoes, I couldn't bear to breathe the same air!'

'Oh, I'll stay, for Dad's sake. I'm supposed to say I'm sorry, but I won't! I can stick it out as long as she can. I don't know about it being a witch who built our house, but I'm pretty certain she's still around. And I know it's a terrible thing to say about your own mother, but she just isn't normal!'

'You should wear your cross – always. That would keep her from harming you.'

'Oh, she'll not hurt me. Twisted as she is, she wouldn't hex her own daughter. It's Jon I'm worried about. He needs the cross more than I do.'

'When Joe and Dave were called up, Mum gave them each a medallion; got the vicar to bless it. Why don't you get your cross blessed? Nothing would be a match for that!'

'How could I, Bess? I'd have to ask the minister, and Mother would get to know. She misses nothing!'

'Then if you've got nothing against C of E, I'll ask our vicar to do it. He needn't know who it belongs to, and I'm sure he wouldn't ask, anyway.'

'I'll do that! I'll bring it tonight! I'm pretty certain Jon'll be on ops, so I'll come to yours instead.'

'And will your mother let you?'

'She'll have to use physical violence to stop me, and I'm stronger than she is! This worm has turned, Bess! But I did so want to see Jon tonight, especially after –'

'After last night, you mean? Was it wonderful?'

'Yes. But Bess, I don't want to talk about it, really I don't. All I can say is that I'm not a bit ashamed of what we did; only sad that it didn't happen sooner!'

'Ooooooh! Hope you didn't get pregnant!' Bessie was too awestruck to be envious.

'I hope so, too, but I'll know on Friday.' She swallowed hard. She would really have to mark her diary now! 'And, Bessie! The kettle's boiling! Do I get my cocoa, or don't I?' Her voice, Rosamund marvelled, sounded very normal and matter-of-fact and not one bit like she really felt inside her; sort of squeezy and elated and just a little bit afraid. 'And you won't tell anyone, will you? You know what they're like round here, for gossip.'

'As if I would! Cross my heart and hope to die if I do,' Bessie gasped. 'I know your mother doesn't like me and I couldn't care less, but don't let her louse it up for you and Jon, love. Be careful, won't you?'

'We will.' Rosamund smiled. 'And I'm glad you're my friend, Bess; I truly am.'

Whilst it was still light enough to see, Rosamund walked openly, defiantly, to the steel-mesh fence and was dismayed to find that what she had feared would happen. They were flying ops, tonight. Up to a dozen from Laceby would join others from aerodromes in Lancashire; all heading south, picking up more squadrons as they flew.

Maybe it would be another thousand-bomber raid; maybe Berlin would be the target again, or Essen or Cologne. The war was far from over, it seemed. From somewhere, even though people said the Luftwaffe was tied up at the Russian Front, Goering had found enough planes to start bombing London again; the worst raid, the papers said, since the blitz of 1941. Tonight, *J-Johnnie*'s crew would fly their sixteenth op, and though Jon had already flown seven before he came to Laceby, he would fly out the thirty with the crew. The crew. Tom, Dick and Harry, Mick, Sammy and Mac. And Matilda Mint!

Rosamund turned disconsolately away, determined tonight, when she heard the first sound of engines, to return and tie a handkerchief to the fence; would say she was going to watch takeoff, and just let her mother try to stop her! She remembered the look in her mother's eyes last night and sent her love to Jon, wrapping it around him in her mind. And the sooner the cross was blessed and round his neck, the better! She hurried away, all at once sickened by the war, wanting an end to it, wishing she had never met, never loved Jon; grateful that she had.

Her mother would have sanctioned the lighting of the sitting-room fire today, and she and Dad would be reading the papers as they always did. It was the only treat her father allowed himself; Sunday afternoons in his favourite chair, feet to the fire. He worked so hard it was the least he deserved, she thought, hoping fervently that the worst was over; that things would soon get back to normal – as normal, that was, as they would ever be in that loveless house!

She was not prepared, for all that, for what faced her when she opened the back door to run, startled, to the kitchen as she heard her mother's moans. She found her sitting at the table, hands clenched into fists, rocking to and fro, sobbing.

'Mother! What is it?'

'I've said so all along, but nobody would listen to me! Well, I was right! They've admitted it at last! There *is* a secret weapon!' She began a demented pummelling of the table top, pulling in her breath noisily, letting it go in anguished sobs. 'Go on, then! Read it, if you don't believe me!'

'Dad . . . ?'

'Dratted newspapers!' Bart flung the *Telegraph* across the table. 'Go on! Front page; read it, lass, then tell your mother she's getting herself upset over summat that might never happen!'

Rosamund shook open the paper, finding at once the column headed 'NAZI'S SECRET WEAPON: RADIO BOMBER'.

> There is evidence now that the Germans' secret weapon is actually a crewless radio-controlled aircraft which, loaded to capacity with explosives, can be accurately directed to its objective.

It would, it seemed, be difficult to shoot down, either by fighters or anti-aircraft fire, but its delivery was its primary weakness, because of its complex launching system.

She ran her tongue round lips suddenly gone dry, and read on.

There were launching sites in Europe, and the article concluded that although the rocket could prove to be serious, there was little doubt that it would never be more than a temporary worry, which could and would be taken care of by the destroying of the launch pads by Allied bombers.

'So?' Rosamund's voice did not sound as contemptuous or dismissive as she intended. 'All right – there *is* a secret weapon and now we know about it! Probably we know where they are all hidden, too. Our lot will have a seek-and-destroy policy – or something!'

She took in her father's ashen face, her mother's demented rocking, her harsh sobs, and felt a strength she never knew she was capable of.

'I think you should go to the doctor, Mother. Tomorrow. You're a bag of nerves and you've got yourself run down. Ask him for a tonic. It's been a long, dark winter and we're all fed up.'

'I've been to the doctor! Went before Christmas and got a flea in my ear for my pains! There's nothing wrong with me, he said. I'm at *that* age, so I'll just have to get on with it!' Her voice rose higher. 'And do you know what else I got for the price of a visit? I was told to count my blessings; that there were women far worse off than I am! But nobody listens to me! That rocket will be the death of us, I've known it all along!'

'Will you stop it!' Rosamund pleaded, sickened at the sight of her mother. 'You are not the only woman they'll be firing those rockets at – if ever they do! You'd think Hitler had your name on every one of them; that they were invented specially to fall on Laburnum Farm, to put paid to your precious privacy! This war hasn't touched you, Mother! I am still at home and you have no sons for the war to take! We never go hungry and we don't sleep in shelters or the Underground night after night because our house has been bombed to rubble!'

She paused, angrily snatching air into her lungs, knowing that what she was saying only made matters worse, but determined, now the flood gates were open, to say it.

'And we don't live in Leningrad, where they've been bombed and shelled for more than two years. We've never had to eat cats and rats, as they have! I don't understand how you can be so selfish, Mother, and I'm going out before I say something I regret!'

She ran from the kitchen, anger churning inside her and puking in her throat. If she let herself, she could be sick, because that was what she was: sick, sick, *sick* of her mother's selfishness, her narrow-mindedness, her total inability to think about anyone but herself!

Jon! Take care tonight because I couldn't go on living if anything happened to you! Especially now she couldn't; not since they had been lovers, a million years ago!

She pushed open the small door of the hay barn then stood, hand on the latch, breathing deeply, trying to stop the tears that choked in her throat; thinking about her mother and if women really did go peculiar when they got to *that* time of life. Was her mother mad, or bad? And for how much longer could her father put up with a loveless marriage; because that was what it was. And their daughter was the child of a loveless conceiving.

The barn was dark, with only a shaft of light slanting through the open door. It pointed across the floor to the foot of the wooden steps leading to the gantry and she turned away, closing the door behind her, because malice spilled out of her and must not be allowed to contaminate this special place.

She looked at her watch. It was too early to begin afternoon milking and she didn't want to go back to the boundary fence. Best she should feed the hens, make sure the arks were secure against foxes; do anything to kill time until milking.

Feeling suddenly limp, as if the rage inside her had drained her of all feeling, she walked towards the paddock. Her mind was in a turmoil of bewilderment: thoughts she couldn't make sense of nor sort into any kind of order.

Last night she had been so sure that nothing that lived or breathed could touch their love, because it had been so right. Yet now she feared for it, because her mother had gone off on a different tack. Last night's angry threats had not worked, so now she hysterically demanded pity and attention, latching on to the bogey of the secret weapon, magnifying it out of all proportion just to cause another upset. Her mother was not mad; she was bad. And she was dangerous and ruthless and until now had never been thwarted nor gainsaid.

Why, Rosamund demanded, had she let her mother's sarcasm get to her last night? Why hadn't she bitten on her anger and let it wash over her, closing her ears to the accusations? Why hadn't she matched cunning with cunning; stood silent and let the innuendoes flow over her head, whilst she hugged her secret to her, keeping their love safe from harm? Yet in her stupidity she put that love at risk, and her mother had wished Jon dead.

All at once the tears came, and she leaned against the dry-stone wall, her body shaking, crying out her anguish, needing Jon's arms around her, whispering that it was all right, kissing away her tears. But Jon was on ops tonight and all she could do was wish him a safe return; wish him at the gate tomorrow night at nine. And she had better pull herself together, or her mother would know she had been weeping, and gloat inside. She fished for a handkerchief, dabbing her eyes, blowing her nose loudly and inelegantly, then squared her shoulders and stuck out her chin.

'And that is the last time, Rosamund Kenton,' she flung at the distant hills, 'that you let her get you down! OK?'

She had stood at the bottom of the cow pasture long after the bombers had thrashed and roared into the sky; waited, fingers entwined in the steel-mesh fence, until the sound of their going could no longer be heard.

Eleven had taken off; she would count eleven back. She *would*! Jon would be at the gate tomorrow night, and everything would come right again.

'I'm going to the village,' she said, forcing her voice to sound firm and ordinary and remembering not to say she was going to see Bessie, because the very name could trigger another tirade of abuse.

'Will you be gone long, lass?'

'No, Dad. It isn't too dark outside.' There was half a moon, and a sky full of frosty stars. 'I won't be long. Just feel like a breath of fresh air.'

'Mind how you go, then.'

'I will. See you.' She smiled briefly, closing the door gently, letting go a sigh of relief.

She was all right now; had managed to avoid her mother's eyes. She had not expected her to speak, because since her outburst she had sat at the fireside, staring into the flames, not even knitting. She was, Rosamund thought as she pushed her cycle across the yard and down the lane to the crossroads, like an unexploded bomb, and she and her father were speaking only when necessary lest one careless word should start that bomb ticking.

She stopped at the six oaks, where she and Jon had kissed, wondering where he was now. Crossing the coast, maybe; giving Harry and Mick permission to test-fire their guns?

She pushed a hand into her pocket, feeling for the small gold cross. It had been given to her on the day of her baptism, but her mother had never encouraged her to wear it, saying that crosses and crucifixes were popish things, and that a string of pearl beads was far prettier.

Now, she would give that cross to Jon; guard him against any evil that might be directed towards him. It was childish of her, she readily admitted it, but if a cross could do no good, neither could it do harm, and it was always better to be sure. And she was being foolish and very wrong, she thought as she gazed, eyes straining into the darkness around her, even to think that Margaret Dacre's soul was still around, much less have taken possession of her mother. Common sense said that witches did not exist, nor ever had, yet those who lived in the wild stretches of Lancashire always kept an open mind. You could never be sure, the old ones said, and that there were more things in heaven and earth than ordinary folk ever dreamed about – or words to that effect.

Ahead of her she could hear voices so she coughed loudly, because it was probably a courting couple. There were a lot of couples about since the aerodrome was built, all grateful for the blackout, she shouldn't wonder. She called a greeting as she passed them, and envied the man and woman who walked close, thighs touching most likely, fingers entwined.

Then she smiled, because she would see Jon tomorrow. They hardly ever flew ops two nights running. It would be all right. It was just, she supposed, that since last night she must never take anything for granted, because to do so would be tempting fate, and she had enough to worry about with the mess at home.

'Take care, darling,' she whispered, then pedalled as fast as she dare in the darkness to Bessie's house.

'Come on in.' Elsie Drake opened the back door, closing it quickly. 'We've got the place to ourselves tonight.'

'Mr Drake gone for a pint?'

'No. He's at work, on lates. Double time for Sundays, though for all the good it does, I don't know why he bothers. Nothing in the shops to spend it on!' She laughed, calling out that Rosamund was here, telling her to go through into the parlour.

'I've brought you some milk, Mrs Drake; thought you might be able to find a use for a drop extra.'

'My word!' she smiled, holding up the large lemonade bottle. 'That's two days' ration for the three of us, Rosamund. We could have had a rice pudding – if those dratted little Japs hadn't collared all the rice!'

She thought tremulously of the days she could have bought half a stone of rice had she been so minded. Now, it was like bananas – to be remembered with nostalgia.

'Hi! Twice in one day! Does your mother know you're out then?' Bessie teased. 'Come and get yourself warm, and tell me the news!'

'There isn't any.' She couldn't tell anyone, not even her best friend, about her mother's hysterics. 'But I've brought the cross. I want it blessing, Mrs Drake,' she offered by way of explanation, 'for Jon. Help keep him safe. Do you think I'm being mawkish?'

'Oh my word, no! Not one bit! But why can't your own minister bless it for you?'

'Because my mother might get to know, and –'

'And she doesn't know about your young man,' Elsie Drake nodded. 'Are you sure you can't tell her? She was young herself, once. Happen she might take it better'n you think.'

'She won't, and I don't want her to know.' Rosamund glanced briefly, gratefully, in Bessie's direction. 'She wouldn't understand. She thinks I'm too young to have a boyfriend.'

'Maybe the pair of you are, but wars change things. Make things seem more urgent. That's when a girl has to be careful, and you both know what I mean,' she said meaningfully, eyeing them over the tops of her spectacles. 'Feelings run high when there's a war on, and it's understandable for a young man to want to know what life is all about.'

'And there are plenty of girls who are curious, too,' Bessie sighed, 'and worried because all the young men are away at the war, and wondering if they'll ever get a husband.'

'They will, if they wait long enough. Now when I was your age, men were very thin on the ground,' Elsie Drake sighed. 'So many had been killed in the Great War, you see, that there were a lot of spinsters around. Thank the Lord there hasn't been the terrible slaughter, this time, and none of that awful trench warfare!'

'But there might be, Mrs Drake. What about when the

second front starts? It's almost certain to be somewhere in France, and they might start digging trenches all over again!' Rosamund whispered.

'In my opinion, the second front – if ever it comes, that is – will be so well organized that our lot will go through France like a hot knife through butter. Things are all mechanical now. They don't have horses pulling their guns and wagons like they did in the last war. Won't take long once that lot in London decide when it's going to be.'

'But there'll be the Japs to settle up with after Europe, Mum. The Americans are helping us and we'll have to help them with those Japs. This war could go on for years yet, and I'll be past it by the time it's all over,' Bessie pouted.

'Past it!' her mother laughed. 'You're only bits of lasses, so don't look so badly done to! And why don't we all have a cup of cocoa, cheer ourselves up!' She was thinking of the lemonade bottle on the slate slab in the pantry; of cocoa made extravagantly with boiled milk instead of water, and the stuff in blue tins They called milk powder! 'Won't be long!'

'Thanks for not telling your mother they know about Jon,' Rosamund whispered when they were alone.

'I said I wouldn't, didn't I? What do you take me for then?'

'A good friend, Bess, and I hope we'll always be friends, no matter what happens.'

'Of course we will! We'll be bridesmaid for each other and stand godmother when our kids are christened! Oh heck, Rosamund! I wish I had a boyfriend – a serious one, I mean. Dancing partners are all very well, but I'd swap Mick any day, for a steady!'

'Being in love isn't all wine and roses, especially when you've got a mother like mine!'

For a moment she was tempted to tell Bessie about the upset over the rockets, and how awful it had been. But she bit on her tongue, because what happened this morning was her mother's business and anyway you didn't admit, even to your best friend, that you thought your mother was going off her head!

'Oh, come on, Rosamund! You told her where to get off,

didn't you – told her about Jon and that you were going to keep on seeing him, no matter what? All you've got to do now is not to let her trample over you any more! And put the cross on the mantelpiece, so Mum doesn't forget it. There's a Mothers' Union service tomorrow – I'll remind her to take it with her.'

'Thanks, Bess. And when we've had our drink, I'll have to be going. Don't want to stay out too long – rock the boat any more than I have to.'

Yet even as she said it, she wondered what new upset would be waiting for her the minute she opened the door, then asked herself yet again if she had been wise to tell her parents about Jon. And even as the thought slipped through her mind, she knew she had been wrong.

But it was too late for regrets.

Rosamund was grateful when she got home to find that her mother was in bed.

'She was past it,' Bart Kenton said. 'Made herself a glass of hot milk and took one of her herbals, and she's sleeping now. I've not long been to have a look at her.'

'I'm sorry I was the cause of it, Dad. I should have kept quiet about Jon, but I'd give anything to be able to bring him home. You'd like him. Even Mum would. His Aunt Charlotte brought him up. She never married. Her young man was killed in the last war. She sent me a photograph of Jon, and I've written to thank her. I'll show you, if you like. Or do you think you'd better not see it in case Mum finds out?'

'I'd like to, very much. But not tonight, lass. I was only waiting for you to come in before I went to bed. I could do with a good night's sleep, an' all.'

'I've said I'm sorry, Dad . . .'

'Nay, Rosamund. It isn't your fault. Maybe the doctor was right, and your mother is going through a funny time. She was always one to keep herself to herself; this war upset all her plans, and she took it personal. She's tried to ignore it, but it won't go away. Bear with her, there's a good lass? She'll come through it, given time.'

'But have we got time, Dad? This war is awful for everyone – especially those with people they love in it. Jon's on ops tonight. I'm worried sick about him.'

'I know. I heard them going. And there'll be a right old din when they come back in the early hours! Best I get myself off to bed before they do! And lass, try not to worry over much? One day, it'll all be over and it'll be a rare old day, when that happens. I know what I'm talking about! Your dad did his share of fighting, don't forget.'

'I won't, and I'm proud of you. Mrs Drake was talking about your war tonight, and the terrible killing. You never say a word about it.'

'Only if I have to. Best forgotten. Put my medals at the bottom of a drawer when it was over, and I haven't looked at them since. But I'll bid you good night, Rosamund. See the fire is safe before you go to bed, and don't forget the lamps.'

'I'll check everything, and, Dad . . .' She held out her arms, drawing him close, laying her cheek on his. Then she stood back, pink-cheeked, because shows of affection were rare at Laburnum Farm. 'I love you very much,' she whispered as he walked, shoulders bent, from the room; said it in defiance of the woman who slept upstairs, and softly, so he should not hear it. ''Night,' she called.

She awoke to Shep's howling. It was as if she was tuned in to the animal; both of them on the same waiting wavelength. She lay still, heart thudding. The dog's keen ears had picked up the faraway sound of engines and very soon she would hear them, too.

She wondered why he didn't make a fuss at takeoff, but lay in his kennel, unmoving, as the heavily loaded bombers roared low overhead. Did he know it was important to waken her so she could listen and count? Dear old Shep, who hadn't barked on Saturday night.

She swung her legs out of bed, feeling for her slippers, then reached for the dressing gown that always lay at the bottom of the bed, wrapping it round her, fastening it tightly, trailing her fingertips along the bedside table from which it was only two steps to the window. Pulling back the curtains she pushed open the window, wincing as cold air slapped into her, reaching for the eiderdown, snuggling it round her. All was darkness, save for a few fading stars. She focused her eyes in the direction of the aerodrome and saw one dim light ahead, then another and another until the sky glowed in two straight long lines. They had lit the runway flares; the bombers were almost home.

She heard the first faraway drone of engines almost at once. A returning aircraft seemed to make a very different sound to one which was taking off. It was a lighter, keener tone and not the aggressive growl they left behind them as they shuddered into the sky. Was it because their bomb load had gone, the fuel in their tanks almost used up, or was it because of the clear morning air? Was it all in her mind? Did the relief she felt make her light-headed?

The first-home Lancaster circled overhead. The first was the luckiest, she supposed; could land at once without waiting and circling. Was it *Johnnie* or *Zebra* or *Sugar*? Did it matter, as long as they all got back?

One down with a roar; ten more to go, two of them already circling. It was going to be all right. Jon would be at the gate tonight. He *would*.

Yet when the bedside alarm jangled a five o'clock reminder that it was time to go to the shippon, only ten bombers had returned and to add to her fears, the runway lights had long since been extinguished.

One not back, nor expected back, it seemed. Automatically, she drew the blackout over the window, then lit the candle, pulling on her clothes with clumsy fingers, wondering what to do. Instinct urged her to get on her bike, go to the village and phone the aerodrome, but would the switchboard there accept her call? They didn't when crews were flying; a security thing. And when that happened no one could ring out either. Even if Laburnum Farm had been on the phone, Jon could not have sent her a whispered, 'Hi! I'm back. I love you!'

There was nothing to do but wait until tonight, telling herself over and over again that Jon was all right. He had to be because they belonged now, and nothing must harm a love so precious.

She fell to her knees, opening the bottom drawer of the chest, taking out Jon's picture.

'Darling – please, if you love me, be there tonight?'

The day dragged. Rosamund went through the motions of milking, but the missing plane was never far from her thoughts. She loaded milk churns, unloaded them at the end of the lane, all the time scanning the sky. She was at the far end of the paddock from where she could look down on a distant, misty aerodrome when she heard what she had been hoping for; the sound of aircraft engines. It came from afar, but it was a Lancaster sound; maybe the missing bomber. She searched the sky until her eyes lit on it, watching it get closer, bigger, dropping lower. Then it was circling, waiting permission to land, and as it flew low overhead on its second circuit, she was able to pick out the squadron markings and the letter C. It *was* one of Laceby's! *C-Charlie* was home and waiting to touch down. They had all made it! Again!

She looked yet again at the mantel clock. Still fifteen minutes to go, but she could stand it no longer!

'I'm going out,' she said shakily. 'I – I need some air – a walk . . .'

'Wrap up warm then,' her father said gently. 'And take the flashlight with you; have a look at the arks whilst you're about it; let those foxes get a scent of you.'

'Good idea,' she smiled, waiting for her mother to protest, forbid her to go. But Mildred Kenton's eyes were fixed on her knitting, her mouth a tight button of disapproval.

Her father nodded and smiled briefly, and she knew it was his way of saying he was on her side. She wrinkled her nose in return and hoped he knew she was grateful to him.

Closing the back door behind her she ran as fast as she dare, blinking her eyes to accustom them to the darkness outside, because Jon might be early and she wanted to be early, too; be waiting when he got there.

She paused at the kennel, bending to fondle the dog. 'Good boy. Don't bark, then?' Shep was on her side, too. At the top of the narrow path that led to the little iron gate she stopped, calling his name softly.

'Rosie?'

She flung herself into his arms and they hugged tightly, not kissing nor speaking; just glad to be together.

'I came early. I couldn't wait another minute,' she whispered at last. 'I'm glad you did, too. Kiss me?'

'Up until midday,' she said breathlessly, tremulously, many kisses later, 'I'd have given all I owned for just one of those. Then I saw *C-Charlie* coming in to land, and everything was all right again. What happened, Jon? Why was he so late?'

'He'd taken some flak; his instruments had an attack of the gremlins. Anyway, they ended up at RAF Waddington – in Lincolnshire. His RT was working, fortunately, and they let him land. They patched him up, got him airworthy, and he shoved off back to Laceby – very relieved, I shouldn't wonder.'

'I'm glad he made it.'

'So were we all. But how long have we got?'

'Not long, Jon. I said I was going out for a blow of fresh air and Dad said I was to take a look at the poultry whilst I was about it. There are foxes about, so it won't hurt to let them get the scent of a human. Checking the arks gives us a few more minutes, but tomorrow night, if you can make it, can you be here early? You know why . . .'

'I can make it for half-seven. But what excuse will you give – Bessie's again?'

'No. I shall just say I'm going out.' She couldn't tell him about Saturday night; he had worries enough, flying ops, without her adding to them.

'Will there be trouble, Rosie? I don't want friction at your place because of me. I'm still willing to risk calling.'

'And I don't want you to – yet. I'll know, darling, when the time is right. And meantime, I'm getting into your aunt's good books.' Change the subject! 'I wrote to her, thanked her for the photograph.'

'Good! But let's do that checking? D'you know something – I've never kissed my girl in a field full of hens!'

'There's a first time for everything.' All at once she was very happy, and slipped her arm in his, snuggling close. 'And, darling — please don't be flying tomorrow night? Be at the hayloft, early?'

'I'll do the washing up,' Rosamund said when supper was finished. 'Then I'll be going out.' Her voice sounded ordinary, because she had the words arranged ready in her mind. 'About half-seven.'

'You went out this afternoon,' her mother said tartly.

'To the village, to post a letter to Jon's aunt. If you'd asked me, I'd have told you.'

'I see. Then if you must go out, I want you in early. Where did you say you were going?'

'To meet Jon.' She was shaking. Telling the truth was much harder than inventing glib lies. 'And I don't know what we'll be doing; probably just walking, and talking.'

She began to stack cutlery and plates on a tray; did it methodically, scraping uneaten scraps into the pigswill bucket, concentrating hard on the simple task to shut out the thinly disguised hostility behind her mother's probing.

'Early,' Mildred Kenton stressed. 'Before the news.'

'I'll try. It'll all depend on what we decide to do.'

She was becoming apprehensive, because her mother was intent on another upset, and it was important she should not allow herself to be goaded into saying something else she might regret. And she had told only half a truth when she admitted to posting the letter, because she had called on Bessie's mother, too, to collect the cross; wrapped it carefully in a clean handkerchief because it was special, now it had been blessed. Now it had become an amulet against ill wishes, and lay in the bottom drawer of the chest, beside Jon's photograph.

'I said *early*, or you'll find the door locked.'

'You may please yourself, Mother. It's your house and your door and your key, and I can always sleep at Bessie's. I'm sure Mrs Drake wouldn't mind.'

She looked at her father for support and saw he was engrossed in choosing a pipe from the rack at the fireside. She glanced back to her mother, looking her straight in the eyes, holding them with her own, throwing out a challenge.

'There'll be no need.' Mildred Kenton was the one to surrender, drop her gaze. 'As you say, Rosamund, this is my house, though you seem at times to forget it!'

'As far as I'm concerned,' Bart jammed a pipe between his teeth, 'I don't see why she can't have the young man call for her! It isn't right he should wait at – have to hang around in the cold.'

'Wait where?' Mildred demanded.

'We usually meet at six oaks, Mother.' Another lie; one her father would recognize because he knew they met at the iron gate – had almost said so.

'I don't approve of that man, and you know it! Meet him where you like, for all I care!' She turned to face her husband. 'But she's not bringing him here, Bart Kenton, and that's my final word!'

'All right! Just stop it, you two! I'm sorry I told you about Jon! I should have gone on telling lies, deceiving you both. But I won't stop seeing him!'

'So do what you want, lady!' The venom was back in Mildred Kenton's eyes. 'You'll come to a bad end if you carry on as you are doing! And when you do, when you get yourself into trouble, just don't bother bringing it home!'

'So you're threatening your own daughter now!' Rosamund gasped. 'You've already wished Jon dead, said you hope his plane crashes, and now it's my turn! Don't dare get pregnant or you'll be kicked out! You are ill, Mother! Not your body, but your mind, and I don't know how Dad has put up with you all these years!'

She ran from the room, feet slamming angrily on the narrow wooden stairs, locking her bedroom door behind her.

Then closing her eyes, she whispered, *God – it's Rosamund Kenton and I'm sorry for all the trouble I'm causing. But I love Jon so much that I just don't know what to do . . .*

Her bottom lip began to tremble and she bit on it hard to stop the tears she dare not let fall. And she *did* know what to do! It had come to her in a flash, as if God had really heard her!

She would say she was sorry for the things she had said, that she didn't mean any of them; would lie through her teeth for the sake of peace and quiet. She understood, she would say, the stress her mother was under, beg her not to be upset; to think of her health, and try to take things a bit easier.

What she would not apologize for was her love for Jon! As far as Jon was concerned, there was no deal! She would grovel, pay lip service if that was what it took; would do it glibly if only to keep the pressure off her father, and ill wishes away from Jon!

Carefully she poured water into the bowl on the washstand. It was very cold, and washing in it had a steadying effect on her. Then she brushed and combed her hair and put on a skirt and blouse, all the time willing herself to be calm. She wasn't proud of what she was about to do, but she didn't have a lot of choice!

She opened the drawer, gazing at the photograph of Jon, slipping the cross into her pocket. Then she blew out the candle and walked downstairs to the kitchen.

'Mum – Dad – I'm going out now. I shouldn't have said what I did, and I'm sorry for it. Don't upset yourselves. I won't be getting myself into trouble, and I'm sorry you're ill, Mother. I'll try to help you more in the house. And I won't be too late in.'

She glanced at her father, begging him with her eyes to understand. Then she forced her gaze to her mother, who looked at her blankly, then turned away to pick up her knitting.

Rosamund went to great pains to close the kitchen door gently behind her, then walked carefully across the darkness of the dairy to take her coat from the peg, buttoning it up, wrapping a muffler round her neck and ears. Then she took the cross from the pocket of her skirt slipping it, for greater safety, into the deep pocket of her jacket. And as she did so her fingers touched something cold and hard.

She knew at once it was the key to the keeping pantry, off the dairy. It had a door that was seldom used, and opened onto the yard. Nor did it have bolts on the inside.

It was her access to the house, Rosamund realized, in case her mother had a fresh fit of pique and locked her out; no one but her father could have put the key in her pocket!

Smiling, she sent him her thanks, walking carefully on cobbles slippery with ice, knowing that though it had hurt her pride to offer it, the apology had been necessary.

She crossed the yard, whispered to the sheepdog, then made for the hay barn. And whilst she waited, she would empty her mind of the things said in anger, because nothing mattered, now, but Jon. He was her reason for being, the axis on which her world spun giddily; her reason for getting up and going to bed, her breathing out and breathing in. Without him she was nothing, and if one night he didn't come back then she would want to die, too.

She thought about the little gold cross, knowing already that Jon wore a medallion on a chain around his neck; had felt it with her fingertips as they lay in the hay. And tonight she would thread her cross there to protect him from evil, though she wouldn't tell him so.

It was a charm, she would say, from her to him; something to keep him from colliding, at takeoff, with low-flying witches on broomsticks. They would laugh about it and he would never know how near the truth her words were.

She was sitting on the wooden steps, chin on hand, thinking how much she loved him, how desperately she needed him to make love to her, when she heard the click of the door latch.

'Jon?' she whispered, switching on her torch. 'Over here, darling . . .'

TEN

February snarled in on a bitter north wind. It was still dark though the early morning sky showed a thin streak of cold yellow light to the east. Rosamund knew her father was already about; could hear him calling the cows, from the foldyard.

'Morning, Dad. Playing up a bit, are they?'

'When did you ever see the dratted cow that didn't? And they say sheep are the stupid ones!'

Rosamund smiled, all at once light-hearted, though she didn't know why. Perhaps it was because she was becoming more relaxed, more sure of herself. After her mother's warning about girls who got themselves into trouble, no more had been said on the matter, which was as well, Rosamund thought, since she hadn't got pregnant! She called back their first loving and how she had wondered if her period would come, and it had. On the exact day. Yet she would not have been surprised if it hadn't; had been ready to accept that a child would have been the natural outcome of so passionate a coupling.

Soon, they would no longer be able to go to the hayloft. Now, blackout curtains were not drawn until seven at night, with total darkness arriving half an hour later. Before long, clocks would be put forward to double summertime, and in June the days would last until almost midnight; long, warm days. She longed for them. After the drear of winter and a blackout that could last for sixteen hours, a sun-filled, flower-bright summer would be heaven.

Things at home, she pondered as she scrubbed her hands in a bucket of blissfully hot water, were not so tense now; as if her mother had finally acknowledged that she must accept what she was powerless to change. Yet for all that, Rosamund could turn suddenly to find the older woman's eyes on her, a strange, watching expression in them.

It no longer seemed important that Jon be allowed to call at Laburnum Farm because she was content with the way things were; they were lovers, married save in the eyes of the Church. And did words from a prayer book matter all that much? Marriage was for the procreation of children – it said so, in the marriage service – and since Jon was making sure they did no such thing, society's approval seemed less urgent.

She dried her hands, then put on apron and milking cap, forcing her thoughts back to reality, trying not to think that tonight *J-Johnnie* would almost certainly be flying its seventeenth operation over enemy territory and that for Jon, if she wanted to be nit-picky and include his first seven, it would be only six off his thirty. A tour of ops, she cautiously admitted, now seemed possible.

From the far end of the shippon she could hear the hiss of milk as it hit the bottom of her father's pail. From each stall came a slow, steady munching, punctuated by snorts and blows and the occasional flick of a tail. She rested her forehead against the belly of the cow and took the udders in her hands, squeezing and pulling rhythmically, imitating the sucking of a calf.

Life was, she thought, full of contradictions; of highs, when she and Jon were together; and lows, when she stood at the steel-mesh fence, counting. Then there were ordinary things like milking on a dark morning, red-nosed with cold, to be set against the delight of dancing with Jon, or waiting at the little gate, counting the minutes until he came.

She was, she had to admit, the luckiest girl ever, and soon she would be the most thankful because even though they never talked about finishing the tour, she knew now that Jon's crew were increasingly confident of making it – and oh, please, they would!

'Bye!' Rosamund called to her parents who sat at the kitchen table, trying to get order into a box filled with bills and invoices and receipts; all the paraphernalia that went with the running of a dairy farm.

Her father lifted a hand without taking his eyes from the papers he was arranging into piles, telling her to be off and not to be late in. He always said it now. It kept the peace and saved her mother saying it; maybe adding some sharp remark that could spark off an upset.

So complicated had the farm accounts become that her parents had taken the minister's advice and sought professional help. Tomorrow, at half-past two, her father would take the shoebox and dump it thankfully on the accountant's desk. Accountants cost money, but Mildred Kenton had said she was sick of form-filling and the like and was no longer able to make sense of accounts for the tax inspector! And Bart had agreed wholeheartedly and was glad to be rid of the worry.

Rosamund made for the iron gate. They waited there now, until it was dark enough to slip into the barn. Impatient to see him, she walked down the lane towards the crossroads, pausing at the signpost which, before its arms had been removed for security reasons, had pointed to Laceby Green on the one hand, and Lancaster on the other. She could just make out the lonely outline of the post in the near-dark, and wondered how long it would be before railway stations had names on them again, and signposts showed people which way to go, and lights shone through windows in the darkness. Perhaps those things were not so far away. Talk of the second front was becoming more and more insistent, and papers printed every scrap of news the Ministry of Information thought prudent to release about it. It was no longer if, but where, and when.

'If you could see what They've got on the south coast! Rows and rows of guns and trucks and tanks and landing craft and Lord knows what else, covered with camouflage netting! You'd never believe it!' Joe Drake had said on his last leave, tapping his nose with a forefinger. 'That lot will wonder what's hit them when we go in!'

But more than that he had not been prepared to say, except that one of the chiefies on his ship was taking bets on where the second front would be. Joe had had a couple of bob on

Dunkirk, because it stood to reason it would be, after what had happened there four years ago.

She waited, listening to night sounds, glad there seemed to have been a news clampdown on anything about rockets, because even mention of the word sent her mother into fits of depression after reminding them she had been right all along, and they hadn't heard the last of those rockets, mark her words they hadn't!

Rosamund blanked out her thoughts and stood, breath indrawn, impatient for the sound of Jon's footsteps, deciding she had waited here long enough; that she would walk to six oaks and meet him there. How desperately she loved him!

'I should think,' Rosamund whispered from the shelter of Jon's arms, 'that we'll soon have to be looking for another place.'

'Anywhere in mind?'

'There's an empty cottage I know of; it's padlocked and the bottom windows are boarded up, but I'm sure we could find a way in.'

'Why isn't it lived in?'

'Their water supply got contaminated and the health people condemned it. Like most places around here, they didn't have mains water, you see.'

'So if you could get an afternoon off or even a couple of hours, we could do a recce, though I'd still give a lot for us to have just one night together.'

'So isn't this enough for you, Jon?'

'No, it isn't! I want you with me always; want you to belong!'

'But I do!'

'I want to call you wife, Rosie; want every man who sets eyes on you to envy me. You're so lovely to love, it hurts like hell to leave you.'

'But it's like that for me too. How do you think I feel when I know you are flying and all I can do is stand there and watch you go, then worry myself sick till you're back?'

'Sorry, sweetheart.' He kissed her gently. 'I shouldn't have said that. What we have now is more than I could ever have hoped for, that night we met, but it doesn't stop me wishing we could be married. Tomorrow! And, Rosie – talking about tomorrow, we're almost certain to be flying, and after that they've slapped a seventy-two-hour leave pass on the crew. I won't see you for ages.'

'Can't be helped.' She tried hard to keep her dismay from showing. 'And at least I'll know you are out of harm's way. You'll be going on Saturday morning, then?'

'No. Leave doesn't start until noon. I'll be getting the two o'clock train from Preston.'

'Then if I could be at Bessie's house, could you try to ring me? I'm sure Mrs Drake wouldn't mind if I gave you their phone number. Bessie's mum is OK; she knows about us. The number is Laceby Green 734; can you remember it?'

'I can. And you're talking too much. Can you shut up just long enough for me to kiss you – very thoroughly?'

The crew of *J-Johnnie* was cock-a-hoop. Back from Berlin, their seventeenth op behind them, and a three-day leave to come. It had been the worst raid ever, but Skip had got them home. Jammy, he was, and a bloody fine pilot, and when they'd got their tour over and done with, they wouldn't mind, they said, crewing up again – after a respectable spell away from operational flying, of course – and doing another thirty! Provided they could do them in *J-Johnnie*, Lord love the old kite, and have Jon Hunt in the driving seat again!

Yet Jon, wise beyond his years, warned them to watch it, and not do their gloating out loud, and though he didn't say as much, he knew that RAF Laceby Green had been lucky in not losing a single crew in the three months it had been up and running; had wanted to remind them that luck was a fickle thing, and that Laceby's could run out at the drop of a hat!

He didn't, though, because when they had had breakfast and shaved and showered and togged themselves up in their best uniforms, buttons polished and stripes gleaming white, they would pile into the transport that would take them to the station, and home, where for three days they could forget flying.

Jon thought about the soft, springy bed with the blue eider-down and wished Rosie could be with him. But the dragon lady wouldn't allow it; come to think of it he wasn't at all sure that Aunt Lottie would either; not actually in her own home!

He was tired. Some of his answers to the debriefing officer's persistent questioning had been short and to the point. He'd made it there, hadn't he; dropped his load and got back? What more did the desk-bound clot want? But he would feel better when he had washed away the sweat of the night and was on the train.

Laceby Green 734. Bessie's place. And Rosie would try to be there tonight and Sunday night, waiting for his call. Come to think of it, it would be the first time he had ever phoned her.

'See you all then.' He picked up his flying jacket. 'Half-twelve outside the guardroom – OK?'

And they chorused back that sure as hell it was OK! They were going home, weren't they, and were off flying for three days and three safe nights? They'd be there, all right, leave passes and travel warrants at the ready!

Poor old Skip. He'd got it bad. Not that you could blame him. Rosie was a real good-looker and pretty gone on him too. Pity she had a mother who could put Boadicea in the shade – or so Mick's dancing partner said!

Ah, well, it took all sorts, didn't they say, and tired but high as kites, they were off on a crafty seventy-two, so what the heck?

Rosamund had been waiting for twenty minutes at the station entrance when the transport from RAF Laceby Green arrived. Two crews were on weekend passes and Jon was the last to get out. He looked tired, she thought; there were rings beneath his eyes and his face was pale. Then he pushed his hair from his forehead with his left hand, and put on his cap. So small a thing; so endearing. Half the time he didn't know he was doing it and it made her eyes prick with little tears because she loved him so much.

'Rosie!' He turned to see her standing there and his smile

was instant and warm. 'How did you manage it?' He held out his arms and she went into them, lifting her lips to be kissed.

'I decided I needed a haircut, and it worked,' she laughed, lacing her fingers in his, smiling into his eyes.

'Don't have it cut too short, Rosie.'

'Not *cut*, darling; just the bitty ends trimmed. And I've brought you six eggs – stolen from Laburnum Farm!'

'*Six!* All at once!' He opened the khaki case of his respirator and she saw that the mask and canister had been removed and the inside stuffed with shirts and socks and underwear. 'My washing,' he explained, wrapping a shirt round the brown paper bag. 'Aunt Lottie will be really glad of these. Wish you were coming with me, darling.'

'Mm. But I'll be at Bessie's tonight and tomorrow night and at least I won't panic so much when the circuits and bumps start.' They had found an empty bench and were content just to sit close, shoulders and thighs touching, until the train left. 'Are you expected, Jon?'

'No, but I've got a key. I don't want to leave you, Rosie. Shall we sit here till Tuesday?'

'Idiot.' She laid her head on his shoulder. 'Remember, you're to get lots of sleep and wear your civvies and relax a bit. And try to get through to Laceby, let me know you've got there safely.'

'Darling girl! I can find my way to Berlin and back in the dark. Getting to Lower Sellow will be a piece of cake! And I think you should go now. The train looks like it's leaving, and I don't want you to wave me off.' He got to his feet, pulling her into his arms, kissing her gently. 'I'll ring you tonight. Don't know what time, but I'll keep trying till I get through. And don't let them cut too much off your hair?'

'I won't,' she whispered. 'See you, Jon. Love you . . .'

She hurried away, resisting the need to turn round for a last look, wanting desperately to be with him; refusing to let herself think how wonderful three days – and nights together – would be.

But at least, she thought tremulously, he would be safe for three days. And nights.

★　　★　　★

Rosamund leaned on the dry-stone wall, arms folded. Ahead lay Beacon Fell and Parlick Pike and, darker in the distance, Fair Snape. So wild and beautiful; miles and miles of moorland, rising and falling, interspersed by stretches of trees to remind that long ago, when the north of England was ungovernable, there had been a great, dense area of trees known as the Forest of Bowland. She was glad that tracts of that forest still existed.

Now the sky was grey, the fells sombre. Only when spring came would the dull green of spruces be laced with flowering rowan trees, the pale, silky green of unfolding beech leaves and wild, white cherry blossom. And in summer, when they collected bilberries, all squashy and purple, the heather would flower and turn the hilltops to lavender pink.

Up here, for as far as she could see, there was no sign of human habitation; no curls of woodsmoke from stout stone chimney stacks; not even the faraway bark of a dog. There were roofless houses in the distance, though, their slates long ago plundered so the elements had eroded window frames and wooden floors, and all that remained were walls and wide, deep hearths covered with moss and weeds. Sad, really, if you thought too much about it.

The cottage called Fellfoot – it couldn't have been given any other name – was the only one that still stood secure, almost hidden between two bluffs of rock. Outside it was a well, filled with rubble, and to the left the polluted stream still ran in a shallow gully, dammed, further down, to make a pond. Dad could remember when ducks swam on that pond, and people lived there. Now the pond was still and grey and calm, the trees around it bare and lifeless as if it waited for summer and the return of wild fowl and water hens.

Fellfoot's roof was stone-slabbed and, because of the weight of it, had been left untouched. Its doors were padlocked, its downstairs windows covered with corrugated sheets. Had it not been for the undrinkable water, people could live there still, Rosamund pondered.

There were no hedges nor fences around the deserted house; only a stretch of dry-stone wall to protect it from the worst of the winter gales. The doorstep at the front gave way not to a tidy, flower-planted path, but to the tussocky grass of the moor. No pigs squealed in the sty; no sheep bearing Fellfoot's mark roamed the hills. Once, anyone living there need never see their nearest neighbour, fifteen minutes' walk away, from one Sunday to the next – unless they wanted to. The windows were of stone; the sheeting had been hammered into it with huge nails. Stout padlocks secured the front and back doors; only the wide, narrow upstairs windows had been spared, to stare, unblinking, to the tops of the fells.

The pale February sun slipped behind a hill to remind Rosamund it was time to go home; go back to Laburnum that smelled of furniture polish and lavender bags and things cooking in Margaret Dacre's kitchen. Laburnum was all the things Fellfoot was not, yet it seemed to Rosamund that when the last family left the wild, isolated farmstead, likely as not for a modern council house in Clitheroe, they left behind a little of their contentment, because she knew it had once been a happy house, where children ran free and paddled in the stream and fed the ducks that nested beside the pond.

She hurried towards home, because already she had wished away the weed-choked gutters, the peeling paint, the unwashed windows. Now, in her mind, the doors and windows had been painted and a red rose climbed the stone walls. Now Fellfoot was her home – hers and Jon's – because a small miracle had brought clean water to it. And the war was long over and their children ran free on the fells and threw stale bread to the ducks that swam there again.

All at once she was at the armless signpost and Laburnum Farm only a few yards away at the end of the dirt road. It was called coming down to earth with a bump, she thought dolefully, because Fellfoot would go the same way as the other ruins, given time, and until then it would mock young lovers needing to be alone, because it was too securely protected for anyone ever to get inside it.

She pushed open the squeaky gate, lingering her hand on it because Jon had waited there so many times, then hurrying because milking began at four and finished before it was time for blackout. Milking. Always, *always* cows to be milked! Yet soon, she thought as she pulled on dungarees and smock, winter would be gone and birds would sing and the evenings would be long and light. It would, she thought gratefully, be like escaping from a damp, dark dungeon into sunlight and warmth.

To indulge herself, and because she wouldn't see Jon tonight, she took out his picture, whispering, 'Hi! Have a good leave. I miss you!' wishing she had a photograph of herself to give to him. But films for the cameras of civilians were almost a thing of the past, because the Armed Forces' – especially the RAF's – need of them came first. Only rarely could one be bought over a shop counter, to be cherished and used only on the most important occasions.

It was a pity, Rosamund sighed, that the last formal photograph she'd had taken was of the class of '37, Clitheroe Grammar School. Rosamund Kenton, staring into the camera, her hair in plaits. And Bessie beside her, whose eyes, even on so solemn an occasion, were bright with mischief. Bessie had always treated life as a giggle.

Dear Bessie. She had answered the phone last night, then hurried to the kitchen, demanding to know if anyone was expecting a call, then closing the door firmly behind her so no one should hear what was being said.

'Hi, darling. I love you.' Jon's voice had sounded deep and husky over the phone. She must remember, Rosamund thought, that the first words of their first ever phone call had been 'I love you'.

'Got to go,' he'd said softly, when pips interrupted the call to warn them their three minutes had only a few seconds to run. 'I'll phone tomorrow night. Love you . . .'

She had felt very alone when she replaced the receiver, longing for Jon, wishing they could be in the hay barn or even at the aerodrome dance. But as Bessie had pointed out, it was no use going to the dance when both Jon and Mick were on leave. No use her doing anything, except to wish for Tuesday night. And on Tuesday night she would be as late in as she wanted, because she wouldn't have seen Jon for four days, nor kissed him, nor loved him.

She put away the photograph then hurried to the shippon and the boring task of milking. It was as well, she thought, that once into her rhythm, she could blank it all out and think of Jon, living again their precious times; recalling his mouth, his smile and every whisper and touch of their loving.

Jon had been gentle, patient, at first; holding back his passion until she had learned to be a part of it, match it with her own. Now she was unashamed of the need in her eyes and her eagerness to couple. Loving Jon, being loved by him, was as normal now as breathing out and breathing in and a million times more marvellous. It was why she knew she had been wrong to wish Jon had not gone on leave; knew it as she awakened suddenly this morning to lay in the darkness, counting.

Two Lancasters had not returned from last night's operations, nor would they. It was on the midday news bulletin: a thousand-bomber raid on Essen and eighty-seven of our planes unaccounted for – two of them from Jon's squadron. War had come to Laceby Green at last and taken fourteen young men. She had thanked God over and over again in chapel; thanked Him for a seventy-two-hour leave pass and that *J-Johnnie* had not been one of RAF Laceby Green's first casualties.

'Shall I start milking, Dad, or put the fodder out?' she called.

'Make a start, lass. I'll see to the feed.'

His reply pleased Rosamund, because she could slip into her own secret world all the sooner.

'How long is it since Fellfoot was lived in?' she asked as she scrubbed her hands. 'I went for a walk towards the tops whilst you were having your Sunday snooze and wondered about it. It must have been a solid little house once.'

'Still is. Built to last. It was when you were a little lass – before you went to school. We had a very dry summer and something happened to the water that supplied the well. They had a boy taken ill and it turned out the water was to blame. The health people shifted them out quicker'n you could say Jack Robinson. The well was filled up and the primer taken out of the pump, an' all.'

'So it's been empty about fourteen years? Such a pity, Dad . . .'

'Aye. But everything depends on water, Rosamund. In the old days, before sewers and sanitation, folk built where there was water. With Laburnum, there was once a stream and that sufficed till they'd sunk a well and set up a pump. Beautiful water we've got; clear as crystal. Hope they'll never bring tap water here. We'd all be badly, I shouldn't wonder, and have to pay for the dratted stuff into the bargain. Were you up there with your young man?'

'No, Dad. He's on leave. I went to Bessie's last night. But I'll make a start. It's grand, isn't it, doing afternoon milking in the daylight?'

She put on her cap, washed the first cow's udders in warm water, then settled herself down to her daydreaming and thoughts of living in a house amazingly like Fellfoot, with Jon – and making love. And of sleeping in a big, soft bed with Jon – and being lovers. And of Tuesday night, and waiting at the kissing gate for Jon – and staying out very late . . .

It wasn't until the milk had been cooled and poured into churns and the herd secure in the foldyard that it happened. Something very ordinary, but which seemed to catch her gaze and hold it and make her wonder why suddenly she should notice a bunch of keys that must have been there for years.

It was hanging on an iron nail by the side of the keeping pantry door. There were many keys on it – at least thirty – and all in different sizes and shapes. Some were old-fashioned and heavy – very much like the one which had found its way into her pocket not so very long ago – and all of them looked as if they hadn't been used in years. Keys. For doors and locks – and padlocks?

She reached for them, surprised they were so heavy, wondering if, amongst them, was one that would fit the lock on either of Fellfoot's doors.

'It's a long shot, of course,' she said to Bessie that night, 'but it's worth a try. Dad had a letter from the accountant. He wants him and my mother to see him on Tuesday. They'll be gone for at least two hours, so I shall go there and see if there's a key to Fellfoot.'

'But you can't, Rosamund! You'd be trespassing!'

'On whose property?'

'It'll be breaking and entering.'

'No it won't! But wouldn't it be just my luck for the door to fall off its hinges when I try to open it?'

'You'll never get in there,' Bessie warned. 'And just supposing you did – what are you going to find?'

'A few cobwebs, maybe.'

'Cobwebs! It could be *filthy*, Rosamund!'

'So we won't know, will we, until we've had a look inside?'

'You really mean it, don't you? You'd go into that mucky old ruin and – and – do *that*? It won't be a bit romantic. Do you expect to find a bed in there, or something?'

'Not even in my wildest dreams, Bess. But Fellfoot isn't a ruin and I'm sure it isn't dirty inside. There won't have been any tramps or roadsters using it either. It looks as if nobody's been in it for years.'

'Well, *I* wouldn't go there,' Bessie spluttered, red-cheeked. 'Not for anything!'

'Not even to be with a man you're crazy about?'

'By the heck, Rosamund Kenton, you've changed, I'll say that for you! Once you wouldn't have said boo to a goose, yet now you're – you're –'

'In love,' she said softly as the phone began to ring. 'That'll be Jon. Talk of angels . . .'

Mildred Kenton sat straight-backed, her silk-stockinged legs dangling inelegantly over the edge of the trailer. She was wearing her winter coat and hat and clutched her bag with both hands as if afraid of falling off – or maybe because her daughter was driving the tractor and in her opinion, inclined to take bends too quickly. Beside her sat her husband in his Sunday suit, relieved to be handing over the complicated business of the farm accounts at last.

'Stop here, please!' Mildred called as they approached the village, because not for anything would she be seen riding behind a tractor! 'This'll do nicely. We'll walk the rest of the way!'

404

Rosamund waited until they reached the bus stop outside the White Hart, then reversed, waving as she went, planning how to use her two-and-a-bit hours. The dinner dishes had to be seen to and a pan of potatoes peeled – and she would have to remember to build up the kitchen fire and leave it safe. After which her time was her own!

Her heart thudded. It always did when she was about to do something she shouldn't, but she could only think that today Jon was due back from leave, that there had been no sign of any circuits and bumps and that it was almost certain they would meet tonight. And when they did, she wanted to be able to tell him she had found a way in to Fellfoot and how it would be a good place to go until the days were warm and they could loose themselves in the wildness and the wideness of the hills and be lovers; just she and Jon beneath miles and miles of sky, and no one to see them. She harboured none of Bessie's doubts about the isolated house. She only wished she could make her friend understand how wonderful their loving was and how it had never seemed, right from the start, that they were doing wrong. There was a war on and you lived for the day; tomorrow never came, thank God, because tomorrow might trail unhappiness behind it, and it was best not to know what was written in your Book of Life.

Parking tractor and trailer, she ran to the house. The big iron kettle on the hob was puffing steam and she emptied it into the brown sink. Dishes, spuds, fire, then off up the fell to the little house! She was so happy she began to sing.

Thirty-three keys lay on the kitchen table, and no two alike. Rosamund discarded the least likely; the old, heavy iron ones that looked as if Margaret Dacre's hand could have turned them. Threading them back on the wire loop, she selected smaller, more modern keys that looked as if they might fit a padlock; there were nine and she slipped them into the right-hand pocket of her jacket.

Then she pulled on gumboots and made for the kennel. She would take Shep with her; a walk was just what he needed when he spent most of the day and night on the end of a chain! She bent to release him and he licked her hand, yapping like an over-excited puppy.

'Off with you then! Seek!'

She watched him go, nose down, tail wagging, sniffing the scent of rabbits, or the vixen, maybe. It was his reward for awakening her each time the bombers returned, and she smiled, loving the creature, loving everything she could see: the rise of land behind the paddock, Parlick, and Beacon Fell to her left and sombre Pendle behind her, where no trees grew and no birds nested; the witches' hill.

She crossed the fingers of her left hand and spat. People around these parts always did that when they spoke of, or even thought about, witches. Then calling to Shep she made for the little stone house, looking at her watch to check the time it would take if she took the fell track. There were easier ways of getting there, but only if you knew the fields and walls and ditches like the back of your hand – and not in the dark!

The narrow road gave way to a track and from there, veering to her right, she looked for landmarks that could be picked out by torchlight; a clump of leafless rowan trees, a huge round boulder, the pointed bluff they called witch-hat rock. Then she saw the sweep of dry-stone wall ahead. Walking slowly, it had taken twenty minutes. She dipped her fingers into her pocket, touching the keys, letting go a deep sigh. Soon, she would know . . .

Only three of the nine keys fitted the padlock on the front door, and not one of them turned. She had done it systematically, placing each discarded key into her left-hand pocket. She tried the three again and again until her fingers became sore, then dejectedly admitted defeat.

She whistled to the dog then made for the door that was lower, stouter, its padlock heavier. Only one key fitted and she pulled in her breath and turned it to the left.

'*Yes!*' She had done it!

She tugged at the hasp and it parted from the lock in a shower of powdery rust. Dry-mouthed, she unhooked it from the chain, which swung with a clatter against the door jamb.

Then she lifted the big wooden latch, put her foot against the door, and pushed.

With a creak it gave an inch and she quickly pulled it shut again, her hands trembling as she wound the chain around the latch and slipped home the padlock, clicking it shut.

'That's it then, Shep.' She slipped the precious key into her trouser pocket, then stooping low, blew the rust from the step, looking for more telltale marks. But her boots had made no imprint in the springy grass, and only a trickle against the door showed that Shep had left his mark against it.

She turned and began to run, slipping and sliding downwards, the dog thinking it was a game and bounding ahead, barking. She did not stop until she reached the armless signpost, then leaned against it because her heart thudded in her ears and she didn't know if it was from exertion or triumph. Then she walked slowly up the lane, past the standing for the milk churns, all the while pulling in her breath, holding it, letting it go in little huffs. By the time she unlocked the dairy door, she was calm again. And by the time she had driven the tractor to Laceby to pick up her parents at the bus stop, thirty-two keys were back on the loop that hung on a nail beside the keeping-pantry door.

She had found a way in to Fellfoot, tonight she would see Jon, and life was wonderful!

Mildred Kenton was in a rare benign mood, partly because the outing had made a break in farm routine and partly because the accountant proved to be both intelligent and charming and assured them they would save more than the cost of his fee by placing their financial affairs in his hands.

When they left, he had seen them to the door, shaken each by the hand and told them he hoped to have a balance sheet ready very soon for their perusal.

'It seems, Bart, that the man is going to be worth all the money he'll charge.'

'Aye. Reckon he knows what he's talking about!'

'The kettle is on,' Rosamund called over her shoulder as she drove. 'It'll just be coming to the boil by the time we get back.' The change in her mother, albeit temporary, pleased her. 'There'll be time for a drink before we start on the cows, Dad.'

'What did you do with yourself, Rosamund?'

'I – we-e-ll – I did all you told me to,' she gasped, startled, because lately her mother seldom spoke to her directly. 'Then I went up towards the tops for half an hour.'

'Walking? Alone?'

'No, Mother.' She had recovered her composure. 'I took Shep with me for company.'

No more was said until they reached Laburnum Farm, when her mother thanked her father for helping her down from the trailer.

Then speaking to no one in particular she said, 'Next time we go to see the accountant, we must ask him if we can afford a car.'

'We probably can, Milly! Cars come cheap now because of the petrol shortage. What we've got to ask ourselves is whether the expense would be justified. The petrol ration goes nowhere; half the time, cars are standing idle with empty tanks! And we've got the pony and trap. Ponies don't run on petrol!'

'Maybe not, but you can't leave a horse and cart outside the accountant's, now can you, and it isn't very dignified, bouncing on the back of a tractor to the village, then waiting for a bus, having folks gawping at you when you get on!'

'It was probably from shock, Mother. You so rarely go to the village.'

'Which is more than can be said for my daughter, who seems rarely away from it, these days!'

Rosamund caught her father's anxious glance, and smiled to let him know there would be no words, because it took two to quarrel and she was much, much too happy to rise to the bait.

'I'll back the tractor up to the cooling-shed door,' she said evenly, 'and then I'll make us a pot of tea.'

Tonight she would see Jon again. Her head was full of thoughts of him, her heart thudded with happiness, and the acid taunt went over her head.

She laughed out loud as she started the tractor. She was learning to cope with her mother's moods, her mistrust. Things that once drove her to tears could no longer hurt her; her luck had changed. She had even found a key to Fellfoot's back door!

'We'll have to stop coming here soon,' Rosamund whispered, because they always seemed to whisper in the hayloft.

'Suppose so, but we've been lucky – even Shep didn't give us away. And like you said, sweetheart, the light nights are coming.'

'So what would you say if I told you I'd found somewhere?'

'The old place, you mean, that's boarded up?'

'And padlocked. Well, I just happen to have a key to the back door!'

'But how did you come by it, Rosie?'

'Magic! I live in a witch-house!'

She told him about the bunch of old keys and finding one that fitted, and how the door had opened just a little.

'I could have gone inside, I suppose, but I thought it best to wait till you were there.'

'Glad you did. You never know what you might have found!'

'You're as bad as Bessie! And it wasn't because I was afraid. I'm sure there's nothing inside. Why I didn't go in was because I was afraid to push the door too far in case it came off its hinges. It hasn't been opened for years!'

'Then wait till I'm with you. Maybe we can get up there in the daylight without anyone seeing us – take a look?'

'We can fork left at the crossroads, come at it from the pond side. The fell track is the easiest way, but we might be seen. I'll try to go there again tomorrow afternoon – find another way.'

'I wish it could be all above board, sweetheart! And what did you tell Bessie?'

'Only that it would be a great place for us to go – if we

could get in. She didn't much favour the idea, but she isn't in love.'

'Do you tell her – *everything*?'

'Of course not! But she wouldn't blab. I trust her. If I were really, really in a corner, it would be Bess I'd want by me – if I'd never met you, I mean . . .'

'I suppose every woman needs someone close. Men aren't like that. We keep things bottled up, most of the time. We only let it go if we've had a few pints or something.'

'Men can't cry either. It seems unfair. Have you ever wanted to cry, Jon?'

'I suppose so. When I've been afraid – on ops, mostly. And sometimes just before takeoff.'

She pulled him closer and laid her cheek to his. 'I'd say it was natural to be afraid.'

'We all are, sometimes, but we don't admit it. And I get the wind up because I've got six other blokes to look out for – one of them married, with a kid. And now it's worse, because there's you.'

'Darling, darling! Sssssh! It wouldn't be pushing my luck if I reminded you that next time *Johnnie* goes, it'll be the eighteenth – and your twenty-fifth. I reckon you're getting the hang of it, Sergeant!'

'Reckon I am.' He heard the teasing in her voice and relaxed and laughed.

'You'll be fine, Jon. We love each other too much for you not to be. And we've got this, haven't we?' She whispered her lips across his eyelids, his nose, his cheeks, then pushed aside the lock of hair to kiss his forehead. 'And it's all right to be afraid. That way you'll get back. Don't ever get complacent, will you, and blow it?'

'I won't. And you're cold, Rosie. Slip your sweater on.'

'Mm. You don't notice the cold, do you, until – afterwards. It's why I can't wait for summer. Imagine how it'll be when the grass is dry and warm, and there's only the sky to see us.'

She kissed the hollow at his throat then took his hand, kissing each fingertip, and he told her to behave herself and not be such an abandoned hussy. And she laughed throatily, indulgently, sure of their love.

'Oh, Rosie Kenton, I do love you!' His brief, sombre mood was over and he knew that if he let himself, he could well imagine finishing the tour with *J-Johnnie*, and being taken off flying for a time; could think about tomorrow without crossing his fingers. 'Do you know how much?'

'Absolutely,' she whispered. 'And I know you'll be flying tomorrow night, but I'll be here, wishing you well, willing you safely home. And it will all come right for us, Jon. You'll do your thirty! I know it!'

'Here's the pond.' Rosamund clicked on her torch. 'Keep to the left of it; it's boggy, in places. It looks a bit ordinary now, but it's a lovely spot in summer. When the trees are green again we'll come to Fellfoot a lot, and no one will know we're here.'

'Have you got the key, Rosie?'

'In my pocket. It's as if we're looking the property over, isn't it, with a view to renting it, or even buying it, though anyone with half an ounce of sense would do it in the daylight. Would you ever consider living in an out-of-the-way place like this, Jon?'

'I think if I got rich, I'd consider it as a holiday place; somewhere we could bring the kids — let them run free. They'd like Fellfoot. No water to wash in,' he laughed. 'Shall we try the back door then? Will I carry you over the threshold?'

'Idiot!' She fished in her pocket for the key. 'Don't drop it or we'll never find it again.'

She shone her torch on the door, and he turned the key and unhooked the padlock and chain, pushing gently on the door. The hinges creaked, and held steady. He pushed again and there was a crackling of dry leaves rustling in the sudden draught of air. And then the door was wide open, and hanging firm.

'I'll go first.'

He sent a beam of light down the passage. The floor was red-tiled; to either side of them a door. He opened the one to the left, and the musty smell he had expected was not there.

Rosamund followed him into the room, sweeping her torch from side to side, picking out an iron fireplace with a stone hearth and mantel. There was an iron bar across it and she knew that once, cooking pots had hung there.

'The kitchen,' she said softly. It was a low, large room with boarded-up windows at either end. 'Do you think we could light a fire, sometimes? There's plenty of wood about. No one would know – the windows are covered up.'

'People might see the smoke in the distance, and wonder about it. Don't think we should risk it.'

She swung her light to the ceiling and the blackened beams, solid and rough. In two of them were large hooks where once lamps must have hung.

'She would do all the cooking on that fire, Jon. No gas or electricity up here. I'll bet that iron oven baked lovely bread. Wonder how many children they had? Dad vaguely remembers it being lived in, but I didn't push it; didn't want him to think I was too interested.'

'It's a huge kitchen. I suppose they'd have had a big table in the middle of it.'

'And a big oak dresser on the wall, with blue and white plates and copper jugs on it, and a rag rug on the hearth,' she said longingly. 'Abandoned houses are sad, aren't they? It's as if this one is waiting for someone to live in it again.'

'I suppose the other room was once the parlour.'

The room to the right of the passageway was a replica of the kitchen, save for the iron fire basket in the ingle, with two high-backed benches built into either side of it. In the corner, their lights picked out a staircase with wide, shallow treads.

'Amazing! It's as if this place has been asleep for years; doesn't even know there's a war on.'

'Lucky little house.' All at once there was a choke of tears in her throat because she wanted to live in it with Jon and shut the war out; shut out everything and everyone. And she wanted to sweep the floors, rip down the sheeting from the downstairs windows, light fires so the flames lit up the room and danced shadows across the uneven walls.

'I'll take a look at the bedrooms. Stay here, Rosie, till I've checked the stairs.'

She waited, hand on the newel post, calling to him to be careful, counting each probing footstep.

'It's OK. You can come up, now. And watch your torch, darling. Keep it low. The windows up here aren't covered.'

'Jon! It's amazing!' The two bedrooms were wooden-floored; each had a little iron firegrate and a stone hearth. 'And it isn't a bit smelly or damp. You could live here, you really could, if it wasn't for the water. Do you like it?'

'Yes, I do. It's a friendly little place. Pity there's no hay . . .'

'The floor won't be too hard. I don't expect a four-poster bed, Jon Hunt!'

'You're a devious wench!' He scooped her into his arms. 'And I love you. Shall we stay here?'

'No. Let's say goodbye to the hayloft, tonight? After tonight, Fellfoot will be our own special place; we'll play make-believe here, Jon.'

'Pretend the war is over and you've magicked a water tap into the kitchen and we're expecting our third?'

'Something like that,' she whispered, kissing him. 'We must lock up carefully, so no one will know we've been.'

'I think we'll take a lease on this property,' Jon laughed, 'for the duration. Would that suit you, darling?'

'It would suit me very nicely. What say we move in tomorrow night?'

'Tomorrow night will probably be out. Let's make it the night after . . .'

They picked their way slowly to the road, being careful not to use their lights too much, because even the brief flaring of a match seemed to look like a beacon in the denseness of the blackout. Then they walked hand in hand past the crossroads and on to the little creaking gate, opening it carefully, making for the hay barn.

She was, she thought, just as happy as ever she could be;

happy about Fellfoot, about Jon, whose tour of ops was going well; happy that they were lovers.

God, this is Rosamund Kenton. Thank you for this happiness – and please, I beg You, don't take it from us . . .

ELEVEN

'Did you know, Skip, that Yank aircrews have only to do a tour of twenty-five? So what's so special about them?'

Apart from the fact, Willie MacBain brooded, that they had better uniforms, better rations, bigger bombers and more pay!

'Can't say I did, Mac, but it makes sense,' Jon shrugged. 'They do all their bombing in daylight, which I wouldn't fancy at all, and those B-17s of theirs are great, heavy kites; not as nippy as a Lancaster. Reckon they deserve a shorter tour.'

They had been unable to get a seat on the Manchester-bound train, but what the heck? They were on seven days' leave; seven nights away from operational flying – who needed a seat?

Mac offered a cigarette; Jon shook his head. His mouth tasted foul; it always did when he was tired. When he got home he would sleep the clock round, smug in the knowledge that last night *J-Johnnie* had flown its twenty-second operation. A nasty one, to Bremen, but short, for all that. Give him Bremen any day; the Americans were welcome to Berlin, which they seemed to have taken over lately.

He shifted his position, and rotated his head. The floor on which they squatted was dirty, but so were most trains these days. And a bit of dirt wasn't all that important when you were going on leave. It was only when you'd had it and were on your way back to war, that you cared.

'Soon be at Manchester.' They changed trains, there; Mac for Glasgow, himself for Chester.

'Aye. I'll sleep all the way to Central, if I can get a seat. Your wee milkmaid didn't see you off at Preston. Are you going off her?'

'Hell, no! She just couldn't make it this time. I'll be ringing her tonight.'

Rosie would be at Bessie's house, waiting. It pleased him to think about tonight and her slightly breathless, 'Hullo? Jon?'

He adored her; adored the way her voice sounded on the phone. She was adorable in every way. He would miss her. Seven nights without loving was a long time.

He closed his eyes and wondered at his luck. One more op to do for his tour, then seven more to finish the thirty with *J-Johnnie*. Few pilots made the magic number, yet it looked as if he would notch up thirty-seven! All down to the St Christopher medallion he wore round his neck with Rosie's little cross. And Matilda Mint and a smashing crew, of course, with luck all over them. And Rosie.

Rosie. It was good to think of making love in the little upstairs room at Fellfoot with his greatcoat spread on the floor . . .

He felt a dizziness, then blinked open his eyes and shook his head. Mac was looking at him strangely.

'Will you tell me, Skip, what put that smug smirk on your face? You looked good and daft.'

'Nearly dropped off.' Jon pulled his tongue round dry lips. 'Like I said – tired.'

The train began to brake and slow. Change at Manchester, then the bus from Chester to Little Sellow – or thumb a lift, whichever happened along first.

He got to his feet, pulling his cap from the epaulette at his shoulder, picking up his respirator. His eyes were gritty, and granted three wishes they would be a mug of tea, the soft, springy bed with the blue eiderdown, and Rosie in his arms. Not making love – he was too damn tired – but Rosie beside him when he awoke in the morning.

'See you, Mac,' he said when they parted. 'Have a good leave.'

The platform from which the Chester train would depart was crowded, as it always was; there would be one mad scramble for seats when it arrived. If it arrived. Sometimes trains just didn't come. He found a pillar to lean on, folded his arms, closed his eyes and thought of a bed with clean, white sheets and a blue eiderdown. And Rosie.

'Hi! You're early! Come in! Guess who's here!' which was a typical Bessie Drake greeting, Rosamund smiled.

'Tell me.'

'Our Dave! Thought he was in the Med, but what do you know? They're back to join the Home Fleet. Dave reckons it's because of the second front.' And wasn't the Mediterranean pretty quiet these days, with Malta safe, North Africa cleared of Axis troops and half of Italy in Allied hands?

'Where is he now?' Rosamund knew how lucky it was to touch a sailor's collar.

'Out, wouldn't you know!' Elsie Drake smiled fondly. 'Arrived out of the blue not two hours ago, dumped his kit, took all the hot water for a bath, then away on the bus to Preston. There's some tea left in the pot – pity to waste it. Want a cup, Rosamund?'

'Please. And close your eyes and hold out your hands.' She placed a newspaper parcel in the upturned palms. 'Careful.'

'Eggs!'

'One each for your breakfast – well, there would have been if David hadn't been home.'

'But can you spare them?'

'Sure. This is the time of year when even old hens lay well. And isn't it light tonight?'

'Oh my word, yes!' The clocks had been moved forward an hour to double-summertime. It wouldn't be dark tonight until almost nine. 'And the apple trees in blossom, and the birds singing their little heads off. Makes a difference, doesn't it – a little bit less of that old blackout?'

'Makes a difference at Laburnum, too. The herd is out to grass now in the day. A lot less work.'

'And how's your young man?' Elsie Drake offered a willow-pattern cup on a rosebud saucer. 'Gone on leave, I hear.'

'Yes. Part of me is glad, because he isn't flying, but I'm missing him already. I – I don't suppose you'd mind if he phoned?'

'Any time at all. No need to ask! How is your mother?'

'Fine, thanks. I'll tell her you asked.'

Her mother wasn't fine, but it was politic not to talk about her delicate condition. Mildred Kenton would not want her hot flushes passed round Laceby Green Mothers' Union! Nor would she tell her that Mrs Drake asked kindly after her, because the name still rankled at Laburnum Farm.

'You'll never guess what Dave brought,' Bessie grinned. 'Just wait till I show you!' She clattered up the stairs then down again, to place her trophies on the kitchen table. 'A film for my camera, a lipstick and a pot of cold cream. And a bottle of whisky for Dad and four tablets of scented soap for Mum! His ship called in at Gibraltar on the way home; he got them there. I'll be able to take a snap of you, Rosamund, for Jon. And when he gets back, I'll take the two of you together, as well.'

'Oh, Bessie — *thanks*!'

She felt a pricking of tears behind her eyes because everybody was so kind at Bessie's house; and because she wanted her mother to be more like Bessie's mother, and laugh sometimes. So she blinked rapidly and sniffed them away, then smiled radiantly, because at that very moment the phone in the hall began to ring.

'Off you go and answer it, Rosamund,' Mrs Drake beamed. 'It's bound to be for you!'

'Hullo?' Heart thudding she lifted the receiver. 'Jon . . . ?'

'So you managed to get through?'

'Yes, thanks. Not as much delay on trunks as I thought.'

'And how is Rosie?' Charlotte Martin knelt on the hearthrug to put a light to the paper and kindling in the fire grate.

'She still loves me. I said I'd try to get through tomorrow, if that's all right?'

'You know it is. And things are — we-e-ll — all right between you?'

She stared at the flames as they licked the firewood. She really shouldn't be asking; it wasn't any of her business, truth known. 'I mean, last time you were on leave you said there wasn't a lot of chance of your getting married and I —'

'You asked me to be careful – take care of Rosie. And I have been, and she's fine. Do you blame us, Aunt Lottie?'

'No. I wish it could have happened for Guy and me, but there you are! When I was Rosie's age, young men were expected to marry the lady first. Only bounders took advantage. Now at least, thank God, there are ways of getting round it. I enjoy Rosie's letters, by the way. She has a way with words, y'know.'

'You think so?' Jon smiled, pleased.

'I know so. Words are my business. Has she ever written poetry – anything like that?'

'Aunt Lottie! Do you know what the crew call her? My milkmaid! Rosie works on a farm – a land girl. She went to grammar school, got her school certs, but I think the only thing her mother had in mind for her was marriage – to a farmer's son. She's the only child. She'll inherit, you see.'

'Money in the family, is there?' Satisfied the fire had taken hold, she went to sit beside her nephew.

'I think they're comfortable, but the house seems the main asset. There are only a couple of acres to it – the rest they had on lease from the local landowner until the Air Ministry plonked the aerodrome on half of it. The house is very old and solid, and much too big for three people. Rosie's folks should have had half a dozen kids. It's a house for children . . .'

'Which the pair of you will have one day – when you get round to marriage, that is – and fill the place up?'

'I doubt it, Aunt. I'm an engineer, not a farmer and Rosie's inheritance is the furthest thing from my mind. I'd marry the girl if they threw her out tomorrow – barefoot and penniless. Wish they would, actually . . .' He laid his arm round the elderly woman's shoulders, pulling her close. 'I've never said thanks – not in so many words – for all you've done for me, Aunt Lottie. I couldn't have had a better mother. You know I love you, don't you?'

'It cuts both ways, Jon. We needed each other. When I took you on I was in a pretty bad way. You filled a gap in my life. Take care of yourself, won't you, and your Rosie? I'm pretty sure you've found the right girl, Jon.'

'I know I have. It's just that I can't marry her yet. I'd still like to meet her parents, but she won't have it. They know about me now, but they haven't asked to meet me. Suppose we'll have to be satisfied with half a loaf.'

'Count your blessings, son! I suppose you'll be going back a day early?'

'Would you mind? I should really be back by noon, Thursday, and there's no telling that we wouldn't be flying that same night. If I go back early, at least I'll see her on Wednesday. Things are hotting up, now – the second front, I mean. A lot of our targets are in France, and the fighter boys are shooting up trains and gun emplacements on the French coast like there's no tomorrow.'

'You think it'll be soon, then?'

'Not quite yet. General opinion is that they'll have to wait for tides – and the right weather. And there's a strong buzz that all leave will be stopped before it happens.'

'Well, that's pretty silly, if you ask me! As good as telling Hitler we're on our way!'

'He knows it already. What he doesn't know is where. Nobody does.'

'Then the sooner it's over and done with the better!' Charlotte Martin jumped impatiently to her feet. 'Now enough of war talk. I'm going to make a pot of tea, then we'll listen to the wireless – OK?'

'Fine! Want any help?'

'I'm perfectly capable of making a pot of tea, thanks all the same!'

So Jon grinned and stretched his legs to the fire, and closed his eyes. And thought about Wednesday night at Fellfoot. With Rosie.

Sunday was bright and sunny. As she waited beside the six oak trees, camera case over her shoulder, Bessie Drake saw her first butterfly of spring. It settled on a bright yellow bog buttercup, and she recognized it as a red admiral. Winter was really gone when butterflies and bees were about, and tadpoles wriggled in ponds. She lifted her face to the early April sun, and closed her eyes, wondering if first butterflies brought wishes with them. She knew there were wishes on first swallows and the first cuckoo call so it wouldn't hurt to include red admirals. She opened her eyes to fix them on the butterfly, but it had gone, and her wish with it!

I wish, I wish, she had been going to say, for a young man who's as good-looking as Jon and dances like Mick, and if you don't mind, who isn't aircrew. Because it couldn't be a lot of fun for Rosie, worried sick every time Jon's Lancaster took off on ops. It was bad enough worrying about Mick, and she wasn't in love with him!

'Why,' she demanded of Rosamund when she arrived, 'couldn't I have met you at the crossroads?'

'Because I want us to go to Fellfoot.'

'But if I take it there, everybody who sees it will wonder why you want a snap outside a boarded-up old house! It would be giving the game away.'

'Nobody's going to see it, I hope, but you and me and Jon. And I don't want the house in it. I want you to take it beside the pond. There's a big flat stone; we sit on it, sometimes, if it isn't cold. It's looking pretty there, now. The willow is in leaf, and the silver birches.'

'So it's a special place, kind of?'

'Every place I've been to with Jon is special. I wish you could fall in love.'

'I'm in no hurry,' Bessie shrugged loftily. 'I'll meet Mr Right one day, and I'll know – like you did. So where do we go from here, then?'

'The devious way. Across the field, up to the paddock wall, then we can't be seen from the house, after that.'

'And how's it going to be when the nights are really light? Had you thought of that?'

'No. But we will. There are more ways than one, to get to Fellfoot; coming down, though, is a bit of a slither. But let's get on, Bess? And I'm ever so grateful for the snap.'

'There are only twelve on the roll. I'll have to eke them out, because I don't know if I'll ever get another. I want one of Dave in his uniform and Joe, when he's next on leave, and if we can manage it, one of you and Jon together.'

'Are you sure you can spare me two, Bess?'

'Sure. So shall we go, then?'

'OK. But keep down, especially when we get to the paddock wall. My mother's got eyes in the back of her head!'

Didn't all witches, Bessie brooded, though she had the good sense not to say it, because she and Rosamund had been best friends since they were eleven, and sat together every day on the school bus. And Rosamund couldn't help it if her mother was peculiar!

'So has my dad,' she said instead.

'So!' Mildred Kenton shook the Sunday paper and folded it to a more manageable size. 'Things are going a bit better, it would seem.'

Germany being bombed day and night, the Russian armies sweeeping, almost unchallenged, into the Crimean Penin-sula, and the Allies poised ready to invade the Continent any day now. And serve Hitler right for starting it, and upsetting everyone's lives! That man had a lot to answer for. She hoped Mr Churchill would have him hanged when it was all over!

Yet what was more gratifying than anything she had read today was a complete absence of news about the secret weapon, secret no longer. She scanned the papers from end to end every day, and there hadn't been a word lately. Talk. That's all it had been, put out to frighten people. Propaganda. Indeed, if it wasn't for the way her daughter was behaving, life would seem half-bearable again, she reluctantly admitted.

Gone were her worries about the farm accounts, and she had finally decided against the purchase of a secondhand car when she realized that the one to benefit most from it would be Rosamund. Once she got her hands on it, heaven only knew where she would be off to! A car would have been very nice, but its disadvantages were obvious. Their daughter had altogether too much freedom already, without offering her more on a plate!

'Where is the girl?' She took off her reading glasses to squint over the top of her paper at her husband. 'Off out with the airman, is she?'

'Last time I heard, she was meeting Bessie at six oaks. Seems David Drake got his hands on a roll of film, and Bessie is going to take a snap of Rosamund.'

'I wasn't told about any snaps!'

'You wouldn't be. The lass doesn't mention Bessie unless she has to, though what you've got against the Drakes beats me, Milly. And the airman went on leave last Thursday, so she isn't with him!'

'Leave! They're always on leave! And why didn't she tell me? Why is it her father gets all the news?'

'Since you ask, I think she's learning how to keep the peace. What you don't know, you can't fret about. And I still think she should be allowed to bring the young man home, or at least have him call for her in a civilized manner. The more you forbid her to see him, Milly, the more awkward she's going to be! It's human nature. Why don't you have a word with her, some time; say you'd like to meet him?'

'Because I don't want to meet him! That man has turned Rosamund's head, and turned her against her parents, an' all!'

'Not against me, he hasn't. Why can't you trust the lass? There are thousands of girls her age away from home. Their parents don't like it, but I'll bet they aren't making a big issue of it. Why can't you accept that Rosamund isn't a bairn any longer; has a mind of her own?'

'Oh, a fine speech, Bart Kenton! All right! Take my daughter's side against me, but I promise you'll live to regret it!'

'Well, now.' He folded his paper slowly, deliberately, then laid it on the table at his side. 'You'll make me wish I'd never seen Rosamund's point of view, then? Is that a threat, Mildred?'

'I – I – Oh, you know what I mean,' she gasped. 'You're twisting my words! I meant that if you don't stop being soft with her, she'll do something we'll *all* regret!'

'Then time will tell, won't it, which of us is right?'

He reached for the paper, indicating that the matter was closed. And Mildred, who recognized the tone of his voice, knew better than enter into an argument. Most times her husband was biddable and kept his opinions to himself, but today she knew he was all set for digging his heels in.

Men! If only her daughter knew the bother she was laying up for herself, she would take more notice of her mother, who only wanted the best for her, when all was said and done!

'I fancy a drink of tea. Will I make one for you, too, Bart?'

'Thanks. A cup would go down very nicely, Mildred.'

It was her way of apologizing, and his of accepting it. The way it always was, he thought, when you married a woman of Milly's ilk. But he'd known how it would be when they were wed; he couldn't have it all ways. Cold she may be, but she had turned herself into a fine farmer's wife. Pity, though, that she was jealous of her own daughter!

'Good! Hold it! Smashing!' Bessie stood, back to the sun, squinting into the camera. 'I'll come just a bit nearer so I get more of your face in. Now one, two, three and smile please! Fine! Is it really lovely, Rosamund – being in love?' she whispered, settling herself on the flat stone.

'It's better than lovely some of the time, and worse than awful when he's flying, or on leave.'

'We-e-ll – I didn't mean that, exactly. What I mean is – is –'

'Making love? Being lovers? Look, Bess, that's got to be between Jon and me,' she said, gently reproving.

'Yes, but aren't you scared of getting caught in there?' She nodded in the direction of the little house. 'And aren't you afraid of getting pregnant? What would you do if something went wrong?'

'Leave home pretty quick, I reckon – after they'd let me marry Jon, of course. It's the only hope we've got of getting married. It's a pig, isn't it? I can't even take him home, yet my mother would have us down the aisle the minute she knew I was pregnant. And when it was born, she'd swear on the Bible it was a honeymoon baby that had come two months early!'

'I think most mothers would. I wouldn't be too afraid of mum if ever I got into trouble, but Dad would be another matter. He can be very narrow-minded! When I asked him why he was so sniffy about me going out with boys, he said he knew what went on in their heads, which doesn't say a lot for him, does it?' she giggled.

Bessie always made a giggle of things, Rosamund thought, joining in with her; couldn't be serious for long, even over an important thing like getting into trouble and having to get married, and hoping there wouldn't be too much talk about it in the village. And trying to convince busybodies that a seven-pound baby really was two months premature!

'I think,' Rosamund said, trying hard to be serious, 'that next time around we'll come back to earth as men!'

'What! Grow hair all over and have to work till you're old 'cause you've a wife and kids to support! Think I'd be happy staying a woman. But you don't believe in reincarnation, do you?'

'I've a feeling Jon does. But he's been to university. You pick up all sorts of ideas there, I suppose.'

'But what if you both came back in another life, and got married to someone else?'

'I don't think we would. We'd recognize each other again, I hope. Come to think of it, I'd like two lifetimes with Jon.'

'My, but you've got it bad, haven't you?'

'Yes, I have,' Rosamund said softly. 'Thank God.'

She lifted her face to the April sun, and thought about Wednesday night, here at Fellfoot. With Jon.

Unusually alert, the crew of *J-Johnnie* drained their mugs of rum-laced tea and gave their full attention to the probings of the debriefing officer, and the woman sergeant who sat at his side, taking shorthand notes.

Skip had done it, the lucky so-and-so; had flown thirty ops! Jammy, that's what! Seven from his last station and twenty-three from RAF Laceby Green. He'd really got some in, knew what it was about; would keep *Johnnie* in the air for another seven, when they would *all* have done their tour! And what was even jammier, that twenty-third op had been a milk run, mine-laying off the Dutch coast, then climbing steadily, making for the skies over Germany to drop Window to upset enemy radar – fine metallic strips that sent radar screens into confusion, helping the main bomber force that followed to reach Berlin without detection.

When finally the debriefing officer was satisfied, and the crew had offered their own observations – maybe that there was a heavier than usual concentration of flak over the Dutch-German border, and that searchlights had appeared where once there had been none, they stubbed out their cigarettes, making a rush for the door, lifting Jon in the air, letting go a great *Ya-hoo*!

'Good old Skip!'

'Congratters, you lucky sod!'

'What say we go to town tonight – drink the place dry?'

'Steady on! We aren't out of the woods yet!' Jon grinned. 'OK, so we're on the home stretch, but watch it! You lot have seven more to do – with me up front!'

'Yeah! Lucky seven! C'mon, Skip. Your bint'll let you off tonight. Tell her it's special!'

'Correction! It isn't special till you've all done your thirty, and Rosie isn't my bint; she's the girl I'm going to marry!'

'Sorry, Skip. Slip of the tongue. Got a heavy date, then?'

'You bet. But right now, all I want is to get my head down.'

Strange that he could sleep like a baby, Jon thought, after an op; how easily, gratefully, the tension slipped from him and all he had to do was close his eyes and think about Rosie, and tonight.

This afternoon, after briefing, he had tried to sleep away the hours to takeoff, but he had thought instead about the Leipzig raid, two nights ago, and seventy-eight of ours lost; one of them from Laceby. So he had pulled on trousers and battledress top, and walked the circumference of the perimeter track in the hope of catching sight of Rosie. But the pasture was empty of cows and there had been no sign of her, because she was probably in the shippon. It had been good, though, to hear birdsong, see trees in leaf again, feel the sun warm on his face. It would be all right, he'd told himself over and over. OK – so tonight would be his thirtieth; so what?

Because the thirtieth is dicey. It's like the first and the thirteenth; it's a bastard.

Yet tonight's op had the makings of a milk run. Every Lancaster he passed was being loaded with mines, and he already knew where he would be dropping them. And dropping Window was a doddle, too. After tonight, smothered in luck, he would go on for another seven. And when that happened, he would persuade Rosie to take him home with her; ask her parents for permission to marry.

She would be nineteen in June. Young to be married, but there was a war on and girls younger than Rosie were in uniform. In wartime they grew up quickly; young men, too. Overnight they were ordered to become men, fly planes, fire guns, drive tanks, hurtle from the sky at the end of a parachute.

Rosie was mature enough for marriage; had parted with her innocence gladly. And if he made it for another seven, he would go to Laburnum Farm, whether she liked it or not, and tell them he wanted to marry their daughter!

'Hey, Skip! Penny for them!' Fingers snapped, a hand passed in front of his line of vision.

'Sorry! Miles away . . .'

They had come to the Nissen hut, their billet since early November. It had been cold in winter and likely would be too hot, soon. The floor was covered in brown linoleum, but it did little to keep the cold from underfoot; their beds were hard, their blankets scratchy. Yet it was a marvellous dump to get back to, with the twenty-third op behind them.

'Here we are again, then! Home sweet home!'

Tom opened the door and, laughing, they followed him. Then they stopped and stared, and all at once there was nothing to laugh about.

At the far end of the hut were seven beds which, until two nights ago, belonged to the crew of *Z-Zebra*. But *Zebra* got the chop over Leipzig, and now someone had stripped those beds, folded the blankets, left clean sheets. Likely as not they had done it quietly, with hardly a word spoken; had emptied the contents of lockers onto beds, then gone on to search trouser and jacket pockets.

All things personal would be set aside and sent, with a letter of condolence, to the next of kin. The station commander would sign the letter, his regret genuine. And likely he would thank God seven times over that his flying days were long behind him.

Greatcoats were never worn on operations, and left hanging behind a door, or beside a bed, and those who came to do what had to be done knew that anything left in the pockets of greatcoats was not to be sent to the next of kin. Because some things you didn't want your mother or your girl or your wife to know about; some things were best disposed of discreetly and kindly, and crews, who knew exactly what would happen if they got the chop, trusted the people who would carry out those last rites.

It had to be that way. Letters left behind – last letters, written just in case – would be posted and even before that happened another Lancaster, fresh from the makers, would fly in to take *Zebra*'s place. And before the end of the week another crew would claim those beds; a sprog crew, with brand-new stripes up, and they wouldn't think about the men whose bedspace they were taking over, because to do that was unwise.

'Flaming Norah!' Sammy hissed. 'Clean as a whistle. They've even swept the soddin' floor!'

Cheers, Z-Zebra and so long. Been nice knowing you!

'Well, whether you are coming or not, Jon Hunt, this gunner is going to drink himself legless, tonight,' Mick jerked, tight-lipped. 'Bloody legless!'

Without another word, they hung flying kit on pegs and got into bed, and not one of them slipped easily into sleep. Instead, they thought how very easily it could have been them – which was stupid, really, when there was damn-all they could do about it.

Rosamund smiled at a drift of bluebells because they were beautiful and because she was high-as-a-kite happy. Summer was almost here, yet winter had been kind, and mild, too. Not once had snowdrifts blocked the lane for days on end, making it impossible for the milk lorry, the egg collector and the postman to get to Laburnum. Jon, too, come to think of it.

Now the squadron took off without a flare path, and she was able to recognize *J-Johnnie*'s markings as she stood at the fence, and though the cockpit was too high from the ground to see Jon as he passed on the way to takeoff, she got a good view of Mick in the rear turret.

'Tail-end to Skip,' Mick would probably say over the intercom. 'Just passed your milkmaid. Did you see her?'

And Jon would almost certainly answer, 'Pilot to rear gunner. Please keep to correct procedure,' in case the brass hats in the control tower or the ops room were switched on to them, but there would be a smile in his voice, for all that.

It was a little after seven. Jon usually arrived early, and Rosamund wanted not to waste one minute of their time together. Tonight would be special, because he would have the smell of success all over him; would know now that to fly thirty operations was possible.

She paused at the oak trees, closing her eyes to recall that there they always stopped to kiss. Memory storing, she called it. Then she climbed the gate and made for the rising ground and the shelter of the paddock wall.

Soon she would see the pond and the little house. Perhaps Jon would not be there yet, and she would sit on the big flat stone beside the pond and watch as he climbed the slope from the main road. It was the way he came now. Because of the light nights, they no longer met at the little iron gate.

She reached Fellfoot's sheltering wall, then looked down. Jon was sitting on the stone, arms round knees, and she paused to look at him, mentally to record his slimness, the fair, unruly hair, the beauty of him. And when he turned and saw her, he would smile with his lips, his eyes, with his entire face, and love of him would slice wantonly through her.

She called his name and he turned and smiled exactly as she knew he would. And need of him took her and she ran to his waiting arms to stand close, not speaking for a few seconds, grateful to be together. Then she lifted her lips, and he bent to kiss them.

'Hullo, you,' he said huskily.

'Hullo yourself, and congratulations. How does it feel to have done thirty?'

'Unbelievable — but it isn't over, quite yet.'

'You wouldn't want to leave the crew, Jon?'

'No. It wouldn't be allowed, anyway. They wanted to celebrate my thirty, but I told them not yet. But when it's *really* over, I'm coming to see your folks, Rosie. I've made up my mind!'

'Ssssh.' She laid her mouth on his, silencing him. 'Shall we sit here, or walk? It's such a lovely evening.'

'We're doing nothing till you've told me why you won't talk about me meeting your parents. I want to, Rosie.'

'Because they wouldn't let me get married if you did; my mother wouldn't, anyway. She wears the trousers, you know, at Laburnum.'

'But how can they say no — or yes — when they haven't met me?'

'Because. That's what my mother always says. Just *because* and no other word of explanation. We can wait, Jon. I know you're going to be all right. I'm so certain you'll all make that last seven, that I can say it without crossing my fingers. So why should we spoil what we've got by telling her we're in love? She doesn't know what love means. She would sneer, and dirty it. Believe me, darling, I know her so well.'

'How can you say that, Rosie? Has there been a quarrel? Was it because of me?'

'No. I watch what I say these days. But she always wants to rule the roost. There are only two ways of doing anything: *her* way and the wrong way!'

'And your father?'

'Oh, Dad's an old love. Sometimes I wish he would stand up for himself a bit more. When he does, Mother shuts up, but he should do it more often. And I'm being awful, aren't I, because you don't have parents . . .'

'I've got a father — I told you. But he doesn't want to know;

was glad enough for Aunt Lottie to have me. He stood his corner till I was through university, then that was it. But as far as I'm concerned, Aunt Lottie is my mother, my next of kin. It says so, in my paybook. I wish you could meet her, Rosie.'

'So do I. But this war isn't going to go on for ever, and I won't always be a minor.'

'You've got two years to go, darling . . .'

'So? Does it really matter? We couldn't be more married, so please don't do anything rash, Jon? Promise you won't – not yet?'

'OK. Promise.' He gentled her cheek with his fingertips. 'Who am I to object if you like being a scarlet woman?'

'I adore it, Sergeant Hunt, and I adore you. And had you thought – the moon will be nearly full tonight, and we've never made love by moonlight? It isn't cold. Shall we walk further up towards the tops, give Fellfoot a miss? There won't be a soul around.'

So they took hands, walking slowly, carefully, in the fading light. To the east, the moon hung low in the sky; a bomber's moon, though tonight it would be their friend, looking down on them, saying not a word.

Beneath their feet the scutchy grass grew thickly, springily, and stretches of heather and ling sprouted new green shoots from winter-withered roots. It would be softer beneath them than Fellfoot floor.

'Are you sure you want to,' he hesitated. 'I mean –'

'*Want* to! Listen! Being with you, making love with you, is all I ever think about! Why, all of a sudden, do you ask?'

'Because we'd be taking a risk, Rosie. I haven't got anything in my pocket. I thought I had, but –'

'So for once, *just one time*, I'm going to get pregnant?' she whispered, her hands sliding down to his buttocks, her lips close to his. 'Darling, *listen*! Tonight is special. I want you to make love to me out here in the wilds, by moonlight! Please? It'll be all right. It *will*!'

'We shouldn't, darling, but I want you so much. Are you sure?'

'Sure I want you? Sure I love you? Yes, and yes! I want us

to be lovers. Tonight. *Now*. I want you to look into my eyes in the moonlight and say you love me, that you'll love me for ever. And when for ever is used up, that we'll come back and find each other, and live it all again. Promise we will?'

'Right now, Rosie Kenton, I want you so much I'd promise you anything. But tell me again it's all right . . .'

'I love you, Jon. I want you. Nothing else matters.' She lifted her mouth to his, clasping him to her.

The moon rose higher in the sky, and when he took her he said, 'I love you, darling. By moonlight, I do so love you.'

TWELVE

Every man, woman and child waited for the second front to begin. The south coast, and inland from it, was now one huge armoury of ammunition dumps, uncountable field guns, tanks and trucks. At ports and hidden in river estuaries were chunky, flat-bottomed craft for the landing of tanks, guns and stores. And soldiers.

Covered in camouflage in open fields and parks were gun carriers, trucks and ambulances, even, ready to be driven to ports of embarkation at the giving of a signal. One more tank, just one more box of ammunition, some said, and the British Isles would sink slowly into the sea.

In a newspaper cartoon, standing above the white cliffs, Winston Churchill brandished a starting pistol, and the sight of it caused thrills and chills in equal measure. Tomorrow, would he fire that pistol, or the next day? Or next week?

The Air Ministry, the War Office and the Admiralty sent out orders, cancelling all home leave for soldiers, sailors and airmen and their female counterparts. In the direst of circumstances only would compassionate leave be granted. This, then, was it, thought men and women of the Armed Forces. Soon, all hell would be loosed, and afterwards – who knew?

Yet still Hitler's planes bombed London and ports on the south coast; shells still crashed viciously on Dover from across the Channel. It was like the last despairing tail-lashing of a condemned monster that had stood astride Europe for four years past, feeding off life and limb and blood; a monster called Swastika.

In the War Cabinet, though none but a handful knew it,

the date for the landings was set. In Berlin, though no one in British Intelligence dare tell how they knew it, Admiral Donitz pronounced that in his opinion, the Allies were not expected to launch an invasion in the near future. In Italy, Allied soldiers neared Rome; in Russia, though Hitler had ordered them to fight to the last man, soldiers evacuated the Crimea in disarray.

In Germany, boys of the Hitler Youth, some of them hardly into their teens, were called into service, whilst mothers with young children were evacuated to the safety of the countryside from bomb-ravished German cities. In Britain, an air of quiet optimism prevailed, as all who awoke to yet another May morning, wondered if this would be the day.

At RAF Laceby Green, *J-Johnnie* had four more operations to fly, and Joe Drake wrote home to say he wouldn't be coming on leave as he had hoped, but that they weren't to worry, because the whole of the ship's company was looking forward to knocking hell out of the Krauts, and the sooner they got their sailing orders, the better. And amazingly, nothing was cut out of his letter by a sharp-eyed censor, save the name of the ship, at the head of the sheet of notepaper.

June came, bringing wet and windy weather and Rosamund and Jon crept thankfully into Fellfoot and listened to the dismal dropping of rain.

'I wish we could light a fire,' she whispered. 'We haven't made love yet by firelight.'

'We will. One day.'

Jon was quiet; on edge. Three ops to go. The squadron should have been flying tonight, he said, but high winds and driving rain were forecast and the back-room boys in the met office said flying wasn't on.

The gales dropped; the night sky was clear again. From the steel-mesh fence, Rosamund watched twelve bombers taxi past to the point of takeoff. Jon's Lancaster was the seventh plane to pass the bottom of the cow pasture. Seven. *J-Johnnie*'s lucky number.

Rosamund waved her handkerchief; Mick, in the rear turret, saw her dimly through the perspex hood, and rotated his guns.

Takeoff was later than usual; a not-too-distant target tonight – most likely France. It seemed very wrong to bomb someone who was your ally, especially as many Frenchmen had escaped from their occupied country and thrown in their lot with the Allies. Those men would be worried sick, she thought, as the first bomber hurtled down the runway; probably be longing to get their feet on French soil again.

Rosamund waited until each plane was airborne, following the seventh with her eyes until it was a dot in the sky, realizing it was almost nine, and time for the evening news.

She began to run because lately she really wanted to listen to it; wanted to hear the invasion of Europe had begun, yet all the time not wanting it to – wanting Hitler to have been killed, and his generals asking for peace. But someone had tried twice already to kill Hitler, and failed.

Her parents, because it was Sunday, would be using the sitting room, and because it was awful weather for June, would have a fire. Her father put a warning finger to his lips as she entered the room to hear the announcer say, 'Early this morning, soldiers of the US Fifth Army entered Rome.'

A unit had crossed the river Tiber, he said, making their way cautiously along the Via di Conciliazione and it was not until daylight, he droned in unemotional tones, that they were able to see that the city had been left undamaged by the retreating Nazis. Thus, as American soldiers marched into Rome, was the first Axis capital city taken.

'One down,' Bart said softly. 'Two to go!'

Paris and Berlin, Rosamund thought, but how soon and at how high a cost? She shivered and knelt by the fire, holding her hands to the glow, thinking of Jon, wishing him safe from harm, and Tom, Dick and Harry, Mac, Sammy and Mick. After this one there would be two more to go; the twenty-ninth, and the last one. The bastard op.

'I'm going out,' she said, when the broadcast was over. 'I – I feel jumpy.'

'Don't we all?' said her mother, knitting needles clicking furiously.

'I'll take the bike to the village . . .'

'It looks like rain. You're going to get wet,' Bart warned.

'I'll take a coat.' She was a farm worker. It wouldn't be the first time she had been soaked through. 'I want to collect some wool Bessie got in Clitheroe for me. I was short of a couple of ounces for the cardigan.' She didn't care any longer about mentioning Bessie's name. It was the least of her worries, she brooded, as she wheeled her cycle down the puddle-filled lane.

So the invasion was one day nearer, and Jon, when he got back – and he *must* get back – would be one op nearer his thirty.

Sunday, 4 June. The Allies had taken Rome. It was a day to ring round in red on the calendar, she conceded, stopping at six oaks.

Calendars. Dates. Red rings. There had been a small, discreet mark in her diary beside Friday, 2 June, the day another period was due – only it hadn't come. Two days late and all because of the worry and tension each time J-Johnnie took off. Yet these last seven months she had learned to live with tension and worry, so why was she late now?

She ran her tongue round her lips and for the first time allowed herself to think calmly about it. She had got the date right. She had checked a dozen times, and if it didn't come tomorrow morning she would know, wouldn't she? And she would know when exactly it happened – that night in the moonlight, and her own fault. She had known about, and accepted the risk. All she had wanted was to lie beneath the sky in Jon's arms, and with hindsight she was forced to admit she would change nothing.

She wouldn't say anything to Bessie about being late; no need to tell her yet. Jon must be the first to know and anyway, it would probably start tonight. Or tomorrow.

Yet deep inside her she knew she carried Jon's child. They had made it together on a moonlit night; a love child. She wouldn't tell Jon yet that she was late. It might still be a false alarm and, anyway, he had two ops still to fly, and nothing must be allowed to distract or worry him. He must finish that tour, and then nothing would matter because for a year he would be off flying, and safe. And anyway, by the time the last two were over and done with, her period would have arrived – of course it would – and she would wonder what all the worry had been about.

Yet still the small, wayward voice inside her said that she had conceived Jon's child; that she *wasn't* late. She was pregnant.

They sat on the floor of the upstairs room in the little deserted house, backs against the wall, watching patterns of silver light change with every cloud that blew across the near-full moon. Was it two months ago that the heather beneath them had been sweet and springy with a different moon lighting their careless, joyous loving. Yet tonight was wet and windy and cold.

'Flaming June,' she whispered disconsolately.

'Hey! Count your blessings,' Jon smiled. 'We were supposed to be on standby tonight, but the met boys gave it the thumbs-down. Right now, we might have been doing the last one. But what is it, darling? You sound sad. Is everything all right at home?'

'Everything's fine. I suppose I'm a bit edgy – you know . . . ?'

'The last one? Me, too. Part of me wishes we'd gone and part of me is glad I'm here. And I suppose the invasion doesn't help, with everyone on the *qui vive* – will they, won't they? Tomorrow? Next week . . . ?'

'What happens, Jon, when a crew finishes a tour of ops?' She chose her words carefully.

'Normally, I suppose, they'd be sent on leave – given time to sober up first, of course. It would be so long, Laceby Green – or wherever – and the crew split up and given cushy numbers, instructing – they having got some in by then and knowing what it's all about. But all leave is stopped because of the second front and God knows when it'll start again. I suppose in our case, we'll keep a low profile until the invasion gets

437

under way if we can. Maybe then they'll decide what to do with us.'

'But they wouldn't say that because of the landings, you'd have to carry on flying more ops?'

'I don't think so, sweetheart. When it happens, I'll have done thirty-seven, and thirty is reckoned to be the limit a crew can do without a break from flying. Even the idiots in Whitehall realize that. The Americans only do twenty-five.'

'So you'll be sent away?'

'Afraid so. A lot of experienced pilots go abroad, usually to Canada or South Africa or Rhodesia, instructing. Sprog pilots have to learn to fly in the dark, and it's considered best they do it some place where there isn't a blackout. Nobody wants a crew that haven't got their wings up stooging round here at night and getting mixed up with a serious bomber stream. A posting to one of the dominions is considered a piece of cake, except in my case I'd be leaving you behind.'

'You'd be safer abroad, Jon.'

But don't go! she wanted to say. Stay, darling! I want you with me more than ever, now. But she bit on her words because Jon mustn't be told until that last op was over.

'And miserable as sin away from you. But stop worrying about things that might never happen – and let's not talk any more tonight about flying. We'll worry about the last one tomorrow – or the next day . . .'

'You'll make it, darling.'

'Without pushing my luck, and quietly, so the gremlins won't hear,' he said softly, his lips close to hers, 'you could be right. So kiss me, and tell me you love me?'

'I love you, Jon Hunt,' she whispered. 'I'll never stop!'

Without anyone knowing, save a few important people in very high places, the Allies had been gathering intelligence for many months. Helped by resistance fighters of the Maquis and by frogmen and divers from miniature submarines, details of defences had been probed and noted and passed on; even seemingly unimportant bits of information concerning the coast of France; pillboxes and machine-gun nests; searchlight batteries and concrete fortifications. Men and women of the French underground army paid special attention to beaches where mines had been laid, and booby-traps buried. If ever a stretch of coastline was charted and monitored and known as well, almost, as Mr Churchill knew the back of his left hand, it was the coast of Normandy, from Caen to Ste-Mère-l'Eglise.

It was as well that Hitler's generals expected the seaborne invasion miles away at the viciously fortified Pas de Calais and that when, in the early hours of the first Tuesday in June, as paratroopers dropped from the sky to blow up bridges and seal off roads and rail junctions, radar reports of activity in that area were tossed aside as worthless. Not even the British were so stupid, said the generals, as to land anywhere when more gales were expected, and rough seas.

Anything could cause radar blips, they reasoned. A flock of high-flying geese or a concentration of migrating birds, though the British and Americans were to be congratulated on causing a diversion around Normandy when it was known that the real landing would be nowhere near there. The 21st Panzer Division was ready and waiting for them at the Pas de Calais!

Could those too-clever generals have known it, the most enormous armada ever of landing craft and supply ships had already left ports on the south coast of England, and watched over by ships of the Home Fleet, were tossing and slamming their way nearer to France. Seasick, and drenched by huge waves, troops were too ill to be afraid. All they wanted was to get their feet on the coast of Normandy where, in view of the worsening weather, they were not expected.

This, they thought with grim satisfaction, was Dunkirk in reverse! Four years ago, the British army had been kicked out of France; snatched from the beaches by civilians in small, fragile boats, whilst Hitler's lot goose-stepped jubilantly along the French coast, and looked through telescopes at the south coast of England, soon to be invaded!

Well, now the Brits were back, and the Yanks with them, thought those storm-battered soldiers. Now it was *our* lot, doing the kicking!

*   *   *

Later that morning, at the Ministry of Information, pressmen were told of a landing in the early hours on the coast of France, and that no more could be released at present for reasons of security. That same message was also sent out by the BBC, and listeners advised not to turn off their wireless sets as further broadcasts might be made.

A mixing of dread and triumph sliced through all who heard it, and many, Elsie Drake amongst them, went quietly to church and begged on their knees for Divine protection for their sons and husbands – and daughters, too.

Mildred Kenton heard the broadcast in the kitchen at Laburnum Farm, and ran to find her husband and daughter, waving her hands, calling, 'It's started! They've landed!'

Bart Kenton closed his eyes against the sight of broken young bodies, and Rosamund stood unspeaking and added her own plea to the great wave of prayer that rose from Britain.

'Who'd have thought it,' Mildred gasped, 'in weather like this? They're taking a terrible risk, if you ask me!'

'It isn't their own lives *They* are risking.' Bart remembered the first battle of the Somme, and the donkeys who sent young lions to their deaths. 'God help those lads of ours,' he said bitterly then, tight-lipped, went on shifting the poultry arks onto fresh grass.

For the first time, Rosamund was grateful that Jon was not a soldier, then regretted it at once, because to mock her thoughts came the distant sound of aircraft engines. They were about to takeoff, she knew it, to fly circuits, landing only when the engineer was satisfied with the sweet-running of the engines, and the navigator had lined up his instruments and they had tested that bomb doors opened and the undercarriage behaved; wheels down, and up.

Then Jon and Dick would go to first briefing, and mechanics and armourers and riggers and electricians would swarm over the twelve Lancasters, dotted around the perimeter track on their standings. And *J-Johnnie*'s crew would be flying their thirtieth op on the first night after the landings, when every squadron of Luftwaffe fighters would be on alert, and anti-aircraft guns and searchlight crews.

'Are you all right, lass?' Bart asked when his wife had left, red-cheeked and breathless, to put on the kettle. 'You look a bit peaky.'

'I'm all right, Dad. I suppose it was just the shock of knowing it has started – and those bombers up there.' She raised her eyes skywards. 'It looks as if Jon will be on ops, tonight.'

'Aye?' He nodded briefly, then went on with the task in hand without saying another word, because all he could think of was that wars were started by old men for young ones to finish. When, in God's Name, was someone going to think on, and put a stop to them?

At one o'clock, they waited for the time signal and the news bulletin. Nothing more had been added to the first, terse announcement of a landing, Somewhere in France. Now, an anxious country needed to know more; be told where and when exactly, and how the soldiers already landed would fare when it was obvious to anyone who looked at the sky, that the weather wasn't getting any better. Bridgeheads had been established and held, repeated the announcer; it seemed it was all they were to be told.

'I'm going out,' Rosamund said when pots and pans had been washed. 'There's nothing else for me to do, is there?'

'No, lass. Nowt that won't wait.' Nothing as important, he thought, as a landing on the coast of France, and a young man who would happen be flying into the thick of it tonight.

'Don't be over long,' Mildred called, and her husband told her to hush, that the girl knew when it was time for milking.

'She's bound to be bothered, Mildred. Likely her young man is off on a raid tonight.'

'Then she should have thought about that. She was warned, but would she listen?'

'When did the young ever listen? Leave her be, woman. There's nothing you and me can do. It'll all be the same, think on, a hundred years from now!'

So she scowled, and raked through the kitchen fire, piling it with logs, glad of its warmth on so miserable a June afternoon. And though she made no reply, she triumphed inside, because her daughter was learning sense and wishing, she shouldn't wonder, that she had listened to her mother in the first place, and bided her time till the war was over. And from the look on her face, it wasn't far from the truth, because a more miserable countenance Mildred Kenton had yet to see!

The girl would be off to the fence like as not; waiting and watching, hanging round and getting herself whistled at by the airmen on the other side of it, Mildred fretted, wishing the aerodrome had never come and that soon they would go away, every last man of them, for there would be no peace at Laburnum Farm until they did!

Rosamund stood at the steel-mesh fence, watching the men and women who worked, less than a hundred yards away, on the bomber that had replaced *Z-Zebra*.

Three crews would be flying their thirtieth op tonight, Jon said, and another its twenty-ninth; the four remaining of the original twelve to arrive last November, at Laceby Green. And that, she thought soberly, meant that in the eight months she had known Jon, eight crews had been lost.

Lost! A stupid word! Nobody had misplaced them! They had been shot from the sky or had crashed into the sea. Fifty-six men; as if seven Laceby aircrew every month had been singled out to die. It was dreadful they should have to live their lives knowing that any day, any night, your name and number could be on the chop list. It must be like waiting in the condemned cell to be hanged, and all the while hoping for a reprieve.

It had happened twenty-nine times plus seven to Jon; thirty-six reprieves. Small wonder aircrew laughed too loudly, sometimes, and drank too much. With all her heart she was glad she and Jon were lovers, even though now she might be carrying his child. A tiny scrap of a thing but it *was* there, she was sure of it, and Jon must get back safely. Oh, please, he must!

Disconsolately she turned away. She had come often to the fence yet not once had Jon been there. And why should he be when there was so much to do before an op; so much to think about? And why should he begin now, on this the final flight?

'Hey! Rosie!'

She turned to see him there. He was wearing a battledress top and was so heartachingly good to look at that she wanted to tear down the fence and fling herself into his arms, beg him not to go!

'Darling!' She swallowed hard on tears that arose in her throat. 'I needed to see you so much, and here you are!'

'I needed you to be here. I've had the jitters ever since briefing and I promised myself that if you were at the fence, everything would be all right!'

'I want to kiss you,' she whispered, twining her fingers through the diamond-shaped mesh.

'I want to kiss you, too.' He pushed his fingers through from the other side, lacing them with hers.

'I shouldn't be here,' he said. 'Security.'

'Didn't think you would be, but I'm glad you are.'

'Can't stay long . . .'

Their lips were just a kiss away, but the fence stood cold between them.

'Good luck, then. Take care. See you tomorrow, Jon, as early as you can make it – the minute you land!'

'Softie.' It was hell, not being able to touch her. 'There'll be debriefing first, and breakfast and I'll need a shower. How would nine suit you – just to say a quick I-love-you?'

'We'll both be so happy we won't be able to say anything at all. Sure you'll be able to make it?'

'I'll be there!'

'Then in that case, I think you should have a night out with the crew. They'll want to celebrate, you said so yourself, and it wouldn't be a lot of fun if their driver wasn't there, now would it?'

'Are you sure, Rosie? They're planning on going to the pub in Laceby – not so far to stagger home – and I'd intended joining them for the last round.'

'I'm sure. Just be there in the morning, so I'll know it's really happened.'

'Fellfoot it is, then. At nine. Don't watch me go, darling, or I'll want to turn round.' Turning round was bad luck.

'I don't want you to watch me either.' The tears were shaking in her throat. 'Let's both just walk away? I love you, Jon Hunt.'

'And I love you, my Rosie. See you, then. At the pond . . .'

She pulled her fingers from his and turned abruptly, straightening her shoulders, sticking out her chin, hissing, 'Out of the way, stupid!' to a cow that stood in her path and gazed at her with curious, moist eyes.

She wished she could weep, yell at the top of her voice, stamp her feet angrily with every step that took her further away from him, but she could not. She only knew she had never felt so miserable, so lonely and afraid in the whole of her life.

The evening was cold. Rosamund waited at the fence in gumboots and duffel coat. Since she'd stood here this afternoon, the wind had dropped only a little, and blew gusts of rain into her face. They shouldn't be flying tonight, she thought mutinously, wishing time could stand still so she needn't see him go.

They, the faceless ones, had still not confirmed where exactly the invasion forces had landed. And that was plain foolish, because surely Hitler's lot had realized it was happening; no one could ignore the amount of men and machines that must still be pouring ashore to support the bridgeheads *They* admitted had been established. And surely the German High Command were at this minute rushing every reinforcement they could from the Pas de Calais where they thought the invasion would be, to wherever it *was*. Had Bessie's brother been right? Dunkirk, perhaps?

The evening was gloomy. In June, nights should be light and bright until well past ten o'clock. She had yearned for those nights in the deeps of winter, imagined walking hand in hand with Jon, their faces to the sun.

The first bomber lurched past her on its unsteady way to takeoff; only when it was airborne would it be a thing of grace and beauty. On the ground, Lancasters were like clumsy ducks, Jon said, and the first of them to go tonight would be *C-Charlie*.

Take care, Charlie. Come back safely . . .

She shivered. The clouds were low. They'd be into them and above them in no time at all at takeoff. Tonight she wouldn't be able to watch *J-Johnnie* until it vanished, small as a sparrow, into the distance.

She turned her eyes briefly to the control tower, wishing for the red Very flare sent up if ops were called off at the very last minute. Tomorrow night might have been a better time to go; by tomorrow June weather might have returned.

There was no red light. Instead, through the gloom, a green light flashed briefly, and *C-Charlie* was on its way down the runway.

She waited, cold and anxious, wishing luck to each Lancaster that passed her. Then she drew in her breath, because the next – the last in the line of bombers taxiing to takeoff – must be Jon's. And sitting beside Jon would be Willie MacBain, and Tom would lie there, face down in the underbelly, even though it wasn't allowed at takeoff. But the bomb-aimer, with his lucky silk stocking around his neck, would be on the lookout for the Waaf who was always there beside the control tower, waving her knickers.

Rosamund pulled a handkerchief from her pocket. Tonight, she hadn't tied it to the fence to hang there, limp and soggy; tonight, she would wave it like mad and even if Jon couldn't see it, Mick would, and perhaps rotate his guns to let her know he had.

Mick to Skip. Just passed your milkmaid . . .

She held the handkerchief high, which was stupid of her when she ought to be drying her tears with it; tears of frustration they really were, because she couldn't prevent Jon going and because she couldn't go with him.

Please, please take care. I'll be with you every minute of the way! And I'll be loving you every mile there and back.

The guns in *J-Johnnie*'s rear turret made a half-circle. Mick had seen her!

The ninth to go thrashed into takeoff and it was suddenly so dark that the runway lights came on. In June, would you believe?

She stood, hands gripping the mesh tightly, as if by doing

so she could stay connected to Jon. Then came the twelfth green light and Jon's Lancaster began takeoff, gathering speed, shining black against the lights, at full throttle now, then all at once airborne and making for the low, grey clouds.

No watching him, loving him, blessing him out of sight tonight. Soon he would be above the weather – with luck. And with skill, of course. Jon was a good pilot; he had to be. Hadn't he just taken off on his thirty-seventh?

She stood there, trying to control the shaking inside her, until the noise of their departing faded and the runway lights flickered and died; until all was quiet and still once more.

Then she sobbed as if her heart would break in two.

'You sound a mite more cheerful this morning.' It was a long time since Bart Kenton heard his daughter singing as she milked.

'I am, Dad. Suddenly everything seems to be going right.'

'The second front, you mean?' They had learned from a late-night bulletin that the coast of Normandy was where Allied Forces had landed. D-Day, they were calling it, and this morning was the beginning of D-Day plus one.

'Mm. And wasn't it great that they landed on Jersey and Guernsey at the same time?'

It had always been a thorn in Mr Churchill's flesh that, if you cared to be technical about it, Germany had actually occupied a part of the United Kingdom, something he vowed they would never do.

'I think we've got a foothold now.' He didn't say it was a pity so many young men were bound to die, because the airman she had taken a fancy to was in the thick of it. Instead, he said, 'Was your young man flying last night?'

'He was.'

'Aah . . .' This morning, as the sky began to lighten in the east, he had pulled aside the curtain to take a look at the weather, only to see his daughter climb the cow pasture gate and head for the high mesh fence. 'And he's back?'

'All of them, and Dad – it was Jon's last op. He'll have a break from flying now. He's been on thirty-seven raids.'

'So that's why you sound so chuffed with yourself?'

'It is! I'm going to slip out at nine to meet him – just for an hour or so. I won't be seeing him tonight. The crew are going out to celebrate, you see.'

'There'll be some thick heads tomorrow morning, then?'

He tipped the last of the milk into a churn, glad for his girl, even though her cheeks were flushed, her eyes too bright and ringed with dark circles. Staying awake half the night, he shouldn't wonder, worrying.

'They deserve a night out. If you'll give me a hand with the churns, I'll take them down the lane, Dad. And I'll wash the breakfast dishes before I go. If Mum asks you where I am, I don't suppose you could tell her I've popped out for an hour?'

'Couldn't you tell her yourself, Rosamund? I know she's not over enamoured with your airman, but you're never going to get her to see your point of view if you don't try to meet her halfway. I think you should at least ask him to call for you when he takes you out. Would be a lot more respectable. I don't like it when you have to sneak off.'

'I'll talk to her, Dad, but not today. And I agree with you; it's time you met Jon.'

They would have to. Tomorrow, probably, he would tell them he wanted to marry her and there would be nothing her mother could do about it, once she knew about the baby. There would be words, mind; bitter accusations flung, but Dad would be on their side.

'Aye. I reckon the time is long overdue. But away with you and see to the churns. I'll finish off here.'

'Thanks. For understanding, I mean, and for being on our side. Because you are, even though you don't say so!'

She threw her arms round him, hugging him, kissing his cheek in a rare gesture of affection, and he wondered how he and Mildred – ordinary folk, both of them – could have produced so beautiful a child. Because this morning she was more than beautiful. This morning, somehow, his lass had become a woman; was so happy, so grand to look at that it was plain to see why the pilot had fallen in love with her.

'Now what on earth was that in aid of?' he smiled.

'Oh, because you aren't such a bad old dad, and because the sun has come out again and because –'

'Because you're going to meet your young man?'

'Yes. And because he'll be taken off flying for quite a time – maybe a year if they send him overseas, instructing.'

'You won't like that, Rosamund?'

'No. But at least I'd know he was safe, and they'll give him embarkation leave if they send him abroad, even though it's been stopped for the invasion forces.'

They would *have* to give him leave, or how could they be married? How long did it take to get a special licence? A couple of days? A week?

'We'll just have to wait and see, won't we?' He touched her cheek gently, then told her to be off, that her mother didn't like breakfast being held up.

Breakfast! She threw back her head and laughed out loud. On this wonderful morning, who needed breakfast?

The sun shone warmly on her face and she smiled back at it. The grass was still wet from the storms, but the sky was clear and high and blue and she wanted to fling wide her arms, tell the hills and fells how crazily happy she was.

Breathless from running, she reached the wall, then looked down on Fellfoot and the pond, and the flat stone beside it. And at Jon, there already, even though there were ten minutes to go before nine o'clock.

Her eyes lingered on the sight of him; Sergeant Jon Hunt, who waited, eyes narrowed against the sun; slim, good to look at. Jon who had flown on thirty-seven raids and was waiting for her just as he said he would be; safe and real and *alive*!

'God. This is Rosamund Kenton,' she whispered. 'Thank you; thank you . . .'

Then she called his name and he jumped to his feet, running to meet her, arms wide, and all at once it was really happening, just as she had daydreamed a million times over it would.

'Darling,' she whispered. 'I think I'm going to cry.'

'No you're not.' His voice was wobbly, too. 'Not until you've kissed me!'

So they kissed until they were breathless and dizzy, then took hands and walked back to the big, flat stone.

'Isn't this a beautiful world? Isn't it just the most marvellous world you ever did see?' She flung wide her arms, taking in the hills, the tender green of new things growing, the willow that trailed in the water. 'And did I tell you I love you, Jon Hunt?'

'You didn't!'

'Then I love you, love you!' She jumped to her feet, calling, 'Listen, everybody! Rosie Kenton loves Jon Hunt!'

'Steady on, softie! You'll fall in!' He pulled her into his arms again. 'Did I tell you that you're very beautiful this morning?'

'Not yet.'

'Then listen, folks!' he shouted at the top of his voice. 'Rosie Kenton is the most beautiful woman on earth! There now,' he laughed, 'the whole world knows about us!'

She leaned close and he wrapped his arms around her, taking her hands, moving a little so his cheek rested on her hair.

'Tell me how it was, Jon? Not the op, but how it felt when you knew you'd made it? Did you want to throw your cap in the air?'

'No. I felt sick. When I realized we were over the white cliffs, my stomach churned. Only they weren't white. They were a kind of pale gold, because the sun was coming up. We just looked at each other, Mac and me – well, we didn't want to push our luck when a fighter could have come at us out of the sun.

'It was Tom, in the nose, who sort of broke the spell. My intercom clicked, then a voice said, very correctly, "Bomb-aimer to pilot. There's a lovely view down there. English trees . . ." Then Dick joined in. "Navigator to pilot. Calculated that was Southampton behind us. Reckon we've made it, Skip!"'

'Was it wonderful, Jon, knowing that you really had?'

'No. That was when I wanted to throw up.' She felt the movement of his lips against her hair. 'Then they all tried to get in on the act – nearly burst my eardrums – so Mac just turned round and yelled, "Will you daft lot stop your blethering? We've still got to get this thing down!" They couldn't hear him because of the engines, but things calmed down a bit after that. I got a bearing from Dick and we were heading for Laceby – sweet as a bird. And *Johnnie* landed like a bird, too; a textbook job. That was when all hell was let loose, and it felt wonderful, Rosie.'

'So tell me.'

'There was a Waaf driver waiting for us, grinning all over her face, and Mac just grabbed her and kissed her. He was laughing; Willie MacBain actually *laughing*! Then Tom took off his helmet, unwound his silk stocking and waved it like a banner. Harry was the quietest of us all. He was really full up. He just said, "Well done, Jon. D'you know something? Looks like I'm going to be around when my kid cuts her first tooth!"

'We all piled into the transport, then Dick yelled, "Hold it! We've forgotten Matilda Mint!" So Mac went back for her, muttering we were leaving our luck behind, and no way was the next crew getting their hands on her!'

'I'm glad you all thought she brought you luck. What have you done with her?'

'She's safe in my locker. And sorry for going on a bit, but I think it's only just hit me that *Johnnie* made it! Thirty pesky ops!'

'And you did thirty-seven! You should get a medal.'

'No thanks. The best reward I could have had was when that tail-wheel touched the runway, and I knew we were down. Moments like that you never forget – like when I first saw you. It was the same wonderful feeling; something that had to be remembered for ever.'

'Me, too. I was at the fence when you touched down. I just whispered thank you to God, and then I started to shake. But do you want something else to store – something to make this morning extra special? Look down there. See the yellow iris left of the willow? Just beside it there's an old bit of stalk . . .'

'Y-yes . . .'

'Just *look*.' She leaned down to place a finger near the brown, rotting wood. 'Ever seen a dragonfly emerge?'

'No. From what?'

'From the sheath it's been living and growing in. Like a chick coming out of an egg, only much more beautiful. It's got its head out already; see those huge eyes?'

'I see it! What's going to happen next?'

'Just watch . . .'

So they bent low over the pond, to see a leg appear; watched, fascinated, as another leg emerged to flail helplessly, then cling to the stem. Bit by bit, as if it were fighting to come alive, it struggled into the sun, fragile and spent.

'That thing it's just got out of is really called its nymphal skin, Jon.'

'Clever girl! Who told you that?'

'Learned it at school. But not many have actually seen it happen. That one is my third.' She turned to kiss his cheek.

'So what happens now? Does it cling there till a duck gobbles it up?'

'It's resting. See – it's trying to spread its wings – they'll have to dry out in the sun, then it'll be able to fly. It won't live long; about three weeks, poor thing. They can fly very quickly, and sideways and backwards, too.'

'Wish a Lancaster could – fly backwards and sideways, I mean!'

'Forget Lancasters, Jon. Keep your eye on the dragonfly. It's got four wings and they're transparent, but when they're dry, they'll shine in the sun.'

'How long before it can fly?'

'About half an hour, then it'll be off.'

'Half an hour to tell you I love you and that I'd rather be with you tonight.'

'No. Tonight will be something more for your memories – the night seven grown men acted like kids out of school because they'd made their thirty ops. And you'll remember your thick heads, all of you, in the morning!'

'You really don't mind, Rosie? Truth known, I ought to be there.'

'Then go! It could be the last time you're all together as a crew. But don't let Matilda Mint get drunk, will you? She can be a right little madam on two port and lemons!'

'Rosie Kenton!' He gathered her to him. 'Do you really know how much I love you? And do you know you have the most beautiful nose I have ever seen, and the bluest eyes? And can you even begin to realize what it means to me to be grounded? I'd look at you and hurt inside, because I had to face up to the fact that any night I could lose you! But now I can wake up every morning for a year, maybe, and know there's going to be a tomorrow.

'And sweetheart – I want us to be married. Are you sure, now I just might have a future, that I can't meet your folks? The invasion has started; the war could be over in Europe before I'm called back to flying. Wouldn't your father help us?'

'I think he will, Jon.' All at once her eyes were anxious, and she took his face in her hands and kissed him gently. 'You see, you're going to have to meet them. Tomorrow. This morning, when I told Dad you'd done your tour of ops, he said you should at least call for me. He thought it would be a way of breaking the ice. And he would be on our side.' She took a deep breath, then finished, softly. 'So can you be at the gate tomorrow morning, about ten?'

'The little creaking gate? You know I can!'

'Ten is when Mother puts the kettle on and we congregate in the kitchen. And I'll introduce you, then tell them we want to be married.'

'Do you think they'll say yes? And why, all of a sudden, do you want this? You were so against it!'

'Things change, Jon. They won't say yes at first, but they'll have to in the end because I'm going to have a baby.' She said it huskily, hesitantly, her cheeks flushing red; all the while expecting a shout of amazement, or of joy; expecting him to gather her close, all at once protective and ask her, incredulously, if she was sure. But instead his face paled and he looked at her as if she had said something in a language he didn't understand.

'Rosie! You can't be!'

'I can. Think back. The night you had nothing in your pocket . . .'

'But how long have you known – suspected?'

'A week Friday, I'll have missed two periods.'

'Then why, for Pete's sake, didn't you tell me before this?'

'Jon! It's all right. It *is*!' She cupped his face in her hands, forcing him to look at her. 'I'm sorry! I shouldn't have sprung it on you so suddenly. But I didn't tell you because you were flying. I reckoned you had enough to put up with just getting there and back, without giving you more to worry about!'

'So all this time you've taken the worry on your own? Did you tell Bessie?'

'No. I reckoned you had a right to know before anyone else.' She gazed steadily into his eyes. 'Tell me you're glad about it?'

'Since you ask, I don't know whether to laugh or cry! But take tonight, for instance – I tell them what's happened and you know what they'll say? "Well, what do you know? Skip's milkmaid is in the family way! Get another round in! Cheers!" Well, maybe Harry would be OK about it – he's got a little girl.'

'So I'm in the family way! But I don't care about the crew, though tonight wouldn't be a good time to tell them. What I want to know,' she said slowly and distinctly, 'is what *you* think about it. I thought you'd be pleased, yet you're acting like it's my fault.'

'It isn't your fault, Rosie. When it happened I should have said, "No, darling. We can't. Tonight, we mustn't . . ." It's me I'm mad at.'

'Why, Jon? I knew the score. You told me you hadn't anything in your pocket, but I didn't care. I wanted you so much that I couldn't think of anything else! I know you warned me and I know it was me persuaded you, but I didn't do it because I wanted to get pregnant. I just needed you to love me! I happen to be crazy about you – it's as simple as that!

'Or is it simple, Jon? Come to think of it, it was always me made most of the running. Was I too easy? Have I only myself to blame?' She was weeping now, big, hot tears that tasted salt on her lips. Her shoulders began to shake and she fished for her handkerchief, holding it to her eyes as if, all at once, she couldn't look at him; couldn't believe what was happening to them.

'Rosie?' His voice was gentle again and he moved her hand from her eyes and kissed away the tears. 'I don't blame you. It's me should be sorry – putting you through all that worry. You should have told me!'

'And if I had, would you not have minded so much?'

'Minding doesn't come into it. All I can think of at this moment is that I've let you down when I should have taken care of you. I'm not proud of the fact that I was too damn stupid to count to ten!'

'I see.' She blew her nose loudly, defiantly. 'And if I admit that I was too damn stupid to count to ten, too, where does that leave us?'

'Still madly in love, I hope,' he whispered. 'Still wanting to be married. Forgive me? I'm getting a bit more used to it now. When first you told me, though, it hit me for six!'

'Me, too, for the first few days. Then I stopped worrying and counting, and all I could think of was for you to do your tour, then everything would come right for us.'

'And it *will*!' Gently he laid a hand on her abdomen. 'Are you all right? Are you being sick, Rosie? Harry's wife was . . .'

'No – at least not yet! My breasts are tender, though. But they're always like that just before a period comes.'

'So you might not be –'

'Pregnant? It could just be a scare, you mean; that next week it'll turn up on time, just like that? No, Jon. I'm having a baby – woman's instinct.'

'Then if you're glad, Rosie, I'm glad, too. I can't believe it, though. You look just the same as always.'

'Of course I do! But will you love me when I'm fat and clumsy?'

'More than ever. I'll love you enough for two. I do already.' He pulled her close and she felt the tension leaving him. 'I want to kiss you, Rosie. And can we still make love? Will it harm it?'

'Of course it won't! And it isn't an *it*. It's a baby! Only a scrap of a thing, mind, but she doesn't like being called *It*!'

'Then hadn't we better call her Scrapofathing?'

'No. Because before you know it, this Scrap is going to be one great big bump. Anyway, I've decided she's Sprog.'

'*She*? You're sure?'

'I think deep down I want a girl, Jon. Sons have to go to war. It's happened twice, in twenty years.'

'A girl it is then. D'you know, darling, I think it's sinking in. We're having a baby!'

'And tomorrow we're going to tell my parents.'

'No! It had better be tonight. Can't we make it tonight, Rosie?'

'No. You're going out with the crew!' All at once she felt very calm; very sure. 'We can tell them tomorrow, and isn't it wonderful to be able to say *tomorrow* without crossing our fingers?'

'Darling, I do love you!' He kissed her gently, as if, all at once, she would break. 'Are you sure about tomorrow?'

'I'm sure. We've got a whole year of tomorrows.'

'Have you worked it out – *when*, I mean?'

'We-e-ll, I haven't seen a doctor yet, and I'm better at arrival times when it comes to cows, but I reckon early January – the second, or the third.'

'It makes it all sound very real, Rosie – our baby is due on the third of January!'

'Sprog *is* very real. All we have to do now is get married.'

'But what if I get sent overseas?' he gasped, dismayed.

'Then it'll be a quick wedding, a brief honeymoon and I'll just have to get on with it! I'll bet half the babies born today will have a father who is overseas.'

'You could be right. But it isn't a lot of fun, is it, for women on their own?'

'Granted. But there won't always be a war on. We can even look forward to the end of it now. The second front is doing well, the storms have stopped, the sun is shining and this is the most beautiful morning! Look at the dragonfly now, our lucky omen, Jon.'

'Rosie! It's fantastic!'

The creature was still there on the withered stem, only now

its wings were firm and dry, and shone in the sun. And as they watched, it began to fly as if it had always known how, and darted to and fro above the pond, its long, slender body flashing like jewels in darts of blue and gold and green.

'Not so long ago, Jon, it looked like a piece of withered skin, yet now it's the most beautiful thing. Everything comes good in the end. OK – so we got Sprog one moonlit night, like a couple of gypsies in the heather. And long ago, when Laburnum Farm was built, Sprog would have been called a hedge child, a by-blow, and even now there'll be raised eyebrows. But who cares? She's a love child and we know almost to the minute when we made her, and where. Say you're glad, darling?'

'I *am* glad. It's just that right now I feel so choked with loving you I can't make you understand how much. But I'll tell you something for nothing: if any man lusts after Sprog the way I lusted after you the minute we met, I'll black his eye!'

'Darling, I'm so happy.' Her eyes followed the darting, jewelled creature as it flew above the pond on wings of gossamer gold. 'This morning will be another always to remember. And when we're very old, I shall ask you if you remember our dragonfly morning when we were young, and so crazily happy. And you'll say, all shakily, "Can't hear you, woman! Speak up, will you? Who's getting a dragon in the morning?"'

And they laughed, because tomorrow was theirs and she wanted the morning never to end; to sit there wondering if she dare break the spell; if they could ever be as happy again.

'You're tired, Jon. Time to go. Take it easy back to camp, then get straight into bed. I'll see you in the morning at ten. Have a good time tonight. You deserve it, all of you.'

Hand in hand they walked down the slope to Laburnum Farm and the little squeaking gate. And he took her in his arms and said, 'It's going to come right for us, Rosie. I'll make it come right. We *will* be married. Tomorrow morning, we'll tell them! I do so love you . . .'

'Be careful! My mother might be upstairs. She could see us from the bedroom window! And by the way, Sergeant Hunt, I love you, too!'

*   *   *

She walked with him to the end of the lane and they kissed again beside the milk churns.

'See you tomorrow at ten,' she whispered.

'Take care, my Rosie . . .'

She watched him walk away because she could hardly bear to take her eyes off him, loving him, wanting him, impatient for tomorrow to come.

At the six oaks he stopped, then turned and waved, and because tomorrow really was going to come and because it couldn't possibly be unlucky any longer, she smiled and waved back.

'Jon Hunt,' she said softly as he disappeared round the bend in the road, 'do you know how much I love you?'

THIRTEEN

J une 8. D-Day plus two. The Allies were pushing forward
and supplies still being unloaded at beaches code-named
Juno, Sword, Gold and Omaha. Everyone listened to every
news bulletin; were impatient for the time when the Ministry
of Information released films for newsreels in the picture houses,
when the sheer magnitude of the landings could be seen and
appreciated and gasped at. Only now it was known as Operation
Overlord, which, in spite of the worst weather imaginable, was
going better than anyone had dared hope.

Rosamund tried not to think of this morning at ten; ticked
off her list of things-to-do-to-pass-the-time-away in her mind.
Milking was over and the cows in the pasture by eight. Now
she must take the churns to the bottom of the lane, collect mail
from the box and the morning paper the postlady obligingly
left with it.

Hastily she scanned the headlines: 'Invasion Troops Thrust
Inland'. It was going well; all at once everything was going well.
The war in Europe could be over by Christmas said the man
in the street, because Hitler was being hammered on all sides!
The gormless man had invaded Russia instead of the British
Isles and look where it had got him, thank God!

This morning at ten, Rosamund thought as a soaring song
of happiness trilled through her, Jon would be waiting at the
gate and they would take the narrow path – that same path
they had taken in the darkness to the hayloft – and walk
hand in hand into the yard. And if all went as she hoped it
would, her mother would glance through the window and
see them. That, she had long since decided, would be the

worst bit over because from that minute on, there would be no going back.

Jon. She must think of Jon and how he was feeling and if he'd got himself into a tizzy and cut himself shaving. Jon, who probably had more to drink last night than was good for him. Jon, frowning at the man in the mirror who, less than twenty-four hours ago, had learned he had fathered a child; little scrapofathing Sprog.

Rosamund backed the trailer into the barn; did it automatically because at this very moment she was only sure of one thing: that she loved Jon so much it was like a lovely ache inside her.

The smell of bacon frying wafted through the open kitchen window. She wrinkled her nose, because this morning she didn't want bacon and egg and fried bread; didn't want to count her blessings because she had more than a week's ration on her plate every morning. This morning, anyone who wanted it was welcome to her huge, privileged breakfast. This morning, she thought longingly of tart green apples, strawberries dipped in sugar, sticks of celery to crunch on.

Jon would almost certainly have not eaten breakfast; would have made do with a couple of aspirins, washed down with tea. She hoped he hadn't told the crew about the baby. She didn't want anyone to know until her parents had been told and everything said that needed to be said – good and bad, both.

She looked at her watch. Eight thirty-five, and five minutes late for breakfast. Egg and bacon and fried bread gone cold. It made her retch just to think about it.

'Sorry I'm late.' She gave no explanation because there wasn't one, and laid the paper at her father's side. 'It says the landings are going well.'

She looked at the plate: the congealing fat, the egg yolk gone hard, and jumped to her feet.

'Forgot to wash my hands,' she called over her shoulder, making for the pump trough in the yard, swallowing hard on the awful taste in her mouth. Then she grasped the handle and pumped it up and down, cupping a hand under the spout, drinking the clear, cold water in greedy gulps.

Her mouth felt clean again. She wasn't going to be sick, she thought gratefully. Tomorrow morning, though, it might be different. Tomorrow morning, she might not make it to the pump trough!

She wondered how she could return to the kitchen, and the bacon and eggs smell; wondered how she would manage to wash the breakfast dishes without wanting to retch again.

Darling, thank heaven that soon you'll be here, and they'll know . . .

As luck – or maybe Divine Providence – would have it, Mildred Kenton said she would see to the washing-up this morning; that Rosamund could fill the clothes boiler with water, instead, then light a fire under it, if she didn't mind.

'Why today?' Rosamund asked, because washday was always Monday; winter or summer, wet or dry.

'Blanket time!' Laburnum Farm blankets were washed each June, hung in the sun to dry and air, then folded meticulously and stored in the big cupboard on the landing, with lavender bags between them. Second front or not, the blanket wash came round as regularly as Christmas. 'The jar is about full.'

Each week, Mildred put a level desertspoon of soapflakes into a two-pound jam jar; pillaged it from the soap ration so that when the sun shone warmly and a gentle June breeze blew from the south-west, she would not be caught napping without soap to wash her blankets. 'And you'd better fill the peggy-tub with water from the rain butt.'

The blankets were laid in a bath of warm sudsy water, outside in the yard, and ever since Rosamund could remember, she had tucked her skirt into her knickers and trod them barefoot. Splosh, slurp, splash. Once, it had been a great game.

Then they were rinsed in rainwater and put through the mangle and there was nothing, Mildred Kenton said every year, as good as the sweet smell of newly washed blankets drying in the sun. Unless it was newly baked bread, of course, or new-cut hay.

'Fine by me!' Rosamund hurried into the unsullied air, frowning to think of Mrs Drake's gas boiler with its polished copper lid. All Bessie's mother had to do was fill it from the kitchen tap – Laceby Green had mains water, too – then turn on the gas beneath it which lit with a satisfying plop.

Rosamund had yearned for comforts such as electric lights, a bath with hot and cold taps and, every washday she yearned especially for a gas-fired boiler. Until this morning, that was. Now she was glad of the time the preparations would waste.

She collected kindling and filled a basket with beechwood, chopped into faggots small enough to fit into the little boiler-grate through its nine-inch-square iron door.

Soon, Jon would be walking across the field behind the aerodrome in the direction of Laceby; the path they had taken, stumbling and laughing in the darkness to Bessie's back yard where the bicycles were kept. Now there was hardly any blackout – no more than six hours of darkness – and the days warm. And at ten, Jon would be waiting at the little gate because this morning they would tell her parents she was having a baby. Out of wedlock.

It was when the boiler had been filled from the pump and wood smoke was curling out of the narrow little chimney stack, that she heard the sound of aeroplane engines. Soon, probably, Lancasters would be doing circuits and she would know the most grateful, thankful feeling because *J-Johnnie*'s engines would not be adding to the roar. Not until a new crew arrived to take it over; not until Jon and Tom, Dick and Harry and Mick, Sammy and Mac had been posted to another station would the new crew arrive.

'I've stoked up the boiler fire.' Rosamund poked her head round the kitchen door. 'Can someone keep an eye on it? I'm going to the fence.'

No sneaking away now; no more deceits nor lies. This morning it would all come out, and standing at the fence watching bombers would be nothing compared to what was going to happen, a little after ten, in the kitchen at Laburnum Farm.

How would it be when they dropped their bombshell? Shock first, then anger, derisively flung. Jon would see her mother at her worst, could be forgiven for wondering if the girl he wanted to marry would grow into a replica of the shrill-voiced shrew that was Mildred Kenton.

It was her father, though, she would feel sorry for; would be truly sad to have shamed and hurt him. For shamed them she would have, and the fragile, self-righteous bubble of smugness her mother had lived in these twenty years past would burst.

Rosamund reached the fence, then stared in amazement. The bombers dotted at intervals around the perimeter of the aerodrome were being made ready for operation flight! There was no mistaking the tractors towing bombs, armourers fitting guns. And no test flights this morning. Something was happening in a hurry, for never before had Laceby's Lancasters been sent on a daylight raid. Almost always the RAF bombed by night and it was American crews who flew missions by day. Something was seriously wrong; perhaps something to do with the landings. She looked at her watch, knowing she might have enough time to wish them all well before it was time to meet Jon.

Over to her left, the ground crews stood around, checks finished; a truck arrived and airmen in flying gear got out. She closed her eyes, thankful that at this moment Jon would be walking past Laceby church, and on towards the left fork leading to six oaks, and Laburnum Farm.

To her right the bomber on the standing that had once belonged to *Z-Zebra* started its engines. The ground crews stood by, watching this first-ever daylight raid; Waaf drivers joined them.

'Come home safely,' Rosamund whispered as each bomber passed the bottom of the cow pasture, her heart thudding in her throat, because really she shouldn't be here. She'd had her fair share of worrying and waiting and counting; didn't have to go through the torture any longer. Jon had finished his tour; made it there and back thirty-seven times; earned the right to be around when his child was born.

Five minutes to ten, and she must go, would have turned there and then from the worry of watching had not a voice inside her commanded *Stay!* She slid her eyes left. One more approaching along the perimeter track. She would wait for one more, and then she must go!

'Come home safely.' She sent her thoughts to the cockpit

high above her, then her head jerked back as her eyes took in the squadron markings on the fuselage and the letter J beside them. *J-Johnnie!* The new crew must already have arrived; taken over Jon's Lancaster. How unfair to throw them in at the deep end!

Then her insides churned and she let go a cry as if a fist had slammed into her abdomen, because as *J-Johnnie* passed her the rear-turret guns made a half-circle, just as they had always done, in salute. And in her mind she heard the words as they crackled from end to end of the bomber.

Rear gunner to pilot. Just passed your milkmaid . . .

'No!' she gasped, and set off with fear at her heels for the little iron gate.

Jon was not waiting there. How could he be? At this very minute, he was hurtling down the runway with Mac beside him, wrestling *J-Johnnie* into the air. For the thirty-eighth time!

God! Why did you let this happen! Why?

She began to run down the narrow path, past the pigeon loft and the hen arks, stopping to lean, breathless and shaking, on the dry-stone wall at the top end of the paddock. Below her in the distance she could see the aerodrome, a sprawl of concrete buildings and huts; could see almost all the perimeter track circling runways that met diagonally at a spot where once five beech trees stood.

Above her, bombers circled, waiting until the rest were airborne. There were two still to go, though she couldn't count those already in the air. Nine, were there, or ten. Had the entire squadron been ordered into the air regardless of the fact that this morning three crews had expected to be grounded?

But *They* could do what They wanted. It didn't matter that Jon should have been at the gate ten minutes ago. If she was able to demand of *Them* why Sergeant Jon Hunt was on a daylight op when he should have been off flying, an old man with a pale, lined face and a querulous voice would ask, 'Who is Sergeant Jon Hunt?'

The sound of engines beat in her head, mocking her misery. They were all in the air now. Very soon they would make formation and head south. Because that was where they were going; south, to join D-Day plus two!

She wrapped her arms around her, hugging herself tightly to stop the shaking. She wished she could weep; cry the anger and disbelief out of her, but she had lost control of her body and her brain. All she could do was to stand helpless, watching Jon fly away from her, and wonder how the Fates could have let it happen.

Or had they meant it to happen? Had they been jealous of such a love and thought that she and Jon must be taught a lesson; a nasty, spiteful lesson?

No! It was nothing like that! Someone in the War Cabinet wanted bombers in the air, *now*, and didn't give a damn who flew them! Surnames and numbers was what aircrews were; puppets; pieces on a chess board. And she was being stupid standing here, frightening herself to death! OK, so Jon was flying again. There was a war on and an invasion, too, and Jon was having to fly just one more time. And when he got back, he would hurry to the gate just as soon as he was able and would hold her close, like always, and say, 'Rosie! I'm sorry. A panic job, but everything is all right, now. And by the way, I love you . . .'

She sucked in a great gulp of air, trying to think straight, calculate the time it would take. It was almost certain this one-off job would be something to do with D-Day. Marshalling yards to be put out of action, perhaps, or a concentration of reinforcements trying to reach Normandy from the Pas de Calais, where they had been waiting for a landing that had happened at some other place.

How long did it take to fly to France and back? Six hours? Then landing and going through debriefing and getting a meal, and Jon would have to shave because he'd be coming to Laburnum, wouldn't he, to meet her parents?

The sky was quiet again. Only echoes of the hasty leaving hung on the air. It was half-past ten, which meant Jon would be at the gate at six, tonight. Or maybe seven? But she would have a better idea once they started to return. From the top of the paddock, in the daylight, it would be possible to see the letter J on the fuselage of Jon's plane as he circled to land. And after that, she would go to the gate and wait for him; wait as long as it took.

The shaking had stopped now, and she hurried past the hen arks, past the hay barn and down the narrow path to the little iron gate – just to satisfy herself he really wasn't there.

But he would be tonight, and the look of him, the feel of him, the taste of his mouth on hers, would tell her that everything was all right at last, and she would love him more than ever, if that were possible.

She turned from the gate and walked slowly to the yard, her stomach hurting all the way up to her throat. And the world closed in on her, reminding her that this was blanket washing day, and the boiler fire needed to be stoked. And she must somehow exist until six o'clock tonight. Or maybe seven. And she wasn't going to be sick; she wasn't!

Not until she made it to the pump trough!

The first returning bomber flew low overhead at a little before four o'clock. Rosamund had been right; something to do with the landings! She pushed wide the gate of the cow pasture, calling 'Cush, cush,' looking for the leader of the herd, giving it a shove in the direction of the shippon, watching as the procession began to form, to follow the leader. They were all right now – could find their way there without her – and she made for the far end of the pasture, reaching the fence as the first Lancaster came in to touch down on the north/south runway, which wasn't usual at all. Normally they used the other one, but then nothing about today was normal.

She tutted impatiently, realizing the bombers would be landing head-on to her, stepping nervously backward as the great machine seemed to be rushing towards the perimeter fence, to the very spot on which she stood.

Then its engines coughed, the propellers stopped, swinging on their own momentum before they were finally still. Then amazingly, the huge plane turned almost in its own length and began to taxi slowly to its own allotted standing.

She saw the fuselage markings briefly. *B-Bertie* was safely down and two – no, three – Lancasters circling, waiting permission to land. Four back, and Jon would be one of them. Jon was the most experienced pilot in the squadron; would be at the gate at six – or maybe seven! It was going to be all right. Tonight they would tell her parents about the baby. She needn't have worried. The entire op, Jon would probably say, had been a milk run!

The pasture was almost empty of cows. A few waited at the gate, tails flicking, heads moving from side to side as if to balance their ungainly bodies on too-small hooves, unwilling to walk through out of turn.

Many of them were big with calf and their milk would dry up when they reached the seventh month of their gestation. That was when they were put out to grass in three-acre field until they calved. Two months' rest, then in calf again! For the first time ever, Rosamund felt pity for the lives the creatures led; wondered how soon it would be before her own pregnancy showed.

She walked through the gateway, giving the last cow through a friendly pat. Then she laid her hands gently on her abdomen, smiling her love for Sprog; tiny, tiny baby inside her; precious love-child.

The sky was clear and blue, and she squinted into the distance. Two more, safely back. It was going to be all right. After tonight, things would start to get better. They *would*.

'It'll be a fine crop this year. Let's hope the weather is kind to us.' Bart leaned on the gate of Wolfen Meadow, surveying grass that was thick and tall and would soon be cut for hay. 'If I had the time to spare I could stand at this spot, winter and summer, and just look at yon view.'

Apart from the top end of the paddock, this was the finest view of all – or used to be, before the aerodrome came. Yet on June evenings such as this, Bart pondered, you didn't have to see the ugly, vulgar sprawl; could look beyond it to the ups and downs of the skyline that changed with the seasons, and the weather.

'And if I had the time to spare, I'd stand with you,' Rosamund smiled, 'but I'm meeting Jon tonight. He should have come this morning, but he had to fly. I saw him go; couldn't believe it at first – not when he should have been grounded.'

'Happen it was summat important to do with the invasion that made them have to fly in the daylight.'

'The first time ever, since they came last November. I worked it out Jon should get here between six and seven – depending on when he landed, of course. I saw the first one down when I was bringing the cows in. Gave me quite a shock. I thought it was going to run into the fence, it came so close. They used the north/south runway, this afternoon.'

'Must have been some reason for it,' Bart nodded. 'That runway, had you noticed, points directly at Laburnum.'

'I had.' She'd noticed most things about the aerodrome. 'Jon didn't turn up at six, so I'll pop off and see if he's arrived. I want to bring him home, Dad. This morning, if he could have been there, he was going to ask you if we could get married, now he's done his tour of ops. And I don't want you to say anything about me being too young, or that flying is dangerous. All I want is for you to hear us out, and be on our side. You will be? If Mum says I can't get married, will you say I can? *Please?*'

Had she the sense to look at her watch when it happened, Rosamund would have known the time was six twenty. But she hadn't looked because it happened so suddenly that all she could do was close her eyes tightly, flinching as the roar above them crashed through her head. Then something big and black flew so low over them that it blocked out the sun for the moment of its passing, and left a dark, frightening shadow behind it.

'*What the hell . . . ?*' Bart gasped. 'What does he think he's doing? Hedge-hopping?'

Rosamund stood petrified, unable to think until the explosion shook her into action.

'Oh, my God!'

Then came a second blast, further away, and her father grabbed her, pulled her to the ground.

'We're being bombed! That was one of theirs!'

'Don't know. It all happened so suddenly. But I hope not. Ours should all have been back, an hour ago.'

Why hadn't she counted them out, this morning? Why had she thought it no longer mattered? For the first time since RAF Laceby Green became operational, she hadn't known how many.

'We'd best get back to the house. Your mother'll be scared to death on her own.'

He rose to his feet and, still holding her hand, he ran, crouching, towards the farm.

The back door was open, and the door to the cellar, and he called, 'Milly? Are you all right?'

Then he clattered down the twisting stone steps to see the beam of torchlight and his wife, eyes wide with shock, crouching beneath the stone slab of the keeping cellar, her breathing coming in harsh gasps.

'Dad thinks it was bombs.' Rosamund dropped to her knees beside her shaking mother. 'Something flew over us, low, but I don't know if it was one of Laceby's. Shall I put the kettle on?'

'No! You're to stay with me! We'll all be killed!'

But Rosamund, unheeding, was on her way to the kitchen, trying to make sense of what had happened. An aircraft flying dangerously low, its underbelly black. But all underbellies were black – Luftwaffe or RAF. Then came the bomb, the explosion. And another explosion.

She filled the kettle at the pump, trying to think, get things straight in her head. Had that plane crashed or had it been a bomb; two bombs? Bombs, she decided, setting the kettle to boil. It had to be, because the alternative was too awful to contemplate.

She reached for mugs from the dresser, her hand shaking so much that it became a complicated task just getting them off the hooks. She set the earthenware pot to warm, then almost ran to the dairy to fill a jug with milk.

When she got back to the kitchen, her mother was standing at the top of the cellar steps, and released from the initial terror that sent her skittering into the darkness, two steps at a time, let go her pent-up feelings in a rage of abuse.

'Damn that aerodrome! There's been nothing but bother

since the day they felled the beeches! I said no good would come of it, but would anybody listen to me? Hadn't you thought, Bart Kenton, that it needn't have been bombs we heard? How can you be sure they weren't rockets; the secret weapon? Hitler's got his back to the wall and he'll stop at nothing now! And the likes of me will suffer! Me, that never wanted this war and do my best to keep out of it! Well, maybe somebody in this house will listen to me, now that it's –'

'Mildred! That's enough!' Bart's voice was so low and controlled that his wife stopped in mid-sentence. 'We can do without the dramatics!'

'And what about the herd?' she rushed on. 'Has anybody thought to see if they're all right! All that noise could've upset them. Next thing you know they'll all abort their calves and a right mess we'll be in, then!'

'Happen.' Bart's eyes snapped anger. 'And there are soldiers fighting in Normandy, and dying, an' all, at this very minute! And all for the likes of you, Mildred Kenton, who never thinks about anyone but herself! So stop your wailing and see to that tea – give you something to think about!'

'Dad,' Rosamund whispered when her mother had slammed, gasping, out of the room and across the yard, leaving a quivering silence behind her. 'Are you all right?'

'Sorry, lass. It isn't often I let fly, but what with the bombs an' all, the last thing I want is your mother adding her tuppenceworth! She's right, though. I'll just nip down to the pasture, see that nowt is amiss.'

'The tea'll be ready when you get back. I'll leave the cosy on it. I'm going to the gate to see if Jon's there.'

'He mightn't have been allowed out – because of the bombs, I mean.'

'Maybe not. But we can't be sure they were bombs and if they were, whether they hit the aerodrome. When you go to the pasture, Dad, can you take a quick look through the fence; see if things look normal?'

'They're all right. Grazing as if nothing had happened,' Bart said when he came back.

'I'll pour your tea, then. And, Dad – I went to the gate, but Jon wasn't there. Mind, it could be as late as seven.' Her hand was shaking as she poured, and hot liquid slopped on the table top. 'Did you get a look at the aerodrome?'

'I did. It all seemed normal. There didn't seem to be any sign of bombing – no craters, that I could see.'

'Yet that first explosion was quite near, for all that.' And the plane had flown over them so low that she wouldn't have been surprised if it had taken their chimneypots with it! 'Pity we never got the phone put in, Dad. At least I could have rung Bessie; asked her if she knows anything about what happened.'

'If we had two telephones, I doubt Bessie'd be of much help. She'll not be home from work yet. Now what say we have a drink of tea, and give over worrying for a bit. He'll turn up, lass, never fear. And he'll have a fair hearing when he does.'

'Bless you, Dad.'

She felt a sudden flush of shame. A fair hearing. But what would he think when it all came out? And what would her mother say; what would Jon think when Mildred Kenton let go her anger in words dipped in disgust?

But nothing her mother said nor did mattered, she told herself as calmly as she could. Nothing mattered but that she and Jon were married. No! That wasn't true. All she wanted was that Jon should be at the gate. *Now!* And he would be, because surely nothing else could go wrong with this day?

'I'm going to the gate again, Dad, and if he still hasn't come, I'm going to the village.'

'But what if he arrives, and you aren't here?' Bart called as she ran through the door.

But his daughter didn't hear him, so fearful was her leaving.

She was standing disconsolately outside the phone box when Bessie got off the Clitheroe bus.

'Hi! What's news, then?'

'Bess! Thank God! I've been trying to ring Jon, but the switchboard won't put me through to him!'

'But they very often don't when something is on.' Only then did her friend's distress register. 'Rosamund – has something happened? What's so urgent all of a sudden?'

'You mean you don't know about it? Two terrible explosions – one of them quite near! Dad and I saw the plane go over. I don't know how it missed us!'

'But there wasn't an alert in Clitheroe. The siren didn't go.'

'It might not have been a raid, but I've got to find out what's happened. What am I to do, Bess?'

'Calm down, for a start! You'd best come home with me – try again on our phone.'

'But what if your dad is in?'

'Then it's hard luck! Now tell me *slowly* what it's all about.'

'Jon was flying today and he shouldn't have been!'

'Well, of course he shouldn't! They were all celebrating their thirty in the pub last night. Dad said he saw them.'

'Yes, but there was an op on this morning. I went to the fence and Jon's Lanc passed me.'

'OK. So maybe it did. But They can't make anybody fly when they've done their tour!'

'Want to bet? *They* do just what they like! And don't say it was a different crew flying *J-Johnnie*, because I know it wasn't! Mick always waves as he passes – he knows where I stand. With his guns, sort of; gives them a half turn. How could a strange gunner know to rotate his guns like Mick always does, and where? It was them, I tell you, or why didn't Jon meet me this morning?'

'You had a date?' All at once Bessie, too, was afraid.

'Yes. This morning at Laburnum, at ten.'

'At *your* place! Have you gone mad?'

'We made up our minds that when he'd done his tour, we'd ask if we could get married. Dad knows about it, said he'd be on our side – well, give Jon a fair hearing. But Jon didn't show this morning, and that's how I'm certain he was flying.'

'And he hasn't turned up tonight?'

'Not this far.'

'How many went this morning?'

'I didn't count, Bess . . .'

'But you always count!'

'Not this morning. Didn't think it concerned me any more.'

'Well, it concerns us both now!' Bessie whispered. 'We'll try once more to get through, then you'll have to get yourself back sharpish, or Jon'll think you've stood him up!'

'Oh, Bess – bless you! Jon *is* all right, isn't he? Nothing has happened?' Her mouth was dry with fear and her tongue made little hissing sounds as she spoke.

'Of course it hasn't! Nor to Mick either!' She opened the door, calling, 'It's me, Mum! Just making a call . . .'

The switchboard answered at once. The Laceby Green operator was very quick dealing with local calls.

'Hullo? Can you put me through to the aerodrome, please?'

'Is that Bessie? I'll try, love, but they've been awkward all day. Don't know what's going on. Ah! There you are! Through, now.'

The operator answered at once and Bessie smiled reassuringly.

'Laceby Green eight-double-eight.' They never said RAF Laceby Green. Just the number.

'Can you give me the sergeants' mess, please?' Bessie drew in a deep breath.

'Could you tell me which one?' The voice was prim and correct. 'We have several.'

'Aircrew mess. Sergeant Jon Hunt.'

She smiled again at Rosamund, who was sitting on the bottom stair.

'I'm not able to put you through to that particular extension at the moment. Sorry.'

'Then who *can* I talk to, love? I only wanted a quick word – see if he's all right.'

'Then perhaps you should ring again later. Ask for the adjutant, or the padre. I can't help you, sorry. Not when it concerns aircrews . . .'

'Hell!' Bessie glared at the receiver. 'She says I'm to ring the adjutant, or the padre.'

'That's exactly what she said to me. I'm worried sick, Bessie.'

'Now don't start thinking the worst! She was only doing her job. She can't give out information willy-nilly – especially about crews. I suppose we're lucky they accepted the call at all. Rosamund! What's the matter with you? Stop staring like that! You look awful!'

'It's Jon. Something has happened, I know it!'

'*What* has happened?' Elsie Drake demanded from the kitchen doorway. 'Who were you ringing, Bessie?'

'The aerodrome. Where's Dad?'

'Not back from work yet. But what's the matter, Rosamund? Aren't you well?'

'She's worried, Mum. I'm worried, too. Seems they were flying today.'

'So they were. Very unusual. And there were two big bangs not so long ago, but the siren didn't go.'

'Rosamund is worried about Jon, Mum. I tried to get through, but the girl on the switchboard at the aerodrome said we'd have to talk to the padre or the adjutant if we wanted information about aircrews. I couldn't get anything out of her.'

'Then would you like me to try?'

'Would you, Mrs Drake? They might take more notice of you.'

'Right, then!' The older woman picked up the receiver with a flourish. 'That you, love? Give me the aerodrome again, will you?' She put a hand over the mouthpiece. 'Don't worry,' she said comfortably. 'Soon get it sorted. Oh, hullo, miss. I wonder if I might have a word with the adjutant? Or the padre? No, of course I don't mind waiting . . .' She smiled at Rosamund. 'Now what's upsetting you, lovey?'

'Jon was flying today, Mrs Drake, and he shouldn't have been. He didn't turn up tonight, either – well, he hadn't, when I left . . .'

'Then I'll see what I can get out of them, though I'm sure

you're worrying over much. Now into the kitchen, the pair of you, and put the kettle on. And shut the door!'

Just in case, she thought, even though the lass was likely worrying over nothing!

The receiver clicked in her ear; a voice said, 'I have the padre on the line. Go ahead please, caller.'

'Ah. Thanks! Good evening, Padre. This is Mrs Drake from Hall Lodge, Laceby Green. I wonder if you can help me? It's concerning Sergeant Hunt. I believe he was flying today . . .' She glanced at the kitchen door, then sat down carefully on the second stair up.

'Can't hear a thing,' Bessie said, ear to the door. 'Mum's whispering.'

'Why did she say we had to come in here, and shut the door?'

'Oh, you know what mothers are like!'

'I know what mine is like!'

'Are you sure you're all right, Rosamund – apart from getting yourself upset about Jon, I mean? You look washed out.'

'And wouldn't you be, in my shoes? Jon on ops when he shouldn't be; then a plane flies over so low I could've reached up and touched it! And then those explosions. I'm worried, Bess; worse than I've ever been.'

'You'll feel better with a cup of tea inside you. Make yourself useful and get me the milk, will you?'

'Is your mother going to be long?'

'As long as it takes. She can be very persistent when she digs her heels in.'

Rosamund pulled out a chair, wishing she didn't feel so dizzy. But it was her own fault. She hadn't felt like eating supper and she had been on the go all day. She was tired, truth known.

'I think I'd better be getting back home, Bess. Jon might be waiting and I don't want Mum to bump into him. Not until I'm there.'

She pushed back the chair as Elsie Drake walked into the kitchen.

'I – I was just leaving, Mrs Drake.' All at once, she didn't want to know what the padre had said, nor look into the older woman's eyes.

'That's all right, love. Bessie and me will set you on your way then.'

'No! It's all right. I've got my bike; left it outside the phone box. I'll be fine – truly.'

'Go and get Rosamund's bike, Bessie, then we'll be off.'

'You don't have to bother, really you don't!'

Out! She had to get out of here! Where she would go, she didn't know; all she wanted was to run and run, because she was afraid, now. Screamingly afraid. Something had happened, but she'd known all along that it had. Ever since the plane flew over, black and sinister, she had known.

'There now! Here's Bessie with your bike! You didn't ought to have left it there. Those lads from the aerodrome are devils for taking bikes.'

They set out for the lane, Bessie pushing the cycle. No one spoke until they were out of the village. Then Elsie Drake whispered, .

'The padre asked me to tell you, Rosamund, and I don't know how to say it –'

'*No!* Not Jon!'

'There's been an accident.' She tightened her hold on Rosamund's arm. 'Jon *was* on ops today. Seems they took a hit over the target. A miracle he ever made it back to Laceby. Flying on two engines, you see . . .'

'Please, I don't want to know!'

She tried to pull her arm free, to run away from bad news, from accidents; away from this awful day. But Bessie's mother held her tightly, then wrapped her gently in her arms. 'I'm sorry, Rosamund. I'd rather have done anything than tell you . . .'

'Jon's been hurt?' Rosamund whispered, her lips so stiff that it hurt to talk. 'And why are you crying, Mrs Drake?'

She knew why, yet still she had to hear the words.

'Not hurt, lass, he's –'

'Aaaaagh!' The ground beneath Rosamund's feet tilted, and she wanted to be sick. No! Not sick! She wanted to die before Bessie's mum told her Jon was dead! She began to retch, but it only made her stomach hurt more. 'I want to die, Mrs Drake . . .'

Bessie was weeping now, her arms around her friend, and they clung to each other despairingly.

'No, you *don't* want to die,' Bessie said fiercely. 'You only think you do!'

'Jon's dead, isn't he? Why can't I die, too?'

'It was a terrible accident, Rosamund. He'd nearly got it landed . . .'

'Don't! Please don't tell me, Mrs Drake? Not yet? Just go with me as far as Laburnum, will you?'

'Remember what she said?' Elsie Drake whispered on the way back to Laceby Green. 'She didn't say we were to take her home. To *Laburnum*, she said. I mean, it's *home* you want to go to, when there's trouble, now isn't it? And she wouldn't let us take her to the door either, and her that unsteady on her feet, poor bairn. But it's my fault. I should have found a kinder way of telling her, but what was I to do? I shouldn't have interfered. It should have been her mother who told her.'

'No. It was better coming from you. And there isn't a kind way to tell anyone that someone they love is dead. Don't take on, Mum?'

'What's to become of her, will you tell me? How will she live with it?'

'I don't know. She was really in love with him, really and truly; and he loved her. It was wonderful to see them together. It just shone out of them.' She reached for her handkerchief, then took a deep, shuddering breath. 'Can we slip into church on the way home, just for a minute? I can't think straight, Mum. It's as if I'm in a whirlpool, and all I want is to be still.'

'Think we'd better.' She reached for her daughter's hand and they walked on in silence. After all, she thought wearily, where else was there for a body to go when the world was such a terrible place and you didn't know how to cope with it? 'We'll say one for that poor young man and his crew, shall we, and for Dave and Joe, and all the soldiers in Normandy?'

'And for Rosamund?' Bessie whispered.

Especially for Rosamund . . .

FOURTEEN

R osamund stopped at six oaks. An hour ago, on her way
to Laceby, she had turned her head away because it was
there she and Jon always kissed, left the mark of their loving.
At six oaks too, Mrs Drake told her Jon had died. She knew
where, now, though she hadn't been to the exact spot; wasn't
yet able to say that last goodbye.

Now, too, she knew all that Bessie's mother had held back;
all the padre at RAF Laceby Green had said; that Jon might
have landed, crippled though his Lancaster was, had there not
been another bomber circling the aerodrome at the same time;
one flown by a wounded, inexperienced pilot. And if Jon
hadn't been forced to take avoiding action, been able to do
one more circuit, he might still be alive. Had there not been
two emergencies in the air at the same time, both might have
landed, the padre told Mrs Drake.

As it was, they touched briefly in mid-air; no more than
the briefest brushing of wing tip to wing tip, but that was
all it took. *J-Johnnie* had deliberately, it seemed, hurtled on
towards the hills, avoiding Laceby village and the aerodrome.
The other Lancaster plummeted earthwards out of control.
Rosamund knew about that because she had been there; seen
it miss Laburnum Farm by the Grace of God, and nothing
else. At twenty minutes past six, on D-Day plus two, the
bomber *K-King* slammed into the ground a hundred yards
from a little boarded-up house called Fellfoot. Seconds later,
J-Johnnie crashed into the hillside, half a mile away. Two crews
died that early June evening, the pilot of *K-King* flying his first
operation; Jon on his thirty-eighth. They had been to bomb

a rocket-launching site at St-Martin-le-Mortier, in France. A daylight, precision-bombing attack. But that was a lifetime ago, and now it was D-Day plus seven, and she had missed two periods.

The letter from Jon's aunt had forced her to drag herself out of her despair; out of the misery of missing him, wanting him, knowing she would never see him again. Nor touch, nor kiss, nor give herself to him. And even though haymaking had started in Wolfen Meadow; even though they were desperately short of labour, she had gone to the village without telling her father.

> . . . Please, Rosie, get in touch? I do so desperately need to hear from you. Is it possible for you to ring? All I know is that Jon's commanding officer wrote, telling me as little as they need. It would comfort me to know more; speak to you . . .

It was why she must see Mrs Drake; ask how much she had really been told, how much she held back, that day she'd spoken to the padre.

'Rosamund, lovey . . .' Elsie Drake had held her closely. 'Sit you down – you'll have a cup of tea?'

'Please. If you can spare it. I want you to help me,' she'd said without preamble. 'Will you tell me exactly how it was; everything the padre told you and not leave anything out? I've got to come to terms with it, you see. I didn't want to. The day I found out, I'd made up my mind to die, too. I didn't know how I was going to do it, but I'd think of something, I thought; something easy, without too much pain . . .'

'Now stop such talk! Of course you can't face things now; don't want to go on living! But it isn't the same as wanting to take your life! Just think on – there'll be young men dying this very afternoon in Normandy, who would do anything on earth to stay alive!'

'I'm sorry. I suppose I had to tell someone I'd thought about it. I won't do it, though. I'm not brave enough. It's just that I don't know how to cope. I know I must try to accept it, but the bombers are always there, reminding me that I won't see Jon ever again. And forever is such a long time to be without him.'

'Eh, Rosamund! If I knew words that would help, I'd say them. But I don't know any, except sorry. And sorry is poor comfort when a lass is near heartbroken.'

'But you *can* help,' she had said eagerly. 'You can tell me everything the padre said to you, not just the kind bits. I want to ring Jon's Aunt Lottie. She wrote to me; asked me to get in touch. She brought him up, has a right to know how it really was.'

So they had sat together on the sofa, arms linked, and Elsie Drake told her what the padre said that late afternoon on the phone; that by his skill – and bravery – Jon had avoided crashing on the village or the aerodrome, even. Done it without thought for himself; that the crew deserved a medal; would probably be given one. Posthumously.

'So that's what the padre told me. All of it, Rosamund. Are you brave enough to tell it to Jon's aunt? You look so pale and poorly, as if the next puff of wind could blow you over. How has it been at home?'

'All right, I suppose. The night I found out I went to bed and bolted the door, and wouldn't open it. I stayed there all next morning, but I knew I had to help Dad. Mother went on and on at me; about how dreadful I looked and that she'd told me, hadn't she, that no good would come of carrying on with *that airman*. She knew Jon was dead, though I don't know how. I hadn't actually told them.'

'Bad news always travels fastest, lass. And I know you and your mother never saw eye to eye over Jon, but if you ever need to talk to someone, there's always me and Bessie. Now drink that tea. Is your head bad? Do you want an aspirin?'

'No thanks. And I'll have to go, when I've had this. I shouldn't be here, really. Dad has started haymaking, so I'll have to get back for milking. I'll ring Jon's aunt tonight; there'll be more chance of catching her in later on.'

'Then drop in and have a word with Bessie, when you do. I hope you won't have too much bother getting through. A trunk call, will it be?'

'Yes. She lives near Chester.'

'And you'll not get yourself too upset, will you?'

'I'll try not. I've never spoken to her before, though I've had some lovely letters from her. She's good with words. She writes for newspapers . . .'

'Then why not phone from here? You might have to wait a long time outside that phone box. Bessie was only saying this morning she ought to come up to Laburnum to see how you were getting on. Kept putting it off, though.'

'I'll see her tonight, tell her. And I'd like the use of your phone. Thank you for being so kind, Mrs Drake.'

'Kind!' she'd snorted as she stood at the front parlour window to watch Rosamund ride away. The lass looked so badly it would bring tears to your eyes! All she needed was a bit of tenderness, though she wasn't likely to get it from that mother of hers!

'She's a witch, y'know!' hadn't Bessie once said, and she'd told her daughter to watch what she said, and that there were no such things as witches!

'Want to bet? You ought to look into her eyes, our Mum! Three hundred years ago, she'd have been in big trouble!'

A tear ran down Elsie Drake's plump cheek. She was so sick and tired of this war; wanted her sons back home alive.

'Poor little lass,' she'd whispered.

'Where have you been, Rosamund! How could you even think of taking yourself off when your father's up to his eyes in hay?'

'I've been to Laceby and I shall be going back again about eight, Mother.'

'To see the Drake girl! Well, you're not to go!'

'I'm going to ring Jon's aunt. I had a letter from her yesterday, and she asked me to.'

'So who were you with this afternoon?'

'Mrs Drake.' She said it tonelessly, her back turned on her mother's anger.

'I see! There's more work here than we can cope with, yet you go gallivanting off. You can't keep away from those Drakes. What has got into you, girl?'

'Nothing, Mother. And would you mind not going on and on? Isn't it enough that you got what you wanted? Serve him right, you said, if his plane crashed. Well, it did, and still you're not satisfied! You haven't once said you were sorry; not one kind word have you offered!'

'So you want me to go round like you, I suppose? Oh, but I wish you could see your face! And don't ask for sympathy from me. I warned you, but you knew best! Well, now you'll wish you'd listened to me, so pull yourself together, miss! There's a war on, or had you forgotten?'

'No. Nor ever likely to, Mother.'

She said it quietly, evenly, holding tight to her feelings. But had Mildred Kenton looked into her daughter's eyes, she would have seen such hatred there that even she would have been afraid.

Elsie Drake knelt in the small front garden, weeding. On the doorstep sat Bessie and Rosamund, fingers entwined. It was too beautiful an evening to stay indoors, waiting, and the door had been propped open so they could hear the phone at the bottom of the stairs when it rang.

Once, Rosamund had jumped to her feet to answer it, but it was only the operator at the telephone exchange, saying how sorry she was to be so long getting the Little Sellow number, but Trunks had gone mad, she sighed, since the invasion started. She would do her best to get through, though . . .

'You wouldn't think,' Bessie murmured, eyes closed, 'that there is a war on.'

The evening was warm, and sunny still; wallflowers and the red rose that climbed round the front door spilled sweetness on the air. The sky was blue, and empty of bombers; on the railings, overlooked by the iron snatchers, a thrush sang.

'Then pretend there isn't,' her mother sighed. She often pretended the war was over, and how it would be when her sons were sent home from the Navy – and it please God they would be.

Sometimes in her daydreamings, Joe arrived first, a civilian again, to be followed three weeks later by Dave; sometimes they walked up the village street together, kitbags on shoulders, shoe toes kicking flapping bellbottom trousers. Once, Dave arrived with a parrot on his arm; another time, Joe had a Wren in tow – one wearing black silk stockings!

Let's-pretend cheered her up when she was low, when no letters had arrived for two weeks, or when she was seriously short of tea or lard, and the meat coupons all used.

She held up a dandelion root, asking if they'd ever seen one that size, and wouldn't Hitler be glad of it, it being common knowledge that the Germans made coffee out of dried acorns and dandelion roots!

It was then the phone rang again and Rosamund got to her feet almost reluctantly, because she knew that this time Charlotte Martin would be on the other end of it, and she didn't really want to talk to anyone about Jon; especially not to someone who loved him, too.

'Your call on the line, now. Go ahead, please,' the operator said triumphantly.

'Miss Martin – Aunt Lottie? It's Rosie . . .'

'Oh, my dear, how good of you to ring! I hoped you would! How is it, for you?' Her voice was soft and sad.

'Just the same as for you. Sometimes I'm angry, sometimes I don't believe it, sometimes I start crying and can't stop.'

'Yes. That's the way it goes. How was Jon – when –'

'Last time we were together? It was nine in the morning and he'd just finished his tour of ops. We sat by a pond, and watched a dragonfly. We were very happy.'

'Good. Is it hurting too much to talk to me, Rosie?'

'No more than it hurts you. He should have been grounded, but there was an urgent op; in daylight. I'd better not mention place names on this line. And he'd have landed just fine, only there were two of them, shot up and trying to keep enough height to land decently. Neither of them made it. The padre at the aerodrome told us how it was. I miss him so, Aunt Lottie.'

There was a small silence then a voice said briskly, 'Now when are you going to come and see me? There'll be times when you can – even on a farm. Will you come? I'd be so glad, if you would.'

'I'd like that. I'll try. What I really want to know is . . .'

Another small silence, then: 'Where is Jon now, you mean?'

'Yes.'

'He – he came home three days ago. The RAF was very good about it, very respectful. They brought all his things, too.'

'Did you – what did he look like?'

'I didn't see him. The coffin was sealed. It was two days ago . . .'

'The funeral?'

'Yes. It's a lovely little churchyard. He seems at peace.'

'Oh God! Why are we talking like this?' Tears choked in her throat. 'Why are we being so civilized? I wake up, mornings, and all I can think is that it's another day without him!'

'Rosie – I know how it is. Guy and I were going to be married. Just ten more days and he'd have been on leave for our wedding.'

'I'm sorry! You *do* know! Twice it's happened to you! What are we going to do?'

'Just keep loving him – loving them both. It would be such a waste of two beautiful young lives if we forgot. It does get better, Rosie. You never forget, but the remembering doesn't hurt so much.'

'I haven't been yet to where it happened. I know where it was, and I *will* go. I'll write and tell you about it when I do.'

'Jon believed in reincarnation. Did he tell you?'

'Yes. And I believe now. I've got to. Maybe next time around we'll be luckier.'

'Try not to get too upset, dear. Ring me any time things get bad, will you? I do understand. And keep writing, won't you? For Jon's sake, don't let's lose touch?'

'We won't. I promise. And next time we speak, maybe it won't be so bad.'

'Not quite so bad. I'll say goodnight, now. God bless you, Rosie.'

'And you, Aunt Lottie. I did so love him. We were both so happy together that morning. I want you to know we were happy.'

'Yes. And I'm glad. Take care . . .'

Rosamund sat unmoving for what seemed a long time, taking in great gulps of air, dabbing her eyes, trying to stop the shaking in her limbs.

The telephone rang again. It was the lady at the telephone exchange, telling her how much the phone call had cost.

'You did ask me to let you know. Two and six, it was.'

'Thank you very much.'

The front door opened slowly. 'You all right, Rosamund?'

'Fine.' She dipped into her pocket, taking a shilling and three sixpenny pieces from her hand, laying the coins beside the phone.

'How was it?'

'She was lovely, Bess. She understands, you see. It happened to her, too, in the last war. And I'm sorry, but I can't seem to stop crying.'

'It's all right. Here – sit by me, and I'll give you a hug.' Bessie was crying, too, and they rocked, arms entwined, on the doorstep.

'If that pesky Hitler was here now,' Elsie Drake, still on her knees, brandished the six-inch long dandelion root belligerently; 'if he was to walk up that path, I'd stick this thing right up his left nostril! And be damned to the rations! I'm going to make us a drink of tea!'

She hurried indoors so they might not see that she too wept with them.

'And where do you think,' Mildred Kenton held up the envelope with 'On His Majesty's Service' stamped on the top, 'this thing has been until now?'

'What is it?' Rosamund did not want a confrontation tonight.

'It's been in the postbox all day; the paper, too! Left there!'

'Sorry.' She hadn't collected the mail or the newspaper this morning; simply hadn't bothered. 'Is it important?'

'Of course it's important! Read it! From the Air Ministry!'

The letter was brief, and addressed to her father, saying that since they had not been able to make contact by telephone, they would assume that Wednesday, 14 June at 1030 hours would be a convenient time at which to call. It was signed by T. J. Thomas (Group Capt. RAFVR) and by Colonel George G. Murray (USAAC).

'What can the American Army Air Corps want with Dad?'

'How might I know? If we wait long enough they'll likely tell us! And how you had the gall to take yourself off – *twice* – to the village when your father doesn't know which way to turn, I don't know!'

'I had to, but I'll make the time up tomorrow.'

'Then in that case, you can start now! There's a bottle of tea on the cold slab; take it to your father, and ask him when he's going to be finished for the night.'

Bart Kenton had just unharnessed the horse when Rosamund got to Wolfen Meadow. 'I'm sorry, Dad, for going off today.' She sat down beside him. 'Won't happen again.'

'You had your reasons, happen.' He took a long drink of the cold liquid, wiping his mouth with the back of his hand. 'Did your mother tell you about the letter?'

'The one I didn't collect? I can't for the life of me think why an American should be interested in you.'

'Not me, Rosamund; more like Laburnum Farm. I did hear they've been asking around Laceby for temporary billets, but I'd got it into my head it was for the RAF. Happen they want your mother to take a few. Lord knows we've got beds enough for ten!'

'And does Mum think that's what it'll be about?'

'She does, and she isn't best pleased!'

'I can well imagine.' Strangers. Forces personnel billeted at Laburnum, even if only as sleeping quarters, was the last thing her mother would want. People in uniform, invading her privacy, bringing the war right into her house! 'Do you really think that's what it's about?'

'Don't rightly know, but if that's all they want, then we should count our blessings, lass. Things might be a lot worse.'

'Like – like what?' All at once, she was apprehensive.

'Like they took the farm next door, remember? Knocked it down. But we'll know soon enough. Tell your mother I'll be done in about half an hour. I've finished cutting; only the horse to see to.'

'He's a beauty.' She reached up to stroke the shire horse they had hired for haymaking. 'Wish we had one.'

'No call, especially now we haven't any arable land. But he's a fine animal; given the choice, I'd have horses before tractors any day of the week. I'll stable him at Laburnum tonight; don't suppose you'd care to walk him back for me, in t'morning? Or ride him?'

'To Hawkhill Farm? I'd like that.'

'That's settled, then. I'll not be long. It's been a good crop, this year. Let's hope the rain keeps off till we get it dried and stacked.'

'I'll make it up to you tomorrow, Dad.' She kissed his cheek as she left, ears straining for the sound of aircraft engines.

But the evening was still, and tranquil. Here in Wolfen, she thought, you might even be forgiven for imagining, for just a few moments, that the war never was, nor had been. Not until you looked down on the sprawl. And anyway, she sighed, the war *was*, and would be, for a long time yet; that same war that gave her Jon, then snatched him from her.

The searing pain took her and she closed her eyes and hugged herself tightly, making little keening sounds, trying not to give way to tears again, thinking instead about the Group Captain and the Air Corps Colonel.

She didn't know why they were coming to Laburnum; didn't care, unless it was to tell her that what happened a week ago hadn't happened at all and Jon was a prisoner of war, Somewhere in Germany.

But things like that didn't happen; not to her, not to anyone. Jon was in the churchyard of a little Cheshire village now, and she would never see him again. All she had to exist on for the rest of her life were memories, and the blessed certainty that she carried his child.

Sprog. Something to remember him by.

When she walked across the yard she was dismayed to find her mother, arms clasped tightly round her chest, sitting on the back doorstep. She moaned softly, her lips moved silently, her eyes were wide and fear-filled.

'Mother! What is it? Did you fall? Are you hurt? Come inside.' Gently, she guided her to the kitchen.

'Fall? Wish I had – broken my neck! But I told you, didn't I; told you both but you'd neither of you listen! Well I was right!' She began to pace the floor, feet slamming. 'It's started – the secret weapon! There were ten of those rockets launched, it said so on the news, and four of them got through to London! They'll be here before so very much longer, aimed at that aerodrome!'

'Are you sure? Four on London?'

'Do you think I'd make it up, then! What am I to do?'

Her voice rose hysterically higher. She looked like a caged animal, trying to escape, yet not knowing where to run. She looked, Rosamund thought, all at once coldly dispassionate, like the selfish woman she was and only a slap to her face would stop the wild blubbering. She longed to raise her hand, but instead she said softly, 'Jon was killed trying to knock out one of those launching sites, did you know that?'

'Then he wasn't much good at it, was he?'

'Mother! You – you *bitch*!' She lunged at her, pushing her backwards into the fireside chair. 'You. You. *You!* Selfish through and through! Well, do you want something to worry about – to *really* worry about?' Her eyes flashed anger, her voice was harsh with contempt. She looked down on her mother and the sight of the wild-eyed, cowering woman gave her pleasure. 'I'm having a baby, Mother. Jon's baby! It'll be born in January, and I don't care. *I don't care!*'

A sudden silence took the room; a quiet so complete that the ticking of the clock sounded loud and menacing as hatred flashed and snapped between mother and daughter like forked lightning.

'Did you hear? Your daughter is pregnant and the child's father is dead; his plane crashed up the fell, where *you* wished it. So wish me dead, too, why don't you?'

'*Aaaagh!*' Mildred jumped to her feet, running out and

across the yard. 'Bart! Bart Kenton! Where are you? Where are you, I say?'

Rosamund followed her progress; saw the waving arms, the stumbling steps of a woman whose control had snapped, whose smug, narrow world had been ripped apart. And in her distress, she ran for comfort to a man she despised.

'*Witch!*' Rosamund hissed, then made for the narrow path that led to the creaking kissing gate and the signpost with no arms. Then she began to scramble and climb, her feet slipping on grass wet with early evening dew; up and up, to where she knew she would find the place where Jon had died; hear, perhaps, if she listened with her heart, his last goodbye.

This was the place, she frowned. It had to be, because all around heather and scutch grass and wild flowers had been trodden into a dark green pulp. There were ruts, too, deeply defined, showing that something heavy had been dragged away. A dead monster; a Lancaster bomber called *J-Johnnie*. After they removed the guns and the ammunition and checked that the bomb bays were empty, they would have removed the wings to make it easier to transport to the makers for repair. If *Johnnie* was considered repairable, that was. She stood there, blinking as the sun began to sink in the sky, disappearing behind the rise of Fair Snape, throwing long, purple shadows.

There was no sound but the call of curlews. Such a lonely, mournful cry in winter, but in summer it changed to a burbling croon as the cock called to his nesting hen that he was above her, and she was safe.

'Where are you, Jon?' she whispered, pleading for a sign, a sound, to let her know he was still there, waiting to tell her he loved her, would always love her, then whisper goodbye.

But he wasn't there, nor *J-Johnnie*, and though she searched the ground, there was nothing left to give her comfort. The RAF had taken away the stricken plane and then the ghouls had come; souvenir hunters, snatching even the smallest piece of metal, not leaving even a nut or a bolt. Jon and Tom, Dick and Harry and Mick, Mac and Sammy had been carried down to the road on stretchers to the waiting ambulances. Their faces would have been blanket-covered; perhaps only the heavy flying boots sticking out awkwardly. And the ghouls would have been there, watching; waiting for the moment the men who had been guarding the wreck piled into trucks and left, when a long transporter took away the fuselage and wings.

Then they would swarm to the place, exclaiming over their petty finds, with not one thought for the crew who had flown *J-Johnnie* there and back thirty-one times, nor for a pilot called Jon Hunt.

She turned abruptly. Jon wasn't here. It was why she was unable to weep, because that was why she had come here; to cry until her eyes were swollen and her throat hoarse. But there was nothing to weep about here; nothing left of Tom, Dick and Harry, nor of Mick, Mac and Sammy. And Jon wasn't here either. Jon was at Fellfoot, sitting on the big flat stone beside the pond. She began to run. She knew the fells and the tops. To the north-west from here she would find the little boarded-up house. It was still light; she would be able to see for another hour yet and even after that, the twilight would linger until past eleven.

It was not as far as she had thought to the pond near which another bomber had slammed into the hillside. The sun lit the bedroom windows of the little house called Fellfoot, shining them into a dazzle of coral. She turned away abruptly, because those windows were mocking her, reminding her that she and Jon had been lovers in those upstairs rooms. It made her wonder if she would ever be brave enough to go there alone. Not physically brave, because it was a kind little house with only happy ghosts in it. But whether she could be mentally brave was altogether different, because memories were harder to deal with than ghosts. Memories weren't just in rooms; they followed you everywhere and if you were lucky enough to sleep nights, they were there in your dreams, too.

The flat stone was cold when she sat on it. She leaned over to trail her hand in the water and it was cold, too. Everything was cold and hostile and lonely-making. Jon was not here either, and the dragonfly, if it was still alive, would be resting until morning came, clinging to a twig or stick, wings folded.

She wrapped her arms around her knees, then lowered her forehead to rest on them, closing her eyes, sending out her love, begging Jon to come. But here, too, were only memories of a golden morning – the dragonfly morning – when they watched a jewelled creature darting across the pond and she told him about the baby.

Such happiness. They had deserved it, she thought. Jon was safe for a year; would be able to have compassionate leave when Sprog was born, if they hadn't sent him abroad, instructing. And in her shining happiness she had deemed that impossible, being sure Jon would be given a UK posting, and she could be with him. They would find lodgings near at hand and she would be there for him to come home to every safe night.

Only there had been one more raid. In daylight. Had news come secretly from the French underground that one of the launching sites was ready to fire rockets; let loose the secret weapon? It had had to be a daylight raid with pinpoint accuracy, and one of Laceby's bombers was shot down over the target; two were hit, and limped home. *K-King* and *J-Johnnie*.

Why hadn't they tried to land on an aerodrome further south? Had they all voted to carry on back to Laceby? They trusted Jon. Skip would get *Johnnie* down! Even with a shot-up radio and two engines gone, he would do it! Only there had been an inexperienced pilot trying to land, too . . .

She gentled her hand across the smooth surface of the big flat stone, then got to her feet. She was cold, and tired. Best get back to Laburnum, face the music, because by now her father would know about the baby. She was sorry about that. She had intended to tell him first, then Bessie. But instead, goaded by her mother's cruelty, it had all come out in a rage of hatred.

She laid her hands on her abdomen as if to assure her child – her child, and Jon's – that it would be all right; that nothing her mother could do or say could harm it. Not even her mother's eyes, ill-wishing, could hurt it either, because she would wrap it round with love – her love, and Jon's – and it would be safe.

'Good night, my love – wherever you are,' she whispered.

Her father was at the iron gate, waiting for her. He looked tired and drawn and she said, 'Sorry, Dad. I'd intended telling you first.'

'It's true, then? There's a baby on the way?'

'Yes. Jon was coming to tell you both, but instead he was flying. You know the rest.'

'Your mother has taken to her bed. She says she wants nothing to do with you if what you say is true. You weren't just saying it to hurt her, Rosamund?'

'No, Dad. Do you want me to leave?'

'That I don't, but your mother says you'll have to; there are places, she says, for people like you. I'm sorry, lass. It's been a long day. Happen when the men have been in the morning, we can all talk about it without losing our tempers.'

'But there isn't anything to talk about,' she whispered, placing a hand over his. 'I won't give the baby up for adoption, if that's what she thinks I'll do. Go away with my shame, will I, then leave the baby behind for some other woman to take? No, Dad.' She tucked her arm in his, guiding him towards the house. 'I'm sorry if I've shamed you and I'll do anything you tell me to, to make up for what I've done. But I'm keeping the baby – even if I scrub floors for the rest of my life.'

'We'll talk about it in the morning,' he said doggedly.

'I'll keep out of her way, as much as I can. I won't look for trouble. And I'll keep out of the village when I start to show.'

'Have you told Bessie?'

'No, Dad. But let me make you a drink and a sandwich.'

'Aye, I could do with something inside me.'

'I love you – you know that . . .'

'I know it – and your old dad loves you – as much as he's allowed to.'

'You'll be on my side, then?'

'As far as I'm able, Rosamund. Now let's leave it, shall we? I haven't rightly taken it in yet. But tomorrow's another day. Let's see what tomorrow brings?'

FIFTEEN

Rosamund called the horse to a stop, leaning against it to manoeuvre it sideways onto the grass verge, placing herself between it and the oncoming car.

The camouflaged car, driven by a woman sergeant, slowed to a crawl and Rosamund held up a hand in thanks.

'All right, old man.' She patted the neck of the huge shire horse. 'Walk on, then.'

That, she thought, would be the group captain and the colonel, ten minutes early. She was glad that by the time she returned they would probably be gone.

She'd got up early and had started milking by the time her father walked into the shippon. She'd smiled, nodding briefly, then looked down at the pail of milk. She hoped he wouldn't want to talk. There was big trouble ahead, she knew it, but not just yet; not until the men had been and gone.

She had been sick again this morning; had run, hand on mouth, head down, to the corner of the cow pasture and vomited into the hedge bottom. Three months, didn't they say it lasted?

'Will you take the horse back to Hawkhill after we've had breakfast, lass?' Her father was standing at her side in the shippon. 'Your mother isn't very well; says she's stopping in bed and wants nothing to do with those men from the RAF.'

Nor with me, either, Rosamund thought, though she had the sense not to say it.

'You'll need breakfast, Dad. I'll make you some before I leave. Will something cold be all right?' She couldn't face the frying pan.

'Something cold will do nicely.'

'When I get back, I'll go straight to Wolfen – start turning the hay, will I?'

'If that's what you want, lass. Are you all right?'

'As right as I'll ever be, Dad.' She stopped pulling and looked into his face; his kind, bewildered face. 'And I'm not going to act up, make any bother. I know we did wrong, Jon and me, and I know there'll be things said at chapel and in the village when it all comes out, and I'm sorry.'

'You aren't the first and you won't be the last,' Bart sighed. 'But one thing at a time, eh? Happen when your mother's feeling better and those men have gone, we'll all of us sit down, civilized, and see what's to be done.'

'Yes. It'll have to be talked about and I'll go away somewhere if that's what you think best, so there's as little gossip as possible. But if the baby isn't welcome, then neither am I. I'm keeping her.'

'Aye, lass. You said. Though how you'll manage, I don't know.'

'Nor me. But one thing at a time, eh, Dad?'

'You're right.' Briefly he had touched her shoulder, then shrugged into his milking coat and no more had been said between them.

When she had taken the churns to the standing, Rosamund was surprised to see her mother, washed and dressed and wearing a clean apron.

'Do you want breakfast?' she'd asked, arranging knives and forks without looking up.

'No thanks. I'll just have a slice of bread – dry, if you don't mind, then I'll take the horse back.'

'It'll want feeding, first . . .'

'Yes. I'll see to it.' But even so, she would be well out of the way before half-past ten. And maybe, when *They* had been and gone there might be other, more urgent things to talk about than what to do about a girl who'd got herself pregnant out of wedlock, and didn't have a man to marry her and make it decent. Because those men weren't on the lookout for billets. She had given it quite a bit of thought and couldn't believe that it took two fairly high-ranking officers to tout for accommodation, personnel for the use of, when lesser ranks could have done it every bit as well. Trouble was, she didn't care what they wanted. All she worried about was when they left, because that would be when hell would be let loose, over the baby. Her mother would want her pound of flesh!

She passed six oaks with her head held high, then took the fork that branched left, and up a steep incline to Hawkhill, a farm more isolated than their own.

'All right, old lad?' Just a steady, half-mile climb to the farmhouse, then straight to Wolfen meadow with a hay fork so she needn't come face to face with her mother again until it was time to eat.

Why wasn't Jon here? Why did They send him on that last op? And how was she to face life without him?

She squared her shoulders, then laid a hand on her abdomen. They would make it, she and Sprog. Somehow.

If she had thought to slip away to the hayfield unnoticed, it hadn't worked, Rosamund thought as her father waved to her from the kitchen doorway.

'I was going to Wolfen, Dad.'

'No! Leave it! Come and talk to your mother.'

'Won't it wait? Isn't the hay more important?'

'Come inside.' He took her arm, urging her to follow him. 'Your mother's in a right tizzy. I'm not right sure what I'm to do with her!'

'Go to Wolfen, Dad. It's me she wants to talk to. We'll thrash it out between us.'

'No! Not *you*! It was those men did it!'

'But what happened? What did they say to upset her?'

Her mother did indeed look ill. She lay in the kitchen chair, eyes closed, her face ashen.

'Mother! What has happened?'

But Mildred Kenton was past speaking and turned her head from side to side. She looked, Rosamund thought, like a helpless, newborn kitten, eyes still blind, mewling for its mother.

'You'd better sit down, lass – if you want it in a nutshell and straight between the eyes, like they gave it to us, that is! They want Laburnum, Rosamund! We've got a month to get out!'

'*Dad!*' Her cry was one of disbelief. 'They *can't*! Haven't they taken enough?'

'It isn't the house; it's the land. The kettle's boiling. Make us a mashing of tea? Happen a drink might help your mother.'

Like an automaton, Rosamund reached for china mugs, the brown teapot, the caddy. Taking Laburnum Farm? But what could They want it for? She poured water into the pot as carefully as her shaking hand would allow. And where were they to go? What would become of the livestock? And the hay! They'd only cut it yesterday!

'I don't believe any of this.' She stirred the teapot noisily. 'I mean – this morning we had a home and land. Then two men come and tell us to get out! Where will we live? Where will you work, Dad?'

'They can put us in the workhouse as far as I'm concerned!' Mildred found her voice. 'If I can't live here, I'd be better off dead!'

'No you wouldn't, Mildred! Pull yourself together! It isn't the end of the world. They'll give us Laburnum back when they've finished with it.'

'I won't let them take my house, Bart Kenton!'

'You can't stop them! *They* can do exactly as They please. We've got four weeks, that's all, and we'll have to be rid of the livestock a week before that. All those years,' Bart choked, 'building up a pedigree herd for it to end up in the cattle market!'

'Stop it! I can't stand any more!'

'Tea, Mother? Tea will help. Sit up straight, and drink it.' Rosamund wrapped her mother's fingers around the mug, guiding it to her mouth.

'Nothing will help!' She pushed aside the mug and hot tea slopped on Rosamund's arm. 'All I want is to wake up and for someone to tell me none of this has happened; that my daughter hasn't got herself into trouble and those men aren't going to turn us out of Laburnum!'

Yes. She would go along with that, Rosamund thought bitterly; would like nothing better than to awaken to a dragonfly morning, and Jon at her side.

'Your tea is beside you, Mother. Don't knock it over.' She placed the mug on the hearth. 'Come outside, Dad? We've got to talk.'

Taking a mug in either hand, she pushed open the door with her foot, crossing the yard to the pump trough, indicating with a nod of her head for her father to sit beside her.

'Tell me? Right from the start!'

'Your mother – she'll be all right on her own?'

'She'll do. What I want is to hear about it without all the drama. Drink your tea, then tell me. And I'm sorry, Dad, that you've got all this to put up with on top of everything else.' She touched his hand as she gave him the mug, lingering her fingers on it briefly. 'There must be someone we can appeal to?'

'There isn't. No appeal. They want the keys in four weeks. I wish I'd had the shotgun handy. I don't know who'd have got it first: me, or them!'

'Please tell me?' She was shaking, and all at once cold.

'Well, they arrived – polite enough . . .' The American had been almost friendly, offering his hand. The RAF officer, Bart remembered, had merely nodded and said they wouldn't come in, thanks. They had merely come to deliver – *this*.

'*This* was a requisition, lass! Laburnum Farm, it amounted to; but you can read it for yourself later.'

'But didn't they say why? Surely it was a bit more than "Get out. We want your place"?'

'They didn't stop long – ten minutes – and most of that went in calming your mother down. What it amounts to, as far as I can see – and I was asked, *told*, to say nothing yet – is that the RAF is clearing out.'

'Leaving Laceby Green!'

'Aye. And the Americans are taking over the aerodrome. The colonel called it an *airfield*; said there'd be those big ones coming. B-17s or B-24s.'

'Flying Fortresses and Liberators . . .' Rosamund's mouth was making clicking sounds when she spoke.

'Something like that. Anyway, they need longer runways, so –'

'So when they've extended them, the north/south one will end up at our cow pasture gate!' The thought hit her like cold water thrown in her face and she said, hoarsely, 'Oh God! They won't pull Laburnum down? It won't go the same way as Fellstead Farm did?'

'They told me not. The house is much higher than the cow pasture, the land rises all the way to the paddock, but you don't need me to tell you that.'

'No.'

'That particular runway is to be extended at the other end. Laburnum won't cop it. It's the east/west one they'll be concentrating on, if you ask me. But our house'll still be too near to big bombers that could overshoot . . .'

'So we're to be cleared out for our own good?'

'Our *safety* the American said. Happen they'll find a use for the house, but I don't reckon it'll be knocked down. I hope not, lass. Would drive your mother out of her mind if that happened.' He rose to his feet, agitated. 'I'd better go to her.'

'No, Dad. I'll stay. Likely she'll want to talk to me about – well, other things, too. Just drink your tea, then get off to Wolfen. At least They've given us time to get the hay dried and stacked. But just tell me, so I've got everything straight before I go inside, where are we to go and what will *you* do? They couldn't make you work in a factory; all you know about is farming.'

'They left me a name and phone number I'm to ring if there are any queries or if I need help of any kind. And we won't be thrown onto the street. They'll find us somewhere to live – requisition it, he said, if they have to.'

'Another farm?'

'No. When I've got fixed up with a job they'll find us a place somewhere near, or that was how it sounded to me. But I wouldn't mind seeing to the hay, Rosamund.' He could think quietly whilst lifting and turning the fallen grass. 'Are you sure you can cope with your mother?'

'I'll do my best. Try not to worry too much?'

She watched him walk away, shoulders sagging, a man who had been pushed to the edge. Where was he to find work? A farm labourer again? Her mother would never live in a labourer's tied cottage. Hell! What a mess! At the kitchen door she touched her abdomen gently, and it gave her the courage to lift the latch.

'Mother! What on earth!'

Mildred Kenton stood at the sinkstone, washing dishes. Flushed cheeks apart, there seemed no trace of the shocked, helpless woman huddled in a chair, ten minutes ago. But for the redness on her arm, Rosamund might have believed that none of it had happened.

'Give me those mugs. I'll wash them. Then you'd better get to Wolfen, give your father a hand. I'll see to the dinner.'

Fear and bewilderment both took Rosamund as she tried to make sense of it all.

'Mother! It doesn't matter any longer about the hay,' she whispered. 'You know it doesn't!'

'It's the best crop we've had in years! Hay is scarce. We'll have no bother selling it! It'll fetch good money!'

'Look at me!' She didn't want to touch her but for all that, Rosamund placed her hands on her mother's shoulders, turning her about so they stood face to face.

'All right!' Suds dripped from Mildred's fingers and she made no effort to dry her hands. 'If I must.'

'Listen! Your daughter is having a baby! *They* want Laburnum Farm! Dad must find work and we'll have to move to only God knows where! What has got into you? You're acting as if nothing has happened!'

'Am I? Thought I was helpless with shock, did you? Well I'm not! I'm over it now, because when you and him went outside to whisper, it struck me that you thought you'd got the better of me – and you haven't. It was my money bought this house, my name is on the deeds, and because of it I can do as I want! So that lot can take Laburnum Farm. I can wait till I get it back! I'll leave, like they want us to and I'll make sure we're given the house that *I* want; somewhere well away from Laceby Green!'

'Oh, why must you always have your own way? Don't you think Dad and me might have a say in the matter?'

'No, I don't! You, Rosamund Kenton, have thrown away any rights you might have had to an opinion. You've got yourself into trouble and you'll do as I say! And so will your father!'

'You shouldn't be talking like this!' Rosamund's words were little more than a whisper. 'You're in shock. Dad and me don't know which way to turn we're so upset, yet all at once you don't seem to care!'

'Nor do I! I'll make sure I get what I want out of those Americans and I'll bide my time till this war is over and we can move back here again. It can't last all that much longer.'

'Not even though rockets are coming thick and fast? Aren't you afraid of them any more?'

Rockets, secret weapons, V-1s, call them what you like, were devastating London and little could be done against them, so difficult were they to shoot down.

'Afraid? No! The invasion troops will soon take the launching sites – it said so on the news. They're all near the coast. They'll soon be put out of action.'

Bewildered, Rosamund shook her head. For two years the secret weapon had haunted her mother, yet now it had become a terrible reality she was suddenly scornful of it! Her mother was unbalanced! She was *mad*!

'So what do you think we should do?' she asked, picking her words carefully, all at once afraid.

'Do? We'll do as I say! I'm not sure yet, but I'll think it out. Maybe all this has happened for the best. We can go further afield, where no one knows us and there'll be none to smirk over your condition. There'll be places you can go to have it, and women willing to adopt it, I shouldn't wonder. They say some are so desperate for a child in their arms they'll take anything!'

'Dad will want drinkings.' Rosamund was shaking so much she could hardly speak. 'You haven't emptied the teapot, have you?'

'No. Strain it off, and put some cold water to it. Turning

hay is thirsty work. Take it to him, then stay there; give him a hand. Dinner's at twelve thirty sharp!'

As she left for Wolfen Meadow, Rosamund turned in the doorway. One last effort; one more attempt to make sense of what was happening in this kitchen.

'I'll tell Dad you're a bit better, shall I, and that you're accepting it? But will you tell me, Mother, what has really made you change your mind?'

'Very well — if I must! I can wait. Like I said, the war is nearly over. I shall think of Laburnum every night when I go to bed and every morning when I get up. And I shall wish harm to everybody in it and every plane that takes off from over yonder. I can do it. When you want very much for something to happen, there are ways. I'll send ill wishes to this place. They'll be sorry they ever set foot in my house. I'll see to it they are!'

Rosamund turned and ran, feet pounding. Her mother wasn't mad! She was evil! She had ill-wished before, hadn't she? *I hope his plane crashes, and serve him right!* Dear God! Margaret Dacre and her mother, both!

She stopped, doubling up, gasping for breath, willing herself to be calm, to think of the baby. Her mother must not be allowed to harm it. And she couldn't, *wouldn't*, tell her father what had happened, what madness had taken place in the kitchen. Her father had had enough; his back wouldn't take another straw!

She sucked in gulps of air, holding them, letting them go in little huffs and all the time gentling her child, sending her love to it. Then, calmer, she picked up the bottle of cold tea and walked to the hayfield.

'I've come to give you a hand.' She shaped her lips into a smile.

'Why have you left your mother?'

'Because she told me to come here. All at once she's — she's fighting mad. Says the war will soon be over and we'll all be back again. I — I think she intends to get all she can out of the colonel.'

'Then all I can say is that it's a rum do!' He closed his

eyes and gulped at the bottle neck. 'You said she was all right?'

'She said dinner at twelve thirty sharp.'

'Well, I suppose we must be grateful for small mercies, though I don't understand her. I've been married to your mother all this time and I'm still no nearer to knowing what goes on inside that head of hers! I hadn't expected such an about-turn. She's up to something! She's got to be!'

'No, Dad. She's met her match; knows she's got to give in so she's trying to do it gracefully – and is going to make sure the Americans pay through the nose for taking her house! Even Mother knows when she's beaten!'

She went in search of a fork, using the time to think. But nothing made sense except the thought that stood out clearly in her troubled mind.

Her mother was wicked. Her mother could ill wish. Already Jon was dead. Was it to be the turn of his child next? Was her mother so evil she could harm her own grandchild?

Yes. She could, and would, and will try her damnedest to . . .

'Help me, Jon?' She looked towards the fells. 'Wherever you are, we need you. Desperately . . .'

'I'm going out,' Rosamund said flatly when supper had been eaten and the table cleared. 'To Bessie's.'

'I see.' Mildred took the iron kettle from the hob, pouring boiling water into the enamelled bowl in the sinkstone. 'Is all done?'

'The churns are in the cooling shed. I'll take them to the standing in the morning. And the hens are fed and the eggs wiped. Dad has seen to the pigs, and there's nothing more we can do in Wolfen until morning.'

'I suppose you're going to blab your head off about what happened this morning; give them something to gloat over in the village. Because once you tell the Drake woman, you might as well tell it to the town crier!'

On the surface, Rosamund thought, her mother looked ordinary; like any other middle-aged farmer's wife busy in her kitchen. But her movements were jerky and her eyes were anything but ordinary. They blazed bright blue, their lids lowered almost to a slit, as if no one must look into them for fear of what they saw.

'I won't be late. Is there nothing more I can do? Are you sure?'

'I'm sure. Get yourself off, but watch your tongue!'

'Don't worry. They probably know more about it than we do!'

Her father was bent over the pump trough, soaping his arms and chest, lathering his hair, and she stood until he had dried his face and blinked open his eyes.

'Going out for a ride?'

'Only down to the village. There's nothing to do, Dad. Why don't you have a sleep?'

'I'd thought to walk over to Hawkhill, settle up for the horse.'

The walk was too far for him, Rosamund frowned, after a day in the blazing sun, tossing hay, and milking cows and all the other jobs that happened every day on a farm; some of them twice a day. Maybe losing Laburnum would be a blessing; maybe to go out to work, get away from her mother more, would do him good – give him the company of other men, too.

But she knew he would be sad to leave. Laburnum Farm had been run down and neglected when they bought it. They had wondered, her father once told her, where first to begin, so much needed doing.

They had had three cows to start with. One in calf, and two milking. And they'd had a breeding sow, half a dozen piglets and a dozen hens. Times had not been bad though they had been lean, and sometimes hungry.

Now, when the herd was one to be proud of and their fields – those left to them – were productive, they must leave Laburnum Farm to fall into a decline again, and only heaven knew the liberties *They* might take with the farmhouse!

'Pass my clean shirt, will you?'

She took it from the door sneck on which it hung, unfastening the buttons, smiling.

'I don't know what's got into your mother.' Bart lowered his voice.

'Nor me. But I think we should take each day as it comes, and be thankful for small mercies.'

'Did she say anything about –' He stopped, embarrassed.

'About the baby? No,' she lied. 'You see, there's nothing can be done about that either. We'll work something out. You're not to fret.'

'Y'know, lass, it's times like this I wish I had a fill of baccy.'

'But you haven't smoked for years!'

'I know. Just a fancy. Off with you now, and don't be over late.'

He watched his daughter go and thought that if she lost any more weight there'd be nothing left of her that a puff of wind wouldn't blow over, poor little lass.

Then his thoughts returned to his wife, who had hardly been out of them since morning. Mildred storming and weeping and acting up was bad enough; Mildred quiet and brooding was altogether something else. He shivered, despite the warmth of the evening and the glow of his freshly towelled body.

Give him tears and tantrums any day. Those he could deal with, or ride out. But Mildred with a grudge he could well do without!

Rosamund turned her head as she rode past six oaks. She wasn't ready to remember anything about the place yet; good or bad.

She looked forward to seeing Bessie and her mother, though she hoped Mrs Drake would be out, or in the garden, because there were things to be said. Her friend must be told, had a right to know, about the baby. Pity she couldn't tell her about the Americans coming to the aerodrome, and the bombers, bigger than Lancasters. But they had been asked not to, so she must keep that bit quiet.

How it would be, though, when finally she said goodbye to Bessie, she dreaded to think. No matter where they went or how nice their new house was – even if it had electric lights, and hot and cold water in taps, and a telephone already installed – nothing could make up for leaving Bessie.

'Ooooh! Am I glad to see you, Rosamund! I've got such news that I'd almost decided to come to Laburnum – brave the old witch – to tell you!' Bessie laughed, holding wide the back door. 'Dad is on lates and Mum is at the WI, so there'll be no one to hear us. Come on in!'

'I've got news for you, too, Bess.'

'Right! Mine first,' Bessie laughed, when they had settled themselves on cushions on the front doorstep. 'I struck lucky in two queues this lunchtime. I got a lipstick, and five ciggies for Dad. And promise you won't tell a soul about what I'm going to tell you?' She dropped her voice, glancing round to make sure no spies skulked in the bushes.

'Promise,' Rosamund whispered back.

'The RAF is shoving off from the aerodrome! We're getting Yanks! How about that, then? Gum and Hershey bars and silk stockings! And you're not to tell a soul!'

'B-but how did you know? Who told you?'

'Dad's drinking pal at the pub. And he'll lose his stripes if it gets out he's told anybody, so keep it shut, all right?'

'I – I don't believe it!' Rosamund didn't. It should have been the last thing she'd have thought to tell Bessie, and now she knew she couldn't tell her about the baby; she really couldn't. All at once a voice warned her not to. Not just yet.

'So what's your news, Rosamund?'

'Exactly the same, would you believe!' Sorry, Bessie! 'And it's true, because we were told this morning. And promise you won't tell a soul –'

'But I know, idiot!'

'No. About us having to leave, I mean. Two officers came, this morning. It's how I know about the Americans. We've got to be out of Laburnum in four weeks!'

'*Whaaaat!* Flaming ruddy Norah! I don't believe it!'

'It's true.' Rosamund dashed tears from her eyes.

'But where will you go? And They *can't* move you out. Farming is war work. What will you do with all the animals?'

'Sell them. And Lord knows where we'll go. Don't tell, will

you, Bess – about us leaving, I mean? Not a soul. Not even your mother just yet?'

'Oh, Rosamund!' Bessie was weeping, too. 'You might be ages getting the farm back! We mightn't see each other for years!'

'I don't think we'll be going far – just far enough so that when people gloat, my mother won't be around to see it, or hear it.'

'But people *won't* gloat! Oh, I know your mother keeps herself to herself and lives in a gentleman's house, but no woman will be glad They've taken her home. They'll be sorry for her, especially as it's such a lovely old place.'

'Mother doesn't think that. When first they told her, she almost collapsed; then she pulled herself together and you'd think it had never happened! She's gone all quiet inside, and determined, sort of. But she frightens me. It's as if she's going to explode any minute.'

'A walking time bomb, eh? But what about you, Rosamund? Are things getting any better? You look so – so – poorly. You mustn't make yourself ill.'

'I'm all right.' That had been the time to tell Bessie about the baby, but instead she said, 'I'm not the only one it's happened to. I've got to learn to be without him.'

'I wish we were blokes,' Bessie whispered. 'We could go to the White Hart and get drunk!'

'Dry your eyes.' Rosamund dabbed her own. 'Your mother will want to know what we've been crying about when she gets back, and I'm not to tell anyone we're leaving, you see.'

'Your mother is barmy. Are you sure it's not her age?'

'Yes. And she isn't off her head, either. She's just plain wicked.'

'Well, I always said she was a witch, only there's no such thing.'

'Even though women around these parts were hanged for witchcraft?'

'That was three hundred years ago. We've got penicillin now, and fighters without propellers.'

'And flying bombs. Very civilized.' Rosamund sighed. 'But

set me home, Bess? Walk as far as six oaks with me? I'm tired and I have to be up at five for milking.'

At six oaks they hugged and said good night. Rosamund closed her eyes, and when she opened them, Jon wasn't there. He would never come to six oaks again. Stupid to think he would, or could.

'Do you think, Bess, that if I stopped eating, I could fade away, sort of . . . ?'

'Rosamund Kenton! Don't ever dare say such a thing again! Don't even *think* it! And I'm coming home with you. Someone needs to tell your mother you aren't well!'

'No, Bess! No! I didn't mean it! I'm tired, that's all. Hay-making, y'see, on top of everything else. I shouldn't have said that. Sorry.'

Of course she couldn't fade away; there was the baby to think of now, nurture inside her and in February, give life to. Jon's child was all that mattered – and keeping it safe from evil eyes.

'You'll always be my friend, won't you, Bessie? Even though we have to go away and no matter what you might hear, we'll still be close?'

'Of course we will, you daft hap'orth! And stop saying things like that or I'll start crying again!'

So Rosamund smiled, and whispered good night, and Bessie stood beside the oak trees and watched her friend out of sight.

Then she began to weep again and for the life of her, she didn't know why. Perhaps something had walked over her grave? Or Rosamund's?

'Oh, damn this war,' she sniffed. 'I'm sick, sick, *sick* of it!'

SIXTEEN

R osamund's nineteenth birthday passed almost unnoticed
save for a card from Bessie. Now it was July and the far
hills blazing golden with gorse, and the hay dried and stacked,
because St Swithin had been kind.

These were precious days; the last Rosamund would spend
at Laburnum Farm. Tomorrow, cattle trucks would take the
herd to market; would arrive at ten, allowing time to milk and
fodder the beasts for the last time. Yet any sentimental tears she
might have let fall would remain unshed because her mother
had claimed the final churns of milk for herself.

'Law or no law, I want that last milking; all of it! I shall put
it through the separator for cream and at least we'll have butter
to take away with us!'

Mildred Kenton had realized there would no longer be ample
milk, eggs and bacon; not when they lived in Skipton. They
would draw the same small amounts of food each week as other
people, and there would be no game from Ned Loftus; fewer
rabbit pies and no bowls of lard from pig-killing.

Yet food was the least of Rosamund's worries, or leaving
Laburnum Farm. Oh, she loved the old creaking house and
the view from the parlour window that stretched into forever.
It was the only home she could remember and no other house,
no matter how many modern conveniences it had, could ever
hold a candle to Laburnum.

She was being very sensible about it, for all that. Already she
was determined that when the time came to leave, she would
walk away without looking back. Jon had looked back, that
morning; had turned and waved, and because she'd thought

he was safe, she had waved back then watched him out of sight.

So when it was time, she would look at Laburnum Farm; at the red roses climbing past the kitchen window and up and up to peep in the bedroom she would have slept in for the last time. And she would photograph the front garden in her memory; poppies and white foxgloves, the hedge tangled with honeysuckle, then turn away for the very last time because she would never come back; not to where she had been so exquisitely happy and so heartbreakingly sad.

Yet even before that, she would say goodbye to the kissing gate; trail her fingers where Jon's hand had touched. And she must say goodbye to six oaks, because the furniture vans were taking the long way round and joining the Skipton road at Clitheroe. Not for anything would Mildred Kenton, sitting beside the driver, risk the stares of smirking Laceby folk. No one, she vowed, would know where they were going. As far as she was concerned, they would disappear from the face of the earth – until the time came to return, that was!

'Those Drakes mustn't know when we're going. I forbid it!'

'But I've got to say goodbye to Bessie!' Rosamund protested. She'd had more kindness from Bessie and Elsie Drake in the space of one day than she could remember her mother offering in the whole of her life.

'Just try it, that's all!' Mildred's eyes narrowed and Rosamund had turned away, in case there was a curse in them.

Then after six oaks, she would go to the steel-mesh fence at the bottom of the cow pasture; send her love to Jon in case some small part of him lingered there still. And she would imagine *J-Johnnie* lumbering past her, and Mick's salute.

Rear gunner to pilot. Just passed your milkmaid!

After that, if she could bear it, she would climb the hayloft steps to the gantry, empty now, the summer hay stacked in Wolfen Meadow with a tarpaulin over it, ready for the farmer from Whitewell to cart away.

She would *not* go to the place they had lain like gypsies and conceived a child, but she would unlock the door of Fellfoot one last time; look at the kitchen and imagine a rag rug on the hearth and an oak dresser with blue and white plates and copper jugs on it. And she would say goodbye to the rooms above in which they had been lovers.

The last goodbye, at nine o'clock exactly, would be on the very last morning. To go there would tear her apart, especially if she saw the dragonfly. Yet somehow she would claw back a small gleam of the shining happiness of the morning Jon returned from his thirty-seventh op; the morning she told him about the baby.

Five minutes she would stay beside the pond, then walk away and not look back, or her wish would be worthless; a wish that one day she might live in Fellfoot because a miracle would make it possible. Live alone with Sprog, who would run free as the wind and know when spring was coming because the buds on the weeping willow would begin to swell, pale green.

'I'm talking to you, miss!'

'Sorry. I was miles away – at Skipton.'

'I said I'm glad I don't live in London. Thought the war was nearly over, those people down there, yet now they're having to be evacuated all over again! It's about time our soldiers got to those launching sites and blew those rockets up!'

'I think that's what General Montgomery has in mind, Mother!' The flying bomb sites, everyone knew now, stretched inland between Calais and Dieppe and further along the coast, on the tip of the Brest Peninsula. 'But the Germans are fighting every yard of the way. They'll hang on as long as they can to keep the launchings going.'

'Have you got everything seen to – your books and things in boxes?' Abruptly Mildred changed tack.

'Yes.' Rosamund winced as a Lancaster flew low overhead, wondering how soon before the squadron left, and where it would go. But it mattered little, because in three days more the furniture vans would come, and the Kentons would be gone.

Her mother had insisted the removers pack everything so they would be liable for any breakages. What it would cost did not matter. The American colonel, eager to smooth the way for the Liberators that would one day fly from Laceby

Green airfield, had co-operated eagerly. And when her father was offered – *offered*, mind – a position as adviser to the Ministry of Agriculture and Fisheries at their regional offices, a house in nearby Skipton was found almost at once for Mildred's inspection.

'About time that lot at the Ag and Fish had someone there who knows a bullock from a cow,' Mildred said, mollified, because a small car was to be made available for Bart's use, 'and a sugarbeet from a swede!'

'It's what I would call a sinecure; a fob,' Bart had shrugged, wondering how he would abide going to work every morning at half-past eight in a car; wearing a collar and tie, an' all!

'Call it what you want! As long as that house meets my requirements, that's good enough for me!'

The Skipton house, Mildred discovered, had a small, square front garden, a front parlour, a dining room and a large kitchen and scullery. At the back was a wash house, a coal house, twelve square yards of grass and a Victoria plum tree.

'We shall need at least four bedrooms,' Mildred insisted, because not one piece of her furniture would she part with. There must be space enough to store it in the Skipton house, so she could keep her eye on it and have it there, to hand, the minute they moved back to Laburnum Farm.

Whatever she asked for, the obliging American made possible. Far more co-operative, she insisted, than the people from the Air Ministry. Colonel George G. Murray addressed her as Ma'am, had beautiful, old-fashioned manners; knew how to speak to a lady! And living in a doll's house in Skipton, she mused, would make a break for a couple of years from the everyday sameness of farming. Two years of living in a town would be just about enough to make her want to return to that sameness; back to her house and her seclusion. Indeed, there was only one cloud on her horizon of near-contentment: a daughter who had brought shame on the family and would have to be a mite less particular when it came to taking a husband. Unless they could keep it quiet, that was; get the child adopted so no one in Laceby Green need ever learn about the fall from grace.

'Have you told Bessie Drake?'

'What about?' How her mother's voice grated!

'You know what about!'

'I've told no one. Only you and Dad, and Jon.'

'*Him!* The cheek of the man!'

'Leave it, Mother! I don't want you to say things about Jon because if you do, I just might tell Bessie when I go to say goodbye to her!' she snapped, suddenly defiant.

'You will *not* be saying goodbye! No one is to know when we are leaving or where we are going. I thought I'd made myself clear.'

'You did, Mother.'

But she would write to Bessie, for all that; give her the Skipton address and the phone number. There was a telephone in the house, her mother had said, and what was more they would keep it, since the people at the Ag and Fish were to pay a proportion of the bill!

'Once the livestock has gone, it won't bother me when we leave,' Mildred grumbled. 'The sooner, the better – get it over with! And I shall make it plain to Colonel Murray that I expect the American Air Corps people to respect my home and not drive nails in all over the place, and keep the front stairs and the panelling in the dining room waxed and polished!'

'I'm sure they will, Mother.'

'You didn't say anything about us having to leave Laburnum?' Rosamund asked of Bessie later that night.

'Of course I didn't! I'm surprised you should ask! Anyway, when are you going?'

'Don't know.' She was lying to her best friend when she knew that tonight might be the last time they would sit in Bessie's little front garden, faces to the evening sun. 'I suppose,' she hazarded, 'it'll come suddenly, once we get everything settled.'

Yet everything *was* settled. Tomorrow, or the next day it would be and sneakily, because of her mother's stiff-necked pride.

'Then before you go be sure to let me know because I've

got something for you. I've been keeping it.'

'But I haven't got anything for you, Bess! I never thought about it, if I'm honest, because there's just nothing in the shops.'

'What I've got for you wasn't bought in a shop, and you're not to ask.'

A book Rosamund thought. One of her school prizes and very precious, because Bessie hadn't won all that many!

'We'll keep in touch, Bess? As soon as I know where we are going, I'll give you the address.'

Then she despised herself, because she was playing into her mother's hands by lying so.

'I'm having a baby, Bess,' she should be saying. 'My mother's glad we're going to Skipton, because she thinks she'll be able to keep it quiet and no one in Laceby will find out. But you're to tell *everyone*!'

Yet she wouldn't, couldn't say it. Best not rock the boat. She would have to fight to keep Sprog, she knew it; no use making things worse.

'Where will your father work?'

'I don't know.'

'Dad gets good money making aero-engines, but I can't imagine your dad in a factory. I like him, you know.'

'So do I. A lot. It's my mother I can't stand. Sometimes, Bess, I think you've been right all along – that she's a witch!'

'I didn't mean it!' Bess giggled nervously. 'I mean, if she really was a witch she would have hexed those men who came to take your house!'

'How do you know she won't; hasn't already?'

'Hey! Watch it!' Bessie had no wish to get herself further into trouble. She'd had enough black looks already from the mistress of Laburnum Farm! 'Let's talk about when the war ends, shall we?'

Once, it had been their favourite game. No more blackout, bombing, and the shops full of gorgeous things. And the two of them, buying clothes and lipsticks – no longer rationed, of course – like there was no tomorrow.

'What do you mean, Bess – when the war ends? It isn't ever

going to end for me. Do you realize that every day I shall get a little older, yet Jon will be young always. And had you thought I might live till I'm seventy?'

'*Seventy*, for Pete's sake!'

'Yes. And still in love with a pilot of twenty-three. Because there won't ever be anyone else but Jon.' She said it softly and without emotion, as if it were already a pointer to the rest of her life.

'Hush. Don't say things like that. They say that time is a great healer . . .'

'And you believe that, Bess?' The most cruel cliché of all!

'No. Not really. But I hope it won't hurt so much in time.'

'I hope so, too, but right now I want to be unhappy; I can't pretend I don't. And it's going to be hell, saying all the goodbyes; there are so many special places I won't ever see again.'

'I'll come with you if you like, Rosamund.'

'No. Thanks all the same. It's got to be just me and Jon.'

She was ashamed of the way the lies slipped out. She didn't mind lying to her mother, but she shouldn't be doing it to the only person she could really trust.

So why didn't she tell Bess about the baby? Hadn't she a right to know? Bess could keep a secret; even one like that!

'And I'll have to be getting back.' The secret would remain untold. 'Somehow I don't trust my mother. It's as if she's on a slow-burning fuse, and any moment there's going to be one almighty blow-up! She's given in too easily about them taking Laburnum. If she screamed and shouted and raved it would be more in keeping.'

'Oh, lovey, I'm going to miss you. When we say goodbye,' Bessie said shakily, 'let's make it into a giggle, shall we? Promise neither of us will cry, till afterwards?'

'Promise, Bess. And we'll keep in touch. We might even be able to ring each other up – if we can get through, that is. Walk with me as far as six oaks?'

'Course I will. And if you promise not to start crying

when we get there, then neither will I!'

'All right.' She would try to remember it as a happy kissing place, and not where she and Bessie and her mother had clung together, weeping. 'I'll have to get used to – to *things*. The worst thing about leaving Laburnum will be leaving Jon behind, really. Because I'm sure, you see, that he's still there, if only I knew how to find him. He believed in reincarnation, and so do I now. If only I could get on his wavelength . . .'

'Let him rest – for a little while, anyway. When the time is right and you can think more clearly, there'll be a way. Only don't go to any of those seances, will you? Just wait for Jon with – with –'

'With my heart?'

'Yes, love.' She linked her arm in Rosamund's. 'Oh heck, I'm going to miss you something awful!'

That, Rosamund thought as she had whispered good night to Bessie at six oaks, was one goodbye over, because she would not pass that way again. She had intended saying – with her heart, of course – 'I love you, Jon Hunt,' but she had not been able to. Instead, as she hugged her friend and whispered, ''Night, Bessie. God bless,' all she was able to do was think of the morning, that *last* morning, when he had turned and waved. She would never see this place again nor Bessie either, who said, ''Night, love. God bless you, too. Always . . .'

She ran off then because her voice had been wobbly; nor had she turned to wave. And when Rosamund saw the small, black van outside Laburnum Farm, she knew her instinct had been right.

Bye, Bessie. See you. One day – maybe . . .

'The van. Who does it belong to?' Rosamund demanded of her mother in the dairy.

'The removal people. They're here to see to the fragile bits. And they'll be here again in the morning to take the first load.'

'Of furniture? So you knew all along when we'd be going!' Once the livestock had gone, she should have known her mother wouldn't want to wait. 'Why didn't you tell me? You said three more days.'

'In the morning, there'll be two vans.' Mildred chose not to answer questions. 'The smallest will take the furniture we'll be using – for the sitting room and the dining room and the kitchen stuff, and beds. You'll go with the driver; see it unloaded, and put in place.'

'But I won't know where! I haven't seen the house!'

'The sitting room is at the front, the dining room at the back, and not even a fool could miss the kitchen and scullery!'

'Why are you doing this, Mother?'

'Because the sooner we go, the sooner we'll be back! And I haven't time to argue with you! I want to get this butter churned.'

'So what about the second van?'

'Me and your father will see to that. It'll be all the furniture that's got to be stored at the new house, because it'll be coming back here one day.'

'You've planned it all, haven't you, right down to the last detail?' So thoroughly, it would have done credit to the most efficient sergeant major!

'With the help of Colonel Murray.'

'So what time will we – will I – be leaving in the morning?'

'About ten. You can sit in front with the removal men. There'll be room enough. And wear your old clothes,' she added obliquely.

'Don't worry. I'll wear my baggiest trousers and sweater. I'm not showing yet!'

'I'm sure I don't know what you mean!' Mildred rotated the handle of the churn furiously, so the lump of butter inside bumped loudly. 'But you're being a mite too flippant about things, though you'll come to your senses before so very much longer! I'll see to it!'

'If you're talking about the baby, there's nothing to be said. Oh, I'll go away to have it – anywhere you want – but I won't leave it behind! If you don't want your grandchild, then you don't want me!'

'So how will you manage? Who's going to take in a girl

with a brat in tow, even as a skivvy! You haven't thought how serious it is, have you? You've got yourself into trouble and brought shame on us all. I'm glad we're leaving, for I don't know what I'd have done if it had all got out and we were the laughing stock of Laceby! So get out of my way! Go and think about it and start acting like a grown-up for a change!'

'There's nothing to think about. I'm keeping Jon's baby if I have to beg from door to door!'

'Oh, get out of my sight! You sicken me! You're no better than a street woman; a whore!'

'Whores do it for money. With me it was love. But you don't know about love, do you, Mother?'

So it was to be tomorrow. At ten. Rosamund stood at the little iron gate, pulling and pushing it on its hinges, listening to the creak. All was arranged. By her mother, to suit herself. But hadn't Laburnum always revolved around her mother's moods?

She gentled the gate with her hands, and smoothed the tops of the iron posts, because Jon had touched them. And because it was the last time she would stand here. And when she was near to tears at the enormity of it, she would walk down the narrow path that ran behind the outbuildings, and open the small door of the hay barn and sit on the gantry steps in case some small part of Jon was waiting there, too. And if he were not, she would cross the cow pasture – the empty cow pasture – and lace her fingers in the steel-mesh fence and call to him with her heart that she loved him and please not to leave her? Not completely?

Tomorrow there would be little to do; no cows to milk, no hens to feed nor eggs to wipe clean. And the day after, the auctioneer from Clitheroe would assemble all the farm implements in the foldyard: the tractor, the reaper, the ploughs and everything from the shippon and cooling house, down to the last stool and pail. They would bring a good price, her mother said, because such things were in short supply because of the war, and farmers had money enough now to buy what they wanted.

So tomorrow, she would get up at the same time; strip her bed and fold sheets and blankets tidily, ready to be loaded into the first van. Then she would go to Fellfoot, because if ever she was to find Jon, surely it would be there?

Then, at exactly nine o'clock, she would chain and padlock the back door, and go to the pond; to the big, flat stone to remember the dragonfly morning.

Tears began to hurt her throat, and she shut the little gate, then ran, head down, to the barn.

'Dear, sweet Jesus, how am I to bear it, will You tell me . . . ?'

The morning was gentle; exactly as it had been on D-Day plus two, when the rain had stopped, and the gales. For just a moment, when her alarm clock jangled her awake, Rosamund lay there, unwilling to admit that this was the day and that tomorrow morning she would awaken in a different room, in a different place, and would think at once about Laburnum Farm and how suddenly and thoroughly they had left it.

So she had four hours before her new life began; when her mother, free from farm chores, would busy herself getting things straight; walking to Skipton High Street and registering their ration books with a new butcher, a new grocer. And for a time, the novelty of switching lights on and off and having a gas stove and a telephone would please her.

Yet when she realized there was no one to telephone because she had few friends; when she remembered the view that stretched into forever and that once she had said she could walk right round the farm in her petticoat, and none would be any the wiser, things would be different!

So who would the scapegoat be then? Rosamund frowned. Her father, who would hate not being a farmer, or herself, who was carrying an illegitimate baby?

She pulled back the curtains, trying not to think that tomorrow or the next day, someone else would be looking at her beautiful view. Maybe, when the Americans came, Laburnum would be used as a billet, or maybe offices. Or perhaps they would just leave it to grow cold and lonely, and couples might creep in and make love.

She felt sad as she crossed the yard, for no tail wagged at her approach. The farmer from Whitewell had taken Shep, along with the hay; needed a decent yard dog, he said; was willing to take the creature off their hands. Dear old Shep, who hadn't once barked as they crept into the hayloft.

She managed, like someone only half alive, to unlock the back door at Fellfoot. She had not been afraid, had even thought it would be here she would find Jon, sitting on the stairs, perhaps, that led off the parlour. Or maybe he would be at the window; watching as she climbed the slope towards him.

But he wasn't there. She would have known had it been so; would have felt his warmth, his love, and the whisper, oh, ever so gently, of his lips against hers.

'Jon?' she called, wanting to hear his whistle, but her cry sounded strange and alone in the emptiness.

She ran down the stairs, through the parlour, and into the kitchen.

'Jon Hunt! Where are you?' She needed him to know she had been to say goodbye!

Yet all she heard was a bomber, flying low above her. Circuits and bumps. Perhaps tonight they would fly their final op from Laceby Green and there would be no one at the fence, nor at Laburnum farmhouse window, to count them out and wish them back.

And she was glad! In Skipton there would be no more chimney-shaking take-offs, no Shep to warn her that soon she would hear the first of the returning bombers. In the new house she would begin to try to forget. No! Never to forget, but to accept that she was alone until Sprog was born. Scrapofathing Sprog, Jon's child.

'Goodbye, little empty house,' she whispered. 'I really did want to live in you one day.'

With Jon and Sprog, of course, and however many more carelessly conceived children they might have had. If Jon hadn't flown that thirty-eighth op.

*   *   *

The big, flat stone beside the pond was cold, but it was only nine o'clock and the sun had yet to warm it, and the water of the pond.

She pulled her knees to her chin, then wrapped her arms around them. The willow was in full leaf now, and two wild yellow water lilies opened their petals to the sun like giant buttercups. A waterhen swam across the pond, its head poking and ducking, but of the dragonfly there was no sign.

Had it lived out its days? Had it flitted, golden and jewelled in the sunshine, a thing of brief beauty, like their loving? Was it golden and fleeting, and gone?

Here Jon waited for her the morning after his thirty-seventh op; here she told him they had made a child beneath a high, bright moon; here they began to make plans, because they had a year of tomorrows, and life was good!

'But you didn't come to Laburnum, Jon,' she whispered. 'That morning, at ten, you were on ops again, and that was the end of it . . .'

The pain was back in her throat. Every part of her ached; hurt inside at the place she had thought her heart should be.

'Darling, why did you leave me? We thought we had made it, but we loved too well, and the Fates were jealous.'

Now, it was over. Soon – in less than an hour – she would leave Laburnum Farm and the hills and the little creaking gate. And the hayloft, and Fellfoot, and the sound of bombers doing circuits and bumps. Only memories to take with her now. Yesterday was a dream recalled; today she was alone, save for the child inside her.

'Jon, where are you? Let me know you are still here, waiting? Give me a sign?'

But the willow did not move, nor the water lilies; nor was there even the slightest rippling on the surface of the pond to comfort her.

'Jon, *why*?' she whispered, but there was no one to hear her. Not even a curlew called.

This was it, then. She took the red rose from her pocket, picked from her bedroom window at sunrise, with the dew on it.

'Goodbye, Sergeant Jon Hunt.' She threw it reluctantly and it floated gently on the surface of the pond. 'See you, my darling – sometime . . .'

Rosamund sat between the elderly driver and the young, strong man who'd said he was waiting his call-up into the Royal Engineers. Leaving Laburnum had not been too difficult. She was glad she had schooled herself into accepting it; into not looking back.

They bumped down the dirt road, past the standing for the milk churns, then turned right at the armless signpost, taking the lane that would lead them to the junction with the Clitheroe road. There, they would turn left again, making for Gisburn, cutting out Laceby Green.

She stared ahead fixedly until she knew the fells were lost to her and it was all right to stop fighting the turmoil inside her.

'Sad to be going, miss?' The driver had seen the tear on her cheek.

'Not particularly.' She had to force the denial out.

'By the heck, but I would be. It's a bonny spot you're leaving.'

'No option. The Americans want it.'

'Thought that maybe you were leaving a young man behind.'

'No.' She flicked away the tear. 'No young man.'

She felt bad about being so short. The driver was trying to make conversation, maybe wanting to be kind. She closed her eyes and leaned her head back and said, 'My young man is dead. On D-Day plus two.'

'Aaah . . .'

No one spoke again until the younger man took the instructions from his pocket at the approaches to Skipton.

'You'll want to turn left at the junction and down the main street, to the church,' he said to the driver. 'Then left again. About a quarter of a mile, and I reckon we'll be there.'

The house was the middle one of a terrace of five; what people called solid-built Victorian. There were no railings around the small, undug square of front garden; no gate, though the iron collectors had left behind the hinges against such times as iron gates were legal again.

The front door was half glass, and in need of painting; the window frames, too. But so did every front door, every window in the land. Paint came only in dull green, black and khaki, and none of it was available for doing up houses.

'Have you got the keys, miss?'

Rosamund took them from her handbag, selecting one which fitted first time. The door opened onto a little lobby with a brown and orange tiled floor. It was dirty, and littered with dead leaves and unopened letters.

'I think the gas will have been turned on,' she said. 'If you can remember where you put the box with the pan and teapot in it, I'll make us a cup of tea.'

In the hall, a telephone stood on the floor. Ahead, through an open door, she saw the kitchen, and a window in need of cleaning.

To her right, an iron cooking range stood dull and rusty, its unused chimney smelling of damp soot. Beside it, in an alcove, was a grey and white mottled stove, with brass taps.

Rosamund turned one and heard a hiss of gas. Then she turned on the tap marked cold, and water splashed out. Colonel Murray had indeed smoothed their way into exile.

Furniture removers knew that the last thing they carried into the van, and the first thing out, if they had any say in the matter, was tea-making equipment. Rosamund closed her eyes and imagined the firegrate blackleaded and gleaming and a fire lit in it to heat the water in its back boiler.

They had brought all their stock of summer-hoarded coal and the last of the beech logs. When the second van arrived her mother would get to work, tutting at the state of things, and by tomorrow dinnertime the kitchen at least would be to her liking.

'Shall us start lifting, miss?'

'No. Not just yet. We'll have a drink first, and I want to have a look at the place. This is the first time I've been here.'

'Then would it be all right if us went outside for a smoke?'

'Fine by me. I'll bring your tea to you. No sugar, I'm afraid. Only saccharin.'

She tried to smile, then wished they hadn't gone out. Whilst they were here, she could hold back the tears, hug the terrible ache to her and pretend she was coping. But alone she could weep, briefly, for Laburnum and the space, and air so fresh it hurt to breathe it in on cold mornings; weep for her lovely hills and the view that stretched unhindered into forever. And for Jon, who would never find her here.

The water in the pan began to bubble and she was surprised how little time it had taken. Wrapping her handkerchief around the handle, she tipped water into the brown teapot, stirring the contents noisily. Then she dabbed her eyes and sucked in a gulp of calming air, insisting silently that it would be all right here; it would! When windows had been cleaned and fires lit and familiar furniture in place. And the floors scrubbed, of course.

She stood unmoving, listening to the silence of a street of town houses in which everyone, she knew, would mind their own business and not ask questions of the new occupants of number 19.

Her mother would like that.

When she slid thankfully into bed that night, every muscle in Rosamund's body ached and she lay, staring through the gloom to the brighter patch that was the window.

When the second furniture van arrived, she had helped her father assemble the beds whilst her mother directed and fussed and supervised the storing of the surplus furniture into two of the bedrooms. It was a miracle it had all gone in, yet even so, Mildred Kenton had then insisted that access be made from door to window, so she might open and close windows when the weather allowed, to keep everything sweet and aired. And in case of incendiary bombs.

The removal men left with relief all over their faces, each pocketing the ten-shilling note slipped by Bart when Mildred's back was turned.

'Everywhere will have to be swept and scrubbed,' she said. 'We'll make a start on the kitchen; get that fire going for some hot water. Have you got the beds seen to, Bart?'

'Aye. Rosamund is making them up.' First things first. At least tonight there would be something familiar about the place, if only their beds.

They had climbed wearily upstairs at ten o'clock that night, Mildred insisting they'd had enough for one day and anyway, best they should get themselves into bed before it got dark. They had not needed to worry about blackout curtains still unhung, and had taken lighted candles to bed, just as they had done at Laburnum. They'd had to, since the electric lights didn't work. They should not have expected them to, since not one of them was fitted with a bulb.

Rosamund lay, hands behind head, trying to accept the strangeness of the room, though at her right stood her familiar bedside table; on it the familiar candle and alarm clock. That much had not changed, though she had not set the alarm for five. No more early milking; no more awakening to Shep's howl to count the bombers home. Gone were wide horizons; now there was a privet hedge grown straggly for want of pruning and clipping to look out on, and twelve square yards of bitty grass her father intended making into a vegetable plot.

She had not knelt to say her prayers. That there was no rug beside her bed yet was excuse enough. And anyway, why bother? God didn't listen to girls who got babies out of wedlock. There were far more deserving cases for His attention. Stood to sense, didn't it?

'Where are you, Jon? Are you still waiting at the iron gate, wondering why I haven't come? Don't you know we've left?' she whispered.

Or had he gone – his reincarnated, searching spirit, that was – to Fellfoot or to the big, flat stone beside the pond? Or was there no life after death, no coming back for a second chance at happiness? Was it all a nonsense?

She hoped not. Finding Jon again in another life was all that kept her going from day to day; that and the baby she carried.

She slid her hands beneath the bedclothes, cupping them on her abdomen, sending her love to the scrap of a thing that lay there.

She began to weep then. Not tears of anger but of resignation, acceptance; tears that came from an ache of loneliness, and the need to be comforted.

'God,' she whispered. 'This is Rosamund Kenton and I'm sorry I doubted. I know there are people far worse off than I am, but just for tonight, help me, please?'

SEVENTEEN

T he last day of September brought cause for rejoicing on the Home Front. Now, the blackout had been replaced by the 'dim-out'. Some street lighting was to be allowed in the coming winter and windows, except for skylights, could be curtained normally again.

The risk of air raids was over; only the rockets, the new deadlier V-2s fell on London and the south coast, yet it was only a matter of time, the War Cabinet pronounced, before the remaining launching sites were found and destroyed and Britain safe from air attacks of any kind.

Another landing had taken place on the south coast of France; now two armies pushed inland in a pincer movement, to meet each other. Paris had been liberated, then Brussels, and newspapers carried pictures of women whose heads had been shaved by patriots, because they collaborated – *slept*, more like, – with Nazi soldiers during the occupation.

In Holland, at Arnhem, a drop by British paratroopers met with such resistance it had failed. There had never been such bravery, said the newspaper, nor so many lives given for a bridge.

It was then, listening to the nine o'clock news and the announcer's always-level voice telling of the disaster, that Rosamund felt a fluttering inside her. Not the churning that happened when she ate something that disagreed with her pregnancy, but a distinct fluttering that became even more insistent when she undressed that night, and lay relaxed and still.

It was the baby, she thought wonderingly. Sprog had quickened and from this time on, her movements would get stronger until they became like a kicking inside her! Her baby – hers and Jon's – was alive and halfway to being born!

The knowledge cheered her and was welcome, because after only three weeks of scrubbing and polishing and rearranging furniture, Mildred had returned to her former self.

'I hate this house!' she hissed. In spite of lights that now switched on and off at will, of a bathroom with hot and cold taps and a life of ease compared to that at Laburnum Farm, she declared she had been a fool to move. 'I can't abide it, here!'

Nor could she abide the sight of her daughter's thickening waistline, nor her husband being out all day, nor the people at number 17, who came in late Friday and Saturday nights, laughing and shouting, straight from the ale house!

She didn't like the people at number 21, either, because they had tried to be friendly, at first, and they shouldn't have, because townsfolk were not supposed to be friendly. And besides, Mildred wanted to keep herself to herself, just as she had been able to at Laburnum Farm.

Bart added to her annoyance, too, by suggesting it was time for Rosamund to see a doctor; that she should be given, as were all expectant mothers, a second ration book – a green one – on which she was allowed orange juice, vitamin pills and a pint of milk a day.

As the holder of such a book, Rosamund would be entitled to go to the top of the line and escape the long wait for a piece of fish, or any other commodity people had to stand and queue for. Wasn't it time something was done about their daughter's condition, because it wasn't going to go away?

To which Mildred ordered him to keep his nose out of what was women's business and that a green ration book proclaimed to all and sundry its owner was expecting and this far, they had managed to keep things quiet.

'Quiet from who?' Bart countered, mystified, because now they knew even fewer people than before.

'From shopkeepers and the milkman, for a start! And don't go coddling her as if she's done something to be proud of, Bart Kenton! When I was carrying, I booked the midwife for June, and that was the end of it!'

'Aye, but you knitted vests and jackets. Why isn't someone knitting for Rosamund's bairn?'

'Because it's none of our business – or won't be. There'll be no fancy layette made for a child that isn't welcome!'

She had gone outside then, into the back yard to glare at a plum tree that didn't have a single plum on it; then at the privet hedge Bart had thinned and cut, and decided it had been better as it was, since it stopped Them-at-the-back from gazing at her washing line from their bedroom windows!

'Come inside?' Bart pleaded softly, in case next door was outside, too, and listening at the dividing wall. 'Don't get upset, woman. There's many worse off than us!'

But she hadn't been interested in the many; only in hating the circumstances in which the war had forced her to live and the shame her daughter carried inside her that was, as her husband reminded her, becoming difficult to ignore. So she had shut the door on the early autumn evening and leaned against it, closing her eyes.

'Where is that girl?' she snapped.

'Rosamund is upstairs. You know she is.'

'Then I'm going to give her a piece of my mind! She's getting overmuch sympathy for my liking; thinks she's getting away with it! Well, she's got to be reminded that she isn't, and as far as I'm concerned, she's not bringing that baby back here!'

'You'll do no such thing!' Angrily, Bart barred his wife's way. 'You're to let her alone! She's not to be made a whipping post because you don't like it here! Neither do I, if you want to know, and I don't like working as a glorified clerk either! But there's still a war on, Mildred, and you and me will come out of it better than most, so just think on! And don't be getting at the lass when my back is turned either! And before you say you'll do what you want in your own house, you might consider that this house belongs to all of us, and that *I* pay the rent every month!'

There was a silence, then Mildred said, 'If you've finished your diatribe, might I be permitted to say that your daughter's child will *not* come back here when she's had it, and that is my final word!'

She reached for her coat then, buttoning it as she went. Banging the front door behind her, she slammed angrily out. She felt like walking until she fell of fatigue at the roadside; walking till she got back to Laburnum Farm, if she had any sense! And what was more, there would be no peace at number 19, until it was established that there was no room in it for a child. She would see to it that they were as unhappy as she was – until they gave in to what was only common sense. And she didn't give a damn who paid the rent now, because Mildred Kenton was still mistress and always would be!

'Was that Mother going out?' Rosamund stood in the doorway.

'Aye. Gone for a bit of a walk. She gets restless here. But she'll be back for the nine o'clock news, never fret.'

'I'm not fretting, Dad. Just wanted a letter posting.'

'Been writing to Cheshire?'

'Jon's aunt. She must miss him terribly.'

'And is it getting any better for you, Rosamund?'

'No. Worse, if anything. This house is too small, too shut in. There's nowhere to run – out of Mother's way, I mean. And when we were at Laburnum, I used to see Bessie.'

'So how is the lass?'

'I don't know, Dad. We went so suddenly there wasn't time to say goodbye.' Her cheeks flushed red.

'But surely you could put pen to paper; let her know how things are going? You and she were close, once.'

'*Once* seems a long time ago, but don't think I like what I did. It just seemed better, at the time, to fade quietly out of the picture. Bessie didn't know about the baby either, but that was the way Mother wanted it, and I was past arguing.'

'But you're feeling a bit better, now? You've not been looking quite so frail lately.'

'I've stopped being sick and the sight of food doesn't turn my stomach like it used to. And, Dad, since we're talking about the baby, I think I'm going to have to see a doctor; I'm about halfway, you see, and things have got to be arranged.'

Bart said he agreed entirely, though he took care not to

add that he'd already said as much, and been met with indifference.

'Do you want your mother to come with you?'

'No. I'd rather go on my own. I know where there's a lady doctor. It's best I talk to a woman, especially as I'll have to ask her about a home.'

'But I thought you didn't want to go to one of those places.'

'No. All I want is not to go to a place where they expect me to leave the baby behind for adoption. I never wanted Mum to have the bother of a confinement.'

She didn't want her mother anywhere near when Jon's baby was being born; would rather be with a stranger.

'You keep saying *her*. What if it's a little lad?'

'It won't be. I'm concentrating on a girl. It'll be hard enough bringing up a child on my own; I don't want it all to be for nothing – rear it for another war to take from me.'

'Then why don't you make a start by seeing the doctor – see that all is well. And I doubt she'll judge you. All she'll be bothered about will be what's best for the bairn.'

'Then I'll go. Promise. And thanks for being so good about it,' she whispered as a key turned in the front door.

'Told you she'd be back for nine,' Bart teased.

'What's that? Talking about me, were you?'

'No. I'd just asked Dad where you were, and he said you'd gone out for a walk, but that you'd be back in time for the news,' Rosamund said softly. 'Think I'll take a walk to the post box; it's good to see windows without blackout curtains. Then I'll make a cup of tea, if you'd like.'

She tried hard to keep her voice light, not provoke her mother to anger, which happened all too often these days because she disliked living in a town and because she was angry about the baby, too; imagined if she ignored it, it would go away.

But the baby wouldn't go away. It was very real.

It was not until the end of October that Rosamund found the courage to make an appointment to see a doctor; had decided it must be when her father was home from work that she would tell them. She would feel safer, if he were there.

'I'm going to see the lady doctor in the High Street,' she said after supper. 'On Tuesday.'

'I see.' Tight-lipped, Mildred pushed back her chair. 'Then be sure you tell her everything; that you aren't married and want somewhere to have it.'

'I'll be sure to, Mother.'

'Tell her it isn't welcome here, because I'm not putting up with a screaming child at my time of life.'

'I don't expect you to. But let me take each day as it comes? Right now, all I can think of is the baby being all right.'

'Then one day at a time won't do, miss, so you'd better get yourself straightened out – now! I want it cut and dried, and understood an' all, that I'm not changing my mind!'

'Be quiet, Mildred!' Bart's face flushed with anger. 'Let the lass have her say, can't you?'

'Very well. Just so long as it's understood!'

'There isn't any more to say, really,' Rosamund whispered, 'except that I shall ask the doctor for a note for a green ration book – I ought to be having vitamin pills and orange juice, and the extra milk. I should do all I can for Sprog – for the baby.'

'*Sprog!* What kind of fool name is that!'

'It's the one Jon and I gave her when I told him. He intended coming to see you the very day he was – the day it happened; was going to ask you to let us get married. Everything would have been all right. Jon would have taken care of us both and it would have all been above board, if only he –'

'If only he hadn't taken advantage and if only you hadn't let him! Well, it's too late now! You fell for a baby so don't expect sympathy from me – or to bring it back here!'

'So where are they to go?' Bart demanded. 'And had you stopped to think that my name is on the rent book and it's up to me who stays here, and who doesn't? Now away with you, Rosamund, and see to the pots and pans. And close the scullery door. Your mother and me have things to talk about!'

'No, Dad!' He was having one of his rebellions again, and

it wouldn't do because he would suffer for it in the long run! 'All I ask is that you let me stay until the baby comes, and I've found somewhere to go!'

'Clear the table, lass, like I told you . . .'

'Oh, yes! Shield your precious daughter! You only do it to get at me!' Mildred flung. 'Well, tell her when she sees that doctor to ask her if she knows somewhere – apart from the workhouse – that takes in sluts like that one, and their brats!'

'*That's enough!*' Bart raised his hand, and without emotion, brought it against his wife's face with a force that sent her sprawling across the floor.

'*Dad!*' Rosamund screamed. '*Stop it!*'

They stood like waxen figures, staring as Mildred, hand to cheek, rose to her feet. Then she walked to where her husband stood, standing toe to toe, almost, thrusting her face into his.

'You'll be sorry for that, Bartholomew Kenton! I swear you will!'

'Happen so, but it's something that's needed doing for nigh on twenty years. I never thought to strike a woman, but you drove me to it! Now get out of my sight; look at yourself in a mirror – at the badness there!'

He turned his back contemptuously and Mildred Kenton left the room without speaking, pausing only to glance at her husband and daughter, each in turn. Then the door closed behind her and they heard the sound of her laughter as she walked upstairs.

'Come here, little lass.' Bart held wide his arms. 'I'm not proud of what I did. It won't happen again.'

She felt the shaking of his body as he held her close, and remorse filled her.

'You shouldn't have done it, Dad, because it's going to cost you! She won't forget it. And I'm sorry for all the trouble I've caused.'

'No use crying over spilt milk. And I'll make my peace with your mother, so don't fret. Now why don't you be off to your bed – you look tired out. And when you wake up in t'morning, it'll be another day. Your mother's bark is worse than her bite, think on.'

But was it, Rosamund thought as she undressed for bed. Perhaps, because she had seemed to capitulate when faced with her husband's anger, all would be well; that the slap she had so deserved would be a lesson to her.

But her father could not have seen the anger, the cold-blooded evil in his wife's eyes as she left the room. And she had turned those eyes on them both for just a second, hadn't she?

And a second was all it took to ill-wish.

Rosamund stood at the landing window, watching her father drive off to work. He made a jerky start; still felt more at ease on a tractor, she shouldn't wonder. Bart Kenton. So gentle, yet who last night had snapped and hit out.

She lifted her chin and walked downstairs in search of breakfast. It was good to feel hungry again. Bread and jam would be fine, and a mug of tea.

'Good morning, Mother.'

'You're sorry, then, for the upset you caused between me and your father?'

'If that's what you want.'

'I *do* want it! I've trouble enough without you adding to it! What do you think it's like for me having to live here, losing everything that's precious to me? Twenty years I gave to Laburnum, then they take it without a by-your-leave! Don't you think I'm near to breaking point, then?'

'It depends what's most important, I would say.' Rosamund said it softly, hesitantly, pleading inside her for there not to be another upset. 'One day the war is going to end and things will get back to normal again. There are a lot of women waiting for it to end. You aren't alone, Mother.'

'But I don't care about other people! Can't shoulder their worries, now can I? I've enough of my own with a daughter who seems to glory in being no better than she need be; getting herself into trouble, then expecting to bring her shame home with her! Well, I won't let you! I've said my say and the matter won't be mentioned again. Just bear it in mind, though, when you're making your plans and think on that bairns cost money to rear, need a roof over their heads, and that this roof isn't available!'

'Mother – can't you give me a chance; give us both a chance? It isn't the baby's fault. If there's to be blame, it's me you must look at.'

'I've looked, and I don't like what I see! But I don't propose to say one more word on the matter. Get yourself something to eat, then do the breakfast dishes. I'm going to walk into Skipton; there's sometimes a fish queue on a Tuesday. Then you can get on with the dusting.' She made for the door, then turned, a pondering look on her face. 'And had you thought, Rosamund, that we could be worrying over nothing?'

'What do you mean?' The words came in a whisper, because the look was back on her mother's face again and her eyes had narrowed into slits. 'What shouldn't we be worrying about?'

'That child. You mightn't have it. You're just coming up to quickening time.'

'And . . . ?' *Oh Jon, help me!*

'Who's to say you won't miscarry – slip the thing?'

'Why, you – you –' She was across the room in a haste of fear, taking her mother's shoulders, flinging her round as she turned to walk away. 'Look at me, Mother! You did it to Jon, didn't you – ill-wished him, said you hoped his plane would crash and serve him right, you said! And now you're doing it again! You want me to lose this baby! I should have realized that's what you've been doing every time you looked at me!' Anger and revulsion churned inside her, her breath came in short, frightened gasps. Wild-eyed, she was looking at Margaret Dacre. 'Well, you'll not harm it! Jon loved me, and there's nothing your kind can do against that!'

'I don't know what you mean, I'm sure.' Mildred removed the clutching hands. 'You're quite mad, girl!'

Her look, Rosamund thought, was one of satisfaction. Her mother was enjoying this; her goading had done exactly what she intended it to do; made her lose her temper, her control, and her body to shake with hate and fear. More upsets like this, and she *would* lose the baby! Not only was her mother ill-wishing, she was piling on the pressure!

Rosamund clenched her hands, breathed deeply, then said, 'You are wicked, and I hope with all my heart that none of your bad blood comes out in the baby. Because I won't let you harm it, nor me! I'll fight you every inch of the way – you and Margaret Dacre both!'

'Mad! Like your father. Given to sudden rages! And I don't know who Margaret Dacre is!'

'Oh, but you do! You saw her name every day above the door at Laburnum! She was a witch, Mother; a witch who got away with it, and she's taken possession of you!'

'Stark, raving mad; that's what you are! That lady doctor should see you now!' Mildred smiled as she spoke. 'Unmarried mothers' home? You'll end up in the madhouse!'

She walked slowly, triumphantly up the stairs and Rosamund watched, horrified; all at once afraid. She must get out – away from those eyes! Head down she flung open the back door, covering her child with fingers spread wide.

Jon! Help us!'

She remained outside until she heard the front door bang, then crept quietly into the house, trying to hold her breath because it was still coming in noisy gasps. Fearfully she looked at the hook in the scullery from which the shopping bag hung. It had gone, and her mother's coat and hat from the peg in the hall. Lifting the phone, she gasped Charlotte Martin's number into it.

'Please! It's urgent! Will you do your best to get it quickly?' she asked the operator.

'Little – er – *Sellow*?'

'It's in Cheshire. Through Chester trunks, I think.'

'I'll do what I can, caller, but you know how things are . . . ?'

Aunt Lottie! She'd said it, hadn't she; asked her to visit? And Aunt Lottie would understand, tell her what best to do to keep the baby.

But Jon's aunt didn't know about Sprog. She was a maiden lady; how would she react? Best not tell her, Rosamund thought – not until she got there.

And when she did, *if* it were possible to go to Little Sellow for a week, she would be open and honest, beg Charlotte

Martin's understanding. She worked for newspapers, didn't she; it would take more than a girl in trouble to shock her. Oh, please it would?

Her mouth was so dry that she drank a glass of water without stopping to take breath. Then she paced the hall, willing the phone to ring, knowing it could take hours; that her mother might well be back from Skipton long before the call came through. If it came through.

She was ready to give in to tears when the ringing shattered the silence, making her jump. She grabbed the receiver, pleading, praying that the operator wouldn't tell her there had been no reply. She hadn't once thought Jon's aunt could be out, standing in a queue – or working.

'I have your number on the line, caller. Go ahead, please.'

'Thank you – oh, thank you! Hullo? Miss Martin? Aunt Lottie?'

'Rosie? Is it Rosie?'

'Yes it is, and please can I come and see you? I've got all the time in the world now we haven't got the farm. You did say I might.'

'But of course you can! Are you all right, Rosie? Have you been running?'

'No! Yes! I was at the end of the garden, you see, when the phone rang. I'm fine. When can I come, please?'

'Whenever you want. Tomorrow?' She sounded pleased.

'No!' It would have to be Friday when her mother went to town to get the rations. She couldn't get away until then. 'Will Friday do? It would be better for me, on Friday!'

'Then Friday it is. You'll be coming by train? I might not be able to meet you at Chester, but there's a bus to Sellow leaves from outside the station. Every hour, on the hour. Just arrive, why don't you? And Rosie, are you sure everything is all right? You sound a little – we-e-ll . . .'

'I'm fine, only suddenly I need to talk to you. About Jon, and about – oh, can I tell you all about it when I arrive?'

'You know you can. I'll be in all day Friday; will look out of the window at bus time. You can't miss Primrose Cottage. Walk towards the church, and it's a white house, on your right.'

'Thank you, Miss Martin. I'll bring my ration book. I won't be a nuisance.'

'I shall look forward to having you. Take care of yourself. See you soon.'

Friday. Three days away; three days to keep her eyes down and her mind closed; three days of keeping the peace, packing her case sneakily, then getting to the bus stop at the end of the road, just as soon as her mother left for town. And be damned if she wouldn't walk to the station, *now*, check up on train times, perhaps buy her ticket.

She ran upstairs to take her Post Office Savings book from the drawer. Friday was when it must be, and until then she would keep out of her mother's way as much as possible, and please, God, she prayed silently, don't let anything happen to Sprog? I couldn't bear to lose the baby, too.

Rosamund packed secretly, a little at a time, placing Jon's photograph, wrapped round with a woolly scarf, in the centre of the case. Then she pushed it beneath the bed, hoping her mother wouldn't get on her hands and knees and find it when she was looking for dust.

Ten-fifteen the train left, they told her when she bought her ticket. Change at Manchester for Chester. Don't let anything happen, *please*, to mess it up?

But wasn't she being just a little bit stupid, taking herself off without so much as a word? What would her reception be like, when she returned? Should she leave a letter, explaining that she had gone to Miss Martin's house in answer to a phone call, inviting her there?

No! There was a phone box outside Skipton station. From it she would ring her father at work, tell him, ask him to understand why she hadn't told them; that because if she did, her mother might forbid it and she didn't want to cause any more rows.

And she would ask him to make it all right with her mother, so there wouldn't be any trouble at number 19 when she got back. And would he try to understand, please, that she had to get away for a little while, and to tell her mother she had taken her ration book?

That ration book, Rosamund thought, all at once calmer, could be the undoing of everything. Her mother took them every Friday, she should have remembered, to the grocer and the butcher to have the food coupons clipped out; would know one was missing.

Yet how could she inflict herself on Jon's aunt without rations? It wasn't right to expect to share what wasn't enough for one, truth known.

She opened the top drawer of the desk, seeing the envelope in which the books were always kept and knew at once there was a chance of getting away with it; if, of course, her mother didn't realize, when she took out the envelope, that it felt just that little bit thinner.

She took the book with her name and identity number on it and slipped it into her pocket, because she really didn't have a choice; must remember, too, to take clothing coupons, identity card and her bank book; take the important things in case she never came back.

And that was a laugh, because she would return, and when she did, when she had unburdened herself to Aunt Lottie and had perhaps been given a little comfort, she would go to the doctor in the High Street, then not think beyond each day until she had to. One day at a time was how it must be. What would happen to her; what it was like birthing a child; where she would go, afterwards, she did not know.

Sufficient that her baby would be born in February, and once she had held it, guided the small searching mouth to her breast, nothing and no one would part her from Jon's child. And she wasn't being deceitful or sly; all she wanted was to see Jon's aunt, ask that she help her get things straight in her mind, because truth known she was at the end of her tether!

The hours passed slowly until Friday morning, then everything became incredibly easy.

'Want a lift, Mildred?' her father asked. 'Save you hanging around for the bus. I can drop you off at the shops.'

So her mother hurried away, not noticing that a ration book was missing or that her daughter was acting a mite strangely.

From the landing window Rosamund watched the car disappear, then dragged her case from beneath the bed, checking that the important things were in her handbag.

Just time to make a sandwich for the journey; with luck she could buy tea at the station buffet. She looked around the kitchen, shaking with apprehension and didn't feel safe until she had heaved her case on the bus, fifteen minutes later, asking for a twopenny ticket to the railway station.

Only a call, now, to make to her father, asking him yet again to be on her side. Three pennies clinked in her pocket, ready to be pushed into the box. Her father worked less than half a mile away; getting through would be easy.

The Ag and Fish telephonist answered at once, and yes, she was almost sure Mr Kenton had not gone out on field-work yet.

'Dad! It's me. I'm at the station, and I'm going to Jon's aunt to stay. Just for a week. Will you tell Mum I've taken my ration book, and –'

'Lass! What are you thinking about? You know what your mother is going to say about going off without a word. Is anything wrong? Why didn't you say?'

'Because I knew there'd be trouble if I did.'

'There'll be that, all right, when she finds out!'

'I know, and I'm sorry you'll have to take the brunt of it, but I've got to get away – just for a few days.'

'Oh, all right. We're about due for a bust-up, anyway. Things have been too quiet, these last few days.'

She heard her father's chuckle, and let go a breath of relief.

'Dad, you're a darling and I'll make it up to you, I promise I will. And I love you very much. Take care . . .'

She replaced the receiver quickly, then walked to the platform from which the Manchester train would leave, the worst over.

She was in good time, could catch her breath then clear her mind of all guilt, because for a week she could talk about Jon, she hoped; tell Aunt Lottie about the baby and beg her to understand the way things were, and to help her, if she could.

And if she could not, then she would have had seven days away from the house her mother hated; from the tension that always shimmered in the air, and most of all, away from her mother's half-closed eyes.

The train was only a little late arriving at Chester, which wasn't bad at all, considering the railways were busier than ever since the invasion. She had time enough to find the bus stop and buses were usually on time; especially little local ones.

She was hungry and her arms ached from the weight of the case. A lady arrived to stand beside her and Rosamund asked if she was in the right queue for Little Sellow.

'You are. I'll tell you when to get off. Pretty country, but half asleep. Not a lot going on there.'

Half asleep. Not a lot going on. Peace and quiet for a week; living in Jon's home, talking about him as if it were the most natural thing in the world to someone who loved him as much as she loved him. Safe, for a whole week.

She recognized Charlotte Martin the minute she got off the bus; not because she was in any way like Jon, but because of the wide smile of welcome, the outstretched arms, the whispered, 'Rosie? Oh, my dear . . .'

'Thank you for letting me come. You didn't think I was cheeky, did you?'

'Not a bit. I've been wanting to meet Jon's girl. You'll be hungry. I managed to get a rabbit, so there's plenty for two. Oh, it's so good to see you!' She lifted the case with amazing ease. 'Not far to go. This is the third bus I've met. Third time lucky!'

Lucky? Yes! Jon's aunt would understand; wouldn't condemn or blame. And she would help her, especially when the baby was born; Aunt Lottie, Rosamund was sure, would know of a place she could go. A kind place.

★　　★　　★

Primrose Cottage was small and higgledy-piggledy and every bit as nice as Jon had said.

'How are you, child – about Jon, I mean.'

'Oh, so-so,' she shrugged. 'In one week's time we'll have known each other a year. Some days I can accept what happened – just about; other days I'm angry about it. Sometimes I cry a lot. But I won't talk about him, unless you want to, and is it all right for me to call you Aunt Lottie?'

'That's my name,' she smiled. 'Give me your coat, then I'll put the kettle on – oh, my God!' She saw at once the pregnancy that was beginning to show. 'Why didn't you tell me? How far on are you?'

'About halfway – maybe a little more,' Rosamund whispered, all at once dry-mouthed. 'Are you shocked?'

'No. But I'm surprised. Jon didn't say a word about it.'

'I only told him when I thought he was grounded. But he had to fly again . . .'

'But he knew?'

'Yes. He was glad about it. He was going to ask my father next day if we could be married, but –'

'Oh, Rosie! Give me a cuddle? I'm so glad! Jon's child!'

Her eyes filled with tears – happy ones, because she was smiling through them – and all Rosamund could say was, 'Bless you for understanding,' before she wept with her.

'I've heard it said,' Charlotte Martin smiled many minutes later, 'that two women can't be true friends until they have shared tears. Does that make us true friends, Rosie?'

'I hope so. I really do.'

'Jon talked to me about the way you both felt, and I understood – had been through the same thing myself in another war.'

'You're a very kind lady,' Rosamund whispered tremulously. 'Thank you for letting me have this week with you.'

'I've put you in Jon's room,' the elder woman said when tears had been dried and tea sipped. 'It's the only spare I've got. Can you bear it, do you think? His clothes are in the wardrobe, and his best uniform. Will it upset you to see his things?'

'I don't know, but I'd like to sleep in his bed.'

'Then you'd best unpack, settle yourself in whilst I see to the supper. The bathroom is next door to yours. Use the top two drawers in the chest. Sure you'll be all right?'

'I'll be fine.'

She hadn't reckoned, for all that, with what she saw when she looked at the bed with the blue eiderdown, and there on it – oh, *no*!

'Aunt Lottie!' She ran to the kitchen, clutching the rag doll. 'Where did you get this? It's Matilda Mint!'

'It came amongst Jon's personal things. It must have been in his locker. Is it special?'

'She belonged to me. I gave her to the crew as a lucky mascot. She hung on Jon's seat. They touched her when they got on the plane. I know she was with them on their thirtieth op. Jon must have forgotten to take her that last time.' She was weeping again.

'Oh dear. I just put it there. Didn't know it was so important.' She offered a handkerchief, and Rosamund dabbed her eyes.

'Sorry about that. It just threw me, seeing Matty.'

'Now see here – how about using my bed? It won't be so upsetting for you.'

'Thanks, but no. I really want to be in Jon's room. And I won't burst out crying again, I promise.'

When the curtains had been drawn against the autumn evening and logs laid on the fire, Charlotte Martin said, 'Feel better for that?'

'Oh, yes! I didn't realize how hungry I was. I've brought my ration book. Is there a Ministry of Food office nearby so they can give me rations for a week off it? I can't eat yours.'

'There is, and I'll see to it for you. It was thoughtful of you to bring it. Food *is* a bit short. You'll be missing the perks from the farm, I shouldn't wonder.'

'We are – eggs especially, and milk. My mother is finding it much harder to manage, and she hates the house we live in now.'

'I can understand it. I'd hate it if someone turfed me out of

Primrose Cottage. But it'll all come right in time, I suppose, and we can at least see an end to the fighting in Europe now. You might be lucky, Rosie; might have a baby born into peace.'

'I hope so. It's why I want a girl. You'll understand . . . ?'

'Oh yes. Guy, then Jon. Seems females have a better chance, all things being equal. But I want to give you something. Are you up to it, after Matilda Mint?'

'Photographs . . . ?'

'Later. What I want is for you to have this.' She held out the cross; the one Bessie's mother had taken to be blessed in church. 'It was yours, wasn't it?'

'Yes. I wanted Jon to have it, help keep him safe from – from harm. He wore it with the St Christopher you gave him, but you'd know that.' She felt the colour drain from her cheeks, a coldness tingling in her fingertips as she looked at it. It hadn't worked against the evil.

'Do you want it back?'

'I – yes, please. He'd be wearing it, wouldn't he, when – when it happened.'

'Yes. The medical people would have . . .' She left the sentence unfinished.

'Thank you.' Rosamund held out her hand for the cross. 'I'll wear it; never take it off . . .' Her voice trailed away because she was fighting tears again.

'That was unkind of me.' Charlotte Martin's eyes were sad. 'I should have waited.'

'No! Seeing it was like seeing Matty Mint again, that's all. So much of Jon is here, you see. His uniform in the wardrobe; it was the one he wore when we went dancing. I touched it, closed my eyes and tried to pretend he was wearing it. And there are all the photographs. It's like he's going to walk in as if nothing had happened.'

'But it *has* happened, Rosie. And you aren't just grieving; there's something else!'

'No! There isn't! Today's been a bit much, that's all!'

'Oh, child! You didn't come here for nothing! As soon as I heard you on the phone, I could tell you were upset. Said you'd been running from the bottom of the garden, yet you told me in a letter that you've only got a tiny, shut-in bit at the back.'

She took the cross that still lay in the upturned, shaking hand, laying it on the table beside the sofa arm. Then she took Rosamund's hands in hers and looked into her eyes.

'I know something is wrong. I couldn't get Jon out of my mind that day you rang me. Did Jon tell you to call me?'

'No! Oh, I don't know! I'd had a row with my mother about the baby. She didn't want me to keep it; said it so often I got so I couldn't stand it. I remember wanting Jon; crying out to him in my mind, sort of, to help us.'

'Seems he did. Your mother may not want the baby, Rosie, but I do! It will be my grandchild, as well as hers! Jon was my son, almost. How could she not want it?'

'Because I've acted like a slut – a whore, she once said. And because I've disgraced the family – well, will have, when it all comes out. I think it was the only comfort she had in leaving Laburnum Farm, when the Americans wanted it – to keep my shame from the village.'

'Rosie! What am I to do with you?' She reached out, pulling her close. 'You're shaking! Sssssh. It's all right. You're with me, now, and Jon is as near as you want him to be. Tell me about it? *All* of it? I love Jon, too, don't forget.'

'You're sure you want it all?' All of it, that was, but her mother wishing Jon dead. She could never tell that. 'You'll think Jon found himself a nutter – and that's a laugh, if you like. Alice Nutter was one of the Pendle witches, like Margaret Dacre who built Laburnum Farm in 1592.'

'What are you trying to say, Rosie?'

'I think a witch built the house we lived in. She didn't get caught, like the others, but local folklore has it she was too high and mighty to let that happen – friends in high places. Anyway, when my mother found I was meeting Jon, she got really angry. Bessie – my friend – didn't like her. It was Bessie first called her a witch, I suppose.

'So maybe I'd got it into my head that my mother *was* peculiar, sort of. My dad is a love. He hit Mother the other night. Imagine? – Dad hitting a woman, and him so gentle.

He'd be on my side, if he dare. He'd love the baby if she would let him, but I suppose he realizes it wouldn't be a lot of use insisting I bring it home. The baby would suffer, too. My mother would ill-wish it. I'd be afraid to leave it alone with her.'

'And you really think your mother is capable of such a thing?' She pulled her closer, laying her cheek on her head, as Jon had once done.

'I don't know. If I said yes, I really thought she was, then you'd think I was mad and my mother bad.'

'I think she is. How did she come to have a lovely daughter like you?'

'Y'know something? I've often wondered how they got me at all! My mother was against – well – demonstrations of affection. *That* sort of thing was for procreation, and to make sure animals paid their way. She made it seem dirty, and it wasn't! Between Jon and me it was wonderful. And I'm so sorry, Aunt Lottie. What must you think of me, saying things like that about my own mother? You must think I'm wicked all through.'

'No. Jon loved – *adored* – you. His face shone, when he talked about you. If Jon loved you, then that's fine by me. But when you phoned, you said you needed to talk to me. Is there more?'

'I rang because I didn't know which way to turn. I thought about Jon – wanted him there to take care of me. Then I found myself ringing you. I wanted to get away from number 19 for a bit and you were the only person I could think of.

'Oh, I know there are homes for unmarried mothers, but I was hoping you'd be able to tell me of some place not as strict as the rest; some place where they'd understand I wanted to keep my baby and not leave her behind for adoption. And perhaps help me to find a job, so I could provide for her. Are there such places, do you know?'

'Yes. There's one I know of.'

'And they wouldn't treat me like I'm no better than I ought to be? Jon was the only one ever. I'm not common.'

'I can guarantee that won't happen.'

'Then will you tell me where it is, Aunt Lottie?'

'Rosie, you don't have to go anywhere. You are welcome here. The baby can be born in Jon's bed, even. Say you will? I wouldn't get possessive of it; wouldn't try to tell you how it should be brought up. But I would like a grandchild. I missed out on the motherhood bit – can I share your little one?'

'Ooooh!' Rosamund's body sagged; all the breath seemed to leave it. 'You can't mean it, and anyway, it isn't possible! Had you thought – nappies, teething babies, the night watch, pacing the floor and someone else's child upsetting your life? I couldn't let you, and I'm still a minor. Dad might agree, but my mother wouldn't. She'd make me come home and things would be worse than ever.'

'Your mother would *not* make you go back home; not when I'd had my say! If what you tell me is true – and I don't for a minute doubt you – then she's not fit to go near the child. And I'm speaking for Jon now. Jon's got rights, too!'

'Then you really mean it? You won't change your mind?'

'The moment I realized you were pregnant, I wanted you here. Would your father give his permission for you to leave home, do you think?'

'I think he might, only she'd make his life a misery.'

'Then he'll have to slap her again, won't he?' She was smiling, as if she were sure it could all come right. 'Shall we go for it, Rosie?'

'What about Dad?'

'There'll be ways of keeping in touch, letting him know you still care about him.'

'Y-yes, there will.' Dad kept in touch with his own father, didn't he? 'But is it right to land him in it?'

'You don't have a choice. The baby comes first.'

'I might never see Laburnum again. My mother wouldn't have me back, if I defied her. It was her inheritance bought it, so she'll see I don't ever get it.'

'And will that matter?'

'No. I love Laburnum, but the baby must come first. As long as I can pay my way, though; I'd have to work.'

'Of course! But that would be in the future. I won't push

you, though. You aren't in a fit state to make decisions now. Sleep on it? There's a whole week to think things out.'

'I'll think very seriously about it.' Shyly, she kissed the older woman's cheek. 'And so must you, too. Think what you would be taking on – perhaps for ever.'

'I've already thought, Rosie. It's up to you now. Pop a log on the fire, will you, and I'll put the kettle on. I think this calls for a cup of tea!'

Later that night, Charlotte Martin walked softly into the little back room, the light from the landing falling on the bed in which Rosamund lay; Jon's bed, with the faded blue eiderdown, and the table beside it with the Mickey Mouse clock on it, long ago broken. And on the walls, group photographs of Jon at school, and at Cambridge; Jon in cap and gown on his graduation day; Jon a man, with wings on his tunic.

He would never come back; never fill the house with his presence again, nor smile at her with his eyes because of the love between them. But in his bed slept Rosie, the girl he loved and who carried his child. Her lashes lay on her cheeks, thick and fair; she looked like a child, vulnerable and frail. And clutched to her, a little rag doll that once flew with Jon into danger and back.

She closed the door quietly, stirred the embers in the grate then took the photograph from the mantelpiece.

'She's come home, Jon, and it's going to be all right. She'll stay here with me and I'll be there for them both. I won't let her go back to her mother. That's what you wanted, isn't it; why you've been nagging me these past weeks?'

She smiled, a commitment made. The young pilot smiled back from the silver frame and for a moment it was as if he were beside her and alive still, and happy. Then he was gone.

But the young were like that, she smiled sadly, proudly. Always impatient. As if there was no tomorrow . . .

One Summer At Deer's Leap

Part Two

Chapter Eleven

I was determined not to let the December grizzle get to me. Trees bare and black, grass scutchy and withered. Not worth looking out on. Roll on Christmas and New Year and the first snowdrop. And making a start on the Deer's Leap books, as Jeannie and I had come to know them, even though the first of the quartet was still nothing more than a synopsis. At the moment, the embryo book was known as 'First of the Deer's Leaps' – no title, yet, though one would be there in the text; a phrase that would jump out and hit me before the book was finished. A phrase with *witch* in it, maybe?

Deer's Leap, and the summer I found it, was never far from my mind. And I had found more than I bargained for – a house I ached to own and the ghost of a long-ago pilot looking for his girl. And me falling in love with him, would you believe, or ready to fall for someone very much like him, if men like Jack Hunter still existed.

A train on the up line crashed past, startling me, and I shifted my elbow from the window ledge.

'Come to London,' Jeannie had said. 'Have a Christmas lunch with me and bring the synopsis of the First of the Deer's Leaps with you.'

There is no messing with Jeannie, but she knows her stuff; likes her own way too when it comes to books, because she knows what she's talking about. Doesn't believe in ghosts either, even though reluctantly prepared to admit there was 'something peculiar' at Deer's Leap, though I wasn't to let it get in the way of my writing!

So I had done as she said; kept my head down and delivered my second novel on time. Only then had I let Jack Hunter back into my mind; Suzie, too. Because there would be no rest for that pilot until he found her, old though she would now be.

The bonus was that she was still alive. She had to be. I had established that beyond reasonable doubt as I read *Dragonfly Morning*. Susanna Lancaster was Susan Smith – Jack Hunter's Suzie. That novel was thought to be her swan song, Jeannie had once said; setting the records straight before she retired from writing. And it was sad that her lover was only a name now on a war memorial. Small comfort, that, to a young woman bringing up a child alone. There must have been a few like her during that war, I supposed, as the train began to slow on the outskirts of Peterborough.

But at least her baby had been born into love, if not into peace, in the higgledy-piggledy cottage in Cheshire. Suzie – *Rosie* – had remained with Aunt Lottie; never seen her parents again. Nor Deer's Leap. Nor had she ever got in touch with Bessie. It was all there in the last four chapters of *Dragonfly Morning*; how a little love child was born three days into January 1945, and how that baby's mother, encouraged by Charlotte Martin, had become Susanna Lancaster – and famous and rich.

When the compartment settled down again after the Peterborough stop, I closed my eyes, trying hard to think about the Deer's Leap stories, and how lucky I was to have had four books commissioned – provided the first was anything like decent. And to keep my mind on them, I concentrated hard on the advance I would soon get. Advance on publication, it's called; a decent payment up front to subsidize the author during the writing, so she needn't starve in a garret.

So I had no money worries, though I wasn't in Susanna Lancaster's league. And now I was back to Ms Lancaster again, and Deer's Leap and Jack Hunter, and it simply wouldn't do!

Trouble was, I would have to return to the beautiful Trough of Bowland time and time again. Research would demand it. And to Pendle witch country too, to steep myself in folklore, because the first of the quartet would be about the building of a house in 1592, and a secret witch called Mary Dobbie, who had lit the first fire on the stone hearth and longed for a son to inherit that house. Margaret Dacre's fictional counterpart . . .

We were slowing again, and I looked out at the close-packed houses, trying not to compare them with Deer's Leap and a view that stretched into forever.

People began to put on jackets, pick up briefcases and walk slowly towards the front of the train so they could be first off; first through the barrier, first in the taxi rank queue.

I didn't get to my feet until all the pushing and shoving was finished, then picked up the plastic bag with a whole parkin in it, and a jar of heather honey for Jeannie, going with the flow following the signs to the underground. I wasn't rich enough yet to splash out on taxis.

'So you read *Dragonfly Morning*?' Jeannie asked on the way to the restaurant round the corner from Harrier Books.

'I did. Do you think it's Susanna Lancaster saying goodbye to her past?'

'Dunno. Fiction, faction or biography – who cares as long as it sells books?'

'You're a cynic.'

'So? It's a cynical world we live in!'

I rather liked the restaurant. It had tablecloths of brown paper, and bright coral napkins. I made a mental note to remember to tell Mum about brown-paper tablecloths for her next WI bash!

'Am I to be allowed to talk about Deer's Leap?' I asked as we settled ourselves at a window table. 'Not World War Two Deer's Leap, though it's never going to be far away. But all four books are going to be motivated by Deer's Leap – haunted by it, in fact!'

'Agreed. But you're not to go poking about, raising ghosts. Only legitimate research allowed.'

'So you are willing to admit that *Dragonfly Morning* was written by Susan Smith and that Bessie Drake is really Mrs Taylor, née Lizzie Frobisher? And that the aerodrome at RAF Laceby Green was really at Acton Carey?'

'All right! And that Laburnum Farm was Deer's Leap! It all fits in! But do you reckon Mildred Kenton could have been such a bitch, Cassie?'

'A bitch *and* a witch,' I said firmly, 'and possessed by the ghost of Margaret Dacre. And I think the immediate vicinity of that house is ghost territory; we-e-ll, if you are like me and Aunt Jane, that is. Some people attract ghosts; some don't. And before I forget, Jeannie . . .'

I dipped into my handbag and brought out a letter I had written to Susanna Lancaster, c/o Harrier Books, with 'Kindly Forward' written in the top left-hand corner, and a first-class stamp in the other. I asked Jeannie to pass the letter to Susanna Lancaster's editor.

'You're still determined, then, to get in touch?'

'I am. Somehow she's got to know that Jack Hunter is still looking for her. And you needn't worry. I haven't gone in feet first. There's only sufficient in that letter to make her curious, and maybe write back.'

'She doesn't have to reply, you know.'

'But she will, Jeannie. She must!'

'That one summer at Deer's Leap was a long time ago; she might want to put it all behind her.'

'She can't, or why did she write *Dragonfly Morning*, will you tell me?'

The waiter was standing there, eyebrow raised, and Jeannie asked him to give us a minute, then shoved the menu at me.

'Chicken Kiev,' I said without hesitation, 'and water to drink, please.' I had twenty miles to drive when I got off the train.

'She wrote *Dragonfly Morning*,' Jeannie said, 'because it was a good story. World War Two novels still sell. The young ones are interested in what their grandparents got up to; to the older generation they are pure nostalgia.'

'And you're saying she wrote Jack and Suzie's story just for *money*? She couldn't have! That book was written from the heart!'

'Maybe. But she could have used memories, Cassie. A lot of authors do. And haven't you just once thought she might have met someone else – married him?'

'No, I haven't,' I said stubbornly. 'She would never have taken second best.'

The waiter arrived with water and a glass of red wine for Jeannie, who put the letter in her handbag.

'You'll see she gets it?' I said, fixing her with a don't-dare-forget stare.

'I'll give it to her editor, and it will be sent on. After that, it'll be up to Susanna Lancaster, so don't hold your breath!'

'And talking of Lancaster – the *place*, I mean,' I said, determined to have the last word on the subject, 'I always thought Susanna took the pseudonym Lancaster because that was where she lived, but when she started getting noticed as a writer she was still at Primrose Cottage, with Aunt Lottie and Kate.'

'Yes. It says in the last chapter of *Dragonfly Morning* that when Charlotte Martin died, she left Primrose Cottage to Rosamund for her lifetime, and then to Rosamund's daughter, Kate. Some time after, Susanna must have gone home to live.'

'As near to Deer's Leap as she dare, you mean?'

'Back to Lancashire. And I know what you are getting at. She could never have forgotten Jack because she took Lancaster – the name of the bomber he flew – as her pseudonym.'

'Yes. And she doesn't live in the house near Lancaster-the-place now.'

'How do you know?' Jeannie's head came up with a jerk.

'Because I knew, from what you had said, approximately where she lived, so I went looking for her.'

'Cassie! You can't do things like that! A writer is entitled to her privacy – surely you of all people realize that?'

'Well, I don't – *didn't*. I'm not in Susanna Lancaster's league, am I? Nobody has yet beaten a path to the door of Greenleas.'

'Well, it'll serve you right when it happens to you!'

'Jeannie, don't go on, so! I found the Regency house with seven steps, but someone else was living there. Susanna had gone, having first warned the new owner there might be fans knocking on the door from time to time. It was a wasted day, except that I took photographs for research, and got you some honey!'

'Then perhaps you'll listen to me next time. I *do* know what I'm talking about, Cassie!'

My reply about me and Aunt Jane not being able to help attracting ghosts was not made, because our food arrived. So instead, I pierced the meat and watched the garlicky sauce spread across the plate. Then I forked chips onto my plate with an easy conscience, because since finishing *Firedance* I've been giving Dad a hand in the market garden, and there is nothing like a spot of good, honest digging to shift the odd pound of flab!

'You won't forget the letter?' was the last thing I said to Jeannie, and she said she wouldn't, and that she hoped I had a good Christmas.

I felt a bit flat on the train going home. I adore London, but when I get to King's Cross and see the York train, I want nothing more than to get on it.

It was impossible to see anything through the dark windows, except the compartment lights reflected back, so I closed my eyes and let the rhythm of the train into my head, putting words to the low, repetitive noise.

Rosie Kenton – Suzie Smith . . . Mrs Taylor – Bessie Drake
. . . Acton Carey – Laceby Green . . . Mildred Kenton – witch,
witch, w i t c h . . .

'Excuse me?' There was a voice, above my head. 'You've
been asleep. Are you getting off at York?'

I blinked open my eyes. The train was almost at a stand-
still.

'Good heavens! Thanks a lot!'

Still feeling a bit gormless, I waved from the platform to
the vigilant lady who smiled from the window as the train
set off again. I hoped I hadn't snored.

York station, decorated for Christmas, made me feel pleased
to be almost home. I took torch and keys from my bag and
made for the car park and the red Mini. Twenty more miles
to Greenleas. I hoped the kitchen would be full of cooking
smells, and that Mum would have the kettle on.

Christmas was over. Dad was pleased because sales of holly
wreaths and decorations and late-flowering chrysanthemums
had been good. I was pleased because, with all the fuss over,
I could get down to the First of the Deer's Leap books and
daydream about an old, empty house and a For Sale board
outside it.

Mum was *not* pleased, and started the first working day
after the holiday by snapping at Dad over nothing. It began
with the needles from the Christmas tree, and the mess
they always made, and that for two pins she would have
an artificial one next year!

Dad had said that artificial, as in growing things, was an
unacceptable word at Greenleas, and any such Christmas
tree would be thrown out!

Whereupon Mum burst into tears and flung the *Yorkshire
Post* at me.

'Look! In the Engagements column! All done sly and
his mother never saying a word about it last night at the
WI!'

> Yardley – Deighton-James. The engagement is announced
> between Piers Yardley of Kensington, London, and Maria
> Deighton-James, of Cromer, Norfolk.

I sucked in my breath, remembering King's Cross station, and the look of love.

'So he did it!' was all I could think of to say.

'Very brief and to the point, isn't it?' Dad jabbed his pipe at the offending two-and-a-bit lines.

'And why, will you tell me, isn't Rowbeck good enough for him?' Mum was still indignant.

'Piers always did like a good address,' I said softly, then burst out laughing.

'And what's so funny, Cassandra?' I always get my full name when Mum isn't best pleased with me. 'They'll all be at it in the village. Everybody thought that you and Piers would make a go of it!'

'Then everybody is wrong, Mum. And *if* anyone remarks on it, you can tell them that Cassie is very pleased for them both.'

'And are you?'

'I am. Truly. Even though everyone thought that he and I were an item. Like I told you – three books . . .' I tapped my nose with my finger, then winked at her. 'You'll get your grandchildren, I promise. And, Mum, Piers was never the right man for me, so get on the phone and ring Mrs Yardley, like you should have done, or she'll think you are jealous!'

'If you're sure, Cassie . . .'

'Of course!' I was never more sure of anything, though for the life of me I couldn't tell Mum why. It was what happened, I suppose, when you had to admit that given half a chance, you could fall in love with a ghost you hadn't even kissed! And who was in love with someone else! I had more interesting things on my mind than Piers's engagement.

I had told myself I wouldn't worry overmuch if it took

Susanna Lancaster a couple of weeks to reply to my letter.

> ... I have enjoyed reading *Dragonfly Morning* so
> much, especially as last summer I spent a month at
> a house called Deer's Leap. I think I slept in Rosie's
> room, too, above the kitchen; the red roses still peep
> in at the window.
>
> Is Deer's Leap the Laburnum Farm of your novel
> and could Bessie Drake once have been called Lizzie
> Frobisher?
>
> I enclose a stamped envelope in case you can find
> time to reply to me. I do hope you will ...

Allowing for the postal rush over Christmas, and given she
wouldn't write back immediately, even though she couldn't
help being curious, I was sure there would be something in
the post by the end of January.

February came, and two chapters of the First of the Deer's
Leaps written and rewritten. It looked as if she wasn't going
to write, I thought, going through the morning post on 14
February. No letter from Susanna Lancaster, and this was
the first time since I was twelve that no one had sent me a
Valentine card! Cassie Johns was turning into a workaholic
spinster! I put on my wellies and jacket, wound a scarf round
my neck, and made for the churchyard.

'Piers is getting married at Easter,' I said. Not out loud, of
course; Mum had already made it plain she didn't want anyone to see me carrying on a conversation with a headstone.
I talk to Aunt Jane with my mind and my heart, though
Rowbeck would think that a little bit kinky, too!

'*So? You never loved him, Cassie.*'

'This was the first year I didn't get a Valentine card either.
Not even one!'

'*Does it matter?*'

'We-e-ll, no. Not really. I feel a bit cast adrift, though ...'

'*On the shelf, you mean? I wouldn't worry overmuch about that, girl. Get on with the next book!*'

'I am. It's taking shape nicely. *Firedance* should be out in October. D'you reckon it'll do well?'

I listened, but there was no reply. She had gone, and without so much as a chuckle. Not a bit interested in my second novel.

'Bye,' I whispered. 'Just thought I'd pop by – say hullo.'

Hullo my left foot! I wanted the right words, like Aunt Jane usually gave out; words of comfort, or hope – like *he* was out there, and it wouldn't be long before I met him. But she had left me hanging, turning off impatiently as if wanting to be rid of me!

She was right, of course. I ought to be working now, not time-wasting, telling Aunt Jane something she probably knew already!

The phone rang as I opened the back door and I called, 'OK! I'll get it!' then ran upstairs to my desk.

'Good morning. Am I speaking to Cassandra Johns?'

'That's me . . .'

'My name is Susanna Lancaster. You wrote to me.'

'Good heavens! Ooooh, thanks for ringing. It's very kind of you – I didn't expect . . .'

'No problem. You mentioned Deer's Leap, and Lizzie Frobisher, and the red roses. I'm curious. Can we meet?'

'*Meet!* Do you live near, then?' This was altogether too much!

'No, but I'm staying in York for a few days. Are you too busy?' Her voice was soft. She sounded amused, sort of.

'Of course not!' Too busy to meet Susanna Lancaster and with her, Susan Smith? 'Where, please – and when?'

'Tomorrow. Short notice, I'm afraid, but I'm leaving on the 11.37 in the morning.'

'Then tomorrow it is!'

'York station – at ten?'

'I'll be there. I'll wait near the flower stall. And you'll know me at once. I've got red hair!' My hand was shaking as I put the phone down.

'Who was that?' Mum asked, conveniently appearing with coffee.

'Susanna Lancaster, would you believe?'

'The one whose books are on TV?'

'The very same! She's in York. I wrote to her and I'm to meet her tomorrow at the station. I can't believe it!'

'What did she sound like?' Mum settled herself on my bed.

'Well – very nice, I suppose. Her voice was low and normal, sort of. I'd expected her to sound like an old lady.'

'Posh?'

'N-no. Well spoken, though. I must have sounded like an oik, but I was gob-smacked!'

'Well, I hope you don't use words like those when you meet her, or she'll think all Yorkshire folk are *oiks*!' Mum put on her button mouth. 'And why did you write to her? Because she's a celebrity?'

'Yes – but mainly because I think she has connections with Deer's Leap. I think she lived there, you see, during the war. Well, I *am* writing about a house that is Deer's Leap in all but name, aren't I?'

I couldn't tell Mum why really I had to meet her. Aunt Jane would have understood, but not Mum!

'As long as you aren't pushy, Cassie.'

'Of course I won't be! I told her in the letter that the Laburnum Farm in her book sounded very much like Deer's Leap – I suppose she was curious. And I did tell her I'm a writer, too, so maybe that's why she said she'd see me.'

'Pity she didn't write. You'd have known where she lives then.'

'Meeting her is better, Mum. Do you think I should take her *Ice Maiden*? Would giving her a copy of my first book be pushy, do you think?'

'No,' Mum said firmly. 'I'd sign it, if I were you, and put a nice message in it – like "Thank you for meeting me", or something . . .'

I wondered if I should write a list of questions I wanted to ask; deciding against it at once. Because I was meeting Susanna Lancaster, not Suzie Smith. I would have to tread carefully, see how things went, before I mentioned Jack Hunter. I couldn't ask her outright if she was really Susan Smith; tell her that Jack hadn't forgotten her. You had to be careful too about upsetting elderly ladies; couldn't fling, 'By the way, there's a ghost looking for you – name of Jack Hunter!' at them.

'Want anything doing in the house, Mum?' I asked as she got to her feet.

'No thanks, love. Best get on with your writing.'

Yet I knew there would be no writing done today. Already my mind was full of Susanna Lancaster and what we would talk about; if she would clam up at the mention of Jack's name, or the baby girl born in Charlotte Martin's house just before the end of the war in Europe.

Yet I felt, somehow, that she wouldn't. Why should she when she had put it in *Dragonfly Morning* for all to read. And besides, girls who got pregnant out of wedlock didn't jump in rivers now.

I pulled on warm clothes and wellies for the second time that morning. Oh, my word! Just wait till I told Aunt Jane!

I was early. Still ten minutes to go. I stood at the flower stall, casting a professional eye over the display. It was bitterly cold, and I wished I had worn a woolly scarf.

This morning, before I left, I had tried to let Jeannie know about Susanna Lancaster, but she was in a meeting so I left a cryptic message, asking them to be sure she got it. *Cassie phoned. She is meeting Susan Smith in York.* She would know exactly what it meant, I told them.

I had footled about a lot, deciding what to wear to meet

a famous author; deciding in the end to dress normally – for February, that was. My best jeans and a chunky sweater, with a silk scarf knotted at the neck. And my best boots, of course.

What would Susan be like now? White hair, blue-rinsed? Slightly stooping? Wearing a camel-coloured coat, the collar turned up against the wind?

Had she married? The last chapters of *Dragonfly Morning* gave no indication of it, but then, after the birth of Kathryn Charlotte, the final pages of the novel were businesslike, almost a resumé, telling about the first short story she had sold to a magazine for three guineas and how, with Charlotte Martin's guidance, she wrote her first book – and never looked back!

Now that daughter would be in her fifties, with children of her own; would have read *Dragonfly Morning* and about her conception on a hillside in the moonlight.

A woman stopped to look at the flowers. She carried a Chanel bag and an expensive-looking grip. Her skirt was long and straight; slit to her calves. Beneath the cape she wore, I could see a rose-coloured sweater, and if it wasn't cashmere, I'd eat my hat! She turned, then saw me, and smiled.

'Miss Johns? Cassandra?'

'Y-yes. How did you know?' I was blushing. I could feel it.

'Your hair – you told me . . .'

'And it doesn't come redder than mine!' I took the hand she offered.

'It's beautiful. Chestnut. Shall we find somewhere for a coffee?'

I picked up her grip, nodding in the direction of the buffet, still not believing how attractive she was. No sign of the blue rinse. Her hair was a soft ash-blonde and simply, expensively styled. Her face was almost wrinkle-free and her eyebrows looked happy-surprised, sort of.

I found us a corner table, then brought coffees on a tray.

'I didn't get you anything to eat,' I faltered, pulling out the chair opposite. She didn't look the sort who ate chocolate biscuits between meals.

'Coffee is fine,' she smiled. Even her teeth were perfect.

'I know why he fell in love with you,' I gasped, my resolve forgotten. 'I was expecting to meet an old – *elderly* – lady, and you're not! And please forgive me? I'm not being pushy, but I feel I know you already – Rosie from *Dragonfly Morning*, I mean.'

'Is that why you wanted to meet me? Well, you are right. I *am* Rosamund Kenton in the story and yes, I lived at Deer's Leap during the war.'

'Jean McFadden gave me your book last August. I've only now got around to reading it. You signed it for me.'

'Of course! I remember Jean. She minded me at a luncheon. How is she?'

'Very well, last time I saw her.'

I took *Dragonfly Morning* from my shoulder bag, opening it at the title page, pointing to the inscription.

> For Cassie, a new author,
> From Susanna Lancaster,
> an 'old' one.

'I'm writing my third book now, but only the first is in print. I brought you a copy – I hope you'll accept it.' I showed her what I had written.

> From a very new author
> to Susanna Lancaster,
> with gratitude.

'Gratitude?' She lifted an eyebrow. 'Will you tell me why?'

'For letting me share your story – yours and Jack's,' I said softly.

'Jack's? But only my family know that *Dragonfly* is more

fact than fiction. I asked their permission before I started to write it.' She looked puzzled.

'I stayed a month at Deer's Leap, babysitting the place, and I fell in love with it. Now I'm all chewed up because it's on the market, and I can't afford it.' It was all I could think of to say.

'You're nothing if not direct.'

'I know! I'm always doing it; saying things before I think. But I'm so mixed up, Miss Lancaster, so gobsmacked at meeting you – and Mum said you'd think I was an oik if I used words like that!'

'Why did you write to me, Cassandra? *Really*, I mean?'

'Because yours was such a lovely love – yours and Jack's – and because I envy it, even though you had each other for such a short time, and –'

'But in the book we were Jon and Rosie. How did you know – guess?'

'Because Aunt Jane and I are sort of psychic, and because – I – I asked questions in Acton Carey – Bill Jarvis and Mrs Taylor. Lizzie Frobisher, wasn't she? I found out about the Smiths at Deer's Leap, and I saw a name on the war memorial and –'

'And, Cassandra?' she prompted. Her voice was gentle, her eyes curious. She didn't seem upset or annoyed at the way I had crashed into her life; her long-ago life.

'I wasn't going to say this – not until I'd had the chance to prove to you I'm not imagining things – but I've got to say it, and I'm so very sorry . . .'

Her eyes met mine, and held them for a second. Then she stirred her coffee and said, 'What are you sorry about, Cassandra?'

'For blundering in. What happened all those years ago should be no business of mine. But I got caught up in it. I didn't have a lot of choice. And I wanted to help him because I found him attractive. But mostly it was because he loved you so much.'

'Like I said, in the book he was Jon – so who told you his name was Jack? Lizzie, was it?'

'No. He told me.'

I was glaring down at my hands because I couldn't bear to look at her. She was so gentle, so beautiful, so very talented that I had no right to be sitting at the same table, let alone clodhopping over her memories.

'Jack was killed more than fifty years ago,' she whispered.

'Yes, I accept that. But he's still looking for you, Miss Lancaster.' My eyes filled with tears and I did nothing to stop them. 'He doesn't know he's dead. I think I'm a medium, you see. People like me attract people like him to us. I met him last year. It was a beautiful day. He was at the side of the lane, near six oaks; wanted to get to Deer's Leap, he said.'

'So . . . ?' She ran her tongue round her lips and breathed in deeply.

'So you think I'm a nasty little piece who's read your book and out to get herself noticed – pretending I saw a ghost who's looking for his girl and who thinks it's still 1944. I'm not, though. I saw him several times, and Beth – Jean McFadden's sister – has seen him, too. Quite a few have, but they don't say anything because they don't want the press nosing around Acton Carey. And I didn't mean to tell you so – so brutally. It just slipped out.'

I fished for a tissue and dabbed at my eyes, disliking myself for what I had done to her and what I'd done to myself, too, because it was obvious she thought I was unfeeling enough to try such a stunt. She just *had* to!

'Dry your eyes, my dear,' she smiled. 'Shall we have another coffee?'

'You don't believe me,' I choked.

'Well – let's just say that it wouldn't be too hard to put two and two together, once you'd read *Dragonfly Morning*, and come up with –'

'Twenty-two,' I said miserably.

'You are a writer, Cassandra – and I shall read your book with especial interest now that I've met you – but we are all the same. We have to be, or we wouldn't be writers. We live with our imaginations, most of the time; live *off* them, too!'

'But there was so much, Miss Lancaster! The way he pushed his hair out of the way, with his left hand; the way he called her Suzie . . .'

'But everything was in the book for you to read. Are you sure you didn't take it all in, then let your imagination take over? And are you sure that Lizzie Taylor didn't mention his name to you?'

'She might have. I'm not sure. But he told me the very first time we met that his name was Jack Hunter. And he called you Suzie . . .'

'Look – I don't think I want another coffee, and it's getting near train time.' She collected up her gloves and bag.

'I'm sorry,' I said, picking up her grip. 'What must you think of me? Please forgive me?'

'Only if you walk with me to the train.'

'Of course I will.'

'I wanted to have a couple of days in York,' she smiled as we walked up the steps of the bridge. 'I'm glad I did. It's so like Chester – unchanging.'

She was trying to change the subject, but I didn't want her to!

'Aunt Lottie lived near Chester, didn't she? I was so glad you went to see her and stayed with her to have your little girl. And I won't say any more about it,' I said hastily, 'because I don't want you to think I'm a pushy, one-book writer, trying to latch onto someone like you. I'm not pushy, even though I came to your Lancaster house, looking for you.'

'Then you would find I had left. I've bought another house. I'm having a few things done to it, and the decorators are in. I'm staying with Kate, meantime. She still lives in Aunt Lottie's house – Charlotte Martin *was* her name. I knew she wouldn't mind me using it in *Dragonfly Morning*.'

'You don't have to be kind to me.' We were standing on platform five now, and soon we would part. 'You're being so decent that I'll be miserable about today for the rest of my life. I'm going to write four books, y'know, starting at 1592. They'll all centre on Deer's Leap, so I won't ever be able quite to forget today. And it'll hurt more because some other woman will look out at the view from that kitchen window. Serves me right, I suppose, for the things I've said to you.'

'That house has made an impression on you – the time you stayed there, I mean.'

'I shall never forget that one summer at Deer's Leap. Even at this very minute, some awful woman could be looking it over, finding fault to try to get the price down!'

'It *is* a lovely house. I can understand you wanting it.'

'Is this your train, Miss Lancaster? It goes to Liverpool, it says.'

'That's right. I change at Manchester for Chester. Kate will meet me there.'

'Why are you being so nice to me?'

'I don't know, Cassandra. Maybe because something inside me wants you to have met Jack, though my sensible side says you were influenced by *Dragonfly Morning*. On the other hand, it might be because I am like my grandson. Like me, he seems to get on well with redheads – but for an entirely different reason!'

'Kate had a son?' The train was standing at the platform, doors open.

'Just the one child.'

'Are you sure I'm forgiven?' I whispered. 'I did so want you to believe me.'

The tears were pricking again and I squeezed my eyes tightly, so they wouldn't come.

'I would like to believe you, but like I said, it was all there in the book to –' She stopped, embarrassed.

'For me to make up a story about, you mean?'

'We-e-ll – yes. If only there was some small thing you could tell me that wasn't in the book; something only you and I could know.'

'There isn't. I've got to agree it was all there in *Dragonfly Morning*. Even the fact that Rosie took a candle to bed. But I met your Jack ever before I read the book, don't forget. And by the way, I liked your father. Did you really never see your parents again?'

'I kept in touch with Dad – on his birthday, and at Christmas. When we could, we spoke on the phone. He died of a heart attack before they got Deer's Leap back. I went to his funeral, but my mother didn't know I was there. It was only by chance I got to know, but at least I said goodbye to him. My mother returned, briefly, to the house when the war was over, but it was never a farm again – never really my Deer's Leap. When she died, she left it to the local hospice, who sold it, I believe to a man who'd won the pools.'

'I'm glad you said a goodbye to your father. I want you to say one to Jack – so he can rest,' I said softly, 'but it won't ever be possible.'

'Cassandra – I do so want to believe you! Isn't there anything at all you can remember?'

'No. Sorry.' All I had hoped for was slipping away from me. 'He was so solid and real. I thought he was all done up for the fancy dress party I was going to. His stripes, the way his hair was cut. I asked him where he'd got his uniform because he looked so authentic. He said they threw the uniform at you; it was only the wings that were hard to come by.

'He was even carrying a respirator; his number was stamped on the front of it, in black, though I don't remember what it was. Maybe you would believe me, if I could. There was a little heart there, too, and S. S. beside it, on the strap and –'

'There was *what*? What did you say?'

'A heart, the size of my thumbnail, and initials, inside the strap. I don't think I read that in the book.'

'You didn't! What colour were they?'

'Well – a sort of purple, I suppose . . .'

'*Yes!* There were no ballpoint pens, nor felt-tips, in those days. We often used an indelible pencil. You moistened the tip on your tongue, and it looked like purple ink. And, oh! I'll have to get on!' A guard, whistle poised, was looking at us pointedly and she made for the nearest door. I picked up her grip and handed it to her.

'I'll ring you tonight,' she called as the doors began to slide shut. 'From Kate's!'

I watched the train go, not believing any of it; that I had found Susan Smith who hadn't believed me until I mentioned something quite unimportant. Initials, and a heart beside them. The sort of thing lovers do – *did* – a long time ago.

I was shaking, but whether from relief or because I was so full up, I couldn't tell. It seemed, now, that all I wanted was to get back to Greenleas and wait for the call – *if* she rang, that was. It would serve me right, I supposed, if she didn't.

And what was Jeannie going to say when I told her?

'My word,' Mum said. 'You know when to put in an appearance! I thought you'd decided to make a day of it. Soup?'

'Please.' I washed my hands at the sink, drying them thoughtfully.

'Well?' she demanded. 'What was she like then? What happened? Was she pleased with your book?'

'She was nice, and really beautiful – elegant. And we talked, and yes, she seemed quite pleased with *Ice Maiden*.'

'And . . . ?'

'Mum! We had thirty minutes! She had to catch a train to Chester – her daughter was meeting her.'

'So what was she doing in York in February?'

'Having a short break, I suppose. She'd always wanted to see it, she said.'

'I'll have another slice please, Lyd, if you're cutting.'

Dad didn't seem one bit interested – but then, he didn't know what I knew; Mum neither.

'And I forgot!' Mum paused, bread knife poised. 'Jeannie rang. She's ringing back, after two.'

'Fine! Jeannie met Susanna Lancaster, too. It was when I was at Deer's Leap for the month. Harriers are Susanna's publishers, too.'

'Yes. You said. But what did you talk about?'

'Oh, this and that. About writing, and about her last novel – and my first one. And she said she once lived at Deer's Leap.'

'Well, now!' All at once, Mum was interested. 'When was that?'

'She and her parents left it during the war – never went back. But it's all in *Dragonfly Morning*. I've finished it now, so I think you ought to read it. It would explain a lot!'

The phone rang, and Mum went to answer it.

'That was the pub.' She sat down at the table again, annoyed at the interruption. 'They've had a lot of bookings for tonight for dinners. Need more sprouts. Can you let them have three pounds? I told them yes, but we don't deliver. They're sending someone to collect them.'

'They can darn well pick 'em, an' all!' Picking icy sprouts on a February day isn't Dad's most favourite pastime.

'So not a lot happened, Cassie?' Mum seemed disappointed.

'You can't say much in half an hour. But she did say she would ring tonight.'

'Why?' Dad asked, being perverse, I suppose, because of the sprouts.

'I don't know! Maybe because she wants to talk some more – maybe let me know she got back to Chester all right. Does it matter? I met her, and she was lovely. You can tell Piers's mother, next time you see her. Tell her your daughter had coffee with the famous Susanna Lancaster!'

'Y-yes . . .' Mum smiled wickedly. 'Make a change from that dratted engagement!'

'I'll wash the dishes for you,' I offered when we'd finished, 'then I've got to get on with some work, catch up on the words.'

'You wouldn't like to pick three pounds of sprouts?' Dad grinned.

'Now how would I be able to type,' I grinned back, 'with frozen fingers?' All at once, I felt good!

Jeannie was on the phone for ten minutes, delighted at what I told her. 'But, Cassie, what are you going to say when she phones? Suggest you both go to Deer's Leap; try to find the pilot? This isn't what I'd call ghost-hunting weather. You could walk up and down that lane for days, and still he mightn't show, and the two of you frozen stiff!'

'Jeannie! I don't know how she's going to take it. Maybe she'll tell me when she rings tonight. At first, you see, she wouldn't buy it, till I told her about the heart and the initials. We had to leave it there. Her train was pulling out. The last thing she said was that she would ring tonight. I'm just praying she'll believe me now. And nothing can happen yet. She's living with her daughter near Chester at the moment. She's bought another house, but it isn't ready to move into, so she won't want to do anything till she's got herself settled, now will she?'

'Did she tell you where the house is?'

'No. I didn't ask. But at least I've got hopes that we can meet again at Deer's Leap, perhaps when summer comes. I want so much for Suzie and Jack to at least say goodbye.'

'Cassie! Be careful! Lancaster might be like me – not able to tune in on ghosts. You saw the pilot the day after Beth and Danny came back from Cornwall but I didn't! What will you do then?'

'I'll worry about it if it happens. I know it will happen, if only I can persuade her to go with me to Acton Carey. She and Jack loved too much for him not to know when she was about.'

'And is she married? Was she wearing a ring?'

'Not a wedding ring. She did have a lovely sapphire on her third finger, left hand, though. Exactly like Diana's . . .'

'Romantic, I suppose. Wish I could meet a bloke like Jack Hunter. The ones I come across are very forgettable! But let me know what happens, will you?'

I said I would, and put the phone down, my elation leaving me, because all at once I knew Susanna Lancaster wouldn't ring again. Why should she?

I felt restless, which isn't good for wordage; began to think I'd have done better offering to pick the sprouts. I closed my eyes and breathed in deeply.

'Cassie!' I hissed. 'Pull yourself together and get some work done! Sitting here agonizing doesn't buy houses!' Not a house like Deer's Leap, it didn't!

Yet even as I switched on the machine, I knew Deer's Leap was sold. It was so beautiful, such a very desirable residence, that it had to be! And if ever Susanna Lancaster and I made it to six oaks or the squeaking iron gate, it was going to hurt like mad just thinking about the lucky cat who had beat me to it!

'Cassandra?'

'Oooh! Thank you for ringing. I'd convinced myself you wouldn't.'

'I nearly didn't – but I'm curious. And I suppose I want to believe you saw Jack.'

'I did.'

'Right! So what happens now?'

'I've been thinking about it a lot – shall we give it a try when the better weather comes? Maybe when you've got settled into your new place, it could be. And I know this is a cheek, but could you possibly make it to Acton Carey; stay a couple of days? The Red Rose does bed and breakfast.'

'Y-yes. I'm sure we could work something out.'

'We must, Miss Lancaster. I only hope we can send some

vibes out – let Jack know we are looking for him. How long, do you think, before you can get into your house?'

'Not too long. In fact, I plan to have the place up and running and well aired by the end of March. I'll have all the time in the world, then.'

'I don't know exactly how we'll manage it, but we'll do our best to be there, for Jack. Wasn't it strange that right at the last minute, I should mention the heart?'

'It was. I drew it on the strap of his gas mask, when I saw him off on leave from Preston station. He told me I'd get him into trouble for defacing Air Ministry property! I didn't put it in *Dragonfly*, though.'

'I think I know when it was. You'd said your hair was in need of a trim; an excuse so you could get away. And Jack told you not to have it cut too short. He liked your hair long.'

'Yes. That was the afternoon the purple heart happened . . .'

'You won't change your mind, will you? When the days start getting warmer, you *will* meet me there – try to find him?'

'I promise. And you'll see Lizzie again, Cassandra. Or should I call her Bessie? She told me you'd been asking questions. She remembered your hair, you see.'

'But when did you meet? *How* did you meet?'

'As a matter of fact, I was in the area, looking at houses. There was one I wanted very much to buy, but I couldn't make up my mind – for all sorts of reasons. So I went to Acton Carey, and saw the war memorial with Jack's name on it, and that settled it for me. I was walking away, just a bit full up, when someone said, "So you're back at last, Susan Smith! Well, you'd better come in for a cup of tea, because I've got something to give you! Kept them fifty-five years; reckoned we'd meet up again one fine day . . ."'

'Oh, how *wonderful*! I liked Mrs Taylor. Imagine Bessie Drake marrying a curate!'

Susanna laughed, and I knew everything was going to be all right.

'He ended up a parish priest, and Bessie – *Lizzie* – came back to Acton Carey, a widow, to retire in one of the vicarage flats – but you know that.'

'You'll be meeting again, I hope?'

'No doubt about it! I gave her a copy of *Dragonfly Morning*, asked her to read it, told her she was in it, too. And that it would explain everything. We keep in touch by letter, and phone weekends.'

'How lovely! And can you and I keep in touch – for Jack's sake I mean? Just the odd letter?'

'We must, or how are we to arrange things? Quite a few weeks, yet, until I move in.'

'Yes. But you'll be busy and I'll be busy, too. The time will soon pass.'

'I'm sure it will. But what if I haven't got your powers; if I'm not psychic, I mean? Would Jack appear if there were negative vibes around?'

'I'm sure he would, because you wouldn't be sending out bad vibes, would you, because you want to meet him again? I met him once when I was with Jeannie, but she didn't see him! She got quite cross with me. But you won't frighten him off, if that's what you are thinking.' I felt so confident, so absolutely sure, that I didn't feel one bit guilty about raising her hopes. She and Jack would meet again, I knew it. 'But this call must be costing the earth! We've been on for ages!'

'Worth it, though! But we'll keep in touch, till we can arrange something. And, Cassandra – you are a writer, so you know the value of punchlines, don't you?'

'Where to end a chapter, you mean? The very last line that's got to be special, so the reader will want to keep turning pages? Yes – I'm learning about punchlines!'

'Then here's a punchline for me to end this call with! I bought Deer's Leap, two months ago, so you'll be able to come and stay in April, won't you? Bye. See you!'

She hung up before I could reply, which was just as well

come to think of it, because I stood for ages looking at the receiver before I put it down.

'Flaming Norah!' I whispered. 'Oh, Aunt Jane! You knew all the time, didn't you!'

Then I ran to tell Mum the wonderful news.

Chapter Twelve

I stopped the Mini at six oaks, telling myself I was back again; thinking how pretty the sloe blossom looked, frothing white in the hedges. And to notice that the oak trees had not broken leaf, yet, and that everything was familiar and precious, like always.

But it wasn't entirely the coming-home feeling that caused me to pull in at the side of the road. I had stopped, truth known, and wound down the window so I could send out messages; let Jack Hunter know I was at Deer's Leap, and that he had better be aware of the fact.

Such a shock, Susanna Lancaster's triumphant punchline; discovering she was the rich bitch who had snapped up Deer's Leap. A happy shock, really, because if I couldn't have it, then it was best that she should.

She was brave, for all that, going back to her green years and all the happiness and heartbreak to be lived over again. Yet I felt nothing but delight, because soon I would see the lovely old house again; drive up the dirt road to the white gate ahead, and beside it the little iron gate, painted shiny black.

Would she be waiting as Jeannie had been, that very first time? And, more important than anything, would I see Jack Hunter at the roadside and would he ask for a lift to Deer's Leap?

Would there be a flock of sheep ahead and could I, should I, tell him his Suzie was back, and would he please not disappear through the rusty, creaking gate. Just this once?

I turned the key in the ignition, then crawled past the spot. He wasn't there, so I sent white-hot vibes through the window, then picked up speed.

Jack wasn't coming, today; nor was there a flock of slow-moving sheep ahead as I rounded the bend to see the cross-roads and the right turn to Deer's Leap, hidden by a hawthorn hedge in new green leaf.

Susanna was not at the white gate, but it had been obligingly opened. I drove through, my stomach making noises, then glanced in the rear-view mirror.

I hadn't realized someone was standing there. Her hair was grey, and permed into tight curls; she had a cigarette in her hand and was still wearing the green cardigan.

'Mrs Taylor!' I grinned. 'Or are you Lizzie, or Bessie?'

'Be blowed if I know. Lizzie, I think, like always. Susan said you were coming, and that I was to be here to meet you. Still asking questions, are you?'

'No. Think I've got most of the answers, now.'

'Ah. Read *Dragonfly Morning*, did you? I quite enjoyed being in a book. Trouble is, I can't tell anybody that it's me Bessie Drake is based on, and that there's more truth in it than fiction. Wouldn't be right, now would it? Not round here. Poor Susan. If she wasn't so rich, I'd feel sorry for her.' She drew hard on the cigarette, then threw it into the hedge. 'Not allowed to smoke in the house.' She pulled down the corners of her mouth. 'I was asked to keep an eye open for you if the lady of the house wasn't back in time. She's having her hair done in Clitheroe.'

'I'm early. Nearly an hour. Y'know, that day we met – when you were cleaning the church – I didn't know I was going to read all about you in a book. Bessie was a lovely character, wasn't she?'

'Spare my blushes, if you don't mind. And can you shift your car up a bit, so Susan can get hers in? I've got the kettle on. She shouldn't be long.'

I opened the boot and took out the potted plants I had brought with me. Not a lot in the garden now the daffodils were almost over, Dad said; and daffodils would be coals to Newcastle, so best take plants.

'What do you think to the kitchen?' Mrs Taylor said smugly, opening the door with a flourish.

'Oh, my word! The old firegrate has gone!'

An Aga stood in its place; a kettle puffed complacently on it.

'Like it?'

I said I did because not too much had changed. Newly decorated, of course, with William Morris-type wallpaper and a new terracotta tile floor. 'I'm glad she has come home. It must have taken a bit of doing.'

'I think it did, but she's got herself together now, I think. And there she is! Away you go, and say hullo.'

I waited on the step, and she smiled and said, 'Welcome back to Deer's Leap, Cassandra.'

'You beat me to it,' I smiled. 'I was going to say, "Welcome home, Susan Smith." I like your kitchen.'

'Wait until you see the rest of the house.'

'You haven't changed it too much, have you?'

'No. Only, shall we say, *enough* . . .'

I knew exactly what she meant, so I asked her if she was sleeping in the bedroom above the kitchen again.

'No. I sleep above the sitting room now.'

'The room with the marvellous view.' I felt so at home I wanted to hug myself.

'That's the one! But I see Lizzie has been making herself useful.'

A teatray was set, and she was putting the cosy on the teapot.

'I'm not staying, Susan. You two'll have a lot to talk about. Give me a ring, when you know what your plans are?'

'I'll run you back home, Mrs Taylor. It won't take a minute,' I offered.

'Thanks, but no. I like walking, and besides, I want –'

'A cigarette,' Susan finished, smiling wickedly.

'As a matter of fact, I do. Nice to see you again, Cassandra.

We'll have a chat, soon. And don't bother to come to the gate with me, Susan.'

'Tell me, please,' I asked when she had gone, 'are you Miss Lancaster or Miss Smith?'

'Susan, I think. After all, we are both writers. And I'm sure Mrs Taylor won't mind if you call her Lizzie.'

'I'm still inclined to think of her as Bessie, and you as Rosamund – Rosie.'

'Whichever! Now let's have that tea, then I'll show you your room.'

'Am I up the back stairs, like before?'

'No. That bedroom is my office, now.'

'So *Dragonfly Morning* isn't to be your last book?'

'I – oh, I don't know! I'd thought it would be, but there is such a buzz of words in my head that I can't be certain.'

'What might it be about – or don't you discuss plots with other writers?'

'I'd like to talk to *you* about it.' She stirred her tea, slowly and for too long, as if arranging the words in the right order before she said them. 'It might be a bit historical. I know you are doing books based on Deer's Leap and it gave me the idea to research Fellfoot – see if there was a story there. Just something to keep me out of mischief once I've got Deer's Leap to my liking . . .'

'Fellfoot? Would you be laying ghosts, perhaps?'

'I don't know. Will you come with me to Fellfoot, Cassandra?'

'Of course I will. I haven't seen it, nor the pond. I'd have thought the place might have fallen down, or been vandalized.'

'Neither. Fellfoot was built solid, but it's in a sad state, for all that.'

'And you think something of Jack might still be there?'

'I did, but there's nothing – not this far. I've been there quite a few times, since I came home.' She sipped her tea and I knew she was arranging words again. 'Do you remember the bit in *Dragonfly* when Bessie said she had something to give to Rosamund before she left Deer's Leap for Skipton?'

'Yes. A parting present, wasn't it? Rosamund thought it would be one of Bessie's school prizes, and quite precious?'

'I was wrong. Lizzie gave it – *them* – to me the day we met again after all those years. She had kept them all that time, would you believe? There was a snap of me, sitting on the big, flat stone beside the pond – and Jack's last letter.

'Young men who flew used to write a last letter; leave it behind to be posted in case they didn't make it back. When first Jack was killed, I used to hope he had written one to me, but nothing came, so I told myself it was because we had both been so confident *J-Johnnie* would make the tour of ops safely, that he hadn't done it.'

'But then came the daylight raid . . .' I prompted.

'Jack's thirty-eighth. He had written a letter long before that last op; even before he knew about the baby, but it was addressed to me care of Lizzie. He thought, I suppose, it would have a better chance of getting to me, the way things were at home. Some day, when we know each other better, I'll let you read it. I had looked over Deer's Leap; been hesitating about making an offer for it, so I walked down to Acton Carey, to look at the war memorial . . .'

'Trying to find an answer there?' I said gently.

'Yes. And there was. I met Lizzie, and she gave me Jack's letter, and the snap. That settled it for me. It was as if Jack was asking me to come back.' Then the remembering left her eyes and she said, brightly, 'Another cup, then perhaps you can get unpacked? Kate isn't coming until after you've gone, but Josh might make it, he said last night when he rang. He's clearing some woodland near Chichester, and it's taking a bit longer than he thought.'

'Is that what your grandson does?'

'I suppose you'd call him an arborist, but he says his work is looking after trees. He loves trees; couldn't have chosen a better career.'

'You love trees, too. It hurt, didn't it, when the beeches were felled because of the aerodrome?'

'It hurt a lot. But Josh intends planting five more for me. Deer's Leap is for him. He intends making the paddock into a nursery for young trees, and there'll be plenty of work around here. He'll live here permanently.' Her eyes lit on the plants on the draining board. 'Are those for me? How lovely!'

'Home grown,' I said proudly. 'Dad thought the viburnum should do well outside. He's seen Deer's Leap. He and Mum visited when I was house-sitting.'

'Then Josh shall plant the little bush. How do I look after the other one? It's a peace lily, isn't it?'

'Water moderately, except when it's in flower. Bright light, but not direct sun. And spray the leaves, occasionally. You're talking to a market gardener's daughter. I'm good with growing things, too!'

'Then you and Josh will have quite a lot in common. I do hope he gets here before you go, Cassandra. But get unpacked, then it'll be time to eat. After, maybe we might take a look at Fellfoot . . . ?'

'I'd like that.' I was touched, truth known, that she was letting me share her memories. 'Is it very much changed? Will I see a dragonfly?'

'No. It's a bit early in the year for them, but the willow is still there, quietly dying. And the pond is almost empty; not as much water about, it seems.'

'Will it be possible to see inside the house, or are the floors unsafe?'

'It's all unsafe now. It has had to be fenced off. If one of those heavy roof slabs fell onto anyone, it could be serious. Fellfoot has a stone roof. It's older, even, than Deer's Leap.'

'Didn't you find it a bit upsetting, seeing it like that?'

'Not any longer. I've been there three times alone. Tonight, after you have seen it, I shall tell it goodbye. But first things first. I'll take you to your room. I think you'll like it . . .'

*   *   *

It was still light when we set out for Fellfoot. The higher we climbed, the more slippery the grass became with evening dew; and I offered my arm to Susan.

At the pond, she took a photograph from her jacket pocket. It was in black and white, faded to sepia, yet even so it did nothing to detract from the beauty of the young girl sitting on a stone with a weeping willow behind her.

'Lizzie had managed to get a film for her camera. Films were very scarce in those days, and precious. That snap was for Jack. You can see how it used to be here. The willow is sickly now because it isn't getting as much water as it should, and the pond is little more than a bog. Even the stone I was sitting on is overgrown. And you won't see a dragonfly, Cassandra. There are no pond insects now for it to feed on.'

'It's very sad,' I said gently, wondering how she could bear to come here.

'Yes, but look! The little house still hangs on.'

Fellfoot was ringed round with a sturdy fence, and on the padlocked gate was a very official-looking notice to warn off trespassers. I was seeing for the first time the house where long-ago lovers met secretly; something from a work of fiction that all at once was very real. The moss-grown roof was still there; the windows still boarded up. Greening around the foundations and up the walls told a sorry story.

'I suppose it never had a damp course?'

'No. Fellfoot is in a fold, you see. When it was built, the rising ground either side sheltered it from wind and the worst of the weather, but now water has started to collect in the dip.'

'So what will happen to it?'

'It will die slowly, like the willow. It's why I won't come back after tonight.'

'Do you want to leave now?' The sky was beginning to darken to the west.

'Yes.' She turned abruptly and walked away without even a backward glance.

'Give me your arm,' I said gently. 'And thank you for showing me the place where you were both so happy. The dragonfly morning, I mean, at the pond, when Jack had finished his tour of operations, and everything seemed to be coming right for you both.'

'Seemed. Yet on the whole, I've had a good life, Cassandra, though I really think the morning Jack and I met here and I told him that . . .'

'That you were carrying Kate,' I finished for her, when her words trailed into silence.

'Yes. That hour we spent here was the most perfect I shall ever know. Over the years, if I get a feeling-sorry-for-myself mood on me, I remember the dragonfly morning, and it comes right again, and I'm glad.'

'Glad you had Kate?'

'Yes. Because of Kate, I didn't quite lose Jack. And I have a grandson.'

'You've got the lot, almost. And as an author, you're a household name. You haven't lost your looks either,' I added, just a little bit peevishly.

'Goodness! Flattery will get you everywhere! But I do cheat a bit. My hair is good, but completely white. I have a blonde rinse on it,' she laughed, in charge of her emotions again. 'And my smile is the result of an orthodontist's skill. But it was always there at the back of my mind, you see. I tried to stay young for Jack; keep things as they were. Foolish old woman, aren't I, because Jack is in the little churchyard near Primrose Cottage. Kate will look after him now that I'm living here.'

'Do you ever wonder how life would have been if that daylight raid on the rocket site hadn't happened?'

'All the time! I don't suppose I'd have become Susanna Lancaster, though; been too busy being a wife and mother. I think we'd have had three children; two girls and a boy.

But once the edge is off the hurt, remembering is quite a comfort. And all my memories of Jack are good ones. I'm luckier than most.'

We had got to the road, and the signpost that once had the arms removed because of enemy parachutists.

'Have you ever tried to find Jack,' I said out of the blue when we were near the iron gate.

'If trying to find him means thinking about him constantly, and loving him and wanting him, still – then yes, I've tried – especially since I came back to Deer's Leap. I have stood at six oaks and beside the kissing gate and in the hayloft – or where it used to be before someone altered the outbuildings around. And I've been to Fellfoot, too, but he isn't there either. I think I'm going to need help if I'm to meet him just once more; ask him to wait a little longer for me. Now you are here, Cassandra, it might happen.'

'So you do believe I have seen him, talked to him?' I said softly, hoping I hadn't made her wish for something that might not happen.

'Sometimes I believe; sometimes I don't. All I really know is that deep down, I want it to be true.'

When we had built up the sitting-room fire, kicked off our shoes and curled up in the big, squashy chairs either side of it, she said, 'Now! Tea, coffee, or a real drink?'

'Do you have any sherry?'

'Dry, medium, or sweet-pale?'

'Medium, please. Are you going to have one, too?'

'I rather think I am,' she smiled.

'To Deer's Leap!' I raised my glass. 'And to Susan Smith, who has come home.'

'Bless you. Deer's Leap is really for Josh. He and I are very close, and he'd like nothing more than for me to live out my days here. But I hope he'll marry, and have the children this old house needs.'

'Josh has a girlfriend?'

'Not a regular one, though I fancy he's dipped a toe in the water a time or two. I think he's ready to settle down, now college is behind him, but I have a strong feeling he'll be like me. When he meets the right one, he'll know at once.'

'What is he like?' This far, I hadn't seen a photograph of him anywhere in the house. Of Jack, yes! Jack on Susan's bedside table; smiling from the desk top, the mantelshelf – yet none of his grandson.

'You'll know – soon, I hope.' She smiled.

'This house doesn't appear to have had many children – not actually born here,' I said, with the First of the Deer's Leap books in mind. 'Margaret Dacre didn't have any, and Jeannie's sister's children weren't born here.'

'Nor was I. I was born in Ribchester – came here as a baby.'

'In *Dragonfly Morning*, Rosie once asked about her grand-parents. Was that bit fact, or fiction?'

'Sadly, it's fact. My mother cut herself off from her parents.'

'Did you ever know why?'

'I've had thoughts about it from time to time. I suppose it's wrong of me, but the only thing that makes any sense is that she was – well – when she was young, someone . . .'

'You mean she was molested! But I thought that sort of thing didn't happen in those days!'

'Oh, but it did! The only difference, as far as I can see, is that if a child complained, or made accusations, it was never believed. They didn't have Childline then. It would account for her coldness; for her leaving home and marrying the minute she came into her inheritance; for a lot of things. To my mother, *that* sort of thing was – dirty. Looking back, I don't know how my father put up with the way things were. I loved Dad, y'know.'

'But you and Jack still fell in love, in spite of your mother.'

'Oh, yes! It was instant! We loved, and were in love! I ached for him; couldn't wait to be loved. Reckon we'd have had more than three children, Cassandra!' She smiled, impishly. 'Kate was my fault, you know. I wanted Jack so much that night, so we were careless – just the once.'

'You must have loved him very much.'

'Did. Do. Always will. I hope we'll get our second chance. I'm depending on it – reincarnation, I mean.'

'Miss Lancaster – Susan!' All at once, I couldn't bear it. 'What am I doing here?' My voice was shaky because a wobble of tears in my throat was getting in the way of my words. 'You invite me, a stranger, to your home, take me into your confidence, open your heart to me – treat me like a friend. *Why*, will you tell me?'

'Because you are like Lizzie. You knew – *know* – Jack.'

'But I'm only here for a week! We might not see him!'

'Then we'll keep trying till we do. You'll have to come here often to do research for your books, won't you? We'll have plenty of chances, and I feel he's very near,' she said gently. 'It's going to come right, I know it. And don't look so woebegone. Don't be sad for me. Jack and I talked about being lovers; decided the risk was worth it. During that war, there seemed to be an urgency to know what love was like, because tomorrow you might be dead. Jack and I got Kate on the hillside, under a full moon, yet I never thought we were doing wrong. We loved so desperately that what society thought about pre-marital sex didn't apply to Jack and me.'

'I suppose there wouldn't have been so much agonizing if your generation had had the pill, like mine has.'

'It would have made a lot of difference, I suppose, but if the pill had been around fifty-odd years ago, I'm almost sure it would have been frowned on. Nice girls were expected to be innocent; nicely reared young ladies weren't supposed to know about birth control.'

'Funny, but losing your virginity doesn't count for much nowadays. Things have changed a lot in fifty-odd years.'

'When I was growing up, Cassandra, the risk of conceiving kept most girls on the straight and narrow until their wedding night. Only those who were madly in love risked it. You had to be utterly besotted, when you thought of the disgrace and trouble there would be if anything went wrong. There was no such thing as a legal abortion, then. You carried the baby, even if it was a rape child.'

'It's a pity you weren't of age until you were twenty-one,' I sighed.

'Pity? It's a crying shame. If I had been of age at eighteen, I think Jack and I would have been married right away! But if you had told me about the freedom girls have these days, I wouldn't have believed you. Oh, how I do go on! What must you think of me, Cassandra?'

'I almost envy you,' I said after I had thought over the question. 'Yes. I really envy you the way you loved. I'm not a virgin. With me, it was curiosity. I wasn't in love with the man. Then I met Jack, who was looking for you, and I was certain as I could be that he was the kind of man I could fall in love with. Only he belongs to you; always will. I found him so attractive I once decided that if I had been around in those days. I'd have given you a run for your money! There now! What do you think to that!'

'It makes me feel rather smug that I have exclusive rights,' she laughed. 'But to change the subject – I think that tomorrow I should ring Lizzie. We could take her for a pub lunch, perhaps?'

'I'd like that.' It would be fun, meeting Bill Jarvis again. 'I'll drive.'

I would have to, though it would mean not having a drink at the Red Rose. Jack Hunter had responded to my car. Even if ghosts don't see in colour, I hoped he would recognize the Mini again.

'And I think that if we go out, we should always use my car. It's a two-door job – so could you perhaps sit in the back, Susan, when we do – leave the front seat available, kind of?'

'Whatever you think best. You are the go-between, Cassandra. I don't think I'm psychic enough to do it alone. But do we always have to drive? The car isn't absolutely essential, is it?'

'No. I think the power of love is way ahead of anything the internal combustion engine can offer. If we are to see Jack, he'll be there, no matter what.'

'I hope so. But then I try to think about it dispassionately and my Lancashire common sense tells me I'm a woman who's had more than her three-score years and ten; who has a close, loving family and is financially secure. What more dare I ask of life?'

'To say goodbye to Jack,' I said softly.

'But why *me*? What's so special about Susan Smith?'

'The fact that she was loved – is still loved . . .'

'There's no such thing as ghosts, Cassandra!' She jumped to her feet, crossing the room to stare, arms folded, out of the window.

'I've seen one.' I went to her side. 'Susan – do you think I'd do anything so completely rotten as to raise your hopes just for the hell of it? OK – so we are both writers and prone to flights of fancy – but I met Jack, I swear I did, or how could I have known about the purple heart?'

She looked long into my eyes, then sighed and whispered, 'How could you indeed? And I want so desperately to see him – just say that last goodbye, y'know . . .'

'I do know.' I laid an arm around her shoulders. 'And it's been a long day for us both. Maybe we should go to bed. I'll bring you a milky drink if you would like.'

'I'd like that very much – and tomorrow is another day, isn't it? Maybe tomorrow we'll be lucky . . .'

I drew back my curtains, got into bed, then switched out the light. My room was smaller than when I was last at Deer's Leap, because part of it had been taken for an en-suite bathroom. It was a very feminine room and had a view right over to the hilltops. I felt so completely at home in it that I half expected Tommy to jump, purring loudly, onto the bed.

I lay still, my eyes adjusting to the brighter rectangle of light that was the window, thinking about Jack Hunter, reaching out with my mind to him, breathing softly so I might hear the howl of a dog called Shep, and the distant sound of returning bombers.

But the silence was complete, so I thought instead about Susanna Lancaster's deep and abiding love; a love that was as strong and fresh as the night they had met. I felt pleased to have gained her trust; hoped that one day I would gain her affection. And Lizzie's, too, because Lizzie – *Bessie* – was a part of the Deer's Leap story, and a long-ago love that would never end.

As the floaty feeling that comes before sleep took me, I whispered, 'Be there for us soon, Sergeant Jack Hunter. Please?'

Susan put down the bright red phone that matched the bright red Aga, then asked, smiling, 'Had a good walk?'

'Great, thanks. I took loads of pictures, for research.'

'You'll have to come back – take more – in summer and autumn and winter, too. There's a special kind of beauty about the fells, when winter is on them.'

'Any excuse at all,' I laughed. 'Just try keeping me away! By the way, I took one of Fellfoot; just to finish the roll off,' I added hastily. 'It probably won't be much good.'

I told lies, too, because I had wished like mad that when the negative was developed I would see a World War Two pilot standing there – waiting for Suzie.

'Can I think out loud, whilst we drink our coffee? Or do you want a break from words?'

'Of course you can, Cassandra. Words are my stock in trade.'

'Then when you said that Fellfoot was even older than

this house, it suddenly struck me that in Margaret Dacre's time, the people who lived there would have been her nearest neighbours. What would you think if I used Fellfoot, too, in the first of the novels? I'm not so far ahead with it that I can't introduce another house, another set of characters.'

'Mm. But don't overload a novel with people, Cassandra – especially when there are three more books to follow, and you might have to take some of the characters into the next book. But go on,' she nodded.

'Do you suppose that Margaret Dacre really was a witch? You know more about local folklore than I ever will. Mind, she'll be a witch in book one, no doubt about it, though I have called her Mary Dobbie.'

'M. D. – 1592. The times I have seen that inscription. But yes, Cassandra. I think she was. When we were young, Lizzie was sure of it, and that my mother was a witch, too – sort of possessed by Margaret Dacre.'

'And what did *you* think, all those years ago?'

'I agreed with Lizzie in the end. It was why I went to Aunt Lottie's house. I was afraid for the baby. My mother had already ill-wished Jack, don't forget.'

'And you could think that about your own mother?'

'There was a lot of Margaret Dacre in her. It would strengthen the storyline of book one if you stressed the witch-craft angle, Cassandra. But you've read *Dragonfly Morning*. It's almost all fact, disguised as a work of fiction. *Dragonfly* just had to be written; for Jack, for Kate and for me, to set the record straight. I don't think, even yet, that I have forgiven my mother for the way she was. But we were talking about your book . . .'

'No. It's OK. I think I've got it straight now. And I'll be careful about cluttering it up – thanks for the advice.'

'You're welcome, as they say! Now tell me – how do you fancy afternoon tea at the vicarage? At Lizzie's actually. She rang this morning and I accepted. All right?'

'Fine.' I had liked Bessie Drake in *Dragonfly Morning*, so

it was easy to like Lizzie. And besides, there were things I wanted to ask her about witchcraft, locally – if being the wife of a parson hadn't changed her beliefs in such matters. 'And there's something else. I think it might be a good idea if you were to keep the photo that Bessie – ooops! *Lizzie* – took at Fellfoot; the one she kept all those years for you. You could show it to Jack – something he would recognize.'

'A sort of passport, you mean? I'll take one of Aunt Lottie, as well. He would recognize her, too.'

'A passport to 1944 and Suzie,' I said gravely. 'Oh, I do want him to be there. I've been sending out vibes like mad. Surely he's got them.'

'And I've been doing much the same, Cassandra. I'm not very *au fait* with vibes, but if longing and love counts for anything I think that between us we shall see him!'

It was such a lovely afternoon that we decided to walk to Acton Carey, though we passed not a soul on the way, and no one stood at the roadside, thumbing a lift.

Lizzie was waiting for us, wearing her Sunday best; had baked scones, she said, to eat with cream and jam and wasn't the weather just lovely?

The vicarage had been converted into four retirement apartments; Lizzie had one on the ground floor, with old-fashioned French windows opening onto what had once, she said, been a croquet lawn.

Easy chairs were arranged with a view of the garden; Lizzie took the one nearest the open window so she could blow her cigarette smoke out, I supposed. A small table was ready laid so that when we had done enough talking, it would be only a matter of lighting the gas under the kettle.

'So – what's news? What have the pair of you been doing at Deer's Leap?'

'I've been wallowing in it,' I smiled. 'It's so good to be back. I've taken photographs and a lot of notes. Grist to the mill.'

'When do you go back, Cassandra?'

'Sunday, unfortunately.'

'I've told Cassandra, though, that she must feel free to pop in any time she wants,' Susan said. 'She is setting four books around Deer's Leap, you know, though she will have to give it a different name.'

Lizzie asked me what the new name was, and I told her Wolfen House.

'Aaaah.' She tapped her nose, nodding knowingly. 'That's what it was called when Walter and Margaret Dacre built it all those years back. One of the fields is called Wolfen Meadow to this day – but you'd know that.'

'I too,' I grinned, 'have read *Dragonfly Morning*!'

'So how will Margaret Dacre figure in your plot, Cassandra?'

'She'll be Mary Dobbie, wife of William. And could you tell me, Mrs Taylor, if Margaret Dacre really was a witch? To the best of your belief, is it fact or fairy story?'

'We-e-ll, put it this way. It's fact when it's talked about by Acton Carey folk, but it's fiction when nosy parkers come asking questions, if you see what I mean.'

'I – I'm sorry. I'm not being nosy – just wanted some research for the book. I wouldn't want to upset anyone in the village.'

'I'm not talking about you, girl! You're well on the way to being accepted, hereabouts. It's the press I'm on about; those who go ferreting around, trying to get a story that'll sell newspapers. Was the same when talk got around about the ghost.'

'Which ghost?' I looked at Susan whose eyes were on her hands. 'Does it haunt in Acton Carey?' I laughed, trying to make light of it.

'*It* is an airman – or so some say. But when you challenge them to say more, they shut up, because they're afraid folk will think them a bit daft. The ghost business seems to catch people's interest from time to time, but we won't have anything to do with it here. Who wants this village turned into a circus, will you tell me? Rumours are quickly put a stop to by mutual consent so the matter dies a natural death – for a time.'

'And have you seen the airman, Mrs Taylor?'

'Of course I haven't! And there's none around here will look you in the face and say they've seen him either – for fear of being thought a penny short of a shilling!'

'You never said anything about it to me, Lizzie.' Susan seemed to have got over her initial shock.

'I'd have got round to it.' Lizzie dipped into her pocket and brought out a cigarette packet. 'What you can't seem to grasp, Susan, is that we have over half a century of gossip to catch up on! She went off without a word,' she glared at Susan. 'Just like it was in the book!'

'Did you enjoy *Dragonfly Morning*?' I asked guardedly, not wanting to talk about the ghost.

'Oh my word, yes! I've started to read it again, digest it properly this time. And not once did I suspect that Susan was pregnant. But there were a lot of things she never told me,' she said huffily.

'The book says it all. I wanted to tell you, Lizzie; I always felt bad about the way we left Deer's Leap.'

'That dratted mother of yours was at the bottom of it! I always said she was a witch, now didn't I?'

'Which brings us back to Margaret Dacre again. Can you tell me any more about her, Mrs Taylor?'

'Questions! Questions! You're forever at it! First it was the girl who lived at Deer's Leap during the war; now it's Margaret Dacre. Very peculiar how she got away with it, to my way of thinking. All the others were hanged! That's what you should concentrate on, young lady. Margaret Dacre would be a fine character to write about, even if she was as wicked as sin!'

'She's already in my book, Mrs Taylor. Mary Dobbie. I told you.'

'Then you do your own ferreting, young Cassandra. I'm

off to put the kettle on. And for heaven's sake, call me Lizzie, why don't you?'

'I didn't know people round here knew about Jack,' Susan whispered anxiously.

'Not about Jack particularly. Just about an airman. Jean McFadden's sister admitted to seeing him. She was in her car, so she put her foot down, she told me. Her husband said it was all nonsense, though. There are people who can see ghosts and people who never will. Like Mrs Taylor said, if talk about the ghost starts up again, it's quickly put a stop to.'

'I wish she'd told me sooner, for all that. But there are a lot of things we've got to catch up on. Why she married a clergyman, for one thing. It just doesn't seem like her, because she's still the same old Lizzie underneath. She hasn't changed.'

'Who hasn't changed?' She was standing in the doorway. 'And what isn't like me?'

'Well, if you must know, I remarked to Cassandra that I can never understand why you married a clergyman, if you want the truth. Sorry, love, but you did ask!'

'Then I'll tell you!' She set the teatray down, then stood, hands on hips, looking at both of us in turn. 'It's simple. He was the first one that asked me, if you must know!'

'But, Lizzie! You were so full of life, and fun. You loved dancing. Remember how you and Mick used to –'

'Yes, I remember Mick – and the pilot of one of the American planes that came here, too, when our lot left. That's something else I haven't got around to mentioning, Susan Smith!'

'I'm sorry,' I whispered. 'We truly weren't being catty. As a matter of fact, I agree with Susan. Bessie Drake wasn't the sort to marry a curate. She was a bundle of fun, in the book.'

'Oh? Well, all I can say is that it happened to me, too. I fell heavily for a pilot, Susan. Stewart, his name was. Flew a Liberator. So I understand about you and Jack. Only I didn't have his child, though I'd have considered myself lucky if I had – and be damned to the village!'

'What happened, old love?' Susan's eyes were wide with sympathy.

'Same as happened to you. He went off on a mission. Americans always bombed in the daylight. Flew in a square formation, with fighter escorts. Stew didn't come back. I married on the rebound, I suppose, though Frank Taylor was a good, kind husband. And for goodness' sake, let's make a start or this tea is going to be stewed black! Give me a hand, Cassandra. And I'll tell you no more about the American until I'm good and ready, Susan, so don't ask!'

'I won't,' came the gentle reply. 'Not until you are ready, I promise.'

It was six o'clock, and a beautiful April evening. We had stayed too long at Lizzie's, eaten far too many cream-dolloped scones. We walked slowly, because we felt relaxed, and happy.

'This is where I last saw Jack.' Susan stopped where the left fork turned out of the village. 'We'd met, at Fellfoot, after his final – what *should* have been his final – op. The crew were going to celebrate that night, and it was only right he should be with them. So we agreed that next morning – at ten – he would come to Deer's Leap and we'd tell my parents I was pregnant and that we wanted to be married.'

'Exactly as it happened in the book?' I whispered.

'Exactly. I was utterly happy. Jack had made it! Within a week we could be married. I watched him go and he turned, and waved. I shouldn't have watched him – bad luck – and he shouldn't have waved, but it didn't seem to matter any more. He was safe from flying for a year, we thought.

'Then he disappeared round that bend and I stood for a while, just loving him and being happy; not caring that in the morning we'd have to face my mother. But he never made it.

Next morning at ten he was preparing for takeoff; an urgent, daylight raid. Every bomber on the station went.'

'So this is a very special place,' I said gently.

'Yes. I think of it as the goodbye place.'

'But you never said goodbye.' I took her hand. 'It's still to come. Let's go home.'

I saw him, I think, before she did. For almost a week I had been willing him to come, but even so it was a shock.

'Susan!' I hissed. 'Can you . . . ?'

There was no need to ask if she had seen him. She stopped, wide-eyed, staring at the figure at the roadside, fifty yards ahead. Her face was deathly pale and she gripped my hand tightly.

'It's all right, Susan. Leave it to me. Just walk slowly; I don't think he's seen us yet. Ready?'

One minute he was there, clear and solid, an airman with three stripes on his arm; yet with the first step we took towards him, he vanished.

'No!' I jerked.

'Was – was it . . . ?' She was still holding fast to my hand, still staring at the road ahead.

'That was Jack.' My voice was croaky, too. 'We missed him by seconds.'

'Or fifty-five years.' Her voice still shook, though the colour was returning to her face.

'Are you all right, Susan?'

'Just about . . .'

'A shock, for all that you were expecting – *wanting* – to see him,' I soothed, still a bit wobbly myself.

'Y-yes. Let's get on home, Cassandra? I need a cup of tea.'

'Brandy,' I corrected, 'and I'm glad it was only a brief encounter, sort of. Next time, you'll be prepared.'

We walked slowly to the crossroads, still clasping hands. When we got to the white gate, I saw she was weeping; big, silent tears. I gave her a couple of tissues, and she dabbed her eyes and drew in her breath.

'A bit better, now?'

'No,' she sniffed loudly. 'I'm still shaking. But oh, wasn't it unbelievable and wonderful? He's here, Cassandra, and *I can see him*!'

'I thought you'd be able to – when the time came.'

'So what happens now?'

'First I put the kettle on, pour that brandy, then we'll have a cup of tea.'

I unlocked the door, then guided her to a chair at the kitchen table. She looked as if she was in control again, but for a couple of minutes she'd had me worried.

She smiled briefly. Her hands were relaxed on the table-top and she was making a visible effort to breathe deeply, slowly.

'A bit of a shock, for all that.' She took a sip from the glass, then another.

'It'll be OK next time, Susan. You'll be fine.'

We didn't talk, after that, until we had emptied the tea-pot.

'I've never forgotten him for one minute.' Susan was the first to speak. 'The slimness of him and the height of him; the way he held his head. He was so straight-backed, you know; so completely wonderful. And he hasn't changed – even from a distance I knew at once he hadn't.'

'Good,' I whispered.

'No, it isn't. I'm Susanna Lancaster. I'm seventy-four and it's Suzie he's looking for – hadn't you thought?'

I had thought. A lot.

'He's been waiting for you, looking for you, for a long, long time. He'll see what he wants to see. He'll see Suzie.'

'You think so?' She ran her tongue round her lips. 'You really, truly think so?'

I didn't know, and that was the God's-honest truth, so because I was Cassie Johns, and stupid with it at times, I said, 'Now see here – who's in charge of this ghost business? And I think another brandy is in order.'

'Just a very small one – and only if you will have one with me.'

I trickled a small one into her glass, relieved I had avoided answering her question, then poured a goodly slurp for myself.

'To Sergeant Jack Hunter,' she whispered, raising her glass.

'And to lovers' meetings.' We touched glasses.

'And will it be journey's end then for Jack?' she asked tremulously.

'We'll see,' I said softly. 'We'll see . . .'

Chapter Thirteen

My last day at Deer's Leap. Early tomorrow, I would be leaving; back at Greenleas in time for ten o'clock coffee, I had decided.

We had shopped at the village store, then called in on Lizzie to say goodbye. We refused coffee – or rather *I* did. I didn't want to dawdle. I'd planned to the minute when the Mini would be passing The Place; at the same time, exactly, as when first I met Jack Hunter. A little before eleven, it had been, and me going to Jeannie's sister's place to a fancy-dress party. On a Saturday too.

I hadn't come under the spell of Deer's Leap then; hadn't fallen in love with an old house, nor a view that stretched into forever. Nor had I, on that first Saturday morning at almost eleven o'clock, met Jack Hunter, given him a lift to the little creaking gate, nor decided he would be good to dance with – very closely.

'Are you sure I shouldn't sit in the back?' Susan asked as I clicked in her seat belt. 'We agreed we'd leave this seat empty.'

'No bother. We'll worry about who is sitting where *if* it happens.'

I had come to the conclusion that manoeuvring over the tipped-forward front seat of a Mini and squeezing into the back isn't a lot of good for an elderly lady – no matter how young and agile she may look. Indeed, my cuddly, middle-aged mother had tried it only once and said never again!

'*If*, Cassandra? This might be our last chance, until you visit again.'

'Then I'll have a better than ever excuse to come back often, won't I?'

'You don't need an excuse.' She laid her handbag at her feet, then relaxed, hands on her lap as if we both knew that Jack wouldn't show, so why get het up about it?

When we got to the bend before six oaks I dropped a gear, not only because the road is narrow there, but because I wanted an excuse to slow down without it seeming obvious.

Call it sixth sense or wishful thinking – whatever it was it worked! He was there again, at the side of the road, and Susan's hand on my knee told me she had seen him too!

'Right!' My mouth had gone dry and I was already pumping the footbrake. 'I'm going to stop. Just sit there. I'll get out first!'

'Then what?'

'I don't know.' I was staring ahead, pulling on the handbrake, afraid to take my eyes off him, willing him to see me, and stay right there. I slid out carefully, then let the door swing shut behind me.

'Sergeant Hunter!' Please, *please*, don't vanish. 'Want a lift? Deer's Leap?'

'Er – yes.' He smiled, and it did things to my heart. 'Good of you . . .'

I walked round to the nearside door, and he followed me. Trying not to meet Susan's eyes I opened it, offering her my hand, helping her out. She did it with absolute grace, swinging her legs elegantly. I was proud of her.

'There's someone I want you to meet,' I said softly.

She took a step towards him, her eyes pleading, then held out her hand.

I wanted to yell, 'No! Don't touch him!' but he didn't take her hand and she let it fall to her side.

'You're on your way to meet Suzie, aren't you, Jack?' I said. It wasn't meant to be a whisper. I'd intended to be completely in control like that first time – because I hadn't known then that he was a ghost. 'Susan Smith,' I prompted.

'Yes, I am.'

He smiled again, as if just to hear her name caused it, and this time it lit up the whole of his face and ended in a crinkling at the corners of his eyes. If I'd had my wits about me, I'd have wondered how it took Susan so long to get pregnant.

'Susan is here. *This* is Susan.'

Her eyes were still on his, so she couldn't miss his look of puzzlement.

'It *is* Susan,' I urged. 'She's been waiting a long time, Jack. You're both going to Deer's Leap, aren't you, to tell them about the baby?'

'Yes. But how did –'

'Jack. It's me, Suzie . . .' She had found her voice, though her words were so soft, so anxious, that I wondered if he had heard them. 'It's been such a long time that I've grown away from you, grown old . . .'

'No.' He smiled politely, hesitantly. 'Suzie is nineteen; not old enough to get married.'

'She never did get married, Jack.' I was homing in on the vibes between them, but I didn't care. 'She's got something to show you, so you'll remember . . .'

I nodded to her, but she was already taking the photographs from her pocket.

'Look – do you know her?' She passed one to him, smiling tremulously.

'Suzie! It's Suzie, at Fellfoot!' he laughed.

'It's the one Lizzie took – I never gave it to you. And do you know who this is?'

'Of course I know!' He took the second photograph. 'That's Aunt Lottie, with a baby.'

'*Your* baby, Jack. That's Kathryn – Kate. She was born in your bed at Primrose Cottage. And I am Suzie, her mother.'

'Jack?' I said softly, and he turned to look at me. 'Try to concentrate? And stay with us? Please don't go?'

'All right. I'll try. But explain, will you? This lady is . . . ?'

'Is Susan Smith. She lived at Deer's Leap when the aerodrome was there, and the Lancasters. But they've been gone a long time – more than fifty years!'

'No! That isn't possible. It's *now* – June 1944. I've done my tour of ops. The baby! Suzie and I want to be married!'

'Sweetheart.' Susan's eyes were gentle, and full of love. If she had felt fear, there was no sign of it now. 'Can't you recognize me at all? Is there nothing about me you remember?'

I took a couple of steps backwards. They needed to be alone, yet I was afraid of taking my vibes too far away.

'Your smile – it's like Suzie's, and your eyes.' He frowned, looking at her throat. 'That cross. It was Suzie's. She gave it to me.'

'And Aunt Lottie wanted me to have it, Jack. It was sent to her with the rest of your – your things. After –'

'After the thirty-eighth.' He said it flatly as if reluctant to remember it, to admit it had happened, even.

'Yes. I saw you take off, from the steel fence. Mick gave me a salute like always. I couldn't believe it. I'd been waiting for you at Deer's Leap. We were going to tell them about the baby.'

'And I didn't show?'

'No. At ten o'clock, when we should have been telling them, you were flying over Deer's Leap. You shouldn't have been sent on any more ops, but –'

'The daylight one. It was a bit dicey. Once we were over France, we had to hedge-hop most of the way. Don't remember a lot.'

'You don't remember getting back to Acton Carey?'

'No. Only thinking, Hell! Only just missed the church! Two engines gone, you see . . .'

'Then what, Jack?'

I wanted to weep. I must remember this happening, keep every word, every look of it in my mind. This was a love scene at its best, with Susan's eyes so tender, and every now and again, her lips trembling into a small smile. And she was young again, and beautiful. This *was* 1944 and I could feel – see, almost – the love that sparked between them like electricity.

'Fellfoot? We went there together, didn't we?'

'I found a key that fitted the padlock on the back door.'

'It was good – our loving.' She was his Suzie again.

'And then Sprog happened!'

'Is that her with Aunt Lottie?' He looked at the photograph again.

'That's Sprog. I left home. I had to. My mother didn't want me to keep Kate. That's why I went to Aunt Lottie.'

'Kate . . .'

'Yes, Jack. She's very beautiful. Would you like to keep the photographs?'

'Please.' He unbuttoned the top, left-hand pocket of his tunic, taking out his paybook, letting it fan open at the middle. Then he laid the pictures inside it, and put it carefully back. 'But something is wrong. Why did I miss Kate? Where have I been? What time is it, Suzie? Am I late?'

'It's ten past eleven. It's a Saturday. And I am seventy-four. We lost each other, darling.'

'Is that why they sent my things to Aunt Lottie?'

'Yes. To your next of kin, like they always did. I've got Matilda. You forgot to take her on that last op. Remember Matty Mint?'

'I remembered her when it was too late. We were cheesed off, having to fly again. All of us had thick heads . . .'

'You'd been at the Red Rose, celebrating.'

'Yes. Celebrating the tour. Got a bit tight, the lot of us. Where is Sprog now?'

He asked it so suddenly that Susan pulled in her breath, all at once off guard. Then she looked into his eyes again.

'She's at home. Home is Primrose Cottage. When Aunt Lottie died, she left it to Kate.'

'Aunt Lottie is dead? When?'

'A long time ago – '85, it was.'

'*Nineteen* eighty-five? Then where are we now? Tell me, Suzie? There are too many blank spaces. Can't seem to . . .' His voice trailed off and he sounded sad and bewildered. I wondered how much it was costing her not to wrap her arms around him, hold him close.

'Kate – Sprog – is fifty-four. She's married and has a son – your grandson. Joshua John Marlow. We call him Josh.'

'So this is . . . ?'

'We're almost at the Millennium.'

'The *what*?'

'The year 2,000, Jack. You've been lost a long, long time.'

Tears filled her eyes. She was going to break down, I knew it, and he would take her in his arms, kiss away her tears. And if he did, if they touched . . .

'Am I dead, Suzie? After I missed the church – when I was trying to land – did I . . . ?'

'They gave you a medal for it. Posthumously.'

'Medals for dead heroes.'

'Kate has it now – your DFM. She's very proud of it.'

'I can't understand any of this. You are so like my Suzie, yet you aren't Suzie, are you?'

'No. There have been a lot of years between. But I still love you. There hasn't been anyone else.'

'Then where am I? And why have you changed into –'

'Into an elderly lady?' She smiled as she said it. 'Because I am a grandmother, now.'

'But this Millennium – such a long way away . . .'

'No, Jack. Very near.'

I took my sleeve across my eyes. I wanted to touch them both, hold them, tell them it would be all right, but I just stood there, hurting all over. Because people like Jack Hunter didn't – *couldn't* – think of the year 2,000, not in 1944, when young men lived each day as it came and with gratitude. Tomorrow never came, so you weren't so crazy as to think of millenniums that were a million tomorrows away.

'So tell me – where am I – *really*, I mean?'

'In the little churchyard near Primrose Cottage, Jack. And Aunt Lottie is beside you, and when it is time for me, I'll be there, too.'

'So we'll have to believe, won't we, Suzie?'

'In reincarnation? Yes. Hope for another time around, another chance. But till then, darling, why don't you go back – to Aunt Lottie, I mean? Wait for me there?'

'You *are* my Suzie. You really are! And I – I'm dead.'

'Yes. After the thirty-eighth. But now I've found you I don't want you to leave me. I want to meet you every night at the kissing gate like we used to. But I'm an old woman, and you are young, still, and you can't stay. You've got to sleep away the years, sweetheart, not wait here for me. Don't you want to sleep?'

'Sometimes – most times – yes, I do. But then I think that I'm meeting my girl, at ten . . .'

'Well, you've met her. Just a little bit late. So what have you got to say to her?' Her voice was full of love and longing. And sadness.

'That I love you, loved you – will always love you.' He whispered it huskily, despairingly. 'I suppose this has got to be goodbye . . . ?'

'For just a little while, Jack.'

'I'll wait, Suzie . . .'

'Then goodbye it is, Sergeant Hunter. I love you. I never stopped. Next time around we'll be luckier, I know it. And can you make it easier for me, darling? Will you hold me, just once more, then go? And don't turn round?'

'Not goodbye, Suzie. So long. See you.' His eyes were sad, but his lips tilted into a smile. 'Second time around, uh . . .'

He held out his arms and she went into them, her face so beautiful that I could hardly bear to see her joy. Then she turned, bewildered, eyes wide.

'Cassandra! Where is he? Why did he go so – so *completely*?'

'I don't know. I think his time finally ran out. But he understood, Susan. He'll rest now.'

'And he won't come back? Not ever?'

'Not to Deer's Leap.' I nodded to the grass at her feet, and the two photographs that lay there.

'But I wanted him to have them!' She picked them up, her hand shaking.

'He couldn't take them with him, Susan. You gave them to him too late.'

'Oh, what a waste of time! I could have said so much more! There's been so much need and love and longing inside me. I didn't even thank him for the letter – his last one!'

'No, but it will keep – for the next time around.'

I gave way to the tears, then; couldn't take any more. I reached out and held her close and I don't know how long we stood there. It was she who finally pulled away, head high.

'That's the second time I've been through it, Cassandra,' she whispered huskily. 'The first time, it was just down the road and I cried myself sick in Lizzie's mother's arms. This time, you were there for me and I'm truly grateful to you. But did I really let him go? What if we don't meet again?'

'You won't – not at Deer's Leap, nor at Fellfoot, nor at the little iron gate. But there'll be another chance. Next time around, you'll both know – just as you did at the dance in the Nissen hut.'

'Yes. We'll know . . .' She walked unsteadily to the Mini, then slid into the front seat. 'They say that when you're miserable and really want – *need* – to get drunk, you can't. They say you've got to be in the mood.'

'You don't want to get drunk, Susan. It's just that you've had the saddest, the most unbelievable experience – the most wonderful one, too – and it's going to take time to get over it.'

'But I don't want to get over it, Cassandra!'

'Get over the shock, I mean.' I started up the car. 'I'll tell you something – *I* won't ever forget it! Are you going to be able to cope alone? Shall I stay a couple more days . . . ?'

'It's kind of you, but no. Kate arrives on Monday, don't forget, and who knows – the wayward Josh might take up residence any day now. I won't tell Kate, though; nor Lizzie. What happened will have to be between you and me – and Jack. And I think that when we get home I'll have a cup of tea, then sit on the terrace, if you don't mind. Just for a while; look at the hills, go over it again, then put it all away. I suppose I'll have to look forward to the Millennium – let 1944 go. It was a good thing, mind, that I was wearing the little cross. I think that in the end, it was the cross convinced him. I've never taken it off, Cassandra, except to have the links and the clasp checked . . .'

We didn't speak until we were at the white gate.

'You are a very remarkable lady,' I said as I helped her out. 'And I'd still like to have given you a run for your money, though you'd have won. Hands down!'

We spent the remainder of Saturday quietly. I packed my case, then put a casserole in the oven – just in case Susan felt like eating.

Then I went to sit beside her and was glad when she smiled and said, 'Will you be a love and bring the sherry and a couple of glasses? It's still quite warm – let's stay here a few more minutes?'

'I envy you this view,' I said as I placed a glass at her side. 'A million pounds wouldn't buy it. And you've got all the lovely summer evenings ahead of you to sit out here and gloat.'

'Yes – and to tell myself that I've finally come home. And said goodbye to Jack. I'm glad I wasn't alone, Cassandra. Thanks for helping me through it. Promise you'll visit as often as you can? I really don't want to lose you. Already you are a part of my past; I'd like to think we could share what's left to me of the present.'

I reached for her hand and held it to my cheek. I didn't say anything, but she understood, and smiled and said, 'Suddenly I'm feeling a little cold. Would you mind if we went inside?'

'Not a bit. Shall I light the fire?'

'Please.' She settled herself beside the hearth. 'This is so cosy, isn't it, and peaceful?'

'Mm. Yet tomorrow I'll be back at Greenleas, and you'll be busy getting ready for Kate. Does she like Deer's Leap?'

'She hasn't seen it yet, would you believe? I bought it without telling her; was afraid she would say I couldn't possibly live here alone. Daughters can be quite bossy, you know. But when I eventually told her, and that Josh was going to live with me and start a tree business, she said it mightn't be such a bad idea, if that was what I really wanted. Pity you'll miss her.'

'What is she like?'

'Tall, slim, fair. Her hair is wavy and she's always complaining that she can't do anything with it. And she's got a lovely smile. She's –'

'Jack's daughter,' I finished for her.

'She is. And as for Josh – oh, *no*! Talk of the devil! Did I say *peaceful*?' From outside came the sustained blaring of a horn, then the banging of a door. 'It's him! It's Josh!'

She hurried outside, cheeks flushed. I followed, to see a very old truck piled high with what could only be Joshua John Marlow's worldly goods.

'Hi, Gran!' He held wide his arms, hugging her tightly and I thought – as far as I was capable of thinking, that was – that the top of her head reached the wings above his tunic pocket – if he'd had wings, which he should have.

'Cassandra Johns, this is Josh Marlow.'

She was smiling, her eyes bright and teasing. She had known, dammit, how uncannily like Jack he was and had deliberately not shown me a photograph of him!

I stood quite still. I know my mouth was open and that

I was gawping like an oik. I felt giddy, too, and my cheeks were burning.

'Cassandra?' he smiled. 'Cassie suits you much better.'

He looked me over very slowly from top to toe, and I hoped he didn't know how much I was shaking.

I tried to focus on his smile, his face, the fair hair that fell untidily over his forehead. And when he lifted his hand – *his left hand* – and brushed it aside, I was ready to fall in a faint at his feet; would have, if I'd known how.

'Hullo, Josh.' I should have said it softly, seductively, but it came out in a strangled croak. 'You are so – so like your grandfather!'

'Think I'm just a bit taller than he was, otherwise the resemblance is uncanny. Gran's been showing you her photographs, I suppose?'

He was still holding my hand – or was it me clinging on like I was afraid to let go? All I was certain of was that at half-past seven on an April evening in what was once the farmyard of long-ago Deer's Leap, I was ready and willing to fall desperately in love.

Then the bright bubble of my wondrous disbelief burst into a million pieces when he said, 'I'm starving, Gran. Haven't eaten since this morning. Any chance of a quick fry-up?'

'Fry-ups give you spots!' Susan said severely, but he grinned, gave her bottom a smack, and told her he was past the spotty age.

'I'll just get my bag – won't bother unloading the truck till the morning.'

'Then drive it into the big stable, Josh, in case it rains in the night. I take it you are stopping, this time?'

Susan was purring like a cat that had got at a dish of cream, in charge of her life again. And besides, she had Josh now, if ever she needed reminding.

'So what do you think to my grandson, Cassandra?' she asked when the truck had lurched off in a belch of fumes.

'Do you really need to ask? But you're enjoying this, aren't you? You knew all along what a shock it would be when I met him!'

'Yes, I did! And serve you right, too, for coveting my man!' she grinned. 'Well, Miss Cassandra Johns, Jack Hunter Mark One belongs to me, never forget, but the Mark Two model is up for grabs – so the best of British!'

She turned, whisking off like an eighteen-year-old to cook a fry-up, leaving me to stand there in a daze of disbelief, wondering how anyone could get so lucky.

I got up early next morning, but Susan was already in the kitchen. A percolator blurped on the stove top; the table was set for breakfast.

'Eggs, bacon, or your usual?' she smiled.

'Just toast, thanks. I'm all ready for the off. This week has been marvellous.'

'It has,' she sighed tremulously. 'Unforgettable.'

'Did you sleep, Susan?'

'Amazingly, I did. But I awoke early and decided to get up. You'll say goodbye to Josh before you go? He's in the yard, unloading. So tell me – having slept on it – have you got over the shock of Josh yet?'

'No. Have you – of seeing Jack, I mean?'

'No. And I hope I never will.'

'Mm. I know exactly what you mean. It's as if Josh was meant to turn up – right on cue, sort of.'

'To remind me always to be thankful, no matter how lonely and difficult it has sometimes been, that I lived my full three score years and ten; that Jack had to settle for a lot less? Fate plays funny tricks from time to time . . .'

'Yesterday was nothing to do with fate. It belonged to you and Jack. It was meant to be.'

'Like you and Josh, I suppose . . .'

'I'd like to think so, Susan. But I still can't get over it. I mean, which woman falls in love with a ghost, then meets his flesh and blood doppelganger? There's got to be a catch in it somewhere along the line. Is there anyone – er – special?'

'Not that I know of. One or two young ladies seem to have flitted into and out of his life, but that's par for the course with young men these days, I suppose. Playing the field is part of growing up.'

'It wasn't for Jack,' I defended.

'Jack had a war to fight; Josh hasn't, thank God. And why did you go to bed so early, last night?'

'Thought I'd better. Reckoned you'd have lots to talk about.'

'Nothing that wouldn't have waited. Actually, Josh seemed quite interested in you. He's got a penchant for redheads, but you knew that, didn't you? I told him you didn't have a steady boyfriend.'

'*Susan!*'

'Ssssh! He's here, now; must have smelled the coffee. All finished, Josh?'

'All done. I don't suppose I could use that barn for my clobber, Gran?'

'Be my guest. Full breakfast then? Cassandra is just about to leave – why don't you give her a hand with her luggage?' She put a large plate in the warming oven. 'On the table in ten minutes . . .'

'It's all right. I can manage. There's only an overnight case. Most of my stuff is already in the boot,' I protested.

'No problem!' He smiled, and I forgave him at once for interfering. I looked at my watch. If I left now, right this minute, I could be on the M6 before the morning rush, though really I wanted to be away from Josh Marlow before I made a complete fool of myself!

'It's been wonderful.' I hugged Susan, and kissed her. 'And I'm going to take you up on your offer to visit.'

'Any time at all – truly. And thanks for – for *everything*, Cassandra.'

'In the boot or in the back?' It was Josh with my case, and I followed him to the car.

'In the back, please,' I said, blowing a kiss to Susan, who stood on the doorstep.

'Got everything, Cassie?' Josh was standing beside the Mini, making it look very small.

'I have, thanks. Nice meeting you, Josh. I hope things go well for you at Deer's Leap. See you – sometime . . .'

'Didn't Gran tell you about the tree planting?'

'The five beeches? Yes, she did.'

'Then I hope you'll be here for that – make an occasion of it. You could give me a hand.'

'I'm well qualified,' I said primly, wondering what had happened to last night's smouldering glances.

'Right, then – take care. Safe journey, Cassie.'

'Thanks. Nice meeting you, Josh.'

Such sparkling conversation! Hell! He wasn't even going to kiss me goodbye! I banged the door then wound down the window, allowing myself one last despairing look, smiling sweetly, though it took a lot of doing.

He smiled back, drat him, and held up his hand.

'So much for Mark Two,' I hissed as I passed six oaks. I felt hurt. Really hurt. There had been such *throb* between us last night, such promise. And the way he'd smiled into my eyes and looked me up and down was so blatant that any girl could be forgiven for thinking she was in with a chance.

Yet maybe he smiled that way at all his women; maybe it was trees that really turned him on!

I got back to Greenleas in time for coffee. Dad was already in the kitchen. I knew because his wellies were at the back door.

'Now then, our lass! Had a good time then?'

'Fabulous, Dad. Deer's Leap was better than ever.'

'And did you do all you wanted to?' Mum was slicing parkin. 'The notes . . . ?'

'And photographs. And I got to know Lizzie Frobisher quite well. If you've started reading *Dragonfly Morning*, Lizzie is Bessie Drake in the book.'

'Well, now! Want it black or white, love?'

'Leave it, can you, Mum? I've got to ring Deer's Leap. You wouldn't believe it – I forgot my handbag; left it in my bedroom.'

'You're getting like our Jane,' Dad said. 'Daffy as they come.'

I went upstairs and dialled from the extension on my desk.

'Cassandra! You're home all right!' Susan answered almost at once. 'And before you say any more – you left your handbag behind! I thought only old ladies did things like that! I found it not long after you'd gone. Said I'd pack it up, send it registered post, but Josh said I'd better not; that it would be safer if he were to bring it. No problem, he said.'

'But it's a hundred miles, there and back!' could feel my cheeks burning, I was so ashamed. 'Look, Susan – tell him not to bother. I can manage without it for a few days. I think it's up to me to collect it.'

'If you're sure . . . ?'

'Absolutely. My own fault, anyway.'

'Then if you really can manage without it, why not come up Saturday, stay the night, then have Sunday dinner with us – meet Kate? Say you'll come? Saturday – supper at six?'

I unpacked, wondering why, when he had been so laid back when I left, Josh Marlow was willing to make the round trip with my handbag. Bored already with Deer's Leap? Surely not! And surely I'd got it right – the instant attraction, I mean – because there *had* been something between us; a kind of surprised recognition with a touch of the what-took-you-so-longs?

Or had it all been in my mind; my over-active author's mind? Had I seen a man so like Jack Hunter that I'd wanted, there and then, to fall in love with him? Jack Hunter Mark Two, and up for grabs, hadn't Susan said?

Yet there was nothing I could do about it until Saturday. Come Saturday, though, I would get to the bottom of it if it was the last thing I did! Would it be a feet-in-first attack or would I play it cool – bored, even?

I decided to forget all about it – to *try* to forget about it – until Saturday, and went downstairs to ask Mum if she wanted anything doing. But as usual she had everything in hand so I said I thought I'd pop along to see Aunt Jane.

'She's all right, Cassie. I took flowers yesterday.'

'I'd like to go, Mum,' I said stubbornly, so she shot me one of her no-communing warnings, then reminded me that Sunday dinner was at one sharp, and she didn't want the Yorkshire puddings going flat, if I didn't mind! Dear, lovely Mum. If she really knew what had happened at Deer's Leap she would have me locked up! It was why I was going to see Aunt Jane, who understood such things.

'Hi! It's me.' I stooped to rearrange the flowers in the marble vase. 'I'm back.'

'*And . . . ?*'

'And it all turned out just fine for Jack and Susan,' I said with my thoughts.

'*That's good . . .*' She didn't seem to be very forthcoming this morning.

'I – I left my handbag behind, would you believe?'

'*Good grief, Cassie! Was that the best you could do?*'

'It seemed like a good idea at the time. I couldn't think of anything else.'

'*There's a man in it, isn't there? My word, he must have been quite something!*'

'He was. *Is.* Name of Joshua and the spitting image of Jack Hunter! What am I to do, Aunt Jane?'

I was really upset. I never thought that falling in love could be so hurtful.

'Do? You'll get yourself up there on Saturday, then play it by ear! You'll think of something. Maybe the handbag scam wasn't such a bad idea . . .'

I heard her chuckle and I knew she had gone, so I let go a big sigh and thought how awful it was going to be, waiting for Saturday.

I was restless all week. Saturday seemed years away and I couldn't concentrate on *First of the Deer's Leaps*, my own fault entirely for letting Josh Marlow put me off my stroke. I'd thought I could handle it, but how wrong can you be?

OK! So falling in love with a ghost was fine, and the agony of knowing I couldn't have him quite delicious, but to meet that ghost again, and him up for grabs with his grandmother's blessing, is altogether another thing. It was putting me off my work and off my food. I had been to the churchyard for a bit of comfort from Aunt Jane, but I couldn't get a word out of her.

Now I knew *exactly* how Susan felt the night she and Jack met, except that she had got to dance with him. Closely! Mind, I knew that Josh would dance well – *really* well – so I closed my eyes, and let it happen. Me, in the clingy green lily-of-the-field frock, arms round his neck. Josh gorgeous in jeans and shirt and dance music from the forties, soft and sensuous. And me not caring that his hands cupped my bottom as we danced and . . .

'*Aaaagh!*' This would not do! I had a book to write and a contract that said it would be delivered to the publisher by the end of January!

By Tuesday I knew I'd got it bad, so bad it was making a nervous wreck of me! Oh, there had been the moment of our meeting; that first eye-to-eye contact that knocked me sideways. And when he looked me up and down with a smile tilting a corner of his mouth, I went to pieces. I had blushed, gawped and squirmed under the impact of that gaze;

made a complete fool of myself, though why Josh hadn't seen through the handbag scam, I'll never know!

The door opened slowly and quietly and Mum's face appeared round it with a have-you-got-a-head-full-of-words-or-can-I-interrupt look on it.

'Hi,' I said.

'Coffee time. Shall I bring one up?'

'No thanks, Mum. I'll come down for it.'

'Anything wrong, Cassie? Got word block, or something?'

'Nothing that a mug of coffee and a slice of parkin won't put right.' Like a lot of Yorkshire mums, mine thinks that food is the cure for most of the world's ills. She cut an extra-large slice which I fell on with great greedy bites.

'There is no wonder, Mrs Johns,' I sniffed, 'that your daughter is too fat!'

'Nah then, lass!' Dad crept into the kitchen on stockinged feet. 'Is summat up?'

(That's Yorkshire for, 'Hullo, Cassandra. Is something worrying you?')

'There is,' Mum said comfortably. 'She's got word block and she's too fat!'

'Oh, is that all?' He slurped two sugars into his mug.

'It's far worse than word block,' I said, when Dad had gone back to the big glasshouse. 'And I've got to tell someone!'

'Deer's Leap, is it?' She settled herself comfortably on the chair opposite. You can't fool Mum!

'Sort of. Susan's grandson arrived on Saturday night, and he's drop-dead gorgeous!'

'Oooooh!' Mum went pink, but didn't say anything because I was sure as I could be she was composing a piece for the engagements column in the *Yorkshire Post*.

'Mother! You aren't listening!'

'Yes, I am. You seem quite taken with Susanna Lancaster's grandson, you said. Tall, dark and handsome, is he?'

'Very tall, *fair* and handsome. He's just like Jon Hunt, in *Dragonfly Morning*.'

'Is he now? And how would you know that?'

'Because I – I've seen photographs of him,' I floundered.

'I'm enjoying that book,' Mum smiled dreamily. 'Just got to the sad bit. Does it end happily, Cassie?'

'Wait and see. But you appreciate what I'm up against, don't you? Men like Josh Marlow shouldn't be allowed!'

'He must be really something if he's put you off your stroke!' Mum clucked. 'I suppose you wouldn't like to come to York with me this afternoon – if you aren't going to be able to write, that is? I'd intended getting the two o'clock bus, but if you're driving . . .'

'Might as well,' I said ungraciously. This wasn't going to be a flow day, nor tomorrow. I felt so jumpy, in fact, that there would be little done in the way of words till I got back from Deer's Leap, on Sunday night. By which time everything would be sorted; came wonderfully right. Or gone abysmally wrong!

By the time Saturday came, I was well behind schedule on First of the Deer's Leaps. I'd made an effort, mind, and chapter three was finished, though it would have to be severely edited before I could be anywhere near satisfied with it.

'You're ready early,' Mum remarked. 'I thought you weren't expected till supper.'

'It'll be all right. Besides, I'm keeping off the M6; thought I'd go A59 all the way – take my time, get there about four.'

That pleased Mum, because she doesn't rate motorways very highly. Boring, she says, and people drive far too fast for her liking!

'Where do you want this?' Dad arrived with a pot of bright yellow ranunculus for Susan. 'Look lovely on her kitchen window ledge. When they've finished flowering, tell her to plant them in the garden, don't forget.'

I said I would, and wedged the plant pot carefully in the

boot. Then I gave Dad a hug, and kissed Mum, who winked and said, 'Mind how you go!'

Yet for all that, I was driving through Acton Carey at two o'clock and hoped Susan would forgive me for arriving too early.

I took the left fork out of the village, then dawdled past six oaks. There were dark green bluebell leaves beneath them, spread out in a carpet. Not long before they flowered, I thought. Bluebells look so lovely in spring. Everything looks lovely, come to think of it, when you are in love. And I was in love!

Jack Hunter wasn't at six oaks, so I stopped a little further on, at the spot where only a week ago, he and his Suzie said hullo, and goodbye. It had been so beautiful, but not the kind of thing you could put in a book, because who would believe it, anyway? Which reader would have any sympathy for a heroine who fell in love with a ghost, and him in love with someone else?

I got out of the car, leaned on the bonnet and relaxed, probing for vibes, wondering if he would appear just one last time. But the air around was sweet with birdsong and I accepted it as a requiem for a lost soul who had gone to sleep at last.

'Bye, Jack Hunter,' I said softly. 'It was terrific meeting you.' I almost added that I liked his grandson, too, but decided it wasn't appropriate, in the circumstances. I drove slowly to the crossroads, then turned into the dirt road, anticipation and anxiety churning inside me.

'Hi, Cassie!' Josh was leaning on the white gate. 'Was at the top of the paddock – spotted the Mini as you passed six oaks. You're early. Gran doesn't expect you till about four.'

'I know. I'm sorry.' Nothing had changed since our first meeting. He was still disturbingly, disgracefully attractive and I wanted desperately to pull my fingers through the hair that fell over his right eyebrow. And I wanted – *needed*

– to ask him why all of a sudden we were being so polite and friendly when it had seemed so very promising.

'Sorry? Don't be. Gran is out – gone shopping with Mum and Mrs Taylor. I volunteered to look after you if you arrived before they'd got back.'

'Then in that case,' I was concentrating hard on unlocking the boot, 'perhaps you could take my case?' I swallowed hard. Not for anything dare I look him in the face.

'Your handbag is locked in Gran's desk, by the way. Are all redheads forgetful?'

'Not usually.' Carefully I removed the ranunculus which had travelled very well, then still not looking at him I said, 'And since you ask, Josh, I had a good journey, I'm very well and really pleased to be here – even if only to collect a handbag!'

'I've bought a new hand-plough,' he said, cheerfully, ignoring my acid aside. 'It was a toss-up between that and changing the truck, and the plough won. I'm planting the paddock with potatoes. Potatoes clean the soil, did you know?'

I told him I *did* know; that I'd known about such things since I was old enough to lift a spade, and would he mind if I put the kettle on as I was desperate for a mug of tea!

'Not at all. I'll have one with you, Cassie. I'll just take your stuff upstairs. Gran said you are in the same room as before.'

'So you're turning the paddock into a nursery?' I'd got myself pulled together by the time he came downstairs.

'Not until it's been ploughed and cleaned. Best make a good job of it.'

'Couldn't agree more.' And why had we got on to such a subject, when all I wanted was for him to say, 'Hi, Cassie. Glad you've come,' or maybe even, 'Hullo, darling. I've missed you,' and then kiss me, because I was still sure, just as Susan had been, that he was the man I wanted.

I covered the teapot with the cosy and allowed myself a clear, dispassionate look at him. And he was every bit as good to look at, every bit as attractive, and I was every bit as smitten – so what had gone wrong? Because since that first head-to-toe appraisal when we met, that first breathtaking recognition, nothing seemed to have gone right!

'How is the book coming along, Cassie?' He spooned sugar into his mug, then stirred it noisily.

Everyone asks how The Book is coming along so I said, like I always do, that it was coming along just fine!

I plopped saccharins, then asked him what kind of seed potatoes he intended planting in the paddock, because I know about seed potatoes, too, and he said he hadn't decided yet. It was real heart-stopping stuff and I was beginning to think it had been a waste of time coming when he said, completely without warning,

'Look – I'd like us to talk before Mum and Gran get back. Shall we stay here or would you rather walk?'

'Walk,' I shrugged. After all, did it matter where he told me he wasn't the faithful type? Because that was surely what it was all about. I'd blushed and stammered and gawped at him doe-eyed, hadn't I, when we met; sent out all the signals? The wrong signals as far as Josh Marlow was concerned!

'I'm going to like living here,' he said as we made for the paddock. 'It's so peaceful. Do you like peace and quiet, Cassie?'

'Yes, I do. And I think Deer's Leap is very special.'

'Gran said you'd fallen in love with the place.'

'I have. Stupid of me. Once, I even had ideas of buying it – one or two novels on, of course – but your gran beat me to it. I'm glad she has come home, for all that. Have you read *Dragonfly Morning*, Josh?'

'Actually – no. Seed catalogues and trade magazines are about my level. Ought I to read it?'

'I think you should. You'd understand, then, how much she loved Jack, and how much it means to her to come back to where they were once so happy together. It was a brave thing to do.'

'She talks a lot about my grandfather. Everyone says I'm like him and when you compare photographs of us both, the resemblance is quite uncanny. But I wouldn't have coped very well with his war. It must have been hell, flying those old bombers.'

'Those *old* bombers,' I said sharply, 'were very remarkable planes. Jack flew thirty-eight ops – missions, they call them now.'

'Look at the view, Cassie.' He held open the paddock gate, closing it carefully behind him, like a real countryman. Then he turned to lean his elbows on it. 'Just looking at all that makes me glad I'm alive, and don't have to fly a bomber.'

I went to stand beside him. Quite close, in fact. Just one more step to my right and our shoulders would have touched.

'So what do you want to talk about?' I stared ahead.

'Handbags,' he finally offered. 'Yours.'

'*Aaaaah . . .*'

'Last Sunday morning, actually. When I went upstairs for your case your handbag was at the bottom of the bed, so I left it there. And I didn't remind you you were leaving without it.'

'Josh! *Why?*' Any minute now he was going to ask me why I had done such a damn' fool thing, and what had I expected to achieve by it. I might have known he'd see through it.

'You were leaving and I hadn't had a chance to get to know you better. I had no idea at the time that you'd be a regular visitor. Thought I could offer to bring it to your place . . .'

'I see.' I didn't see, actually; didn't feel anything but relief. I felt my cheeks go red.

'OK, Cassie! So I shouldn't have! But it was all I could think of at the time!'

'But, Josh! This is 1999, for heaven's sake!' I was shaking, and my mouth had gone suddenly dry. 'Couldn't you have asked me for my phone number? Couldn't you even have gone completely mad, and kissed me goodbye? Did you really have to pull a stunt like that?'

'Oooh, Cassie Johns! If that doesn't take the plate of biscuits!' Aunt Jane, pushing her nose in!

'So it was stupid of me, and now I'm in the doghouse because you've had to come all this way to get it! Reckon I'd be annoyed, too!'

'But I'm *not* annoyed! Didn't I just say that I like being at Deer's Leap? There's no problem, Josh – honest!'

'You're sure? Then can we start again, Cassie?'

'From where, exactly?'

All at once, my conscience was beginning to bother me and I was on the point of blurting out that it was six of one and half a dozen of the other when Aunt Jane hissed, '*Don't dare tell him, idiot!*'

So I said nothing and looked down at my shoes and offered up a thousand thanks for my undeserved good fortune.

'So how about from the beginning, Cassie – it's as good a place as any.'

'When your gran introduced us, you mean? From when you looked me over and undressed me – *blatantly*, if I might say so!'

I tried to say it flippantly, but the shaking was still there inside me.

'From there would do very nicely,' he said, turning to face me. 'Did you mind being blatantly undressed?'

'In front of your gran? You might have waited till we were alone!'

'Like now, Cassie?'

I took a step away from him because he was much, much too close and because any minute now I was going to panic and run!

'Look, Josh! Before we go any further, there is something I've got to tell you!' It came out in a rush, because I was playing for time to pull myself together before I blew everything! 'This is cards-on-the-table time, and if you don't like what I'm going to tell you, then it's up to you to say thanks – but no thanks! You see, when we first met, that was it for me! I found you attractive, disturbingly attractive, and I didn't mind one bit being metaphorically undressed! But even though this is 1999, you've got to know that I'm really old-fashioned at heart. I'm a romantic. I want to be married and have children, and stay married! I'd even, if I haven't frightened you off completely, that is, like nothing better than to be plain, old-fashioned courted! Now what have you to say to that?'

'Couldn't agree more!' He reached for my hand, lacing his fingers in mine. Then he tucked my arm in his, which rather pleased me, because running is out when a man has got you in a half-nelson – or as near as makes no matter! And come to think of it, running with knees turned to jelly is equally impossible!

'That's all you've got to say!' I squeaked. 'I've just set out the rules, and you agree! Why? Do you think I'm a pushover, or something?'

'Well, *are* you, Miss Johns?'

He was smiling at me, very tenderly and possessively; just as Jack smiled at Suzie, and I could have hit him for being so gorgeous! But the fight had gone out of me and anyway, it was time to give in.

So I just smiled back and whispered, 'A pushover? Oh, *no*! But if you were to kiss me, perhaps I could make an exception in your case.'

So we kissed long and urgently, as if we had both been waiting ages for that very moment and there were years and years of kissing and touching and holding to catch up on. And it was so dizzy-making it left me breathless.

'This is crazy!' he laughed. 'We are so right together, yet I don't know the first thing about you except that you are very beautiful and kiss like no girl has kissed me before! And that Gran,' he said, all at once serious, 'adores you!'

'Does it have to make sense? Can't we just agree to fall in love like there's no tomorrow, and take it from there?'

He gathered me close, and laid a cheek on my hair, and I felt myself relax because it seemed so absolutely right to stand there in his arms, and wonder at the amazing peace of it.

'So we're in love,' he said eventually, soberly, pushing me a little way from him, looking into my eyes. 'When did it happen, Cassie?'

'I don't know.' I smiled, almost certain it had its beginnings in Acton Carey – or was it Laceby Green, in the blackout? – and that more than half a century on, it was happening again. Yet how could I tell him I had been in love with him since the day I gave a lift to a pilot who wanted to get to Deer's Leap, when Jack and Suzie's secret wasn't mine to tell? Not even to Josh. 'Perhaps another kiss might help?'

We kissed, more gently this time; a kiss of commitment, as if we both knew that all our tomorrows stretched safely ahead of us, and out and away beyond the hilltops into forever.

'That was the car. They're back. What do we tell them, Cassie?'

'Nothing, just yet. Let's keep it secret for a little while longer – wallow in it?'

He took my hand and we walked, unspeaking, towards the house, to where Lizzie and Susan were unloading shopping bags. I knew Kate at once by the fair, wavy hair so like that of her father. It even flopped over one eye and I half expected her to brush it away with an impatient left hand.

'Hullo, Cassandra!' Susan called, mouthing a kiss because her hands were taken up with plastic bags. 'And what have you two been up to?'

'Don't ask!' Kate tutted, pushing a tissue at Josh. 'Wipe your mouth, for goodness' sake! It's all over lipstick!' Then she smiled at me with Jack's smile and held out her hand. 'Hullo, Cassandra. Lovely to meet you!'

She said it as if she really meant it, and I stood there, so crazily happy it just wasn't true.

It was then I thought I heard Aunt Jane's chuckle, but my head was so full of wedding bells I couldn't be sure. Come to think of it, I didn't think I would ever be sure of anything ever again.

When Kate and I had cleared away the supper things, I went in search of Josh but found Susan instead, leaning arms folded on the big white gate. I went to stand beside her and whispered, 'Penny . . . ?'

'Hullo, dear. I was thinking about the beech trees. They'll be delivered next week in tubs. We can't put them back where they once were –'

'At the point where the runways cross – *crossed*?'

'Mm. Josh thinks we should make a feature of the dirt road – put a decent drive down and plant the trees either side. That way, they would be near, yet not too close to the house for their roots to become a nuisance – we-e-ll, that's what the expert says,' she grinned.

'I like the idea. Three one side, and two the other? And had you thought of planting a rowan tree – keep witches away?' I teased.

'I just might do that, Cassandra! This gate will be moved to the bottom, near the road, where the standing for the milk churns used to be. About time there was a decent approach to the house. This bit of dirt road can be very tricky if it rains a lot, or if it freezes hard in winter. I speak from experience!'

'I think it would look really good – given a couple of years to get things established. The hedges will have to be thinned and cut back, and spring bulbs planted, maybe, and –'

'I'd forgotten you were brought up to gardening, Cassandra! You'll have to help Josh with it; give him a hand with the beech trees, too. I'd like that. Full circle, sort of. The young ones putting back what the old ones allowed to be destroyed.'

'No fault of yours, Susan. There was a war on.'

'Yes. A war. And at least I shall replace the trees. Would you like to walk with me across the cow pasture?'

'Please. Are you going to show me the steel-mesh fence?'

'How did you know? Anyway, there is no sign, now, of it ever being there, but I know exactly where it was. And I'm not being an interfering old busybody – I really care, you see – so will you tell me something, Cassandra?'

'About who? Or what? And is it all right for us to be here?' I shut the gate behind us as Susan must have done so often in her young years.

'Yes. I know the farmer who rents this land. And we aren't walking through growing crops.' Around us, ewes grazed with their lambs. They looked at us curiously as we walked, then went on cropping grass. 'And you don't have to tell me about you and Josh, but I would so like to think you could get fond of each other. Might you, perhaps?'

'No,' I said gravely and firmly, looking down at the grass.

'Oh! And I was so sure there was something there. It seemed to me you've hardly taken your eyes off each other since you got here. You like him a little, though?'

'*Like?* Listen – I'm besotted with the man! I'm in love with him, too! And please don't tell him this, will you, but I left my handbag behind on purpose. Josh doesn't know. Devious of me, I know, but you did say the Mark Two version was up for grabs!'

'And Josh . . . ?'

'The feeling, I am very glad to say, is mutual.' Then all at once I felt a shiver and stood stock-still in the middle of the field. 'Susan! It's just hit me – how everything has fallen into place! I was meant to come to Deer's Leap and to fall in love with the place. And I was meant to meet Jack, and read *Dragonfly Morning*! It must have been preordained, sort of. It's spooky, if you think too much about it.'

'No, dear. Just written down for us all at the moment of our birth – in our Book of Life,' she said matter-of-factly. 'I was meant to meet Jack and conceive Kate. And it was written in Jack's Book of Life that he would never live to see her.

'But I shall love Jack again in another life, I know it, and till then I have Kate and Josh, and you. I have come home, to Deer's Leap and met Jack again, and told him I love him still. And had you thought, Cassandra, that if ever you and Josh decide to tie the knot, you'll get Deer's Leap, one day – though not as you had planned.'

'Josh and I *will* make a go of it. I told him I'm really old-fashioned underneath, and that I want to be married and have children. And he said it was fine by him! I had to get things straight between us, you see, before we jumped in with both feet!'

'Then I won't ask another word about it, but I shall expect to be the first to know, Cassandra, when you name the day! And you'll be so good for Deer's Leap. You've got what it takes to put paid to Margaret Dacre – let her know just where she stands!'

'Oh, I will! There'll be children at Deer's Leap, I promise you! And Susan – can I please call you Gran, like Josh does? It would make me feel I really belonged, if you wouldn't mind?'

'I'd like that.' She kissed my cheek gently, then said, 'This is the place, Cassandra; this is where They put the steel-mesh fence. And about ten yards to the other side of it was the perimeter track and the hard-standings for the bombers. They're gone, now, but Lizzie told me that when there's a dry summer, you can make out where it all was all those years ago.'

'Beth told me. The grass yellows where the track was, she said. Beth saw Jack, too.'

'Then perhaps one hot dry summer you and I will come here, Cassandra, and see the outline of it. And I shall imagine I am young, and that *J-Johnnie* is going to taxi past to takeoff, and that Mick will rotate his guns and say –'

'"Rear gunner to Skipper! Just passed your milkmaid!"' I finished for her.

She dabbed her eyes and sniffed away a tear. 'It was written in your Book of Life that you would read *Dragonfly*

Morning. And there is that grandson of mine, come looking for us!'

Josh was standing at the gate of what was once the cow pasture, a hand held high.

'Why is it that my stomach turns over every time I look at him?' I gasped. 'What's with the man, drat him!'

'He gets it from his grandfather, I shouldn't wonder. Looking at Jack did things like that to me, too – right from the minute we met. Seems it runs in the family!'

'Shall we go, Gran?' I pulled her arm through mine and we walked away from where a steel-mesh fence once kept lovers apart, to where Josh waited.

And I was so very thankful that he won't be flying ops, tonight. Nor any night.

I'll Bring You Buttercups
Elizabeth Elgin

WHEN LOVE SURVIVES WAR

It is 1913 and Rowangarth, Yorkshire is a rural arcadia for sewing-maid Alice Hawthorn and young gamekeeper, Tom Dwerryhouse. For Julia Sutton, daughter of Alice's employer, it is also a time of unfolding love for the handsome doctor Andrew MacMalcolm. But with the outbreak of war their lives will be changed for ever.

As Tom and Andrew volunteer to fight for King and Empire so too do Alice and Julia as VAD nurses at the Western Front. All find trials that will test them to the limit. For all, passion and hope must be tempered by heartbreak, and sorrow.

Those who survive the torment of the trenches return to their homeland as very different people. For Alice it is a reluctant return as one of the aristocratic Sutton family . . . Will she find peace and fulfilment once again?

Weaving love and friendship with breeding and brass, *I'll Bring You Buttercups* is a halcyon and shimmering page-turner, rich in drama and content. An enchanting novel, brimming with freshness, vitality and emotion, it echoes with the author's unique voice.

ISBN 0 586 21696 0

Daisychain Summer

Elizabeth Elgin

THE FOUNDATION FOR THE FUTURE

The legacy of the Great War has haunted and changed the lives of both Upstairs and Downstairs society. For spirited and resourceful Alice Hawthorne, ex-sewing-maid, ex-Lady Sutton and now happily married to gamekeeper Tom Dwerryhouse, fortune shines on that union and brings forth an adorable daughter, Daisy.

Meanwhile brilliantined bounder Elliot Sutton has been ordered to mend his ways by his adoring yet dominant mother, Clementina. Will marriage to Anna Petrovska, the beautiful Russian aristocrat, produce a much needed Pendenys heir?

What lies in store for Daisy Dwerryhouse and her childhood friend, Keth Purvis? Will the relationship with the brother she never had progress from a platonic one to a much deeper emotional level?

As the years roll on, there's a new generation of Suttons who must look life in the eye and find out if the secret sins of one generation taint the fate of the next.

Shot through with ecstasy and pain, this panoramic account of love, life and social change is a tribute to the author's unique imagination.

ISBN: 0 00 647887 5

Where Bluebells Chime

Elizabeth Elgin

A Nation United in Conflict

Blackouts, munitions, kitbags and rations once again pepper daily life. Daisy Dwerryhouse, the spirited daugher of gamekeeper Tom and his wife, ex-sewing-maid Alice, finds herself apart from her true love, Keth Purvis. Joining-up fever is infectious. Daisy is now a Wren, based in perilous Liverpool; Keth involved in secret war work in America. Will their mutual passion survive such a divide, as well as the tribulations and untold dramas of a world at war? Britain fights with desperate stubbornness, as the stench of undignified death and the snarl of enemy fighters touch Rowangarth. For Daisy and Keth, and for all the Suttons, these are years of danger and change: a bewildering time when a nation cannot even begin to hope for an end to the conflict.

Told with the author's consummate voice, this panoramic account of a bygone era and its society is dramatic, page-turning, and a superbly crafted experience.

ISBN: 0 00 649622 9

Windflower Wedding

Elizabeth Elgin

OUT OF THE DARKNESS COMES LIGHT

1942: Britain is in the midst of the darkness, the fear, the horrendous bloodshed of war. For the Sutton clan, it is a time of dread that all Europe shares, of fear for the future, and, oddly, of consummation and hope.

Daisy Dwerryhouse still waits for her Keth and for the wedding she and all in Yorkshire's Rowangarth long for. But Keth is on a secret mission in France, so dangerous that the big question is: will the wedding ever happen?

Love is in the air, too, for Sebastian. He has found the woman of his dreams, the landgirl Gracie, but she swears that she will not fall in love in wartime. Can he change her mind?

Drew is besotted by the spirited Kitty: he will inherit Rowangarth, and their future seems assured. Are they ships that pass in the night, rocked by the waves of war?

For all the Suttons, these are years of changing horizons, of loss, and, ultimately, of finding. This grand saga of a family at war reaches a triumphant conclusion.

ISBN: 0 00 649884 1

All the Sweet Promises
Elizabeth Elgin

CROSS MY HEART . . .

Vi's life is shattered by the arrival of a letter telling her that her husband is missing in action. Then, when her Liverpool home is destroyed in an air raid, the WRNS becomes her only reason for carrying on. For upper-class Lucinda, who sees life mapped out along a predictable route of engagement, marriage and motherhood, joining up provides a means of escape. And for the lovely Jane, there is little choice when she gets her call-up papers. Their backgrounds couldn't be more different, yet together they will share their finest hours.

Beautifully written and wonderfully evocative, *All the Sweet Promises* is the compelling story of three young women as they enter the WRNS during the dark days of the Second World War, and of the men, both British and American, with whom they find love. Deeply moving and poignant, it captures the unique spirit of love and adventure, of promises made in the heart, and broken on the rack of war.

ISBN 0 586 20804 6